"You could have[...]

There was no mistak[...]
Kelly reacted immediately. "Don't expect [...]
fall in line when you bark an order. I'm not some
damsel in distress to feed your knight-errant
complex. I—"

The words stuck in her throat as he loomed over
her, big and dangerous. His hands landed on
either side of her head, bracketing her body and
trapping her in the bed.

"I'm bigger than you," James whispered, his
breath warm on her cheek. "And stronger." His
fingertips traced her arm, leaving goose bumps
in their wake. "It's my job to protect you. And if I
have to, I'll use my body."

She saw the intensity in his eyes and felt the
emotional currents swirling around them.

Did he care about her? After everything that
happened, did he still harbor feelings for her?

There was only one way to find out....

Dear Reader,

This is my first book, and I couldn't be more excited!

As a science nerd, I spent a lot of time in school. While I enjoyed it, I also needed a break from the dry, factual world of science, so I turned to romance novels as my escape. What started out as a hobby quickly turned into a (mild) obsession, and I decided to try writing romance, as well.

Fast-forward a few years, and here we are. I had a blast working on this book, as it combines my two loves: science and romance (they're not as incompatible as you might think). I hope you enjoy James and Kelly's story—they have a lot to overcome, but if anyone deserves a happy ending, it's this pair.

If you get a chance, please stop by my blog and say hi. You can find me at laralacombe.blogspot.com, as well as on Facebook and Twitter. I'd love to hear from you!

Take care, and happy reading!

Lara

DEADLY CONTACT

—

Lara Lacombe

HARLEQUIN®ROMANTIC SUSPENSE

Recycling programs
for this product may
not exist in your area.

ISBN-13: 978-0-373-27848-0

DEADLY CONTACT

Copyright © 2013 by Lara Kingeter

This edition published by arrangement with Harlequin Books S.A.

For questions and comments about the quality of this book, please contact us at CustomerService@Harlequin.com.

® and TM are trademarks of Harlequin Enterprises Limited or its corporate affiliates. Trademarks indicated with ® are registered in the United States Patent and Trademark Office, the Canadian Trade Marks Office and in other countries.

Printed in U.S.A.

www.Harlequin.com

LARA LACOMBE

I earned my Ph.D. in microbiology and immunology and worked in several labs across the country before moving into the classroom. My day job as a college science professor gives me time to pursue my other love—writing fast-paced romantic suspense, with smart, nerdy heroines and dangerously attractive heroes. I love to hear from readers! Find me on the web, or contact me at laralacombewriter@gmail.com.

For my family, of course.

Special thanks also to Rachel Burkot, Patience Bloom, Jessica Alvarez, the members of the CompuServe Books and Writers Community, and the members of the North Texas chapter of RWA.

Last but not least, thanks to Sarah, Tara, Jacqui, Adrienne, Jill and Laura. You saw the early draft, and you didn't run away screaming. You guys are the best!

Chapter 1

Washington, D.C.
April

Where is she?

James nursed his beer as he kept one eye on the television mounted on the wall behind the bar. His spot at the corner table afforded him a view of the entire place, and although he wasn't a huge fan of golf, the highlight reel from the Masters Tournament was the most interesting thing going on at the moment.

He glanced at his watch as he set the bottle down and reached for a handful of peanuts. Kelly wasn't usually late, but maybe she'd had a long day or had gotten stuck in traffic. It was raining, and D.C. drivers tended to lose their minds when any kind of precipitation fell from the sky. Whatever the reason, if she didn't get there soon, he'd start drinking the beer he'd ordered for her. He'd be doing her a favor, he decided, as no one liked warm beer.

"Ready for another, James?" Danny called out, pausing in his obsessive wipe down of the already clean bar.

He shook his head. "Not yet, thanks. I'll work on Kelly's first."

"Shouldn't she be here by now?"

As if on cue, the door opened with a blast of humid air and Kelly dashed in, wearing a frown as she brushed the raindrops off her jacket. She waved at Danny as she walked over to the table, then sat with a sigh and reached for her beer. James raised a brow as she gulped down the brew, draining the bottle in one go. She set it on the table and turned to gesture for another, but Danny was already there, handing her a fresh one and wearing an expression of amused surprise.

"Want me to keep them coming?" Danny offered. Kelly nodded, and Danny shot James a meaningful look before he returned to the bar. *Keep an eye on her tonight.*

James nodded. *I will.*

They had been meeting at this bar every Friday night for the past six months, a tradition that had started after they'd met at a friend's party. She had looked strangely familiar to him, so he'd struck up a conversation. It turned out they had gone to the same college and had even shared some mutual friends, but by some quirk of fate they hadn't officially met back then. After finding out she lived in a nearby neighborhood, he had suggested they meet up for drinks sometime. She'd taken him up on the offer, and they'd quickly developed a solid friendship.

Normally, Kelly was fun and easygoing when they got together, having only one or two drinks each time. He'd never seen her drunk, but if her current mood was any indication, he would tonight.

She set the bottle down with a loud *thunk,* then wriggled out of her jacket and hung it on the back of her chair. Facing him again, she smoothed a hand over her auburn hair and tucked the stray strands behind her ear.

"You are not gonna believe the week I've had," she said, her hazel eyes flashing as she reached for the bottle. He opened his mouth to respond, but she continued, not missing a beat. "My boss is driving me crazy."

"I figured as much," he said, sensing a rant in his future. "What's he done now?"

Kelly rolled her eyes and took a sip. "What *hasn't* he done is the better question. Remember that project I was telling you about?"

He closed his eyes and tried to recall the conversation. "Vaguely," he said slowly as the details came back to him. "But I didn't really understand what you were saying. You got a little jargon-y on me there, and you know I didn't take any biology in college."

She grinned at him, amused as always by his lack of scientific knowledge. "Yeah, sorry about that. Anyway, I'm not getting the results he expected, so he pulled me into his office today and reamed me out. Said I was a bad scientist, and if I couldn't do the job he paid me to do, he'd find someone else."

"Can he do that?"

She bit her lower lip and nodded. "Yeah. Technically he'd have to show cause, but since his grant is paying my salary, the university won't really ask too many questions if he decides to fire me. It's his lab, and the investigators have total authority over their labs. But you know what the worst part is?" She leaned forward, and he caught a whiff of her honeysuckle perfume as she moved. "The data are correct, and he's wrong. He just won't admit it."

"What's he wrong about?" James was genuinely curious, but he didn't hold out hope that he'd understand her project or results. He'd never been very good at science in school. Philosophy and law fascinated him much more. He'd take a criminal over a lab report any day.

She launched into an explanation of her experiments, and to her credit, she did try to dumb it down for him. He listened intently, occasionally interjecting an "uh-huh" or a nod to encourage her. He loved watching her talk, the way she gestured and moved, her body language communicating just as much as her words. With her bright eyes and flushed cheeks, she was a sight to behold.

She finished her beer and signaled to Danny for another. "Anyway, it's a big mess and it all kind of came to a head today. Sorry to vent to you."

He reached across the table and placed his hand over hers. "It's no problem—that's what I'm here for."

She smiled at him as he pulled back, then cleared her throat. "Enough about me and my crappy day. How are you? What's new with you this week?"

"Not much to tell," he said, nodding at Danny as the bartender set down fresh bottles. "I'm still working on the pipe-bomb case, and Carmichael is breathing down my neck for results."

She winced in sympathy. "Any leads?"

"Yeah, a few." He shrugged, wanting to tell her more

but knowing he shouldn't really talk about the details of the case. "I think it's going to turn out to be one of the kids."

Her eyes widened as she sipped her beer. "Why would a kid bring a pipe bomb to school?"

"To show off. To scare someone. Because they thought it would be cool. Why do teenage boys do anything?"

"Good point."

"I'm just glad it didn't explode," he said, running a hand through his hair. "The last thing we need right now is more tension, and you know an explosion at a local school would freak people out."

Kelly shook her head as she watched him. "Why did they bring you guys in on this in the first place? Shouldn't the D.C. cops have handled it?"

He sighed, suddenly tired. "It all comes down to appearances. The police don't want to be accused of not taking the threat seriously, so they ask the FBI to join the investigation, to make sure they're not missing anything. Since we don't want to be accused of the same thing, we conduct a full investigation, even though this really is a matter better left to the locals." He shook his head. "It's all very circular, and at the end of the day, I'm not sure it really makes a difference."

Kelly studied him a moment, her head cocked to the side. "Are you saying you're tired of working for the bureau?"

"No. Maybe. I don't know." He shrugged, raising his bottle to his lips for another swallow. "Some days I feel like I'm really making a difference, and then other days I feel like I'm just spinning my wheels."

"Not to be a Debbie Downer, but I'm pretty sure everybody feels that way at one point or another, regardless of their job. I know I do."

He nodded, picking at the label on his bottle. She was right, of course, but lately he'd had a string of bad days, making him question if he was really doing any good at all. He should probably take a vacation, get away for a few days and clear his head.

Kelly clapped her hands, jerking him out of his thoughts. "You know what we need? Irish car bombs."

He shuddered in mock horror. "Please don't say *bomb* too loudly."

She grinned back at him. "We're in a bar. I'm pretty sure Danny isn't going to call the police when I place this order."

A moment later, Danny appeared at the table with the requisite ingredients. James stifled a groan. Irish car bombs were a sneaky drink—they tasted like a chocolate milk shake, and more than once he'd been seduced into drinking several of them. It was only after he stood up that he realized how much of a wallop they packed.

"Ready?" Kelly asked, holding up her shot and reaching across the table to clink glasses with him.

Her expectant grin had him smiling in return. One car bomb couldn't hurt, and it was a good way to celebrate the end of the week. "Ready."

The dual *thump* of the shot glasses hitting the bottom of the pint glasses signaled the start of the race, and they both chugged the frothy mixture. He set his glass down first, wiping the bubbly residue off his lip with the back of his hand. An instant later, Kelly set her glass down as well, saying that she'd let him win.

"Not likely, princess," he said, grinning at her. "I'm a car-bomb champion from way back."

She laughed, her tongue darting out to lick the foam off her lips. The action sent a zing of awareness through his system, and an unbidden thought popped into his mind: *God, she's beautiful.*

He'd found her attractive from the start, but since he'd been buried in work and she had been, too, he hadn't tried to strike up anything more than a friendship with her. By the time his schedule had cleared up, they'd been friends for so long he didn't think she'd be interested in anything more, and he wasn't willing to risk ruining that friendship by telling her he wanted to take things to the next level.

He wasn't pining for her, exactly, but he hadn't been on a date since they'd met. He probably should find someone in order to get over these less-than-platonic feelings. The trouble was, he wasn't interested in anyone else.

"I demand a rematch!" she said, her eyes shining and her heart-shaped face pink from laughter and alcohol. He smiled at the sight, enjoying the view. "Are you ready to take me on again?" she demanded with a giggle.

He shook his head. "Not tonight, I'm afraid. I don't want to risk losing my title."

"Next week, then," she declared with a regal nod. "You'd better be ready."

"Next week," he said, reaching out a hand to seal the deal. "It's on."

She grasped his hand and gave it a firm shake, then picked up her bottle and drained the last of her beer.

After signaling Danny for another round, she leaned back in her chair and closed her eyes.

"Don't tell me you're tuckered out already," he teased. "It's not that late yet."

She opened one eye and shot him a grin. "I'm old—I can't help it."

He snorted. "Yeah, right."

They fell into an easy conversation, teasing affection underlying their exchanges. James felt a flush of pleasure every time he made Kelly laugh, loving the uninhibited sound of her giggle. He always enjoyed their time together, the way he could let down his guard and talk about anything with her without fear of being judged. She made him laugh, she made him think, but most important, she made their time together fun, something that was in short supply in his life.

After two more drinks, she let out a loud sigh, reaching back for her purse and pulling out her wallet.

"It's been fun, as always, but I'm gonna head home." She dropped several bills on the table, then stood and grabbed her jacket.

James hurried to stand, as well. "Let me walk you to the Metro," he said, digging out his wallet and dropping some money on the table. He caught Danny's eye and gestured to the money on the table before hurrying to catch up with Kelly.

She stopped by the door and blew the bartender a kiss. "'Night, Danny. See you next week."

"Good night, Kelly." He waved at her. "You stay close to James, now, you hear?"

She whirled around, almost bumping into his chest, and reached out to link her arm through his. "Is this close enough?" she asked.

Danny nodded. "That'll work. You two be careful."

"We will," James said, escorting Kelly out the door.

The rain had stopped sometime earlier, and the streetlights reflected off the puddles, making the sidewalk glow. The air was clean and crisp with the scent of rain, and he hoped the walk combined with the fresh air would help sober her up.

She stumbled over a crack in the sidewalk, jerking on his arm to stay upright. "Guess I'm a little tipsier than I thought," she said with a giggle.

"That's what happens when you drink car bombs," he replied. "Here, let me help." He placed an arm over her shoulder to steady her, meaning to keep the gesture as platonic as possible. His good intentions flew out the window, though, when she snaked an arm around his waist, fitting her body snugly against his side and hooking a finger into his belt loop.

She was warm and soft, and he liked the feel of her pressed against him. Her fingers on the waistband of his pants had his thoughts going off in an entirely inappropriate direction, and he tried to rein them back in to safer territory.

He spent the rest of the walk mentally reciting FBI rules and regulations to keep from fantasizing about the woman under his arm. It wasn't a foolproof method, but it did prevent his thoughts from getting too far out of line. He nearly sighed with relief when the lighted Metro sign came into view, signaling an end to this most exquisite torture.

They paused at the top of the escalators, and she turned to smile up at him. "Well, James, I hope you have a good night." She stood on tiptoe to press a smacking kiss against his lips.

It was too much. He had behaved himself during the walk, but the feel of her lips against his caused him to lose his tenuous grip on self-control. Before he realized what he was doing, he grabbed her by the waist and lowered his mouth to hers.

She let out a little "Oh!" of surprise, and he had a split second of doubt before she relaxed against him. Her lips moved under his, and he felt her tongue swipe across his bottom lip; the sensation made his knees wobble.

He deepened the kiss, tasting Guinness and whiskey, reveling in the silky smoothness of her mouth. She pressed closer and he tightened his hold, his hands traveling from her hips to her back, anchoring her into place.

Her hands skimmed down his back, one of them reaching around to squeeze his butt. His hips arched forward in response, and she made a purring sound low in her throat when she felt his erection.

A rude shove forward, accompanied by a muttered "Move!" had him pulling back. A steady stream of people was pouring out of the Metro station, darting around them with various degrees of success. Keeping his hand on her back, James stepped to the side, pulling Kelly with him to take them out of the pedestrian traffic. He had forgotten they were in public, and given her sound of protest and dazed eyes, he'd bet Kelly had forgotten, too.

"My place?" he said, the words flying out of his mouth like bullets from a gun, unstoppable and just as dangerous.

She nodded enthusiastically, with no hint of hesitation or reluctance. Her eyes were clear and bright, her mouth curved up in a sexy smile that made him want to lean in for another kiss.

His condo was about two miles away—too far to walk, especially given the state he was in. He grabbed her hand, leading her toward the curb, and flagged down a taxi.

Kelly reached for his hand after they'd settled in the backseat and the car started to move, pulling it into her lap and turning it over to trace patterns in his palm with her fingertip. He leaned back into the seat, closing his eyes and enjoying the feel of her touch. It had been a while since he'd been with anyone, and he hadn't realized until now just how much he missed being touched. Not necessarily in a sexual way—he just missed feeling someone else's body against his, missed the comfort that only came when skin touched skin. He'd read somewhere that babies who weren't touched regularly failed to thrive, and he understood all too well how that could happen.

Moments later, the car pulled to a stop in front of his building. He fished out a bill for the cabby and helped Kelly to her feet, placing a hand at the small of her back to guide her into the building.

She stood close to him in the elevator, the faint scent of her perfume making him want to bury his nose in her neck to get a better whiff. Honeysuckle and something else warm and subtle. Whatever it was, it was deeply appealing, and he couldn't wait to run his nose over her body to find where exactly she had applied it.

He ushered her into his condo, their progress momentarily halted by the two cats sitting at the end of the foyer, wearing identical expressions of bored superiority. They mewed at him, then turned and headed for the kitchen, confident he would follow along to feed them.

"You have cats," she said, a smile in her voice. "Why didn't I know this?"

He shrugged, at a loss. "It never came up?"

"That's true. I certainly never expected the big, bad FBI agent to have cats. A dog, maybe, but cats? I'm impressed. What are their names?"

"The black one is Edgar, and the orange one is Eliot. They're brothers, believe it or not."

She stared at him for a beat, then threw back her head and laughed. The rich, throaty sound had warmth spreading through his chest, and he reached out to touch her again.

"Let me guess," she said. "Eliot Ness and J. Edgar Hoover?"

He nodded with a grin, leaning down to kiss her. She stood on tiptoe to bring her mouth closer, but she stopped when she heard another meow from the direction of the kitchen, this time louder and more insistent. "I think they're hungry," she said.

He cast her an apologetic look. "I'm sorry. Do you mind if I feed them real quick? They'll leave us alone if they're full…." He trailed off, feeling suddenly self-conscious.

"No problem. I grew up with cats, so I understand. I'll just take the opportunity to use your bathroom."

"Down the hall, to your right," he said. He watched her disappear into the bathroom, then turned and headed for the kitchen.

He wrenched open the cabinet door, grabbing two bowls with one hand as he pulled open the drawer and reached for a spoon with another. After hastily pulling out two cans of food from the pantry, he pulled the tops off and dumped the food with a *splat,* the cats winding around his legs as if to urge him along.

He set the bowls down and stroked each cat once, then left them to their dinner and headed into the living room to wait. He sat on the couch, then stood to pace the room.

I can't believe this is really happening. His stomach fluttered with anticipation, his fingertips tingling with the desire to touch her smooth skin again. Just the thought of running his hands and lips over her body had his heart pounding double time. It was a wonder she hadn't heard it in the elevator.

Was he doing the right thing? She seemed to want this, too, if her earlier responses were any indication. She'd returned his kisses eagerly, her hands roaming his body with abandon. Warmth flooded his system as he recalled the feel of her gripping him, pulling his hips against her, arching into him and rubbing against the bulge in his pants. She'd been refreshingly direct in her response, and he couldn't wait to pick up where they'd left off.

Was it because she was drunk though? He frowned at the intrusive thought, but he couldn't dismiss it out of hand. He wanted to take things to the next level, but only if she was fully on board. He wouldn't take advantage of her intoxication to sleep with her, no matter how badly he wanted her. All the signs were there, but could a woman who had consumed six drinks really consent? He'd worked enough cases in his days as a police officer to know that alcohol and sex were a dangerous combination. He glanced down at his crotch with a sigh, willing his arousal to recede. He should probably set her up in the guest bedroom and go to sleep alone, after taking a cold shower. It would be a disappointing end to the evening, but probably best for all involved.

Resigned to his fate, he walked back to the couch and sat down. It would be okay. They could laugh, blame their kisses on alcohol and go back to the way things were. Safe. Easy. It was the right thing to do, he knew, but he couldn't help but feel disappointed. Now that he knew how she felt in his arms, what she tasted like, it would be hard to go back to being just friends.

I'll do it, though, he thought with a sigh, stretching out his legs in an attempt to find a comfortable position. Better to have Kelly as a friend than not at all.

Kelly stared at her reflection in the mirror, amazed that her heart hadn't pounded right out of her chest. What was she doing? James was her friend—was she really about to have sex with her friend? Yes, the man was gorgeous, with his dark brown hair, bedroom eyes and strong, square jaw, but he was her *friend.* It had been so long since she'd been friends with a man that she didn't want to risk jeopardizing their relationship just so she could scratch an itch.

But…he had kissed her. Technically, she supposed she had started it. She hadn't meant to take things that far—she'd just wanted to feel his lips against hers, and if he'd pulled away she could have blamed it on the alcohol. She'd been shocked by his reaction, to say the least.

She blushed as she recalled where her hands had been, how she'd reacted when she'd felt his response to her. It had been so long since she'd felt desirable and beautiful, and the attention of this attractive man had gone straight to her head. Even more amazing was the effect she seemed to have on him, as well. She ran her hand down to her belly, rubbing the spot where he had pressed firmly against her. *He wants me,* she marveled, a shiver dancing over her skin at the thought.

She drew her hand up, running the palm over her ribs. Her injuries had long since healed, but the ghost of the pain was never far away. All it took was a look, an accidental touch or a whiff of cologne and she was back to that awful night, broken and bleeding and oh-so-scared.

She frowned at her reflection, not liking the direction of her thoughts. She took a deep breath and tried to focus on something pleasant, stuffing the memories and insecurities back into the box where they belonged.

"James is not Gary," she said softly. "He won't hurt me."

Neither did Gary at first.

She shook her head at the errant thought, firmly dismissing it. *No.* James was not Gary. James was a decent man, her friend—nothing like Gary. She had to start trusting people again, and James was a good place to start.

Her mind was made up, but despite her resolve, she couldn't ignore the tight ball of nervous energy in her stomach. She pressed her hand there, taking a deep breath and blowing it out slowly. Her lips curved up in anticipation as she imagined kissing him again, running her hands over his chest and lower....

After one last look in the mirror, she walked out of the bathroom and into the living room. He stood when she entered and offered her a seat on the couch, then resumed his place as she settled onto the cushion.

He was warm, and this close she could smell the spicy citrus of his cologne. She inhaled deeply, resisting the urge to press her nose into his neck to get closer to the source. She'd always loved his smell, and soon it would be all over her. Goose bumps broke out on her skin at the thought, and she rubbed her arms absently.

"Are you cold?"

She shook her head. "No. Just thinking."

"Thinking gives you goose bumps?" he asked, smiling.

"Some thoughts do."

He swallowed with an audible gulp, and she felt her lips twitch as she fought to contain a grin.

"Kelly, are you sure?" His voice was husky and deep and danced along her skin like a touch.

This was it. This was her chance to back down. She could say *No, I was just kidding,* and they'd laugh it off and go back to being friends. And she'd go back to feeling damaged and alone.

No. Not this time. Gary was gone, and she wasn't going to let him affect her anymore.

"I'm sure," she said, leaning forward to press her lips to his.

He was still for an endless moment, as if giving her one more chance to change her mind. Then he pulled her to him with a groan, deepening the kiss as he ran one hand down her back in a caress.

It was several minutes, or maybe hours, later when he rose, pulling her to her feet and tucking her hand into the fold of his elbow. They walked down the hall, past the bathroom and into a large bedroom. Her gaze tracked around the room, her eyes landing on the huge, mission-style bed that took up the center space; the spread and pillows were in shades of dark brown and hunter-green. A matching bedside table, corner chair and dresser completed the room. It was neat and composed, a perfect reflection of James.

He led her to the bed, then pressed her gently down as he kissed her. She was so caught up in the delicious sensation of his mouth against hers that it wasn't until she felt the warmth of his hands on her bare shoulders that she realized he had undone the buttons of her blouse and was sliding it off her body.

She pulled away from the kiss, breathing hard. He moved closer, but she put a hand on his chest to forestall him. "Wait. There's something you should know." It was now or never—she needed to tell him. Her mouth dried up at the thought, but he deserved to know.

He sat back, looking at her with an indulgent expression. "What's that?" he asked, leaning in to press small kisses along her collarbone. She helpfully lifted her chin to provide him with easier access, shivering as his lips feathered across her skin.

I was attacked by my boyfriend. She wanted so badly to say it, but the words stuck in her throat. How would he react once he knew? She couldn't handle it if he pushed her away, not right now. She was so tired of feeling damaged.

Chickening out, she said, "It's been a long time for me, and..."

"And?" he asked, trailing his tongue up the side of her neck.

"And I'm probably a little rusty," she finished, gripping his shoulders with a moan as he found a sweet spot.

He pulled away to look down at her, a smile quirking up the corners of his mouth. "Would you believe it's been a while for me, too?"

Her gaze traveled over his strong jaw, broad shoulders and trim waist. "No," she drawled. "I have a hard time believing that."

A flush rose on his cheeks and he flung himself down next to her, lying on his back with his head pillowed on his hands. "It's true," he said, looking up at her, sincerity in his eyes and voice. "I haven't slept with anyone in about a year."

"Really? You look like a guy who would have no trouble finding a willing lady." She lay down next to him and propped her head on one hand, facing him.

"Not so much," he replied. "Besides, I've been so crazy with work, I just haven't really had time for a relationship."

"I can understand that," she said, and he laughed.

"I know you can," he said, reaching over to tuck a strand of hair behind her ear. "You're just as big of a workaholic as I am."

"Guilty as charged."

He reached for her, and she moved willingly until they were pressed flush together. "I'm off duty now," he whispered, using his teeth to slide her bra strap off her shoulder.

She gasped, her fingers moving to his hair. "So am I," she said, ending on a moan when his hand found her breast.

"What a coincidence," he said, rolling her onto her back and rising over her. "Now, no more talking, Doctor."

She reached up to his shirt, making quick work of the buttons and pushing it off him. The feel of his bare

chest against hers sent sparks of tingling warmth shooting through her limbs, and she fumbled to get her bra
off, wanting nothing between them.

He stood for a moment to shuck off his pants, and
she took the opportunity to wiggle out of hers. She
reached for him as he came back, but he gently moved
her hands above her head. "It's my turn now. You can
have a go later."

"Promise?" she whispered as his hands and mouth
did delightfully wicked things to her body.

He made a sound of assent, not bothering to pause
in his ministrations. He worked his way back up to her
mouth, ending with a smacking kiss. "Yes. Just lie back
and enjoy yourself."

She did.

The tree branches outside James's bedroom window cast moving shadows across the ceiling in the
pale gray light of approaching dawn. Kelly watched
them flicker and move in the wind, swaying back and
forth in a hypnotizing dance that was oddly soothing.

She wasn't sure how long she'd been awake—long
enough for the sky to fade from inky-black to smoky-
pearl—but James slept soundly by her side. His breathing was deep and rhythmic as he slept the sleep of the
satisfied, and she smiled knowing she'd been a part
of that.

Last night had been wonderful. James was a con-
siderate and skilled lover, and her skin still tingled in
remembrance of his touches. She turned her head to
look at him; his outline was fuzzy in the dim light.
He slept on his stomach, arms stretched out, his face
relaxed and so beautiful. Despite her presence in his

bed, he'd had no problem dropping off to sleep. She
envied him that, his trust in her, his surrender in her
presence. She had been like that once, too, until Gary
had changed everything.

No, she thought firmly. *I will not let him ruin this
moment for me.*

Too late, though. As usual, the thought of her ex-
boyfriend made her heart beat a little faster, and her
stomach tightened. She focused on her breathing in
an effort to keep from drowning in panic. In…out…
over and over, she counted her inhalations until the
fluttering in her chest subsided and she felt somewhat
normal again.

James stirred, turning and stretching out a hand in
her direction. She moved away carefully, not wanting his touch right now but not wanting to wake him,
either. His hand landed on the mattress next to her
and curled gently before relaxing again. His skin was
dark against the pale sheets, the color of it warming
as the light improved.

Such beautiful hands, she mused, tracing the long,
graceful fingers with her eyes. Strong and capable but
still elegant, with dark hair trailing from his forearm
to dust across the back. Would they ever fist in anger
or be used to hurt? She didn't think so, but she'd been
wrong before.

Gary's hands were much different. Wide-palmed
with thick, blunt-ended fingers, she'd always thought
his hands were the ultimate example of practicality.
Still, they had brought her pleasure, at least at first.
Eventually, sex with Gary had become more like a
race to the finish, a contest she had rarely won. He'd
never put her pleasure before his own, never watched

her fall apart with warm, focused eyes and a smile of male satisfaction. Never held her close and stroked her gently, whispering dark, seductive words in her ear as she came back down to earth.

She knew now that Gary had never truly cared about her. He had been her first, though, and she'd been too naive and unsure to really stand up for herself. *You control your orgasms, babe, not me,* he'd pointed out. *I can't make you come—only you can do that.* Maybe he was right. After all, hadn't she read the headlines of women's magazines in the grocery store checkout line? Take Charge of Your Sex Life! Lose Your Inhibitions and Take Back Your Pleasure! There had to be some truth to that. She just needed to work harder, that was all.

Still, she couldn't deny there was a little voice inside her head that said, *This isn't how it should be.*

She'd tried to rationalize that voice away, with varying degrees of success. Passionate, no-holds-barred love affairs made for great movies, but how often did that happen in real life? Never, as far as she could tell. So she convinced herself that things were all right, that real adult relationships weren't perfect and this was about as good as it was going to get.

But then the abuse started.

He'd never left visible bruises—he was too smart for that. No, he preferred to target her elsewhere. A pinch here, a sharp poke there. It had begun slowly, small events that could be explained away. *I'm so sorry, baby. I just don't know my own strength,* he'd say after a particularly forceful slap on her bottom. Or *You're just too sensitive. Maybe you should see your doctor, make sure you don't have a clotting problem or some-*

thing after she'd pointed out the bruise left behind from one of his pinches. He always had an excuse at the ready, always turned it back around on her. He was so convincing that she had started to think the problem *was* her, not him.

After months of these "love taps," he'd graduated to outright hitting. The first time, he'd slapped her face during an argument over holiday plans. The shock of it had kept her frozen in place, and he'd taken advantage of it by pulling her close. *I'm so sorry, baby. So sorry,* he'd soothed, running a hand down her back. *I'm just really stressed at work, and I don't know what came over me. It won't happen again.*

It had escalated quickly. A few weeks later, Gary had come home drunk and randy. Exhausted, she'd begged off, which had sent him into a rage. Two broken ribs and multiple bruises later, she'd gotten a restraining order and cut him completely out of her life.

That had been almost a year ago. For the first several months, she'd looked over her shoulder constantly, always expecting Gary to turn up and hurt her again. It was only after meeting James that she'd begun to relax a little. He was a strong, calm presence, and he made her feel secure. He'd offered friendship, with no pressure or expectation of something more.

Until now.

The shadows on the ceiling blurred as she blinked back tears. She couldn't do this. Sleeping with James had been a mistake. He would want more from her than she could give now that they had taken this step. She wasn't ready for that—given her history with men, she didn't think she was capable of having a normal relationship, whatever that was.

She had to leave now, before he woke up. She didn't want to tell him face-to-face, because then he'd ask questions and want an explanation, one that she wasn't able to give. A lump of shame formed in her throat at the thought of telling him about her past. She'd told only one other person about Gary, and her friend's look of pity and disgust was burned in her memory. She did not want to see that expression on James's face.

Moving cautiously, she eased out of the bed and began to gather her clothes. It was still early; the birds had only just begun to greet the new day with sporadic chirps. James would probably sleep in after last night's activities, but she still tried to be as quiet as possible as she moved around the room. After spotting her socks over by the doorway, she retrieved them and sat gingerly on the edge of the bed to put her shoes on.

She felt a twinge of guilt as she tied her shoes, but she ruthlessly pushed it down. Leaving was the best thing she could do, both for her and for James. She was damaged goods, and he deserved better. In fact, he'd probably thank her for this later. No one wanted to be saddled with an emotionally unavailable woman with trust issues. Better to make a clean break now, before things got complicated.

Her heart couldn't take another blow.

James woke in stages, rubbing his eyes against the pale pink light of dawn that flooded his bedroom. His jaw cracked in a yawn as he stretched, reaching across the bed to pull Kelly into his arms so he could bury his nose in her hair.

His hands came up empty.

Awake now, he sat up in the rumpled bed to find her sitting on the edge, tying her shoes.

"Kelly?" Her name came out as a croak, so he cleared his throat and tried again. "Everything okay?"

He reached over and placed a hand on her shoulder. She stiffened at the contact, so he withdrew, alarmed at her reaction. What was wrong? Had he hurt her last night? He quickly reviewed his memories of their encounter, but came up blank. She had been an eager participant, and he had made sure she was satisfied before seeing to his own pleasure. Surely she would have told him if he had done something wrong?

His stomach dropped as another thought dawned. Did she regret sleeping with him?

She finished tying her shoes and sat for a moment, not looking at him. The silence between them grew heavy as he took in her appearance—hair pulled back, fully dressed, shoes on. She was leaving, and he was certain she would have left without a word had he not woken up in time to catch her.

She stood, turning to face him with a heavy sigh. "James, I was just—"

"Leaving. Yes, I can see that." Not wanting to have this conversation while naked and lying down, he grabbed the blanket and wrapped it around his hips as he stood. "Any reason you were sneaking out?"

She looked down, her cheeks flushing a pretty rose. "I wasn't sneaking out. I was just leaving quietly."

"Uh-huh." He ran his hand through his hair, wincing inwardly as he felt the bed-head spikes. Putting his awkward appearance firmly out of his mind, he summoned his best interrogation voice. "Why are you leaving?"

She was silent for several seconds, then spoke in a near whisper. "I just think it's best if I go."

He took a step forward but stopped as she took a small step back. "Kelly," he said gently, "I don't want you to go. I'm sorry if I've said or done anything to give you that impression."

She looked down at the floor again, chewing her lower lip.

"Last night was special to me," he continued, slowly moving to stand in front of her. He reached out and tilted her chin up with a finger, and his gut twisted when he saw the glitter of tears in her eyes. She was clearly upset, but he couldn't for the life of him figure out what he'd done.

"James, please," she pleaded in a choked voice. "Don't make this harder than it already is."

He frowned down at her in confusion. "What's going on here? I thought we had a great time last night."

She nodded, dashing away tears with the back of her hand. "We did. Last night was—it was amazing. I just have to go now." She moved to walk past him, but he grabbed her arms to keep her in place. She didn't resist his hold, but she wouldn't look at him, directing her gaze at his belly button.

"Kelly, what is this about? Have I done something?" Exasperation crept into his voice as she shook her head mutely. "Then why are you running away? Do you regret sleeping with me? Because if that's the problem, we can go back to being just friends."

A ghost of a smile flitted across her lips before she shook her head again. "I don't regret it," she said softly. "Please understand that I need to go. It's nothing you did." She met his eyes then, holding his gaze as she repeated her assurance. "You were wonderful. But I can't stay, and please don't ask me why."

He held her a moment longer, searching her face for a sign or any expression or gesture that would explain her desire to leave so suddenly. She bore his gaze with a neutral expression, as if simply waiting for him to give up his scrutiny. Seeing that she wasn't going to tell him anything, he released her with a sigh.

"I don't know what's going on with you this morning, but you clearly don't trust me enough to tell me."

She bit her lip at that, and he knew his words had hit home. He studied her for another moment, hoping she'd fill the silence and tell him her reasons for running away, but she remained quiet.

He stepped back, giving her space to move. She waited until he sat on the edge of the bed before walking to the doorway. She paused at the threshold, and a flutter of hope flared to life in his chest. Had she changed her mind?

"I'm sorry, James," she said, her voice wavering. "You're a great guy, and—" Her voice broke, and she swallowed hard before continuing, "And you deserve better than me."

Then she was gone, leaving him staring after her in silent confusion.

Chapter 2

September

Professor George Collins strode through the parking garage toward his car, whistling cheerfully as he fished for his keys. He was looking forward to the promise of the weekend, ready to spend some quality time with his wife. Ruth's oncologist had given them the good news about her remission on Monday, and they were going to a B and B in Annapolis to celebrate. The doctor's words had lifted a weight off his shoulders, and for the first time in months, George felt as if he could breathe again.

He stopped next to his car, fingers still searching for the keys. Damn things must have slipped to the bottom of the bag again. He really should just keep them in his pocket so—

"Evening, Professor."

He froze at the smooth voice behind him. Fear skittered across his skin like ants on parade, and his bag fell from his shoulder, hitting the ground with a dull thud. His mouth suddenly dry, he swallowed convulsively a few times as he turned to face the man he had hoped to never see again.

His visitor cut a dashing figure in black slacks and a tan overcoat, a newspaper folded under his arm. His blond curls were perfectly tousled, and his wire-rimmed glasses lent him an academic air. No one would give this man a second look, much less think of him as evil. George, however, had come to think of him as the devil.

And it seemed the devil had come to collect.

"I thought we had a deal," the man said calmly.

George forced himself to make eye contact. "What do you mean?"

"Did you see the headline this morning, Professor?"

George shook his head mutely in response, not trusting his voice a second time. He knew the man already thought him weak, and his quavering voice would only add to that impression.

The man unfolded the newspaper with a snap as he stepped forward. George resisted the urge to step back, instead fixing his gaze on the print in front of him.

Food Poisoning at Local Restaurant Kills One, Sickens Ten.

He looked up to find the man staring down at him, blue eyes blazing. "I don't see the problem—it clearly worked."

The man let out a sigh. "Not well enough. You told

us it would sicken hundreds, not just ten people. Furthermore, the mortality rate is unacceptable."

"Wait just a minute," George began, the affront to his professional pride getting the better of his fear. "How can you say this is my fault? Maybe you guys didn't distribute it properly or store it correctly. I told you after I supplied you with the bug that it was your show. It's not my fault if you didn't follow my instructions."

The man took another step forward, forcing George back against his car. His bravado drained from his body like air from a balloon as the man leaned over him.

"We followed your instructions to the letter, Professor," he hissed, his breath warm on George's cheek. "We did everything you said, and yet it did not work."

"But it did," George protested weakly. "People got sick."

He jumped as a gloved fist landed next to his head.

"As I said, not enough people were affected. We cannot use this as a weapon if it will be thought of as a natural outbreak." The man pulled back slightly and reached into his coat.

George let out a sob as his knees gave out, and he fell to the ground. Gulping for air, he tried to focus on Ruth, but he couldn't conjure up her face. All he could think was that he was going to die here, in the parking garage, shot by the devil.

The man rolled his eyes and withdrew his hand, holding out a business card. "I knew we shouldn't have used you," he muttered, reaching down and pulling George roughly to his feet. George leaned back against the car, not trusting his legs to hold him. He silently agreed with the man—he was not cut out for this. He had agreed to provide the bacteria in exchange for money to pay for Ruth's treatments, but as soon as he had made the deal, he'd regretted it.

"Here's how it's going to work, Professor. You're going to give us another sample. I want you to call this number when it's ready for pickup." He pressed the card into George's sweaty hand and continued, "You're also going to come with us, so that there are no mistakes this time."

"What? No, I can't—"

"Yes, you can. And you will." He reached into his jacket again, this time pulling out a photograph. "She's looking much better, your wife." He turned the photo around, and George blinked in shock as he recognized Ruth emerging from her doctor's office, holding his hand. The picture had been taken as they'd left her appointment on Monday. "It would be a shame if something were to happen to her."

George crumpled at the threat, knowing this man wouldn't hesitate to hurt Ruth. "I'll do it," he whispered, hating himself for the weakness that had made him agree to the deal in the first place. "But I need time to modify the bacteria."

The man stepped back with a satisfied smile. "I thought as much. Enjoy your weekend in Annapolis with your wife, but don't keep me waiting. You have five days to deliver my product, or I will take it out on her."

George watched him walk away, despair settling over him with every breath he took. He dropped to his knees and dry heaved, then leaned back against the car, gasping lungfuls of exhaust-scented air like a landed fish. There had to be a way out of this. His thoughts raced as he tried to come up with a solution. Maybe he could take Ruth and leave, flee the city and never come back. But no, they knew about the B and B, which meant they probably had him under surveillance.

They'll find me. Of that he was certain.

He briefly considered going to the police but quickly dismissed the thought. He was an accomplice. Even though he had modified the bacteria to be less lethal, he was still involved. At times, the guilt of that knowledge was overwhelming, but he wasn't willing to leave Ruth. She was still so fragile, and he knew the authorities would not hesitate to put him in jail, away from his wife.

Picking up his bag, George struggled to his feet, feeling every one of his fifty-five years. For Ruth's sake, he was going to have to cooperate with the monster. He pulled out his keys and climbed into the car. His hands shook so badly that it took him three tries to get the key into the ignition, but he finally started the car and pulled out of the parking space.

This will be the last time, he promised himself as he drove, merging onto the freeway as he headed home to his wife. *The absolute last time,* he repeated.

But no matter how many times he said it, he didn't believe it.

Caleb stood in the shadows, watching as Dr. Collins slowly picked himself up off the ground. The man was obviously flustered, and the pinched expression on his face communicated his distress as clearly as any words.

"Thank God he didn't piss himself," Caleb muttered, shifting slightly from side to side and shoving his hands into his coat pockets.

Collins had looked as if he'd seen a ghost, and in a way, he had. Caleb prided himself on staying behind the scenes, away from prying eyes. To be visible was to make yourself a target, and he had no intention of painting a bull's-eye on his back. The fact that he'd had to make this little visit today was a nuisance but not a huge risk. Besides, some messages had to be delivered in person.

Given the fear that had entered Collins's eyes at the mention of his wife, Caleb figured he'd made his point.

He waited for Collins to speed out of the garage before heading to his own car. He hadn't bothered to forge a university parking pass—there were no guards or security cameras monitoring the area, so he wasn't worried about being seen. Besides, there were so many students coming and going every day, no one was likely to notice or remember the nondescript black sedan he drove.

He slid into the driver's seat with a sigh. *Someday,* he promised himself, *I'm going to upgrade this POS.* He glanced up at the dog-eared picture taped to the sun visor. The sporty, sleek roadster winked back at him, taunting him with the promise of speed. It was a beautiful car, all curvy, graceful lines and paint so glossy that it looked wet. A car he deserved, and one he would have—just as soon as he retired. A car like that was for a man who wasn't afraid to show off, not one who had to live in the shadows.

His cell phone buzzed against his chest. He pulled it from his pocket and glanced down at the display, gritting his teeth as he recognized the glowing white number. *Damn him!*

"I told you not to contact me."

There was a pause, as if his caller hadn't expected such a harsh greeting. He heard the man suck in a breath.

"I don't think this is working out."

Caleb took off his glasses and pinched the bridge of his nose. *God save me from whiny CEOs....*

"And why is that?" he asked, working to keep his voice calm and even.

Dr. Glen Wilkins, CEO and heir extraordinaire of Wilkins Pharmaceuticals, lowered his voice. "Because I don't think—"

"Are you alone?" Caleb snapped, his patience running thin. Customer or not, Wilkins shouldn't be calling if he had company.

"What? Yes, of course I am."

"Then speak up," Caleb commanded. "I can't hear you when you whisper like that."

Wilkins cleared his throat. "I was saying I don't think your methods are acceptable."

"Is that so?"

"Yes. Did you see the paper today?"

Caleb glanced over at the newspaper lying in the passenger seat. "I did. What's your point?"

"People are *dying*," Wilkins said. "Doesn't that bother you at all?"

Caleb rolled his eyes. The old man was such a hypocrite. "You hired me to do a job, did you not?"

"Yes, but—"

"And you knew my reputation, and the reputation of my organization, when you contacted me." It wasn't a question. Wilkins had received their information from another satisfied customer, a regular practice in his line of work. There was no way he hadn't known the score when he'd picked up the phone that first time.

"Well, yes."

"So why are you getting cold feet now?"

"It doesn't seem to be working," Wilkins said, his voice taking on a whiny edge that made Caleb's fillings ache. "Drug sales haven't improved in the wake of the outbreaks. I thought you said people would be clamoring for our medication!"

"I did say that," Caleb replied, not liking the man's petulant tone. "Do you remember what else I said?"

There was a pause, as if Wilkins was trying to recall their conversation. "I don't know."

"I told you to be patient. This isn't going to happen overnight."

Undeterred, Wilkins tried another tack. "I thought we were just going to make people sick. I didn't know people were going to die!"

"Oh, please," Caleb retorted. "Enough with the false concern for your fellow man. The only reason you're upset is because dead people don't buy antibiotics."

Wilkins sputtered at that, but Caleb ignored him. "You need to give this time to work. An outbreak here, an outbreak there—soon the authorities will piece it together and then it will be national news. People will be clamoring for your antibiotic, just like everyone stockpiled Cipro after the anthrax mailings."

"And you're sure this won't be traced back to me?"

"As sure as I can be. It would help if you would follow my instructions and didn't contact me again."

Wilkins ignored the warning. "How much longer? We need to start turning a profit quickly, or the company will have to fold. I can't let that happen—my grandfather built this company, and I'll be damned if I let it die on my watch. We're the largest employer in town. If we have to close, the town will collapse."

Caleb sighed, his fingers itching to reach through the phone and strangle the old man. He was probably sitting in his mahogany-paneled office, swirling his fifty-year-old Chivas Regal and pondering how to spend his next bonus check. If the company did go under, there was no way he was going down with the ship, and his "concern for the employees" act was wearing a bit thin.

"I'm putting the final pieces in place now," Caleb said, his thoughts drifting back to Collins. "I can't give you an exact schedule, but soon."

Wilkins harrumphed, evidently displeased with such a vague answer. That was just too bad. There was no way Caleb was going to share sensitive information, especially with someone as hotheaded as Wilkins.

"Let me remind you that I am in charge of this operation," he said coolly. "I am speaking to you now as a courtesy, but I do not report to you."

"You listen to me, you little snot," Wilkins shot back, anger making him brave. "I paid for your services, and I want to know what's going on. Do you know what I can do to you if you don't cooperate with me?"

Caleb laughed. "Nothing. You can do nothing to me."

Wilkins sputtered. "Now, see here—"

"What would you do, Mr. Wilkins? Turn me in? I doubt it—you know if you did, I'd sell you out before the lock clicked into place on the cell door. Do you think you can kill me? You can try, but I should warn you, I'm very well connected. What does that leave you?"

"You must have family," Wilkins said, his voice now low and threatening.

Caleb felt a dull throb in his chest at the mention of family, but he ignored it. "Sorry to disappoint, but they're all dead."

"You're not as untouchable as you think. I can come up with something."

"You're welcome to try," Caleb agreed. "In the meantime, let me do my job and stay out of my way."

Wilkins paused, clearly weighing his options. "Don't try to double-cross me, boy."

Caleb ignored the insult, knowing a careless tone would get under the man's skin more than any verbal retort. "Wouldn't dream of it. Don't call me again."

He hung up before Wilkins could respond, feeling a small, childish spurt of satisfaction at having gotten the last word. The man was a dinosaur, a throwback to the days of the three-martini lunch, when deals were sealed with cigars and handshakes. He was used to being in charge, accustomed to having his minions defer to his every word, but Caleb refused to play the game. Wilkins might be the customer, but that didn't mean he was right.

He leaned over and pulled a D.C. city map out of the glove compartment, unfolding it across the steering wheel. Time to pick out the next target....

"Reynolds!" Kevin Carmichael stood in the doorway of his office, his summons a loud bark that carried over the hum of activity in the room. James made eye contact and held up his hand, silently asking for a few minutes. Carmichael narrowed his eyes at the delay but nodded and turned back into his office, allowing James a chance to finish up his conversation.

"Uh-huh. Yes. Well, I appreciate the call, and we will definitely keep an eye open….You, too. Have a nice day." He hung up with a sigh and rubbed his eyes, taking a moment before heading into Carmichael's office. It was only noon, and already the day was dragging.

"Any new leads?" Thomas asked, looking up from some paperwork.

James shook his head. "Mrs. Gerard was just telling me that she remembered a suspicious-looking young man hanging around by the salad bar that night and asked if we had checked him out yet. Based on her description, it sounds like she's talking about the busboy who maintained the salad bar."

"And he's already been cleared."

"Yeah." James sighed. "The kid is a straight-arrow honor student, and there's nothing to suggest he knew anything about the tampering. She's just being a drama queen."

"Were the surveillance tapes helpful at all?" Thomas held out the dish of jelly beans on his desk, and James took a few, popping them into his mouth before answering. As far as lunches went, it wasn't the greatest, but it would do in a pinch.

He shook his head, swallowing the fruity glob of sugar and reaching for a few more. "No. Unfortunately, the angle of the camera didn't cover all of the salad bar, so we can't see the end with the cottage-cheese bin. No one remembers anything out of the ordinary or anyone behaving strangely, so we really don't have any good leads."

"Sounds like these guys are pros."

"Well, they did their homework, that's for sure." James grabbed a notebook and pen and stood, knowing he couldn't put off Carmichael's summons any longer. "Thanks for lunch."

Thomas grinned up at him. "Anytime, man."

He wended his way through the maze of desks and rapped lightly on Carmichael's partially closed door, then pushed it open after the other man beckoned him in.

"Any news?"

James sat in the metal-framed chair in front of Carmichael's desk, stretching out his legs in a vain attempt to find a comfortable position. "Just Mrs. Gerard turning in the busboy."

"Sanders? Was that his name?" At James's nod, Carmichael snorted. "That kid is as innocent as they come."

"I know, but in her mind, any young man who wears a hat indoors is clearly suspect."

"Doesn't she know that's part of the uniform?"

James jerked his shoulder up in a shrug. "Probably not, and I wasn't about to waste time trying to explain it to her."

"Good. I have more important things for you to do."

James leaned forward and uncapped his pen. "What's up?"

Carmichael pulled a folder off the top of a precariously balanced stack of papers on the corner of his desk. "We got the lab report back from the science guys. They've identified the bacteria and have started characterizing the modifications."

"Tell me we have something," James said, feeling a surge of adrenaline at the possibility. He'd been working this case for weeks without a break, and he was exhausted and out of leads.

Carmichael's smile was pure satisfaction. "We do."

James grinned, his annoyance with Mrs. Gerard fading in the face of this good news. This could be the information he needed to break the case wide open.

Carmichael passed the lab report across his desk, and James took a moment to skim the printout. It was full of scientific jargon, which immediately made him think of Kelly. She'd know just how to translate these findings into plain English. He felt a pang of longing and regret, and firmly pushed thoughts of her out of his mind.

He had tried to get in touch with her a few days after their encounter, but she'd never returned his calls. It was clear she wanted nothing to do with him, so he'd left her alone. He wasn't going to chase her down and demand an explanation, but he couldn't deny her actions had stung. This was not the time to think of her, though, not when things were finally starting to look up.

"There are only four labs in the country that work with this particular strain of bacteria," Carmichael said, his voice interrupting James's musings.

"Three of them are on the West Coast," James murmured. "But the last one…this one is local," he said, looking up at Carmichael. "Do we think this is a neighborhood job?"

"Yes. The guy who runs the lab has been conveniently out of town for the past couple of weeks, which is pretty suspicious. We've sent field agents in California to check out the other labs, but I think this is our guy. I want you to head over there this afternoon."

"Since the guy is out of town, is there anyone in particular we need to talk to?"

Carmichael nodded. "Yeah, there's a postdoctoral fellow in the lab who seems to run things. A doctor." He shuffled through some more papers, pulling out a Post-it note and squinting at the writing. "Dr. Jarvis. Bring him in for questioning."

James sucked in a breath, his stomach dropping. "Dr. Jarvis? Dr. Kelly Jarvis?"

Carmichael frowned and checked the note again. "Don't know about the Kelly part, but yeah, Dr. K. Jarvis. Do you know her?" He raised narrowed eyes, and James fought to keep a neutral expression on his face.

"If it's Kelly Jarvis, then yes, I know her. We used to be friends." What the hell had she gotten herself into? The Kelly he knew would never participate in something like this, but maybe she'd changed in the past few months.

He sucked in a breath as a new thought hit him. Was that why she'd left? So he wouldn't discover her involvement? He gritted his teeth as he reevaluated their encounter in a new, ugly light. *You deserve better than me,* she had said before leaving. Was that her guilt talking?

"Used to be? What happened?" Carmichael's question snapped him back to the present.

James deliberately relaxed his jaw, hoping the other man hadn't noticed his agitation. If Carmichael thought there was something personal between him and Kelly, he'd yank him from the case. He hadn't worked this long and hard to be benched in the final stages of the investigation.

He shrugged, trying for nonchalance. "We just fell out of touch," he explained, hoping Carmichael wouldn't press for more details. It was mostly true—after that night, they hadn't spoken again.

"At this time, she doesn't appear to be involved."

James felt a swell of relief, and some of his anger faded. It must have showed on his face, because Carmichael studied him intently for a beat. "If there is a conflict of interest here, I need to know about it now."

James shook his head before the other man had finished talking. "No. No conflict at all. Like I said, we used to be friends, but we're not now. Hell, that may even help us. Since she knows me already, she'll probably be more likely to talk to me."

Carmichael nodded thoughtfully. "Maybe. But if something comes up, I want to know about it. I won't have this investigation put in jeopardy."

"I understand." James stood, wanting to leave and compose his thoughts before bringing Kelly in for questioning.

"Reynolds."

He stopped at the door and turned back.

"You've done a great job on this investigation so far," Carmichael began, sounding a little uncertain.

James frowned. What was he trying to say?

"Thank you, sir."

Carmichael nodded. "You're a great agent, and I know part of what drives you is your...family history," he finished delicately.

James drew up his shoulders, waiting to see where

Carmichael was going with this. Why the hell was his boss bringing up the subject of his father?

"What I'm saying is, if you have to withdraw from this investigation for personal reasons, I'll understand. You've already proven yourself to me, and I don't want to risk this case in any way."

James met his gaze, resisting the urge to tell the other man to go to hell. Bobby Reynolds had tarnished the family name by taking bribes and botching investigations for the highest bidder, but James would never risk a case—he wasn't his father. "I understand, sir," James said stiffly. "I'll be back with Dr. Jarvis in about an hour."

Carmichael looked as if he wanted to say more, but he settled for a nod. "I'll let the rest of the team know."

James left the office and walked to the men's room, which was blessedly empty. He splashed water on his face and swallowed a handful; the cool liquid relaxed the tight muscles of his throat. What kind of mess was Kelly in? And more important, did she even know, or was she truly innocent in all of it?

He blotted his face dry with a square of paper towel. Up until five minutes ago, he would have sworn Kelly didn't have it in her to fall in league with a terrorist group. But if history had taught him anything, it was that people weren't always who they seemed to be. His father, his friend Steve…both of them seemingly good people who had made all the wrong choices. Was he going to have to add Kelly to that list?

He glanced in the mirror and straightened his tie, then brushed his hair back into place. He looked calm and professional, his outer image at odds with the emotional turmoil this new lead had created. He had worked hard to put his disappointment and anger toward his father behind him, and he hated that it had popped up again after a few words from his boss. *Get it together.*

He was too close to breaking open the case to let his emotions get the better of him now.

Kelly pushed away from the microscope and stretched, arching her back as she reached up to massage her aching neck. She had been looking at slides most of the day, and although it was only two in the afternoon, she was heading home early. Two weeks of burning the candle at both ends had caught up with her, and she was exhausted.

She switched off the microscope and began gathering up her slides as thoughts of a hot bubble bath and a glass of wine danced in her head. It wouldn't be the same as drinks with James, but it would do in a pinch.

She shook her head as a pang of longing hit, the way it always did when she thought of James. She missed him, missed their regular Friday night conversations. More than that, though, she missed his friendship.

Not for the first time, she regretted walking out on him five months ago. The irony of it all was that in the months since she'd left, she'd come to realize that not all men were Gary in disguise, just waiting to hurt her. James especially didn't deserve that kind of suspicion. She'd obsessively gone back over their interactions, looking for any sign that she'd been right to leave, but in the end, she could only conclude that he was a genuinely kind and decent man.

Yes, she had been scared of what their night together had meant, but she had ruined things by running away.

She had treated him badly, and she carried the regret with her on a daily basis.

Lost in her thoughts, she moved on autopilot as she placed the glass slides in their cardboard folder, paying little attention to the order in which they were stowed. After the last slide went in, she snapped the folder shut and grabbed her notebook.

She stepped into the hall, eager to get everything put away and to duck out before someone asked her a question. With Dr. Collins, the lab head, on vacation for the past couple weeks, Kelly was the de facto group leader. Normally she didn't mind helping out the other lab techs and graduate students, but today she was tired and wanted nothing more than to be left alone. She moved quickly and kept her head down as she walked, trying hard to look unapproachable as she entered the main lab.

She noticed the shoes first. A pair of brown men's dress loafers, to be exact, right in the middle of the aisle. Shoes that nice were *never* found in a research lab, and she frowned as she raised her gaze up suit-clad legs, a trim waist and broad shoulders. Her eyes finally landed on a face she never thought she'd see again.

Her body flushed hot then cold as she stared at James in openmouthed shock. She took a half step forward, wanting to touch him, to hug him, but his stern expression stopped her. With his mouth pressed into a thin line and his arms crossed over his chest, he looked rather forbidding and not at all happy to see her.

They stared at each other for a few seconds until she shook herself free of the moment. She had to take control of the situation. Faking a confidence she didn't feel, she asked "Can I help you?" in what she hoped was a professional tone. What the hell was he doing here? Why, after all these months, had he come to find her?

He arched a brow, disbelief plain on his face. "That's all you have to say to me? 'Can I help you?' Are you kidding me?"

She tried to keep her voice aloof, wanting to seem unaffected by his presence. "I don't know what you mean."

He took a step toward her and she reflexively stepped back, her shoulder bumping into the door frame.

Dammit, she thought. *Act normal.*

It had been over a year since she'd been hit, but whenever she felt anxious or upset, her nerves got the better of her.

While her mind knew that he wouldn't hurt her, her body was taking no chances. He was a powerful presence when he was angry, his eyes bright and his body tense as he stood in front of her, staring at her with his angular features arranged into a fierce scowl. Her heart thumped in her chest and nausea gripped her stomach in a sickening fist. *He won't hit me.* She wiped a slick palm down her thigh. *He's not Gary.*

After what seemed like ages, James's expression changed. His eyes grew considering as he stared down at her, and she had the sneaking suspicion he knew. Not all the details of her past, but enough to suspect something. He took a step back to give her more room, and she slowly exhaled, trying not to look too relieved at the return of some personal space.

He held her eyes for a moment, then looked down with a sigh, running his hand through his hair. He turned away, and she caught a whiff of his cologne. *Oh, God, he still smells the same….*

"So, why are you here?"

He snorted and shook his head. "Just business, is that it, Kelly?" For a split second, he dropped his guard and she watched as confusion, hurt and anger danced across his face. The weight of guilt settled on her shoulders and she swallowed hard, hating herself in this moment for having hurt him.

"I—I thought after what happened…" she stammered. "I didn't think you'd want to see me again."

"You know, I could have forgiven you for running away," he said slowly. "But when you didn't return my calls…" He shook his head and looked down. "Well, I suppose it doesn't matter now."

Pushing down her regret, she repeated her earlier question. "What are you doing here?"

The question roused him from his introspection. He drew himself up, his professional mask back in place. "I'm working a case, and I need your help."

He needed her? What could she possibly do to help him? She didn't know anything about the law. Although, given the way things had ended between them, he probably wouldn't have turned up here unless it was absolutely necessary. "What do you need from me?"

"I need you to come to the office with me, and we'll talk there."

"But…I have plans," she sputtered, thinking longingly of the bubble bath and wine. After this shock, she'd need to add some chocolate, too. It was only fair.

"Going out for a drink?"

Ouch. She supposed she deserved that, but it still stung. "No," she said, struggling to keep the hurt out of her voice.

A quick flash of what may have been guilt passed over his face, but before he could say anything, she held up her hand. "Just let me get my bag." At his nod, she turned and walked over to her alcove of an office, taking a moment to shut down her computer. She stood with her back to him while the machine powered down, trying to arrange her features into a neutral expression. The last thing she wanted was for him to see her confusion and the attraction she still felt for him. First things first—figure out why the FBI wanted to talk to her, then deal with the shreds of her relationship with James.

She put the laptop in her desk drawer and grabbed her bag. "Let's go," she said, walking over to stand next to him.

They moved down the corridors in awkward silence, and he led her to a black sedan parked by the front door.

"How did you get this spot?" she asked, wanting to say something, anything, to break the tension. "I'm surprised security didn't tow your car."

"Being an FBI agent has its privileges," he commented, waiting for her to slide into the passenger seat, then shutting the door firmly. He was careful not to touch her, and given the set of his jaw, she supposed he was still angry, but whether at her or the situation, she didn't yet know. Probably a combination of both.

She was hyperaware of him as he drove, all her senses tuned in to the man sitting next to her. She thought back to the last time they had been in a car together, how she'd taken his hand in hers and stroked his palm. She doubted he would welcome such a gesture now.

"So why do you want to talk to me?" she said, hoping she could get him to open up a little.

He took the next exit and slowed as they approached

a red light. "It's nothing to worry about," he replied, glancing over at her after the car stopped. "Just standard procedure."

"Standard procedure for what?" she pressed.

"We'll be there soon," he replied, accelerating away from the intersection. "All your questions will be answered shortly."

She sat back in the seat, dissatisfied with his response. Her stomach felt as if it were being squeezed in a vice, and she tasted the coffee she'd had at lunch. Why would the FBI want to talk to her? She wiped damp palms on her pants as she considered what James had told her, which wasn't much. *Standard procedure* was vague and gave her no clue as to what they wanted with her. Of course, given the way their reunion had gone, he probably wasn't interested in easing her mind.

She stared out the window at the downtown buildings, absently watching the people walking past. She hadn't done anything wrong, so it was unlikely the FBI was investigating her. As far as she knew, she didn't know any criminals, but who could really say these days? She watched enough late-night TV to know that people weren't always who they seemed to be. Wouldn't there be some sign of trouble, though? Her thoughts tumbled around and around, spinning like a centrifuge, getting her nowhere.

"Don't worry." She glanced over to see James watching her, his dark brown eyes looking like pools of melted chocolate. "You're not in trouble."

"I know," she said, her voice ringing with a confidence she didn't feel.

He didn't bother to mask the sarcasm in his tone.

"Right. That's why I can practically hear you worrying."

She dropped the act with a sigh. "Can you blame me? I've never been questioned by the authorities before, and you've got the cloak-and-dagger act going on."

"Fair enough. It's just easier to explain everything back at headquarters, so you don't have to repeat yourself over and over again to the different members of the team." His voice was deep and soothing, and she let the comforting words wash over her. She wanted so badly to touch him, to apologize with her body for the hurt she'd caused him. Even now, after messing things up so badly, he was still kind to her. Her stomach sank as she realized once again what a good guy he was and what a huge mistake she'd made when she'd left and turned her back on him.

He pulled into a parking space and cut the engine, then turned to face her. She refused to look at him, not wanting him to see the guilt and regret she was sure were written on her face. "We're here," he said softly.

He unbuckled his seat belt and moved to get out of the car, but she placed a hand on his arm to stop him. "James," she began, then paused to swallow the lump in her throat. "I never meant to hurt you," she whispered.

"I'm not going to lie," he said softly. "Waking up to find you leaving was a disappointment. But…" He drifted off, staring out the windshield as if fascinated by the sight of the other parked cars. "But I think I know why you did it."

She nodded, not wanting to correct whatever assumptions he'd made about her motivations for leaving. She wasn't ready to have that conversation with

him, and she especially didn't want to tell him about
Gary while sitting in a car in the FBI parking garage.

"Is there anything you want to tell me before we go
in, Kelly? Anything at all?"

His tone was resigned, as if he knew he was about
to hear bad news. What was going on?

"No," she said, frowning at him. "What's this about,
James? I thought you said I wasn't in any trouble."

He sighed, the sound of a man with the weight of
the world on his shoulders. "You're not. Come on. Let's
go. They're waiting for us."

James climbed out of the car and took his time ad-
justing his suit jacket, carefully smoothing the wrinkles out and reaching up to straighten his tie. Seeing
her again had thrown him for a loop, and he needed to
get his equilibrium back.

He'd been angry after she'd left, the sting of rejection quickly piercing the morning-after glow. He had
thought their encounter was something special, the beginning of something new and exciting, but she clearly
hadn't felt the same way. It hurt to know she hadn't
cared about him the way he had about her, but more
than that, he missed her friendship. He'd thought he
was over it by now, but seeing her again had brought
all those feelings rushing back.

It seemed his heart didn't care that she might be involved with terrorists.

The sound of the car door slamming behind him
shook him from his musings, and he turned to find
Kelly standing with her arms wrapped around her
waist, her eyes on the ground. A lock of auburn hair
had slipped from her ponytail, making him want to

push it behind her ear to keep it out of her face. Despite the brave front she tried to present, she looked so small and scared standing there alone. An ember of protectiveness flared to life inside his chest, along with the urge to tuck her against his side and comfort her with a hug. He squashed the desire like he would an invading bug—he had a job to do, and he had neither the energy nor the time to worry about what she was feeling. He'd made that mistake before.

"This way, Dr. Jarvis." He gestured with his arm as he rounded the front of the car, indicating the bank of elevators to the far right. She waited for him to reach her side before falling into step with him. They walked to the elevators in silence, the only sound the echo of their footsteps in the garage. James fished his ID badge out of his jacket pocket, scanned it in front of the card reader and pushed the button to call the elevator.

While they waited, he glanced at Kelly out of the corner of his eye. She stood ramrod straight, her shoulders set and her jaw clenched. It seemed his earlier reassurances in the car hadn't relaxed her for long.

"There's no need to worry," he said, turning to look at her fully. She glanced up at him, brows drawn together in a slight frown. Again he felt the urge to comfort her, to reach up and run his finger over the wrinkle between her eyebrows, to smooth away the line. Instead he shoved his hands into his pockets with a bit more force than necessary.

"I can't help it," she said a little sheepishly. "I'm a worrier—it's what I do."

They stepped onto the empty elevator car in unison, and he swiped his badge again before pressing the button for the eighth floor. "We're just going to ask you some questions as part of our investigation. You're not under any suspicion, and this isn't going to be an interrogation."

"No bright lamps shined into my face and a 'good cop, bad cop' routine, then?" she asked with a weak smile.

He appreciated her attempt at humor in the face of her fear. "You watch too much TV," he replied and was rewarded with a quick grin before her lips returned to a thin line.

"Sometimes my imagination gets the better of me," she admitted, her voice trailing off as the elevator doors opened and he guided her out of the car.

She hesitated, seemingly taken aback by the activity in front of her. The floor had an open configuration, making it one large room with the desks arranged in rows, forming a maze of sorts. The space buzzed with life as agents spoke on the phone, typed or moved about the room. Afternoon light streamed in from the wall of windows on the right, while the left wall was dominated by a map of the greater D.C. area and posters of the FBI's most wanted.

James directed Kelly to the back of the room, walking her through the maze of desks and agents. Her head swiveled from side to side as they moved, and he could tell she was taking it all in. For the most part, the agents ignored them, a few raising their hands in a wave or acknowledging him with a quick nod. He returned their greetings with a nod of his own and steered Kelly into one of the conference rooms lining the back wall.

"Have a seat." He pulled out a chair and she sat down, folding her hands and placing them on the table.

"Can I get you something to drink?"

"Do you have Coke? I could use the caffeine."

"Sure thing. I'll be right back." He walked out of the room and turned right, snagging a Coke from the group fridge in the corner of the room. On his way back to the conference room, he stopped at Kevin Carmichael's office and rapped on the door.

"Yeah?"

James stuck his head in and found his boss behind his desk, jacket off, shirtsleeves rolled up, wearing a sour expression, as if he had just taken a sip of bad coffee. His salt-and-pepper hair stuck out in multiple directions, and he was even now reaching up to run his hand through it for what had to be the millionth time today.

"Dr. Jarvis is here," he said, and Kevin's expression morphed from disgusted to pleased.

"Excellent," he said, standing up and rolling his sleeves out. "She's in the conference room?"

"Yes. She's a little nervous, too," James added.

Kevin paused in the act of putting on his jacket. "Why do you think that is?" he asked, slowly sliding the suit coat into place. "Think she has something to hide?"

James shook his head. Although he wasn't convinced she was completely innocent, going after her with guns blazing was not the way to get her to cooperate. "I think she's just worried about being here. She's not used to dealing with the law, and I don't think she has any idea of what's going on."

"We'll see about that," Kevin muttered, moving toward the door.

James held up a hand. "Um, Kevin?" The older man stopped, a puzzled look on his face. James gestured to his own hair, moving his hand around to pantomime the frazzled mess sitting atop the other man's head. Kevin reached up and winced, then spun around and grabbed a comb from his desk drawer.

"Thanks," he said.

James nodded. "Meet you in there?"

"Yep. I'll just be a few seconds."

James returned to the conference room and placed the can in front of Kelly. She looked up with a grateful smile. "Thanks," she said quietly as she reached for the can and popped it open. She took a swig, closed her eyes and let out a sigh. "Perfect," she breathed.

James swallowed hard and took a seat across from her, trying not to stare at the smooth column of her neck as she took another sip of her drink. She had a small freckle at the base of her throat, right where her neck met the arch of her collarbone, and he had the sudden, vivid memory of pressing his lips to that spot.

He shifted slightly in his chair, dropping his gaze to the tabletop. He hadn't slept with anyone since their encounter, had been too busy and exhausted with work. His body remembered their night together, though, and was flaring to life at being so close to her again.

He glanced back up in time to see her lick her lips as she set the can down, and he almost groaned. Where the hell was Kevin? He didn't need this distraction in the middle of a case. He absolutely, positively could not get involved with this woman again, with her silky hair, hazel eyes and delicate features. No. He refused.

"Well," she began, her voice quiet. "Are we waiting for someone?"

As soon as the words left her lips, Kevin breezed into the room carrying a manila folder, his earlier disheveled appearance transformed into that of a polished professional. He pulled out a chair at the head of the table and sat, then scooted forward and rested his arms on the tabletop. Other people streamed into the room as he got settled, taking the remaining seats around the conference table. Kevin shot Kelly a dazzling smile, and she smiled in return, the expression freezing on her face as he fired his opening shot.

"So tell me, Dr. Jarvis. How long have you known your boss is a terrorist?"

Chapter 3

Kelly stared at the man sitting at the head of the table, blinking in shock. She must be hearing things. There was no way he had actually asked that.

"I'm sorry," she said, shaking her head in an attempt to clear her thoughts. "What did you just say?"

He leaned back in his chair and regarded her with a serious expression, all traces of his earlier smile gone. "I asked you how long you've known George Collins is a terrorist."

"But…" she sputtered, at a temporary loss for words. James had told her repeatedly that she was not a suspect of any kind, but apparently this agent thought she was guilty of something. Had James lied to her, or was he just out of the loop? She glanced across the table to find James watching the other man, a slight frown on his face. Was he surprised by the question, too?

"Who are you?" she said, wanting not only his name but a few seconds to gather her thoughts.

"My apologies." He sounded anything but contrite. "I'm Special Agent in Charge Kevin Carmichael." He introduced the other people in the room, but she didn't absorb their names.

Kelly traced the tab of the soda can with her finger as she spoke. "What makes you think George is a terrorist?" She glanced up to see Agent Carmichael lean back in his chair, a satisfied smile on his face.

"Do you read the paper, Dr. Jarvis?"

She frowned at the non sequitur. "Not as often as I should. What does that have to do with anything?"

He opened a manila file folder and pulled out a piece of paper. He pushed it across the table and Kelly read the headline: Food Poisoning at Local Restaurant Kills One, Sickens Ten. She skimmed the article, which detailed an outbreak of food poisoning in a District deli restaurant.

She frowned. "I don't understand," she said, pushing the article back across the table. Agent Carmichael carefully placed it in his folder before meeting her eyes.

"That outbreak was not your garden-variety cluster of food poisoning—the Health Department found that the causative agent was *Bacillus cereus*. The same bacteria that Dr. Collins works with."

"There must be some mistake," Kelly interjected. "The strain of *Bacillus cereus* we work with isn't associated with food-borne illness. In fact, it's actually used as a probiotic. People take it to help regulate their digestion, stuff like that."

"Exactly," James responded, drawing Kelly's attention. "That's why we got involved."

"The FBI? That doesn't make sense. Why wouldn't the CDC get involved?"

"Because the evidence suggested this was a crime, as opposed to a natural outbreak," James said.

"What evidence?"

"The bacteria was only found in the cottage-cheese bin of the salad bar, and only for the bin put out for consumption after 6:00 p.m. The Health Department tested the supply of cottage cheese found in the kitchen that was used to refill the bin, and there was no evidence of bacterial contamination. Also no evidence of the bacteria in the kitchen or any other area tested." Agent Carmichael paused, and Kelly gestured for him to continue. "Taken together, these facts suggest the cottage-cheese bin was dosed with the bacteria sometime after six, making this a deliberate event."

"I still don't understand," she said. "Even if someone drank a culture of our *Bacillus cereus*, it's unlikely they'd get ill. It's not considered a pathogen."

"This particular bacteria had been modified to express the anthrax toxin. This was a calculated bio-attack, designed to look like a natural outbreak of severe food poisoning," James said.

Kelly sat in silence, absorbing the news. A chill skittered down her spine, and she rubbed her hands over her arms in an attempt to smooth away the goose bumps that popped up on her skin. How many times did something like this happen? How many times was a supposedly accidental or natural event really a deliberate attempt by others to harm?

"Why do you think Dr. Collins has anything to do with this?" she asked, still not clear about his alleged connection to the event. "We're not the only lab that works with *Bacillus cereus.*"

Agent Carmichael glanced meaningfully at James. Kelly didn't understand what that look was supposed to convey, but apparently James did because he piped up. "That's true," he allowed. "But we contacted all the labs that regularly work with this bacteria, and they all told us the same thing—the strain identified in the outbreak was obtained from Dr. Collins's lab."

"Furthermore," Carmichael broke in, "their stocks are all accounted for. No missing vials. No suspicious activity."

"So you think it came from our lab," Kelly stated. It wasn't a question. She wouldn't be here if they didn't think the bacteria came from George's lab. However, that didn't necessarily mean George was at fault—any number of personnel could have accessed the bacteria and passed it along. She told them as much, but Agent Carmichael and James both shook their heads.

"The bacterial modifications suggest someone with know-how engineered this strain. Our experts tell us this isn't something a rotation student or glass washer would be able to do."

"Wait a second," she said, her brain finally kicking in. "You said the bacteria was modified to produce anthrax toxin?" At their nods, she continued, "So these people essentially had intestinal anthrax, which has a high mortality rate. But only one person died." They studied her silently, and she raised a brow, waiting for them to catch on. When they didn't speak, she let out a sigh. "Is it possible you made a mistake and that the bacteria wasn't modified at all?"

Carmichael shook his head firmly. "I wish it were

that simple. The lab showed that the gene for the anthrax toxin had been mutated to produce a less virulent form. Do you know how to do that?"

Kelly mutely nodded in the affirmative.

"Does anyone else in your lab know how to do that?"

She shook her head. No. She was the only postdoc; the others were graduate students, whose projects didn't include molecular biology, or undergraduate rotation students, who performed the most mundane of tasks.

"Were you aware that Dr. Collins's wife has cancer?"

Kelly jerked back in her chair, Carmichael's words hitting her like a blow. Ruth was sick? Why hadn't George said anything to her? Granted, he wasn't the most demonstrative person, but over the past several months their relationship had warmed somewhat, to the point that she would have expected him to tell her something major like this.

"I take it from your reaction Dr. Collins hadn't shared that news with you," James remarked drily.

"No, he hadn't," she whispered.

Carmichael opened his file folder again and withdrew another piece of paper. "This is a summary of account transfers made to Dr. Collins. As you can see, he received a substantial amount of money two months prior to the event and again one day after. I think you can appreciate that the timing is suspicious."

Kelly stared at the numbers in front of her, not really seeing them. Even she had to admit that this did not look good for George.

"We think Dr. Collins provided the modified bacteria in exchange for money, which he used to pay for his wife's chemotherapy." Carmichael leaned over the table, his voice low and urgent. "We need you to help us catch him, so we can find out who he's working for."

The weight of disappointment settled in Kelly's stomach, and she found it hard to breathe. In her heart of hearts, she knew Carmichael was right. It all made sudden, horrible sense: George's distractedness of late, the worry in his eyes. He had even snapped at her when she had arrived at the lab early on a Saturday and found him digging in the freezer. He had brushed it off, saying she had startled him, but now she realized he had probably been retrieving frozen stock and hadn't wanted anyone to know.

The worst part was, she could understand why he had done it. George doted on Ruth, loved her with everything he had, and everyone knew it. The fact that his devotion had been exploited for destructive purposes made it much more horrible.

"Can't you identify where the transfers came from?" she asked, gritting out the words from between clenched teeth. "How do you have access to his bank account anyway?"

A small smile flitted across Agent Carmichael's face. "The Patriot Act has substantially expanded our investigative freedom," he said. "That's neither here nor there, though. The transfers came from a Swiss bank account, and unfortunately, we can't determine the account owner."

"Why do you need me?" Surely they could figure this out on their own or use someone else. George hadn't confided anything to her, and she really had no idea how she could help them.

"Kelly," James said softly, leaning forward. "George trusts you—by all accounts, you run his lab. That gives you insight into his behavior, his habits, which means you can help us identify what he might do next or where he might be now."

"What do you mean, where he might be now? He's on vacation—has been for the past week and a half."

James shook his head, and Kelly felt her stomach drop. "He's not on vacation, Kelly. He's on the run. And we need to find him before the bad guys decide he's outlived his usefulness."

It was three hours before they finished questioning her. Kelly had lost track of time in the windowless conference room, but seeing the orange evening light streaming through the windows of the main room made her realize how late it had become.

She felt raw and exhausted, as if she was coming down with the flu. Agent Carmichael had questioned her over and over, going through one set of questions and then asking them again, sometimes changing up the order or the precise way he asked them. It was as if he was trying to catch her in a lie, except she honestly didn't know anything. He hadn't seemed satisfied with that, but it was all she had to give him.

James touched her elbow, making her jump. "Sorry," he murmured. "Let me take you home."

She didn't want to spend any more time in the company of the FBI, but she was too rattled to take the Metro home. James guided her out of the room, but before she had taken two steps into the main office, Agent Carmichael called out and they paused.

"If you think of anything, Dr. Jarvis, don't hesitate

to call." She looked back to see him stand and reach for the papers spread out on the conference table. He formed piles before tucking them back into the manila folder. He glanced up at her and she nodded. He held her gaze for a beat before turning back to his papers, accepting her response.

James touched her arm again, and they moved to the elevator. He waited until the doors shut before turning to look at her. "Are you doing okay?"

She barked out a laugh. "Am I okay? What do you think? I just spent my afternoon getting interrogated about the behavior and motivations of my boss, and you people don't believe me when I tell you that I have absolutely no idea what's going on."

"You're not in trouble," he said quietly. She looked up to find him regarding her with a serious expression, his dark brown eyes radiating reassurance. She found herself wanting to trust him, to believe his words, but she shook herself mentally. He had told her that she wasn't a suspect, but his boss clearly felt otherwise. That meant trusting him would most likely be a mistake.

"Forgive me if I don't quite believe you," she scoffed.

They walked in silence through the parking garage. Kelly gave him directions to her apartment and then turned to look out the window. The silence in the car was thick, but she didn't feel like talking. Unfortunately, her stomach betrayed her, emitting a loud rumble as James turned north onto Wisconsin Avenue.

"Hungry?"

It was pointless for her to deny it as her stomach rumbled again. "Yes."

"Feel like a hamburger?"

She almost laughed at the question because it was so normal compared to the ones she had spent the afternoon answering. "That sounds good."

"I know a place. We can stop in for a quick bite before I drop you off, if you're up for it," he offered. When she didn't respond right away, he continued, "I thought it could be a peace offering."

She smiled, unable to help herself. She wanted to clear the air between them, and dinner would be the perfect opportunity to start fresh. "That sounds nice," she said, feeling some of the tension leave the car.

He maneuvered into the right lane and turned into a nondescript shopping center. He parked in front of a storefront marked Buddy's, and a small neon sign indicated the place was open. Tinted windows hid the interior, but as she climbed out of the car, she caught a whiff of hot grease, and her stomach growled in appreciation.

The interior wasn't anything to write home about, but apparently she was the only person in D.C. who didn't know about the place, as it was packed full of diners. Families with young children and couples on dates sat at the booths lining the room and occupied the tables in the center, filling the air with the buzz of conversation.

The crowd and the heat of the grill made the place warm, and Kelly pulled her hair into a ponytail as she and James made their way to the counter to order. She studied the menu in silence, reading the choices again and again so she wouldn't have to look at James. She didn't know what to say to him and was starting to regret agreeing to dinner. What exactly were they supposed to talk about? *Sorry I wrecked our friendship and stomped on your feelings* wasn't exactly the most eloquent thing to say, even if it was the truth.

Kelly claimed an open table after picking up their sodas while James went to get napkins and condiments. She sat and sipped her soda, idly tracing the red checkerboard tablecloth with her fingertip. It had been one crazy day. If even half of what the FBI had told her was true, George was in way over his head.

James placed the napkins and condiments in the middle of the table, and Kelly pushed his soda toward him as he sat down. "Thanks." He picked up the drink and took a sip, watching her across the rim of the cup.

"Long day, huh?" he asked.

"You could say that."

He opened his mouth but was interrupted by the arrival of their food. The teenage waitress placed cheeseburgers and fries on their table.

"Can I get you anything else?" she asked, her eyes on James as he shrugged out of his suit jacket and flipped his tie over his shoulder. He glanced up with a polite smile. "No, thanks."

She let out a small sigh. "Okay. Well, my name's Staci, with an *i,* so let me know if you need anything?"

He nodded, and Staci-with-an-i walked back to the counter, casting one last look behind her as she went.

Kelly couldn't blame her. He was an attractive man, and she watched with growing awareness as he rolled up his shirtsleeves to reveal warm golden forearms dusted with dark hair. It was soft, she knew from experience, and her skin tingled with remembered sensation.

Shaking her head to clear her thoughts, she squirted ketchup on her bun and waited for him to take a bite of his burger before asking, "Why did you lie to me today?"

He coughed, then finished chewing and took a sip of his soda. "What makes you think I lied to you?" he asked, wiping his mouth with a napkin.

"Well, for starters, you told me I wasn't in any trouble."

"You're not," he said, sounding confused. "Why do you think you're in trouble?"

She dipped a fry in ketchup and popped it into her mouth. "Your boss certainly acted like I've done something wrong."

He shook his head and picked up his burger again. "That's just the way Kevin is. He questions everyone like that."

"Guilty until proven innocent?" she asked, taking her own bite. The burger was juicy and hot, and she had to quickly dab at her chin with a napkin to catch the drip.

"Something like that. He's a little old-school about interrogations."

Silence descended over the table as they concentrated on their food. She studied him from under her lashes. She'd forgotten what nice hands he had—broad palms, long fingers, short, squared-off nails. She hadn't forgotten what those hands could do to her, though, and her face heated as the memories invaded her thoughts once again.

"I have a confession to make," he said, dragging her out of the past and back to the table.

"What's that?"

"I don't really understand all the science behind these attacks. How could someone modify bacteria like that to make them more dangerous?"

Kelly lifted one shoulder as she chewed. "It's not that difficult," she said, reaching for her drink to wash down the food. "All you need to do are basic genetic manipulations."

"Such as?"

His gaze was direct, and her stomach fluttered at having his dark brown eyes on her again. His expression was one of genuine curiosity, and she warmed a bit at being the center of his attention.

"Well, if you know the genetic sequence of the toxin—and we do, since it's been published—then all you have to do is design a vector with that gene and transfer it into the bacteria. The bacteria take care of the rest."

His brows drew together in a puzzled frown. "What do you mean?"

She pulled a pen from her bag and confiscated a napkin. "It's like this," she said, sketching out a diagram as she spoke. "Bacteria will incorporate new genes into their chromosomes through a process called recombination." She quickly illustrated the process for him, proving once again why she had always failed art. James was a quick study, though, and seemed to grasp what she was saying despite her obvious lack of talent in the drawing department.

"And you said the genetic information is widely known?"

She nodded. "Sure. It's been published. Anyone with an internet connection can access the database."

His eyes widened. "There's no security in place?"

"Not really. It's not publicized or anything, but the data are out there."

"Unbelievable," he muttered, leaning back in his chair.

Kelly returned to her meal while James crumpled his wrapper. "Do you know if George accessed this data?"

"No. But I'm sure you could check his computer."

James nodded in response, his eyes narrowing the slightest bit before his expression returned to the neutral, professional mask he wore. It was a tiny slip, easily dismissed, but something told Kelly he wasn't as confused by the science as he'd said. She was willing to bet he'd known all this before, and he had merely wanted to see how she'd respond to his oh-so-innocent questions.

No longer hungry, she put down the remainder of her burger. It was time to go. She'd been lulled into thinking this conversation was like countless others they'd had in the past, but that wasn't the case. Her boss was aiding a terrorist group, and James was interested in her because he was the lead investigator, not because he was her former friend and lover. It had been so easy to forget, but the fact that her hormones were happy to see him again didn't mean he felt the same way about her.

James collected her trash as they stood, then placed his hand at the small of her back to guide her out the door. Her skin burned at the contact, despite the layers of clothes that separated them. What she wouldn't give to be able to turn around and press against him! She knew from experience that her nose fit perfectly into the hollow of his throat, and she wanted nothing more than to embrace him now, to inhale deeply and draw the citrus-spice essence of him deep into her lungs.

Despite their past, despite the fact that she had wrecked things between them, he still meant the world to her. He'd always been a calming presence in her life and had made her feel safe. Now that her world was turning upside down, she needed him more than ever.

But given her earlier mistakes, would he be there for her?

Caleb winced and held the phone away from his ear as the voice on the other end rose in volume. Dr. George Collins was missing, and his employers were not happy.

"Where the hell is he?" the man bellowed.

Caleb fought to keep his tone calm. It would only increase his problems if he yelled back at this man. "I'm not sure right now. I'm working on it."

"How did he get away? I thought you had him under surveillance."

"I did—" Caleb began.

"Then how did you lose him?"

He took a deep breath, wishing he could just hang up the phone. He didn't need this. It wasn't his fault George had slipped away. The men who were supposed to watch the scientist had failed, and they would be dealt with. Truth be told, Caleb was surprised—he hadn't thought the mousy little man had had it in him to run.

"It hardly matters now, sir," Caleb ground out, hating the need for deference but knowing it would help soothe the other man's ruffled feathers.

It did. His voice lowered to a normal level, and Caleb put the phone back to his ear.

"What are you going to do about it?"

He walked to the mini-fridge and pulled out a sampler bottle of vodka, frowning at the label. It wasn't his usual brand, but it would do. "I have some leads," he said, filling a glass with ice and pouring the alcohol. He took a bracing sip and continued, "He has a timeshare in Florida, and I've sent men to check if they've holed up there."

"What about other family members?"

Caleb loosened his tie and sat on the bed, placing the glass on the nightstand. "He and his wife didn't have children, and his brother died three years ago."

The man made a dissatisfied sound in his throat. "Any nieces or nephews?"

Caleb frowned as he kicked off his shoes. "One niece, but they're not close."

"Well, keep that in mind. We may need to use her if he doesn't turn up soon."

He read between the lines. *We* actually meant him, and he didn't relish the thought of getting his hands dirty like that. His job was to procure the bacteria and work out the details of the project, not to torture an innocent woman in the hopes of drawing out her uncle.

"I don't think it'll come to that," he said, flipping through the folder on the bed.

"What makes you so sure?" the man asked skeptically.

"I've got a better lead," Caleb said, pulling out a picture. "She's a postdoc in his lab, and by all reports, he trusts her. She may know where he is. And do you want to know the best part?" he asked, unable to resist taunting this man a little.

"Do tell."

"She's got the know-how to complete the project. So

even if we never see Dr. Collins again, we can still finish what we started." He tried to keep the satisfaction out of his voice, but it was hard. He had done a damn fine job of salvaging the operation, and he deserved a little appreciation.

There was a pause as the man digested his words. "That's good," he said softly. "But make no mistake, Caleb. You will find Dr. Collins, no matter what it takes. I don't like loose ends."

Caleb swallowed the last of his vodka, hating the twinge of fear that danced down his spine at the implied threat. "What if he can't be found?"

"Then I'm going to blame you." His tone was casual, as if they were discussing something as simple as the weather. "You're a good operative, Caleb. You've done a fine job for us over the years, but you're getting soft. You know how this operation works—failure must be punished." He paused, took a sip of something and crushed an ice cube before delivering his final blow. "Don't make the mistake of thinking you're irreplaceable."

A click and the sound of a dial tone saved Caleb from needing to reply. A good thing, too, because his tongue had gone thick and clumsy at the threat. He had seen the things that happened to people who failed, knew just what his "punishment" would involve.

He took a deep breath, then stood and walked back to the mini-fridge and pulled out another bottle. Scotch this time. He wasn't picky now; he just wanted the release it would bring. He poured it into a fresh glass and took a hasty gulp, concentrating on the burn as the alcohol made its way down his throat. Warmth curled in his stomach, and he returned to the bed and stretched out, enjoying the heavy feel of his limbs as he moved.

He would fix this. He would find the professor and make him pay for this behavior. In the meantime, he pulled out the picture of the woman again and studied it, squinting to bring the image into focus. She was pretty enough, he supposed, with her auburn hair, hazel eyes and heart-shaped face. He could turn her, he thought, blinking against the glaring light of the bedside lamp. He could be very persuasive and charming when the occasion called for it, especially around women. He'd have her eating out of his hand within an hour. And if she resisted? Well, he'd just take her.

He traced a finger along the curve of her cheek. "You're mine," he murmured. "Whether you want it or not, you're mine now."

He reached over and placed the picture carefully on the bedside table, then switched off the lamp. The movement made him slightly dizzy and he lay back against the pillow, liking the pleasant spinning sensation. After a moment he closed his eyes, ready to surrender to the darkness.

Time to get some sleep. Tomorrow was going to be a big day, after all.

For both of them.

Chapter 4

Saturday dawned clear and bright, a direct contrast to Kelly's mood. She hadn't slept well; her thoughts had kept her awake for most of the night. She went over every interaction she'd had with George in the past month, trying to identify any sign that she had missed. Aside from the Saturday he'd snapped at her, there was nothing to indicate he was unduly worried. Either the FBI was wrong about his involvement or he was a very good actor.

She frowned at the thought of the FBI as she walked into the kitchen and grabbed a Coke from the fridge. Despite telling them everything she knew, she suspected she hadn't seen the last of them.

She had invited James inside last night, which had been its own brand of torture, and had given him her key to George's office. She didn't think George would be stupid enough to leave incriminating evidence lying around, but he said they had to check it out.

Having him in her apartment had made her feel more...aware. Not nervous per se, but she had watched him take in her living room, had seen the way his gaze rested on the pictures on her bookshelves and the pile of folded clothes on the couch. He wasn't overt in his assessment, but she was willing to bet he could describe everything he had seen in great detail, right down to the crooked painting hanging on the wall.

She headed to the bedroom, stripping off her T-shirt as she walked. Her eyes felt as if they'd been rubbed with sandpaper, but there was no point in going back to bed—she'd never get any sleep with the sun streaming into her room. Time to get cleaned up and go into work. If she had to be awake, at least she could be productive.

Forty-five minutes later, she unlocked the lab and settled in at her desk. As she waited for her computer to boot up, she heard footsteps in the hall and a door unlocking. That was unusual, but not alarming. Sometimes people came in early on the weekends, wanting to get their work done so they'd have the rest of the day free.

Her ancient computer was taking its time about coming to life, so she decided to walk down the hall and say hi to the other early bird.

She stepped out of the lab, expecting to see another lab a few doors down with the door open and lights on. Instead, she found George's office door open and heard the sounds of rummaging. It seemed the FBI had gotten an early start on their search.

She stood in the hall for a moment, debating what to do next. Should she poke her head into George's office and say hi? It was probably James conducting the search, since he was the one who had the key, and after their reunion yesterday it would be rude to ignore him. On the other hand, she really didn't want to get involved in this investigation any more than she already was.

In the end, her manners won out. She walked down to George's office, rapping her fingers on the partially closed door as she pushed it open. "Good morning…" she said, the words trailing off as she realized James was not the person digging in the office.

The man straightened from behind George's desk, pushing his wire-rimmed glasses up on his nose with a gloved finger. "Good morning," he responded politely. "You must be Kelly Jarvis."

He didn't appear threatening, but the hair on the back of Kelly's neck stood up and she could feel her heart thumping. "That's right," she said slowly, unsure of how much to reveal. "What's your name?"

"Caleb," he said, sending her a smile. He had dimples, she noticed, but there was something about his eyes that made her uncomfortable. Despite his friendly appearance, they remained cold and assessing.

"Are you with the FBI?" she asked. "I didn't see you yesterday." She watched him carefully, saw his smile slip a bit when she mentioned the FBI. *Interesting.* "Of course, there were so many new faces, I may have just missed you."

He nodded, then said, "I have trouble with names and faces, too, especially when I meet a lot of people at once." He rounded the desk and moved to stand in front of it, a few paces away from her.

She backed up a step, not liking him so close. He

hadn't answered her question, but she decided not to press. Whoever this man was, he didn't belong here, and she didn't want to provoke him.

"Well, I just came to say hello. I'm down the hall if you need anything." She gestured vaguely with her left hand, backing out the door at what she hoped was a reasonable, non-suspicious speed.

"Actually, there is something you can do for me," Caleb replied, advancing on her.

She didn't stop moving. "What's that?"

Quick as a flash, his arm snaked out and his fingers wrapped around her wrist in a painful grip. He yanked her toward him, close enough that she could smell the stale coffee on his breath.

"You're going to help me make things right."

James tugged on the glass doors of the research building, letting out an impatient huff when he discovered they were locked. Kelly hadn't said anything about needing a key to get in, but then again, he had told her he would swing by on Monday.

He dug in his pants pocket, fishing out the key to Collins's office. It was a long shot, but maybe…

No luck. He cupped his hands around his eyes and pressed them to the tinted glass, squinting to see inside the building. There was a reception desk in the middle of the foyer, but the chair behind it was empty. Either the security guard was making his rounds or no one was on duty today. Considering it was a Saturday, the regular guard was probably off, which meant no one would be around to show him in.

"So much for getting an early start," he muttered, stepping back to consider his options. He didn't see any other entrances to the building, but there had to be a side or back door. It was probably locked, though, so if he went off on a search for other entrances, he'd miss out on an opportunity to be let in if a student or professor arrived.

He should really call Kelly. She'd be able to get him in and could probably escort him right to Collins's office. Since he didn't know the layout of the building, he was going to have to roam around the sixth floor until he found the right room. Kelly could save him a lot of time and trouble, but he didn't want to contact her. It was probably just paranoia on his part, but the less she knew about the investigation, the better.

He let his thoughts drift back to yesterday afternoon, replaying the montage that had been running on an endless loop in his mind since last night. Kelly had seemed genuinely shocked at the implication that Collins was involved with a terrorist organization, but he knew from experience how good her acting skills were. After all, hadn't she seemed to be attracted to him, only to give him the cold shoulder the next morning? He wasn't going to forget that little performance anytime soon.

Still, the Kelly he'd once known—or thought he'd known—would never have gotten involved in something like this. At least not willingly. He knew from experience that people were capable of doing almost anything for money. Collins had signed up to pay for his wife's chemo treatments. Did Kelly have some kind of debt hanging over her head?

She appeared to live within her means, if her apartment was any indication. It was a small place, in an okay neighborhood—not a luxury suite or dump, but a decent apartment in a quiet, older building. She didn't have a big-screen TV or any expensive computer or electronic equipment that he'd seen, but that could have been in another room. The place had been rather sparse, with the light coating of dust giving it a semi-neglected feel. He'd gotten the impression that she used the apartment mainly for sleeping and showering, which fit what he knew of her workaholic tendencies.

He knew she didn't have a car, either, so she certainly wasn't blowing money on creature comforts. Did she have gambling debt? She didn't seem the type to play the ponies, but anything was possible. He made a mental note to check on her financial records, but he suspected everything would be in order.

That left family. Were her parents in trouble? Had she gotten in with the wrong crowd trying to help them out? He knew scientists in her position weren't well paid, and short of winning the lottery, she didn't have many options to increase her salary. She certainly had the know-how to engineer the bug, given her detailed explanations last night. Helping Collins in return for part of the money would be an easy way to make a quick buck, and since Collins wasn't around to confirm her involvement, she was on the verge of getting away with it.

The thought drew him up short. Since when had he decided she was part of this? The rational side of him realized his emotions were clouding his judgment, making him hypercritical of her motivations and actions. Just because she'd broken his heart...

He sucked in a deep breath, shaking his head. No, not broken his heart. He refused to believe he'd been in love with her. She'd disappointed him, that was all.

And despite his disappointment, he owed her the benefit of the doubt, at least until he discovered otherwise. All suspects were innocent until proven guilty, and she was no exception. Granted, he didn't usually have such a personal history with the suspects in an investigation, but it couldn't be helped.

Just because his best friend had turned out to be a traitor didn't mean Kelly was, as well. He wouldn't let his experiences with Steve cloud his judgment here.

He rubbed absently at the center of his chest, the thought of his late friend triggering a familiar ache. Despite the intervening years, James remembered that night with terrible clarity. It had been a scorcher of a day, and he was sitting under the fan in his tiny apartment in Silver Spring, drinking a beer and watching the Orioles game. The knock on his door had been rapid and insistent, announcing his visitor's agitation as clearly as words.

He'd opened the door to find Steve looking as though he hadn't slept in days, and smelling like it, too. "Can I come in?"

James stepped aside and gestured him through the door. "Have a seat, man. Can I get you anything?"

Steve shook his head as he parked it on the couch. James sat in the recliner, taking in his uncombed hair, stubble and wrinkled clothes. What worried him most, though, were the white lines of strain around Steve's eyes and lips. Deciding he could use a beer after all, James grabbed a bottle from the fridge and returned to his chair, holding it out for his friend, who took it with a sigh.

This is it, he thought, his stomach dropping in anticipatory dread. *He's in over his head, and he needs me to bail him out.*

He would do it, too, he realized grimly. He didn't have much money in the bank, but if it would get Steve out of trouble, he'd fork it over.

He watched in silence as Steve peeled the label off his bottle with fumbling fingers, letting his friend come up with the words in his own time.

"I screwed up," he blurted, his leg bouncing a rapid tattoo as the last of the label flaked off and fell to the floor. "It's bad—really bad." He looked up at James then, despair shining in his eyes.

"I'm sure it seems that way now," James began, trying to inject reassurance into his voice. "But whatever it is, we can fix it."

Steve shot up from the chair and began to pace, prowling the room like a caged animal trying to find an escape. "No, man. You don't understand. It's over. They're gonna kill me."

"Who's going to kill you?" James felt the fine hairs on the nape of his neck rise, and he instinctively glanced at the door. Was Steve being followed?

"The Cartel. Internal Affairs. Take your pick." Steve flopped back into the chair, his features arranged in a mask of misery.

James's stomach twisted as his dinner threatened to reappear. The rumors were true, then. Steve was dirty. He took a healthy swallow from his bottle, trying to wash the bitter disappointment away.

"I think you'd better tell me what's going on."

With a heavy sigh, Steve told him how he'd gotten sucked in, how it started out small, selling dime bags on the side, but then he'd been tapped to launder money for the Cartel. Now IAB was onto him, and if they didn't get him, the Cartel would kill him for turning against them.

James sat quietly, digesting the news, not sure how to respond now that he knew his best friend was a crooked cop, a drug dealer and a liar.

"Will you help me?" Steve's voice was quiet but thick with emotion.

Help him? Help him break the law again so he could ride off into the sunset with his drug buddies? James felt a hot spurt of anger, wondering how Steve had been so stupid to get involved. Yeah, narcs walked a fine line, but most of the guys were good, clean cops. It could be done.

He bit his tongue to keep from yelling, his throat tightening on the words he wanted to scream. For the first time in his adult life, he wanted to hit someone, wanted to feel the painfully satisfying crunch of knuckles against nose, the warm gush of blood on his fist.

How could Steve do this to him? Steve knew that his dad had been a crooked cop, knew that James had entered the academy wanting to restore his family's name. There was no way James could risk getting involved in something like this, especially when certain factions in the department were watching him closely, just waiting for him to screw up like his father.

Steve may have thrown away his career and reputation, but James wasn't about to do the same.

He must have been silent for too long, because Steve rose with a sigh. "Forget it," he muttered, starting toward the door. "I should have known Saint James wouldn't get involved."

James bristled at the old high-school nickname, his

anger rising at Steve's insinuation that he was a Goody Two-shoes.

"Why'd you do it?" he called after Steve. The other man stopped, then turned to face him.

"I thought you were smarter than that," he continued, watching as Steve's face turned from pink to a mottled red.

"You think you're so great, don't you, Reynolds?" Steve took a menacing step forward, but James held his ground. "You think you're so damn perfect," he hissed, getting in James's face.

"No," James said evenly. "I just want to know why you threw your life away."

Steve held his gaze for a beat, then stepped back, shaking his head. James looked down, searching for something to say, which kept him from seeing the punch until it was too late. Steve's fist connected with his left eye with enough force that he stumbled back. He fell to the floor, clutching his face in reflex.

Steve moved forward, sending James scrambling back until he met the couch. He grabbed for a handhold, something he could use to leverage himself up in case Steve was going to strike him again, but the pain and shock of the blow was disorienting and he couldn't convince his legs to work.

Steve loomed over him, leaning forward until his face was inches away. James regarded him warily out of his good eye, his hand cupped protectively over the left side of his face.

"Go to hell." Steve didn't yell the words, but he didn't have to. The contempt and hatred came through loud and clear.

James sat motionless as Steve stood, spun on his

heel and stalked out the door, slamming it so hard it bounced back open. He was still sitting there when two agents from Internal Affairs stopped by for a "chat."

That had been the last time he'd seen his friend. Steve had been found dead two days later, shot in the back of the head, execution-style. James often wondered if he could have prevented it, if only he'd stepped forward to help.

Or maybe he would have been killed alongside him.

The crunching sound of footsteps on the gravel path brought him back to the present. He shook his head to clear the memories and turned. Hopefully someone was coming who could let him into the building. A young man rounded the corner, headphones firmly in place, head bopping along to some faint techno beat that grew louder as he approached. James winced, feeling sorry for the kid's eardrums.

Without giving him a second look, the student dug his keys out of his backpack and unlocked the door, swinging it wide so James could enter after him. "So much for security," he muttered as he followed in the wake of the soon-to-be-deaf student. The kid peeled off down a hall to the left, leaving James standing in the foyer searching for the elevator.

He found it, a little ways down the right hall. As he reached forward to push the call button, he noticed the sign for the stairs a few doors down. Hoping the exercise would help clear his mind, he pulled open the door and started up the concrete steps. He'd focus on searching Collins's office now, and when he was finished, he'd head back to the office to do a little more digging into Kelly's family situation. He might even pay her another visit this afternoon, see how she responded to his questions.

Sometimes a person's reactions told you more than their answers ever could.

Kelly let out a strangled scream, twisting as she struggled to free herself from Caleb's grip. His other hand grabbed her arm to hold her in place.

"Stop that!" His smooth smile was gone now, replaced by an angry snarl that matched his cold eyes. He gave her a little shake that had her teeth clacking together. "I'm not going to hurt you."

Yeah, she'd heard that song before. Her thoughts raced as she struggled to recall the instructions of her self-defense instructor. *It doesn't matter how big they are. They're all vulnerable. Go for the eyes, the neck or the groin.*

His eyes and neck were out, as he had both of her arms pinned. That left his groin. Right now her legs were free, but how long would that last?

Oh, God, she had one shot at this. She had to make it count. She stopped struggling, hoping he would relax his grip. He didn't, but his expression softened. "Good—" he began.

She drew her knee up hard, landing a solid blow between his legs. His breath rushed out in a wheeze, his eyes big and round in a face that had gone a little green.

She jerked away, but he held on, his fingers digging into her arms. "You little bitch," he huffed out, blinking back tears. Letting out a frustrated cry, she stomped hard on his foot. He grunted, and she felt his grip loosen just a little bit.

It was enough. She twisted and pulled, coming free

to land in a heap on the floor. She scrambled to her feet and managed to get a step in before she felt a hand on the back of her neck. He had grabbed her again.

"No!" She kept moving forward, felt his fingers slip and scrabble for purchase. He ripped a hank of hair from her ponytail, bringing tears to her eyes. She ducked her head down to keep her hair out of reach and wriggled out of her jacket, picking up speed as she left it behind.

She heard his angry cry and his footsteps pounding down the hall after her. She didn't stop to look back, knowing the move would cost her time. She rounded the corner, frantically searching for another open door, any sign of occupancy that meant she wasn't alone.

A cart was pushed against the wall up ahead, piled high with lab glassware waiting to be cleaned and sterilized. She grabbed one end as she dashed past, flinging it behind her in the hopes it would slow Caleb down.

She rounded another corner and headed for the stairwell, desperate to get away. If she could just reach the stairs… A satisfying crash and the sound of breaking glass behind her told her that the cart had done its job. Good. Hopefully, he was hurt.

She slammed into the stairwell doors, risking a glance behind her before they shut. Before she could turn her head back around, she ran headlong into something solid. Strong arms banded around her as she was picked off her feet, and she screamed, wiggling and fighting to get away.

"Kelly? Kelly! It's James!" He shook her briefly as he spoke. She heard the voice over the pounding of her heart, recognized it from somewhere, but it took a few breaths for her to realize who held her. He kept talking, and she forced herself to concentrate on his words. James. It was James, her friend. James, the FBI agent. She was safe. All the fight went out of her at this realization, and she rested her forehead against his shoulder.

Before he could set her back on her feet, she started babbling, "Oh, thank God you're here! There's a man, Caleb, in George's office, and he grabbed me and started chasing me. He tripped over the cart and I think he might be hurt."

His lips pressed together in a thin line, and he drew his gun from the holster at his waist. "Stay here," he said in a tone that brooked no argument. He pushed open the stairwell door, checking the foyer before stepping out into the open.

Kelly stood in the stairwell landing, her sides heaving as the gasped for breath. Her heart was still pounding, but the adrenaline rush was gone, leaving an acrid taste in her throat. She swallowed hard, fighting down a wave of nausea. Her knees felt as though they were knocking together, so she moved to the stairs and collapsed, wincing as a spike of pain shot up her tailbone.

Please, please, please, she thought, not really knowing what she was hoping for. Was it for Caleb to be caught? For him to be gone, so she wouldn't have to see him again? For James to be safe? If Caleb hurt James, there would be no stopping him from coming after her. And since he had crashed into the cart, he'd probably be angry.

She reached a shaky hand out to the railing and pulled herself up. She had to know, one way or another.

She couldn't just sit here. If Caleb was coming back, she needed to move.

As she approached the doors, she heard footsteps in the foyer, heading her way. She scrambled back to the stairs, heart in her throat. She walked up a few stairs and pressed herself against the wall, out of sight. If it was James, he'd call to her. If it was Caleb…at least she'd have a head start.

The footsteps paused at the doors and she held her breath. She watched a slice of light grow on the floor as the door opened; the uncertainty of the moment made her want to scream in frustration. After a split second that felt like an hour, she heard his voice.

"Kelly?"

The breath whooshed out of her as she descended the steps and poked her head around the corner. James stood in the doorway, solid and strong, his presence a comfort after the crazy events of the morning.

He studied her for a moment, his serious eyes taking everything in. Suddenly self-conscious, she attempted to straighten her shirt. The sleeve and neck had gotten hopelessly stretched when she had shrugged out of the jacket, but she tried to reposition it so it wasn't falling off her shoulder. She reached up to smooth her hair back, and his gaze zeroed in on her shaking hand.

She saw the moment he realized she was physically unhurt, watched the lines around his eyes soften and his mouth relax. If he said something comforting, she would lose it, so she spoke before he could. "Did you get him?"

He shook his head, and her stomach dropped. "No, he was down the back stairs and probably out the building before I got here."

"So he's still out there."

He came forward and rested a hand on her shoulder. His palm was warm through her shirt, and she focused on that spot, trying not to think about Caleb and the fact that he was free to find her again.

"Maybe not for long."

Her brows drew together in a frown as she looked up at him. "What do you mean?"

He stepped back toward the door, beckoning her to follow with a wave. "C'mon. I'll show you."

Ignoring her still-roiling stomach, she followed him across the foyer and down the hall, stopping at the glass-cart crash site. The cart was lying on its side, and a halo of broken glass littered the floor around it. Closer inspection revealed that the metal frame of the cart was actually dented—he must have hit it while running full speed.

James stood next to a pile of glass fragments, hands on hips. "Nice job with the cart," he said, giving her an impressed look. "Quick thinking on your part."

"Thanks," she murmured, placing a hand on her stomach. "Why are we standing here?"

"Because of this," he answered, squatting down and pointing to the glass. She bent for a closer look and saw the smudges of red he was indicating. There was a smear on the tiles, along with a few crimson drops. Blood.

That did it. The stress of the morning combined with the sight of Caleb's blood on the floor had her stomach pressing the eject button. She straightened, clapping a hand over her mouth to keep the rising bile contained.

James rose quickly, grabbed her shoulders and

steered her away from the glass. "Don't you dare puke on my crime scene!"

He pushed her into the bathroom, and she made it to the toilet just in time. When she was finished, she sat back on her heels and blotted her mouth with some toilet paper. After a moment, when she was sure the vomiting portion of the program was over, she rose and walked to the sinks. She splashed her face with water and rinsed out her mouth.

Squashing the rising embarrassment that came from almost puking on another person, she walked out of the bathroom to find James leaning against the wall, phone to his ear.

He wrapped up his conversation and turned to face her. "Sorry about that," he said, tucking the phone into his pocket. "I'm a sympathetic vomiter, and I thought it would be better if one of us wasn't hunched over a toilet."

She waved off his explanation. "I'm actually glad you didn't stay," she confessed. "I really don't like people to see me that way."

"I can understand that," he said. There was a beat of silence. "Why don't you walk me through what happened? I've got a team on the way to collect evidence, but it would help if I can tell them where to start."

She nodded, leading him back to George's office. "He was standing behind the desk when I first saw him. I'm pretty sure he was going through the desk drawers, so you'll probably want to dust for prints or whatever it is you guys do."

"I'll be sure to let the team know, Serpico." His wry tone had her raising one eyebrow in his direction, causing him to hold up his hands in surrender. "Okay, not quite ready for teasing yet."

"You'll be the first to know," she replied, hating the quaver in her voice.

"Hey," he said. She turned aside, trying to surreptitiously wipe away a stray tear before he could see. "Hey, it's okay." He placed his hands on her shoulders and gently turned her back to face him. She looked down, refusing to meet his eyes until she got her emotions under control.

"I'm sorry," he said, reaching up to smooth a hand over her hair. The kind gesture had her crying even harder.

"You had quite the scare this morning, and I can only imagine how you feel after the revelations of yesterday." He tugged on her shoulder, and she reluctantly stepped closer. She stiffened when he put his arms around her, but after a beat she surrendered to the hug, enjoying the feeling of being held, of literally having a shoulder to cry on. Still, her pride insisted that she say something.

"I'm f-f-fine," she sputtered, hating the show of weakness that was leaving a wet spot on his shirt.

"I know you are," he replied. "But in my experience, shocks like the ones you've experienced have a way of taking a toll on the body, and you have to release the tension somehow."

"How do you release it?"

He paused, then gave a small shrug. "I generally go for a run, then I sit on the couch with a beer and a big bowl of popcorn and watch *The Goonies*."

She pulled back with a small smile. *"The Goonies?"*

"Yeah. It's my favorite movie."

"I've never seen it."

He tsked in exaggerated disappointment. "For shame. You'll have to watch it sometime. Nothing better for relieving stress."

Maybe we could watch it together, she thought. She slammed the door to that line of thinking, but she couldn't quite ignore her growing awareness of how his body felt pressed against hers. His hand was moving in lazy strokes up and down her back, and his mouth was pressed to the top of her head, his breath warm against her hair.

It felt so good, so *right,* to be in his arms again. The casual strength he displayed while holding her affected her on some primal, instinctive level, and despite the fact she'd just been attacked, she felt her body respond to his touch. Her breasts grew heavy against his chest, and anticipation raced through her limbs with a delicious shiver.

One of his hands drifted up to rest on the back of her neck, and his thumb stroked the sensitive skin just under her hairline. Her nipples hardened at the contact, causing Kelly to suck in a breath. She was mortified at her brazen response and prayed James couldn't feel it, although given the fact she was practically glued to his chest, there was little chance of that. *For crying out loud,* she mentally scolded herself. *He's just trying to be nice, and I'm acting like some oversexed floozy.* Time to end this hug before she embarrassed herself further.

She leaned away and wiped her cheeks, and he released her, letting her take a step back. "Thanks," she said quietly.

"Don't mention it," he replied easily. If he'd felt her

arousal, he wasn't going to comment on it, a fact that made her pathetically grateful. "Ready to continue?"

She nodded and turned back to the office, then stepped inside to point out the drawers she had seen Caleb touch.

She could do this.

He had to stop touching her. All his cool, professional detachment went out the window when he touched her, and he needed to stay focused, now more than ever.

She was connected to his investigation—hell, she might even be a suspect—and he had to treat her as such. FBI agents did not go around holding suspects, no matter how much they might want to.

It was difficult to let her go. Despite the fact that only fifteen minutes ago he'd been questioning her involvement in this case, she had been attacked, and his protective instincts had flared to life. Still, he could keep her safe without touching her. Needed to, in fact, because touching her was a surefire way to distract him, and he had to be on top of his game right now.

It was when she'd started crying that he'd given up the battle.

The fact that his thoughtless teasing had set her off was what really tipped the scales. He had forgotten that she wasn't one of the guys, wasn't used to dealing with this kind of thing every day. Joking around was just the way they all got through it, but a civilian wasn't as jaded.

So he had pulled her into his arms, trying to ignore the way she fit against him, the way her head tucked perfectly under his chin. The feel of her breasts pressed against his chest had nearly made him groan. The sensation short-circuited his brain and muted all rational thought. He was back on that damp sidewalk again, holding her close, drowning in the scent of honeysuckle and that indescribable note that was just *Kelly*.

He should have kept his hands on her back, but he hadn't been able to resist touching her, needing that skin-to-skin contact to reassure himself she was really fine. So he'd moved his hand up to rest on her neck, the softness of her skin affecting him like a drug. When her nipples had hardened against his chest, it had taken every ounce of self-control he possessed not to kiss her or to slide his hands around to cup her feminine weight. His thumbs had ached with the memory of rubbing over the rigid peaks, and he was desperate to touch her there again, craving the contact like a starving man longed for food.

He'd almost sighed with relief when she'd pulled away, knowing he wouldn't be able to keep the hug platonic much longer but not wanting to push her away if she was still upset.

She had pulled herself together quickly; he'd give her that. You'd have to look closely to see that she had been crying, and no one would guess that she had lost her breakfast mere moments ago.

His doubts about her innocence were quickly fading in light of this turn of events. If she had been involved, she would have cooperated with the guy, not run away. She certainly wouldn't be trying to help him now. No, he decided. She probably wasn't a part of this world.

He watched her round the desk, pointing out the things she had seen her assailant touch. A cold ball of anger had settled in his stomach at the thought of him grabbing her, chasing her down the hall. He had felt the burn of satisfaction when he'd spotted the blood on the floor. Not only was the bastard injured, but now they had his DNA.

She stopped speaking, her hand flying to her forehead, a stricken look on her face.

"What's wrong?" he asked, wondering what she'd seen that caused this reaction.

"I just remembered." She shook her head. "He was wearing gloves. There won't be any fingerprints." She looked up at him, her face a mask of despair.

Damn. That was unfortunate, but nothing they couldn't overcome. He tried to inject reassurance into his voice as he said, "That makes things a little more difficult, but not impossible. We'll get his DNA from the blood, see if he's in the system. We may also get some clues from what he was looking at—it may tell us where he's going or what he wanted."

She nodded, still wearing a worried expression. "I'll have them dust for prints anyway," he continued. "Maybe he's been in here before, without the gloves."

She pursed her lips in thought, drawing his gaze to her mouth like a moth to a flame. "Maybe," she said slowly. "But I don't recall seeing him before."

His phone rang, stalling his response. He pulled it from his pocket. "Agent Reynolds."

Kelly wrapped her arms around her waist while he took the call and she looked around George's office. Hopefully she would notice something that would help them.

"That was my team," he informed her, pocketing the phone. "They're here. I'm going to meet them at the elevator bank. Do you want to come with me or stay here?"

"Actually, I was hoping to go back to the lab, if that's okay. I do have some work to get done today."

He admired that she was trying to carry on with her plans, but that wasn't going to happen. "I'm afraid that after the team takes possession of the scene, you're going to need to come with me back to the office." Her brows came down in a scowl, and her mouth tightened into a line. He held up a hand to block her inevitable protest. "We need to debrief you, and you need to work with a sketch artist so we can get a good image of this guy."

She sighed, but he held her gaze, refusing to back down on this. "Fine," she said quietly. "Let me go turn off my computer and get my bag."

"Sounds like a plan," he said, happy to have avoided an argument. "I'll meet you in the lab in a few minutes."

He turned to go, but her hand on his arm stopped him. He looked down to find her staring up at him, gratitude shining in her eyes.

"Thank you," she said. "For everything."

He swallowed past the sudden lump in his throat, determined not to draw her into his arms again. "You don't have to thank me," he replied. "It's my job."

Her face shuttered, and she snatched her hand away as if burned. "Of course," she said flatly, brushing past him to walk down to her lab.

He let out his own sigh. *Great.* Now she thought he didn't care about her. Nothing could be further from the truth, but maybe this was for the best. If she thought he was aloof, she might stay away from him, and he might be able to keep his tenuous grip on his self-control.

It wasn't the best solution, but he'd take it.

The meeting with the sketch artist took a lot longer than Kelly had anticipated. She wasn't used to describing faces in such detail and didn't really have a sense of how to talk about his features. Handsome but cold-eyed wasn't too informative. She quickly grew frustrated with her descriptive shortcomings, but the sketch artist was a study in patience, guiding her through the process with professional ease. Kelly had to admit that the final product was a close rendering of the man who had chased her.

"This is basically him," she said slowly, studying the image. The eyes weren't quite right, but she didn't think the coldness in them could be adequately captured on the page. Everything else was pretty close.

"How on earth did you get this based on my crappy descriptions?" she asked the artist, thoroughly impressed with the woman's skill.

A quick smile prefaced her reply. "I've been doing this awhile," she said, packing up her supplies. "You did a great job."

Kelly snorted and shook her head. "Not really, but that's kind of you to say."

"Hey, we have a good likeness, so that's all that matters." With a final smile, the woman left the room, handing the page to Agent Carmichael as she walked through the office.

He glanced down at the image in an offhanded way, but then he froze and Kelly noticed his eyes widen as he took in the drawing. He masked his reaction quickly, but he held the paper closer to presumably get a better look at the sketch. *Interesting.* It seemed Agent Carmichael recognized her attacker.

She wasn't the only one to notice this development. James walked over and spoke quietly to the older man, and they conferred with each other for a moment, heads down, both faces absorbed by the image on the paper. What was going on here?

She couldn't hear their conversation, but their urgent gesturing and facial expressions fed her growing sense of unease. She shifted in her chair, trying to get comfortable, wanting to be anywhere else at the moment. If both James and Agent Carmichael recognized this man, then it was quite likely that she had landed in the middle of something big, and she did not want to get mixed up in trouble.

She sighed, and as if they had heard her, both men looked up to stare at her at the same time. *Oh, no.* Those intense, thoughtful expressions did not bode well for her. By unspoken consent, they started forward, marching in step until they reached the conference room. Carmichael entered first, taking his customary seat at the head of the table, and James trailed behind, quietly shutting the door before sitting down across from her.

There was a beat of silence, and then James spoke. "This is the man who chased you today?"

"Yes."

More silence. "Are you sure?" Carmichael asked.

She turned to meet his eyes, not appreciating his skeptical tone or expression. "Yes," she repeated, an edge to her voice.

James and Carmichael exchanged a loaded look,

stretching Kelly's patience to the breaking point. Enough of this cloak-and-dagger routine—she had a right to know what was happening, especially since it involved her.

"What is going on?"

Carmichael refused to meet her eyes, while James looked down and sighed. Fed up with being kept in the dark, Kelly slammed her palm down on the conference table; the loud *thwack* caused both men to look at her in alarm.

"Last chance, gentlemen. I'm tired of being kept in the dark. Either you tell me what's going on, or I walk out of here and I'm not coming back."

"You said his name is Caleb?" Carmichael asked, holding up the sketch and waving the paper slightly.

"Yes. That's what he told me, anyway."

"We've been tracking him for a while but never had a name until now," James said, his gaze sliding to Carmichael as if silently asking how much to share.

"How can that be?" Kelly asked. "If you don't know his name, how are you tracking him?"

"We have a grainy image taken from another suspected bio-event," Carmichael said, apparently deciding to share.

Kelly felt her jaw drop. "There was *another* bio-event? When? Where?"

"Nine months ago," Carmichael informed her. "In Richmond."

"Was it the same organism?"

James shook his head. "Different bacteria, but the same M.O."

"So you think the two events are related." It wasn't a question. Similar methodology and the same guy shows up again? She didn't have to be an FBI agent to know this was probably not a coincidence. The only question was, did George have something to do with the first event, too?

She swallowed, dreading the answer but needing to know just the same. "Do you think George played a role in the first event?"

"Not at this time," said Carmichael.

Her shoulders slumped, and the tension in her muscles eased with this news. It was bad enough that George was involved in the most recent event, but at least he hadn't been a part of it from the beginning.

"We think Caleb is the go-to guy for this organization, the one the higher-ups use for their dirty work," James said, tapping the sketch with his forefinger as he spoke.

"What organization?" Kelly said. "You know who's responsible for these attacks?" Her voice rose at the end, and James held up a placating hand.

"We have our suspicions but no proof," he said, his tone soothing.

"You can bet if we had solid evidence, we'd have already moved on it," Carmichael interjected, his face a mottled red. "I don't appreciate the implication that we aren't doing our job."

She met his gaze, refusing to be rattled by his angry expression. "You know what I don't appreciate, Agent Carmichael?" She held up her fingers as she spoke, ticking off her statements. "Being hauled in for questioning and treated like a suspect, being chased by a psychopath and being kept in the dark about matters concerning my safety!"

"You're perfectly safe!" Carmichael fired back. "There's no reason to suspect that you are a target."

"No?" she asked with a brittle laugh. "This man knows my name! Don't you think it will be the work of a moment for him to find out where I live or the fact that I live alone? Do you honestly think I'm safe at home when he's out there?"

"She's right, Kevin," James said quietly. "We need to put her into protective custody until we nab this guy."

"She's not in any danger," Carmichael insisted. "There is no indication that Caleb or his group wants her for anything."

"Aside from the fact that he chased me?" Kelly asked, unable to keep the incredulity out of her voice. Was this man kidding?

Carmichael turned to glare at her again, and James held up his hand, shooting her an imploring look. *Let me handle this, please.*

She lifted a shoulder in a shrug. *Be my guest.*

James returned his attention to Carmichael, holding the other man's gaze. "Think about it, Kevin. With Dr. Collins gone, the group needs someone who can provide them with the bacteria or manipulate the stuff they already have. She's the only one in Collins's lab with those skills, so it stands to reason she'd be a target."

"I'm not convinced the group hasn't moved on, like they did last time. I think they're still refining their techniques, and this was another practice run."

James nodded agreeably. "Could be. Doesn't mean that we shouldn't be careful, on the off chance they're still here."

Carmichael set his jaw, clearly not convinced. James

laid a hand on the man's shoulder, and the pair stood and moved a few steps away. He lowered his voice, but Kelly could still hear his next words. "If we put her in a safe house, we can watch her. If she is involved, they'll come for her, and we can scoop them up."

Kelly tried not to react to his statement, pasting a bland expression onto her face and pretending she hadn't heard. Inside, she was reeling. James's words were like a physical blow, a punch to the gut that made her stomach drop. Did he really not trust her, or was he just putting on a show for his boss? She reviewed their interactions, searching for clues as to his real feelings. Her chest felt hollow as she realized she didn't know if James believed she was innocent.

After a moment of thoughtful silence, Carmichael sat with a loud sigh. "Fine. She gets put into protective custody." His eyes cut to Kelly, then back to James. "I want her to stay in the safe house 24/7. No walks, no trips to the grocery story, no phone calls to friends. Nothing. Got it?"

Kelly nodded woodenly, not trusting her voice. All this time, she'd thought James was on her side. Despite their past, he had seemed to believe her, trust her side of the story. And now? Now she wasn't so sure. Was he lying to his boss or to her? She'd always known he was smart, but she'd had no idea he was capable of such duplicity.

"Good call," James said, in a tone that suggested Carmichael had done something amazing. She seized on this bit of flattery the way a drowning man might cling to a life preserver. Surely James was just trying to get his boss to cooperate?

"I'll go start the paperwork," Carmichael muttered. "I'm only going to authorize this for three days, though," he warned, glancing at Kelly as he walked to the door. "I'm still not convinced she's in danger, and I'm not going to waste man-hours and departmental resources for no good reason." He paused in the doorway, giving James a meaningful look. "Unless something happens to change my mind, she goes back home at the end of the week."

James nodded, managing to get out a "Yes, sir" before Carmichael left the room, slamming the door behind him.

He turned back to face Kelly with a loud exhale, and she saw the lines of strain on his face as he briefly dropped the pleasant expression he'd held while talking to Carmichael.

"This is bad, isn't it?" she said quietly, unable to ask the real question weighing on her mind: *Do you trust me?*

His eyes were serious as he met her gaze. "Truth?" he asked. She almost laughed at the irony of his response, but she settled for a nod.

"It's not great," he admitted, running a hand through his hair. "Despite what Carmichael says, I think you are in danger, and I'm glad he agreed to put you in the safe house."

"Thanks for that." She placed her hands in her lap, linking her fingers together like a schoolgirl.

He didn't respond, making her wonder if he'd heard her. She could tell by his unfocused gaze that he was lost in thought. Gathering her courage around her like a cloak, she said his name. He didn't reply, so she tried again, louder this time.

"James?"

"Hmm?" He raised his eyes to meet hers, his gaze clearing as he focused on her.

"What you said before, to Carmichael." She paused, sucked in a breath. "Do you really believe I'm somehow involved in this?"

His expression changed then, becoming guarded as his professional mask dropped into place. "Truth?" he asked again, raising a brow as if daring her to respond.

She nodded, holding her breath as she twisted her hands together in nervous agitation.

"I honestly don't know."

Chapter 5

The warm orange glow of the setting sun peeked through a crack in the drawn curtains. George could see a sliver of the parking lot through the gap, which meant others could potentially see into the room. It was a risk he wasn't willing to take.

He set his book on the bedside table, got to his feet and walked over to adjust the curtains. A tug here, a pull there and the gap was closed. He absently smoothed his hands over the rough fabric, pushing it down as the vent from the wall unit sent out a gust of air that caused the drapes to billow slightly.

After a moment, he turned back to face the room. Ruth sat in the chair by the desk, over in the corner of the room. She was ignoring him, as usual; while she was physically present, it was clear that mentally she was very far away. She had become so removed that there were times he forgot she was there at all.

He cleared his throat to break the heavy silence between them. Nothing. She didn't respond in any way—not a flicker of the eyes, a tilt of the head or a purse of the lips. It was as if he was in a vacuum, for all the attention she paid him.

He tried again. "Are you hungry?"

"No."

Ah, so she *had* heard him. It was a start.

"It's almost dinnertime."

Silence.

"It's important you eat. The doctor said you need to keep your weight up."

Gray eyes lifted, met his. Then dropped back to the book on her lap.

"Does anything sound good to you?"

She turned the page, leaned forward to see better.

"I was thinking maybe I'd get us some takeout from that Indian place around the corner. I thought the food was pretty good, didn't you?"

When she still didn't respond, he stepped forward. She tensed, but didn't otherwise acknowledge him. *Oh, Ruth. How can I fix this?*

He reached out, his hand hovering just above her shoulder. It had been almost two weeks since he had touched her, since he had uprooted her life and yanked her out of their home. She should be sitting in her favorite chair by their bedroom window, not hunched over the desk of this second-rate motel.

She'd been quiet and withdrawn ever since he'd checked them in. Her silences had gotten longer and longer with each passing day, making George feel more and more alone. Nothing he said or did seemed to draw her out of her cocoon, and he was beginning to worry she would never emerge again.

But she's still alive. It was a thought he'd had on more than one occasion, but it no longer brought him comfort. Sure, she was breathing, functioning, eating, sleeping—all the things living people did. But she wasn't talking to him, didn't try to interact with him at all. She was slipping away, and he didn't know how to hold on to her.

At first, he'd assumed her silent treatment was due to anger. Ruth had never been one to hold a grudge, but then again, he'd never made such a colossal mistake before. He'd become defensive and had wasted a lot of breath trying to justify his actions. *I did it to save you,* he'd told her, half pleading for understanding, half being self-righteous about the risks he'd taken. *And I'd do it again, too!*

Ruth hadn't responded to this declaration. She'd merely flipped off the light and rolled over in bed, giving him her back.

As the silences stretched on and the days added up, George had realized that she wasn't angry, but rather disappointed in him.

"You know," he said, striving to keep his tone light, "at some point you're going to have to talk to me again. We can't spend the rest of our lives in silence."

She sighed then, a long-suffering sound that suggested she might be all too happy to forgo conversation with him.

"Ruth." It came out sharper than he'd meant, but his frustration was growing. "Ruth," he repeated, even more forcefully. She looked up at him, her expression flat and disinterested.

"How long are you going to punish me?" George knelt down next to her chair and grabbed one of her hands. If he could just make her understand… He hadn't meant to hurt anyone; he'd only wanted to save her.

"I'm not punishing you," she said quietly, her voice so low he had to lean forward to hear the words. "But I have nothing to say to you. I don't know you anymore."

His heartbeat picked up and he squeezed her hand, as if the force of his touch could convince her he hadn't changed. "Yes, you do. I'm still the same man I always was. I'm still your George!"

She stared at him for a moment, her gray eyes scanning his face. The heaviness in his chest grew as he watched sadness creep into her gaze. She extracted her hand from his and turned back to her book. The loss of her touch left him feeling cold and empty.

"Ruth?" he whispered, her name a shaky plea for understanding, for contact. For their marriage.

She didn't bother to look at him again. "Go get your dinner."

The drive to her apartment was quiet. James seemed lost in thought, and Kelly wasn't interested in making conversation. His earlier admission had left her feeling shaken and alone, and she didn't trust herself to speak to him.

Wanting a distraction, her thoughts turned to the morning attack. How did the man know her name? What did he want with her? Did he know where George was? What was the motive behind the bio-attacks? Would there be another? Where? When? So many questions, but no answers in sight.

She glanced at James from the corner of her eye. The rapidly setting sun outlined his profile, casting the side of his face in shadow and making it impossible for her to see his expression. Why didn't he believe her? How could he possibly think she was involved when she'd clearly run from the man who had tried to take her? Maybe this was some holdover from her walking out on him earlier—she'd hurt him then, so he didn't trust her now. But really, couldn't he see all the evidence pointed against her involvement?

He pulled into her apartment complex and found a spot by the door. "Pack a week's worth of clothes," he advised as they walked into the building and approached the elevator.

"I thought this was only approved for three days," she said, confused by his directions.

"It is, but if we have to extend it, I don't want you coming back here," he explained as they walked down the hall to her apartment.

They approached her door, but before she could reach out to insert her key in the lock, James put a restraining hand on her arm. She shot him a questioning look, and he reached up to put a finger to his lips.

"Let me go first," he whispered. "There might be someone waiting."

Her frustration flared to anger at his words. Why would he care if there was a second attack? It wasn't as if he believed her anyway. Or did he think she was going to give some kind of signal to whoever was watching if she went first? That was probably it. He wasn't concerned for her safety—he just wanted to make sure she couldn't communicate with her henchmen. *Jerk.*

She shook off his hand and shoved the key into the lock, giving it a savage twist that had the metal digging into her fingers. Ignoring James's muttered curse, she shoved the door open and reached for the light switch.

James placed a hand on her shoulder and pulled her back, keeping her from stepping into the apartment. "Dammit, Kelly, I told you—" His next words were lost as a movement inside the apartment caught her eye. There was a sudden bright flash and a muffled pop, and she was slammed back into James's chest. They fell into the hall, landing in a heap on the tiled floor.

James reacted quickly, rolling her off him and tugging her down the hall, away from the door. He pushed her up against the wall by the elevator, wincing as he moved. She stared at him dumbly, her mind struggling to process what was happening. A wet patch was spreading on his shirt and she reached out to touch it, amazed to find it warm.

He clapped a hand over her fingers to stop her tentative exploration. "Listen to me," he said, punctuating the words with a little shake. "Stay here. Don't move." His eyes drifted down, and he took her outstretched hand and pushed it onto her shoulder, igniting a burning flare of pain that had her seeing stars.

She heard movement, felt the air stir. When her eyes focused again, he was down the hall, gun drawn as he stepped into her dark apartment.

The pain in her shoulder was a constant throb, and a sticky, cooling warmth coated her fingers and was spreading across her shirt. *Blood.* She knew it even before she pulled her hand away to find it stained red.

"Oh, God." Tears began to fall as she put her hand back over her shoulder, trying to plug the leak. Her heart galloped in a pounding rhythm that left her gasping for breath. *Air.* She needed air, but no matter how hard she tried, she couldn't fill her starving lungs.

Her vision blurred and grayed, and she felt herself slide across the wall until she hit the floor. Her hand fell away from her shoulder and landed in front of her face; her fingers were stained an absurdly cheerful red. She tried to force her hand back into place, but her arm was strangely numb and wouldn't cooperate.

So this is dying, she thought, her world shrinking down to a pinpoint that gradually faded to black.

James crept through the dark apartment, leading with his gun as he moved. He felt like a hot poker had been jammed into his side, but he ignored the pain, trying to focus on the job at hand. There was a gunman on the loose, and he knew that a distracted agent was a dead agent.

The kitchen was clear, as was the living room. He started down the hall, making a quick check of the small bathroom before moving on. Kelly's bedroom was ahead, and it was the only place the perp could have gone.

Stepping carefully, silently, he approached her bedroom, ears straining for any indication of the assailant. He had to know he was cornered and would likely be waiting to shoot James as he walked into the room.

James paused outside the room, not willing to risk it yet. "FBI," he shouted out. "Drop your weapon and approach with your hands up."

There was no response, but he hadn't really expected one. "I repeat, drop your gun or I will shoot you."

Still nothing. He could see gray light in the room—

probably from a streetlamp—but there was no way to know how big the room was or where the perp could be hiding. He had the advantage from his position in the shadowed hallway, but the longer he waited, the more time the shooter had to regroup and replan.

A faint scratching sound came from within. If the gunman was moving, he'd be distracted. James decided to risk a quick glance, and he poked his head around the door frame, scanning the room before pulling back again.

Nothing. The room appeared to be empty. Fighting a sinking feeling of dread, he risked another, longer glance. When he saw no apparent threat, he stepped into the room, clearing the corners and checking the shadows for any sign of an intruder.

The room was empty; the curtain billowed in the breeze from the open window. The fabric grazed the surface of a desk, disturbing papers and pens and re-creating the scratching sound he'd heard. Frustration and anger welled up as he stalked over to the window. The shiny black of the fire escape mocked him as he approached.

He should have remembered the fire escape, should have moved faster. He'd wasted precious time being overly cautious, and now the shooter had gotten away. His instincts told him to chase after the guy, but he knew there was no way to tell where the perp had gone. He had too much of a head start and was likely far away by now.

Besides, he thought, pressing a hand to his side. *I'm not in any shape to run right now.*

Neither was Kelly. His heart had skipped a beat when he'd seen the blood on her shirt, but it looked like a flesh wound, nothing more. She was lucky. A few inches to the left, and she would have been dead in his arms.

He dug his phone out of his pocket as he made his way back through the apartment. "It's Reynolds," he said, then explained the situation in a few terse sentences. "I need an ERT and a bus. I've got two casualties." He relayed the address, then snapped the phone closed and stepped out into the hall. Time to deal with Kelly and give her the dressing-down she deserved for ignoring his instructions.

Oh, God. His anger evaporated as he took in the scene.

She was slumped over, lying on the floor in a crumpled heap. Her outstretched hand was limp and bright with blood, but she wasn't moving. Why wasn't she moving?

Heart pounding, he rushed over and dropped to his knees next to her. "Kelly! Kelly, wake up." The words were a strangled croak, so he tried again, reaching out to roll her onto her back.

She moaned faintly at the change in position. He ran his hands over her body, searching for another wound. Was the injury more serious than he'd thought? Had he missed something? He'd never forgive himself if he'd left her to bleed out in the hall....

She was starting to come around, her eyelids fluttering as he continued his search. "Kelly, I'm here," he said, hoping his voice would help bring her back. He didn't find any other injuries, so he turned his attention to the bright red blossom of her shoulder.

Gingerly, he peeled back her shirt to expose the wound. There was a small hole in her skin, a neat, round thing that was oozing blood. Relief washed over him at the sight, causing his hands to shake. It was just a through and through, no arteries involved. *Thank God.*

"James?" she whispered, her voice wobbly. She blinked up at him, her eyes hazy with pain. He sat with his back to the wall and gently gathered her into his arms, cradling her against his chest.

"I'm here, baby," he said, pushing a strand of hair off her face. "You're safe. I've got you." He pressed his mouth to her forehead, feathering soft kisses across her brow. He wanted to squeeze her tightly, but knowing that would only cause her pain, he fought to keep his hold gentle.

"My shoulder hurts." She frowned, concentrating. "You're hurt, too."

At the mention of his own injury, the pain in his side roared to life again. The adrenaline rush had kept him from feeling it before, but now that things were calming down, his body was wasting no time in communicating its displeasure with the events of the evening.

"I'm fine," he assured her. Although he hadn't looked yet, the injury felt like a flesh wound. He shifted slightly, the fabric of his shirt sticking to his side. No fresh bleeding, then, which was a good sign. The bullet had likely passed through her shoulder and grazed him, making them both damn lucky to be alive.

"I'm sorry," she whispered, a tear leaking from the corner of her eye. "I should have—"

"Hush," he told her, wiping the drop away with the pad of his thumb. "Just rest now." Time enough to yell at her later. For now, he needed to get her to a hospital, make sure she really was going to be okay. Once he knew she was safe and whole, then he'd talk to her about following directions.

The muted wail of sirens sounded, a beautiful symphony that grew louder by the second. The cavalry was here.

The ambulance ride to Shady Grove Hospital seemed to take forever. Kelly lay on the gurney, trying not to moan at every bump in the road. It felt as if the driver was going out of his way to hit every pothole, but maybe it was just the speed that made the ride feel so rough.

James sat next to the paramedic, having refused to ride in the second ambulance. "We stay together," he'd said, his tone and expression brooking no argument. He had deigned to allow the paramedics to check his wound, and he sat now with his shirt open, his hand pressed to the white strip of gauze taped along his side.

She didn't know how he could just *sit* there, so stoic and reserved. Her shoulder was screaming and his side had to be, too, but he gave no outward indication of feeling any discomfort. He winced slightly when the driver hit an especially rough patch of road, but otherwise he could have been made of marble.

After what seemed like an eternity, the ambulance pulled into the emergency bay. A moment later the doors at the end opened, bringing fresh air tinged with diesel fumes into the back. Kelly gritted her teeth as the paramedics jostled the gurney out and onto the pavement. She knew they were trying to be careful, but her pain was overwhelming. Her whole consciousness was focused on her shoulder and the throbbing that kept time with her heart.

They wheeled her into the emergency room, James trotting alongside. He looked like an avenging angel, with his hair mussed and his hands bloody. There was a streak of red down the side of his face where he'd wiped his hand in a moment of distraction, and his eyes were bright and focused. He had the look of a man who would mow down anyone or anything that got in his way, and she saw several orderlies and nurses jump back as they rolled her down the hall and into an exam room.

A triage nurse approached and began her examination with brisk, efficient movements. She asked a few questions, but Kelly only heard about half of them. Her tongue was thick in her mouth, and she wanted nothing more than to close her eyes against the bright overhead lights.

She was cold, so cold, and she reached down, fumbling for a blanket that wasn't there. James pulled the sheet over her legs, telling her to lie back and relax.

She felt a sharp sting in her hand and looked over to find a nurse taping down a needle. She saw a few drops of blood on her skin, and then she was back in the tunnel, her vision narrowing down to a pinprick of light before finally going dark.

When she came around again, a young woman in a white coat was standing over her.

"Welcome back," the woman said. "You gave us a bit of a scare there."

"Sorry," Kelly replied automatically.

The doctor laughed. "Don't worry about it. I'm Dr. Mahoney, and I'll be stitching you up today."

"No more blood," Kelly mumbled.

A blond eyebrow went up. "Oh, you're one of those, are you? Good to know." She moved around the bed to a cabinet, took out a blue cloth and returned to the head of the bed.

"I'm going to clean this out and stitch you up. The bullet didn't hit anything important, which makes you very lucky."

Kelly grunted in response. With her shoulder on fire and every breath painful, she didn't feel too lucky at the moment.

"I'm going to need you to lie on your side so I can access both sides of your injury."

Kelly sucked in a breath and moved as instructed, stretching out her arm to pillow her head. The position was very much like the one she assumed while sleeping, but there was little chance of her dozing off while being stitched up.

"You're going to feel a little prick...." Kelly winced at the sting in her shoulder as the doctor injected something to numb the area. After a few more pokes, the pain began to ease, and Kelly exhaled in relief.

"Lidocaine's a wonderful drug, isn't it?" the doctor said.

Kelly could only nod in response, her limbs relaxing as the pain left. She sank more fully into the bed, not realizing until that instant how rigid her whole body had been.

The woman ripped open a package, took out a wandlike instrument with a sponge on the end and squeezed. There was a quiet cracking sound, and the sponge turned a dark orange. "Any shellfish allergies?"

"No."

"Great." Dr. Mahoney set about wiping Kelly's

shoulder, moving in an ever-expanding circle. She reached the margins of the numbed area and continued outward; the liquid was cool on Kelly's skin.

"Do you want your, um, friend to stay?"

Kelly stiffened, unaware that anyone else was in the room. She tried to sit up, but Dr. Mahoney put a hand on her side. "Stay down, please. I don't want to have to resterilize the area."

"I'm not going anywhere." There was a screech of wood on tile as James dragged his chair across the floor, then pulled it around to the other side of the bed. He sat down and glared at Kelly, as if daring her to ask him to leave.

She glared right back, not appreciating his attitude. Why was he here? He had his own injuries to deal with. And why was he so angry? It wasn't as if she had known there was an intruder in her apartment.

He probably thinks I set this whole thing up! She felt her face heat at the thought and bit her lip to keep from crying out in frustration. Was that his problem? He had said he didn't trust her, but surely he knew she'd never do something like this.

She closed her eyes against the prickle of impending tears. How had they gotten to this point? She'd gone from being his friend to his lover to a suspect in his investigation. Quite an evolution, and one she wasn't sure she could reverse.

Dr. Mahoney's voice brought her out of her thoughts. "You can't stay if she doesn't want you here."

There was a moment of tension as James and the doctor faced off, gazes locked in silent battle. James might be the big, bad FBI agent, but the young doctor appeared to have a spine of steel and she wasn't about to back down.

"It's fine," Kelly said, wanting to defuse the situation. James looked as if he was close to his breaking point, and the last thing any of them needed was for him to get into an argument with the doctor. Besides, if she made him leave, he'd probably think she was trying to hide something.

"Are you sure?" the doctor said in a low voice.

Kelly nodded. "Yes. He can stay." James nodded once and leaned back in the chair, apparently satisfied with the outcome.

"Thank you for asking," she murmured.

Dr. Mahoney winked at her, then draped the blue cloth around her shoulder. A flap covered the side of her face, effectively blocking Kelly's view of the proceedings. Probably for the best.

She heard the metallic tinkle of instruments as the doctor went to work on her shoulder. "Want to tell me what happened here?" Dr. Mahoney asked, a tugging sensation accompanying her words.

Kelly's stomach fluttered a bit in warning. She squeezed her eyes shut, swallowing hard.

"There was a gun," she gritted out, focusing on the memory of the shooting as a distraction from the sounds accompanying the doctor's movements. "He fired as we walked in."

"I see." More tugging, then pressure. "You're lucky his aim wasn't better. A few inches to the left, and he'd have hit your heart."

"James got shot, too."

"Is that right?"

Kelly opened her eyes to see James frown at her,

as if he was annoyed she'd brought it up. "It's just a scratch," he said gruffly.

"Why don't you let me be the judge of that?"

He harrumphed in response but didn't press the issue.

There was a brief period of silence as the doctor worked; then she spoke again. "All right," she said as she set down her tools. There was the rip of a package and the smell of rubbing alcohol, and Kelly felt a pressure on her shoulder as the woman rubbed the Betadine stain from her skin.

"I'm just going to tape this up, and you'll be good to go."

She worked quickly, applying bandages and taping them into place. She whisked away the drapes and helped Kelly sit back up, then tugged off her gloves.

"Is it safe for me to look?"

"Yep. I'm all done."

Kelly turned to see a neat white square on her shoulder. She studied it for a moment, fascinated by how such a small thing had caused so much pain. She reached around to find a matching bandage on her back. Two holes. She felt like Swiss cheese.

"You're all set," the doctor said, laying the chart on the bed as she spoke. "That lidocaine is going to wear off soon, so I'll have a nurse bring you some more Dilaudid, and I gave you a shot of antibiotics to prevent infection. Do you have any questions for me?"

Kelly shook her head, her thoughts still too scattered to focus on forming an intelligent question. "Not right now. Thanks for taking care of me."

Dr. Mahoney smiled, making her look even younger. Kelly idly wondered just how old the good doctor was,

but decided it would be too rude to ask. "You're welcome. See your primary-care physician to get those
stitches out next week, okay?"

"I will."

"Good." The woman turned to face James, who was
still scowling in the corner. "Now let's have a look at
you."

"I'm fine," he repeated, making no move to leave
the chair.

"You have a gunshot wound," the doctor replied.
"The law requires me to examine you."

The corner of his mouth quirked up in what might
have been a smile under different circumstances. "Doctor, I work for the FBI. Before that, I was a D.C. cop.
While the law requires you to report a gunshot wound,
it does not require you to examine said wound without
the consent of the patient."

Dr. Mahoney shrugged. "It was worth a shot, no pun
intended. Are you sure you don't want me to look at it?"

He nodded.

"Suit yourself." The doctor turned to leave.

"James." Kelly said his name softly, knowing that if
she pushed him, he'd push right back. "Please?"

He held her gaze for a long moment, emotions that
she couldn't identify flashing through his eyes. Finally, he sighed.

"All right."

He stood with a wince, slowly unbuttoned his shirt
and tugged it off with careful, deliberate movements.
He kept his eyes locked on her face the entire time. Determined not to look away, she maintained eye contact
with him, a task that grew increasingly difficult as the

shirt dropped to reveal a wide expanse of golden skin and the dark curls that dusted his chest.

She'd seen that chest before, been intimately acquainted with those shoulders and arms, the flat belly that tapered to slim hips. She'd used her tongue to trace the line of hair from his belly button to his...

She swallowed hard, trying to keep her face impassive as they played this silent game of chicken.

If he was affected by her subtle perusal, he didn't show it. He merely raised a brow, silently asking if she liked what she saw. She almost nodded, but she stopped herself just in time. Yes, he was gorgeous. Yes, she was still attracted to him. Yes, she'd love to jump him right here, right now, Dr. Mahoney be damned. But she refused to admit her appreciation for his body when he had made it clear he didn't trust her.

Dr. Mahoney stepped closer, reaching out to grab a corner of the tape holding his bandage in place. She glanced up. "It'll hurt less if I just rip it off."

He nodded. The tape came free with a few firm tugs to reveal an angry red gash tracking along the side of his rib cage. Kelly sucked in a breath at the sight, wondering how he was still standing. Her injury was in a much smaller area, and before the pain meds, she'd barely kept it together.

Dr. Mahoney probed along the margins with her gloved fingers, eliciting a wince from her patient. "Looks pretty clean," she muttered as she examined him. "Still bleeding, though." She was right—even now a few drops of blood welled up and began a downward trek across his skin.

Satisfied, the doctor pressed a fresh square of gauze to his side. "Hold this for me."

James obliged, and Dr. Mahoney straightened. "You need stitches," she pronounced, removing her gloves with a snap. "I'm going to grab another suture kit. Be right back."

She left before James could respond; the soft squeak of her shoes on the floor faded as she walked out.

The silence in the room was a thick blanket pressing down on them. Kelly fiddled with the edge of the bed sheet, folding it over and over again to form an even pleat as she cast about for something to say that would ease the tension between them.

"I should move." She pushed herself up with her uninjured arm, swinging her legs over the side of the bed. "The doctor will probably want you to lie down so she can stitch you up."

"You're fine." James held out a hand to stop her, but he was careful not to touch her. "Just stay there. I can sit on the end of the bed." He made no move to approach the bed, a fact that wasn't lost on Kelly.

"Look," she said, unable to keep the bite of temper out of her voice. "I don't know what's got you all twisted up, but I'm a little tired of being treated like some kind of pariah."

James merely raised a brow, and his cool aloofness added fuel to the fire of her anger. "Who's treating you like a pariah?"

"You are," she bit out, her jaw clenched so tightly it was a wonder her teeth didn't crack. *Damn this man!* "It's not my fault we're here." She crossed her arms over her chest, ignoring the twinge of protest from her shoulder.

He took a step forward at that, glaring down at her. "Actually, it is your fault." His words were short and

YOUR PARTICIPATION IS REQUESTED!

Dear Reader,

Since you are a lover of romance fiction – we would like to get to know you!

Inside you will find a short Reader's Survey. Sharing your answers with us will help our editorial staff understand who you are and what activities you enjoy.

To thank you for your participation, we would like to send you 2 books and 2 gifts – **ABSOLUTELY FREE!**

Enjoy your gifts with our appreciation,

Pam Powers

SEE INSIDE FOR READER'S SURVEY

For Your Romance Reading Pleasure...

YOUR READER'S SURVEY
"THANK YOU" FREE GIFTS INCLUDE:
▶ 2 Harlequin® Romantic Suspense books
▶ 2 lovely surprise gifts

PLEASE FILL IN THE CIRCLES COMPLETELY TO RESPOND

1) What type of fiction books do you enjoy reading? (Check all that apply)
○ Suspense/Thrillers ○ Action/Adventure ○ Modern-day Romances
○ Historical Romance ○ Humour ○ Paranormal Romance

2) What attracted you most to the last fiction book you purchased on impulse?
○ The Title ○ The Cover ○ The Author ○ The Story

3) What is usually the greatest influencer when you <u>plan</u> to buy a book?
○ Advertising ○ Referral ○ Book Review

4) How often do you access the internet?
○ Daily ○ Weekly ○ Monthly ○ Rarely or never.

5) How many NEW paperback fiction novels have you purchased in the past 3 months?
○ 0 - 2 ○ 3 - 6 ○ 7 or more

YES! I have completed the Reader's Survey. Please send me
the 2 FREE books and 2 FREE gifts (gifts are worth about $10) for
which I qualify. I understand that I am under no obligation to
purchase any books, as explained on the back of this card.

240/340 HDL F5DT

FIRST NAME	LAST NAME

ADDRESS

APT.#	CITY

STATE/PROV.	ZIP/POSTAL CODE

clipped. "And believe me, we will talk about your behavior. But not now."

"My behavior? Just who the hell do you think you are? I'm not a child you can scold when I don't do what you want. That's not how this works." She gestured between them, her movements jerky but forceful. She leaned forward, pointing at him. If he'd been just a step closer, she would have poked him in the chest. "And for the record, your behavior has been lacking, as well."

A polite cough from the door cut off whatever James was about to say. Dr. Mahoney stepped into the room carrying a bundle wrapped in blue fabric, which she placed on the rolling tray next to the bed.

"Why don't you come sit down for me?" She patted the end of the bed. "This won't take long."

With a final glare at Kelly, James sat down, making sure to arrange himself as far away from her as possible. *Fine.* She didn't want to touch him anyway.

Kelly stared down at her lap as Dr. Mahoney patched James up. Why was she letting him get to her like this? So he still harbored doubts about her innocence. After the way she had walked out on him before, could she really blame him for not trusting her? Maybe she was being too hard on him, but a small part of her was disappointed that he thought she could be involved. After all, walking out on someone was a far cry from terrorism, and he should know her well enough to realize she would never do something like that.

She couldn't deny she'd been keeping secrets from him. She'd never told him about Gary or about the fact that she'd started seeing a therapist after their night together. She had finally gotten to a point where she felt secure again, and then this nightmare had started. It wasn't James's fault she was involved, but it did hurt to know he didn't think of her as being on his team.

"These the two GSWs?"

Kelly looked up to find two uniformed police officers at the door. The older man sported a mustache and a frown, while his partner looked impossibly young, his cheeks pink and smooth and his eyes wide.

"Yes," Dr. Mahoney responded. "Just give me a minute to finish, and then they're all yours."

"We'll be right outside the door," the older man replied. He nudged his partner, and the pair stepped out into the hall, their shadows casting dark lines on the floor.

"Good," James muttered under his breath. "I need to talk to them."

"I imagine they're quite interested in what you have to say," the doctor said. Kelly heard the snip of scissors, followed by the rip of tape. "After all," she continued conversationally, "it's not every day we see an FBI agent involved in a shoot-out."

"Glad I could provide some entertainment for you," James said wryly.

Dr. Mahoney winked at him as she stepped back, and James grinned at her. A small spark of jealousy kindled to life in Kelly's chest as she watched the pair—the pretty blonde woman and the dangerously handsome man. *Mine,* she thought as she watched him button his shirt.

No, not anymore, replied the voice of reason. *You had your chance.*

James spared her a glance as he stood. Her thoughts must have showed on her face, because he paused, studying her as if trying to read her emotions. "I'll be right back," he said slowly, frowning slightly before he turned and stepped out of the room.

"Looks like you're all set here," Dr. Mahoney said, tossing the debris into the trash can in the corner. "I'll start the paperwork, and we'll get you on your way."

"Thanks," Kelly replied absently. Where was she supposed to go? She couldn't go home, not with what had happened tonight. There was no way she was going to stay in that apartment now that Caleb and his thugs knew where she lived. She shuddered at the thought of him in her home, her space. She didn't really spend much time there, but it had always been a kind of refuge for her. Now Caleb had ruined that. She'd never feel safe there again.

Would James still take her to the safe house? What was the protocol after someone had been shot at? She idly wondered if he'd have to take her someplace new or if his original plan was still good. He was probably looking forward to dropping her off and having someone else deal with her. Maybe a little separation would do them both good.

What exactly did a safe house look like? she wondered, leaning back against the stiff, undersize hospital pillow. More important, was there a bathtub? She sighed, wanting nothing more than to wash this night off her and climb into a soft bed. Surely that wasn't too much to ask.

She shifted a bit, gasping as the movement sent a sudden spike of pain down her arm. Hadn't the doctor said something about pain medication? Where was the nurse?

As if summoned by her thoughts, a young man in brown scrubs stepped into the room. "Ready for pain meds?" he asked cheerfully, holding up a paper cup as he approached.

"Yes, please," Kelly replied, leaning forward to sit up.

After verifying her identity, he passed her the pain pills. They were small and white and went down easily, a fact Kelly was grateful for, seeing as how the cup of water the nurse had given her only held a few sips.

"Sit tight," the nurse said, gathering up the trash as he moved to the door. "Buzz me if you need anything."

"Thanks," Kelly called out, but he'd already moved on.

She glanced around the empty room, at a loss. After spending the day with James and other members of his team, she suddenly felt very lonely.

"Now what?" she whispered to herself.

Chapter 6

"Let me get this straight."

Mitchell, the older cop, flipped his notebook shut and eyed James dubiously. "Even though there were no serious injuries, you want us to go back to the station and report this as a double homicide?"

James nodded, trying not to look too desperate. "That'd be great."

"And why would I want to create all that paperwork for myself?"

James could tell by the set of his jaw that Mitchell wasn't in a mood to cooperate. Not that he blamed him. He remembered well the reams of forms that accompanied a murder investigation, all needing to be filled out in triplicate on the antique typewriter with the sticky keys.

"I know it's a pain in the ass. When I worked in the

106, we had the crappiest typewriter in the city. I always had to pull the forms out and start over."

Mitchell's brows shot up. "You were a D.C. cop?"

James nodded. "Yeah. Seven years on the job."

"The 106, you said? That's district one, right?"

James nodded again. "You got it."

Mitchell eyed him up and down, a new respect in his gaze. "That's a tough area."

James shrugged. "Aren't they all?"

That earned him a laugh and a slap on the back that made his eyes water. "True enough. So." He stepped in closer, lowering his voice. "You gonna tell me why you want me to file a false report?"

James took a second to weigh his options. If he refused to talk, Mitchell might very well refuse to file the report, which would complicate an already bad day. Better to risk the information getting out, especially if it bought him a few hours' time.

"I'm working a sensitive case right now," he said, pausing slightly before saying the magic words. "It's a national-security thing. I need the perp who took a shot at us tonight to think we're dead."

"I see." Mitchell nodded thoughtfully. "And this would really help you out?"

"Oh, yeah," James assured him. "You have no idea. And to make things easier on you, you don't even have to file the paperwork. You could just go back to your car, check in with dispatch and let them know the two GSWs were DOA. Then you have a quiet word with your captain when you get back to the station." He rubbed his palms together in a pantomime of washing his hands. "That's it."

Mitchell broke into a wide smile. "I think I can handle that."

James held his hand out for a quick shake. "Good man. I really appreciate it."

"Good luck to you." Mitchell tucked his notepad back into his pocket. "You ready, kid?"

The younger cop, who had remained silent during the discussion, nodded. "Say, how'd you go from being a cop to an FBI agent?"

James swallowed hard, forcing down the painful memories the innocent question had stirred up. "I worked a joint case with the bureau, and they recruited me." It wasn't a lie, exactly, but it wasn't the whole truth, either. After Steve's death, he had needed to leave the force, and luckily, the bureau had been hiring.

"What about your partner?" The kid's eyes cut to Mitchell, who was listening to the exchange with barely concealed curiosity.

"My partner was retiring, so it was a good time for me to make the jump."

The young man nodded, seemingly satisfied with his answer. "That's cool. Saved you having to break in a new partner." He shot a sly grin at Mitchell, who chuckled.

"Let's go, wiseass. We've still got a lot of night ahead of us."

The pair nodded at him and wandered away. James exhaled slowly. One thing taken care of. How many fires were left to put out?

He caught sight of a blond ponytail rounding the corner and hurried after it. Getting the hospital to co-operate was next on his growing to-do list.

He found the doctor standing at the nurses' station,

jotting something down on a patient's chart. Crap, what was her name?

"Um, excuse me?"

She glanced up at him, did a double take. Then she smiled, the expression transforming her from harried professional to beautiful woman.

"Hello there," she said. "Did you need something?"

"Yes, actually, there was something." He laid a hand on her arm and gently guided her to the doorway of an empty patient room. It wasn't the best option, as far as privacy went, but it was better than nothing.

"I need a favor," he began.

She didn't say anything, but her smile slipped a little. If he didn't know better, he'd say she was disappointed.

"I'm working a case," he went on, talking quickly to hold her attention. The last thing he needed was for her to be pulled away on an emergency before he could finish explaining what he needed her to do.

"So do you think you can sit on her chart? Maybe keep it out of the general circulation, so anyone snooping around wouldn't know she'd been here?"

She let out a sigh. "I suppose I could misplace it for a few hours, if that's what you're asking."

"That'd be great. But only if it doesn't get you into trouble."

She smiled up at him again. "Nah. It's no big deal."

"I appreciate it." He gave her arm a squeeze, and her smile grew warmer. *Uh-oh.*

"There's one more thing," he said, feeling like an ass. He didn't want to take advantage of her seeming goodwill toward him, but he wasn't done asking for favors yet.

"Yes?" she said, moving infinitesimally closer.

"Can you keep her overnight?"

She blinked up at him. "Your friend?"

He nodded, holding his breath.

Her blond brows drew together in a frown. "That's a little tougher to swing. She's not seriously injured, and we need the bed."

He cast about for something he could say to convince her. "She did pass out several times tonight, though. Could you admit her for observation or something?"

The doctor pursed her lips and exhaled, causing the stray strands of hair that had escaped from her ponytail to flare out. "I suppose you want me to admit her under an assumed name, too?"

He grinned. "Now you're getting the idea. I think Jane Doe has a nice ring to it, don't you?"

"Well, she didn't have an ID on her when she came in," said the doctor. "I suppose it wouldn't be too much of a stretch."

"I owe you," James said sincerely.

The corner of her mouth quirked up. "Normally, I'd take that as my cue to request drinks and dinner as payback. But something tells me you're not available...." She trailed off, watching him closely.

He fought to keep his expression neutral. "Not exactly," he admitted.

"Figures," she muttered. "It was worth a shot anyway. Tell your friend I said she's a lucky girl."

"What makes you think it's her?"

She shot him a look that was pure feminine amusement. "Please. I heard the two of you arguing. It's clear from the way you fight that you both care about each other."

Well, that much was true. Most of his anger had stemmed from fear—the fear that Kelly was seriously hurt, the fear that she'd come so close to being killed tonight. The fear of losing her had cut through the tangled thicket of his emotions and laid bare the fact that he still had feelings for her. That realization had only made him more frustrated than ever, and it had caused him to lash out.

The doctor was watching him, clearly expecting an answer. "It's complicated," he said, not knowing what else to say. How could he explain the situation to a relative stranger when he couldn't even explain it to himself?

"It usually is," she replied, the ghost of a smile flitting across her face. "You've both had a crappy night, and I imagine you're short on sleep. Will you be staying with her tonight?"

He nodded. No way was he going to let her out of his sight. Besides, they were both supposed to be dead, so he couldn't very well go gallivanting around town.

"I'll try to get her a bigger room so we can roll a cot in alongside the bed."

James shook his head. "No need. I can't sleep anyway. Save it for someone who can use it."

She shrugged. "Suit yourself." A shrill beep had her reaching for the waistband of her scrubs. She read the number with a frown, then reattached her pager to its holster. "Gotta run. I'll start on that paperwork when I get a minute."

"Thanks, Doc."

She sent him a distracted wave as she rushed off

down the hall, leaving him standing alone in the doorway. Time to get back to Kelly. He'd been gone for too long, and even though it was unlikely she was in danger here in the emergency room, he didn't feel comfortable leaving her alone. He still had some calls to make, but he could do that from the room.

First, though, he had to talk to her about the shooting. She had deliberately ignored his instructions tonight, putting them both in harm's way. He had to make her understand that when he told her to do something, it was for her safety and she needed to listen to him. But how? She clearly wasn't in the mood to hear him out, and he didn't want the conversation to devolve into another argument.

With a deep sigh, he began the walk back to her room, mentally practicing his speech as he moved down the hall. He was just going to come right out and say it, no beating around the bush. She generally appreciated honesty, and he was going to give it to her. If she didn't like it, too bad. He wasn't a fan of getting shot, so they were even.

"Kelly, we need to talk." He stepped into the room, the words sticking in his throat as he drew up short at the sight that greeted him.

Kelly lay back in the bed, her hair spread out in a reddish halo on the pillow. Her face was pale but relaxed, her lips parted slightly, as though she was inviting a kiss. Her chest rose and fell in an even cadence under the starched white sheet, the only movement in the otherwise still room.

She made quite a picture, all delicate lines and muted colors. He rubbed at his chest, where a curious warmth had blossomed. Seeing her like this, with her guard down and looking vulnerable, reminded him of how things used to be between them. Back when his heart didn't ache every time he was around her, and she didn't look at him as if he'd just kicked her puppy. He wanted to get back to that place with her, but it seemed as if for every step forward, they took two steps back.

Today was a perfect example. They'd shared a moment this morning, at her work. But he'd said or done something to push her away, and admitting he didn't fully trust her had only made things worse. Now they were both injured, and he knew things were about to get a lot more complicated.

He walked over to the chair with quiet, careful steps, then gingerly settled onto the seat. She needed her rest tonight. Tomorrow and its tough conversations would come soon enough.

He could wait.

Kelly wasn't sure what woke her.

She didn't even know she had fallen asleep, as she'd had no dreams to mark the time. She opened her eyes to find a room, dark and unfamiliar, with long shadows reaching across the floor to grab at her toes. She shifted, trying to sit up so she could get a better view of things, only to gasp as a burning spike of pain shot down her arm.

Her shoulder. That was right. She'd been shot. Was she still in the hospital? Why would they keep her there overnight, when the doctor had told her she was fine?

There was a soft rustling beside the bed, and she turned to see a shadowy figure sitting in the chair, his face hidden from view. She jerked away with a strangled cry, her heart kicking into a frantic rhythm.

The figure moved, reaching out to lay a warm hand on her arm. "It's okay, Kelly." James spoke quietly, giving her arm a gentle squeeze.

"James," she breathed. "You scared me. For a second there I thought—"

"I know," he said softly. "I'm sorry. I didn't mean to frighten you. I thought you were going to go back to sleep."

"My shoulder hurts too much for that right now." She groped for the button to raise the head of the bed, pushing herself up into a sitting position to better talk to James. Being flat in the bed next to him felt too intimate.

"Should I turn on the light?"

"No. Dark is better." She didn't want him to see her like this. While the doctor had done a good job of cleaning her shoulder, she could feel a crust of dried blood on her neck and chest and could only imagine how scary she looked.

"How long have you been here?" He shifted in the chair as if he was uncomfortable, but since hospital chairs were not designed for comfort, that didn't tell her anything.

"Not long," he said softly. He looked up, but the dim light from the streetlamp outside her window didn't provide enough illumination for her to see his face. "I thought it would be better if we stayed here overnight."

"Because he's still out there?"

"Yes."

"And you think he's still a threat."

James didn't reply, but he didn't need to. Kelly wasn't stupid. She was no tactical expert, but a hospital was a busy place—lots of witnesses and even the odd guard or police officer roaming around. It would be harder to attack someone in a building that never slept. Still, knowing that James thought they were in danger sent a chill through her body. She wanted to curl up in a ball and shut the world out, but she knew that wasn't an option.

"Did you get a good look at the shooter?"

James shook his head, confirming her suspicions. "He was already gone by the time I entered the apartment. Out your bedroom window and down the fire escape. We're dusting for prints, but…" He didn't have to finish. The man had probably worn gloves, and even if he hadn't, who knew how many layers of fingerprints were on the fire escape?

"Do you think it was Caleb?"

Another head shake. "Could be, but I doubt it. Based on what we know about him, he usually hires this kind of thing out. He went after you at the office today because you were right there in front of him, but he doesn't like to get his hands dirty."

Wonderful. More people after her. She absently fingered the edge of the gauze bandage on her shoulder. She'd been lucky tonight but probably wouldn't fare as well during a second encounter.

James caught her gesture and cleared his throat. "I don't think he meant to shoot you," he said quietly. "I think he was aiming for me."

"What makes you say that?" His head was down again, and she watched him run a hand through his hair.

"It makes no sense for them to shoot you. You can't help them if you're injured or dead." He sat up in the chair, and the dim light filtered through his mussed hair. "Me, on the other hand, they don't care about. If I'm out of the picture, you're easier to take."

"But how did they know you'd be with me?"

"They probably didn't. I'm thinking the guy was going to use the gun to make sure you cooperated this time. But then he heard us talking in the hall outside your door, and he changed his plans."

"Shoot first—ask questions later?"

"Something like that."

"So it's probably a good thing I walked in first." She tried to keep her voice neutral, but a note of self-righteous smugness crept in. "If you'd gone in first, you'd have walked right into a bullet."

"No, I wouldn't have. I would have entered the room using a tactical approach, something I wanted to do before you butted in and got yourself shot." His hand tightened on her arm before he released her to lean back in the chair. "If you had just listened to me, none of this would have happened."

"Oh, so this whole thing is my fault?"

"Yes! You could have gotten killed tonight! Do you realize that?" His voice was low, but there was no mistaking his anger. Kelly was glad it was dark so she couldn't see his face. It was easier to be brave in the dark.

"Maybe if you weren't such a jerk, I would have listened to you." She heard the pout in her voice but didn't care. She was too tired and in too much pain to be diplomatic about things.

"What the hell are you talking about?"

"I am so tired of being treated like crap by you. Even though I was attacked yesterday morning, you made it clear that you don't trust me. What else do I have to do to prove I'm not involved in this?"

"That's not what this is about."

She gritted her teeth. He was so damn *calm,* which made her want to scream. Taking a deep breath, she continued, "You expect me to just fall in line when you bark out an order. Well, guess what? I'm not a child— I'm a grown woman, and I can take care of myself."

"All evidence to the contrary," he muttered.

"Listen, I'm not going to play some damsel in distress to feed your knight-errant complex—"

"You have no idea what you're talking about."

"Yes, I do. I—"

The words stuck in her throat as he suddenly loomed over her, big and warm and dangerous. His hands landed on either side of her head, bracketing her body and effectively trapping her in the bed without actually touching her.

She fought the urge to panic, her muscles tensing up as she instinctively prepared to defend herself. *He won't hurt me,* she repeated silently, hoping it was true.

He raised a hand and she flinched, sucking in a breath. He paused, then gently pushed back a strand of hair from her forehead. She could feel his gaze on her, studying her, watching her, but she refused to meet his eyes. Even in the dim moonlight, she was certain he'd be able to see her fear.

"I'm bigger than you," he whispered, his breath warm as it drifted over her cheek. "And stronger." His fingertips traced down the line of her arm, leaving goose bumps in their wake. "It's my job to protect you, using my body if I have to." He found her hand and lifted it up to press against his chest. His heartbeat was a steady, comforting rhythm in her palm, and she felt her muscles begin to relax. "This has nothing to do with your abilities, or whether or not I trust you, or with some knight-in-shining-armor thing. When I tell you to get behind me, it's because I know there's danger ahead and I want to keep you as far away from it as possible. It's as simple as that."

Kelly swallowed around the lump in her throat as a flock of butterflies took up residence in her stomach. Slowly, so slowly, hardly daring to breathe, she let her eyes drift over until she met his stare.

His eyes were twin pools of darkness, their normal golden brown appearing silvery-gray in the shaft of moonlight that fell across his face. Still, there was no way to miss the intensity of his stare or the emotional currents swirling underneath his apparent stillness.

Did he care about her? Could he? After everything that had happened, maybe he still harbored some feelings for her. Maybe he didn't hate her after all. The thought made her heart swell with hope, only to crash back down to earth a second later. Maybe she was wrong, and he was willing to sacrifice his body to keep all his charges safe.

But…the spark of hope flared back to life as a new thought occurred to her. He had held her earlier, and he was practically on top of her now. Surely he wouldn't do those things if he felt nothing for her. Surely he wouldn't throw himself in front of danger for just anyone. Right?

Only one way to find out.

"James," she whispered. His hand fell away, but she kept her palm pressed to his heart, which had started beating faster. She wanted to take her other hand and cup his face, but she couldn't move it. She settled for tipping her head forward the barest inch instead.

"James," she said again, his name both a plea and a question.

His tongue darted out to wet his lips as he ducked his head, bringing his mouth closer to hers.

Kelly closed her eyes, parting her lips slightly in anticipation. Her skin tingled where he had touched her; waves of sensation spread over her as she waited for his kiss.

There was the barest flutter across her lips, soft as the caress of a butterfly wing. She leaned forward, wanting to trap this feeling, to prolong the contact between them, but she met empty air.

Confused, she opened her eyes to see James standing over the bed, looking down at her with a troubled expression.

"James?" she asked, unsure of what to say. Why had he pulled away?

He didn't respond, but as she looked up at him, she could see him rebuilding his defenses, brick by brick, until his expression was once again that of the professional, detached agent.

"You should go back to sleep," he said, his rough voice the only indication he'd been flustered just a moment ago.

"I'm not tired," she said softly.

He ignored her. "I'll call the nurse, get you another dose of pain meds."

She sighed, knowing a lost cause when she saw one. "Don't you need any? You were shot, too."

"I'm fine."

"How is that possible? You have a huge wound along the side of your body—that's got to hurt."

"It's only a flesh wound. I've had worse."

She snorted, which had him lifting an eyebrow. "You sound like you should be in a Terminator movie or something."

Was that a smile playing at the corner of his mouth? "You need to rest, and you can't do it in pain. I'll be right back."

He left the room, his steps quiet as he moved. Kelly leaned back against the pillow, pressing her fingers to her lips in a vain effort to re-create the feel of the gentle whisper of his kiss.

He's still there, she thought, the realization making her almost giddy. The old James, her best friend and onetime lover, the man she cared about and had never really gotten over, was still inside this new, harder man. He seemed to be buried deep, but she'd seen a glimpse of him tonight and she wanted more.

It would take time, she knew, to earn his trust again. Time to break down the walls he'd erected to keep her out. But now that he knew for sure she wasn't involved with Dr. Collins or the terrorist organization, she could work on repairing the damage to their relationship.

They'd shared something special before, something she had thrown away in a moment of fear and weakness. She didn't know if the embers of their connection still burned inside him, but she knew she had to try to find out.

She wasn't going to give him up so easily this time.

James watched Kelly sleep, taking a small measure of comfort from the even rise and fall of her chest. She slept soundly, telling him that her pain was under control, at least for the moment.

He sighed and ran a hand through his hair, shifting in a vain attempt to find a comfortable position in the Naugahyde chair. Today had been one of the worst days of his life, both personally and professionally.

Carmichael had been livid after hearing that Kelly had been shot. He had blamed James for not taking the proper precautions, and James had had to bite his tongue to keep from pointing out that Carmichael hadn't considered her to be a target. Truth be told, James thought Carmichael was more upset by the shooter's escape than the fact that Kelly had been injured.

He stared at the white square on her shoulder, remembering the feel of her blood on his hands. He could have lost her tonight. Just a little bit lower, and the bullet would have hit an artery. He shuddered at the thought of her bleeding out under his hands, him powerless to stop it.

Bad enough that she had been injured on his watch. He didn't think he'd ever forget that flash of fire, the thud of her hitting his chest. The look of shocked confusion on her face as she tried to process what was happening. His heart had skipped a few beats when he saw her lying in the hall, still and so very pale.

Much as he hated to admit it, she'd gotten under his skin again. After she had walked out, he'd worked hard to get over his disappointment, and he had grudgingly accepted that she wasn't going to be a part of his life. It wasn't the first time he'd lost someone important to him, and although it never got easier, he knew it was a part of life.

Now, after only two days of being around her again, his feelings were as fresh and as strong as ever. Not even his initial suspicions regarding her involvement had been enough to keep his heart from beating a little faster when he was around her. Now that he knew she was innocent, his feelings were threatening to overwhelm him.

He was in serious danger of letting his emotions control his behavior. He'd let his anger have free rein earlier, and he had scared Kelly without meaning to. He thought back to the way she'd flinched when he'd raised his hand, the memory of her reaction twisting his gut and filling him with shame. Did she honestly think he was capable of hurting her?

Kelly stirred, shifting positions with a sigh. A strand of hair had fallen across her forehead, and he moved to push it back behind her ear, his hand stalling just before he touched her. He needed to keep his hands off her. Bad enough that he had kissed her earlier. His fingers drifted across his lips, a poor substitute for the softness of her mouth. He had been so tempted to lean in and deepen the kiss, wanting nothing more than to gather her into his arms and pour all his confusion and frustration and relief into the contact. It had taken all his self-control to pull away. Some primal part of his brain had known that if he started something, he wouldn't be able to stop.

While he wanted to feel her under him again, he wasn't about to scratch that itch in a hospital bed. Especially not when things were still so murky between them. Better to keep things on a professional level, for everyone.

James leaned back in the chair, gritting his teeth

as he considered his options. Kelly was definitely a target; that much was certain. She needed protection, but he couldn't keep her by his side 24/7. A safe house was out—he wasn't about to let others do the watching for him. Besides, he wasn't convinced Caleb didn't know the locations of the safe houses. Given today's events, he wasn't about to take any more chances with Kelly's life.

That left one alternative, one he knew she wouldn't be happy about. His apartment. It was the only place he was confident was secure, where he'd be able to keep her safe. Taking her home with him was completely against protocol, but what Carmichael didn't know wouldn't hurt him. Besides, given Carmichael's earlier behavior, James didn't feel a need to provide a detailed update on Kelly's position. The fewer people who knew where she was, the more protected she would be.

He'd need to leave a convincing trail, something for Caleb and his men to follow that would keep them off her scent. Having the officers and the doctor report them as DOA had bought them a few hours, but Caleb would see through that and would start looking for her again. Who could he trust to help him keep Kelly safe while he led the bad guys off course?

Right away, a name popped into his head: *Thomas*. No question about it. The man was an excellent agent, but more important, he knew his way around a computer. In the few months they'd been sitting next to each other, they'd gotten to be friends of a sort, and he knew he'd be able to trust Thomas with this little secret.

Satisfied that he now had the makings of a plan, James shifted again, leaning to the side and propping his head on the corner of the chair back. It would be several hours yet until morning, and he needed to be sharp for tomorrow. Closing his eyes, he deliberately pushed out images of Kelly, bloodied and moaning in pain, and tried to focus on the rhythmic sound of her breathing. Gradually, his body relaxed and he drifted off into a light, unsatisfying sleep.

Chapter 7

It was ten in the morning before they released her. James wasn't quite sure why it took so long, since the doctor poked his head in around seven and pronounced her fit to leave. Apparently, discharges required a lot of paperwork.

Thomas was idling by the entry, pointedly ignoring the glares from the valet parking attendants as he read the paper. He glanced up when James tapped on the window, moving quickly to unlock the doors. James carefully maneuvered Kelly into the backseat. The nurse had given her another dose of pain medication just before her discharge, and she was clumsy with drowsiness.

He slid in next to her and clapped Thomas on the shoulder. "Good to see you, man. Thanks for coming."

Thomas checked the mirror as he steered away from the hospital. "No problem. How you doing?"

James leaned back against the seat as he considered the question. His side was starting to ache something fierce, and the sleepless night was catching up to him. He wanted nothing more than to fall into bed and sleep for a week, but that wasn't going to happen.

"I've been better. Been worse, though."

"I hear that."

Kelly gave up the battle to stay awake and slumped against his shoulder. He lifted his arm and wrapped it around her, securing her to his side. She let out a little sigh and snuggled closer, and her hand reached up to rest on his chest. Her touch made his stomach flip-flop, and his breath caught in his throat.

He must have made some sound, because he looked up to see Thomas watching them in the rearview mirror, his brow raised in silent question. James frowned and shook his head slightly, which caused the other man to roll his eyes, his disbelief coming through loud and clear.

James knew how they must look cozied up in the backseat together, her head on his shoulder and his arm draped over her. He couldn't deny that he still wanted her and that this forced proximity was wrecking havoc with his emotions. He didn't think Thomas knew about their past, but the other man clearly thought there was something going on between them now. The trouble was, James didn't think he could make a convincing argument that Kelly was just another asset.

Deciding discretion was the better part of valor, he changed the subject. "Can you lay a fake digital trail?"

Thomas met his eyes briefly in the rearview mirror again. "Sure. Why?"

"She's still in danger. I want to steer Caleb away from her so I can keep her safe."

"Why not just put her in a safe house?"

James shook his head even though Thomas wasn't looking at him. "I'm not convinced the locations of our safe houses are secure. This guy has been one step ahead of us the entire time, and I'm not about to drop her into his lap."

"Fair enough." They stopped at a red light, and Thomas turned around to look at them. "Where exactly am I taking you guys, then?"

James met his gaze, determined to keep his expression neutral. "My place."

Thomas shook his head and faced forward again, but not before James saw the faint smile on the other man's face.

"Playing fast and loose with the rules, I see."

"You got a better idea?" James shot back. He knew he sounded defensive, but at the moment he didn't care.

"No, no," Thomas replied, holding up a hand. "This is your op, so we'll do things your way."

"Thanks," James muttered.

They spent the rest of the drive in silence, interrupted only by James giving Thomas directions to his condo. Traffic was light, and it wasn't long before Thomas pulled into the parking garage and killed the engine.

"Let's get you both upstairs," he said, climbing out of the driver's side.

James glanced down at Kelly's peaceful expression. She was totally relaxed, warm and boneless against his side, and he hated to disturb her. She was still too pale for his liking. Hopefully she would go back to sleep once they got her upstairs, since she clearly needed the rest.

"Kelly," he said softly, shaking her a little.

She opened her eyes, only to stare up at him with an unfocused gaze before her eyelids slowly lowered again.

He tried another time, saying her name a little louder. "We're here, baby," he added.

She blinked up at him once more. Then her face lit up with a beatific smile that hit him like a punch to the gut. "James," she breathed.

He couldn't help but smile back. "Hey," he whispered.

She reached up with her hand, cupping his face in her palm and pulling him down. Before he realized her intention, her lips were pressed against his, warm and soft.

His brain short-circuited at the contact, all rational thought deserting him as he let himself get caught up in the sensation of her mouth. She kissed him with drowsy abandon, her lips parting and her tongue darting out to administer teasing licks.

More, he thought, needing to taste her. He slid his tongue into her mouth, kissing her deeply as he sought the contact he craved. He'd been so lonely the past few months, but now she was here, with him, and it felt so right to be kissing her again. Better than ever before.

She arched up, pressing herself against his chest, and he groaned at the feel of her breasts. What he wouldn't give to feel them again, to let the soft weight of one fill his palm as he caressed her. His hand moved of its own accord, sliding down her back and around her side. Just a few more inches…

The sudden tap on the glass next to his head poured cold water over his heated arousal. Kelly jerked back with a gasp, her hand covering the wet sheen of her lips.

"Who is that man?" she asked, her face flaming. She looked down, fiddling with her clothes—something James had come to realize she did when nervous.

James cleared his throat before responding, feeling a little embarrassed himself. Christ, he had just been making out in the backseat of a car with an asset in front of another agent! Could he possibly be any more unprofessional?

"That's Special Agent Thomas Kincannon. I work with him, and he picked us up from the hospital."

Kelly nodded, still not looking up. "I see."

"Uh, why don't you give me a minute? I'm going to talk to him, and then I'll take you up."

"Okay."

He climbed out of the car and took a few steps to stand by Thomas, who had thoughtfully walked away and was standing with his back to the car.

"Sorry," the other man said as James approached. "I wanted to give you guys privacy, but it looked like things were heating up rather than winding down."

James ran a hand through his hair. They had been heating up indeed. "No, it's no problem. I'm glad you knocked."

Thomas cast a quick glance over his shoulder. "She okay?"

"Yeah. Just a little embarrassed."

Thomas nodded his head. "Anything you want to tell me?"

James let the question hang there for a moment. Did he want to share the details of his past with Kelly?

No. But Thomas deserved an explanation, and it was probably the only way to avoid getting written up and taken off the case.

"We were together once. A few months ago. We used to be friends."

"Used to be?" Thomas's voice was neutral, but James could practically *feel* the other man's curiosity.

"Yeah. It didn't really work out." And that was all he was willing to say about the subject. No way was he going to rehash the details while standing in a parking garage, of all places.

"Well, if what I just saw back there is any indication, I'd say you might want to give it another shot."

James shook his head. "I don't think so. That was probably the painkillers talking, not her."

Thomas snorted. "Think what you want, man. But I've been around women on painkillers before, and they've never tried to suck my face off like that."

James narrowed his eyes at the other man, which had Thomas raising his hands with a laugh. "I'm just saying."

"Look. Could you maybe not report this? I need to stay on the case, and I don't want Carmichael to pull me because he's pissed about our...contact."

Thomas smiled, the expression making him look like a mischievous choirboy. "What contact? I didn't see any contact."

James stuck out his hand, relief lightening his mood considerably. "Thanks. I owe you one."

Thomas shook it. "You owe me several, but who's counting?"

"Fair enough." James turned to head back to the car, but Thomas's hand on his shoulder made him pause.

"Why don't you give me your keys, let me check out the apartment before you bring her up?" He nodded in the direction of the car. "That'll give her a few minutes to get over her embarrassment at being interrupted."

James fished the keys out of his pocket. "Thanks. I appreciate it."

"No problem. Grab the bag out of the trunk on your way up, would you? I stopped by her place before heading to the hospital and grabbed some clothes for her."

James shook his head. "I hadn't even thought about that. I'm glad you're here, picking up the slack for me."

Thomas grinned. "We'll let this one slide, seeing as how you got shot and all." With that, he turned and headed into the building.

James walked back to the car and slid into the backseat again. Kelly glanced up at him, her expression guarded. Clearly, their moment of intimacy was over.

"Where are we? Is this a safe house?"

"Not exactly," he hedged, searching for the right words to explain his plan.

She raised a brow, clearly expecting him to elaborate.

"I've brought you someplace safe. Someplace off the grid."

"And that place would be where?"

He was just going to have to tell her. "My place."

"What?" The word was a shrill outburst that made him wince. "You've got to be kidding me! How is this place safe?"

"First of all, I had the police report you as dead and the hospital admit you under a false name. Second—" he held up another finger "—Thomas is going to lay a false trail for the bad guys to follow. And finally—" up went the third finger "—no one will think to look for you here. It's completely against protocol, and I have a reputation for doing things by the book. My team, with the exception of Thomas, doesn't know where you are, so on the off chance there is a mole, they won't know where I've stashed you. Add to that the building security and the fact that either Thomas or I will be with you at all times, and you're going to be pretty safe."

She glared at him as she sat with her back against the opposite door. "Please. Your address is public record. Do you honestly think they won't come looking for me here?"

He shrugged. "How will they find you? After we get you inside, you're not leaving until the danger has passed."

"So now I'm your prisoner?" Her tone was icy and deadly calm. The lingering warmth from their earlier kiss vanished, leaving a decided chill in its wake.

"It's not like that." He scrambled, knowing he had fumbled the presentation. She was truly angry now, and he had to work fast to ensure her cooperation.

"I'm not going to let another man control me," she continued, ignoring him. Her jaw took on a stubborn set as she folded her arms across her chest.

"Another man? What do you mean by that?"

Her composure slipped for an instant, her cool facade cracking the tiniest bit. Even though he knew it wasn't fair, James pounced on the momentary display of weakness.

"Who's tried to control you before, Kelly?"

"No one." She shook her head, rallying to rebuild her defenses in the face of his question.

"Did someone hurt you before?" he pressed. A se-

ries of memories flashed by as he spoke: the way she'd
stiffen if he touched her without warning, how she'd
moved away when he'd approached her in the lab, the
way she'd chafed when he'd given her instructions, her
flinching away when he'd raised his hand. Moments
that had nagged at him but he hadn't examined at the
time. Now a picture was forming in his mind as things
clicked into place. Had someone physically abused her?

"Kelly, I—"

"Let's go," she said, twisting around to open the
door.

He quickly climbed out of the car, staring at her
over the roof. She wasn't looking at him; instead she
focused very intently on the door to the building. She
was clearly trying her best to ignore him, which meant
he'd touched a nerve.

He collected the bag from the trunk and motioned
her forward. Falling into step beside her, he said softly,
"This discussion isn't over."

She didn't break stride or look at him, but he saw
her shoulders stiffen. "There's nothing to talk about."

Oh, yes, there was. But he was content to wait.

For now.

Caleb paced the hotel room, limping slightly from
the wound in his thigh. He had underestimated Kelly
yesterday, and her little stunt with the cart had slowed
him down. The shard of glass he'd pulled out of his
leg had been long and lethal-looking, but fortunately
it had missed vital parts. Now the pain was a welcome
distraction from his thoughts.

Could this operation go any worse?

He didn't think so. His plan had been simple: take

Kelly in, using the gun if necessary. When he'd heard the FBI agent's voice in the hall, he'd adapted, intending to take him out so Kelly would be easier to grab. A good plan, but the execution had been sorely lacking. Not only had he missed the FBI agent, he'd hit Kelly instead.

She had looked pale and groggy this morning as she'd left the hospital. He'd kept his distance, using binoculars to watch the agent escort her to a car and help her into the backseat. Then he'd climbed in next to her, putting a proprietary arm around her shoulder as a redheaded man drove them away.

She wasn't dead, which was the good news. The problem was, he'd tipped his hand when it came to her, and she was now under heavy guard. If the grim look of determination on the FBI agent's face had been any indication, it would be even more difficult to get to her now. He'd put out feelers, having his men check all the known safe-house locations, but that was eating up precious time. Time he didn't have.

His boss would be calling soon.

Think, he had to think. Had to come up with a way to salvage things so he wouldn't be blamed. He sank down onto the bed, fisting his hands in the scratchy bedspread. Maybe it was time for him to disappear. After all, if a middle-aged scientist could dodge the organization, maybe he could, too.

A blast of cold air from the wall unit danced over the back of his neck, causing him to shiver. No, running wasn't the answer. It would only anger his employer, and it would make things much worse for him in the end. He took a deep breath, deliberately relaxing his hands. He smoothed out the wrinkles in the spread, trying to clear his mind of the thoughts whirring around, zinging to and fro like a flock of birds.

He had two options: find Collins or try to get Jarvis again. After his bungled kidnapping attempts, he probably wouldn't be able to get close enough to grab her. Besides, based on what Collins had told him, she really didn't know about the project. Oh, he could bring her up to speed, but that would take time, and she would likely refuse to cooperate. He could "convince" her, but he didn't have the luxury of time. Besides, he mused, it would be a shame to mar that pretty skin of hers....

Better to focus his energy on finding Collins, he decided, massaging his temples with his fingertips to stave off a burgeoning headache. But where would the man go? They had eyes on his home, had checked nearby hotels and had even gone so far as to check out his niece's place in New York. So far, nothing.

He'd spoken with George's friends, all four of them. From all accounts, Collins was a quiet man who was never far from his wife's side. She was the key, Caleb decided. He'd threatened her to ensure Collins's co-operation, but he should have taken her to make Collins stick around and finish the job.

They couldn't have gone far, Caleb mused, rising to pace the room. She was still frail and weak and probably had trouble traveling. Collins would have to take her someplace comfortable, someplace close to help in case she needed it....

His head pounding in earnest, Caleb reached for the bottle of aspirin on the nightstand. He shook two pills into his palm and swallowed them dry, wincing at the bitter taste. He screwed the cap back on and reached to put the bottle back, but he froze before he set it down.

Help. Medication. She was probably still on medication. Not stuff that you could get over the counter, but prescription medication.

Collins would have to stay by some kind of pharmacy, so he could get his wife's drugs. No way would he make her do without, even if they were on the run. Caleb felt a spurt of satisfaction and reached for the phone. All he had to do was find out where Collins had last picked up his wife's drugs, and then he'd have him.

Fifteen minutes later, he hung up the phone, a wide smile pasted on his face. Things were finally looking up.

Kelly was quiet on the elevator ride up to James's apartment. She didn't trust herself to speak, afraid that her voice would wobble or she would say or do something to tip James off. He was already suspicious after her little slip in the car, and she had no intention of filling him in on the sordid details of her past with Gary.

Why was Gary still ruining her life? No, that wasn't right. If she'd learned anything in therapy, the better question was why was she continuing to let Gary influence her life. She knew that remaining silent gave him a kind of power over her, one that she didn't want him to have, but she couldn't just open up and talk about that time in her life. It was still too painful, a sore spot that had finally scabbed over but throbbed just the same.

She wasn't ashamed. She knew she'd been a victim. She hadn't deserved his abuse, and she recognized on a rational level that the problem was with him, not her. Months of therapy had helped her let go of the idea that she was damaged goods, but that didn't stop people from looking at her with pity when they found out.

She still remembered the look on Charlie's face when she'd told him. He'd been a graduate student in George's lab, and they'd worked together for a few years. He'd met Gary before and had liked him, but he hadn't pressed for details when Kelly had told him about the breakup.

She and Charlie had been friends, at least in the context of work. Late nights and weekends spent in the lab had resulted in the development of a close work relationship, and it wasn't unusual for them to grab a bite to eat together when their experimental incubation periods coincided.

It had been during one such fast-food dinner that she'd told him the truth. He'd been bemoaning his most recent breakup, the latest in a long line of casual relationships. Charlie had always had high hopes for finding a girlfriend, but his dates were usually sacrificed on the altar of science, something Kelly could relate to all too well.

"Whatever happened with you and Gary?" he asked, crumpling his hamburger wrapper before moving on to his fries. He glanced up at her, his eyes impossibly large behind the thick lenses of his glasses. "He seemed like a great guy."

Kelly fidgeted with a fry, dipping it in ketchup and tracing a design on the wrapper. "Sure," she said, debating how much to reveal.

"Did he get tired of playing second fiddle to the lab?"

And there it was. Her out. She could lie and say *Yes, we broke up because I was never available.* But why should she protect him like that? He was the bad guy, not her, and she shouldn't have to pretend that he was an awesome person who had gotten tired of waiting around. Not anymore.

She took a deep breath. It was now or never. "Actually, I broke up with him because he hit me."

Charlie froze, his hand halfway to his mouth. After a second, he lowered it, his Adam's apple bobbing as he swallowed hard. "Wow. That's, uh, wow. I'm so sorry to hear that."

He looked her up and down, as if trying to see the bruises that had faded long ago. Kelly resisted the urge to shuffle in her seat, instead watching as Charlie's expression morphed from shock to pity to apprehension. He cleared his throat again, his eyes darting wildly about the semi-deserted restaurant, and she realized with growing disappointment that he was feeling embarrassed and uncomfortable.

She changed the subject quickly, and they headed back to the lab to finish up. The revelation shouldn't have changed their friendship, but it did. Charlie grew increasingly distant, always finding excuses to avoid her company, and when he did have to spend time with her, he treated her with kid gloves, as if she was a fragile piece of china he was afraid of dropping. She eventually gave up trying to have anything more than superficial interactions with him, and she could tell her presence bothered him.

He'd wrapped up his studies quickly after that, pressing forward to graduate a few months later. She'd been happy for him, but sad that her confession had cost her a congenial relationship with a coworker. One more thing Gary had ruined.

"This way." James's voice roused her from her

thoughts, and she shook her head to clear it of the memories. There was nothing to be gained by living in the past, especially when the present held dangers that required her full attention.

She moved mechanically down the hall, mentally slamming the door on Gary and all he represented. James stopped outside his door, reaching out to rap smartly against the wood with his knuckles.

She frowned at him. "Why are you knocking on your own door?"

"Thomas is inside, making sure the place is clear. I don't want to spook him."

There was a faint shuffling from within, and James called out, "It's us."

"Door's open" came the muffled reply.

James motioned her behind him, and she was all too happy to comply. With careful, measured movements, he opened the door and pushed it in, his hand resting lightly on the butt of his gun. She felt her eyes widen as she caught the gesture. Why did he need his gun if his partner was inside?

He stepped into the entryway, still on alert. She caught sight of a shock of red hair around the corner. James saw it, too, and visibly relaxed. "Everything okay?"

Thomas stepped into the entryway, holstering his own weapon. "All clear. You're good to go." He looked past James and met her eyes. His face creased with a broad smile as he stepped forward, his hand outstretched.

"Thomas Kincannon. Nice to meet you."

Kelly shook his large, warm hand. "Kelly Jarvis. Thanks for picking us up."

"No problem." He jerked a thumb back at James. "This guy doesn't ask for many favors, so I have to take advantage of it when he does."

Kelly smiled. His friendly demeanor put her at ease. "Keeping score, huh?"

He winked at her. "You bet."

James returned to the entryway, his hands now empty. "Kelly, I put your bag in the guest room."

"My bag?" What was he talking about? She hadn't brought anything.

Thomas cleared his throat. "That was my doing. I took the liberty of stopping by your apartment before I picked you up at the hospital. I grabbed a couple of changes of clothes for you, just enough to get you by for a few days."

Absurdly touched by the thoughtful gesture, Kelly reached out and squeezed his hand. "Thank you," she said, staring up into his bright blue eyes. "I really appreciate that."

"My pleasure," he replied.

She dropped his hand and turned to walk into the apartment, catching a glimpse of James's face as she moved. He looked distinctly unhappy, but before she could wonder about it, his expression smoothed back into neutral detachment.

He's probably tired and sore, she thought as she made her way down the hall. *I know I am.*

True to his word, James had placed the duffel bag on the foot of the bed. She unzipped it and began to pull out the clothes Thomas had packed for her. *Might as well hang them up,* she figured. Given James's earlier response, she could be there awhile.

At the bottom of the bag were several pairs of panties. She felt her face heat as she realized Thomas had been in her underwear drawer. It was bad enough he'd seen her kiss James. The fact that he now knew she preferred bikini briefs brought a fresh wave of embarrassment that had her quickly stuffing the items in question into a dresser drawer.

"Get over yourself," she muttered. Given his clear blue eyes and fallen-angel smile, she was willing to bet Thomas had already seen his fair share of women's underwear.

With a sigh, she placed the now-empty duffel bag in the closet, then cast a longing look at the bed. A nap seemed like a fabulous idea, but first she wanted a bath.

She gathered up a change of clothes and made her way to the bathroom. She could hear the low murmur of voices from the den but couldn't make out what they were saying. *Probably working on the computer,* she figured, pulling a towel from the cabinet in the bathroom.

Slowly, carefully she stripped off her shirt. The nurse had given her a dose of Dilaudid before she'd left the hospital, and while it kept the worst of the pain at bay, sudden zings shot down her arm when she moved a certain way. Hopefully, a good soak would help her to relax.

The water was almost too hot to bear, but Kelly gritted her teeth and sank in. *The better to burn off all the hospital germs,* she thought, raising a pink hand and reaching for the soap. She washed around her shoulder, trying to keep the stitches dry as she rinsed off the dried blood and residual iodine. Then she leaned back against the wall of the tub and closed her eyes.

James wasn't going to be content to ignore her earlier verbal slip. He'd backed off for now, but she knew it was a temporary truce at best. He was probably just waiting until they were alone again to start up the questions.

She was running out of reasons not to tell him. James deserved to know why she'd walked away from him before, why she'd been so afraid. She recognized that, but she didn't want to get into it when they were both distracted by the issues of George and Caleb and everything else going on. This wasn't like discussing what to have for dinner; it was a conversation that required time and focus, things neither of them could spare right now.

She absently rubbed her stomach, which was feeling decidedly queasy. The voice of doubt whispered in her ear as she pondered her options. What if she told him, and he responded like Charlie had? She couldn't deny that she still had feelings for him, still wanted him. Could she take the chance that he would walk away when he found out she'd been used as a punching bag? Would he believe her when she told him she was over it and wanted to start fresh, with him?

I have to try. She'd resolved to rebuild their relationship, and to do that, she had to be honest with him. It was the only way they could move forward. She'd let her fears hurt him once—she wouldn't, couldn't, do it again.

Now she just had to figure out how to tell him.

"Hello, Professor."

George sucked in a breath, the hair on the back of his neck standing at attention as a cold chill slithered over his skin. Surely he was hearing things. There was no way—

"You're looking good."

He squeezed his eyes shut, refusing to acknowledge the voice from his nightmares. This was clearly a hallucination brought on by lack of sleep. If he ignored it, it would go away. He opened his eyes, focusing on the bottle of sleeping pills he'd plucked from the pharmacy shelf. Were these the maximum doses? Because he really needed to get some rest.

"I must admit, I'm impressed it's taken me this long to find you. Of course, I haven't been giving it all of my attention."

"Go away," George muttered. A small part of him recognized he was on his way to acting like one of those crazy homeless people who paced the streets, talking to themselves, but he was too tired to care.

Just one night, he thought desperately. *Just one good night of sleep. That's all I need.*

The price of his constant vigilance was exhaustion, but every time he tried to sleep, his brain kicked into high gear, churning out what-ifs and terrifying scenarios that ended with Ruth being hurt or killed and him being tortured for information. Ruth's disappointment in him wasn't helping, either. He obsessed over ways to win her back, his plans growing increasingly far-fetched as his fatigue heightened.

At this point, he was almost willing to turn himself in to the police just so he could relax enough to rest.

He jumped when a hand landed on his shoulder, squeezing hard enough to make him wince. He turned around, the protest dying on his lips as he came face-to-face with the devil once again.

"You," he managed, swallowing hard to push down the lump in his throat.

The man merely smiled in a predatory way, which only made George's stomach flop ominously. "Me," he said, his tone perfectly polite.

"But how did you...? I don't understand." George shuffled back a step, bumping into a woman, who frowned at him as she moved down the aisle.

"Watch where you're going," she muttered as she wheeled her cart away.

The man waved his hand, as if he couldn't be bothered with silly details like how he'd hunted them down. George had known it was only a matter of time, but he hadn't expected to be found so soon. He'd hoped for enough time to develop a plan, at least.

"If I didn't know better, I'd think you were trying to renege on our agreement." He said it pleasantly enough, but the man's eyes were cold and dead. George had the sudden realization that if not for the witnesses in the store, this man would cheerfully kill him and not think twice.

"Ruth wanted to redecorate, to celebrate beating cancer," he stammered, the lie tripping off his tongue before he realized what he was saying. "We're just staying at the hotel until the renovations are done."

The man shook his head. "Do you know how I can tell when you're lying, George?" He took a step forward, and George's heart leaped into his throat. "Your lips are moving. Now." He reached out, brushing his hands lightly across George's shoulders. "I suggest you stop lying, and tell me how you're going to make this up to me."

"I can still get you the bug," George said, taking another step back. "I'll get it for you, and we'll be even."

The man rolled his eyes. "How are you going to do that? Your lab is being watched. If you go back, you'll get picked up." He raised a brow over the rim of his glasses. "I assume you're still interested in staying out of jail and with your lovely wife?"

Absolutely. Even though Ruth wanted nothing to do with him right now, he still needed to stay by her side. Once this danger had passed, they could go back to being the way they were before and pretend as if this whole thing had never happened.

George cast about for something—*anything*—to say to buy him some time. The way the man was watching him made him viscerally uncomfortable. Right now, George felt a bit like prey, while the hunter in front of him merely waited for his opportunity to strike.

"I have a postdoc," he offered, wiping his palms on his pants. "She could get the bug out of the freezer and bring it to you."

A spark of interest flared in those dead eyes, so George went on, warming to his subject as he spoke. "She knows where everything is, and I trust her to bring the right stuff. I can tell her to meet you somewhere to give you the stuff. Will that work?"

The man seemed to be considering his suggestion. His eyes narrowed for a moment; then he nodded slightly, his lips curving up in what might have been a smile.

"That could work," he said, cocking his head to the side. "But you'll do exactly as I say."

George nodded quickly. Anything to distract him. His breath came a little easier now that it seemed the man wasn't going to hurt him. "Of course, of course. Whatever you want."

With a decisive nod, the man raised his arm out in a sweeping gesture. "Well, then. Shall we?"

George gulped, unsure of what he was meant to do. "What?"

"You can't call her here, Professor. We need a little more privacy for this conversation."

Oh, God. No. He couldn't go with him. He was as good as dead if he walked out of the store. His heart thumped madly as he searched for a reason—*any* reason—to stay put.

The man still held his arm up, but his tone was steely when he spoke again. "Professor," he said quietly. "I'm not going to hurt you. But if you don't do what I say, I will make life very unpleasant for your wife."

George stepped forward mechanically, his legs stiff and uncooperative. He jumped when the man's hand landed on his shoulder.

"There's a good lad," the devil whispered in his ear as they walked to the front of the pharmacy. "Let's hope you can clean up the mess you made."

Chapter 8

"How's it looking?" James set a beer by Thomas's hand, then carefully lowered himself into the chair he'd dragged over to the desk. He flipped off the cap of his own bottle and took a long swig; the bubbles tickled their way down into his stomach.

Thomas leaned back and ran a hand through his hair. He reached for the bottle and toasted James in silent thanks.

"Looking good, actually. I've got her showing up at the safe house in Herndon. Close enough to be believable, but far enough away that if anyone actually goes to check it out, it will waste their time."

James considered the screen as he sipped his brew. He wasn't quite sure how Thomas had done it, but he wasn't going to ask too many questions. Ignorance was bliss, as far as this kind of thing went.

"Will you be able to tell if anyone shows up there?"

Thomas nodded. "Yeah, if they break in, it will trip the alarm."

James frowned. "But they won't need to break in. They can just look at the house and see that it's empty."

"Not exactly," Thomas said, a sly grin playing at his mouth. "Remember Fisher?"

"Mark Fisher?" James said, shaking his head. "What does he have to do with this?"

"We play poker together twice a month. He lost last time. A lot." Thomas lifted one shoulder. "I told him I'd forgo his debt if he'd spend some time at the Herndon house tonight, make sure everything was in order."

James smiled, his appreciation for Thomas growing by the minute. "Remind me never to play poker with you."

The other man just laughed. "Hey, it's a living."

They sat in silence for a few minutes. Thomas typed away while James enjoyed the feeling of sitting in a comfortable chair in familiar surroundings. For the first time in days, his brain slowed and he let himself relax, sinking deeper into the cushion as the tension drained out of his muscles.

He heard the groaning of the pipes and the sound of running water in the background. Kelly must be getting cleaned up. He needed a shower as well, but he was feeling fine where he was for the moment. He'd get to it later.

She'd shut down quickly, he mused, thinking back to their earlier conversation. As soon as he'd asked about her past, she'd thrown up a wall so high and thick it was a wonder she could see to walk. If that wasn't a red flag, he didn't know what was.

But how to get her to talk? He swallowed another mouthful of beer as he considered his options. Given her behavior, he was pretty certain she'd been hurt in the past, and not your run-of-the-mill bad-breakup kind of hurt. He was willing to bet she'd been hit. In his experience, people didn't shy away from physical contact unless there was some history of abuse.

He rubbed his chest with his free hand, absently trying to massage away the ache that had formed at the thought of Kelly bruised and battered. He closed his eyes, calling up the image of her naked body and seeing their encounter with fresh eyes. He didn't recall any scars on her smooth, pale skin, but they may have simply healed. Besides, abuse wasn't always physical....

He let out a breath, suddenly exhausted. His side throbbed and his limbs felt heavy, weighted down with guilt and responsibility and worry. He needed to know what Kelly was hiding—had to know—but he couldn't find out tonight.

"You got any food in this place?"

"Ah..." James switched gears, trying to remember the last time he'd been to the grocery store. Was it last week? No, he'd worked late all last week, which left no time for shopping. Maybe it had been the week before....

His head was starting to ache, so he gave up trying to think. "No. There's a Thai place around the corner, though. Want me to order in?"

Thomas leaned back and stretched his arms over his head. "God, yes. I'm starving."

James dug his cell phone out of his pocket. "I suppose I can buy you dinner. Any special requests?"

Thomas rattled off a list of food that made James's

eyebrows shoot up, and the total the restaurant relayed back had him rethinking his offer. He hung up, then eyed the other man up and down.

"How are you not five hundred pounds?"

Thomas shot him a grin and shrugged. "My excellent metabolism?"

James snorted. "Whatever."

"Don't hate me 'cause I'm awesome." Thomas turned back to the computer and began typing again. "I'm almost done here. What comes next?"

James shifted in the chair. "I'm not quite sure." He tipped the bottle back, swallowing the now-warm dregs with a wince. "I'm still working on that part."

"You at least need to check in with Carmichael."

"Yeah."

"You don't trust him." It wasn't a question, but James still felt the need to respond.

"I don't think he's dirty. I just think he's incompetent."

Thomas huffed out a laugh. "Glad I'm not the only one," he muttered.

"Doesn't matter." James shrugged, reaching forward to set his empty bottle on the desk. "We're stuck with him."

"For now." Thomas picked at the label on his bottle, refusing to meet his eyes. His tone was quiet, almost confessional, and James wondered what, exactly, the other agent knew.

He decided to probe a little. "You've heard differently?"

"Just rumors. I overheard him on the phone the other day. He was saying something about covering his ass if this op blows up in his face."

Disgust was a bitter aftertaste in his mouth. "Figures."

"What should we do?"

It was a good question, one James wished he could answer. Unfortunately, all his energies were focused on keeping Kelly safe and solving this case. He didn't have the time or the inclination to figure out how they should deal with Carmichael.

"We solve this case," he said, his voice strong despite his fatigue. "That's all we can do."

Thomas nodded, his expression thoughtful. "Do you think we can?"

James didn't hesitate.

"Absolutely."

Kelly's phone rang while she was putting on her shirt.

Getting dressed was proving to be more difficult than she'd anticipated. While Thomas had been kind enough to grab some clothes for her, he hadn't thought to bring any button-down shirts. As a result, Kelly had to contort herself in impossible ways to get her arms through the sleeves of the T-shirt without moving her shoulder too much.

It was proving to be a slow, painful process, and the shrill ring of her phone wasn't helping any.

She jerked the shirt down with a vicious tug, then grabbed the phone off the bed.

"'Lo?" she mumbled, trying unsuccessfully to straighten the shirt. It had gotten twisted in the struggle and was bunched uncomfortably on one side.

"Kelly?"

"What?"

"Kelly, are you okay? You don't sound good."

The voice was familiar, setting off a tingle of recognition in the recesses of her drug-addled brain. It sounded like… But surely it couldn't be…

"Who is this?" It came out a little sharper than she had intended, but she was tired and in pain. If this wasn't important, she wanted to go to bed.

There was a pause, followed by a heavy sigh. "It's George."

She was silent for a beat, certain she had misheard. "George Collins?"

"The one and only," he said, a hint of amusement in his voice.

Kelly fought to shake off her annoyance as her mind kicked into gear. Where was he? Why was he calling her? Did he know that the FBI was searching for him? What should she do?

"Sorry, George. I've got a cold, and I'm kind of high on decongestants right now." She tried to sound casual, hoping he'd believe her. "What's going on?"

"I'm extending my vacation," he said, sounding as if he didn't have a care in the world. "Ruth and I are back in town to regroup, and then we're taking off again."

"That's great," she said, trying to sound happy for him. "Where are you going?"

"Oh, here and there," he responded airily, as if the details were of little consequence. "I'm calling because I need you to do me a favor."

"Okay," she said slowly, wondering what he was getting her into.

"I'll be seeing a collaborator on this next leg of my vacation, and I promised I'd give him a vial of modified *Bacillus* for use in his experiments. I don't want to come into the lab to get it because I know I'd get bogged down in work and I don't have time for that. Would you pick it up for me?" He paused, and when she didn't respond right away, he rushed on. "I'd meet you somewhere to get it, of course. Wouldn't ask you to do *all* the work." He finished with a forced laugh, sounding nervous for the first time.

He must know the lab was being watched, but was he trying to evade the FBI or Caleb's shadowy organization? Either way, he seemed to think she wouldn't be in danger. Or maybe he just didn't care. "Sure, George. I could do that for you."

"Excellent!" he said, sounding relieved. "I'll call you back later with the details, all right? Ruth needs me for something now. Talk to you later!" He hung up before she had a chance to respond, leaving Kelly shaking her head and staring at the phone in her hand.

What had just happened? George clearly wanted a strain from the lab, but why? Was he going to develop it in some way, to buy his safety from Caleb's group? He must know that the terrorist group and the FBI were after him, which explained why he didn't want to come out of hiding. Where was he now? The FBI thought he was on the run, but it sounded as if he was back in town.

She sank onto the bed, overwhelmed by the onslaught of worries George's request had triggered. She rubbed her forehead as she tried to rein in her galloping thoughts, forcing herself to take deep breaths past the tight feeling in her throat.

"This is a good thing," she muttered, massaging her temples. This could be the break James needed to solve the case. Maybe they could trace the call when George contacted her again to find out where he was hiding.

The thought that this could all be over soon loosened the band around her chest, and she sucked in air. Her life could go back to normal, and she could focus on rebuilding her relationship with James.

She indulged in a moment of fantasy—the two of them cooking dinner together in his kitchen. Sharing a bottle of wine, cozied up on the couch with his cats and watching a movie together. He'd put his arm around her, and she'd snuggle against his side, safe and warm. They'd go to bed later and make love, slow and sweet. She'd fall asleep in his arms, her heart light and her body sated.

Could they ever have that kind of relationship? Could James see his way to forgiving her for walking out on him? She had more questions than answers, but she knew one thing for certain: they could only move forward after putting this ugly mess behind them.

Now that George had made contact, they were one step closer to doing just that.

Kelly opened the bedroom door to the tantalizing aroma of hot food. Her stomach rumbled in appreciation as she walked into the den. Two empty beer bottles sat on the computer desk against the far wall, and she heard the low rumble of male voices in the kitchen, accompanied by the clinking of plates and silverware. Clearly, dinner was about to be served.

James entered the room, a stack of plates in his hands. He stopped when he saw her. "Oh, good. I was just about to come grab you. Hungry?"

She nodded. "What can I do?"

"Nothing. Just have a seat." He nodded toward the couch, so she took a corner spot. James set the plates on the coffee table, then headed back to the kitchen. Thomas chose that moment to enter the room, carrying a large bag, which he deposited next to the plates.

"Hope you like Thai," he said with a friendly smile.

"It smells wonderful," she said truthfully. Her stomach, having been neglected all day, was roiling and gurgling in anticipation of food, and she was suddenly ravenous. She helped Thomas pull foam containers from the bag as James returned with glasses of water.

She waited until she'd eaten a bit before breaking the news of George's call, figuring that once she told them, she wouldn't be able to finish her dinner because of their onslaught of questions. The men had already cleared off most of their plates with a few large bites, so now was as good a time as any.

Kelly set her fork down and took a deep breath. James shot her a concerned look. "Don't like the food? I could order you something else if—"

She cut him off. "No, the food is great, thanks. I need to tell you guys something."

Now Thomas was looking at her, his fork poised halfway to his mouth. Having both men focused so intently on her made Kelly's stomach flip, and she pleated her napkin while she tamped down her discomfort at being the center of attention.

"Kelly?" James's voice was soft, gentle even, and she realized they were both waiting for her to say something. She felt her face heat, but when she looked up, she could see James wasn't upset or impatient. His expression was calm and open, interested but not annoyed. This wasn't the first time he'd made her feel secure, and she relaxed, knowing that she didn't have to deal with George alone. James was here, and together they'd figure out what to do.

"George called me," she said, keeping her gaze on James's face. His eyebrows shot up, but he didn't say anything.

The clang of silverware on ceramic interrupted the silence, and she looked over to see that Thomas had dropped his fork. "George Collins?" he asked, his voice heavy with disbelief. "As in, the George Collins who is a person of interest in this investigation?"

"Yes. He called about twenty minutes ago. He wants me to retrieve a sample from the lab and bring it to him."

"Did he say where?" She swung her gaze back to James, who had placed his plate on the coffee table and was now leaning forward, his elbows on his knees.

"Not yet. He's going to call me back soon with the location."

James shot a meaningful glance at Thomas, and she saw the other man nod in return.

"What? What does that look mean?"

Both men were silent for a moment, then James spoke. "It means this is a setup. He's putting things in motion and will call you back when he's sure he's covered his bases. You'll show up to give him the sample, and you'll either be killed or taken."

Fear trailed a cold finger down her spine as James's words sank in, and Kelly tasted bile at the back of her throat. Swallowing hard, she asked, "Can't you stop him?"

"Yes." She glanced at Thomas, who had resumed eating. "Once we find out where he wants to meet, we'll scope the place out and put a team into play. Simple as that." He shrugged, then stuffed a forkful of noodles into his mouth.

She turned back to James, needing his reassurance. "Thomas is right," he said, shifting to dig his phone out of his pocket. "We'll get there before he does and scoop him up. But first—" he flipped open the phone and began punching numbers "—we need to set up a trace on your line. Maybe we'll get lucky and find George's location so we don't even have to worry about setting up a meeting."

Kelly remained quiet while James made his phone call. She used her fork to trace designs in the remnants of sauce on her plate. She was still hungry, but her throat felt so tight that she didn't want to risk choking on a bite of food. Thomas sat beside her, chewing happily, completely oblivious to her anxiety.

James hung up and placed the phone on the coffee table, then picked up his plate and twirled another forkful of noodles. She watched in amazement as he popped the bite into his mouth and went back for more, as if he hadn't a care in the world. *I could get killed, and they're acting like it's no big deal!*

"How can you eat at a time like this?" Kelly pushed her plate away so she could stand, then began pacing the room. "I'm about to crawl out of my skin with worry, and you guys are just sitting there like nothing is going on!"

Both men stared at her again. Only this time, they wore identical looks of bewilderment. "I'm hungry," Thomas pointed out, as if that simple statement should explain everything.

"I'm hungry, too," she shot back, hugging herself

as she moved around the room. "But I can't eat or I'll puke."

James set his plate aside and walked over to stand in front of her. He placed his hands above her elbows to keep her still. "You need to calm down. It's not worth getting so worked up when we don't know what's going to happen next. Collins will call you and we'll make our plans, but in the meantime, we've had a long couple of days and we need all the energy we can get. There's no sense in letting this ruin our dinner."

For the first time, Kelly noticed the dark circles under his eyes, the lines of strain around his mouth. He'd been working nonstop for the past few days, and how long had he been working before he'd come to her? Weeks? Months? Who knew how long this case had consumed his every waking moment. And now, to top it all off, he was injured. She knew he hadn't taken any pain medication at the hospital, and she doubted he'd slept at all last night. He had to be exhausted.

"You're right," she said, feeling a prickle of guilt as she realized his food was getting cold. "After all you've been through, you deserve a hot meal at least. I'm sorry I kept you from it."

He tugged gently until she was pressed against him, her nose buried in the hollow of his throat. "Don't apologize." His voice was low and warm in her ear, and she closed her eyes, savoring the feel of him and the faint citrus-spice smell of his cologne that a night in the hospital hadn't erased.

James rubbed circles on her back with his strong hands; the gesture felt comforting and familiar. She wanted nothing more than to stay like this, wrapped in his arms and pressed against his solid chest. But she knew that no matter how long she shut out the world, Caleb and Collins and the rest of this mess would still be waiting for her. Better to deal with it now.

So she pulled away with a shaky smile. James gave her uninjured arm a squeeze before releasing her completely. She sat back down on the couch and reached for her plate, feeling as if she might be able to stomach a few more bites.

She chewed mechanically, not really tasting the food as she replayed her conversation with George. He had seemed so normal, so completely oblivious to the magnitude of what he was asking her to do. He sounded as if he needed her to pick up a cake for a lab member's birthday, rather than retrieve and bring him a vial of a deadly bacteria.

Was he really that clueless? Did he really not appreciate the severity of what he'd done? Maybe he didn't think he'd done anything wrong. Maybe he figured saving Ruth had been worth it. After all, if she'd been in the same situation, Kelly couldn't say with 100 percent certainty she wouldn't have been tempted.

He may have seen it as delivering a product, nothing more. If he didn't ask what it was being used for, he could convince himself that he hadn't done anything wrong. She wanted to believe that was the case—that George had been willfully blind to what was going on, simply because he was desperate to pay for Ruth's treatments. The alternative was too painful to consider.

She jumped as something touched her sleeve. "Sorry," Thomas said with a sheepish smile. "I didn't mean to startle you. I just wanted to grab your plate."

She looked down to find it was empty. When had

that happened? Shaking her head, she released her death grip on the fork and passed it over. "Thanks."

"Least I could do, seeing as how I'm the only uninjured person in this place." He gathered up the detritus of their meal with efficient movements, then carted it all into the kitchen. After a moment, she heard the water running and the faint sound of singing.

She glanced over at James, who shook his head with a smile.

"Is he always like this?"

"Pretty much." James stretched his legs out with a sigh, then patted the cushion next to him. After a second of hesitation, Kelly slid over until they were sitting side by side.

"You doing okay?" he said softly, his dark brown eyes searching her face.

She felt his gaze like a touch, featherlight on her features. The sensation made her heart stutter-step, so she nodded, not trusting her voice at the moment.

"Is there anything you want to tell me?"

Kelly closed her eyes, knowing that this was her opportunity. She could tell him all about Gary and her past, expose all her secrets so they could move on. She wanted to do it. She needed to do it. It was time.

She opened her mouth, but Thomas chose that instant to really turn up the volume on his kitchen concert. Who was she kidding? They couldn't talk with someone ten feet away, even though he was clearly trying to generate a noise complaint from the neighbors.

"Just wondering when George will call back," she said, trying to keep her tone light.

Was that disappointment in his eyes? Before she could examine his expression too closely, her phone rang.

She froze and her heart leaped into her throat.
It was time.

James sat up and leaned forward, placing his hand
over the phone. Thomas stopped his god-awful singing
and appeared in the doorway, his expression focused
and determined.

Kelly looked scared to death. She glanced at him
with wide eyes, biting her bottom lip so hard it was a
wonder it didn't bleed.

"Get him to commit to a location and time for the
meet," James said, willing her to stay calm. "Don't ask
too many questions, though. We don't want to spook
him." At her nod, he lifted his hand. "You'll be great."

She sent him a wavering smile, took a deep breath
and answered the phone.

"Hello?" She frowned slightly. "Nothing's wrong,
other than the fact I don't feel good. I have a cold, remember?"

James held his breath, hoping George would accept
Kelly's excuse. Her voice was strained, but hopefully
she could convince him she was just grumpy from
being sick.

"No, it's okay—I can get the vials for you."

James scooted forward to the edge of his seat, as
if getting closer would help Kelly pin George down.
Thomas moved to sit on her other side, and the pair
of them strained to hear the other man's words. Kelly
angled the phone away from her ear so he and Thomas
could hear George's side of the conversation, too.

"…appreciate it," he heard the other man say. "I
would ask one of the graduate students, but you're really the only one I can trust."

"I understand," Kelly soothed, doing a great job of sounding normal. "Where are the vials stored?"

George relayed the location, which she scratched onto a napkin.

"Okay," she said, looking at James while she spoke. "When and where do you want to meet me to pick these up?"

George was silent for a beat, and James felt his palms grow damp with sweat. He knew. Somehow, he had figured out Kelly was with the FBI.

"George?" Kelly asked when the silence stretched out. "Did you hear me?"

"Yes, dear. Sorry, I just had a thought there for a moment." He cleared his throat. "Let's meet at the science museum tomorrow at four, shall we? I know how much you like to visit that one."

"Sounds good to me," Kelly replied. "That'll give me time to duck in and see the new exhibit before they close for the day."

"Splendid," George replied absently. "See you by the elephant, then?"

They said their goodbyes and she hung up, looking at James with doubt in her eyes. "Did that seem too easy?"

"Maybe," he said, glancing over at Thomas. "Or maybe he's telling the truth."

Thomas snorted. "Doubt it. Let's see if we got a trace." He flipped open his phone and made a call, stepping out of the room to talk.

James absently rubbed his side while he considered the motives behind George's choice of meeting place. The museum was a busy, public place. Did Collins think he would be able to slip into the crowd and evade detection? That he could get past all the FBI agents and police that would be in place? Unless he didn't know he was a wanted man.

Maybe he wasn't afraid of the law at all, but rather Caleb and his lot. Meeting in such a crowded location did ensure a certain degree of safety. Caleb probably wouldn't risk causing a huge scene in the rotunda of one of the busiest locations on the Mall, and he bet George was counting on that.

The crowd was going to be a problem. While the mass of people might help keep things from getting violent, James and the rest of the team couldn't risk their safety if things went south. They could flood the museum with plainclothes police and FBI agents, but the chances of a civilian getting hurt were still too great. They couldn't just close the museum, though, or George would know something was wrong. How could they secure the premises without giving away their plan?

Ultimately, it wasn't up to him. Carmichael had the final say on any operational plan, and, given Thomas's earlier revelation, James didn't trust the man to do the right thing.

He glanced up as Thomas stepped back into the room. "No dice on the trace. He used a burn phone."

James wasn't surprised by the news. Of course it couldn't have been that easy. "Which means it probably wasn't his."

"You thinking Caleb?"

"Yeah. Collins doesn't strike me as sophisticated enough to know that he should use a burn phone, much less where to get one."

"Agreed."

James stood and ran a hand through his hair. "We need to get our people in place to secure the museum ASAP. I'd bet my pension that Caleb will be there tomorrow, and we need to be ready to take them both out."

"You know that's not our call."

Frustration welled up, making him flush hot and then cold. He shot a glare at Thomas, who held his hands up in surrender.

"I'll head to the office, see if I can't talk some sense into him face-to-face."

James nodded, his temper cooling a bit. Kincannon was a good agent and probably the only one who could convince Carmichael to do the right thing. "Probably better if you talk to him," he said drily. "He'd only yell at me for getting shot, and then I'd have to strangle him."

"I'll check in with you later," Thomas said, heading for the door. "See you at the office."

"Watch your back," James cautioned as he followed a step behind. "I don't like any of this."

"One way or another," Thomas said in a low voice, "this is going to wrap up tomorrow."

"Yes, but at what cost? We can't sacrifice civilians, and you know as well as I do that the museum is going to be crawling with kids. We've got to figure out a way to protect them."

Thomas cut him off with a slash of his hand. "I'm on it. I'll get the rest of the team together, and we'll figure it out. Meantime, you get some rest. You're beat to hell, and we're going to need you tomorrow. If you want to worry about something, worry about taking care of her." He jerked his head in the direction of the den. "She's not looking so hot."

"She's tougher than she looks."

"Maybe, but people can only take so much." Thomas opened the door and stepped into the hall. "Stay by your phone."

James locked the door and headed for the kitchen. After dumping cat food into bowls, he returned to the den to find Kelly curled up at the end of the couch, staring off into space.

He recognized that stare. He'd even done it himself a few times. It was the gaze of a person who was shocked to their core, teetering on the edge of despair and desperation. And was it any wonder? Her whole world had been turned upside down: she'd been shot, and her boss had just asked her to aid and abet the commission of an act of bioterrorism. She was due for a breakdown, and it was a testament to her strength of character that she hadn't folded yet.

God, he wanted to hold her. Wrap her in his arms and tell her everything was going to be all right. She looked so lost and lonely, and it tugged at his heart, making him want to tell her things he had no business saying. Things he had no business feeling, especially not when she still wasn't being completely honest with him.

He knew she wasn't involved with Caleb and his organization, but she was hiding something. Something that scared her, if her reaction to his probing was any indication. Now that they were alone, maybe he could get her to talk....

She didn't look at him when he sat next to her, but

he knew she was aware of him by the way she tensed slightly.

After a moment, she spoke, her voice rough and low. "Are you really going to take him out tomorrow?"

He mentally winced, cursing his earlier choice of words. If he had to, yes, he absolutely would kill Collins, especially if it meant keeping Kelly or any other innocents safe. That didn't mean he had to rub it in her face. She had worked with the man for a while, and it was understandable that she'd be upset at the thought of his death.

"Hey," he said softly, waiting until she met his eyes. "We're not going to hurt him."

"What if he makes you?" she asked, her eyes bright with unshed tears.

James handed her a napkin that Thomas had left behind in the cleanup, which earned him a wobbly smile of thanks. "He won't."

She shook her head, as if doubting his words. "I thought I knew him," she said, dabbing her eyes with the napkin. "I never figured him for the kind of person who would do something like this."

"I understand," he said. She snorted, and he replied, "No, really, I do. You think you know someone, and it hurts to find out you were wrong about them. It makes you question your judgment, and you start second-guessing yourself."

Recognition dawned on her face. "That's exactly it!" she said, sounding relieved. "I'm thinking about all the people I know, wondering what horrible things they're all capable of."

"That'll fade with time," he assured her. "You probably won't trust people as easily anymore, but you will get to the point where you're not always waiting for them to do something bad."

Her eyes were round as she studied him. "It sounds like you speak from experience," she observed, her voice soft. "Who betrayed you?"

"What makes you think I've been betrayed?"

She merely stared at him, wearing the expression of one who has reached the finish line and is waiting for everyone else to catch up.

He looked at his lap for a moment, then back up at her. "He was a good friend."

"Want to talk about it?" Her voice was soft, the tone understanding.

He sighed quietly, the corners of his mouth pulling down in a frown. "Before I joined the FBI, I was a D.C. cop for a few years," he said slowly, feeling his way back into a story he hadn't told in years. "One of my best friends from high school went through the academy with me. We were so excited—we were going to save the world, that sort of thing." He laughed, shaking his head. "We were so damn naive."

"Were you partners after the academy?"

"No. I worked in the gang unit, and he was assigned to narcotics. Our paths did cross, though, as you might expect," he drawled, arching a brow in her direction. She smiled faintly.

"Quite."

"Everything was fine for about a year and a half, and then Steve's demeanor changed completely."

"How do you mean?" she asked, tilting her head to the side.

"He went from being a frugal guy—never really bought anything for himself, drove the same car for ten years, that kind of thing—to suddenly spending money like it was going out of style." Suddenly restless, James grabbed the remote and turned it over and over in his hands.

"I asked him about it," he said, putting it back on the table. "He said he had to dress the part, or else the dealers would make him for a cop. I didn't press for details. I think I knew even then that he was dirty, but I didn't want to confirm it."

"I can understand that," Kelly said softly. "If you don't have proof, you can pretend nothing is wrong."

"Exactly." He shook his head. "I remained firmly entrenched in my denial over the next several months, while Steve continued to burn through money. It all came to a head one night in July."

He told her about their fight, about his refusal to throw away his own career to help out a friend. The way Steve had stormed out, never to be seen again. Looking back on it, there were so many things he would have done differently, but that was the gift—and the curse—of hindsight.

James jerked when a hand landed on his arm. He looked up to find Kelly watching him with knowing eyes. "I know you did the right thing," she said, giving his arm a gentle squeeze.

"Yeah, well, I'm not so sure." He paused, recalling the crime-scene photos of Steve's body. "It doesn't matter," he said, shaking his head to clear his thoughts. "What's done is done."

Kelly's hand was warm on his arm; her thumb moved back and forth with gentle strokes that sent shivers of awareness across his skin. He turned to face her, and the way she was staring at him, her eyes dark and heated, had his mouth going dry and his heart pounding. Then she parted her lips, her pink tongue darting out to leave behind a shiny gloss on her mouth, and he nearly groaned aloud.

Unable to stop himself, he reached out to cup her face and ran his thumb along her bottom lip. She nipped at it, biting him gently, sending a tingle of awareness shooting up his arm and into his belly. She closed her eyes and leaned closer, pressing herself against him and snaking her good arm around his waist.

In the dim recesses of his brain, he heard his conscience telling him to stop. A split second more, and he would have listened to that voice. But then Kelly stretched up and captured his mouth with hers, letting out a little moan of satisfaction that nearly undid him.

She broke the kiss and stood over him, her mouth swollen, her eyes shining. Slowly, deliberately, she lowered herself onto his lap until she was straddling him, her hand clutching his shoulder. He gasped as she settled over his erection. The pleasure of the contact forced his eyes closed. For a moment, he couldn't think, couldn't breathe, and then he became aware of her hot mouth trailing kisses across his neck.

He felt her fumble at his belt buckle. *Yes, yes!* He reached up to grab her shoulders, remembering too late her injury. Her slight gasp brought him back down to earth, and he opened his eyes.

"Oh, God, I'm so sorry. Did I hurt you? Did I make it worse?" He fought to steady his breathing as he eyed her shoulder. It didn't look as if the wound was bleeding again, but he had obviously caused her pain by touching it.

She smiled, pushing a strand of hair off his forehead.

"It's fine." She leaned down to press a gentle kiss to his lips. "I'm fine." She moved in again, but he pressed a finger to her mouth, stopping her.

"What are we doing here?" he whispered. It felt so good, so right to have her in his arms again, but if she was going to regret this in the morning, it wasn't worth it. Then an ugly thought occurred to him, making him suck in a breath.

"Are you doing this because you think you owe me?"

She reared back, almost falling off his lap. He clamped his hands on her hips to keep her in place. "Owe you?" Two pink spots appeared high on her cheeks, and he had the distinct impression that if she'd had a free hand, she would have slapped him. "Do I look like a prostitute to you?"

He definitely knew the correct answer to this question, but the fact that she had asked it did not bode well for him. "No, of course not—" he began.

"I was not going to sleep with you because of any feeling of obligation on my part." The words were clipped and sharp as she struggled to slide off his lap. With a sigh, he helped her to stand, missing the warmth of her body after she moved away. She glared down at him for a beat before her eyes slid away. The angry set of her mouth relaxed before she spoke, the words almost a whisper. "I just wanted to connect with you, that's all."

He blinked up at her in disbelief. "You want to connect with me? I seem to remember you walking away the last time we 'connected.'"

She winced, and he knew his words had struck a nerve. He felt a prick of guilt at upsetting her, but being so close to her again had dredged up the hurt feelings he still carried from her earlier rejection. It was small of him, but he wanted her to have a taste of that same rejection.

"I made a mistake," she began, not looking at him. "I see that now."

He snorted. "A mistake? A mistake is forgetting to put the clothes in the dryer. That's not what you did. You basically set our friendship on fire and then walked away without looking back."

"That's not true—"

"The hell it's not!" He stood, not wanting to have this conversation while she towered over him. "Not only did you run away, but you refused to return my calls. I could have dealt with it if you didn't want to keep sleeping together—it would have hurt my feelings, but I would have gotten over it. What killed me was the fact that you cut me out of your life entirely." His throat tightened at the admission, his emotions threatening to boil over and erupt out of him like an exploding volcano. It was too much, so he turned away and headed for the door.

"Wait." Her voice stopped him before he could leave the room. "You want to know why I left? I was scared."

He turned to face her. She stood a few feet away, her chin up and her left fist clenched at her side. She blinked back tears as she met his gaze, and his heart lurched at the sight. "I was afraid, so I took the coward's way out and ran."

"What were you scared of?" he asked hoarsely.

She took a deep breath, as if preparing herself for battle. "You."

He almost laughed. He frightened her? Not possible. He'd never been anything but gentle with her, especially that night. "What did I ever do to scare you? I've never hurt you, and I never will."

She took a step forward, her eyes locked with his. "I know that, but you have to understand." She paused, tucking a strand of hair behind her ear. "When I was in graduate school, I had an abusive boyfriend. His name was Gary." She stopped a foot away, close enough that he could smell the almond soap from her bath. "It's taken me a long time to get over what he did to me, and after our night together, I was afraid you'd want more. I wasn't ready for that."

He swallowed hard, not knowing what to say. It all made horrible sense now.... He thought back to that morning, how she had refused to offer an explanation for leaving, just saying he deserved better. His stomach twisted, threatening to expel his dinner. God, the thought of her being used as a punching bag... He had suspected, but having her confirm it was so much worse. What kind of man did that to a woman? His hands clenched involuntarily at the thought of the faceless Gary who had hurt her. Kelly noticed the gesture and her eyes widened, but she stood her ground.

Cursing himself for scaring her, James forced his hands to relax. "Kelly..." His voice was a croak, so he cleared his throat and tried again. "Why didn't you tell me?"

She frowned up at him, her frustration evident. "Because of the look on your face right now. That combination of disgust and pity? I couldn't bear to have you look at me like that."

"How am I supposed to look at you?" He ran a hand through his hair, unsure of what she wanted from him.

"You tell me you had an abusive boyfriend, and I'm not supposed to be upset?"

"I didn't want you to think of me as broken."

He sighed heavily, at a loss for words. She held his gaze for a beat, then looked away. "I don't think you're broken," he began, testing the words out as he spoke. "But I wish you would have told me this before. We could have worked through it together."

She shook her head firmly. "This was something I had to do on my own. It took me months of therapy to even get to this point."

He nodded. "I can respect that, but still. You have to know I wouldn't have pushed you into anything you weren't ready for."

She smiled at that, and a spark of hope flared to life in her eyes.

"Well…" she said quietly, dropping her gaze to the floor. "What if I told you… What if I said that…" She raised her head to look at him, her cheeks pink. "I think I'm ready for something more, now, with you."

He stared down at her, disbelieving. She wanted him now? She'd just revealed a former abusive relationship that she was clearly still getting over, and she wanted to take things to the next level? Impossible. It was the stress of her situation talking, he decided. Near-death experiences often made people horny, he knew, and that was exactly what was happening here. There was no other explanation.

"You don't want me," he said, shaking his head. "You're scared, and you want a distraction. That's all."

Her expression morphed from hopeful to angry, her brows drawing together and her lips forming a white line in her already pale face. "You're wrong," she bit out. "Don't tell me what I'm feeling, James. I know I made a mistake before, but I want to move past it now, with you. You are not a distraction—you're so much more than that."

"Tell me this," he said, holding up a hand to stop her. "If I hadn't showed up in your lab two days ago, would you have called me? Would you have still wanted to start something new with me?" He waited for her to respond, and when she remained silent, he continued, "That's what I thought."

He turned back to the doorway, pausing at the threshold. "You say you're ready to move on, but you couldn't even trust me enough to tell me about your past. There is no room for secrets like that in a relationship."

He walked out before Kelly could respond, his side on fire and his heart heavy.

Chapter 9

Kelly sat on the bed and absently rubbed her shoulder as the light from the window illuminated the room, gradually changing from gray to pink to a warm yellow as the sun rose more fully in the morning sky. She had spent a sleepless night tossing and turning as much as her injury would allow. They would be leaving in a few hours, which meant she still had a good chunk of time to spend alone with her thoughts.

How had it come to this? Not for the first time, she wished for a do-over, to go back and change the outcome of that fateful night, when their friendship had changed forever. Her heart ached when she recalled the look on James's face as he had explored her body, the way his hands had been both teasing and gentle, their mutual sounds of pleasure. They had shared an extraordinary night, but dawn had brought insecurities and fear, and she had left, hoping to spare herself the pain of exposing her past. She had thought she was making it easier for both of them.

She knew better now.

She rose and paced to the window, her toes digging into the plush carpet. She stood in the sunlight and closed her eyes, hoping the warmth would burn away the memories of last night. James looking at her with an expression of shock and dismay before his face shuttered and he rebuilt the walls to keep her at arm's length. She should have never kissed him, never given in to her selfish desire for contact. She should have known the truth would only push him further away.

In an ideal world, she would have told him about Gary over dinner, or maybe while snuggling on the couch. He would have asked her questions and held her close as she told him about that painful episode from her past. He would have been supportive and caring, and she would know he really cared for her.

Instead, she had blurted out the truth in the heat of an argument, catching him off guard and making a wreck of things. Then, to top it off, she'd told him she wanted another chance, a statement that had practically sent him running for the door. No one could accuse her of having good timing.

Maybe it's for the best, she thought, blinking back tears. It wasn't as though either of them really had time for a relationship anyway. She worked constantly, and now that George was in such a fine mess, she was going to need a new job. This was the perfect opportunity for her to move away, get a fresh start somewhere. Maybe she could find work in Houston, be closer to her family.

Besides, it was his loss. Despite what he might

think, she was ready to move on. She'd thought he was the one, but his actions last night had indicated otherwise. She didn't need a man who would back down in the face of her past. She deserved a good man, one who would be proud of her strength and the things she had overcome.

But he is a good man.

She couldn't deny the truth of that thought. James had been by her side since this whole mess with Dr. Collins had started, despite his personal feelings. Given their history, it would have been so easy for him to recuse himself from the investigation, but instead he had jumped right in, putting his own hurts aside to keep her safe.

He took on so much responsibility, she mused, thinking of his reaction to her getting shot, the way he had swept her off to the safety of his apartment rather than risk leaving her in someone else's care. Maybe he was overreacting a bit, but as he had talked last night she'd seen how the ghost of Steve haunted him still. A chill raced through her at the thought of how close she had come to being another casualty in his life, and she rubbed her hands over the goose bumps on her arms.

Was it any wonder he'd pushed her away? He was probably feeling overwhelmed between the case, seeing her again and the massive amount of guilt he carried around. It was a wonder he hadn't collapsed yet; the fact that he was still functioning must be due to an excess of sheer stubborn will.

The sound of the shower running down the hall drew her out of her thoughts. James must be awake. She should get cleaned up so they could leave on time.

She just had to get through today, and then life could go back to normal.

Whatever that was.

The water was almost too hot to bear, but James forced himself to stand under the jetting spray until his skin was red and prickly with pain. He usually preferred a more temperate shower, but this morning he wanted the distraction. Better to focus on the physical discomfort than spend another minute thinking about Kelly and how badly things had ended between them last night.

How had this situation gotten so messed up? She'd made it clear months ago that she didn't want a physical relationship with him, and, given her history of abuse, he could understand her reluctance. But how was he supposed to believe she'd gotten over her past in the few short months they'd been apart?

I think I'm ready for something more, now, with you. He rubbed gritty eyes and reached for the soap, lathering his body with efficient movements. Her words had haunted him all night, and he still didn't know what to make of them. Was she serious? Did she really want him, or was it the stress of her situation talking? He stepped back under the spray for a moment, grabbed the shampoo and poured out a dollop into his palm.

Once again, her face appeared in his memory, her expression both scared and hopeful as she revealed what had to be a painful secret. It reminded him of Steve and the look on his face when he had asked for help so many years ago. He had turned his friend away then, and the action haunted him to this day. Was he making the same mistake again?

But did they really have a chance? A spark of hope flared to life in his chest, but he wasn't ready to believe quite yet. Despite her brave words, she was emotionally damaged. A person didn't go through something like that and come out unscathed. He didn't want to punish her for her past, but the thought of getting involved with someone so fragile, so...vulnerable made his stomach tighten.

Maybe he was a coward, but he wasn't sure he could give Kelly the commitment she needed. He knew from his days as a street cop that domestic-abuse victims needed stability and support as they rebuilt their lives. If he got involved with Kelly and he couldn't handle her issues, he'd never forgive himself for hurting her again.

Tired of being alone with his thoughts, he rinsed the shampoo from his hair and wrenched the faucet to the right, letting the cooler water sluice over his body for a moment before he turned the shower off. He grabbed a towel and quickly dried off with jerky impatience. He had to focus on the job today, find a way to get Kelly out of his mind so he could finish this operation. Distractions would only complicate matters, and he couldn't afford to have things unravel at this late stage.

His career, and Kelly's life, depended on it.

Kelly drew up short as she entered the kitchen. James was standing at the window, his back to the door, phone to his ear. Mentally scolding herself for letting him affect her, she walked over to the counter and dropped two pieces of bread into the toaster, then moved to the fridge and pulled out a Coke.

James glanced over his shoulder at the hiss of the can opening and met her gaze briefly before turning back. His voice was too quiet for her to make out the conversation, but he was probably talking to the FBI about today's plan.

The toast popped up and she busied herself smearing butter and then strawberry jam across the warm surface. She heard James snap his phone closed, and she turned to put the butter and jam back in the refrigerator, buying herself a few seconds before she had to face him. It was a cowardly thing to do, but she needed the extra time, however brief, to compose herself.

He was standing by her breakfast after she shut the fridge door, eyeing her soda with a faint smile. He looked up as she approached.

"You never did like coffee," he said softly.

"No. I don't. Some things never change."

"Kelly…" His mouth turned down at the corners, and his brows drew together. He looked like a man about to deliver bad news, and she wasn't in the mood for it this morning.

She held up a hand to stop him. "What's the plan for today?"

He met her eyes for a beat. When she didn't look away, he nodded once in acknowledgment of her desire to put yesterday behind them. "That was Carmichael."

She nodded and took a bite of toast. He set the phone down on the counter next to her plate and retrieved a mug from the cupboard.

"We're going to rendezvous at headquarters in an hour. We're going to put a wire on you and give you the vials. Then I'm going to drop you at the Metro station so you can travel to the museum and meet George." He poured coffee and doctored it with a little sugar before turning back to her.

The toast stuck in her throat, and she took a swig of soda to wash it down. "You're actually going to give me the vials he wants?"

He shook his head. "No. Not the real ones. Those are safe in our lab. We're giving you decoys. They'll look the same, so he shouldn't suspect anything."

She nodded, feeling marginally better. "What do I do after I give George his vials?"

"You walk to the information desk, where I'll be waiting. We'll walk out together, and I'll take you to a secure location until we pick up George and Caleb." He sipped the dark brew, watching her over the rim of the cup. "Simple, really."

Kelly set down her toast, not really agreeing with his assessment. "Maybe for you," she muttered. He made it sound so easy, but any number of things could go wrong. What if George didn't show up? What if he recognized the vials were fake? Would they hurt him when they picked him up? It was hard to feel sorry for the man, but she didn't want him to get hurt, no matter what he had done.

What if George hurt her? Her stomach twisted as a wave of nausea hit. As far as she knew, he wasn't a violent person by nature, but desperation could drive a man to do things he normally wouldn't. She would be an easy target, given her earlier injury. Her shoulder was still too sore to allow for much motion, making her easy pickings if George's thoughts did indeed turn toward the use of force.

Would James even care if she were injured during this operation? She stole a glance at him from under her lashes. He was staring into his coffee cup with a look of abstract concentration, and she knew he was miles away. Probably mentally rehearsing the upcoming take-down. She envied his ability to turn off his emotions and focus on work, and she wished she could do the same. Her lack of sleep and last night's argument had left her feeling raw and gritty, and her feelings were too close to the surface to be ignored.

Or maybe…maybe he didn't have any emotions to turn off where she was concerned. After all, he had walked out and left her standing alone in the middle of the room last night without even a moment's hesitation. She had shared her darkest secret, laid her heart bare for him, and he had told her that her feelings weren't real and turned his back. Not exactly the actions of a man who cared about her.

Stop thinking about it, she chastised herself. Nothing good could come of her mentally rehashing their argument, and it was using up energy she couldn't afford to burn. Determined to focus on the day ahead, she finished her soda and tossed the empty can into the recycle bin.

First things first—get this meeting over with and then figure out the rest of her life.

"Ready to go?" she asked James, who nodded and drained his coffee cup.

A few more hours, and it would all be over.

The FBI office was a study in controlled chaos, with agents moving about the room in what looked like a carefully choreographed ballet. One group was standing by a large map, inserting pins and drawing what looked like different routes out of the city. Another group was clustered around a table, and as they walked by, Kelly saw that they were looking at plans of the museum, marking off exits. She watched one man pick up a file folder of papers and walk it over to the other side of the room, typing on his phone all the while. It was a wonder no one crashed into each other, but she supposed they had done this before.

The room had a lived-in look, with empty coffee cups scattered on flat surfaces and the occasional candy-bar wrapper or half-eaten bag of chips punctuating the detritus. The air was stale and warm, and most of the agents were down to their shirtsleeves, their hair mussed and the dark circles under their eyes testifying to the general lack of sleep.

"Don't these people ever go home?" Kelly muttered under her breath.

James glanced over, and she felt her face flush as she realized he'd heard her. "Not when we're this close," he said grimly.

He led her back to the conference room she'd come to hate, and she settled into what she thought of as her chair.

"I'm going to round up the rest of the team," James said from the doorway. "Will you be all right here for a few minutes?"

He'd been gone for only a few seconds when Agent Carmichael walked into the room, carrying his usual bundle of papers. She stifled a giggle as the image of Linus and his security blanket popped into her head, causing the older man to glance at her with a frown. "Is something wrong?"

She shook her head. "No, not at all." Except for the fact that she was losing her mind. Clearly the stress of the situation, combined with her exhaustion and the pain pills, had put her on edge, and rather than focusing on the very real issues ahead of her, her brain was throwing up cartoon references. *Wonderful.*

The rest of the team filed in, and she recognized some of the faces from her interview two days ago. James entered last, shutting the door behind him before taking the seat across the table from her.

Carmichael cleared his throat, drawing the eye of everyone in the room. "Okay, people, this is it. You already know the plan, but we're going to go over it one last time before heading out. I don't want any mistakes out there. We've already had one close call—" he glared meaningfully at James, who stared impassively back at him "—and we can't afford another one. I want to wrap this thing up today. Are we clear?"

Heads nodded, and a collective murmur of assent floated up from the table. He turned and fixed Kelly with a gimlet stare, making her want to squirm in her chair. "Are you ready for this?"

She met his gaze unflinchingly. "Yes," she said, pleased that her voice didn't waver. "I want to get this over with." Her eyes flickered to James before returning to Agent Carmichael. If he noticed the brief lapse in her attention, he didn't react. "I just want my life to go back to normal."

The older man nodded as if pleased with her response. "And it will, just as soon as you do this one thing."

He glanced down the table and nodded at a woman sitting a few seats away. "Caroline is going to get you wired up as soon as we're done here, and then Thomas—" he gestured to the redheaded agent, who gave her a wink "—will walk you to the Metro station."

"What about the vials?" James had said she would

be given duplicate vials, but she hadn't seen anyone carry anything in with them.

Thomas reached into his jacket pocket and pulled out two small plastic vials, which he slid across the table to her. She examined them closely, surprised to find that the labels appeared to be written in Dr. Collins's even script and the liquid inside was the right color and consistency of a bacterial culture—a thick, milky yellow substance that slid lazily around the tube.

She set them down and turned to Carmichael, who was watching her closely. "These look real." He smiled at that, his shoulders relaxing subtly. "But," she continued, "they need to be frozen. If I hand him tubes of liquid, he'll know they're fake."

"Are you kidding me? He's not even going to see them—we're going to scoop him up before he gets a chance to look at them."

Kelly stood her ground. "He'll expect me to bring him frozen stocks. If I don't walk in carrying tubes on ice, he'll know something is going on and he may not even approach me. Do you really want to lose him because of something so simple?"

Carmichael glared at her. "What do you suggest?"

She shrugged. "Just give me a foam cup of ice to carry, and I'll drop the tubes inside. I can stick a straw in it so it looks innocuous, but George will see what he wants to see."

James frowned at her. "I don't think you're allowed to bring a drink into the museum. How are you going to get in the door with that?"

"I'll stick it in my bag," she said simply. "No metal, so it won't set off the detectors."

Carmichael nodded slowly as he considered her suggestion. "Works for me," he muttered, then motioned to Thomas. The other man quickly rose from the table and returned in short order with a cup of ice, which he handed to her. She nestled the tubes inside.

The meeting progressed quickly from there. Carmichael sketched out where everyone would be stationed, what they were to look for and how they were to approach George. The goal was to apprehend George with as little disruption as possible. It wouldn't do to frighten the tourists. Kelly shook her head. If they only knew...

"Is there another problem?" Carmichael asked, having seen her movement. She looked up to find the room watching her. The agents wore expressions ranging from expectant to irritated to pitying.

"No," she said with another shake of her head. "My shoulder is just a little sore, that's all," she lied.

Carmichael's gaze tracked over her shoulder, and she fought the urge to pull the neckline of her shirt up higher to conceal the small strip of bandage that remained visible. It wasn't obvious, but she did feel self-conscious about it and she hoped George wouldn't notice.

"Any questions?" he asked the group. When none were forthcoming, he stood. "Let's be safe out there," he ordered before turning and leaving the room.

The rest of the team stood and began to gather their papers. A woman approached—Caroline? Was that her name? She placed a hand on Kelly's good shoulder. "If you'll come with me?" she asked in a surprisingly husky voice that suggested she was either a heavy smoker or suffering from a cold. "I'll get you wired up in the bathroom."

Kelly nodded and followed the petite woman out of the room, resisting the temptation to look back for James. From this point on, she was on her own, and she needed to get used to it.

Caroline placed a small box on the bathroom counter and turned to face Kelly. "I'm going to affix the wire near your bra, so nothing will be showing. The main part is a microphone, and it will transmit your conversations to us." She opened the box and pulled out the item in question, which looked like a small earbud. Kelly gingerly lifted her shirt to allow Caroline to tape the microphone in place between her breasts. Next came a small, flat black box that Caroline hooked on the waistband of her jeans at the small of her back, tucking it inside Kelly's pants so that nothing was showing.

She stepped back and circled around Kelly with a critical eye, presumably checking to make sure nothing looked out of place. Seemingly satisfied, she nodded and gathered up the now-empty box and tape.

"You don't need to worry about talking into your shirt or anything like that," she informed Kelly. "The microphone is pretty powerful, so just speak in a normal volume—no need to yell."

"Is it on now?"

Caroline shook her head. "Not yet. I'll turn it on right before you leave to get on the Metro. Speaking of which." She glanced at the door. "Thomas should be ready to escort you in a few minutes."

She held the door open, waiting for Kelly to step through before falling into step behind her. It was a few steps from the bathroom to the main office. Unsure of where to go next, Kelly stood against the wall, trying to stay out of the flow of traffic while she scanned the room for Thomas. Caroline touched her arm. "I'm going to let Thomas know you're ready. Stay here?"

Kelly nodded, absently fingering the wire wrapped around her torso. Was it really invisible? Caroline seemed to think she looked normal, but she didn't *feel* normal. The wire was thin, but what if her shirt slipped or caught on it, and George saw it? Worse, what if the unit malfunctioned and didn't transmit? Would the FBI still be able to make their case if they couldn't hear what he said to her?

Her thoughts were interrupted by the appearance of Thomas. The agent walked over to her with a reassuring smile, his dimples winking in his stubbled cheeks. "Get any sleep last night?" he asked.

Kelly snorted. "Not exactly."

She glanced past Thomas's shoulder to see James watching her from across the room. Her stomach did a little flip as their eyes met, but he quickly looked away. Letting out a small sigh, she bit her lip and focused on the man now standing next to her. *Message received.*

Thomas looked her up and down with a critical eye. "Are you feeling okay?"

She gave him a wobbly smile. "I guess. I'm not sure how I'm supposed to feel right now."

"I can remember my first operation. We were taking down a smuggler in the airport. I was so nervous that things would go wrong, I puked in the car on the way over." He grinned at her. "I have yet to really live that down."

She smiled back as the butterflies in her stomach relaxed at his confession. "I don't think I need to throw up, but if there's any blood, all bets are off."

"There won't be any blood," he assured her. "This is going to be a cakewalk."

First James and now him. Did these men not understand what a big deal this was? "If you say so," she replied.

He placed a hand on her good shoulder, and she felt the warmth of his palm through her shirt. "I'm not trying to dismiss the seriousness of what you're about to do, but you need to know that you'll be safe at all times. We have two agents in the museum who will be watching you, plus eyes on all the entrances and exits. As soon as you give Collins the cup, we're going to scoop him up."

She raised her eyebrow at the rhyme, and he chuckled softly. "I'm not a poet, all right? Cut me some slack." He bent his head so he was at eye level with her. "Despite my cheesy delivery, the message stands. You're going to be fine."

A movement on the other side of the room caught her attention, and she shifted her gaze to see James watching them, his jaw tight and his shoulders tense. He relaxed a bit when Thomas removed his hand, but he still didn't look happy.

Thomas glanced over his shoulder to see what she was looking at. James quickly looked away, but not before Thomas saw the expression on his face. He turned back to Kelly with a speculative gleam in his eyes. "Interesting," he muttered.

Her face felt warm, and she knew she must be as red as a tomato. "I—I don't know what you mean," she stammered.

Thomas studied her for a beat, then shrugged. "Now is not the time. Let's get you on your way."

He guided her toward the elevator bank, and she took a few steps before stopping. "Wait! My transmitter has to be on." She turned around to search for Caroline, gasping when she felt the back of her shirt jerked up. Thomas flipped the switch on the transmitter, then tugged her shirt back into place and turned her back around to face the elevators. He hadn't actually touched her, but she saw his wicked grin and wink and knew he was taunting James.

She wanted to tell him not to bother, that James didn't have feelings for her, but as he had said just a moment ago, this wasn't the time. Besides, she didn't feel like telling the whole humiliating story, especially to one of James's coworkers.

No matter how handsome he was.

The elevator sped them down to the street level, and Thomas paused in the foyer, out of sight of the door. He raised his wrist to his mouth and muttered something. After a beat, he placed a hand on the small of her back. "We're good," he said softly, escorting her out the door.

She walked purposefully toward the Metro station. Thomas dropped in behind her after a few steps. She was tempted to look back and make sure he was still there, but she knew it was important that they appear to be strangers. She'd just have to trust he hadn't left her alone.

The sidewalks weren't overly crowded, but there was a steady stream of people walking around—the usual combination of tourists, businessmen and the homeless who wandered the same patch of sidewalk day in and day out hoping to encounter a generous soul.

Kelly rode the escalator down into the Metro station, standing on the right to avoid being trampled by the people in a hurry. She made her way onto the platform, fighting the urge to check for Thomas. *He's there,* she told herself, wiping damp palms on her pants. She hadn't seen anyone suspicious-looking, but that didn't mean she wasn't being watched. She could only trust that Thomas would do his job and keep her safe.

Where was James? She knew he was supposed to meet her inside the museum after she handed the vials to George, but where was he now? Would he be watching her the whole time, like Thomas? Despite the way things had gone last night, she'd still feel better knowing he was around. He was so…calm, always composed and put together. She felt safe around him, and she had missed that in the months they'd been apart. The events of the past few days had been stressful, but in spite of all the chaos, she had enjoyed just being around James again.

Too bad it couldn't last.

Her heart in her throat, Kelly merged with the crowd to spill out of the station. Blinking in the sunlight, she walked across the Mall to the Natural History Museum. A Girl Scout group was gathered on the white marble steps, their green uniforms a bright splash of color in the crowd. Large banners hung from the building, advertising the latest IMAX movie and special exhibit. Normally, she looked forward to coming here; she always enjoyed spending an afternoon wandering the halls and reading the placards mounted next to specimens. Now, instead of the usual pleasant anticipation, she was struggling not to vomit.

She took a deep breath, gathering her courage to climb the stairs. There were so many children running around with harried parents chasing after them.

Everyone was enjoying the beautiful day, seemingly without a care in the world. These families had no idea how close they were to danger, that there were people out there bent on hurting them. In one small way, she could do something to make sure they maintained that innocence. As difficult and scary as this was, she could help. The thought gave her the resolve she needed to finish the climb up the stairs, and she stepped inside the museum with her head held high and her jaw set.

Game on.

Chapter 10

George stayed in the shadows by the stairwell, trying hard to blend into the wall and avoid being trampled by the seemingly endless parade of children and families marching by to get to the dinosaur hall. Where was she? She should be here by now.

His heart pounding, he glanced at his watch and scanned the center of the museum again. Kelly wasn't tall, but her reddish hair should stand out in the crowd. Was she coming? He had tried to sound so normal on the phone, but maybe she had picked up on his nerves....

He wiped his damp palms on his pants, swallowing hard in a vain effort to keep his nausea under control. This was all his fault. He should have taken Ruth and run, left the city and never looked back. It was no wonder they'd been found—he hadn't done a good job of hiding.

He felt a prickle of guilt at using Kelly to get out of this mess. Caleb had been all too happy to agree when he'd suggested getting her to bring the vials. He clearly had something planned, but George couldn't figure out what.

There was a lot he found confusing lately. Like how Caleb had insisted he call Kelly twice to set up the meeting, when only one conversation was really needed.

"It's not your concern," the other man had said dismissively. "Just do as you're told."

And so he had played his part, his knees knocking throughout each conversation with Kelly. One slip and he knew Ruth would be killed, in a very painful, drawn-out way, if Caleb was to be believed. It wasn't something he'd been willing to test.

Even now, he couldn't truly focus on the task at hand. His mind was back at the hotel room, where Ruth was no doubt reading a book or sleeping, completely oblivious to the danger she was in. Caleb had men on standby, waiting for his signal.

The hairs on the nape of his neck prickled as he recalled Caleb's cold, smug voice. "Get the vials from Kelly, and your wife will be left alone. Fail to do this..." He had trailed off at the end, the silent threat to Ruth all too clear.

A flash of red caught his eye, and he rose on his tiptoes to see over the heads of the crowd. *Is that... Yes!* Kelly was there. She was standing just inside the museum, her head swiveling back and forth as she searched for him.

He stepped forward, pausing to let a large group of kids pass by before making his way over to the elephant in the center of the rotunda. She was walking over to the elephant as well, but she hadn't seen him yet. He raised a hand to draw her eye and saw her head nod in recognition. A tight smile formed on her face, triggering a niggle of fear in his chest. Why was she looking at him like that? Did she suspect something?

As she approached, he saw she was walking a little strangely. She held her right arm close to her side, as if it was giving her pain. A man bumped into her, causing her features to tighten as her face went pale, and he realized she was injured. How had that happened? He'd never questioned Caleb's interest in Kelly before, but now he wondered if she'd been a target all along.

Deciding to play it cool, he pasted a large smile on his face as he stepped forward to greet Kelly. "Great to see you," he said, trying to fake a confidence he didn't feel. "Thanks so much for bringing the vials. I knew if I went into the lab, I'd get tied up in work, and Ruth is eager to set off again." He forced a laugh, hoping she was buying it. "You know how determined she can be."

Kelly nodded and opened her bag. "No problem." She rummaged a moment, then pulled out a foam cup and held it out for him. "I figured you'd want them kept frozen, so I packed them on ice for you."

His heart pounding, he reached out to take the cup. Two small tubes were nestled inside, their innocuous-looking golden content his salvation. He breathed a sigh of relief, knowing it was almost over.

He glanced up to thank Kelly, and the smile froze on his lips as he noticed her expression. She wore a look of sad resignation, as if she was disappointed in something. Or someone. She darted a quick glance to the right, then looked back at him. A prickle of unease danced across his skin as she took a step back. It was time to go.

He opened his mouth to tell her goodbye, but before he could speak, all hell broke loose.

It was true. Despite all the evidence against him, Kelly had harbored a small spark of hope that somehow George was innocent and this was just a big misunderstanding. Seeing his look of abject relief as she'd given him the tubes had made her realize how naive she'd been.

She risked a quick glance around, hoping to see one of the FBI agents in the crowd. They were supposed to be in the museum, but she didn't see anyone nearby. Her stomach tightened at the thought that she might be alone. Where were they?

She took a step back, wanting to get away from George as soon as possible. Just being so close to him made her skin crawl. Her part of the operation was finished, and the sooner she got out of there, the better.

George seemed to pick up on her discomfort; the smile faded from his lips. He opened his mouth to say something, but only a strangled sound escaped. His features twisted in horror as he glanced over her shoulder.

Before Kelly could turn to see what had scared him, she felt a sharp poke in the ribs and stiffened. She tried to step away, but a strong hand clamped onto her arm and squeezed, sending pain shooting up her arm and into her shoulder. Her knees went weak, but before she could fall, she was pulled into a solid body and felt a warm breath at her ear. "We meet again, Dr. Jarvis."

Oh, God. Oh, no. Fear sent cold spikes through her body, and her heart threatened to pound out of her chest. How had he found her? How had he gotten past the FBI agents? She glanced up and met George's eyes, silently begging him to help her. He thrust the Styrofoam cup back into her bag and shook his head, slowly backing away as if afraid to make any sudden movements.

"You bastard," she hissed at him. He'd probably set this whole thing up, promising her in exchange for his safety. "You won't get away with this." She could have bitten her tongue the minute the words left her mouth. The last thing she needed was for him to suspect the FBI was nearby.

"I'm sorry," he whispered before turning and walking away. He merged quickly with the crowd, disappearing from her sight and leaving her alone with a psychopath.

She took a deep breath, preparing to scream. Yes, it would scare the families in the museum, but it would also alert the FBI agents, who could help her. Before she could even emit so much as a squeak, she was spun around and found herself face-to-face with Caleb.

His mouth quirked up in a smile. "Not a good idea, Doctor. You don't want to draw attention to us. Believe me." He opened the flap of his jacket, and she saw a remote tucked into the breast pocket of his shirt. She snapped her mouth shut with an audible click, her gut turning to water as she realized why he would be carrying such a device. Was he wired, or had he set up a bomb nearby?

"Be a good girl and smile for me," he urged, tucking his free hand into his jacket pocket. She stared up at him in disbelief, certain she had misunderstood. He gave her arm a warning squeeze. "Smile." She forced the corners of her mouth up, and he regarded her with a bemused expression. "You could at least try to make it look natural," he said with a sigh. "But that will do for now."

His hand still wrapped around her arm, he steered her into the depths of the museum. She glanced wildly around as he forced her past the dinosaur skeletons, hoping to catch a glimpse of one of the FBI agents. If they were around, they were certainly staying in the shadows. Despair washed over her as she realized they had probably all moved to close in on George, thinking she'd be fine once they picked him up. There was no way anyone could have foreseen Caleb would come out of hiding, especially not when the risk of getting caught was so high.

"Where are you taking me?" she gritted out from between clenched teeth. Her only hope now was that the FBI was listening. If she could get him to tell her where they were going, there was a good chance the good guys could get there first.

Caleb chuckled close to her ear. "Now, Dr. Jarvis, surely you don't think I'm that stupid? In fact—" He reached down and pulled the back of her shirt up, then yanked out the pack attached to the waistband of her pants. With another sharp tug, he pulled the wires free from her shirt. "Much better," he said, dumping the wire over the rail of an exhibit as they passed.

"Now it's just you and me."

James scanned the museum, his heart pounding so loudly he had trouble hearing the voices of his team.

They had picked up Collins without incident, but since Caleb was on the scene, all bets were off.

It had taken all his willpower not to rush over when Caleb had grabbed Kelly. Only repeated orders from Carmichael, liberally laced with threats, had kept him standing by the information desk with his thumb up his ass. If he went charging in, he'd likely botch the whole operation and possibly get Kelly hurt in the process. Her safety wasn't worth the risk, but he hated sitting around when he could be doing something to put this whole thing to rest.

"We've lost her." The voice was tinny in his ear, snapping the last of his control.

"I'm on the move," he said as he began to walk through the rotunda. He hadn't seen them come by him, which meant they had likely gone in the opposite direction.

"Negative," Carmichael commanded. "Stay in place, Reynolds. We need to let this play out."

"She is not a bargaining chip," James snapped, reaching up to lower the volume on his earpiece. Carmichael's squawking faded from his attention as he scanned the exhibits. It was darker in the halls; the lighting was strategically placed to highlight the bones and other artifacts on display while leaving shadows in the corners.

He glanced at the faces of the tourists as he passed. No one looked upset or distressed, which meant if Kelly and Caleb had come this way, she wasn't putting up a fight. Caleb must have threatened her to ensure her cooperation. Maybe even hurt her, he thought grimly, picking up speed as the crowd thinned.

He caught a glimpse of blond curls up ahead, just

rounding a corner. He drew his gun from the side holster, holding his hand down by his side in an effort to
keep the civilians from noticing. He heard a few startled gasps as he moved by, but he couldn't take the time
to reassure them now.

He rounded the corner, narrowly avoiding a colli-
sion with a stroller. Stepping to the side, he glanced
up and saw Caleb and Kelly a few paces ahead, moving quickly. They were heading for a service corridor,
and he hung back to let them enter the hall. Better to
confront Caleb in a nonpublic area of the museum,
where there was a lower chance of innocent casualties.

He grabbed the heavy door before it slammed shut
and drew the gun up to aim at Caleb's back. "FBI!"
he boomed, his voice loud and echoing in the cement
corridor.

Caleb reacted immediately, whirling to the side and
pulling Kelly in front of him to act as a shield. James
scanned her quickly, checking for injuries. She seemed
unharmed, and relief at seeing him shone on her face
as she held his gaze. He gave her a brief nod before
turning his attention back to Caleb.

"Let her go, Caleb," he began, slowly stepping forward to close the distance between them. Caleb stepped
back, dragging Kelly with him while his hand reached
up to press a knife against her throat. She stiffened and
whimpered when he pressed the blade on her skin, and
James halted.

"Very good." Caleb smiled as if he were a teacher
praising a particularly clever student. "You shouldn't
have followed us," he continued, dragging Kelly back
step by step.

"I couldn't just let you walk away," James responded,

risking a small step. He stopped at Caleb's raised brow, hating that he had to yield to this man.

"Such a good little fed," Caleb taunted, pausing for a beat to sneer at him. "So dedicated. You even walked her home." He jerked on Kelly's arm as he spoke, and her face went white. "I was supposed to hit you, you know." His tone was conversational, a man telling a story.

James's stomach lurched at Kelly's pained expression. The bastard was hurting her again, and he was powerless to stop it. With Caleb's knife at her throat, he couldn't get a shot off in time, and if he missed...

"I'm here now." Maybe he could keep him talking, distract him until he made a mistake. Just one tiny mistake, that was all he needed to end this. "Why not try again?"

Caleb shook his head. "Oh, no, we're past that now." His expression turned considering as he watched James. "Although I must say, if we had time I would like to finish this. Can't have you turning up over and over again."

"What's wrong with now? I've got time." Keep him talking; keep him engaged.

James inched forward, his eyes never leaving Caleb's. If he kept his focus on Caleb, he could almost ignore the fact that Kelly was trapped with a knife at her throat, something he had to push aside in order to function. Emotions were the enemy right now.

He chanced another half step forward, saw Caleb's eyes flicker down and then back up. "That's far enough," he warned, tightening his grip on Kelly.

"Just let her go, and you and I can settle this," James

suggested, trying hard to keep the anger and fear for Kelly out of his voice.

Caleb scoffed. "Do you honestly think I'm stupid? The minute I let her go, you'll shoot me."

James shook his head. "No. I just want to talk to you. I find you very intriguing." It was a long shot, but he was rewarded by a spark of interest in the other man's eyes.

"Really? Why is that?"

James scrambled to come up with something suitably flattering, digging deep for those psych classes he'd taken at the Academy. "I've been studying your movements for so long, trying to figure out where you'd strike next. I feel like I practically know you."

Caleb's mouth twisted in a smug smile. "Kept you on your toes, did I?"

James nodded. "Oh, yes," he said, trying not to choke on the words. "You've been a true challenge. I imagine we'll teach a course about you someday."

"The one that got away?"

"That depends," James said slowly. "You know the FBI doesn't want civilian casualties. If you let her go—" he nodded at Kelly "—I might be willing to look the other way while you escape. Keep the game going and all."

Caleb appeared to consider his offer, but his gaze snagged on the gun and his eyes narrowed. "You'd put the gun down?"

"Naturally."

The other man nodded. "Do it."

James opened his hand to turn the gun to the side, then slowly bent down to place it on the floor. He stayed in a crouch, his right hand loose by his ankle and the pistol concealed by his pant leg.

Caleb smiled. "Thank you," he said courteously.

"Now you let Kelly go."

"You know what, Special Agent? I've changed my mind." Keeping the knife at Kelly's throat, he reached into a pocket and drew out a remote. Before James could draw his gun and stand, Caleb pressed a button and the ground shook as a concussion rocked the building. Plaster rained down from the ceiling, and the glass doors of the large display cases lining the wall shattered, sending sharp splinters everywhere. James threw his arms over his head and hunched his shoulders, drawing into himself for protection as debris rained down.

Muted screams sounded in the museum while the lights flickered in the hallway. He fleetingly wondered what had exploded, but before he could gather his thoughts, a second blast rocked the building. This one brought him to the ground and he landed hard in the piles of glass; pain shot from his knees as the shards dug into his skin.

After a beat, he raised his head. A lone fluorescent light shone midway down the hall, casting a weak glow over the aftermath. Cracks ran along the walls, and fine particles hung suspended in the air, shaken free from the walls and ceiling. He coughed violently to clear the dust from his throat, but his mouth and nose still felt coated with the chalky, foul substance.

He gingerly got to his feet, bracing himself for another explosion. As he squinted down the hallway, his heart skipped a beat with fear that had nothing to do with the destruction surrounding him.

Kelly was gone.

Chapter 11

"Get in."

Caleb roughly shoved Kelly into the car, pushing her across the passenger seat to the driver's side. He kept the knife pressed against her ribs, and she briefly considered throwing herself out the driver's side door. How badly could he hurt her if she was moving away from him? She might get cut, but his reach wouldn't extend out of the car. He would have to get out to chase her, and that would give her time to make a break for it. Only a few seconds, but it might be long enough to draw attention to them....

As if he'd read her mind, Caleb lifted a brow. "Don't even think about it." He reached into the glove compartment as he spoke, drawing out a small, lethal-looking black gun. So much for plan A.

Sirens screamed down the street, wailing past them

as police cars and fire trucks converged on the museum. The scene was utter chaos as pedestrians ran in multiple directions, some darting out into traffic in an effort to get away from the museum. There were a few car wrecks on Constitution Avenue, effectively stopping traffic and keeping the emergency-responder vehicles from getting too close. Kelly watched in a kind of detached fascination as one of the ambulances hopped the curb and drove right up to the museum steps.

"Drive."

A poke in the ribs brought her back to reality. Caleb leaned over and started the car. "Just pull out and drive slowly. Don't try to draw attention to us, or I'll blow the car up."

She stared at him in horror. He patted his jacket pocket with a small smile that had goose bumps popping up on her arms. He was serious—the car was rigged, and he'd have no problem pressing the button, even if it meant his own death. He was truly crazy.

"Why are you doing this?" she whispered as she put the car in gear and pulled away from the curb, heading away from the museum.

"I have no other choice."

She shook her head, not understanding. There was always a choice.

"You think I'm worried about dying?" He laughed, a harsh, grating sound. "Trust me, dying in a car bomb would be preferable to what they'll do to me if I don't fix this." He scanned the road ahead, his voice dropping until she had to strain to hear him. "But I did fix it. I fixed it, and I deserve a reward."

"Who are you talking about?" She drove carefully, keeping an eye on the throngs of people running along the sidewalks. More emergency vehicles flashed by, giving her hope that the police would try to pull them over. She couldn't stop for fear that Caleb would blow up the car, but if the police gave chase, Caleb would be forced to change his plans and she might make it out alive. With that in mind, she slowed a bit, knowing that the faster they got away from the scene, the slimmer the chance of getting help.

"I know what you're doing," Caleb said. "It won't work. Drive faster." He poked her in the ribs with the muzzle of the gun.

"If you shoot me, we won't get anywhere," she gritted out from between clenched teeth. "And since you seem to need me for something, it's in your best interests to keep me alive."

"Alive? Yes," he agreed, his tone conversational. "Whole? Not so much."

He was so calm, so utterly composed and resolute. She knew without a doubt he wouldn't hesitate to injure her to ensure her cooperation, and she shuddered to think what he'd do. She stepped on the gas, and the car punched forward. Out of the corner of her eye, she saw Caleb lean back into the passenger seat, a small smile playing at his lips. *Bastard.*

Her hands were slick on the steering wheel. She wiped her palms on her pants, one at a time, her mind whirring as she struggled to process the situation. How had Caleb planted bombs without being caught? Security was so tight around the Mall, it was a wonder he hadn't been seen. How had this happened?

And how many people had he just killed or injured? Was James one of them? She sucked in a breath as a wave of nausea hit her at the thought of James lying in that concrete corridor, alone. He'd been on the floor when she'd last seen him, curled into a ball with debris raining down. She'd heard glass breaking as Caleb pulled her down the hall, and God knew what else had fallen or crumbled onto James. He could be hurt, passed out from a blow to the head or even dead. Would anyone know to look for him? In all the chaos, it would be easy to overlook one FBI agent who wasn't even supposed to be there.

She had to find a way to save him. He had come to her rescue before, when Caleb had shot her outside her apartment. Now it was time for her to return the favor. No matter what happened between them, she loved him. Besides, she realized with cold clarity, she was probably going to die today anyway. Caleb was all too willing to hurt her, and he seemed to be on his own suicide mission. If he was going to take her with him, she might as well go out with a bang.

She fought to contain a hysterical giggle at the unintentional pun, then glanced over to find Caleb staring straight ahead, the gun in his hand pointing more at her legs than at her ribs. Good. If he stayed relaxed, maybe she could pull this off without getting shot again.

The Lincoln Memorial was coming up fast on the right. As quickly as she dared, she pressed on the gas, wanting to build up speed before they came to the wall of concrete barriers erected around the famous landmark. Caleb didn't comment, so she pressed harder on the pedal, the engine vrooming as the car shifted gears to accommodate her demands.

"Watch your speed," he snapped. "I don't want you drawing attention to us."

She nodded but ignored him, keeping her foot down

as they approached the towering marble structure. She gripped the steering wheel hard, then took a deep breath. *I have to get to James.*

She heard the *click* of the gun being cocked. "I said—"

She wrenched the steering wheel to the right, slamming the passenger side into the solid white barricades that lined the road. The force of the impact jerked her hands from the wheel and sent them flying. Her head slammed against the window, setting off fireworks behind her eyes. The car scraped along the concrete for an agonizing eternity before bouncing off. A split second later, she was slammed forward as they hit the curve of the barricade, and then the car rocked back as it stopped, pinned in on the passenger side and the front by white concrete.

Dizzy, her head pounding and her heart racing, Kelly shook her head and glanced over. Caleb had a hand to his forehead as blood streamed down his face. The gun was nowhere to be seen. She fumbled for the seat-belt buckle, letting out a small cry of triumph when her fingers connected with the button. Wriggling gracelessly out of the restraint, she yanked on the door handle. It wouldn't budge. She pulled again, desperation mounting as she heard Caleb's awareness returning. If he pressed that button…

The lock! It took her several attempts to get her fingers to cooperate, but she finally flipped the door lock over and yanked on the handle again. This time the door opened, and she half fell, half crawled out of the car. As she struggled to her feet, she risked a look back. Caleb's door was blocked by the concrete fence, so he'd have to crawl over the seats to get out.

She limped forward, her entire body lit with pain. James. She had to help James.

Two police officers ran toward her, their guns drawn. She angled for them, holding her arm close to her body to keep from jarring her shoulder. "Please," she sobbed. "He's got a gun!"

"Stop right there!" The officer pointed his gun at her and she stopped, confused. Why was he pointing a gun at her? She wasn't the danger—Caleb was!

"Show me your hands," he instructed. Gingerly, she let go of her injured arm and held up her left hand. "Now the other one."

She tried to lift her right arm, bringing a fresh wave of pain that nearly brought her to her knees. "I can't," she choked out. "I can't raise my arm."

The man nodded at his partner. While he kept his gun trained on her, the younger officer walked toward her, his expression grim.

"Why are you doing this to me?" she cried in frustration. "I'm not the dangerous one—he is!"

The younger officer looked back at his partner. "Who?" the man asked.

Just as Kelly opened her mouth to answer, a loud bang rang out behind her. A white-hot poker struck her side and she stumbled. The ground rushed up to meet her. Pebbles from the asphalt dug into her cheek and she felt a growing pool of wetness form underneath her body.

Popping sounds split the air, and she watched with a growing sense of detachment as feet raced by her head. "Don't step on me," she mumbled, lacking the energy to move out of the way.

Someone grabbed her shoulders and flipped her

over. She squinted up into the face of the young officer. His expression was now one of horror. *Poor kid.* Protecting the monuments had probably never been this much trouble before.

"James," she croaked.

He leaned down, his face inches from hers. "You hang on, okay?" he said, his voice wavering a bit. "The ambulance is on the way." His hand found her side, and pain knifed through her as he applied so much pressure it felt as if he was trying to push between her ribs.

Black spots danced before her eyes. "Help James," she repeated, needing him to understand what she was telling him. "He's in the museum. He needs help."

He nodded, clearly humoring her. "All right, we'll help him. You just worry about staying here. I'll take care of James."

She felt a flicker of annoyance at being dismissed but was too cold and too tired to snap at the young man. His partner would come back soon, and she could tell him.

She closed her eyes against the bright sunlight. She'd rest for a few minutes, wait for everyone to calm down, then explain why they had to get to the museum and help James.

Sirens joined the cacophony of voices and noise. Hands pulled at her shirt, lightly slapped her face. There was a great pressure on her side as a loud voice called out, "Wake up. C'mon, open your eyes."

She moaned, moving her hands to try to cover her side, but they were pushed away and held down. Then she was rolled onto her side while fingers probed her back, poking painfully at the wetness there. Urgent voices spoke above her head, but she couldn't make out the words. She felt as if she were underwater, hearing sounds that were fuzzy around the edges.

She tried to speak again but something came over her face, blocking her words. The world spun as she was raised into the air and moved; then a shadow blotted out the sun. It was cool in the shade, quieter, too. Maybe now she could rest.

An annoying tickle registered in her mind. There was something she had to do…something important.… She grasped for the thought, but it drifted away, like water draining from a cupped hand.

The harder she fought to remember, the faster the idea slipped away. She chased after it, catching an elusive glimpse of dark brown eyes before surrendering with a sigh and slipping into the quiet depths.

Kelly.
Oh, God. Kelly.

His heart pounding, stomach twisted into knots, James picked his way through the debris in the corridor as he traced the route Caleb had taken. His eyes stung from the dust in the air, and he absently wiped his face with his palm, puzzled to see blood on his fingers when he drew his hand away.

He paused when he reached the door at the end of the hall. It was unlikely Caleb was hanging around on the other side, but he wouldn't do Kelly any good if he walked into a bullet. Holding his gun with a firm grip, he kicked the push bar and stepped through the swinging door into another exhibit hall. Glancing around, he saw no sign of Kelly or Caleb in the eerily empty space.

Keeping the gun in his right hand, James reached

to turn the volume up on his earpiece, wincing at Carmichael's loud voice.

"—is Reynolds? Has anyone seen him?"

"I'm here," James said, feeling guilty that he had waited to check in with the team. They were likely worried about him, thinking him injured or even dead.

"Where have you been?" Carmichael barked, his fury coming through loud and clear as he punctuated the question with a string of expletives. Oh, yes, there would be hell to pay for this. It might even cost him his career.

But with Kelly in danger, he just didn't care.

"I intercepted Caleb. He's taken Kelly as a hostage."

"We know." The older man's voice was laced with frustration, but James knew he was just upset at losing Caleb again. He didn't care that Kelly was in danger or that Caleb might have killed her by now.

After making his way through the museum, James headed for the exit. "I'm coming back in," he reported. "Did we get Collins?"

"Yes. He's being questioned now."

That was something, at least. Maybe the professor would know where Caleb was taking Kelly. A small spark of hope flared to life in his chest as he pushed through the crowd milling around the museum. A police officer moved to intercept him, but he flashed his badge and kept walking. Legs pumping, he covered the blocks back to headquarters, his mind churning with possible scenarios and options. There had to be a way to find her before it was too late.

The thought of Kelly at Caleb's mercy made his throat tighten with panic. As long as he thought she was useful, he'd likely keep her alive. If she refused to cooperate…

I'll find her, he thought fiercely, firmly pushing the alternative out of his mind. He didn't want to consider his life without Kelly in it. His earlier fears of getting involved with her now seemed like flimsy excuses, the rationale of a man looking for any excuse to run away.

He'd spent his life running—working hard to distance himself from his father's actions, walking away from Steve in his friend's darkest hour. Did he really want to spend the rest of his life keeping people at arm's length? Kelly had offered him a chance, one he had stupidly rejected. If—no, *when*—he found her, he wouldn't make the same mistake again.

Too keyed up to wait for the elevator, he took the stairs two at a time. He reached the top, panting but still feeling as if he had nervous energy to burn, and pushed into the office.

He saw Thomas from across the room and nodded. The other man's eyes widened, and he strode quickly through the office, grabbing James by the arm and tugging him in the direction of the bathroom. "We need to talk," he said, his voice low and urgent.

James tried to tug free, but Thomas tightened his grip. "Now."

James entered the bathroom first, whirling to face Thomas. "I can't do this now—Caleb has Kelly, and I'm running out of time!"

Thomas studied him for a beat, his eyes sweeping across his face and down his body. James looked down as well, for the first time taking in his dusty, bloody clothes. His face began to sting, and he risked a quick glance in the mirror. Wincing, he took in the fine cuts on his face, red and oozing, and the larger gash on his forehead. That must have been where the blood had come from earlier, he realized.

He walked over to the sink and splashed water on his face; the coolness soothed his irritated skin. Thomas held out a wad of paper towels, which he accepted with a grunt of thanks. Patting his face dry, he turned to face the other agent.

Thomas looked fine, he realized with a sense of relief. "Was anyone hurt?"

Thomas shook his head. "Just a few bumps and bruises. Nothing major."

The tight fist in his chest eased a bit when he heard the rest of the team was okay, and he quickly pushed away the fissure of guilt that he hadn't thought of them before.

"I think you need stitches," Thomas said, nodding at his forehead. James pressed the paper towel against the gash, then drew it away to see fresh blood. "Stay here. I'll be right back."

Thomas stepped out, giving James an opportunity to make a more detailed survey of his appearance. A fine white dust covered his clothes and hair, making him look like an old man caught in the snow. Keeping one hand pressed to the cut on his forehead, he dampened some paper towels with the other and began to brush at his shoulders and hair in a vain attempt to clean up. While he was successful in removing the top layer of dust, fine white particles had become embedded in the fabric of his shirt, and no amount of rubbing would dislodge them. It was the same for his hair; he was able to shake out some of the powder, but only a thorough washing would render it clean again.

Thomas returned with a first-aid kit, which he unpacked on the counter. Ripping open an alcohol square, he approached James with an apologetic expression. "This is gonna sting."

James hissed at the burn as Thomas dabbed his skin. "What happened?" he asked, wanting a distraction.

"I grabbed Collins after the meet and rushed him back here. He was babbling about Caleb, but I didn't pay much attention since I figured he was just trying to distract me. It wasn't until I got back here that I realized Caleb was in the museum and had grabbed Kelly."

"I saw him take her from my position next to the information desk." His hands clenched at the memory. "Carmichael told me to stand down, but I couldn't let them walk away without knowing where he was taking her."

"He's pretty pissed about that," Thomas said, the corner of his mouth quirking up. "I've never seen him so riled up."

James smiled as the image of Carmichael with a full head of steam popped into his mind, but he quickly sobered. "It's all my fault," he said quietly.

"What?"

"The bomb. I cornered them, tried to bargain for Kelly. I thought he was going to cooperate, but then…" He shook his head, the words trailing off.

Thomas squeezed the edges of the cut together and began to apply butterfly bandages. "He was going to detonate them no matter what."

"How many people were killed?"

"So far? None."

James jerked his gaze to Thomas's face, searching for signs of deceit. "How is that possible?"

Thomas finished up, wiping stray blood from around the cut. "He set the charges in an empty area of the museum that was undergoing renovations. No one was around, and the bombs themselves weren't that big. It looks like he was going for panic, which he definitely achieved." He crumpled up the empty bandage wrappers and tossed them into the trash, then turned back to face James.

"That was a hell of a stunt you pulled, turning off your comm like that."

James took a deep breath, knowing he owed Thomas, and the rest of the team, an apology. "I'm sorry," he said, meeting the other man's level blue gaze. "I didn't mean to play cowboy. I just went a little crazy at the thought of Kelly being at Caleb's mercy, and I couldn't handle playing by the book."

Thomas nodded, his expression at once stern and sympathetic. "I know you have feelings for her, but you put us all at risk. How do I know it's not going to happen again?"

"You don't," James said, the words out of his mouth before he had a chance to think. "If I have to choose between Kelly and following the rules, she's going to win, every time. And know this," he said, now choosing his words carefully. "When you guys go after her, I won't be content to sit on the sidelines. I'll stay out of your way, but I will be there."

Thomas shook his head. "Not my call, man. I think you're an integral part of the team, but Carmichael wants your head. After today, he'll probably have you riding a desk for the next thirty years."

"Then maybe I shouldn't check in with him just yet," James said slowly.

Thomas grinned, his eyes sparkling with mischief. "Well, that's one way to play it. I do have a lot going on right now, and the fact that I've seen you will probably slip my mind...."

"No," James said firmly, shaking his head for emphasis. "Under no circumstances are you to cover for me. I don't want you risking your ass for me. Just because my career is over doesn't mean yours has to be."

Thomas opened his mouth, but before he could voice a protest, his phone rang. He fished it out of his pocket and held it to his ear. "Kincannon."

He listened for a moment; then his eyes widened and flickered to James. "Uh-huh. Good. Yes. I'm on the way." He snapped the phone closed and stared at James, one eyebrow raised. "I think we've just caught a break," he said, his voice practically vibrating with energy.

"What happened?" Was Kelly involved? Had Caleb let her go? Did they have a lead?

"There was an accident by the Lincoln Memorial. Some lady drove a car into the barricades. The guy she was with crawled out of the car and started shooting, so the cops took him down."

James reached for the counter, squeezing the edge so hard he thought his hand would break. "Caleb and Kelly?"

Thomas nodded. "I think so. They're at the hospital now. His injuries aren't critical, so we can talk to him as soon as we get there."

"And Kelly?" The words barely made it past the lump in his throat.

Thomas's face fell and his brows drew together as he pressed his mouth into a line. "She's in surgery."

* * *

James was climbing out of the car before Thomas had put it into Park. He slammed the door and quickly made his way to the hospital entrance, his long strides eating up the distance in record time. He ignored Thomas's shouted cry to wait up, pushed through the double doors and made a beeline for the information desk.

"Kelly Jarvis," he demanded without preamble. "Where is she?"

The older woman manning the desk blinked up at him, her large round glasses giving her the look of a sleepy owl. "I'm sorry?"

Gritting his teeth, he started to silently count to ten but only made it to five. "I'm looking for Kelly Jarvis," he repeated. "I need to know what room she's in."

"Are you family?" Her brow arched, and her pink-painted lips pressed together in what must have been her don't-mess-with-me look.

He fished in his pocket for his badge and flashed it at her. "Where is she?"

Thomas appeared at his side, frowning. "You couldn't wait a minute?" he muttered. James ignored him while the woman leaned forward, making a show of inspecting his badge.

Thomas graced her with a smile, his dimples winking. Her features softened a bit in the face of such attention, and he went in for the kill. "Sorry about my friend here, ma'am," he said, pulling his own identification from his jacket. "We're here to question the two patients brought in about an hour ago. They were involved in a car accident by the Lincoln Monument, and they were both shot."

Her face lit up with recognition. "Oh, yes!" she said, nodding. "Quite the event. Let's see...." Her fingers moved across the keyboard at an agonizingly slow pace, and James fought the urge to leap over the counter, grab the keyboard and search the records himself.

"The man is in room 684, and the woman is still in surgery," she reported.

James opened his mouth to speak, but Thomas stepped on his foot. "Where will they take her when she's done?"

She frowned, studying the screen. "Usually surgical recovery is on the sixth floor, so she'll probably be there. You should check in at the nurses' station, though."

Thomas smiled at her again, making her blush. "We'll do that. Thanks so much for your help today."

She patted her curls, simpering. "Elevators are down the hall, to your left."

They turned from the desk and headed down the hall, finding the elevators exactly where she said they'd be. James pressed the button repeatedly, knowing it wouldn't make a difference but needing something to do with his hands.

He glanced over at Thomas, who stood with his hands in his pockets. "How do you do it?" he asked.

Thomas looked at him, brows drawn in confusion. "Do what?"

"Have every woman within a five-mile radius falling over themselves to help you?"

Thomas grinned. "Just my natural charm, I guess." He smoothed a hand through his hair, brushing the strands back into place. "It helps that I'm handsome."

James snorted, making Thomas grin even wider.

"You'd be amazed at how far *please* and *thank you* will go," he said, raising a brow. "You don't always have to bark at people, you know."

They stepped into the elevator, and James stabbed the button for the sixth floor. "When I know Kelly is safe, I'll stop barking."

Thomas sobered at that. "I know you're worried, but they have the best surgeons in the city here. She'll make it."

The knot in James's belly tightened. "I hope so," he whispered.

She had to survive. He couldn't even think about the alternative. He had too much to stay to her, too much to show her, for her to leave him now.

He forced himself to walk at a normal pace to the nurses' station, then let Thomas ask the questions. Kelly's surgery was wrapping up, the charge nurse informed them, and she should be moved up to the floor in about an hour.

Thomas took one look at his face and tugged him away from the nurses' station, pulling him into an empty room. "There's nothing you can do right now," he said in a low, urgent tone. "You need to pull it together."

James nodded, knowing the other agent was right. He wasn't doing anyone any good by freaking out right now. Besides, they had a job to do. He'd worked this case for too long to pass up the opportunity to question Caleb.

Taking several deep breaths, he forced his brain to switch gears. Stuffing his feelings for Kelly and his nervous anxiety into a box, he worked to focus on the task at hand—finding out who Caleb worked for and what they were planning next.

Thomas was watching him closely, studying his face for signs of trouble.

He met the other man's blue gaze steadily. "You're right. I'm ready. Let's do this."

After a beat, Thomas nodded. "He's down the hall. I don't have to remind you how important this is, so if you start to lose it, step out of the room. The last thing we need to do is hand his lawyer an excuse to get him off."

"I won't blow it," James said firmly. He owed it to himself—and Kelly—to finish this, once and for all.

Chapter 12

Pain wrapped around her like a blanket, consuming her consciousness. She fought to dive back into the blissful darkness, but her awareness of her body grew with each breath; her side and shoulder throbbed to the beat of her heart.

She had to be dying.

She became aware of a steady, droning beep nearby, the sound at once annoying and familiar, a metric to measure the passage of time. Breathing carefully, she began to count along with the sound, the diversion a way to keep her mind off the pain.

Her eyelids were heavy, so heavy, but she managed to open them a crack. White. Everything was white. It took a second to register she was staring at ceiling tiles. She briefly considered trying to move her head to gather more information, but she decided against it. There would be time for that later.

Soft footsteps sounded nearby, coming closer. With a concerted effort, she opened her eyes again to focus on a figure in blue standing next to the bed. It was a woman, pressing buttons on a pole-mounted box by Kelly's head. After a few seconds, she turned toward Kelly and ran her gaze along the bed. When she met Kelly's eyes, she smiled.

"Oh, good, you're awake." Her voice was soft and kind, and she stepped closer to the bed, bringing her head down near Kelly's.

"How are you feeling?"

Kelly tried to respond, but her voice came out as a croak. She tried to swallow but couldn't muster up enough spit to lubricate her throat. Seeing her difficulty, the nurse brought a straw to her lips. She drew up cool mouthfuls of water, and the liquid soothed her sore throat.

"I hurt everywhere," she whispered.

The nurse set the cup back on the table at the side of the bed and frowned slightly. "It's not quite time for another dose of pain meds," she said, glancing at her watch as she spoke. "But I'll page the doctor and see if we can give you something else to help."

Kelly closed her eyes. "Thank you," she said softly.

"I'll be back in a few minutes. Press the button on the headboard if you need me before I return."

Kelly nodded weakly, and the movement sent spikes of pain through her head. She winced and started to raise a hand to her head before thinking better of it. Extraneous movement was not her friend right now.

As the pounding in her head receded, her thoughts turned to puzzling out her situation. What had happened? She was clearly in a hospital, but why? She dimly recalled a car and the horrified face of a young man hovering over her. Had she been in an accident? Maybe the nurse could tell her when she returned....

There was a rustling sound from the other side of the room, a shifting of fabric as someone moved. Steeling herself, she slowly turned her head to find a figure slumped in the chair by the bed. His head was down, his chin resting on his chest, but she'd know that dark hair and lean build anywhere.

"James!"

Her voice was low and scratchy, but his response was immediate. Jerking his head up, his hand darted into his jacket as his eyes searched the room. After a beat, he focused on her, the exhaustion lining his face fading as he met her gaze.

She drank in the sight of him, the relief at seeing him whole and unharmed washing over her and temporarily pushing away the pain. She remembered now— the museum, the bombs, Caleb dragging her away. Her overwhelming drive to get back to James, to make sure he had survived. And he had. By some miracle, he had made it through unharmed.

Mostly unharmed, she amended, her gaze snagging on the gauze taped to his forehead. The white bandage made a startling contrast to the warm gold of his skin, giving him a rakish air that in other circumstances would have been dangerously attractive. He caught her stare and raised a hand to his head, gingerly touching the bandage with his fingertips.

"It's nothing," he said softly as he moved closer to the bed and took her hand. She curled her fingers around his palm, reveling in the small contact of skin against skin. She wanted to throw her arms around him and bury her face in his neck, but given the way she felt right now, she'd settle for this.

His fingertip gently skimmed over her cheek, and she realized with a mild sense of astonishment that she was crying. "Shh…" he whispered, leaning in to press a soft kiss on her forehead. "It's all right. You're safe. We have Caleb, and he's never going to hurt you or anyone else again." He smoothed his free palm over her hair; the gesture was protective and comforting at the same time. She closed her eyes and focused on his touch, taking deep breaths so that the familiar spice of his skin replaced the astringent hospital smell that lined her nostrils.

"What happened?"

James leaned back to face her, but before he could answer the question, a tall man in a white coat walked quickly into the room, his head bent over a chart. He stopped at the foot of the bed, absorbed in reading, his graying hair mussed as if he'd been running a hand through it. James shifted off the bed and back into the chair, still keeping hold of her hand. The doctor looked up at the motion, a small frown drawing his brows together at the interruption. Then he turned his focus to Kelly, tucking the chart under his arm as his gaze raked over her.

"I'm Dr. Keenan. I understand you're in pain," he said, the phrase more of a statement than a question.

"Yes."

"Can you tell me where you're hurting?"

"My left side." She moved her hand over the spot as she spoke. "And my shoulder. Mostly my side, though."

He walked to the side of the bed, forcing James to let go of her hand. Stopping between them, he drew the sheet back and lifted up her gown. She felt her face heat at being so exposed, but he carefully tucked the gown and sheet around her so that her modesty was preserved.

She glanced down, horrified to see her skin marred by an angry red line bisected by black stitches. "What happened?"

"You were shot," he said shortly, pressing the periphery of the incision with thick, surprisingly cool fingertips. The pressure was uncomfortable but not agonizing. The wound didn't appear to do anything in response to this attention, and seemingly satisfied, the doctor dropped her gown and replaced the sheet over her torso. He then moved to her shoulder, prodding around the joint in search of what she could only assume was some medical clue. She winced when he hit a particularly sore spot, and he nodded at her reaction.

"The bullet nicked your spleen," he continued conversationally as he finished the exam. "You're very lucky—you almost bled to death. Fortunately, you got here in time and we were able to stop the bleeding. You lost part of your spleen, though." He shook his head, as though he was disappointed she had been so careless with her organs.

Her head was reeling. *Shot?* She remembered crashing the car into the concrete barriers, but shot? And now she was missing part of her spleen? *What the hell?*

Her tongue felt thick in her mouth, making speech difficult. Why couldn't she remember getting shot? What else did she not remember? Nausea gripped her stomach, and she felt a clammy sweat break out across her forehead.

Oblivious to her inner turmoil, the doctor retreated

to the foot of the bed again. She dimly registered James reclaiming possession of her hand, but she was too upset to answer his gentle squeeze.

"It's not time for your Dilaudid yet, but I'll have the nurse give you some morphine," he said. "That should take the edge off this pain you're feeling now." With that announcement, he turned and stepped toward the doorway.

"Wait," she croaked before he could leave the room. He obligingly stopped, but he looked at her with an expression that clearly communicated she was on borrowed time.

"I don't remember getting shot," she confessed, tears leaking from the corners of her eyes. "Why don't I remember?"

He shrugged as if this was nothing to worry about. "It's not uncommon for people to experience short-term memory loss after undergoing general anesthesia," he said, already edging toward the door again. "If you don't remember things after a few days, follow up with your primary-care physician." Then he was gone, leaving her staring at an empty doorway.

"His bedside manner leaves a lot to be desired," James muttered.

She wasn't able to stop the strangled laugh from escaping, and the sound was loud in the now-quiet room. James gifted her with a small smile, almost as if he was indulging her, and she laughed again. Hysteria bubbled up her throat like champagne bubbles, sending her into fits of giggles. Her side ached with the movement, but she couldn't stop laughing, her body taking over like some kind of macabre autopilot.

James's expression morphed into one of concern

as her fit continued. After a second, he climbed up onto the bed beside her and gathered her into his arms, rocking her slowly as she laid her head on his shoulder. Gradually, the cackling spasms eased, giving way to tears again.

What was she going to do now? Caleb and George were gone, leaving her safe, albeit injured. Would she recover, or would her injuries leave her with permanent health issues? She knew the loss of a spleen left people vulnerable to infections, but would she be all right with only part of the organ? She wished the doctor had been more forthcoming with information, but he'd been in quite a hurry to leave. Hopefully, the next one who came along could give her some answers, like when she could expect to return to work.

That thought nearly made her groan. In all the excitement, she hadn't really considered the effect George's actions would have on her career. She had been so focused on finding and stopping him that she hadn't had time to think about what her next steps would be. With George under arrest and probably headed for jail, she didn't have a job anymore, and it was unlikely the university would help her find another position. Besides, who knew if anyone would hire her, tainted as she was by her mere association with George. Maybe she should move back to Houston so she could be close to her family again. She could use some unconditional support right now....

James gently stroked her hair as he held her. He was such an amazing man, and she loved him; her heart was breaking with it. What was he doing here? He'd made it very clear he wanted no part of a relationship with her. For him to come here now and be so supportive and wonderful really wasn't fair. It made her want things she could never have, and she had enough to deal with as it was.

He deserved someone good and whole and uncomplicated. Someone who would trust him without reservation, someone who hadn't been damaged by life. She was none of those things, and based on their conversation last night, he knew it. She couldn't make him happy, and maybe he had done them both a service by pushing her away before she could hurt him again.

She leaned away from him. His hands drifted down her arms as she disentangled herself from his embrace. His warm brown gaze tracked over her face, but she refused to maintain eye contact. What she had to say was hard enough.

"I think you should go."

She caught a flicker of confusion before his features smoothed out again. "Are you tired?"

She shook her head. When he continued to stare at her, she let out a small sigh. "You can't just come here and hold me when I cry, James."

He narrowed his eyes at her, but his voice was even when he spoke. "Why not?"

"Because it isn't fair to me." Did he really not understand?

Now he was frowning at her, regarding her like a particularly puzzling specimen under the microscope. "Not fair...?" he repeated, the words trailing off at the end.

"I know you don't want me," she gritted out, hating that she had to explain everything in such detail. Why was he being so obtuse? "You made it clear last night you don't want a relationship with me, so I think it's best if you go."

"Kelly—"

"Just go, James." She turned away, not trusting herself to look at him. If she saw his face, the tears she was trying so hard to blink back would spill over, undermining her words. She needed him to leave, now, so she could fall apart in private.

He was silent for a long moment. She heard the rustle of movement as he stood, then the whisper of her name, part question, part plea. She closed her eyes and bit her lip, holding in the words she so desperately wanted to say.

He let out a heavy sigh, then walked away. It was only after she heard the door click shut that Kelly allowed the tears to fall.

"I love you," she whispered to the empty room.

Given the severity of her injuries and the fact that this was her second gunshot wound in three days, the doctor wanted to keep her under observation for a little longer. Since she didn't relish the thought of going home to an empty apartment that had recently doubled as a crime scene, Kelly didn't protest his decision. On the contrary, she was slightly relieved to know she wouldn't have to take care of herself for at least a few more days.

At first it had been wonderful. She'd slept, woken to eat, then slept some more. She hadn't felt so well rested in years. But now, on the third day of hospital existence, she was trying not to go insane.

Daytime television wasn't doing it for her, and the library cart kept skipping her room, so she was left at

loose ends. She filled most of the afternoon by counting all the ceiling tiles and making up stories as to the
origin of the mysterious discoloration on the floor tiles
outside the bathroom door.

And when she wasn't searching for distractions, she
thought of James.

While she tried to focus on other things—like her
job, or lack of one now—her mind always circled back
to James. She kept dreaming of him, smelling that po-
tent combination of spicy citrus and warm skin, hearing the soothing deep murmur of his voice. She'd
woken yesterday with his name on her lips, so sure he
was there that she had actually cried when she'd opened
her eyes and found the room empty.

Sending him away had seemed like the right idea at
the time, but now she wasn't so sure. She couldn't shake
the fear that she had just thrown away her one chance
at love. Was she ever going to find another man who
accepted her, flaws and all? Who wasn't scared of her
past, who wanted to build a life with her?

And what if she didn't? Better to be alone than to
be with someone who treated her with kid gloves all
the time, as if she was some fragile piece of china that
would break if jostled. She didn't want someone who
would try to protect her from life; she wanted someone who would be a true partner, someone she could
rely on when needed and someone who would rely on
her in turn.

Once upon a time, she'd thought James could be that
man, but his first instinct had been to shut her down.
He'd denied her feelings, writing them off as adrenaline, saying she really wasn't ready for a relationship.
Maybe he was right.

It had been one of the hardest things she'd ever done, but cutting James out of her life had been necessary. She needed to move on, not get emotionally entangled with a man who would never see her as more than a tragic figure, someone to be pitied and coddled.

So she gathered up the pieces of her shattered dream and tucked them away, determined to rebuild her life and find another image to keep her warm at night.

"Am I interrupting?"

She glanced up to find Thomas standing in the door-way. Her stomach fluttered a bit—was James with him?—but she pasted on a smile.

"Not at all. Come on in."

He smiled at her; his bright blue eyes and coppery hair were a striking contrast to the muted gray of his suit. He looked as if he'd stepped out of a catalog, making her acutely aware of the hospital-green gown she wore and the fact she hadn't properly washed her hair in several days.

"You look great," he offered as he walked over to the chair and sat.

She resisted the temptation to snort in disbelief. "Thanks."

"No, really, you do. You forget—the last time I saw you, they'd just wheeled you out of surgery. You were very pale and unconscious, so I'm happy to see you awake now. You're starting to get your color back, too," he added, relaxing in the chair and lifting one ankle to rest on the opposite knee.

"Your flattery is wasted on me." He grinned at her, and she couldn't help but smile in return.

"How are you doing?" Concern had replaced the teasing note in his voice as his eyes searched her face.

"I'm still trying to piece together what happened." Her memory had been returning in fragments, little snippets of sounds or images, and while she was gradually filling in the gaps in time, there were still large chunks missing.

"What do your doctors say?"

She shook her head. "Nothing helpful. Just that this happens to some people, and I may remember getting shot or I may not. They're not too worried about it."

He shrugged. "Then maybe you shouldn't be, either. Honestly, it would be great if we had your side of the story to compare to what Caleb has told us, but you've done quite enough already."

Her skin prickled at the mention of his name, making her shudder slightly. "I'm so glad you caught him."

"All thanks to you. If this science thing doesn't work out for you, you could always join the bureau." His dimples appeared as he grinned at her. The smile turned slightly wicked as he added, "We have some new openings."

"You do?"

"There's been a—" he paused, as if searching for the right word "—reorganization in the wake of the operation. A few heads have rolled."

"But you caught both Caleb and George. Isn't that a success?"

"Sure, but Caleb set off two bombs in the museum." He held his hands out, palms up, moving them up and down in a pantomime of a scale. "Even though no one was seriously injured, the brass tends to frown on that kind of thing."

"Is James in trouble?" She held her breath, hoping the answer was no.

"Oh, yeah, but not as bad as some," he informed her cheerfully. "Carmichael was asked to retire, and believe me, he did not take it well. You should have seen—"

If Thomas didn't stop babbling about Carmichael and tell her what was going on with James, she was going to lose it. "What about James?" she interrupted, trying to steer him back on course.

He regarded her with wide eyes, the very picture of innocence, but she caught the way the corner of his mouth twitched up. He was teasing her. The nerve of the man!

"James got his hand slapped for the stunt he pulled at the museum, but it's nothing major. He's been working double-time, chasing down leads Caleb has given us."

She let out her breath in a relieved whoosh. "So his job is safe?"

"As far as I know."

"That's good."

Thomas frowned, tilting his head as he regarded her. "I'm surprised he didn't tell you this already."

She looked away, her fingers fumbling on the blanket. "I haven't seen him in a few days. I asked him to leave."

Thomas raised a brow as he studied her. "I see."

Kelly rushed to explain, feeling her face heat. "I wanted him to work on the case, not waste his time here," she lied, hoping she sounded more convincing than she felt.

"Well, whatever you told him didn't work. He's come to the hospital every day."

It was Kelly's turn to frown. "No, he hasn't. I haven't seen him."

"You mean…" He trailed off, shaking his head. "What an idiot."

She stared at him, watching realization dawn on his face. "What?"

Thomas looked up, his bright blue eyes narrowing slightly. "You really haven't seen him?"

She shook her head. "No. But there have been times I could have sworn he was here. I just thought I was going crazy."

He leaned forward, putting both feet on the floor. "I'd be willing to bet he's visited but hasn't wanted to wake you." He shook his head as if puzzled by this behavior. "No wonder he's been so moody lately," he muttered, almost to himself.

Kelly felt a flare of curiosity at his words, but she ruthlessly tamped it down. James wasn't a part of her life anymore, and she shouldn't have asked about him. She was only torturing herself. She didn't need to hear about how he was or wasn't doing.

"How's the investigation going?"

If Thomas noticed her desperate attempt to change the subject, he didn't comment.

"Pretty well. Dr. Collins was singing like a bird until his lawyer showed up and explained that he really shouldn't tell us everything he knows without some kind of deal in return. Now the legal eagles are arguing over immunity or some such nonsense." He lifted one shoulder in an eloquent shrug. "It's fine, though. We got enough out of him to break open a few new angles."

"What about Caleb?" She suppressed a shiver at the thought of those cold eyes.

Thomas sat forward. "He's talking, too, and you're not going to believe this—he was hired by the CEO of Wilkins Pharmaceuticals."

"What?" She shook her head, convinced she had misunderstood. "Why?"

Thomas rubbed his fingers together in the universal pantomime for money. "The company is circling the drain. An outbreak of bioterror events would send people scrambling for their antibiotics."

"Please tell me Wilkins is under arrest, too!"

Thomas nodded. "The guys from the Jersey office picked him up a few days ago. He's been quite vocal about his distaste for our accommodations." The corners of his mouth turned up in a wry smile.

"And how is Ruth?"

His smile faltered a bit as his gaze slipped to the floor. "She's dead."

The unexpected news hit her like a slap. "What? How? Did Caleb—"

Thomas shook his head. "It looks like a suicide. She was found in the hotel room, a bottle of sleeping pills next to the pillow. She didn't leave a note."

"Oh, my God," Kelly murmured, shivering as a wave of sadness swept over her. She hadn't really known Ruth well, but the older woman had always been kind to her. The thought of her swallowing a handful of pills in a dingy hotel room was disturbing, to say the least. No one should have to spend their last moments alone like that.

"Does George know?" He must be devastated. Ruth was his world, the reason he'd gotten involved in this mess to begin with. For her to kill herself like that must have destroyed him.

"He's not doing too well. He spends a lot of time asleep in his cell, speaks only when spoken to. They have him on suicide watch."

Kelly shook her head, blinking back tears. How did it come to this? People sickened and killed by the bacteria, injured by the bomb blast. James shot. She was lying in a hospital bed, for crying out loud. And now two lives ruined, all because of one bad decision on the part of a desperate, misguided man doing what he thought was needed to save the love of his life.

They sat in silence for a few minutes, alone with their thoughts. Finally Thomas stretched out his legs and gave her a rueful smile. "Let's move on to some happier news."

"What did you have in mind?" She wiped away a stray tear with a sniffle. Thomas was right—no sense dwelling on things that couldn't be changed.

"For starters, the nurses told me you're getting discharged in the morning."

"They did? That's news to me. Why did they tell you first?"

"I have a way with the ladies," he said, waggling his brows and giving her a flirtatious wink. She couldn't hold back a giggle and reached over to press a hand to her side when it ached in protest.

"Anyway, do you need a ride home?"

She blinked at him, taken aback by his offer. "I hadn't actually thought about it. I guess I do. It's not like I have a car here or anything."

He stood, shot his cuffs and smoothed down his tie. "Great. I'll stop by tomorrow morning."

"Are you sure you don't mind?"

He shook his head as he walked toward the door.

"Not at all. Besides, it's kind of tradition for me to pick you up from the hospital." With a wink he was gone, leaving her alone but smiling.

Three weeks later...

"You are a moron."

James glanced up in surprise as Thomas plopped down on the neighboring bar stool and ordered a beer.

"Excuse me?"

The other man turned to face him. "You heard me. You're a moron."

"I don't remember inviting you out tonight."

"You didn't. I came as a favor to you."

James turned back to his drink. "Thanks, but no thanks. I don't need company."

"Sure you do." Thomas nodded at the bartender as he set down his drink; then he picked it up and took a long sip. "Someone has to help you pull your head out of your ass."

James tightened his grip on the sweaty glass, determined not to let his temper get the better of him. Thomas was just trying to goad him, and he wasn't going to take the bait.

He turned to stare at the other man, who was scooping up a handful of mixed nuts from one of the bowls that were placed at intervals along the bar. As far as he knew, Thomas had never been here before, and he was already making himself at home as if he owned the place.

Knowing he wouldn't leave until he'd said his piece, James decided to try to speed the process along so he could go back to drinking in silence.

"You obviously have something to say to me, so why don't you just get it out?"

Thomas chewed thoughtfully for a moment, then cleared his throat with another sip. "Are you usually this grumpy when you drink?" The corner of his mouth tugged up as he fought to contain a smile, which only made James's mood darken further. He did not feel like cracking jokes and laughing tonight.

"Only when I want to be left alone. Don't try to change the subject. Why are you here?"

All traces of humor left Thomas's face as the other man gave him a level stare. "Because you're making a huge mistake."

God save him from this cryptic conversation! "Could you just get to the point?" The game would be on soon, and he wanted to finish his drink in peace and head home to his empty apartment to watch it.

"It's probably escaped your notice, but you've been a royal pain in the ass lately." When James opened his mouth to respond to this nonsense, Thomas glared at him and kept talking. "Don't bother to deny it. Ever since the operation at the museum, you've been a jerk. People are tired of being treated like crap, and you need to cut it out."

James gritted his teeth, biting back a retort. He so did not need this right now. With the office in an up-heaval over all the personnel changes and his personal life in the crapper, the last thing he wanted was to listen to Thomas go on and on about how he wasn't playing well with others. As far as he was concerned, they all needed to stay out of his way and let him do his job. Was that so much to ask?

"Message received," he said coolly, taking another sip of his beer. "Now run along."

Thomas rolled his eyes. "For the love of all that is holy, would you just get over yourself and call her?"

James coughed as his beer went down the wrong pipe. After clearing his throat and wiping his eyes, he glanced at Thomas. "What did you just say to me?"

"I said call her."

James decided to play dumb for the moment. "Call who?"

Thomas merely stared at him, waiting. After a moment James looked away, giving up the pretense. "She doesn't want to see me."

"What makes you say that?"

James ran his finger along the edge of the soggy cardboard coaster. It felt disturbingly slimy, but it was better than looking at Thomas.

"She asked me to leave."

"When?"

"While she was in the hospital."

"I didn't know she saw you."

James looked away, unable to meet the other man's eyes. Technically, Kelly hadn't been awake for most of his visits. He'd gone by her room every day, needing to see that she was okay so he could focus on the investigation into Caleb's organization. Creeping into her room while she was asleep had made him feel like a stalker, but since she'd made it clear she wanted nothing to do with him, it was the only way he could check on her without upsetting her.

James nodded, deciding not to tell Thomas the whole sordid story. "Yeah. I was there when she woke up. She asked me to leave."

"Interesting," Thomas muttered.

James huffed out a laugh. "Sure. Whatever. Anyway, I'm not going to call her because she doesn't want me to."

"I don't know about that," Thomas said, sounding dubious.

James glanced at him. "What's that supposed to mean?"

The other man lifted his shoulder in an easy shrug. "Just that I think she misses you. A lot."

His stomach flip-flopped at that, but he refused to get excited about the possibility that she wanted to see him. She'd been very clear in the hospital. Still, his curiosity wouldn't allow him to stay silent.

"You've talked to her?"

Thomas nodded, taking another sip from his glass. James waited for him to elaborate, his impatience mounting as the other man remained infuriatingly silent.

"And?"

Thomas met his gaze. "And what?" he asked, his tone oh-so-casual. He looked for all the world like another clueless guy, but James caught the slight twitch at the corner of his mouth and knew he was being played.

"How is she?" he bit out, his pride taking a backseat to finding out about Kelly. Even though she didn't want him in her life, he still cared about her. More than he wanted to.

"Like I said, she misses you. I think you should talk to her."

James mulled this over for a moment. Did she really want to see him again? Could she have changed her mind? Maybe she had reconsidered all the things she'd said in the hospital.

Or was Thomas just setting him up? He didn't think the other man had anything to gain by sending him in to get his heart ripped out, but maybe he was misreading her signs....

"Did she actually say she misses me?" As soon as the words left his mouth, James winced, knowing he sounded like a fumbling teenager. It couldn't be helped, though. If he was going to talk to Kelly again, he wanted some kind of assurance he wouldn't be shot down. He didn't think he could handle being rejected by the woman he loved a third time.

"She didn't have to," Thomas replied, choosing not to comment on James's sophomoric question. "I can just tell by the way she acts."

Jealousy was a hot flame in his chest. He'd seen her? Spent time with her? When? Where had they gone? Had it been a date? He narrowed his eyes at the other man, considering him in a new light. He'd seen the way women reacted to Thomas, how he'd lay on the charm and have them eating out of his hand. Had he done that with Kelly? Was she another notch on his bedpost now?

His thoughts must have showed on his face, because Thomas held up a hand. "Whoa. It's not like that, man, so dial it back a notch. She's just my friend."

"I've never known you to be just friends with a woman."

"Well, I am with this one. Besides, she doesn't want me. She wants you, if you'll ever man up enough to go after her."

James turned back to his beer. "It's complicated."

Thomas groaned. "Gimme a break. Life is complicated. Why should this be any different?"

"Because it just is."

"That's where you're wrong. I used to think you were a smart guy, but you're clearly not. My mistake." Thomas stood, drained the last of his beer and threw a bill on the bar. "You have a chance here, something most people don't get. Kelly is an awesome woman, and if you don't try to make it work with her, you're going to regret it for the rest of your life." He clapped James on the shoulder, then walked away.

"Thomas?"

The redhead stopped at the door, turning back to look at James with one brow raised.

"She's okay? Really?"

Thomas sent him an exasperated smile. "Ask her yourself," he replied, a subtle dare in his tone.

James turned back to the bar, his thoughts swirling. Maybe Thomas was right. No, scratch that. There was no maybe about it—he *knew* Thomas was right. He'd been thinking about Kelly nonstop since the accident, to the detriment of his job performance. And okay, yes, he'd been a little snippy with everyone. It was hard to be cordial when he'd spent his time reliving their conversations over and over again, obsessively looking for any sign that Kelly might be willing to forgive him.

Walking away from her after she'd told him about Gary had been a huge mistake. He'd been overwhelmed at the time, but it didn't matter. She had needed him, and he had turned his back on her, just like everyone else she'd ever worked up the courage to tell. She deserved so much better than him, but maybe, just maybe, she'd give him another chance to make things right.

He realized now that if he didn't talk to her again, didn't try one last time, he would spend the rest of his life carrying around the regret and guilt of letting her go without a fight. After all, if he put himself out there and she rejected him, he could move on, secure in the knowledge that he'd tried everything. But if he didn't even attempt to win her back, he'd never be able to get rid of the ache in his chest that had become his constant companion since the morning she'd walked out on him all those months ago.

He had to talk to her. She might not roll out the welcome mat for him, but he was going to tell her once and for all how he felt about her. If she laughed in his face, so be it. At least he'd know for sure, which was a damn sight better than wondering.

He just hoped it wasn't too late to turn things around.

Kelly frowned at the shirt in her hand, weighing her options. It was her favorite shade of green, but she'd bought it almost six months ago and the tags still fluttered from the sleeve. She should probably throw it in the donation pile, but it was just so pretty....

"All right, you can stay," she muttered, resolving to wear the shirt soon as she hung it in the large wardrobe box camped out in the middle of her bedroom. She was almost done packing up her closet, and then it was on to the bookshelves.

She was getting close to finishing up, which was a good thing since the movers were coming tomorrow and she still needed to do a quick clean of the bathroom and kitchen. No way was she going to lose her security deposit because the place needed a professional cleaning after she moved out.

Her apartment, already small to begin with, was now a cramped maze of cardboard boxes, with half-finished rolls of packing tape and stacks of newspaper adding to the overall aesthetic. She hated the claustrophobic feel and was looking forward to settling into her new place. It was a little bit smaller, but the amazing view of the Potomac more than made up for the loss of space.

So she had set about packing up her belongings, getting rid of things she no longer needed or hadn't used in years. Thomas had driven her to the local Goodwill on several occasions so she could drop off loads of stuff that she didn't want to take with her. Hopefully, someone else could use her leftovers.

It felt good to purge her home like this. Clearing out all the unwanted items really felt like a fresh start, something she needed to do to move on with her life.

She'd known in the hospital that she couldn't stay in this apartment. Not after the shooting. She only had to close her eyes to see the shadowy figure standing in her den, his arm raised. And even though she knew it was impossible, every once in a while she'd catch a whiff of gun smoke and cordite, and she'd be taken back to that awful night. It had taken her several days before she'd been able to sleep at night, and even now she slept fitfully; every little noise jerked her awake, her heart threatening to pound right out of her chest.

Moving was the best thing for her to do, even though it was an exhausting process made even more tiring by the fact that she still wasn't back to feeling 100 percent. The doctor had told her to take things easy for a while, and she would—just as soon as she got settled into her new home.

She pulled another shirt off the rack and froze. It was the shirt she'd worn the night she and James…

Kelly tossed it in the donation pile as if it was a lit firecracker. One of the benefits to being wrapped up in the move was that she hadn't had time to think of James. But seeing that shirt again hit her like a punch to the stomach, and she squeezed her eyes shut against the flood of memories.

She'd made the right choice. She had. Yes, it still hurt, and yes, she missed him something fierce, but in the end, they weren't meant for each other.

So what if she felt as if a part of her was missing? As if she had a hole in her heart that was never going to heal? Loving someone meant you did what was best for them, and it was clear she wasn't what was best for James. It was the truth, and she just had to keep repeating that until she accepted it.

Which she would. Eventually.

With hands that shook ever so slightly, she lifted the shirt from the donation pile and smoothed out the wrinkles. Then she hung it in the wardrobe box. She couldn't just throw it away. It was still a good shirt, even with all the painful memories that seemed woven into the fabric. Maybe one day she could even wear it and not feel as if her heart was breaking all over again.

Maybe.

The doorbell rang, and the harsh sound made her jump. She shook her head as she wiped a stray tear from her cheek. It was just the pizza. She had to get her nerves under control and stop thinking that every noise, every unexpected sound was a threat. Her therapist had told her it would take time to feel safe again, but she was tired of being afraid.

She walked to the door, wishing for the umpteenth time she had a peephole. It was a little thing, but it made a huge difference to her peace of mind. With a deep breath, she reached out to lay a hand on the baseball bat she'd taken to leaving by the door. The wood was smooth and cool under her fingers, and although it probably wouldn't do her any good, it made her feel better to know she had some means of protecting herself.

It's fine, she told herself, reaching out to lay her hand on the dead bolt. Knowing that if she didn't act now her insecurities would get the better of her, she flipped back the lock and twisted the doorknob, pasting on a false smile as she opened the door to get her dinner.

Except it wasn't the pizza delivery guy standing on her threshold.

She blinked in sudden confusion at the sight that greeted her.

Her dinner had arrived, all right, but rather than some pimply teenage boy, it was James who held the thin rectangular box in his large hands.

Kelly caught her breath as she drank in the sight of him. He looked amazing, standing there in a T-shirt and jeans, his broad shoulders nearly the width of her door. His hair was a little longer, the ends curling up at his neck and over his ears. He probably hadn't had time to cut it lately, if the stubble darkening his cheeks and the dark shadows under his eyes were any indication. She knew from Thomas that they'd all been working overtime lately, but seeing James looking less than his usual polished self really drove the point home.

His dark eyes were focused intently on her, as if he was waiting to see if she'd run. He shifted on his feet, and she caught a whiff of his soap and detergent. She nearly groaned aloud as memories washed over her, making her knees weak and her stomach flutter. *God, he still smells the same.*

His lips curved up in a tentative, almost shy smile. "Hey," he said softly. His voice was husky in the silence, and Kelly felt goose bumps break out across her skin as a thrill of awareness swept through her.

Feeling suddenly parched, she swiped her tongue across her lips to moisten them. His eyes zeroed in on the movement, then flicked back to meet hers.

"Hi," she replied, feeling like an idiot as she stood there gaping at him like a love-struck fool. Why was he here? What was she supposed to say to him?

"Can I come in?" he asked, his expression simultaneously hopeful and guarded.

When she didn't respond, he held up the pizza box. "I brought dinner."

She nodded dumbly, stepping aside to let him enter the apartment. "How did you know I wanted pizza tonight?"

He stepped past her, careful not to brush against her as he walked in. "I ran into the guy downstairs and offered to bring it up."

"Oh." So that explained it. Releasing her hold on the bat, Kelly shut the door and reached for her purse. "Let me pay you."

"No need," he said quickly. "But I hope you don't mind if I have some with you."

She shrugged, hyperaware of his eyes on her. "Be my guest."

He looked around her apartment, taking stock of the stacks of boxes and the empty shelves. "When are you moving?"

"Tomorrow."

Something flashed in his eyes at the news, and he swallowed hard before turning away to set the pizza on her coffee table.

He took a deep breath and squared his shoulders. "Where—" It came out as a rasp, so he cleared his throat and tried again. "Where are you going?"

She debated lying to him for a split second. She could tell him she was moving across the country and that she'd never see him again. With one word, she could make sure he was completely cut out of her life, that her heart was protected. It would be so easy.

But the way he was looking at her now, his big brown eyes almost pleading, gave her pause. He deserved the truth. Besides, she didn't have the energy to lie.

"Alexandria."

His shoulders slumped at the word, and he briefly closed his eyes as he exhaled loudly. Then he gave her a relieved smile, and the fatigue and worry on his face disappeared for a moment. "That's great."

"Why are you here?" Being this close to him again was distracting. She could practically *feel* her resolve weakening every time he looked at her, and God help her if he tried to touch her. She'd worked hard to build a wall around her heart after sending him away in the hospital, but seeing him now and hearing his voice again made her realize she still had a lot of work to do if she was going to get over him.

His smile slipped a bit at her blunt question. "I was hoping we could talk."

That was…surprising. And unexpected. He was supposed to just go away so she could mend her broken heart in peace. Didn't he understand why she had asked him to leave? Did she really have to spell it out for him?

She bit her bottom lip. "I don't really have anything to say." She spoke slowly, feeling her way through the murky conversational waters.

James took a step forward, his expression earnest. "That's okay. You can just listen to me." He gestured back to the pizza. "Do you want to eat while I talk to you?"

She shook her head. A nervous flutter had taken up residence in her stomach at the sight of him, and she didn't trust that food would stay down right now. Better to hear what he had to say without the added worry of throwing up on him.

James ran a hand through his hair and exhaled slowly, bowing his head to stare at the floor. It was clear he was nervous, but why? He'd made his feelings clear, so what was left to say?

As the silence dragged on, Kelly realized she was going to have to prod him a bit to get him to start talking. "James?" she said softly. "I still have to finish packing."

"Right." He jerked his head up to meet her gaze and straightened his shoulders, a man preparing for battle. "It's like this." There was a faint rasp as he ran his hand over his chin, clearly searching for words.

"I messed up."

She blinked at him. "What?"

"I messed up," he repeated helpfully. "The night before the operation, when you told me about...about Gary, I messed up. Although—" his tone became thoughtful "—if you really want to get technical about it, I suppose the first time I screwed things up was the morning after we slept together."

Kelly shook her head, not trusting her ears. "I don't understand."

"For starters, I should have gone after you," he replied. "I could tell you were upset, and I should have made a point of finding out why and helping then, instead of letting you go without a fight. That was my first mistake."

When she didn't respond, he continued, "I told you about Steve, about how I had trusted him and been let down. When I found out you were connected to my investigation, I made the mistake of thinking you were going to do the same thing. I shouldn't have assumed the worst when it came to you. I know you well enough to know you'd never do that, but I let my insecurities cloud my judgment. I'm sorry for that."

Satisfaction was a warm glow in her chest. Even though it didn't matter anymore, it was nice to have confirmation that he had acted like a jerk. "Thank you," she whispered.

He nodded. "When I finally pulled my head out of my ass and recognized you weren't involved, I was hopeful we could try again. I can't tell you how good it felt to know you still had feelings for me, too." His voice broke, and he looked down, taking a deep breath as if to compose himself.

Kelly felt a tug on her heartstrings at this display. James had always been so calm and composed—she'd never seen him look so vulnerable before. She ached to wrap her arms around him and pull him close, but she sensed he wouldn't welcome her touch right now. She could tell he still had things to say.

He glanced up with glassy eyes, and he blinked several times and cleared his throat before speaking again. "And then I ruined everything."

Kelly blinked back her own tears at this admission. She'd spent the past few weeks thinking James hadn't understood how much his rejection had hurt her, but it seemed she was wrong. He did recognize that his words had cut her deeply. Another section of the wall she'd built around her heart crumbled.

"I don't know how to apologize for the way I acted after you told me about Gary. I can't imagine how difficult it was for you to tell me about that, and I pushed you away when I should have supported you. I'll never forgive myself for that."

It took a few tries for her to find her voice, and when she spoke, it was thick with emotion. "It's okay," she said, stepping close to lay her hand on his arm. "I should have worked on my timing. I just kind of dropped it on you with no warning in the middle of another discussion. That wasn't really fair to you."

He covered her hand with his own, his touch warm. "Stop being so nice," he chided, his mouth curving up in a teasing grin. "I'm not done prostrating myself yet."

She let out a wobbly laugh. "There's more?"

His expression turned serious again. "Oh, yeah. Do you have any idea how many years were taken off my life when Caleb took you, and then when I found out you'd been seriously injured?"

Kelly raised a brow at that. "It wasn't exactly fun for me, either. I couldn't think straight at all—I was so worried about you—"

"About me?"

She gave him a little shove. "Yes, about you! A bomb had just gone off, and the last I saw, you were on the ground covered in debris. I had no idea if you were still alive, if you were hurt, if anyone would know to look for you."

It felt good to rail at him, even if the events in question had occurred weeks ago. She'd been carrying the stress ever since that awful day, and the release of all her pent-up emotion made her feel curiously light.

James reached up to push a strand of hair behind her ear. "The important thing is, we both made it out alive. And in the past few weeks, I've realized that I don't want to go on living without having you around."

Kelly caught her breath, not daring to hope. Was he saying…? Did he really mean…?

"I want you, Kelly," he said, his voice whisper soft. "I love you, and I want to be with you."

The words fell on her like warm rain, soothing and gentle, healing the cracks of her heart.

"I know you asked me to go," he continued, rushing now. "And I will, if that's what you want. But I wasn't going to let you go without a fight this time, so here I am, telling you in no uncertain terms that I think we should try again."

She opened her mouth to respond, but he cut her off. "You don't have to answer now," he practically begged. "Take some time to think about it if you want. But I just want to say that I've learned from my mistakes, and if you take me back, I'm going to spend the rest of my life making it up to you."

All her earlier doubts evaporated in the face of his declaration, and the love she'd deliberately locked away expanded to fill the empty space left behind.

A giddy laugh bubbled up as she gave herself permission to believe his promises. Never in her wildest imaginings had she thought she'd get a happy ending like this, but maybe that was her problem. No matter what her therapist said, she still had trouble believing she deserved to be happy.

Well, she wouldn't think that anymore. No longer would she settle for second best or put herself down because she mistakenly thought it was the right thing to do. She was going to reach for her happiness with both hands, grab it tight and wrestle it to the ground so it couldn't get away.

Starting now.

She stared up into the dark eyes of the man she loved, putting all her emotions into her smile.

"I love you, too," she said, reaching up to lay the palm of her hand on his cheek. "Now let's get started on our second chance."

* * * * *

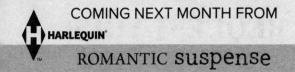

COMING NEXT MONTH FROM

HARLEQUIN®

ROMANTIC suspense

Available December 3, 2013

#1779 COLD CASE, HOT ACCOMPLICE
Men of Wolf Creek • by Carla Cassidy

Detective Steve Kincaid had no idea his latest case would bring the alluring Roxy Marcoli into his life, along with a danger from his past that could destroy them both.

#1780 COLTON CHRISTMAS RESCUE
The Coltons of Wyoming • by Beth Cornelison

To solve the crimes at the Colton ranch and protect Amanda Colton's infant daughter, Slade Kent goes undercover. But to earn Amanda's trust and love, he must risk his heart.

#1781 SEDUCED BY HIS TARGET
Buried Secrets • by Gail Barrett

Nadine Seymour's worst nightmare comes true when she's kidnapped by the powerful family she's hidden from for years. Will the sexy, enigmatic rebel be her salvation or her undoing?

#1782 COVERT ATTRACTION
by Linda O. Johnston

A rugged FBI agent. A determined U.S. Marshal. Both undercover, unaware of the other...at first. Can they work together to uncover a deadly conspiracy while fighting their sexual attraction?

HRSCNM1113

REQUEST YOUR
FREE BOOKS!

2 FREE NOVELS
FROM THE SUSPENSE COLLECTION
PLUS 2 FREE GIFTS!

YES! Please send me 2 FREE novels from the Suspense Collection and my 2 FREE gifts (gifts are worth about $10). After receiving them, if I don't wish to receive any more books, I can return the shipping statement marked "cancel." If I don't cancel, I will receive 4 brand-new novels every month and be billed just $6.24 per book in the U.S. or $6.74 per book in Canada. That's a savings of at least 22% off the cover price. It's quite a bargain! Shipping and handling is just 50¢ per book in the U.S. and 75¢ per book in Canada.* I understand that accepting the 2 free books and gifts places me under no obligation to buy anything. I can always return a shipment and cancel at any time. Even if I never buy another book, the two free books and gifts are mine to keep forever.

191/391 MDN F4XN

Name _____ (PLEASE PRINT)

Address _____ Apt. #

City _____ State/Prov. _____ Zip/Postal Code

Signature (if under 18, a parent or guardian must sign)

Mail to the **Harlequin® Reader Service:**
IN U.S.A.: P.O. Box 1867, Buffalo, NY 14240-1867
IN CANADA: P.O. Box 609, Fort Erie, Ontario L2A 5X3

Want to try two free books from another line?
Call 1-800-873-8635 or visit www.ReaderService.com.

* Terms and prices subject to change without notice. Prices do not include applicable taxes. Sales tax applicable in N.Y. Canadian residents will be charged applicable taxes. Offer not valid in Quebec. This offer is limited to one order per household. Not valid for current subscribers to the Suspense Collection or the Romance/Suspense Collection. All orders subject to credit approval. Credit or debit balances in a customer's account(s) may be offset by any other outstanding balance owed by or to the customer. Please allow 4 to 6 weeks for delivery. Offer available while quantities last.

SPECIAL EXCERPT FROM

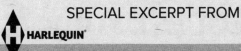

HARLEQUIN®

ROMANTIC suspense

When Liz Marcoli went missing from her home,
Detective Steve Kincaid had no idea that investigating
the disappearance would bring the sexy Roxy Marcoli
into his life, along with a danger from his past that
could destroy them both.

Read on for a sneak peek of

COLD CASE, HOT ACCOMPLICE

by Carla Cassidy, available December 2013 from
Harlequin® Romantic Suspense.

"I need to buy a gun," she said as Steve pulled out of the
Roadside Stop parking lot.

He nearly snapped her neck with his fast stop. He turned
in his seat and frowned at her. "You are not getting a gun.
You can be anything you want in the world, but you can't be
a gun owner. You'd wind up shooting a customer or yourself
by accident."

"Or you," she said, knowing he was right.

"There's always that, too," he agreed.

"It sucks being a target of somebody and not knowing who
they are or why they want to hurt me."

"It's odd that whoever it is hasn't succeeded yet. I mean,
instead of just locking you in the freezer, why not stab you to
death or beat you with something?"

"I know. I thought of that already."

He turned down the lane that was Amish land. "It makes me wonder again if maybe the attacker is a woman."

Roxy frowned. "I just can't imagine any woman who would want me hurt or dead." She turned and looked out the window, where young and old men in black trousers, long-sleeved white shirts and wide-brimmed straw hats worked in the fields.

Steve drove up to a modest white ranch house with a huge dairy barn behind it. "This is Tom Yoder's place. He's the bishop, and we need to check in with him before we speak to anyone else."

He pulled to a halt before the Yoder house and cut the engine. He unbuckled his seat belt and then turned to look at her. "And, Roxy, just for the record, you should never have to change a thing about yourself for any man. You're perfect just the way you are."

He didn't wait for a reply, but instead turned and got out of the car. It was at that moment Roxy realized she was more than a little bit in love with Detective Steve Kincaid.

**Don't miss
COLD CASE, HOT ACCOMPLICE
by Carla Cassidy, available December 2013 from
Harlequin® Romantic Suspense.**

SEDUCED BY HIS TARGET
by Gail Barrett

For victims of violence, Nadira al Kahtani is
a savior in surgeon's clothing. But this time
it's Nadira who must be saved...from her own
corrupt family. Rasheed Davar—a rebellious
CIA agent seeking to avenge his wife's murder—
could risk his undercover mission to save her.
But will he? Things are heating up off
Columbia's coast, and Rasheed can't deny
the mounting tension. Nadira is beautiful.
She is brave. And she's just the kind of
high-stakes hostage who could lure him
directly into terrorist crosshairs.

Look for the conclusion in the
Buried Secrets miniseries
next month from Gail Barrett.

DAVID FISHER

HARD
EVIDENCE

HOW DETECTIVES INSIDE THE FBI'S SCI-CRIME LAB
HAVE HELPED SOLVE AMERICA'S TOUGHEST CASES

A DELL BOOK

Published by
Dell Publishing
a division of
Bantam Doubleday Dell Publishing Group, Inc.
1540 Broadway
New York, New York 10036

In several instances names, dates, or locations have been
changed to protect privacy, ensure security, or to avoid
influencing ongoing judicial proceedings.

ISBN: 0-440-22236-2

Reprinted by arrangement with Simon & Schuster

Printed in the United States of America

Published simultaneously in Canada

June 1996

10   9   8   7   6   5   4   3
OPM

to my father, Irving Fisher, who
taught me the things that matter

CONTENTS

PREFACE

Perhaps no government agency has been more written about than the FBI. Countless books, movies, and television programs have documented the Bureau's fight against crime. But one important aspect of the FBI's operations is virtually unknown: the extraordinary work that is being done by its forensic department—the FBI Criminal Laboratory.

Several years ago, when I was writing about organized crime, I became friendly with Special Agent Joe Pistone, who is better known as "Donnie Brasco," the guise in which he spent six years working undercover in the mob and was responsible for the convictions of almost one hundred leaders of organized crime. In conversation with Pistone one evening, the subject of the FBI's crime lab came up, and, on impulse, I asked if it was possible for me to gain access. To my surprise, a week later he took me to the FBI Headquarters Building on Ninth Street and Pennsylvania Avenue in Washington, D.C., and introduced me to the fascinating world of scientific crime detection—sci-crime, as I began to refer to it. I spent the next two years exploring that world. This book is the result.

For a writer, walking into the FBI crime lab was like discovering an unexplored gold mine, a mine so rich it was difficult to believe that other people had not been there before me. I spent months inside the lab, learning how the cutting edge of science and technology is applied to the

investigation of a crime. I conducted almost two hundred hours of interviews with the men and women who have worked on every major criminal investigation of recent years, including the people who helped uncover the mysteries behind the destruction of Pan Am Flight 103 over Lockerbie, Scotland, and the bombing of the World Trade Center in New York, and the men who did the ballistics investigation in the Kennedy assassination—the first interview they had ever granted a reporter. I spoke to the man who discovered James Earl Ray's identity through a partial fingerprint, and to the people who helped convict the Atlanta Child Killer, Wayne Williams, on the basis of a few slender hairs and fibers. These are the people who often find out what they will be doing at work by reading the morning headlines. As I was told by one examiner, "We have a piece of every major crime in this country."

Few people know about the capabilities of the FBI crime lab. It is, simply, the finest crime lab in the world. And if its work has gone unheralded, it is perhaps because the evidence it has uncovered speaks quite loudly for itself. I was particularly engrossed by the process of detection. How does a partial fingerprint, a spent bullet, a drop of blood, a hair fiber, a piece of bone, a shard of metal or glass, a dab of paint, or an empty bottle lead to the person who committed a crime? The latest and most sophisticated technologies are vital to this process and, as I discovered, many of them were created or adapted to this work in the FBI lab. But ultimately it is the expertise and experience of the men and women who employ these technologies— along with the gut feelings, hunches, educated guesses, and often pure persistence of all great detectives—that have cracked even the toughest cases.

This book is their story: the role their work has played in solving every conceivable type of crime—rapes, murders,

serial killings, product tampering—crimes that have made headlines around the world, crimes that might otherwise have gone undetected or unsolved. It is crime detection of the highest order.

1

A World of Wonders:
Inside the FBI's Sci-Crime Lab

From a drop of water, the logician could infer the possibility of an Atlantic or a Niagara without having seen or heard of one or the other. So all life is a great chain, the nature of which is known whenever we are shown a single link of it. Like all other arts, the Science of Deduction and Analysis is one which can only be acquired through long and patient study, nor is life long enough to allow any mortal to attain the highest possible perfection in it.

SHERLOCK HOLMES
In Sir Arthur Conan Doyle's "The Book of Life"

Not long ago investigators had to find the smoking gun to convict a suspect. Now all they need is the smoke.

On December 16, 1989, federal court judge Robert Vance opened a small box that had been mailed to his home in Mountain Brook, Alabama. When he lifted the lid the box exploded, killing him instantly and seriously wounding his wife. Two days later Savannah, Georgia, attorney and alderman Robert Robinson died in his office when a second package bomb exploded as he opened it. That same day a third bomb was discovered during a routine screening of packages mailed to judges in the Atlanta federal courthouse. A fourth package bomb was delivered to a female employee of the NAACP legal counsel in Jacksonville, Florida. She left it on her desk and went to run some errands, intending to open it when she returned later that afternoon. But her car broke down as she drove back

to the office and had to be towed, so she went home. On the news that night she heard of the explosion in Savannah and realized that the package on her desk was similar to the one that had killed Robert Robinson. The next morning she called the Jacksonville bomb squad. And she lived.

Fearing a concerted attack on the judicial system of the United States, local, state, and federal law enforcement agencies immediately began intensive investigations of the bombings. The FBI designated the murders a major case, meaning they took priority over all other cases. In the Bureau most cases are referred to by a description number; major cases are given code names to facilitate communications. Because this case began with the murder of Judge Vance by a package bomb, it was known as VANPAC; it eventually became one of the most massive investigations in FBI history, a year-long manhunt that involved hundreds of agents. More than six thousand people were interviewed and millions of documents were examined. But the case was finally solved on the third floor of the FBI headquarters building in downtown Washington, D.C., in the finest crime lab in the world.

The crime lab is that place where science meets murder. It's where the wonders of modern science and space-age technology are used to transform clues into hard evidence. Killers may live to tell their stories; there is only the evidence to speak for their victims. But those often invisible bits of evidence can speak loudly to those who know how to understand them. Dead men do tell tales. No one disappears without a trace. There is no such thing as the perfect crime.

The VANPAC investigation ultimately involved just about every unit in the FBI crime lab, but the head investigator was soft-spoken Kentuckian Tom Thurman of the Explosives Unit. As a first step, the unopened package bombs received in Atlanta and Jacksonville were rendered safe, a nice way of saying that an aimed explosive was fired into

the packages to separate the components. They were blown into pieces; essentially the evidence remained but the bombs could no longer function. When Thurman examined the remains of the four bombs, it was obvious to him that the same person had made them.

Each bomb was constructed inside a carton about the size of a shirt box, and each consisted of a steel pipe filled with smokeless powder that would explode when a current generated by two C batteries ran through a lightbulb filament (the bulb had been removed) to a homemade detonator. The only thing that prevented the circuit between the power source and the detonator from being completed was a thin piece of cardboard between two sheets of aluminum foil. When the cover of the box was lifted, a string attached to the lid was stretched taut and pulled out the cardboard, allowing the two sheets of foil to make contact, completing the circuit and triggering the bomb.

Apart from their construction, there were several other similarities between the bombs. Square end plates were bolted to both ends of the pipes. Everything inside each box had been painted with black enamel. The packages had been wrapped in brown paper. And threatening letters were found inside those bombs that hadn't gone off.

Pieces of each package bomb were sent to the various units in the crime lab for examination of any evidence that fell within their area of expertise. The DNA Analysis Unit attempted to develop a DNA profile of the bomb maker from the saliva used to moisten the mailing labels and stamps. The Hairs and Fiber Unit tried to determine where the string had originated, and knots tied in that string were examined by the lab's knot experts to see if they could be associated with a specific profession or region. The Materials Analysis Unit proved that the black enamel paint in each box was identical. It also attempted to identify the manufacturer of the adhesives and determined that ordinary telephone wire had been used in the circuits. The Elemen-

tal Analysis Unit was able to make a positive association between the nails used as shrapnel in all four bombs, providing additional proof that they had been made by the same person, and was also able to identify the specific press in Taiwan on which the nails had been fabricated. The Latent Fingerprint Section found a partial print on the letter inside the Jacksonville bomb and began trying to put a name to it. In the Chemistry/Toxicology Unit examiners set out to identify the source of the explosive, smokeless powder, as well as the primer material. The Document Section began a search for the typewriter on which the threatening letters had been written and for the manufacturer of the cardboard boxes. And the Explosives Unit dissected the remnants of the bombs, trying to trace any single piece to a source that might lead to the bomb maker.

Documents made the first hit. The typewriter on which the letters had been typed had a distinctive flaw: at some time in the past a broken type bar had been replaced with the wrong typeface. It was very easy to spot, and since three bombs had attacked the legal system, the judicial files in four states were scoured for documents written on that typewriter. Amazingly, among tens of thousands of pages, examiners at the Atlanta courthouse found what they were looking for: a threatening letter that had been typed on the same machine.

The letter had been written several years earlier by a resident of Enterprise, Alabama. Officers from the VANPAC task force descended on the small town, trailed by newspaper and television reporters, and several lab examiners flew there to look for the smallest clue that would connect this suspect to the bombings. "We searched every square inch of his house and business," Tom Thurman remembered. "We even drained his sewage system to see if he'd flushed pieces of the typewriter down there. But we didn't find a single thing that would connect him to the bombs. The suspect told us he'd sold a lot of typewriters

out of his junk store and this had probably been one of them. So we had to start from scratch again.''

In Chem/Tox, unit chief Roger Martz quickly identified the explosive used in the bombs as common Hercules Red Dot smokeless powder, but identifying the primer material was much more difficult. ''There are as many as a hundred different primers available,'' Martz said. ''The sample we got from the bombs contained two percent aluminum, and in all my research I found only one primer with two percent aluminum. It was CCI primer for small-arms ammunition, and since it isn't commercially available in bulk, whoever made the bombs had to have bought a large number of primers and opened them up by hand to remove the explosive material.''

Agents began canvassing retailers throughout the South, looking for someone who might have sold several pounds of Red Dot smokeless powder and a large quantity of CCI primers to an individual in the period just before the bombs were mailed. But the first solid break in the case came from a conversation Thurman had had with an agent of the Bureau of Alcohol, Tobacco and Firearms while the two men were in Enterprise. ''He told me that if we couldn't connect the suspect in Enterprise to the bombs,'' Thurman said, ''we should look at a guy named Moody from Georgia. ATF records indicated that Moody had built a bomb in 1972 that had several characteristics in common with the VANPAC bombs. So when the search in Enterprise failed, we turned our attention to Walter Leroy Moody.

''Moody had been convicted of possession of a bomb in 1972, although he had not been convicted of actually making that bomb. He had served time in prison for possession and that could have been when his hatred of the judicial system began. Our investigation now focused on Moody, and we searched his house looking for anything that would link him to the bombs. We even picked up the floor in a room that had recently been totally redone. We didn't find

a thing. We found every color and type of paint imaginable, except the black enamel. We found every type of tool, except what was used to make the bombs. It was as if Moody knew what we would be looking for and had taken those things out of the house. We never found a single thing in that house that we were able to connect to the bombs."

After a long search, ATF found the original photographs of Moody's 1972 bomb. It was a pipe bomb with square endplates bolted to it and it was in a corrugated paper box. It was powered by a flashlight battery, the initiator was a lightbulb filament taken from inside a bulb, and it was triggered by opening the box, which tightened a string. A threatening note was included with the bomb, and telephone wire was used for the circuits. In short, the package bomb found in Moody's possession in 1972 was virtually identical to the four 1989 bombs. "One means we use to identify a bomber is through his 'signature,'" Thurman explained. "People learn how to make bombs one way, and no matter how sophisticated they get, they'll continue to repeat certain techniques. That technique is almost as unique as a fingerprint, and it makes very strong evidence that two or more bombs were made by the same person or group. When I saw all this, I smiled and said, 'Yeah, this looks really good.' But before I would testify that the signature of the 1972 bomb compared strongly to the VANPAC bombs, I wanted to do a little more work. I wanted to compare the damage.

"ATF built us a demonstration bomb duplicating Moody's bombs. We constructed a room similar to Judge Vance's office on our range at Quantico. We used bobber targets, cardboard cutouts, to represent Judge Vance and his wife. Then we opened the box. Remotely. It blew our room apart and destroyed the bobbers. You look at the photographs of the bomb scene and compare them with the results of this test and it's about as close as you can get.

When I saw this I said, 'Now I can testify that the same person made all of these bombs.' "

Meanwhile, other lab units were also getting results. Agents in Atlanta found the store in which Moody had bought four pounds of Hercules Red Dot smokeless powder and a thousand CCI primers about a week before the bombs were mailed. Had Moody not been identified by his signature as a bomb maker, it is possible he would have been found through this search.

Moody's wife eventually admitted that she had purchased some supplies for him. She also claimed that he had ordered her to drive to Covington, Kentucky, to make copies of his threatening letter. Latent-print examiners in the Identification Division were able to identify the partial print found on one of the letters as that of a part-time employee of the copy shop, made while he was loading the machine. That print supported the rest of Mrs. Moody's confession.

Walter Leroy Moody was convicted and sentenced to seven life terms plus four hundred years in prison. Primarily due to the work done in the FBI crime lab, VANPAC was closed.

Crime labs have existed for more than a century, for most of that time relying on the basic tools of science and technology to provide support for the detective in the field. But in the last two decades this world has been revolutionized, and today the most sophisticated instruments are used to answer the ancient question at the heart of every crime: Who did it?

The crime lab is not a place for testing theories or conducting experiments. It's practical, and it's often brutal. It's a place where every test may change someone's life forever. "We deal in violent crime here," DNA Analysis unit chief Dave Bigbee explained matter-of-factly. "After you've been here awhile you think you've seen every pos-

sible thing that one human being can do to another. And then the next case comes in. In one case we got, a woman went out shopping and left her two children with her boyfriend. He raped her twelve-year-old daughter and strangled her to death, then sodomized the nine-year-old boy and killed him by driving ten-penny nails into his skull with a brick." Truly, the lab is not a place for testing theories.

No one knows how many hundreds of years ago the principles of science and technology were first applied to crime solving. But the use of science to develop evidence and solve crimes, which is traditionally known by the rather prosaic term "forensic science," but now might more appropriately be referred to as sci-crime, evolved slowly. Until recently detectives didn't believe in it at all. They wanted the gun and not the smoke; they wanted evidence they they could see with their own eyes and hold in their hands.

Investigators would come upon a crime scene and turn on the lights as brightly as possible, literally trying to shed some light on the crime. No more. Since the 1970s the world of crime detection has changed completely and forever. Now these same investigators will turn off the lights at a crime scene and use lasers and ultraviolet and infrared light; they'll conduct chemical tests, and they'll use special vacuums to try to get just a glimpse of the invisible world where a crucial piece of evidence might be found. "Gone are the days when we'd go to a crime scene and pick up whatever we could see," FBI special agent Dale Moreau said. "Nowadays we're more interested in evidence we can't see."

The FBI's Scientific Crime Detection Laboratory, as it was originally known, had its origins in 1928, when scientific evidence presented at a hearing in the controversial Sacco and Vanzetti murder case impressed Bureau of Investigation director J. Edgar Hoover, although by that time

the Bureau was already conducting basic handwriting and bullet comparisons and blood-type testing and had established a national fingerprint file. In 1931, Agent Charles Appel reported to Hoover: "The Bureau should be the central clearing house for all information which may be needed in criminological work." On November 24, 1932, the lab was officially opened in a converted lounge, chosen because it had a sink.

The concept of scientific crime-solving immediately caught the public's fancy. "Aroused by the ever-increasing menace of the scientific-minded criminal schooled in the fine arts and inventions of organized crime," reported Rex Collier in the Washington, D.C., *Evening News* three months after the lab opened, "the United States Bureau of Investigation has established a novel research laboratory where government criminologists will match wits with underworld cunning."

Perhaps that was a slight overstatement. Appel was the lab's only full-time employee and the lab was equipped with a borrowed microscope, ultraviolet lights, a drawing board, and a "helixometer," a device that supposedly allowed examiners to look inside gun barrels, but that was used almost exclusively to impress visitors. If the lab needed to examine a package suspected of containing explosives, an X-ray machine was borrowed from another government bureau. Appel soon added a comparison microscope, test tubes, wax and plaster to make moulages (impressions of shoeprints and tire tracks), and what he proudly described as "an X-ray mirror, which is transparent from the back only and is an improvement on the old spy hole system."

The lab grew gradually, adding both equipment and personnel. In 1938, for example, examiners began conducting lie-detector tests on the "newly perfected" polygraph machine. A year later they started doing microchemical and spectrographic exams. "I sometimes wonder just how we

were able to accomplish as much as we did," said Dr. William Magee, who joined the lab as its first full-time chemist in 1939 soon after receiving his doctorate, "particularly in light of the fact that we didn't have much scientific backing. By the time I got there, we had a spark-source spectograph which allowed us to analyze a specimen to find out what it was, and we had the first infrared spectrometer in any crime lab, and a pretty good comparison microscope for firearms and hairs and fibers exams.

"But we made do with what we had. In those days if any guys were doing dynamite work, they would take an extract, put it on an anvil, and hit it with a hammer. If it went poof, it was dynamite. We also had an animal room in the old Justice Department building where we kept the rabbits we used in our blood testing. If we got a questioned blood specimen, we'd mix it with rabbit serum and if the blood was human, within say twenty seconds a cloudy ring would form at the interface of those two liquids. Generally speaking, if it were not of human origin, it wouldn't be of any interest to us."

To Dr. Magee's disappointment, Hoover showed very little interest in the lab except as a public relations vehicle. "I felt he should have had some little feeling about the value of science to crime detection, but he apparently saw otherwise and felt that he could entrust that to some of his lieutenants. I worked there from 1939 and I only saw Hoover twice, once when they brought in the eight captured Nazi saboteurs and then when they were making the movie *The House on 92nd Street*. I just wondered how a guy could be a scientific backer if he didn't know the value of what we were doing to the consumer. Things were as right as they could be under the circumstances, but I'll tell you, it was a lonely time down there."

Crucial to the lab's success has been the ability to evolve as the nature of crime has changed and to find means of incorporating advances in science and technology into its

investigative procedures. For many years, for example, Serology was a minor unit limited to determining whether a blood sample had come from a human being or an animal, and if from a human, to which of the four known blood groups the donor belonged. This was "class evidence," meaning it could apply to any one of a large number of people, and had little value to detectives. But the Serology Unit expanded rapidly in the 1970s, when scientists discovered elements in blood and other secretions that made it possible to match a sample to a much smaller number of people. And this once-quaint unit became one of the most important in the lab; the name was changed from Serology to DNA Analysis, when technology made it possible to extract DNA from human cells and link it to a specific person.

In fact, more advances have been made in the past two decades than throughout all of sci-crime history. Twenty years ago there were only three methods of developing latent fingerprints. Today at least forty techniques are used, including lasers and superglue fumes, and prints that once would have remained invisible are now being used to prove that a specific individual was involved in a crime.

From that converted lounge with a single borrowed microscope, the FBI lab has become the single most important law enforcement facility in America. "Almost every case I work is the biggest case, or the most important case, or the most heinous case in the history of that particular community," metallurgist Bill Tobin of Elemental Analysis said. "We get the most visible cases in this country, and we get them every day. If it's on the news, we're probably going to see some part of it in here."

"This is simply the mother lode of criminal investigation," former lab director John Hicks said flatly.

The FBI lab was established to provide impartial investigative services for all federal agencies in criminal and civil

matters, and all local and state law enforcement agencies in criminal matters, and to do so absolutely free of charge. There is never a fee for requesting an examination. This is America's crime lab.

There are only two requirements placed on submitting agencies: First, they must accept the results of the examination as final; they can't go shopping for a crime lab that will issue the report they want. So when they submit evidence to the lab, they confirm that it hasn't been examined by another lab and they agree not to take it elsewhere if they are not satisfied with the results. Second, they agree that those results will be made available to the suspect, even if they show he is innocent. "Sometimes we have to tell prosecutors things they really don't want to hear," said Dwight Adams of DNA Analysis. "I did the DNA examinations in New York's Central Park jogger case, in which a young woman running in the park was gang-raped, smashed in the head with a rock, and left to die in the dirt. The NYPD eventually arrested twelve people and submitted their blood samples, as well as semen found on the victim's body and clothing. Well, the result I got eliminated all twelve of them as the contributor of that semen. It didn't mean they weren't there; in fact, some of them confessed and implicated others. It just meant the prosecutor was going to have a much harder time proving they were there. When I called the prosecutor and told her, if you can actually hear silence, that's when I heard it. I'd been told by police that there were more than thirty individuals involved in the attack, so it's likely the semen came from one of those unidentified people still out there. The prosecutor didn't like what I told her, but everybody knows when they submit something to us they're going to have to live with the results."

In some of the lab units as many as a third of all examinations result in a negative conclusion, meaning the suspect can't be linked to the evidence. As Linda Harrison, a

chemist in the DNA Unit, pointed out, "Evidence is neutral. If it matches it matches, if it doesn't I say it doesn't. We don't get paid in here based on the number of people we put in jail. I want to see the guilty guy go to jail and the innocent guy go home."

As an additional service to contributors, agent-examiners will testify to their results during the trial, also completely free of charge. Many people in the sci-crime lab have testified several hundred times. "Only once, in all the trials in which I've testified, have I been taken by surprise," Latent Fingerprint chief Danny Greathouse remembered, "and that was the first question I was asked the first time I testified as an expert witness. I'd been in training for several years, I'd been through endless moot court sessions, so I knew I was prepared. But the first question the defense attorney asked me was, 'Mr. Greathouse, can you get a latent fingerprint off a sponge?'"

"I knew that question had absolutely nothing to do with the facts of the case, so I assumed it was a trick question and that he was trying to show the jury that I wasn't an expert. But I couldn't figure out what the trick was, so I said, 'Well, I don't know that you can. I don't think it's possible.' He said okay and sat down.

"After the trial he came over to me and explained why he'd asked that question. 'Oh, it didn't have anything to do with the case,' he admitted. 'It was just something I'd always wondered about.'"

From less than a thousand examinations in 1933, by the beginning of the 1990s the FBI lab was routinely handling almost twenty thousand cases annually, consisting of about two hundred thousand pieces of evidence on which almost a million examinations were performed. And all to answer that one question: Who did it?

There are only three possible ways to solve a crime. The person who committed the crime can confess. It happens. The victim or witnesses can identify the person who com-

mitted the crime. That also happens. And finally, information can be obtained through physical evidence, hard evidence, that can be used to link a specific person to the crime or the victim. And that's what happens most often.

Hard evidence is the silent witness. It's always there, always. Every lab examination begins at the crime scene, and no investigation can be any better than the quality of the work done there. A crime scene is simply a mystery waiting to be unraveled, a complex puzzle in which, out of a multitude of items, only one thing need be found. It might be as obvious as a bloody palmprint or a discarded piece of chewing gum. It might be a strand of hair, saliva on a telephone mouthpiece, residue on a curtain, a burnt match, a blank sheet of paper. Anything found at a crime scene might provide the single clue needed to break the case.

When Pan Am Flight 103 exploded over Lockerbie, Scotland, killing 271 people, there were millions of pieces of debris; it was a piece of plastic no larger than a thumbnail that led directly to the bombers. The strongest evidence against Atlanta child-killer Wayne Williams was several hairs and fibers. A partial fingerprint on a forty-year-old postcard was enough to prove that a Detroit archbishop had worked for the Nazis during World War II. Several barely visible green specks led directly to a woman who murdered two people by putting cyanide in Excedrin capsules. Michele Sindona, the Vatican's banker, was convicted of the largest bank fraud in American history because he habitually put a dot inside the bowl of the number 9.

The FBI receives so much mail each day that the headquarters building, at Tenth Street and Pennsylvania Avenue, has its own zip code: 20535. On the average, more than six hundred pieces of evidence are submitted to the FBI lab for examination every day. Physical evidence, hard evidence, consists of anything that might help solve a crime. It might

be trace evidence, something so small that only traces of it can be found: a speck of paint; lead that a bullet has left on a bone; human cells from a drop of blood. Or it might be as large as a skull, or a chunk of wall that has to be lifted into the building by crane. Once the entire contents of a suspected serial killer's apartment arrived by van. "It's always something different," said Kelly Hargadon, a chemist in the Materials Analysis Unit, "always. You never know what it might be. When I open up a case for the first time it's as exciting as opening up a present."

It can also be very sad. "One submission that'll stick in my mind forever was an ordinary blanket," Ken Nimmich, chief of the Scientific Analysis Section, said. "A murdered child had been wrapped in it, and when I opened it up I could see the outline of the child's body. The decomposition products had stained an outline on the blanket. In here we're used to seeing blankets with bloodstains on them, but this . . ."

The lab issues general instructions to contributors about how to properly wrap and submit evidence: Human organs should be sent in plastic or glass containers by United Parcel Service, private express mail, or special delivery. Bullets should be sent by UPS, registered mail, or private courier. When a submission arrives in the Evidence Control Center, it's logged into a computer and given a number that will identify it as long as it remains in the lab. Major cases, like VANPAC, are given code names. The bombing of Flight 103 over Scotland became SCOTBOM. Depending on the nature of the submission and the type of examination requested, the ECC will designate a primary investigative unit, the unit that will be responsible for the evidence while it is in the lab. The package will be hand-delivered to the unit chief, who will assign it to an agent-examiner.

The agent-examiner runs the case in the lab. He or she may decide to send the evidence to various other units for examination, but just like the detective working the case

back at the precinct, he or she makes all the decisions. A single piece of evidence may be examined by six or seven people.

Every examiner is assisted by a physical-science technician, who prepares the evidence for the examiner to conduct the actual testing or examination. The technician may scrape a garment for hairs and fibers, prepare paint samples for microscopic comparisons, even run chemical tests. Many technicians have advanced degrees in their fields, but they haven't completed the rigorous program of study, training, and on-the-job experience that enables them to qualify as an expert in that discipline so they don't testify in trials.

Included with every submission is a letter from the contributor describing the contents of the package, the facts of the case, and what types of examinations are being requested. What do the contributors want to know? What information do they believe will be valuable to their investigation? Typically, contributors ask for an identification, a comparison, or some other information that will allow them to move forward with their investigation. What is this thing? Where could it have come from? What type of gun should we be looking for? Can you determine what make and model of automobile this paint speck, found at the hit-and-run scene, came from? Or they want to know if an item from an unknown source, the Q or questioned item, matches a specimen whose source is known, the K. Is the Q, strands of hair found in the victim's hand, identical to the K, samples taken from the suspect's head? Did the piece of tape used to bind the victim's hands come from the roll found in the suspect's car? Was *this* signature forged by the same person who prepared *those* documents?

Often evidence has to be examined by several different units, and because some tests are destructive, the order in which they are performed is crucial. So part of every examiner's training is learning what all of the other units do,

how they work, and what impact their tests will have on evidence. A blood-soaked shirt might be sent to DNA for the primary investigation, but even before looking at it, the DNA examiner will send it to Hairs and Fibers because hairs and fibers fall off easily and important evidence might be lost. A gun might have human tissue in its barrel, so Firearms will send it to Chem/Tox, but people in the Chem Unit know not to clean the barrel with a sharp object because that might destroy marks useful to Firearms. Latent Prints is last, because many of the liquids and powders they use to try to develop prints will destroy the materials needed by other units to conduct tests—blood, for example. So while each unit is independent, the lab really functions as a whole.

The first thing a primary investigator does when he gets a case is read the accompanying letter to find out what the case is about and what the contributor wants to know. "Sometimes they're pretty confused about what they want," Firearms Unit chief Jack Dillon said, "so we'll call them up to find out what they're trying to prove. Often we can suggest some better ways of doing it."

A lot of requests seem to be inspired by TV detectives. Contributors see Columbo getting results from a crime lab and assume that the FBI lab can perform the same miracles. "We got a package of charred bones in here one day," Chem/Tox chief Roger Martz remembered, "and the contributor wanted us to tell him all sorts of things about the victim. These were charred bones, there wasn't much we could do with them, but the contributor had seen Quincy do something on TV so he knew it was possible."

"On TV detectives are always drawing positive conclusions based on information that they couldn't possibly have gotten from the evidence and that wouldn't stand up in a courtroom," Lee Waggoner of the Document Section said. "I wish it was as simple as it is on TV."

"This is where we really become detectives," Agent-

examiner Wayne Oakes of Hairs and Fibers said. "Most other crime labs tend to get very straightforward requests: 'This is the gun. This is the bullet from the autopsy. Was that bullet fired from this gun?' But in here it's more often, 'Please conduct all appropriate examinations.' They might ask us to make a comparison, but we're always going to suggest more if we think it's logical. There is absolutely no pressure on us to limit ourselves to examinations requested in the submission letter, and that's precisely where all our training and experience become invaluable.

"For example, I may get pieces of duct tape that had been used to bind the hands of several murder victims with a request that I compare them to see if they came from the same roll. The police want to tie all the killings to the same person. That's all they're asking for. But when I examine the tape I may see some blue fibers the police didn't notice. I'll examine them and call the submitting officer and tell him, 'I just want to alert you that there were a number of carpet fibers on that tape you sent me. Here's what I'm guessing might have happened. I can't testify to this, it's just a gut feeling based on my experience. But I'm seeing blue carpet fibers on two pieces of tape that match. They're tri-lobel nylon carpet fibers, the type usually found in automotive carpets. My guess is that the man you're looking for has used this roll of tape and he's laid it on the floor of his car. So I'm guessing your suspect has a blue car. Don't dismiss a good suspect because he's driving a brown car, but this makes sense to me. When you develop a suspect, make sure you get me a known carpet sample.' After doing this every day for more than ten years, I'm not afraid to give the guy my gut feeling, but I always remind him it isn't an affidavit, it's a lead."

The first investigators hired to work in the lab were scientists, given the title "examiner." During training they were known as junior examiners. But as the lab expanded in the late 1930s, it became difficult to recruit qualified

people, so rather than hiring scientists and training them to be detectives, the Bureau assigned agents with scientific backgrounds to the lab and taught them the necessary skills. Until recently it was strict Bureau policy that every examiner had to be an agent and had to have worked in an FBI field office for several years before joining the lab. But as the science and technology needed in the lab have become more complex, that requirement has been relaxed, and experts from a variety of fields are being brought into the lab.

While the examiners work as scientists, they think like detectives. "Before I look at the evidence, I'll read the facts of the case, then sit back and think about it," said mineralogist Chris Fiedler of Materials Analysis, one of the first non-agent examiners in the lab. "I'll try to get a feel for the case. For example, if I know the crime took place in a certain type of physical environment, I'll think about what I should be finding even before I open the evidence. If I don't find it, then I know something's wrong and we get started on a whole different track."

There are more than three hundred county, city, state, and federal crime labs in the United States, serving more than a million law enforcement officials. Most of these labs perform basic examinations and are staffed with criminalists—people with expertise in several sci-crime disciplines—rather than specialists. But FBI lab philosophy is that the more experience you gain in one area, the better you get at it. The more bombings you investigate, the better you will understand bombs. As Bill Magee remembered, "When I got here in 1939 there was one other chemist, but he was one of those jack-of-all-trades types. The decision was made right about that time that we weren't going to operate that way, we were going to specialize. Even in those days we believed we really couldn't do metallurgy one day and hairs and fibers the next."

"It's really necessary to specialize," Documents exam-

iner Jim Lile said. "I know a lot of smaller labs can't afford it, and some of them do excellent work as far as they go. But the scientific knowledge we need to have is growing daily, and even when you're working in only one area, it's sometimes difficult to keep abreast of it."

In every case the objective of the work done in the lab is to use evidence to prove a crime was committed, to associate a known suspect with the victim or the crime scene or prove his innocence, or to develop information that will help law enforcement agents identify a suspect. That's the lab mission, a benign, almost ordinary one. And the lab itself is a quiet place, where efficient people go about their daily business as they might in any large corporation. Visitors walking through the lab might see men and women wearing white lab coats and staring intently into sophisticated microscopes, or mixing chemicals, or preparing samples for some of the most sensitive instruments of modern science. They might see people standing around a coffeepot and laughing softly, or sitting in small groups discussing a problem. On the surface, the place would look and feel like a research laboratory with a thousand different experiments in progress.

But this is a crime lab. And the things examiners see when they look into the microscope make it very different. The examiner leaning over the comparison scope might be looking at a bloody bullet taken out of the President of the United States. Some of the chemicals might be used to analyze specimens in the rape and murder of three Oklahoma Girl Scouts. The samples being prepared for the mass spectrometer might be slices of the liver of a Miami man who went into convulsions and died after drinking a cocaine-laced bottle of a popular malt liquor.

"Every day we get bloody clothing with bullet holes or stab wounds, rocks covered with blood and hair and brains, bloody cinder blocks that were dropped on people, not to mention the bloody weapons," Dave Bigbee said. "You

just can't imagine what we get in here. A broomstick that was crammed up a rape victim's vagina all the way to her throat. We had a case in which a young girl was kidnapped by a motorcycle gang, tied to the back of a motorcycle, and dragged around for a while, and then they killed her by pouring sulfuric acid down her throat. We got her torn shirt that was covered with acid burns, and as I held it, I couldn't help thinking that there was a human being in it not long ago. So I can't help wondering how people can do this to other people. I wonder about it every day.

"I got a call from a prosecutor who wanted us to expedite a rape case and I caught myself asking him, 'Is this a normal rape?' Of course it wasn't; no rape is normal. People call us and tell us it's a homicide, it's very important, and we have to tell them, 'Okay, we'll put you over there in the 'expedite' stack with the other five hundred homicide cases we're working.''

"What gets to me is not so much looking at the bullet," Gerald Wilkes of Firearms said, "but that the transmittal letter will have a synopsis of the case. Some of them you just never forget. I worked a Florida case in which two guys killed four people in two different pizza-shop hold-ups. One of these guys eventually confessed. He said that they'd taken three people in the back of the place, raped the woman in front of her husband and then killed her, and then his partner had put the gun up to the guy's head and told him, 'Smile if you see this coming.' Then he shot him in the head. No matter how many homicides you work, you never, ever get insensitive to that."

Linda Harrison of DNA refused to see the motion picture *The Silence of the Lambs,* even though its hero was a female FBI agent. "Once you've worked on a case in which you cut out blood mixed with semen from Pampers that came off a two-month-old baby, you don't want to see that kind of stuff. I do this every day; I don't need to be reminded of it."

This is the world of the crime lab. But, oddly enough, while examiners might get deeply involved in a case, and while the work done in the lab might lead police to a suspect or might enable a prosecutor to get a conviction, quite often examiners never find out how the case was resolved. They don't know if the crime was solved or if a suspect was convicted. Results like that are just not part of the process. Submissions come in, examinations are made, submissions go out. Next case. Unless an agent testifies in a trial, there's rarely any communication from the agency or prosecutor reporting the results of the case.

But even with all that brutality, most of the people working in the FBI's sci-crime lab find it extremely rewarding. "Every day is different," Firearms Unit chief Jack Dillon said. "Every time the phone rings it could be a drop-everything-and-go-for-it case that no one could have anticipated."

Metallurgist Bill Tobin of Elemental Analysis has turned down offers of as much as three times his civil service salary to work in the lab. "Money isn't everything," he said, "and this is just such an exciting and stimulating place to be. Even when I was working in the field, I found that maybe two out of every ten cases would be good ones, the other eight would be dogs. Here, when I watch the television news at night, I see what we're going to be doing in here the next day."

Or, as former Firearms Unit chief Bob Frazier said, "This is the place where you get the case of a lifetime every week."

2

The Little Green Specks of Death:
The Chemistry/Toxicology Unit

Having sniffed the dead man's lips, I detected a slightly sour smell, and I came to the conclusion that he had poison forced upon him.

SHERLOCK HOLMES,
in Sir Arthur Conan Doyle's *A Study in Scarlet*

A baby is dying and no one knows why. A severed head arrives with rotting tissue clinging to it: How did this person die? An airplane carrying sixteen parachutists dives into the ground: Murder, or mechanical failure? The last tears of a murder victim are collected in a vial: Were drugs involved in this killing? Why did two people die minutes after taking a common pain reliever? A small trunk washes up on a deserted beach: Is the caked white residue inside it the remains of a man who disappeared five years earlier? Several hairs are taken from the head of the mayor of Washington, D.C.: Has he been using cocaine?

Deadly things often come in very small packages—sometimes things one five-thousandth the size of the period at the end of this sentence, yet powerful enough to kill within seconds. Things that by virtue of their size and nature are intended to remain secret. Sci-crime chemists are detectives who search for clues that will never be seen, and the FBI's Chemistry/Toxicology Unit is where investigators in search of hard evidence literally analyze the thin air.

Sci-crime chemistry began a thousand years ago, with the search for a reliable means of detecting the presence of

poison in a body. For a time it was believed that the heart of a person who had been poisoned would not burn. Even as late as the beginning of the nineteenth century respected scientists believed that the body of an arsenic victim would not decay. It wasn't until 1840 that American courts even permitted the introduction of scientific testimony, finally deciding, "[The chemist's] opinion is in fact his testimony to a law of nature."

Sci-crime chemistry was very much an embryonic science when the FBI lab was founded 1932. It was six months before the lab even conducted a chemical examination. The Physics and Chemistry Section, as it was then known, did mostly bloodstain and firearms exams. They used rudimentary instruments: simple microscopes and ultraviolet lamps. Small animals were kept in an animal room and used to provide blood samples needed to make sera for testing. It was the most basic chemistry, and only rarely did chemical evidence play a pivotal role in an important investigation. Typical of the kind of examinations done by the Chem Unit was a Camden, New Jersey, case in which a commercial laundry was suspected of defrauding the government by charging the Navy for dry-cleaning blankets while simply tumble-drying them. To prove his case, the lab's first chemist, Dr. William Magee, marked several blankets with invisible chemical "tags" that were sensitive to chemicals used in the dry-cleaning process. When the blankets were returned these tags were still there, proving that the blankets hadn't been dry-cleaned.

During World War II the entire Chemistry Section, basically Dr. Magee, was active in espionage and sabotage cases. When eight Nazi saboteurs were caught through tips provided by an informant, Magee figured out how to materialize invisible writing known to be on their handkerchiefs, writing that provided the names and addresses of other German spies.

Probably the first significant criminal case in which sci-

crime chemists provided vital evidence was the November 1, 1955, bombing of United Airlines Flight 629. Forty-four people died instantly when, for no apparent mechanical reason, a plane leaving Denver's Stapleton Airport exploded eleven minutes into its flight. Although sabotage was suspected, there had never been a confirmed case of sabotage of a civilian aircraft in aviation history, and no one knew how to prove that there had been a bomb aboard that airplane.

Smoke was still wisping out of the engines when Dr. Magee arrived at the crash site. "After examining literally thousands of tiny pieces of wreckage," he remembered, "I found that some of the small pieces had an unusual appearance—they were kind of a blackish-gray color. What I couldn't figure out was why only these pieces. I packed up a box about the size of a small coffee table and shipped them back to the lab. When we analyzed them we discovered that these deposits consisted primarily of sodium carbonate, along with small amounts of nitrate and sulfur.

"We had no idea what the heck they were doing there. Sodium carbonate is normally found in scouring powder. There was no logical reason for it to be on those parts of the airplane. So we sat down and tried to reason it out. We began by asking ourselves what we were looking for. If there had been a bomb on that airplane, what type of explosive might have been used? And what evidence of that explosive might we find? Gradually, things began to make sense. When dynamite explodes the heat of the blast frees sodium atoms. Sodium atoms like to combine with something—something like carbon dioxide, to form sodium carbonate. Once we'd figured it out, it seemed so obvious. We were looking at the residue of a dynamite explosion; we were holding in our hands the proof that there had been a bomb on that plane.

"Today, the first thing investigators search for when an airplane goes down or a bomb goes off is explosive resi-

due. But we were working on the first case of sabotage in modern aviation history. We were the people who discovered it would be there.''

McGee also found traces of manganese dioxide, which could not have come from any parts of the plane. He surmised that it had come from the battery used to detonate the bomb. Tiny pieces of battery wire found in the wreckage were later matched to wire discovered in the home of a suspect named Jack Gilbert Graham. Graham had purchased several large flight-insurance policies for his mother, who had perished in the crash. McGee's work contributed to the arrest and conviction of Graham, who was executed in 1957 in Colorado's gas chamber.

Working in a sci-crime chem lab is rather like searching through a million-piece jigsaw puzzle to find the one piece that doesn't belong. The search may take a lifetime and never be completed; or, with the proper equipment, it can be done in minutes. There are literally ten million organic chemicals, and each of those ten million can be combined with one or more other chemicals to form an infinite number of mixtures. And at some point every case will require that a specimen be analyzed and its composition determined. Once, the lab was limited to those examinations that could be conducted with a microscope. But now, using an array of sophisticated instruments, much of the work is done on samples so small they can't be seen even with the most advanced optical equipment. Generally a hundred-nanogram specimen—a nanogram is one-billionth of a gram—is sufficient for the lab to identify an unknown substance or detect the presence of a specific drug or chemical. In fact, because cocaine has become so ubiquitous in American society, these instruments were finding drug residue on almost all currency submitted to the lab for testing. So the Chem Unit was actually forced to make these instruments *less* sensitive to the presence of cocaine, meaning

more of the drug has to be present to obtain a valid positive result.

The sci-crime community is far too small to support the development of specialized equipment for its unique needs, so almost all of the instruments used in the chem lab have been adapted from other industries. The instrument that revolutionized sci-crime chemistry and toxicology is the mass spectrometer, which was developed for use in the petrochemical and pharmaceutical industries. The mass spec gave the lab the ability to analyze smaller samples than had ever before been possible. Every one of those ten million organic chemicals has a unique structure, meaning that each consists of a different combination of basic elements. By measuring those properties, the mass spec is able to provide a molecular "fingerprint" of an unknown substance, making it possible to identify every chemical present by comparing these results to known "fingerprints."

The thing that sets the FBI's chem lab apart from all others is that the work done there has a direct impact on someone's life or freedom. If the chem lab makes a mistake, people may die. So the only rule about equipment is that examiners use whatever it takes to get the right answer as quickly as possible. In several cases, doing that has meant adapting a tool to a purpose for which it had never been intended.

A new kind of deadly crime, product tampering, dominated the headlines in 1982 when seven people in Chicago died after taking Tylenol tablets that had been laced with cyanide. Throughout the country extortionists began threatening manufacturers, warning them that unless they made substantial payments their products would be poisoned. Most of these threats were never carried out, but in New York City investigators discovered several bottles containing poisoned Tylenol capsules. Merchants immediately took thousands of bottles of Tylenol off their shelves, but it would have taken months to examine every single bottle to

find those that contained poison. A quick, simple, and perfect method had to be devised to check the bottles, and none of the sophisticated instruments in the lab was capable of doing that job.

"We needed a quick way to scan those bottles," said Roger Martz, who joined the Chem Unit in 1974 and became its chief in 1989. "The answer came from basic chemistry. Potassium absorbs X rays, so potassium cyanide, the poison, would show up on an X ray, while acetaminophen, the main ingredient in Tylenol, would not. So I suggested we just use an X-ray machine. We didn't even have an X ray in the Chem Unit, so I dummied up a bottle with cyanide and brought it over to our mail room, where all incoming packages are screened. Sure enough, the cyanide showed up inside the bottle as a big black blob. It was very easy to pick it out.

"The biggest X-ray machines anybody knew about were the screening devices used at airport security checkpoints. Roger Aaron, the unit chief at the time, flew up to New York and set up the screening process at the airport. We were able to examine thousands of bottles in a matter of hours, and found several other bottles that had been poisoned. So we may have saved some lives, but we were never able to find the person who'd done it."

Desperate situations call for unique and creative measures. The Chem Unit faced a somewhat similar problem in 1990, when a young man in Miami collapsed after drinking a bottle of a popular coffee-flavored soft drink named Pony Malta. He was rushed to the hospital, but he lapsed into a coma and never regained consciousness. Tests showed he was suffering from acute cocaine poisoning, and an examination of the residue in the bottle proved the Pony Malta had been laced with cocaine. Apparently drug smugglers had dissolved cocaine and brought it into the country as part of a large shipment of the soft drink. After the shipment had cleared customs they planned to reclaim the bot-

tles and chemically transform the contents back into crystal cocaine. Each bottle had a street value of almost $5,000. But something had gone wrong, and the poisoned bottles of Pony Malta had been mixed in with ordinary bottles and delivered to stores throughout the Miami area.

No one knew how many bottles contained a lethal dose of cocaine or where they were. The problem was how to pick out those bottles from the thousands of bottles in warehouses and on bodega shelves. In this case X rays wouldn't help, because they cannot distinguish between Pony Malta and liquid cocaine.

The unit got help from Dean Fetterolf, a chemist working in the lab's research unit in Quantico, Virginia. Fetterolf suggested they try a device called a dielectrometer, which is used primarily by engineers to locate imperfections in materials or beams inside walls. A dielectrometer works a little like a microwave; it sends out an electronic impulse and records the amount of energy that is absorbed. It doesn't matter how much energy is absorbed; as long as the reading remains constant, the substance it is examining is uniform. But when there's a change in that substance, when the impulse hits a wall beam or a hollow spot in a concrete block, the reading changes. It won't identify what's there, just that the substance has changed. Fetterolf believed that those bottles of Pony Malta laced with cocaine would have a different density than those with plain soft drink. And he was absolutely right. Within days thousands of bottles had been scanned and forty-five poisoned bottles had been found. Once again, lives had been saved. In this case though, the drug smugglers were captured.

As sophisticated as many of the lab's instruments are, they are only as good as the people who use them. Machines can only answer those questions that are asked, and the most important aspect of identifying an unknown substance is posing the right question to the right instrument.

The chem lab staff has grown to match the capabilities of their instruments. Currently there are six agent-examiners and seven chemists. "We don't prize formal education as much as an individual's ability to think creatively," explained Agent-examiner Tom Lynch. "We do things here that nobody has ever tried to do before, and a lot of times we're very successful."

While everyone in the unit is capable of doing traditional sci-crime chemistry, just about everybody has a specialty. Unit chief Roger Martz is the virtuoso of the mass spectrometer, creating new ways of exploiting its capabilities. Bob Forgione decided to become a toxicologist when he realized he couldn't hit a curveball. Tom Lynch has a doctorate in bacteriology and does most of the unit's work with microorganisms and cell cultures. Ron Kelly is an expert on explosive residues. Jordan Burnett specializes in ink analysis. Debbie Wang has become an expert on sugars in all forms. Brian Donnelly and Henry Schlumph are expert toxicologists. And Pete Lewis, who joined the unit in 1959, before any of the fancy machines showed up, works the arson cases.

To each other, they are "Bub." No one remembers where that nickname came from, or even what it means, but if you work in the Chem Unit you're a Bub.

Every case begins with a delivery to Roger Martz from the Evidence Control Center. Depending on the facts of the case, Martz assigns it to the proper person. After that, there is no specific or best way to work. The investigators open the packages and just look at the submissions. They see what there is to see. They look for anything unusual, anything unique. They begin at the very beginning.

They simply look at it; they never touch or taste it. "When I started here in 1972," Bob Forgione remembered, "I didn't even use bulbs to suck up biological fluids. I'd just stick a straw in it and suck it up halfway, then transfer it to different funnels for testing. I tried to be very

careful, but that's the way it was done. There's a word I would use today to describe that method: risky."

There is potential danger in every submission. Just after Tom Lynch joined the unit he received what appeared to be ordinary white powder, from a Florida police force. Vandals had thrown plastic eggs against the wall of a McDonald's, and when a worker began cleaning up the mess he was burned. The police wanted to know what the powder was. "I must have touched it with my hand, then wiped my eye," Lynch said, "because the next thing I knew my skin was stinging, my eyelid was burning, I'm turning beet red, and I can't stop coughing. I ran to the sink and doused my head in cold water. I later found out this powder was solid tear gas. Solid. Ordinarily tear gas is diluted in an aerosol, but this stuff was pure. I'm lucky, it could have been a lot worse."

The Chem Unit staff would prefer not to smell submissions either, but sometimes that's not possible. Body parts are supposed to be shipped to the lab frozen in dry ice, but on occasion they have thawed out before getting there, and the stench of rotting tissue permeates the lab for weeks. Besides, catching the scent of a case can prove to be the beginning of solving it. In arson cases, for example, the smell of fumes is often the first clue to the presence of an accelerant. Certain poisons and pesticides have readily identifiable scents. And there are cases in which the lab is specifically requested to identify an unknown odor.

Weeks before Christmas in 1989, a strong odor was detected coming from Cabbage Patch Kids dolls being sold in California; a local laboratory identified the smelly substance as a potentially very dangerous organic pesticide. Suddenly, terrified parents became convinced that their children were being poisoned by their dolls, hundreds of which were delivered to the Chem/Tox Unit to be examined. The lab overflowed with Cabbage Patch dolls, their insides hanging out, their heads gone, sitting on closet

shelves or hanging upside down. A row of smiling heads lined a long shelf.

It was quickly determined that the odor came from the dolls' stuffing. They had been made in Taiwan, and their manufacturer, rather than using the high-grade filler mandated in the United States, had stuffed them with shredded rags that had obviously been used to clean up grease and oil. The odor came from these rags. But tests proved that they were perfectly safe, and that children couldn't have been poisoned by the defective dolls.

Sometimes just looking at a submission provides a vital clue. One of the most important cases worked in the Chem Unit began in 1986, when a Seattle housewife named Sue Snow woke up one morning with a headache and took two capsules of Extra-Strength Excedrin. Within seconds she was unconscious; within minutes she was dead.

Initially doctors believed Sue Snow had died of natural causes, perhaps a brain aneurysm. But during the autopsy the assistant medical examiner, Janet Miller, detected a faint aroma, a smell that reminded her of bitter almonds. It was the telltale scent of cyanide, a fast-acting poison that kills by locking oxygen out of the blood cells. Detecting this aroma requires a certain genetic sensitivity; Janet Miller was the only person in the room able to smell it. Samples of Sue Snow's tissues were sent to a local toxicologist, who found evidence that she had died of cyanide poisoning.

Detectives searching her home found several more poisoned capsules in the Excedrin bottle. Consumers were immediately warned to stop taking any Excedrin capsules. Four years earlier, when seven people were poisoned in Chicago, people had been told to flush their Tylenol down the drain—and when they did, all the potential evidence went down the drain with it. This time police began collecting Excedrin bottles from a four-state area. Eventually 740,000 capsules were turned in. Using the experience

gained in the New York City case, these capsules were screened at an airport security gate X-ray machine. Two more poisoned bottles were discovered.

While this frantic search was going on, a second victim was found. After Sue Snow's death was reported, an apparently distraught woman named Stella Nickell called police and told them her husband had died a week earlier—just moments after swallowing several Extra-Strength Excedrin capsules. Bruce Nickell's death had been attributed to emphysema, but when authorities tested a sample of his preserved blood serum they found evidence of a massive dose of cyanide. Bruce Nickell had been the killer's first victim.

Two additional bottles containing poisoned capsules were found in Stella Nickell's trailer home. The contents of all five poisoned bottles were examined by a Seattle chemist, who found nothing beyond the cyanide in the capsules, then sent them to Roger Martz in the sci-crime lab.

"We knew the poison was cyanide," Martz remembered, "so our objective was to try to give the agents in the field a clue as to where that poison might have come from, or if they'd developed a suspect, find a way to link it to that suspect."

Other lab units examined the bottles for fingerprints, toolmarks, anything that might provide a lead. They found nothing. Martz began his examination by pouring the contents of each capsule into a beaker, and just looking at it, seeing what he could see. "I immediately noticed several small specks of a green material that didn't seem to belong there," he explained. "I found those specks in all five bottles. Identifying the cyanide was basic chemistry, and there was no way to trace it to a source. But these green specks were unique. I wondered what they were, I wondered what they were doing there, and I wondered what they might tell us about the killer."

Incredibly, the examiner in Seattle who had first looked

at these capsules couldn't possibly have seen the green specks: he was color-blind.

Martz found that 99 percent of the green specks consisted of sodium chloride, common salt. That didn't surprise him; many consumer products use compounds like sodium chloride to add bulk and carry the active ingredient. It was the mysterious 1 percent that intrigued him.

Analyzing that 1 percent on the mass spectrometer, he discovered that it consisted of four relatively common chemicals, but he couldn't figure out what those four chemicals comprised. Even a new computer program that listed the chemical composition of thousands of products failed to identify it. "I couldn't find a single product that consisted of just these four chemicals. But what I did find out was that they were all herbicides. Herbicides in Excedrin?"

While Martz couldn't identify a specific product, with the help of Debbie Wang he learned that two of the chemicals were used almost exclusively in algicides, products that killed algae in fish ponds and aquariums. But what were they doing in a poisoned bottle of Excedrin? For a time he suspected these green specks were the killer's signature. In many cases criminals want to claim credit for their work, so they leave the same sign at each crime they commit.

Meanwhile, Seattle investigators began focusing on Stella Nickell. They discovered that three life insurance policies had been taken out on Bruce Nickell's life the previous year, policies that would pay Stella Nickell $175,000 if her husband died accidentally. Insurance companies consider death by poisoning to be an accident.

Martz finally became convinced that those green specks, whatever they were, came from an aquarium product. So in his free time he began going to pet stores and reading the labels on their fish tank cleaners. Many products contained one or more of the chemicals, but none included all four.

Then, one Saturday afternoon, Martz picked up a package of an expensive fish-tank algicide named Algae Destroyer. "And there were my four chemicals," he said. "I opened up the package, and it was full of green tablets identical in color to my specks. I just stood there staring at those green tablets. I immediately notified our field agents what to look for."

When an agent in Seattle read Martz's report, he remembered something he had seen in Stella Nickell's trailer: a large fish tank. Agents descended on pet stores throughout the Seattle area carrying photographs of several women, one of them Stella Nickell. A clerk in a suburban shop immediately picked out her picture and remembered that he had special-ordered Algae Destroyer for her. And then the clerk remembered something else; in addition to the algicide, he had sold Stella Nickell a mortar and pestle to mash the tablets into tiny green specks.

The evidence against Stella Nickell was adding up. She failed a lie-detector test. Agents in the lab's Identification Section found her fingerprints in several books about poisons she had taken out of a local library. The Document Section found that Bruce Nickell's signature on two of the insurance policies had been forged.

Stella Nickell had murdered her husband by putting cyanide inside Excedrin capsules. But when the coroner mistakenly ruled that he had died of natural causes, depriving her of the accidental-death benefits in his life insurance policies, she had to kill someone else to make it appear that a cold-blooded killer was on the loose. One *was:* Stella Nickell. She had prepared the poisoned capsules in the mortar and pestle she had previously used to pulverize the algicide, unknowingly providing the evidence that linked her to the killings.

Nickell became the first person in American history to be convicted of murder in a product tampering case and is currently serving a ninety-year sentence.

* * *

Poisoning cases are the most dramatic and, in many ways, the most difficult of the crimes worked on by the Chem/Tox Unit. What makes them so difficult is the extraordinarily large number of readily available toxic substances. The first rule of toxicology is that the dose is the poison. A poison is simply anything that's harmful to the biological system. In sufficient amounts, that can include just about anything. Water can be "toxic," for example: people drown. Household painkillers like aspirin are fatal in large doses. But generally when a poison is used for criminal purposes it's disguised in food or drink, and it's usually given in small doses.

Most units in the sci-crime lab deal with the evidence from crimes already committed. The person has been killed or the money has been stolen. But the Chem/Tox Unit gets cases in which people are dying, and the ability to determine what's killing them can make the difference between life and death. Lives really are at stake. In a California case, for example, two infant children of a foster mother had died mysteriously, and the third child was very sick. And no one could figure out why. After extensive testing, the only clue the hospital could find was the extremely elevated sodium content of the baby's urine. A nurse became suspicious when the foster mother insisted on preparing the baby's formula, and she submitted a sample of it to the Chem/Tox Unit.

"We had a baby dying for no apparent reason," Bob Forgione remembered. "I was not sure where to start. Should I look for arsenic? Cyanide? Drugs? Maybe pesticides? All we knew was that too much sodium was coming from somewhere, so I began by trying to figure out where. I took five grams of the formula and added an acid to it to see if it contained any toxic metals. What happened was totally unexpected. It started foaming up all over the place. Well, that told me there was a carbonate in there. I thought,

I know I've got sodium and I know I've got a carbonate; maybe it's something as simple as baking soda, sodium bicarbonate. It's not a drug, it's not a metal or a volatile, it's not cyanide or pesticide, but in sufficient amounts even baking soda would kill a baby.

"I did a dialysis, a separation technique, until I got a crystalline material. I looked at it under an X ray and, as I suspected, it was baking soda. It was simple and clever; the baby would drink it and excrete the carbonate, leaving nothing but an excess of sodium. The police immediately took the child away from the woman—that probably saved the baby's life—and indicted the woman. I believe she was prosecuted and convicted but, you know, sometimes we never find out exactly what happened in these cases."

Poison has long been a choice weapon for killers. It's simple to use, very effective, difficult to detect, and often impossible to trace back to the killer. In France, white arsenic was once so popular among the rich and powerful that it became known as "inheritance powder." Poisons kill in two ways. "Acute" poisons are substances, such as cyanide, that are toxic enough to be deadly in one small dose. "Accumulative" poisons, such as arsenic and thallium, are not fatal in small amounts; but the body is unable to eliminate them, and those small doses eventually add up to a lethal amount.

Normally, the first clues to the presence and the type of poison are the victim's symptoms. For example, stomach cramps and vomiting might indicate the presence of a heavy metal like arsenic. Dizziness and nausea are symptoms of a volatile compound, perhaps carbon monoxide. Someone who is comatose, with no signs of an external injury, might have taken a sedative or depressant. A maniacal state can be caused by iodine or PCP, angel dust. People who kill with poisons are often aware of these telltale symptoms and try to disguise them.

In a classic eighteenth-century New York City murder

case, the killer poisoned his girlfriend with morphine, a narcotic that is easily identified because it causes the pupils of the eyes to contract. He then attempted to hide this symptom by putting drops of atropine in her eyes, a drug that causes the pupils to dilate, or become enlarged. So the easily recognized symptom of murder by morphine was not present, and the attending physician attributed the woman's death to a stroke. But the curiosity of a reporter and the existence of a witness who had seen the killer putting something in the victim's eyes led to an autopsy, which revealed the murder.

Almost a century later in New York the former chairman of a college anthropology department devised a seemingly foolproof plan to get even with a federal judge who had sentenced him to prison years earlier for making drugs in a college laboratory. John Buettner-Janush sent the judge a box of expensive chocolate candies, candies that would kill. He filled several pieces of candy with atropine, which in addition to dilating the pupils will also cause a very rapid heartbeat, and others with pilocarpine, which regulates the heartbeat. If the judge ate both pieces, he would be dying of atropine poisoning, but would have a normal heartbeat, making proper diagnosis very difficult. Buettner-Janush sent the candy to the judge for Valentine's Day; the judge's wife ate a piece filled with atropine and collapsed. Fortunately, hospital technicians noticed that her pupils were dilated and were able to save her life. The box of candy was sent to the Chem/Tox Unit.

Nick Vertullo and Bob Forgione got the case. "I like to feel that if it comes across my bench," Forgione said, "I'll not only detect the poison, but I'll tell you how much is in there and what was the intent. Was it to kill, or make someone sick, or just someone clowning around?

"When I broke open the candies, I saw what looked like a lump of gooey white filling. I wondered, had the poison been added to that gooey white stuff, or was that gooey

white stuff the poison? Sometimes things are so obvious we tend to overlook them." Using an infrared spectrometer, an instrument that measures the ability of a substance to absorb energy as a beam passes through it, then identifies it by comparison to known standards, Forgione discovered he was looking at a large lump of poison.

The Latent Fingerprint Section was able to lift a partial fingerprint from the box, and by comparing it to the prints of felons previously sentenced by the judge, they were able to identify the suspect. In Buettner-Janush's home detectives found several boxes of the expensive chocolates—and equipment for manufacturing his own candy. It turned out to be more than enough evidence to persuade Buettner-Janush to plead guilty to two counts of attempted murder.

Sometimes the key clue is revealed in the letter written by the submitting agency outlining the facts of the case. In a North Carolina case, for example, an emergency room nurse would bet his colleagues on heart attack calls that the victim was not going to survive—and he won too many bets. Part of this nurse's job was preparing the adrenaline solution injected into a heart-attack victim's heart to restart it. A sample of this solution was sent to the Chem/Tox Unit with a letter asking that it be analyzed to see if it was composed of the prescribed mixture. Using liquid chromatography, a technique in which the different chemicals in a compound are separated by being adsorbed in other solutions to which they have a greater affinity, it was shown that there was absolutely no adrenaline in the original solution. It was just plain water. So each time one of the other nurses thought they were giving someone a potentially life-saving injection, they were inadvertently allowing him to die. The suspect was convicted of murder and given the death sentence.

Submissions in cases where poison is suspected come in every conceivable form. When a real estate agent was accused of murdering his elderly clients to gain control of

their property, the unit received a half-eaten jelly doughnut. It turned out to contain a lethal dose of thallium. In a particularly gruesome case, the submission came in labeled "Q1 chainsaw, Q2 victim's head." But the most common submissions are the "biologicals": blood, urine, and, if the victim has died, body parts. A sample might be several hundred grams of brain. A chunk of liver. A slice of lung. The best place to find a poison is in the liver, the so-called garbage pail of the body, but because that organ is available only after a victim has died, tests have been developed to identify poisons in blood samples. A poison can also be detected in urine, but it's difficult to determine the amount of the poison present in the system as a whole.

Although cutting human body parts into thin slices for testing sounds kind of gory, for the Bubs in the Chem/Tox Unit it's just part of the job. "If a person has been murdered," Bob Forgione explained, "then we're his last resource. If we don't find out what happened, the truth is going to be buried with that person." Body parts generally arrive frozen, because they decompose rapidly after death and chemical changes can mask the presence of certain poisons. In a 1975 case, for example, a nurse in a Michigan veterans' hospital was accused of poisoning patients by giving them lethal doses of pancuronium, a muscle relaxant, through their intravenous tubes. Several bodies had to be exhumed. As their coffins were being opened, Forgione remembered, "All the scientific training I had meant nothing, because the first thing I looked to see was if there were fingernail scratches on the top of the coffin."

Forgione and Roger Aaron spent the next six months in the lab trying to isolate pancuronium from the numerous other chemicals present. After many attempts to separate the poison failed, they decided to try thin-layer chromatography. This is a technique based on the principle of migration. As water will move slowly up your pants if you stand still in a puddle, a chemical will move from a beaker up a

plate of metal or glass coated with a solution for which it has an affinity. Each chemical will stop at a certain spot, and by comparing this "band" to known results, the examiner can separate, then identify a chemical. The pancuronium wouldn't migrate. Perhaps it wasn't present. So the technique was reversed. Every other chemical in the beaker was made to migrate, leaving the pancuronium at the bottom. Its presence was readily confirmed by several sophisticated techniques, proving that these patients had been murdered. The nurse was indicted for murder and found guilty, but that conviction was reversed on appeal. These murders remain unsolved.

Some poisons are much easier to find in human remains. The heavy-metal poisons, for example, can be found in bone, hair, even fingernails, hundreds of years after the victim's death. When historians suspected that President Zachary Taylor, who died in 1850, had been murdered with arsenic, his body was exhumed to be examined by a private toxicologist. Reporters asked Roger Martz what the FBI intended to do if these tests indicated that Taylor had been murdered. "Piece of cake," Martz responded. "If tests show he was poisoned, what we'll do is dig up the suspects and give them polygraph tests."

The tests indicated that Taylor had not been poisoned with arsenic.

There is no prescribed testing procedure to follow if the symptoms or clues don't indicate the presence of a specific type of poison. "You start with common sense and intuition," Roger Martz said.

"You start by ruling things out," Brian Donnelly added. If, for example, a body is found in a forest, it doesn't make sense to begin by testing for carbon monoxide.

A complete screen usually begins with a test for common volatile compounds such as alcohol, methanol, chloroform, Freon, and anesthetics—about fifty of which can be found in products from dry-cleaning fluid to airplane glue.

When teenagers die suddenly and seemingly for no reason, volatiles are often the cause. Different volatiles actually become fads as young people discover new and inexpensive ways to get a druglike high. For a while, the volatile of choice was airplane glue. More recently, teenagers were killing themselves by spraying Pam into a plastic bag, then inhaling it.

After volatile compounds, the next chemicals tested for would be easily obtainable poisons, the inorganic ions like cyanide. Then come tests for heavy metals—poisons like arsenic, mercury, lead, copper, and cadmium. No single test or instrument will identify every unknown, so dozens of tests are conducted over periods of time as long as several months.

Assuming there are no volatile or obvious poisons or metals, the next test might be for the presence of carbon monoxide, a common, silent killer. Following that, the lab would test for the whole class of drugs: the opiates, narcotics like heroin, which produce a state of calm; stimulants, like cocaine, which produce a rush of energy; hallucinogens, like LSD and designer drugs; and ordinary household medications.

The list of potential killers grows longer. Not a drug? Then there are the herbicides, pesticides, and rodenticides—weed killers and bug poisons and rat killers. And finally, if every test is negative, if there is absolutely no evidence that a poison is present, a sample is fed to the house mouse. The "mouse spectrometer," kept in a tidy cage near the front door of the lab, is particularly useful in product-tampering cases, where an unusual substance that might not show up in a general screen has been used. Most of the white mice have died peacefully of old age; only once in fifteen years has a mouse died from an undetected poison.

In many tampering cases the extortionist will put a common rodenticide into a package, then reseal it and threaten

the manufacturer. Rodenticides are generally green pellets and are easy to spot, so their purpose in a product is to show the manufacturer he is vulnerable, rather than to hurt anyone. To test for the presence of a rodenticide after it has been ingested, the gastric contents of the victim are ground up, put through a chemical process to isolate and concentrate the active ingredient, then presented to several instruments equipped to recognize them. That's the way it's supposed to happen.

But it didn't. In a bizarre extortion case, an executive at a major commercial food supplier received a letter warning that rat poison would be put in the company's products if they didn't cease using animal fats. To prove he was serious, the letter writer included samples of the poison he intended to use. Debbie Wang had the case. The sample consisted of several green pellets and they appeared to be a rodenticide, but every test proved negative. "I'd tested for every known rodenticide, I'd searched our computer files, but we'd never seen this one before," Wang said. "I didn't want it reported out of the lab as a negative so I decided to feed it to the mouse. I expected the mouse to die, but I knew its death would justify the extensive exams that were required."

Four days after being fed a sample, the mouse did die. Working with the field agent assigned to the case, Wang contacted governmental and private-industry experts on pesticides. Because rodents quickly develop an immunity to most pesticides, new products are continually being developed. An expert suggested one of those new products, Quintox, and the manufacturer supplied a sample. As Wang discovered, the active ingredient in Quintox, the chemical that actually killed the mouse, was vitamin D_3, which produces test results similar to cholesterol. In fact, the D_3 had shown up in tests, but had been ignored because it was not harmful to human beings.

Most of the submissions to the Chem/Tox Unit are iden-

tified rather easily, and sometimes the work becomes routine. But the universe in which this unit explores is ten million organic chemicals large, and occasionally a small package arrives containing something that has never been seen before, something that can kill people. Then the routine is forgotten, and all the sophisticated instruments and the combined years of experience are put to work identifying this "Q," this unknown. The people who work in the lab are chemists, applying the principles of science, but they are also detectives.

Occasionally the Chem/Tox Unit works espionage cases for government agencies. One morning a syringe containing a blue liquid arrived. The accompanying letter asked the same question asked every day: What is this stuff? But what made this stuff different was that it had been used in an assassination attempt.

Whatever the stakes, the procedure is always the same. Start by looking at the sample. See anything unusual? This was a blue liquid. Apply common sense: The case isn't one of a housewife attempting to kill her husband, so the substance is probably more exotic than a rat poison. Use the instruments. Sometimes everything proceeds smoothly, everything works just the way it's supposed to, and the identification is made quickly.

A small amount of the blue liquid was evaporated and left an oily residue. The mass spectrometer identified the residue as a compound called fluoroacetic acid. Fluoroacetic acid, with minor additions, is known by the trade name Compound 1080 and is an extremely toxic substance. This was a highly concentrated poison. The unknown blue liquid had been positively identified in about half an hour.

But most of the time it isn't quite that easy. In 1982, a gravely ill Florida man named John Wesley Gentry was rushed to the hospital. Although Gentry's illness was never identified, he recovered. But several weeks later, he returned with the same symptoms. Trying to find the source

of his illness, the hospital analyzed all the medication he had been taking at home. Among the assortment of pills were some vitamin C tablets that had been given to him by his live-in girlfriend, a woman named Judy Buenoaño. The hospital tests produced an odd result. Whatever these tablets were, they weren't vitamin C. In fact, they weren't any easily identifiable chemical. The tablets were submitted to the lab with a request that they be identified.

Roger Martz began his examination by running the standard screen for all unknowns. The Chem Unit maintains a database of 65,000 mass spectrum "fingerprints." Whatever it was, it wasn't one of those 65,000 common chemicals, yet it was something a woman in Florida could easily obtain. After additional testing, Martz suspected it might be a polymer, a substance made by linking similar molecules. The most common polymer is probably polystyrene, which is used to make everything from coffee cups to insulating packing material. To identify a polymer examiners break it down to individual components; this is a difficult process.

It took Martz a week to identify the substance. It was a polymer, paraformaldehyde, something he had never seen before. The questions then became, Where did it come from? and, more important, Could it be linked to a specific person?

As Martz worked in the lab more facts about the case began to emerge. Somebody certainly wanted Gentry dead. After the poison had failed to kill him, a bomb blew up his car. He'd been seriously injured, but had survived. And Judy Buenoaño, who had given him the paraformaldehyde, had a deadly past. One of her children, a paraplegic, had drowned in a canoeing accident. Both her husband and another boyfriend had died mysteriously. In all three deaths Buenoaño had been the beneficiary of large life insurance policies. And four months before Gentry became ill, Buenoaño had insured his life for $500,000.

Linking the paraformaldehyde to Buenoaño meant finding the source. Florida investigators began by searching her home and sending Martz the twenty-five beauty products they found there. Martz tested every one; none contained the polymer. Then detectives went to the beauty salon where she worked and emptied her shelves. And there they found a bottle clearly labeled "Poison." It contained tablets used to make the disinfectant in which combs and brushes were sanitized. Paraformaldehyde. It had been right there in front of them all the time, clearly marked. Fortunately for Gentry, Buenoaño had been putting the powder in 250-milligram capsules, not a large enough dose to kill anyone. Buenoaño had made a common mistake. She had ignored the very first rule of poison: The dose is the poison.

Although poisons are often used to contaminate consumer goods in product-tampering cases, not all contaminants are poisonous. Everything from ground glass to razor blades has been found in products. In product-tampering cases the first thing the lab has to do is identify the substance found in the product to determine if it's dangerous. If it is, the public must be warned immediately and the product must be removed from supermarket shelves. But if it isn't, law enforcement personnel can quietly follow through on the extortionist's demands and try to break the case.

Because product-tampering cases endanger so many people, when they come into the lab they are given priority attention. There's a lot of pressure on everyone to identify the contaminant as quickly as possible. While one agent-examiner is officially assigned to the case, everybody knows what's going on and contributes to the effort. Several people go to lunch together in the Bureau cafeteria almost every day, and their conversation often focuses on difficult cases. It was over such a lunch one day that a particularly baffling case was solved.

A large supermarket chain in Kansas City had received a neatly typed, well-written letter from an extortionist threatening to inject mercury into produce unless he was paid a substantial amount of money. To prove he was serious, he told the supermarket chain where to find a grapefruit and an orange that he had poisoned with mercury. These fruits were flown to Washington by Kansas City agents and hand-delivered to the Chem/Tox Unit for examination.

The letter stated that mercury had been injected into these fruits. Bob Forgione examined them—mercury can easily be identified with a scanning microscope—and found a hole slightly larger than a pinhead in each one. There were faint marks around these punctures; when he cut open the fruits, he noticed a long red stain inside. Something *had* been injected into them—but, to his surprise, tests showed that it wasn't mercury.

Forgione was perplexed. The extortionist had specifically written that he was using mercury. Everything else in his letter had been precisely as he had stated. So why wasn't the mercury showing up in tests? Forgione explained his problem at lunch. After thinking about it, Henry Schlumpf suggested, ''Maybe he's using the red mercury from a thermometer.''

That didn't seem to make sense. Wherever it came from, the mercury still would have tested positive. Then Debbie Wang corrected Schlumpf. ''They don't use mercury in thermometers anymore,'' she said. ''It's just a red dye in some sort of carrier.''

Forgione returned to the lab and broke open three ordinary thermometers, draining the red liquid indicator out of them. He ran the standard test for a volatile substance, putting the liquid in a closed container and heating it, then analyzing the escaping gases on the gas chromatograph. The red liquid turned out to be a kerosene-based product containing a red dye. Forgione then tested the unknown liquid and got the same result. The extortionist had used

the red liquid from an ordinary household thermometer, mistakenly believing it was potentially deadly mercury.

There was no way to trace that liquid to a suspect, but the knowledge that it was not dangerous gave law enforcement officials time to try to develop a case without worrying that an innocent person might die. In this case that extra time didn't matter; the extortionist was never heard from again.

The Chem Unit works a lot of drug cases. Drugs can be the cause of a crime, and the unit is often asked to determine whether a suspect might have been under the influence of drugs when a crime was committed. Or drugs can be the motive for a crime and may be present on some item connected with the crime. In every case the objective of the Bubs is to determine whether any drugs are present, and if so to identify them.

Usually this is a time-consuming but not particularly difficult task. Finding and identifying a drug, like finding and identifying any other chemical, is a matter of separating it from other chemicals and then presenting it to the right instrument. The best place to find evidence of drug use is in blood or urine, but the presence of a drug can be detected in every tissue in the body. One day, for example, a human skull arrived from Alaska. A farmer's dog had found it in a field and brought it home. It was actually only a partial skull; the jaw and teeth were missing, and it had no hair and almost no skin covering, although there was some frozen tissue clinging to it and a patch of mummified skin around the base. From experience, it was assumed that animals had attacked the body and carried away the pieces. This was all that had been found. Alaska police wanted any information that might help them identify the victim or determine how he or she had died.

There wasn't too much to go on. It was a partial skull with only a bit of tissue. It could have been anyone, it

could have been lying frozen for years. The tissue was thawed, liquefied, and tested. And it contained a substantial amount of cocaine—so much, in fact, that it was probable that this person had died of a cocaine overdose. That turned out to be vitally important information. Police in the area had suspected that a couple rumored to have hosted several large drug parties was involved in the death. At least partly on the basis of the lab report, these people were questioned extensively, and they eventually admitted that the victim had indeed died of a cocaine overdose, and that they had disposed of the body by dumping it in the woods, assuming the animals would find it and devour it.

Sometimes the unit doesn't even need tissue samples. For example, insects feast on dead bodies, leaving only bones. But Brian Donnelly, working with Wayne Lord, an agent and noted entomologist, developed a mass spec method of identifying the drugs that had been in a victim's body by examining the insects that ate it. In a Connecticut case the partially decomposed mummified body of a woman had been found about a year after her death. Using dead maggots, beetle fecal material, and fly pupa cases removed from the site, Donnelly was able to confirm the presence of antidepressants, antihistamines, and cocaine in her body.

In the "Q1 chain saw, Q2 victim's head" case, a woman in Houston, Texas, had been raped and murdered, and her body had been cut up with a chain saw. Decomposing pieces had been found in several locations. Houston police knew the identity of the victim; what they needed was confirmation of an informant's claim that she had taken a large amount of cocaine shortly before her death. They submitted both decaying body organs and vitreous fluid from her eyes to the lab. If a body has been embalmed or exhumed, if it has decomposed, or if it has been burned, sometimes the only viable source for drug testing is this liquid from the eyes. It's always a very small amount, but it doesn't

decompose and the presence of drugs can be detected in it. In the Houston case the lab was able to confirm the presence of a high level of cocaine, allowing police to link the victim to a group of men attending a drug party that had gotten out of hand.

The primary method of detecting drugs in a living person remains urinanalysis, although that test can detect most drug use only within the previous seventy-two hours. But in 1987 Roger Martz got a San Diego case in which a suspect was caught driving across the Mexican border with a substantial amount of cocaine hidden in his trunk. The suspect claimed that he had been asked by a friend to drive the car to San Diego, knew nothing about the cocaine in the trunk, and had never personally used cocaine. The Hairs and Fiber Unit was able to associate several human hairs in the trunk with the suspect. San Diego police wanted Martz to prove, by finding evidence of cocaine in the suspect's hair, that the man was lying about his drug use.

There had been some research done into extracting drugs from human hair, but no one had been able to develop a method of finding cocaine in a single strand. By adapting several different mass spectrometer techniques, Martz was able to identify the presence of cocaine in the suspect's hair. Since hair grows approximately half an inch monthly, he was also able to prove that the suspect had been using cocaine for a long time, thereby destroying his defense.

No one yet knows how long cocaine residue will remain in hair, but using Martz's method the Smithsonian has found cocaine in the hair of a five-thousand-year-old mummy. Certainly the most publicized case in which this method was used was the arrest of Washington, D.C., mayor Marion Barry on drug charges. On tapes made before Barry was arrested, an associate was heard to warn him, ''If you ever get caught, say that you didn't inhale, say that you blew it out. They can't prove otherwise.'' In

fact, urine testing could prove that Barry had used cocaine within the past three days, but it was important to show that he was a habitual drug user, not simply a man who had gotten caught in the wrong place at the wrong time. The only way to prove that was to examine his hair samples.

Within an hour of Barry's arrest, urine and hair samples were delivered to the lab. Tom Lynch and Henry Schlumpf did the actual examinations. "Usually by the time we analyze a submission, the person has been in jail or in the hospital for a few days, and we don't find much," Schlumpf said. "We rarely get clinical samples. So this was the biggest positive we'd seen in a live person. More than one political career hinged on this exam, but as far as the chemistry was concerned, it was done exactly the same way as we would work any other case." The urine sample confirmed that Barry had used cocaine recently—and, perhaps more important, a segmental examination of his hair showed he had been using cocaine regularly as long as the hair on his head had been growing. There was no question of a political setup; Barry was an habitual cocaine user.

The largest number of different drugs the Chem/Tox Unit has thus far identified in one person was fourteen, which included everything from codeine to cocaine. In that case the probable cause of death was ruled a drug overdose. But in many criminal cases, defense lawyers will claim that their client acted under the influence of drugs, and was therefore incapable of understanding what he or she was doing. So in drug cases the Chem/Tox Unit runs a general screen, and reports both the drugs that the suspect tested negative for—the drugs that weren't there—and those that were present. For example, the only drug John Hinckley was taking when he attempted to assassinate President Reagan was Valium. And when Charles Manson's disciple Lynette A. "Squeaky" Fromme tried to shoot President Gerald Ford, the only drug found in her system was an antihistamine, which would not have af-

fected her actions at all. But in the case of one killer, it was the absence of drugs that proved to be most important.

On Memorial Day, 1989, a New Jersey man taking therapeutic drugs prescribed by his psychiatrist went berserk. The night before he had seen the movie *Field of Dreams,* in which the main character believes that a voice is giving him instructions. The New Jersey man heard a voice, too, only it didn't command him to build a baseball field. He believed that God was telling him to prove how much he loved his mother by killing her. And God also told him that if he did this, God would protect him by making him invisible. So he stabbed his mother to death.

The suspect's brother came home and saw what had happened. The killer was shocked by the fact that his brother could see him—he was supposed to be invisible—and stabbed his brother to death. After that he went on a rampage, running through backyards, stabbing his neighbors. When he was captured, he told authorities the entire story. He was sane enough to realize that if he could be seen, perhaps God hadn't really spoken to him, and he was crazy.

Obviously his defense was going to be insanity. He was under psychiatric care and was supposed to be taking tranquilizing drugs. The question of whether he was in fact taking those drugs when he committed the murders became significant. If he had been, it would be difficult for his attorney to plead insanity. In this case it was the absence of drugs that was important. In addition to blood and urine samples, the police even submitted a partially eaten powdered doughnut to the Chem Unit, believing that the white powder on top might be a hallucinogen.

This was a complex drug analysis because therapeutic doses are generally so small they won't show up in standard screens. So the unit had to create new standards; they had to determine the minimum amount of a drug that can be detected in blood. Tests can detect as few as five na-

nograms of a drug per milliliter. In this case a screen sensitive enough to detect one nanogram per milliliter was developed. And found nothing. There were no drugs of any kind in the killer's system when he committed the murders. In this case it was the absence of the drugs that controlled his behavior that made him crazy.

While the bulk of drug tests conducted by the Chem/Tox Unit focus on human drug use, examiners are often asked to try to find drug residue on objects or assist in finding new methods of detecting hidden drugs. For example, drug dealers often keep their records in complex codes, basically long lists of numbers. Sometimes the only way to connect these written records to drug transactions is to actually vacuum the papers and find excessive drug residue on them.

Drug smuggling is probably the most common and profitable of all major crimes, and smugglers have become extremely sophisticated in their methods. Drugs are chemicals and can be treated like any other chemicals. Chemists working for drug dealers—so-called jungle chemists—have succeeded in adding liquefied cocaine to other chemicals to make plastic, then molding it into common items. The cocaine becomes part of the chemical structure of the item. Theoretically, smugglers can mold any item at least partially out of cocaine. For example, plastic plumbing fixtures, identical in appearance to normal fixtures, were found to consist of 20 percent cocaine. It normally costs dealers approximately $5,000 to ship a kilogram, 2.2 pounds, of cocaine into the United States. But dealers were able to ship 350 pounds of plumbing fixtures, which included about seventy kilograms of cocaine, for about $100. Once these fixtures had cleared customs, drug chemists here would have simply reversed the process, liquefying the fixtures to extract the cocaine. Dealers have impregnated large fiberglass bathtubs with cocaine, and in 1991 plastic dog cages were found to have cocaine incorporated into their chemical makeup. Cocaine could just as easily be

part of the chemical makeup of the foam packing chips in a box—or, for that matter, part of the box.

Drug-sniffing dogs can't detect drugs being smuggled this way. Standard chemical tests won't find it. But the Chem/Tox Unit has helped refine a sort of miniature ion spectrometer—an instrument originally developed by the U.S. space program to analyze alien atmospheres—so that it can be used in the field to detect drugs, explosive residue, and even environmental pollution. This instrument, which weighs about seventy pounds and costs about $70,000, vacuums particles off the surface of an object and can determine within four seconds if cocaine is present. It will even find the drugs in dust.

As the capabilities of the Chem/Tox Unit have expanded, so has the variety of cases in which it has been asked for investigative assistance. In a Tennessee case, for example, a paralyzed, elderly woman in a hospital was raped and sodomized by two men visiting a patient in another room. The only evidence to connect anyone to the crime was spittle found on the floor by a nurse. Two suspects were arrested in the hospital parking lot and a pouch of mentholated chewing tobacco was found on one of them. Tom Lynch was able to confirm the presence of mentholated tobacco in the spittle, and while it wasn't possible to connect it directly to the suspect, he was able to state that it was consistent in every way with the tobacco found in the suspect's pocket. It made very strong circumstantial evidence.

In another rape case the victim said that during the struggle the rapist had spilled Coca-Cola on the floor mat of his car. Three months after the crime was committed, the police developed a suspect and submitted a floor mat from his car to the lab to see if it could find any evidence of Coca-Cola on it. Fortunately, the Bubs had been saving soft-drink cans for recycling. By testing the residue in some of the older cans, examiners were able to show that the stain on the mat was consistent with Coca-Cola, provid-

ing important supportive evidence for the victim's testimony.

Several times every year the unit gets cases in which a woman claims that a man gave her an aphrodisiac, then raped her. The submitting agency wants the lab to identify the substance she was given. Whatever it turns out to be, it's never an aphrodisiac. Thus far there is no such thing, although in one case the Chem Unit did identify a very rare chemical, an extract of the blister beetle, which has been used as an aphrodisiac in animals because it irritates the skin on contact. Of course, it's also highly toxic.

There is no such thing as a magic elixir to cure cancer either, although in an age-old scam a self-proclaimed guru was selling his homemade medicine for a thousand dollars a bottle, claiming it contained ground-up diamonds and pearls. How do you prove that something is nothing? By identifying what it is, and showing that it is a common substance with no medicinal powers. Gem experts in the Materials Analysis Unit found neither diamonds nor pearls, but didn't know what the bottles contained. Tests in the Chem Unit identified the "medicine" as a food product consisting of sugar and carbohydrates; this magic elixir was probably apple butter. Very, very expensive apple butter.

And, so far at least, there are no fuel additives that will allow you to drive a hundred miles on a gallon of ordinary gas, although there always seem to be people willing to invest in such a product. To support fraud cases, the Chem Unit has to identify the components of the substance and verify that it will not do what promoters claim.

Although investigation of airplane crashes is the responsibility of the Federal Aviation Administration, on occasion the Chem/Tox Unit will be asked to analyze a substance to help determine the cause of a crash. When an airliner taking off in a snowstorm crashed into Washington's Fourteenth Street Bridge in January 1982, for example, there

was speculation that the crash had been caused by ice on the wings. The Chem/Tox Unit, given a sample of the antifreeze used to de-ice the wings, provided the FAA with its chemical composition. This was simply a matter of determining the percentage of antifreeze in the mixture, important information for the FAA. In 1989 when a Drug Enforcement Agency plane crashed into a mountain in Peru, sabotage was suspected, so Roger Martz joined officials from several federal agencies on a journey to the crash site, a fourteen-thousand-foot-high mountaintop. Generally, sci-crime chemists wouldn't be involved in this type of investigation, but Martz was asked to search for any evidence that the fuel had been contaminated or that the pilots had been drugged. Martz was unable to find anything wrong, and the crash was eventually attributed to pilot error. But the investigation of a crash in Georgia provided very different results.

Sixteen members of a parachuting club were killed when their plane crashed, and after a Georgia laboratory reported finding sugar in the fuel tanks, the FBI was called in. The pilot was believed to have been connected to a drug-smuggling operation, so the possibility of sabotage was very real. Sugar in an engine might cause an in-flight failure by clogging filters and starving the engines of fuel, causing the plane to crash. Tom Lynch, who is a pilot, was sent to Georgia to investigate. "The case agent who drove me to the site told me that his SAC [special agent in charge] wanted to know what had caused the plane to crash by the end of the day," Lynch remembered. "I sort of laughed to myself and told him I really didn't think that was possible."

The fuel ports had been smashed, so Lynch had to cut a hole in the wing tank. Using a pipette—a long glass tube with a rubber bulb on top to create suction—he drew a sample. "As soon as I looked at it, I could see something

was wrong. I saw two distinct layers; one layer appeared to be fuel, but the layer beneath it looked like water.''

Lynch learned that the plane was used almost exclusively to take up parachutists and then land. The pilot usually carried the minimum amount of fuel required by the FAA for this type of flight. Although the plane could carry as much as 360 gallons, he rarely put more than sixty gallons in his tanks. Each time he landed he would replace the fuel he had consumed from fifty-gallon barrels kept at the field. Lynch focused on those fifty-gallon drums. ''I had to use long tubing to get to the bottom of the barrel, and as soon as I started pumping out liquid, I realized I was pumping water. I don't know how many gallon jugs I filled until I finally got to fuel. I didn't know if there was sugar in there or not, but once I saw what was there, I didn't think it really mattered.

''Oil floats on water. So all the fuel was at the top of the barrel. The bottom third of the drum was filled with water. So it was pretty clear in my mind that water was a major factor in this crash. From witnesses I learned that the plane had climbed steeply up to about fifteen hundred feet, and then suddenly nose-dived straight into the ground.''

The drums had been carelessly maintained. Some were incompletely covered or had holes in their lids. Water, Lynch believed, probably rainwater, got into the drums and sank to the bottom. Someone lifting the lid to inspect the contents would have found the drum filled with fuel. But the airplane's tanks were filled from a hand pump that took fuel from the bottom of the barrels. Without anyone realizing it, a substantial amount of water was being pumped into the tanks. The plane had sufficient fuel for takeoff, but eventually its turbines were getting water rather than aviation fuel from the fuel lines, and flamed out. The passengers, the parachutists, were standing in the aisle because they would be jumping within minutes. When the engine stalled and the nose dropped, the parachutists fell forward

toward the cockpit, changing the plane's center of gravity. Even if the pilot had been able to restart his engine, he probably wouldn't have had time to pull the plane out of its fatal dive. The disaster was an accident.

Lynch didn't even need the entire day to tell the agent the cause of the crash.

While most of the other lab units make cases by linking hard evidence found at the crime scene to a specific suspect, the Chem Unit is rarely able to do so. This is because of the unstable nature of chemicals, which change as their environment changes. Although it's almost impossible to trace a drug sample to its source, for example, occasionally the Chem/Tox Unit can prove a small amount came from a large cache by comparing the type and percentage of the other substances mixed with the drug. And on occasion the unit has been able to match substances on a chemical level. In those cases it isn't even important to identify the substance, simply to be able to positively associate a sample that can be linked to a suspect to a sample found at the crime scene. For instance, a poacher in Alaska was shooting legally protected animals from a plane, then landing to retrieve their carcasses. Alaskan police obtained a sample of engine oil the plane left in the snow, and asked the lab to match it to oil obtained from the suspect's plane. In this case it was possible to make a positive match because the oil was unique; it was a home blend, a mixture of a synthetic oil and a natural oil, and was not commercially available in this mix.

Sometimes it's an additive or pollutant that makes it possible to match oil to a specific vehicle. Oils may be pure when they are put into an engine, but they change rapidly. If an engine is dirty there is a buildup of nitrates, or the owner might alter the composition of the oil by mixing it with additives. So it's possible to match two samples of oil from the same engine if the car hasn't been driven too far between the times the samples are obtained. In several rape

cases, for example, the Chem Unit has been able to show that oil found on the street in front of the victim's home came from a specific car. In a hit-and-run case the suspect claimed that his car had been in the shop having the oil changed. On the basis of nitrate accumulation in that oil, Roger Martz was able to prove that it hadn't been changed in at least four thousand miles, thereby destroying the suspect's alibi.

Even under ideal conditions it's difficult to match oil to a source unless it contains something unique. Again in Alaska, thieves were hooking up their own oil tankers to the Alaska pipeline and stealing thousands of gallons of oil. Authorities asked the Chem Unit to add a unique chemical, a "tag," to this oil that could be used to positively identify it. Martz told the agents to add a halogenated compound called chlorobenzene, which is never found in oil and could be identified on the mass spectrometer. Agents dumped several gallons of this chemical into the oil, then waited. Eventually a drop in pressure at a specific point indicated oil was being siphoned from the pipeline, and police arrested a suspect after he had driven away. They took a sample from his truck and sent it to the lab for verification that this was the stolen oil. It seemed like a simple case.

"And that's when I learned that most halogenated compounds can be detected on the mass spectrometer," Martz remembered with a bit of embarrassment, "but not all of them. Not chlorobenzene, for instance. This is what's called a real dilemma. One of the sayings in our unit is that the only exact science is hindsight. So after trying to figure out what to do, we tried to rig up another instrument, an electron capture detector, to identify the chlorobenzene. That piece of equipment wasn't intended to be used that way, but we had no choice. We had to make up a whole new set of standards, then we said a lot of Hail Marys and turned it on. Fortunately, it gave us outstanding results. The

oil in the truck was identical to the oil in the pipeline. There was no question about it: this was the guy.''

The ability to trace a specimen to its source by comparing their chemical components also provided important evidence in a civil rights case in which a police officer was accused of kicking a suspect. Debbie Wang was able to positively identify a smudge found on the victim's clothes as black shoe polish, strongly supporting the victim's statement.

Perhaps the most publicized case in which the Chem/Tox Unit was able to trace a submission to its source was the controversial Tawana Brawley case. In 1987, a black New York State teenager named Tawana Brawley claimed she had been kidnapped and raped by several white police officers. Soon after she was reported missing, she was found by residents of her family's former apartment complex, partially clothed, with feces smeared on her body and racial epithets written on her torso and clothing. The case immediately attracted national attention for its racially sensitive, as well as sensational, nature.

From the beginning of the case Tawana Brawley was protected by advisers, including the Reverend Al Sharpton, who refused to let her testify before a grand jury. Without her cooperation, law enforcement agencies were limited to the physical evidence, and there was very little evidence to support the girl's story. Initially the Chem Unit received a standard "rape kit"—physical evidence taken from the victim's body in the hospital. Nothing in that kit proved sexual intercourse had taken place, although it was certainly possible that the rapists had used condoms. But within a few weeks a substantial amount of additional evidence was submitted to the sci-crime lab. Working with examiners from the Hairs and Fiber Unit, Tom Lynch was able to identify the fecal matter found on Brawley's clothes as coming from a dog. But then he was asked to identify

the substance used to write racial slurs on her body and clothing.

Using infrared spectrophotometry, Lynch was able to identify the substance as charred cotton, which could have come from anywhere. Then, working with Dennis Ward of the Elemental Analysis Unit, he began comparing the particles found on her sweatshirt, the charred cotton, with a variety of items found in the family's former apartment. Eventually the investigators were able to show that these particles came from a cotton washcloth that had been burned. But much more important, identical particles were also found beneath Tawana Brawley's fingernails, as well as inside a pair of gloves found at the scene. Dog fecal matter was found on the outside of those gloves.

Using all that information, Lynch helped piece together a probable scenario. Testifying to the grand jury, he said that the particles from the towel found beneath Tawana Brawley's fingernails indicated that she had written on her own body, then put on the gloves—that was where the particles found inside the glove came from—and spread feces on her clothing. "I can't state positively that it happened this way," Lynch concluded, "but the evidence would be consistent with this."

Only after Lynch's testimony was made public did Reverend Sharpton claim that Tawana Brawley's kidnappers had forced her to write on herself. "When I heard that I knew we'd hit the nail right on the head," Lynch recalled with great pleasure. "I always have doubts, I'm not God, I follow my instincts and I follow science, but I wasn't there so it was impossible for me to know for certain what really happened. But when Sharpton made this statement, I just knew we had it right."

Sometimes the inability to make a positive comparison becomes important evidence. In a Providence, Rhode Island, civil rights case, prison authorities claimed that a man returned to his cell after being fingerprinted, made a noose,

and hanged himself. If that was true, the Chem/Tox Unit should have been able to find some ink residue on the noose. A detailed examination for ink turned out negative. There was no ink on the noose, and that made it extremely unlikely that the prisoner had tied his own noose and committed suicide.

From the early days of the sci-crime lab, when the primary function of the one chemist was to analyze gunpowder residue, the responsibilities of the Chemistry/Toxicology Unit have expanded to include all the natural sciences, including biology and bacteriology. If a case involves something that once lived, it will eventually come to this unit. In the notorious "Sea Will Tell" case made famous by writer and lawyer Vincent Bugliosi, an elderly couple disappeared while sailing the world on their yacht. Eventually a younger couple was found sailing the boat. They were convicted of theft, but for five years there was no trace of the original owners. It was as if the sea had swallowed them up. And then a trunk was found on a deserted beach. Circumstantial evidence connected the older couple to that trunk. Several bones were found nearby, and prosecutors needed proof that the body had been inside that trunk. Hairs and Fibers was able to find several human hairs in the trunk, but there was no way of proving when or how those hairs got there. Then the trunk was sent to the Chem/Tox Unit with a request to find whatever there was to be found.

Roger Martz, pleased that "once in a while I get to use my biology degree," found a small amount of a white residue in the trunk. It was caked into a corner and there wasn't very much of it, but it shouldn't have been there. After running numerous tests, he was finally able to identify it as adipocere, a product formed when fatty tissue decomposes under anaerobic conditions—that is, in a place without oxygen. Under the sea, for example. This finding proved that something that had once been alive had been in

the trunk; the presence of cholesterol proved that it hadn't been sea life, but a human being.

But that wasn't all. Working with experts from the Smithsonian, Martz was able to identify material found on the bottom of the trunk as the shell of a worm that grows only on the underside of a submerged object, a worm that lives six months before shedding its shell. Martz testified in the murder trials of both the young man and woman, explaining to the jury how he had proved that the trunk had been in the ocean for at least six months, and maybe as long as five years, and that it had served as the coffin for a human being. The man was convicted of murdering the older couple. The sea had told its story, but the Chem/Tox Unit had served as its translator.

3

Putting the World Back Together:
The Explosives Unit

Anyone's safety depends principally on the fact that no-body wishes to kill them. . . . We have come to depend on what has been called the good will of civilization.
AGATHA CHRISTIE, *Murder Is Easy*

This is how a bomb works: A power source causes an initiator, which might be heat, shock, or friction, to start a reaction in an explosive substance. With a flash and a bang the explosive substance breaks apart its chemical bonds, releasing gases that take up a much greater space than the original solid or liquid. This detonation begins the instant the circuit between the three components—power source, initiator, and exposive substance—is completed, and takes only a microsecond. All other bomb parts—the casing and timers and relays and switches and shunts—are simply used to control the time and the place of the explosion.

This is how a bomb causes damage: The gases are released as a powerful pressure wave, which rips apart anything that confines it. The positive phase of this wave moves as fast as thirty thousand feet per second until it's equalized with the surrounding pressure. It smashes through anything in its path. This positive phase creates a vacuum, which draws the gases back as a negative phase. (Thus, there might actually be more shattered glass on the same side of a window as the bomb than on the far side.) Many more people are injured by fragments and debris

sion had been caused by a bomb, and then determining the type of explosive used in that bomb.) In addition to the residue, one of these fragments was identified as a portion of a commonly available six-volt battery. Evidence of a power source and an explosive had been found in the wreckage of Flight 629, proving it had been destroyed by a bomb.

Investigators discovered that a man named Jack Gilbert Graham had recently purchased several large travel-insurance policies on the life of his mother, Daisie King, who had died in the crash. During a search of Graham's home a piece of copper wire with yellow insulation was found in the pocket of his work shirt; this was exactly the kind of wire that had been found at the crash site and determined to have been part of the detonator. A store clerk remembered selling dynamite and blasting caps to a customer who looked like Graham. And while Graham denied putting anything in his mother's suitcase, his wife admitted he had put a small gift—supposedly, a set of artist's tools—in the luggage as a surprise. Finally, Graham confessed, telling psychiatrists, "The number of people killed made no difference to me. It could have been a thousand." Although he later recanted this confession, he was found guilty of first-degree murder and died in Colorado's gas chamber.

The world was suddenly and forever a less safe place.

In the 1960s rudimentary bombs were used by segregationists fighting integration in the South. In a particularly heinous crime, six little girls were killed when a black church was bombed in Birmingham, Alabama. It was to investigate these bombings that an explosives unit was created in the Firearms Unit. While the primary job of its members was to develop evidence against bombers, they also actively participated in "substitutions," undercover operations in which dummy materials were substituted for real explosives. "What they'd do," explained Chris Ronay, who served as chief of the Explosives Unit for seven years

beginning in 1987, "was dig up caches of dynamite and take it to a garage somewhere, and Fred Smith, who was the lab's explosives expert, would empty out the real powder and replace it with a mixture of peanut shells and anything else he could find, smooth out the wax cover with an iron, then rebury it and begin surveillance. They made several good cases that way."

The bombs became more sophisticated in the 1970s, but the technique remained the same. Ronay remembered working a covert operation against the terrorist group FALN one cold Chicago night. "We went into one of their safe houses and replaced about two hundred detonators with sugar. Those people never knew we had been there until we testified against them at their trial."

The Explosives Unit became independent in 1972, primarily in response to the growing number of terrorist and antiwar bombings. While on occasion the unit will still perform covert operations, its primary objective is to develop evidence from bombs that can be used to identify and convict the bomb maker. The FBI retains jurisdiction in all cases of terrorism against Americans and when bombs are used against federal employees, on federal property, or in federally insured banks. Members of the unit don't work on bomb detection, they don't disarm bombs, and, except for demonstration purposes, they don't detonate bombs. They rarely see a live bomb at a crime scene, and if they encounter a live bomb they are supposed to contact a police bomb squad to dispose of it. Their job is simply to find the guys who make the bombs.

No university teaches explosives; there are no degrees in this subject. The only way to learn is through experience. Examiners study old cases and learn from the people who investigated them; they go to bomb scenes and blow up things in a controlled area to see what type of explosive causes what kind of damage. "You learn by trial and er-

ror," Ronay said, then added with a smile: "Although hopefully not too much error."

"If you want to know what certain explosive charges will do to an automobile," explained Fred Smith, the unit's first chief, "then you blow up a lot of automobiles."

The Explosives Unit is one of the smallest in the lab, comprising only seven agent-examiners and an equal number of technicians, but in their investigations these "bombers," as members of the unit refer to themselves, often rely on the talents of other lab units, from chemistry to fingerprint identification.

Each investigation begins with the discovery of a bomb. Surprisingly, it doesn't really make too much difference whether the bomb has gone off, although the job gets a lot more complicated after the bomb has blasted itself into pieces. There are basically four paths to follow in a bombing case: Identify each of the components of the bomb and try to associate them with a specific individual or individuals who bought them or made them. Compare the way the bomb is constructed—the bomber's signature—with bombs found in the past that have been linked to known individuals. Identify evidence found with the bomb that is not actually part of it—the van used to transport it, perhaps, or a latent print found on wrapping paper—and trace that to the bomb maker. Or find the motive for the bombing—perhaps revenge or extortion—and use traditional crime-solving methods to develop a suspect and link him to the bomb.

When a bomb is found intact it's simple to prove that it's a bomb: if an object has a power source, an initiator, and an explosive charge, it's a bomb. But after an explosion has occurred examiners often have a very difficult time proving it was caused by a bomb. Explosives explode, sometimes by accident. So the first determination that has to be made after an explosion is whether it was an accident or a crime. In 1947, for example, the French freighter

Grandcamp, which was filled with the fertilizer ammonium nitrate, exploded in the harbor of Texas City, Texas, killing 561 people and injuring another three thousand. An investigation revealed that a fire had started in the cargo hold and the ship's hatches had been shut to deprive it of oxygen. Instead, this trapped the escaping gases, and the pressure continued to build up until the entire ship was turned into a huge bomb and exploded, virtually destroying the entire city. In 1989, as a United Airlines jumbo jet took off from Honolulu, the baggage compartment doors suddenly blew off, leading to speculation that a bomb had been hidden in a suitcase. In fact, the latches had simply failed to secure the door.

It's the firm policy of the FBI not to declare that a bombing has taken place until they can prove it. Tom Thurman, who headed the American team investigating the bombing of Pan Am Flight 103 on December 21, 1988, recalled in his soft Kentucky drawl, ''When we first heard about it we might have believed it was a bomb, but until we had proof we couldn't say it. I remember asking someone from the National Transportation Safety Board, 'Has there ever been an instance where a commercial airliner with a proven track record has essentially disintegrated at cruising altitude for no apparent reason other than a bomb?' I pretty well knew the answer, but I wanted to make sure that everybody understood that before we could say there was a bomb, we had to prove it.

''We spent that first day walking over the hillsides through the mud. At the end of the day we had a meeting. People were reporting in from various sectors what they were doing and what they'd found. As I walked into the operations center someone handed me a piece of broken metal maybe three inches wide and eight or nine inches long, and asked me if it had any meaning. I knew instantly. It had what we call pitting and cratering. These are marks that look like inverted mushrooms and they're made in

metals by superheated gases when an explosion occurs. That's the only time you see them. I took one look at this piece of metal and said, 'Okay, now we know we had a bomb.' "

After a bomb has gone off it's imperative that the bomb scene be preserved. The clues that may eventually lead to the identification of the bomb maker are right there; it's just a matter of picking up all of them. As a British police inspector ordered at Lockerbie, "If it's not a rock and it's not growing, put it in the bag."

Every bomb scene is unique. Debris from Pan Am 103 rained over 845 square miles of Scottish countryside. A French DC-10 exploded above the Sahara Desert in 1989, scattering wreckage over 265 square miles, and every inch had to be searched in heat that reached 142 degrees. In 1976 a car bomb blew up former Chilean diplomat Orlando Letelier right in the heart of downtown Washington, D.C. The World Trade Center was crippled by a bomb that destroyed five levels of the parking garage, knocked out all power to the buildings, and left huge slabs of concrete hanging precariously above tanks filled with potentially explosive Freon.

Somewhere in the Scottish countryside, or in the sweltering Sahara, or in the rubble-filled crater, are the remains of the bomb. There is a common misconception that the bomb destroys itself in the blast. Not true. As much as 95 percent of a bomb will survive detonation, although it will be shattered into thousands of pieces. And finding those pieces is often the key to solving the crime.

The investigation can only be as complete as the crime-scene search. Finding out what type of explosive was used, the size of the bomb, where it was placed, and how it was transported are the first steps toward discovering who made it and who planted it. Everything found at a bomb scene can help answer those questions. How far certain objects are found from the seat of the explosion might help deter-

mine the size of the bomb, and the size of the bomb would limit the means used to transport it to the scene. Everything matters: the sound of the explosion, the color of the flash and smoke, the smell in the air, the direction of the soot on the wall, the type and extent of the structural damage.

"I knew within two hours after entering the World Trade Center what type of bomb we had and how big it was," recalled Dave Williams, who was in charge of the investigation at the scene. "I was able to determine where the seat of the explosion was from the way debris had been thrown, the type of damage done to the concrete and steel, the pitting and cratering, the fact that there were flash burns on one side of a pillar but not on the other. You have to look at everything and put it all together.

"The extent of the damage told me, from experience, that the velocity of the explosion was somewhere between 14,000 to 15,000 feet per second. Different explosives detonate at different speeds. Anything faster or slower would have done a different type of damage. C-4 or TNT would have shattered the steel, for example. So, from the velocity, I knew it pretty much had to be a fertilizer-based product.

"We're pretty familiar with the capabilities of fertilizer-based explosives, so from the extent of the damage I was able to estimate that we had about twelve hundred pounds of explosives. So how do you get a twelve-hundred-pound bomb into that building? It isn't going to fit comfortably inside a car. The height of the garage door limited the size of a truck. So we guessed it had to have been carried in a one-ton van or truck. That gave us a direction: it told us we should be looking for the remains of that type of vehicle in the crater."

Much valuable information can also be learned from the damage done to the bodies of the bomb victims. For example, when a car in which two civil rights workers were riding suddenly exploded on a suburban Maryland street in

the late 1960s, the initial assumption was that they had been murdered. But the passenger's arms had been blown off from just below his elbows and his legs had been shattered, while a wide strip of skin across his groin was almost untouched by the effects of the blast. Those injuries told a story. Imagine yourself sitting in a car and leaning forward from your waist. As you do, a protective area is formed in your midsection. So from this body damage it seemed obvious that the passenger was leaning forward, his arms down in front of him—perhaps trying to pick up the bomb—when it went off. The bomb had to have been in plain sight, so the people in the car knew it was there, which suggested that rather than being victims, in fact they were transporting this bomb.

Almost precisely the same type of body damage made it clear to lab examiners that a bomb had caused the crash of a commuter airplane in North Africa in 1988. Twenty-eight people had been killed when the plane crashed less than three minutes after takeoff. Because several Americans were among the victims, the Federal Aviation Agency and the NTSB had investigated, but neither agency had been able to determine the cause of the crash.

By the time examiners from the Explosives Unit arrived in North Africa, every victim had been identified—except one. One man couldn't be identified and his body had not been claimed. He had made his reservations under a fictitious name. No one had reported a friend or relative missing. And when lab examiners looked at the body the reason for that became frighteningly clear.

The body had been torn apart symmetrically. Both arms were severed inches above the elbow. Both legs were gone from slightly below the pelvis, but the femurs showed pressure coming up from underneath and slightly behind the legs. There was no damage to the chest area and the penis was still there. That was significant. Previous exams done on individuals known to have been bending over bombs as

they detonated had shown that the belly had hung over and protected the penis. So in this case that made it obvious that this unidentified person had been right on top of the bomb.

His head was missing, with the exception of his scalp from the top all the way down the back. Both ears were still there; it was perfectly symmetrical, meaning he was looking directly at the bomb when it went off.

This person has never been identified. But shortly after the lab determined that the crash had been caused by a bomb, a terrorist organization claimed responsibility. While it's not possible to determine if this was a suicide-bombing or an accident, there was no question that the individual was carrying a bomb. And the likelihood exists that this was one of the first suicide-bombings of an airplane in history.

When one of the big guns aboard the battleship U.S.S. *Iowa* exploded while being test-fired in 1989, killing all forty-seven members of its crew, a Navy investigation concluded that a homosexual sailor despondent over the end of a love affair had planted a bomb in the gun, although there was very little substantive evidence to support that conclusion. In fact, the explosion also could have been caused by what is called an overram, in which powder is pushed too far into the breech. If the explosion had been caused by a bomb, the crew would have had no warning; if it had been caused by an overram, they probably would have heard a crackling sound, like hot oil being poured into a frying pan, seconds before the gun blew up, and would have had a chance to react. Indeed, a split second before the blast the turret commander had reported, "We've got a problem here." In the explosion his lower jaw had been completely severed by a swinging chain, indicating his mouth was open, perhaps shouting an order; this meant he was aware of the situation. The body of the sailor who purportedly had planted the bomb was found with his upper torso and

face missing, indicative of the fact that he had been looking directly into the gun barrel, just about the last place he would have been looking if he had known there was a bomb there. Although there was no way of proving conclusively that the blast had been caused by an overram rather than a bomb, the Explosives Unit could not affirm the Navy's conclusion, and after an additional investigation, including work done by the Elemental Analysis unit, the Navy officially withdrew its report and issued an apology to the family of the accused sailor.

At the beginning of a bomb-scene search the entire blast area is divided into numbered grids, and each piece of debris is tagged to indicate exactly where it was found, then either discarded or bagged for further inspection. Large rolling magnets and vacuum cleaners are sometimes used in searches, but inevitably the work comes down to people crawling through the scene and sifting through tons of debris by hand. Three mesh screens of increasing fineness are set down, with the coarsest screen on top, and the debris is shoveled through. Before a bomb-scene search is concluded, every single piece of debris will be looked at to determine if it was part of the bomb or was close to the center of the explosion.

Because any single piece can be the one that leads directly to the bomb maker, no piece can be overlooked. When Orlando Letelier was murdered in downtown Washington, D.C., for example, fire trucks raced to the scene to extinguish his burning car. So, later that night, lab examiners went to the firehouse and inspected the truck tires for debris they might have picked up. Jagged fragments from the car and bits of a tin pin that had been taped to the underside of the car body to hold the bomb in place were found wedged into the treads. Other tiny fragments found at the scene were identified in the lab as being part of a paging-system receiver, meaning the bomb had been detonated by remote control. That directed the investigation

toward bomb makers known to use radio-controlled devices.

Separating the remains of the bomb and pieces that had been close to the bomb from the millions of tiny fragments of metal and plastic and electronic components found when a plane crashes or a car explodes is extremely time-consuming but not, according to Thurman, as difficult as it might seem. "Explosive damage has a very distinct look," he explained. "Bomb fragments will have jagged edges and they might be coated with residue or soot. Depending on the force of the explosion, they'll probably be a little smaller than debris resulting from a crash. If people know what to look for, bomb damage isn't hard to identify."

Without question the largest, the most complex, and probably the most successful bomb-scene search in history was conducted in the area surrounding Lockerbie. The work done on the ground in the months following the explosion of Flight 103 led directly to the identification of the people who put the bomb on that airplane. And the most important piece of evidence turned out to be a tiny fragment of that bomb, about half the size of a thumbnail, that was found among the millions of pieces of wreckage resulting from the crash.

"Paul Schrecker of this unit and I arrived in Lockerbie thirty-six hours after the plane hit the ground," Thurman remembered. "Everybody in this business has his own way of starting an investigation. I like to walk through the scene, just looking, trying to get a sense of what happened. It looked like a war zone. There were still a lot of bodies in the fields, some of them still strapped in their seats. The plane had blown up at thirty-one thousand feet and we had crosswinds of a hundred and thirty miles per hour up there spreading wreckage over eight hundred and forty-five square miles. I've been at a lot of bombing scenes. One of the most important things you have to do is maintain com-

plete professionalism; you don't want to focus on the human tragedy. But this—four days before Christmas, these people just trying to get home—it was impossible not to be affected by it.''

That piece of metal, found the first day, turned out to be half of the skid rail of the luggage container in which the bomb had been planted. It was taken to a lab outside London, where a chemist found unconsumed residues which he identified as the explosives PETN and RDX. The only explosive in the world known to contain a combination of PETN and RDX is called Semtex. In the past Semtex has been used mostly by terrorists, so this led Thurman to believe that the bombing was a terrorist act rather than murder for revenge or personal gain. Investigators couldn't eliminate that possibility entirely, but when they found the Semtex they began concentrating on terrorists.

''The search continued Christmas morning,'' Thurman remembered. ''It was very foggy and as we walked through the fields we could barely see ten feet in front of us. But incredibly, one of the guys found the other piece of the skid rail that had been ripped apart by the bomb. The odds against us finding those two pieces so fast can't be calculated. It can't happen. What was so important about it was that it told us that the bomb had been in the baggage area rather than in the passenger cabin. The next thing we wanted to find out was exactly which luggage container it had been in. Knowing that might tell us where it had been put aboard the airplane.

''Almost immediately we started putting the airplane back together. In a hangar at Farnborough Royal Air Force Base south of London, a wire frame had been set up, and as each piece arrived from Lockerbie it was hung where it belonged. And gradually the plane came together. As more and more pieces were hung, we started seeing some abnormal bending and crunching of the metal around the baggage area. Then, about seven hundred inches back on the

left side of the aircraft, we could see soot and residue, and finally there was a big hole.

"From Pan Am's cargo manifest we learned that Container AVE4041PA had been right where the hole was. At the Longtown Army Depot in northern England the baggage containers were reconstructed. The sides of these containers had identification numbers stenciled on them, so it was easy to identify AVE4041PA. Its sides were badly fragmented. All the bases were recovered, and they were all ripped and torn. Like the others, the base of AVE4041PA had a hole in it, but what was different about it was that the sides of this hole were bent down at almost a ninety-degree arc. So within a few weeks we knew what type of explosive had been used, the container in which it had been planted, and where it was on the airplane."

While investigators were reassembling the baggage containers, they found a small piece of plastic circuit board that had been damaged by explosive forces rather than in the crash. Eventually they learned it had come from a radio that had been made for European frequencies. "That didn't surprise us," Thurman continued. "We'd been expecting to find it. Several weeks before the bombing, the West Germans had raided an apartment being used by a terrorist organization known as the PFLP-GC, the Popular Front for the Liberation of Palestine-General Command, and arrested thirteen people. In the trunk of the leader's car they found a quantity of Semtex and a Toshiba radio equipped with an altimeter fuse—and the only place an altimeter fuse is any good is on an airplane. When the plane reaches a certain altitude the bomb is detonated. Information gathered from members of this terrorist cell indicated that several other bombs had been made—and no one knew where they were. When this plane blew up it was natural to assume that one of these bombs had been used. So almost all of our attention was focused on the PFLP-GC."

The bomb that had been found in the trunk had been

built inside a Toshiba radio. Investigators took the piece of circuit board recovered at the crash site to Toshiba and the company confirmed that it had come from one of their radios, but not the same model as had been used in the other four bombs. "That surprised us," Thurman explained. "The PFLP-GC had used a large radio with one speaker; this fragment had come from a cassette radio that was long and narrow. It was completely different. But that still didn't stop us from believing that the PFLP-GC might be involved in this. It just seemed like too much of a coincidence.

"We knew the size of the radio and, from suitcase fragments found in the wreckage, we knew exactly what type of suitcase it had been put in. What we did then was try to recreate the damage done to the container by the bomb. That would tell us exactly how much explosive was used and specifically where the bomb had been in the container. Under the same conditions explosives will act pretty much the same way every time; they'll cause the same damage. In this case the size of the bomb was limited by the size of the radio. So we got several baggage containers from Pan Am, suitcases—identical to the one in which the bomb had been carried—from Samsonite, and radios from Toshiba that we packed with Semtex. We filled these containers with luggage that we got from Pan Am and other airlines, bags that were lost or never claimed. If you've ever lost a piece of luggage on an airplane, there's a chance either we've blown it up or somebody else has. This gives us a random collection of baggage that's as close as we can come to what probably was in the actual container. Then we blew them up, two at a time.

"We were trying to come as close as possible to duplicating the damage to the actual container as well as the one next to it. That means breaking the lower skid rail in the same place, creating holes in the sides about the same size, and inflicting comparable damage to the neighboring con-

tainer. To do that we bracket the explosions; it's just like targeting a mortar. We try one thing and if we get too much damage or too little, we add or subtract until we arrive at exactly what happened. It took us fewer than ten tests to reach the point at which we were satisfied we'd come as close as possible. And we felt confident that we were able to determine within two or three inches precisely where the bomb was located in that container. Knowing exactly where it was on the plane made us believe that the bomb had originally been aboard Air Malta Flight KM-190, which had connected with Pan Am 103 in Frankfurt, Germany.''

At that point the forensic work was being done in England. After several months of work investigators felt they knew the size of the bomb, how it had gotten on the plane, and where it had been located. Then things slowed down: there wasn't too much else to be done. But in Scotland, examiners continued to go over every item found at the bomb scene.

Early in 1990, more than a year after the crash, an English detective examining the clothing that had been in the suitcase with the bomb found a tiny piece of green circuit board, maybe half the size of a thumbnail, embedded in a shirt. In an explosion fragments travel very fast and get very hot. When they hit a fabric such as polyester, the fabric will melt right around it and form sort of a protective cocoon. Investigators in England compared the fragment to the Toshiba radio and realized that it did not come from there. At that point, they determined that this piece had probably come from the timing mechanism used to detonate the bomb.

''From the millions and millions of pieces into which that plane had been shattered we finally had a piece of the bomb,'' Thurman remembered with satisfaction. ''It was the only piece of the bomb we ever recovered. Investigators in Europe tried hard to figure out where this circuit board

had come from but couldn't make a positive identification. So they sent us a photograph of it. It was made of fiberglass, and a circuit pattern was printed on it. The first thing I noticed when I looked at it was that it had an unusual curved notch in it. I knew from experience that a lot of travel alarm clocks have a similar notch, which allows some component to fit in snugly.

"I'd investigated several cases in which bombs had been triggered by alarm clocks, and to me, this looked like it might have come from that type of timer. I asked an agent on Malta to buy one copy of every travel alarm clock he could find and send them to me. I got about twenty clocks, plus some other hard devices, but none of them matched up. Truthfully, we were at a standstill.

"We asked other resources in the Washington area knowledgeable in bombing investigations to try to identify that circuit board. Someone I knew at one of these resources told me that the construction reminded him of the timers used in two bombs recovered in the African nation of Togo in 1986 after a failed coup attempt. 'You have them here?' I asked. He went into their files to check and returned a few minutes later carrying two bombs. When we opened up the back of one of the timers, the first thing we saw was a green circuit board. We checked the circuit patterns and they matched pretty closely. I was trying very hard not to get too excited. 'You got a microscope and a screwdriver?' I asked.

"We took the timer apart and examined it under a microscope. Bingo! Professionally, this is the greatest feeling I've ever had. Finally, finally, we had something substantial that could lead us to the bomb maker. I immediately called the case agent, Ed Marshaman. 'Ed,' I told him, trying to be as calm as possible, 'you're not going to believe this, but we've identified the timer. I'm holding an identical timer in my hands right now.'

"We'd found the needle in an 845-square-mile haystack.

Now we had to exploit it. I took the timers back to our lab to see if we could identify the maker, and under very high magnification, on a second circuit board I found some printing that had been scratched out. Jerry Richards, in our Special Photography Unit, was able to bring it up a little with infrared photography. We could read the letter 'M,' then either a '5' or a 'B.' I thought it might be 'M580,' which is a type of circuit board. But when we checked with the manufacturer in Japan, we were told it wasn't their product. Eventually we learned about a Swiss company, Meister et Bollier, known as MEBO AG, that makes very high-quality timers for many different and legitimate purposes.

"MEBO's managing director positively identified that piece of circuit board from the photograph. Between 1985 and 1986, he told us, MEBO had delivered twenty of these timers to a Libyan official." Then in December 1993, he changed his story, claiming that he had been mistaken when he told investigators that these timers had been delivered only to Libya. In addition to the timers supplied to Libya, he said, several more were sold to East Germany. The Stasi, East Germany's secret police, were known to have extensive contacts with Syria-based Palestinian terrorists. This led to speculation that the United States ignored possible Syrian involvement in the bombing to secure that country's cooperation in Operation Desert Storm and in the release of hostages being held in Lebanon.

But once the initial connection was made between the timers and Libya, substantial additional evidence was developed that further implicated Libyan intelligence agents. "Some of the items of clothing recovered from the Samsonite suitcase were traced back to a clothing store in Sliema, Malta, named Mary's House," Thurman continued. "Mary's House was located just a few feet down the block from the Libyan embassy on Malta, and the owner identified photographs of a known Libyan intelligence

agent named Abdel Basset Ali Al-Magrahi as the person who'd bought the clothing found in the suitcase. He remembered one pair of pants in particular, he said, because they were so ugly. He remembered Abdel Basset so well because he'd bought a lot of unrelated clothing. He didn't even care what size they were. Obviously he wanted to make sure the suitcase looked legitimate in case it was opened up and inspected."

Agents on Malta learned that Abdel Basset had arrived on the island on December 20, the day before the bombing. He was met there by a second Libyan intelligence agent, Lamen Khalifa Fhimah, who had been the station manager on Malta for Libyan Arab Airlines. That position gave him access to the airline baggage system, allowing him to bypass normal security checks. Investigators eventually obtained Fhimah's diary, in which he had written, "Abdel Basset is coming from Zurich. . . . Take tags from Air Malta." In retrospect, the meaning of that reminder seemed ominously clear: the bomb would be put aboard an Air Malta flight that connected to Pan Am 103.

Basset and Fhimah were indicted in November 1991. Even in the face of worldwide economic sanctions against his country, Libyan ruler Mu'ammar Gadhafi has refused numerous requests from Western nations that he allow these men to be extradited for trial. "I don't think anyone will really be satisfied until they've been tried," Thurman concluded, "but we feel very comfortable with our conclusions. This was entirely a forensically driven investigation, made possible by the fact that two pieces of plastic, neither of them longer than two inches, were found among literally millions of pieces of debris in the largest crime-scene search ever conducted. That eventually led us to the clothing, which was key to ID'ing the suspect."

Being able to specifically identify a component of a bomb allows investigators to link it to other bombs, often

y unrelated cases—an important step in tracking the bomb maker. To assist in this identification the Explosives Unit maintains an extensive Explosives Reference Collection, perhaps the most complete collection in existence of bits and pieces that might be used in an explosive device.

When the unit was established in 1972, the entire collection consisted of one four-drawer file cabinet and about twenty items found on German saboteurs who landed on Long Island during World War II. It has since expanded to fill dozens of large cabinets and includes two computer databases. The physical collection consists of samples of any type of device that might be used in a bomb: common and exotic batteries from around the world; detonators and detonating cords; inert fireworks and road flares and dynamite wrappers; all types of blasting accessories; shunts and plugs and relays and delays; timers and locks; wires and tapes; road flares, which are often used to simulate sticks of dynamite in hoax bombs; radio-control devices ranging from model-airplane controllers to garage-door openers, which are commonly used to trigger remote-controlled explosives; and a long list of items carried by Radio Shack, which is known in the explosives community as the Bomber's Store because just about everything needed to make a bomb, besides the explosive, can be bought there. The oldest item in this collection is a blasting cap dating back to 1922.

Other file cabinets overflow with catalogues and manuals that allow investigators to determine exactly which company made the particular quarter-inch pipe used in a pipe bomb or where a certain part recovered from a car bombing belongs on a 1991 Chevy van. In addition to these hard files, in 1978 the unit initiated a computerized Bomb Reference File, which enables investigators to link bomb parts, bomb-design techinques, bombers' political affiliations, and the geographic locations of different cases. If, for ex-

ample, a pipe bomb filled with Red Dot smokeless powder, detonated by an alarm clock and bearing a distinctive diamond-shaped toolmark, goes off against the side of a foreign airline office in Miami, these files can be searched for any other cases in which bombs with similar characteristics have been found.

Old bombs don't just blow away. Inert bombs, bombs that have been rendered safe, hoax bombs, and the recovered parts of detonated bombs are regularly submitted to the lab for examination. When that inspection is concluded the bomb is either added to the reference collection or returned to the submitting agency. Incredibly, even with all the safeguards built into the system, on occasion live bombs have inadvertently been sent to the lab. When a car was blown up in a southern state in 1987, for example, local police found several items at the scene that apparently had been dropped by the bomber in his haste to get away. Among those items was an ordinary flashlight. Because latent fingerprints are often found on batteries, police sent the flashlight to the lab, where Tom Thurman examined it. "When I looked at it," Thurman remembered with a trace of an embarrassed smile, "I found that the bottom end was sealed, so I tried to take off the top part, where the bulb is, to get to the batteries. It wouldn't move, and I assumed that the batteries had corroded and frozen up the parts. That happens. So I got out a hacksaw, put the flashlight in a vice and cut off the end. I was careful not to cut near the batteries because if there were any latent prints, I didn't want to ruin them.

"Thank goodness for that. When the end fell off, powder came pouring out. I knew what that meant as soon as I saw it—this was a live bomb. 'Oh boy,' I thought, 'oh boy.' Then I took a deep breath. Actually, I took several deep breaths. The flashlight contained two batteries and a pill container filled with smokeless powder. If someone had turned it on, the current would have caused it to deto-

nate. But the bomb maker had used too much epoxy. He'd glued the switch closed. Of course, the bomb maker couldn't try it after he'd assembled it, so he never realized it wouldn't work.

"We found out later that the bomb maker had been abusing his wife and was trying to kill the doctor who'd advised her to leave him. It was the doctor's car he'd blown up. But he not only wanted to kill the doctor, he wanted to hurt anybody else who came along, so he built two bombs. We got the second one. I don't believe it would've killed me if it had gone off, but it would've taken off my hands or blinded me. We were very lucky on that one, very lucky."

Only once has a member of the unit been injured while examining a bomb. Dave Williams had his finger cut open when the fuse of an antique hand grenade that had been used in an Akron, Ohio, bank robbery turned out to be live. "Basically," Williams remembered, "the way a hand grenade works is that the striker hits the primer, which shoots a flame into the detonator, causing the grenade to blow up. When I X-rayed this device, I saw that the detonator had been removed, so the worst thing the grenade was capable of doing was shooting a flame out the end. I didn't even think that could happen. The grenade had been used as evidence at the robber's trial, and had been handled by a lot of people before we got it in here. A bomb technician in Ohio had inserted a paper clip as an added safety precaution.

"Just to be extra safe, though, I examined it in a stainless steel tank. I was cocking the striker back to put in a stronger safety clip when it slipped. The striker went through the paperclip, hit the primer, which flamed and for some reason the entire cowling blew apart. I knew immediately my hand was gone. I can't describe how good I felt when I pulled my hand out of the tank and saw that it was just laid open. I was real lucky. Without that tank I cer-

tainly would've been blinded, and I might have been killed.''

Every bomb is designed to fulfill the specific objective of the bomb maker, and that may require the inclusion of timers and primers and safety fuses and an assortment of other devices. That's what makes bombs different. And every bomb, every single bomb, has to be put inside some sort of container or carrier so it can be delivered to the target. In cartoons bombs usually say ''Bomb'' on the side. In real life, for obvious reasons, they're always packaged and transported in something that will disguise their purpose. In many cases the bomb maker has been identified through clues developed from these materials rather than from the bombs themselves. That is precisely what happened when terrorists bombed the World Trade Center in New York City.

Dave Williams was planning to spend the afternoon of February 26, 1993, playing golf when his pager went off. There had been a large explosion in the parking garage beneath the World Trade Center. While authorities there believed a transformer had blown up, unit chief Chris Ronay wanted him to go to New York, just in case. Williams had joined the Explosives Unit in 1978 as a technician, with a degree in zoology, and after becoming a special agent in 1982 had spent almost five years working in the field before returning to the lab. Although he had a lot less than the average twenty years' experience held by other examiners in the unit, he had been around long enough to know from initial damage reports that this didn't sound like a transformer explosion.

The bomb had gone off just after noon on Friday. Williams walked into the crater for the first time Saturday morning. ''It was surreal,'' he recalled. ''It was like walking into a bizarre cave. The explosion had ripped through five levels of the parking garage. Slabs of concrete as large

as basketball courts, eighteen inches thick, were just hanging in midair, and they'd suddenly break loose and fall several stories and the whole building would begin to shake. Steel beams were broken and twisted. There had been sixteen hundred cars in the garage when the bomb went off, and their alarm systems had been activated. Wherever you looked headlights were flashing and lights were blinking and all you could hear were sirens and bells and whistles. Their electrical systems were sparking and starting pockets of fire, there was smoke everywhere, and some of the bravest people I've ever seen were risking their own lives to search through the rubble for victims. In two seconds one of the most modern buildings in the world had become a dark, dangerous cavern.

"The building was still moving. We put a spacer in a half-inch crack and walked a hundred feet, and by the time we got back the spacer was gone and the crack was six inches wide.

"I knew we had a bomb the moment I walked in. When I came down the ramp, I saw big pieces of debris that had been thrown more than seven hundred feet from the seat of the blast, and there just wasn't enough natural gas or methane in there to generate that kind of force. In the unit we have a policy of not attributing an explosion to a bomb until we have physical evidence of that bomb, but . . . When I was asked about it by [New York State] Governor [Mario] Cuomo I told him, 'If it looks like a duck and walks like a duck, it's a duck.' We found out soon enough that this was the largest improvised explosive device—meaning somebody made it, as opposed to a military bomb—that had ever functioned in the United States."

Within hours of the explosion, an extremely reliable informant in New York identified specific Serbian nationals as the bombers. On the basis of that information, the Bureau obtained court permission to set up extensive surveillance of these people. As it turned out, the informant was

wrong; the Serbs had nothing to do with the ...
They were actually diamond thieves, and the eviden...
veloped in the bombing investigation enabled the Bureau to
bust a major diamond-laundering operation.

"Although every bomb scene is different and every
bombing is unique," Williams continued, "we try to follow some general guidelines. The first thing we do is get
organized, get set up for the long haul. At this point there
was still a tremendous amount of confusion. Headquarters
in Washington thought New York had put me in charge of
the bomb scene, while New York thought Washington had
put me in charge. In fact, when it came right down to it, in
the middle of all the confusion I stood up on a chair and
shouted, 'Listen up everybody. My name is Dave Williams
and I'm in charge here. From this point on the FBI laboratory is coordinating this crime scene investigation. . . .'
Everybody went to work and we never had another problem.

"People have asked me how I felt. Incredibly excited,
obviously. And nervous. But I couldn't let anyone know I
had some doubts. I'd been taught that if I looked or acted
overwhelmed people would question my capabilities. So I
maintained my composure.

"The first thing I needed to know was when I could get
people in there to try to find the bomb, so I had the structural engineers do a damage assessment. The World Trade
Center was not in imminent danger of collapsing from the
bomb damage, but it was endangered for other reasons.
The twin towers and the twenty-two-story Vista Hotel rest
on twenty-four-inch steel columns spaced about twenty-
five feet apart. These columns were held in place by the
one-foot-thick reinforced-concrete floors on each of the
five levels of the garage. Well, those concrete floors
weren't there anymore. Now we had a one-hundred-fifty-
foot-wide, seventy-foot-deep crater cutting through five
stories of the building. And just to complicate matters, we

had a snowstorm with high-velocity winds. Those columns were swaying back and forth freely. They were dancing, and their lateral movement was seriously weakening the massive concrete foundation, the wall that kept the groundwater from the nearby Hudson River out of the basement. By Tuesday morning that foundation was close to failing, and if it had we would have had the Hudson River in the basement. In my opinion, if that had happened Tower One would have been on the ground by Wednesday. The structural people prevented that from happening by installing wind-shear braces on the columns to hold them in place. It took about a day and a half before it was even relatively safe to get in there and start looking to see what we had.

"We began by looking for residues that would enable us to determine what type of explosive was used. We had people hanging from cranes taking swabbings off the walls, for example, because this can be very important. If we were looking at C4, a plastic explosive, for example, someone would have had to obtain a tremendous quantity of it to cause this amount of damage so we'd look for thefts of government supplies.

"The problem was that we didn't find any residues. What we did find was an unusually high percentage of nitric acid and urea. Eventually we found out that the explosive was a mixture called urea nitrate, a homemade explosive. In more than seventy thousand bombings or attempted bombings worldwide since 1971, the only other time we'd seen it used was in Rockville, Maryland, in 1988. Four college students were making a pipe bomb and it had exploded, killing all of them. What made it difficult is that the explosion breaks down urea nitrate into urea and nitric acid, both of which are very common in nature and could have come from anywhere. We didn't have any means of proving it had been used as the explosive.

"Looking at the way the damage was spread out, the force hadn't been directed right or left or up or down. That

meant the explosive was probably just laid in some large container. When you have a homemade explosion like that and it's got some fluid on it, it's pretty sloppy, so we assumed it had been in a cardboard or wooden box or in some type of trash can. In fact, several trash cans would have been needed to carry that quantity of explosive.

"So now we were looking for a vehicle large enough to hold several trash cans. An attorney asked me how we could prove the bomb had been inside a specific vehicle. I told him that if you blow up a balloon until it bursts, the spit is going to be found on the inside. It's that simple."

Identifying the vehicle in which the explosive device has been carried had provided significant clues in many previous car bombings. When terrorists destroyed the Marine Corps barracks in Beirut, Lebanon, in 1983, killing 241 Marines and fourteen civilians, investigators traced the truck that had carried the bomb back to a small faction of Shiite Muslims.

"We were especially worried about pockets of gas those first few days," Williams continued, "so we had strict orders that everyone working in the crater must maintain visual contact with other people at all times. That way if somebody got into trouble we could get help to them. Early Monday morning, while chemists were taking swabbings to try to identify explosive residue, Joe Hanlin of the Bureau of Alcohol, Tobacco and Firearms, and Don Sadowy of the NYPD bomb squad found a large piece of a vehicle that either had been carrying the bomb or was very close to the blast. That was obvious from the particular type of damage. It was a big piece of the rear frame rail that probably weighed close to three hundred pounds. They put it on a gurney and carried it out. I was furious. When I saw them bringing it out, I started chewing their tail for leaving the chemists in the crater.

"It was the first piece that got us in contact with the bomb. I wasn't happy about the way they'd brought it out,

but just by looking at it you could tell it had been very close to the explosion and was going to be very valuable to us. Finding that piece so quickly was the kind of luck that comes with experience, but without that kind of luck you're going nowhere."

Every vehicle has a VIN, a vehicle identification number, which the manufacturer stamps into the metal at the plant. The VIN numerically describes that particular vehicle. It's the vehicle's birth certificate. It's always in plain sight on the dashboard, but every vehicle also has a confidential VIN, or C-VIN. It's the same number, but it's stamped in three other places; for security purposes those places differ from vehicle to vehicle. The reason is that if you steal a car, you'd have to dismantle it to find those numbers. And just by luck, the piece that was carried out of the crater had a clearly visible C-VIN. An NYPD detective cleaned off the soot with a toothbrush and added some fingerprint powder, and the number came right up.

That number was immediately put into the National Criminal Intelligence Center computer—NCIC is the national clearinghouse for criminal information—and it popped right up. It was identified as a Ford Econoline van owned by the Ryder Rental Agency. It had been rented in Jersey City by a man named Mohammed Salameh and had been reported stolen the day before the bombing.

"I don't think anybody was surprised to discover that the van had been stolen," Williams explained, "but what did surprise us was the name of the person who'd rented it. Mohammed Salameh was known to the New York office of the FBI. He was someone they'd been interested in for a long time. So when his name came up on the computer, there was instant recognition. This wasn't a coincidence.

"Salameh had contacted Ryder to get his four-hundred-dollar deposit back. People have wondered why he'd risk coming back for only four hundred dollars. My personal opinion is that these people intended to knock down the

tower. And, not knowing any better, they believed the van would be totally destroyed in the explosion. They certainly didn't know we could identify it. So we had agents waiting for Salameh when he showed up at the Ryder office. At first we were going to follow him, hoping he might contact the people he was working with, but reporters got wind of this and descended on the scene. Fearing that all this activity might scare Salameh away, the decision was made to grab him while we had the chance. I was conducting our nightly meeting at the bomb scene when I got a phone call and was told that an arrest had been made. I guess I was stunned. It was a tremendous feeling—but now we had to prove that he'd done it.''

The most difficult aspect of any investigation is identifying a suspect. Once Salameh was arrested, the Bureau began applying all the other techniques used to connect an individual to a crime. Because it was William's responsibility to coordinate all evidence for the lab, he stayed involved throughout the entire investigation.

Salameh's personal records, phone bills and things like that, led agents to Nidal Ayyad and Mahmud Abouhalima, who'd helped him buy the chemicals and make the bomb. When the details of the arrest were made public, the owner of a Jersey City storage facility contacted the Newark FBI office and said that the day before the bombing he'd seen four men loading a Ryder van. He'd checked their storage space and discovered a whole lot of chemicals. At the site investigators found about three hundred pounds of urea, 250 pounds of sulfuric acid, about a dozen bottles of nitric acid, two fifty-foot lengths of hobby fuse, a pump, a light blue Rubbermaid thirty-two-gallon trash can, and six two-quart bottles of a substance that looked a little like onion soup, but turned out to be homemade nitroglycerin. Sitting in that storage area was everything needed to make another three-hundred-plus-pound bomb.

''What was incredible is that homemade nitroglycerin

becomes unstable under seventy degrees Fahrenheit,'' Williams explained, ''and this stuff had been stored in an unheated area all winter. Let's say that when we moved it out of there our pucker factor went way up.

''The hobby fuse told us we were looking at a nonelectric burning-type detonating system, meaning they just lit it and got out of there. I'd estimate it had been about a twenty-minute delay.

''Eventually we found pamphlets and a videotape describing exactly how to make urea nitrate and we were able to connect that material to a fourth suspect, Ahmad Ajaj. Urea nitrate is pretty stable. It passes the Coyote test, which is named after Wile E. Coyote from the Road Runner cartoons. You put stuff in a cardboard box and jump on it. If it doesn't blow you up, it passes the test.

''We located the lab where they'd mixed this thing. It was in an apartment in a wooden building in Jersey City. In one room we found acid burns on the rug and it looked like they'd had an acid reaction which had splattered on the ceiling. We also found some nitroglycerin on the floor. These people were definitely not experts. I'm firmly convinced that if these guys hadn't planted the bomb when they did, they would have ended up all over Jersey City in a lot of little pieces.''

Records found in Ayyad's house showed he had purchased three tanks of hydrogen from AGL Welding Supply in Clifton, New Jersey. In an explosion, hydrogen acts as an accelerant. The remains of three hydrogen tanks with ''AGL Welding'' stamped on their sides were found in the debris. The Materials Analysis Unit showed that specks of blue plastic found on the remains of a rear post from the van were consistent with the blue trash can found in the storage area. The evidence was piling up.

''After the bombing, a letter was received at *The New York Times* from a group calling itself the Fifth Liberation Brigade, claiming responsibility for the destruction of the

World Trade Center and threatening other attacks,'' Williams continued. ''When we arrested Ayyad his computer was removed from his desk at the Allied-Signal Company. Our Computer Analysis Response Team was able to retrieve material from the computer's hard drive. In files that Ayyad had tried to delete, they found words from that letter verbatim, proving it had been written on that computer.

''The letter had been mailed in a gummed, stamped envelope. Our DNA Unit was able to develop a DNA profile from the saliva used to seal the envelope. I took saliva samples from the four suspects; you just swab the inside of their cheeks to get some cells. Their attorneys told them exactly what we were doing, and compared to the other suspects, when I touched Ayyad's mouth it was as dry as cotton, which is what happens when someone is extremely nervous. There was no question in my mind that the DNA test would confirm that Ayyad's saliva was on the envelope flap. That's what happened, proving he'd written and mailed the letter. The evidence against these four men was overwhelming. Each of them was sentenced to two hundred and forty years in prison.

''For me, it really was the case of a lifetime. Or at least until the next case of my lifetime comes up. In looking at the deaths and injuries and the damage, I won't say this was fun, but it was incredibly fascinating. It was exactly what I'd spent my career training to do. For weeks we were running on adrenaline, we were working twenty-three hours a day and the other hour I was too excited to sleep. And when we started making those arrests . . . oh, what a wondrous feeling that was.''

A bomb is made to do one thing only: explode. It functions only once and it is successful only if it destroys itself. A bomb can never be tested so sometimes, fortunately, it malfunctions. In the entire world of sci-crime, a world completely dependent on the immutable laws of science,

this is the one place where fate makes a difference. "We've seen all kinds of things in here that we can't explain," unit chief Ronay said, "so we just accept it thankfully and remember it. In the early 1980s, for example, a terrorist group called the United Freedom Front was responsible for bombing the Capitol building, as well as several buildings in New York City, among them the IBM building. We found one of their bombs consisting of five cartridges of dynamite in a briefcase in the Honeywell building in East Rutherford, New Jersey. It just hadn't gone off and there's no one who can tell you why. Maybe there was a bad contact on the timer, maybe a loose connection; when you look at it there's no reason it didn't explode. We don't do a lot of experimentation. We make a bomb safe by tearing it apart, and once that's been done it's almost impossible to figure out why it didn't work."

The history of the Explosives Unit is replete with stories of bombs that didn't go off. When President George Bush was visiting Tokyo, a small bomb was found on the grounds of the American embassy in a building overlooking the President's helicopter landing pad. This bomb used a windup clock as a timer—and the hands of the clock had stopped just a sixteenth of an inch from completing the circuit and detonating the bomb. There was no apparent reason for it to have stopped. Maybe it hadn't been wound enough, maybe it had been overwound, perhaps it was just fate, but it simply stopped, the width of an eyelash away from going off.

In the late 1970s and early 1980s, a series of powerful bombs were planted in Puerto Rico. Some of them went off, but others that seemed to be identical did not. These bombs used a pocket watch as a timer. Watches and clocks are easy to convert to timers. Two wires are attached to the clock, one to a moving hand, the other to a pin or screw stuck in the face at the precise instant the bomb maker wants his device to go off. One of these wires is connected

to the power source, the other to the detonator. When the moving hand makes contact with the metal pin the circuit is completed, the current can go from the power source to the initiator, and the bomb goes off. In the Puerto Rican bombs that did not explode, the hour hand seemed to be making contact with a metal screw. As far as experts could determine, the only thing that prevented those bombs from detonating was a thin layer of black paint on the side of the hour hand, perhaps a thousandth of an inch thick, that had acted as an insulator. Apparently the battery wasn't powerful enough to overcome the resistance in the paint, and many lives were saved by that thousandth of an inch.

Sometimes a bomb maker's mistake prevents the device from detonating. One morning a Missouri state trooper working undercover in a narcotics investigation went out to his car and found a hose leading from his gas tank to a can. Believing someone had tried to siphon gas, he picked up the can to throw it away. As he did, the top of the can came off, exposing almost a thousand feet of detonating cord—a high explosive that looks something like clothesline—four batteries, four detonators, and four clothespins. When he had lifted the top of the can, the clothespins had snapped closed, which should have completed the circuit and caused the bomb to go off. But it didn't. The examiners discovered why. The bomb maker had incorrectly wired his device; it was in series rather than in parallel, and thus there simply wasn't a strong enough current to cause the detonator to explode.

In 1984 a cleaning attendant found an unclaimed bag on a Pan Am jumbo jet that had just landed in Rio. Inside the bag was a bomb, which was later proved to have been made by Abu Ibrahim of the terrorist May Fifteenth Organization. The plastic explosive PETN had been molded into strips thin enough to fit beneath a seat cushion. When a passenger sat down, a pressure-sensitive switch initiated a time delay, which should have eventually detonated the

PETN. The best guess was that this one had been flying around the world on this airplane for at least a week, and had survived several hard landings without detonating. Other bombs made by Ibrahim had functioned perfectly. But whoever had planted this one had unknowingly broken off a small piece of plastic from the arming switch, which had gotten jammed inside the bomb and prevented the circuit from closing. Just a tiny piece of plastic, but it was lodged in the bomb and probably saved many lives.

In 1974 an extortionist who had toppled three power transmission towers and damaged eight others with bombs in the Pacific Northwest was threatening to black out a four-state area unless he was paid a million dollars. He planted his bombs in remote areas serviced only by helicopter and used a novel time-delay system, designed to give him plenty of time to backpack out of the region before his bombs went off. His homemade timer was a half-gallon can filled with water. His two wires, one connected to the power source and the other to the detonator, were jabbed through the bottom of the can, and a sheet of tinfoil floated on the water. He punched a tiny hole in the can, causing it to slowly drain. As the water leaked out, the foil descended until it made contact with both wires, beoming a bridge between them, completing the circuit and detonating the bomb. This time he had overlooked one thing: the weather in the Pacific Northwest. The water in the can froze, and the bomb sat for several weeks until it was discovered.

For investigators, getting a bomb intact is like finding the Holy Grail, only more valuable. The fact that bombs are so easy to make, and that there are an infinite number of ways to make them, means that each one is unique. As Dave Williams pointed out, "Fusing systems and explosive devices are limited by three things: the imagination of the bomber, his finances, and his skill." Even if given exactly the same components, two men—bomb makers are almost

exclusively male—will not make the same bomb. Bomb makers develop their own style, their own technique. They like to use a certain explosive and a certain detonating system and a certain type of time delay or power source. For some bomb makers, making a bomb is an art form, and their productions, like those of great artists, bear their unmistakable handiwork. Their signature. No matter what subject van Goh painted, his style was unique and identifiable. But the same was true of Mohammed Rashid, who made his bombs for a terrorist group, and Leroy Moody, who murdered two people with his letter bombs, and the killer known as Unabomber, whose deadly craftsmanship has plagued law enforcement for more than a decade.

"For most of my career I never used the word 'signature,' " Fred Smith remembered. "But as time moved on, I realized there truly are signatures in bomb making. If I learn one technique, that's all I know. I may make the most reliable bomb in the world, but I only know how to make it one way. Well, when a bomb has four or eight, whatever, points of construction that are the same as other bombs, it's appropriate to conclude that the same person made all those bombs or that they were made by someone following his instructions. To me, that's a signature."

The lab introduced the concept that bombs could be linked by a signature in the early 1980s, and after initial resistance the courts have accepted signatures as evidence. A signature can be the construction, the design of the circuitry, the materials used, including the explosive, even the method used to deliver the bomb. In an extremely controversial case, President Clinton ordered an air attack on Iraq after a bomb found during former President Bush's visit to Kuwait was identified by its signature as having been made in Iraq. It was a large bomb, eighty pounds of explosives, and it was hidden in the false bottom of a vehicle, between the gas tank and the floorboard. It was connected to three types of initiation systems; one was radio-controlled, so it

could be detonated from a distance; the second was a time delay; and the third was a suicide switch. This was a serious attempt on the life of the former president. Intelligence agents learned about the bomb before it could be detonated, and even with that information the vehicle had to be searched three times before the device was finally discovered.

The signature was found in the modifications to the circuit board. The method used to add and remove wires, the locations and skill used to solder the controls, and the type of insulation were identical to other bombs that had been positively identified as having been made in Iraq. After the air attack on Iraqi targets, reporters questioned the evidence that had caused this bomb to be attributed to Iraq, but members of the Explosives Unit felt quite confident in their conclusion that it had been made by the same people who made other Iraqi bombs.

While in that case the signature enabled investigators to link two bombs to a common source, in some instances a signature can be used to specifically identify the bomb maker. In the VANPAC case, for example, it led authorities directly to Leroy Moody. In a 1992 case, the lab received reports about a bank-robbery team operating in seven states. After bypassing the alarm system, the robbers would flood the top of the vault with water, then put a small amount of nitroglycerin in a condom or balloon and blow open the safe. If the money started burning, the water would extinguish the fire. As Paul Schrecker, who joined the lab in 1972 as a clerk and later worked there nine years as a firearms examiner before transferring to Explosives in 1986, explained, "We looked at this description of the evidence and we knew we'd seen it before. It went back to a case we had in the late seventies. It's pretty unusual for two people working completely independently to come up with the concept of putting nitro in a condom and using water to prevent a fire. So we did some research and found out that

several suspects had served time in prison with the people responsible for the earlier bombings. Obviously they'd shared the technology in prison. That certainly told us we had the right people, and helped us make the case.''

Perhaps because bomb makers operate internationally, agents in the Explosives Unit maintain closer contact with their counterparts around the world than any other lab unit does. They worked particularly closely with Northern Ireland's explosives experts on matters involving the Provisional Irish Republican Army, PIRA, an organization that regularly placed bombs in public places as part of its political strategy and received substantial financial and technical support from sympathizers in the United States. In one major case solved through international cooperation, the FBI learned through correspondence from a known IRA member that a Boston resident named Richard Clark Johnson, a brilliant electronics engineer with a top-secret security clearance, was making highly complicated proximity fuses and triggering mechanisms for IRA bombs. "He had quite an operation going," Ronay said. "He was building very sophisticated devices for their homemade surface-to-air missiles and bombs. We were able to connect him to bombs found in Northern Ireland through his signature. You could lay down one of the circuit boards we found in his lab on Cape Cod right next to an unexploded bomb recovered in Northern Ireland, and anyone could see that the handiwork was exactly the same. He might just as well have signed these things 'Richard Clark Johnson.' '' On the basis of this signature, in addition to other evidence found in his lab, Johnson and several of his associates were convicted of making bombs for the IRA.

Sometimes the components of the bomb become a signature. A tiny piece of gold-plated wire found in the body of a Japanese boy killed on a Pan Am flight to Honolulu turned out to be the big, bold signature of Abu Ibrahim. "It was part of the leg wire of an E-cell battery timing de-

vice,'' Tom Thurman explained. "At first it didn't mean too much to us, but when we started seeing other devices with the same type of wire, it became important. We determined that the May Fifteenth Organization used this type of timer to the exclusion of any other group. Eventually we were able to compare the damage to the Japanese boy's body and to his seat and the airplane to several similar bombings, particularly the 1986 bombing of a TWA flight from Rome to Athens in which four American citizens were sucked out of the airplane. We were able to show that these bombs were made virtually the same way, that they were the same size and had been placed in precisely the same manner. More than twenty bombs were traced to this organization from the signature, and when we caught the individual who had planted them, Mohammed Rashid, we were able to successfully prosecute him.''

The explosive substance can be the signature. There are thousands of substances that will explode when "hit" by the proper detonator, and any of them can be used in a bomb. "We have a program in which we'll analyze any foreign explosive sample submitted to us," Paul Schrecker said. "Different groups use different explosives. If it's a plastic explosive, for example, we'll analyze the nonexplosive component. What type of plasticizers are in there? What kind of oils? What kind of dyes? Semtex consists of eighty-six percent RDX and PETN, but the ratio of those two explosives has gone all over the map. Finding the same ratio of RDX to PETN in a Semtex sample enables us to determine if we've seen that particular explosive before. It's that much of a signature. We can say that a sample recovered in Germany matches a cache found in Northern Ireland and start working backwards. It's a big step toward identifying the source of the bomb.''

Finally, the damage done by the bomb is a punctuation mark in the bomb maker's signature. The fact that explosive damage can be recreated is extremely useful. For ex-

ample, when the body of a somewhat shady show-business entrepreneur named Roy Radin was found decaying in the Mojave Desert with his face blown off and eight holes in the back of his skull, a coroner ruled he had been shot in the back of the head with a shotgun. But an informer claimed that Radin had been shot with a smaller gun, and that an M-80, a small firecracker-like explosive, had been put in his mouth and detonated, causing the damage. To verify the informer's story the Explosives Unit constructed a twenty-five-pound head of clay and tried to duplicate the damage. The first M-80 was placed in what would have been the mouth cavity; it blew apart the entire clay head. The second charge was laid across the lip area—and it came very close to duplicating the damage done to Radin's head. It was enough to support the story told by the informer, which gave substantial weight to the rest of his testimony.

When a man named Michael Townley became a suspect in the bombing-murder of Orlando Letelier in Washington, D.C., he readily confessed that he had worked with Cuban operatives in making and placing the bomb under a contract with the Chilean government. Authorities believe he confessed to save his life, knowing he would have become a target if the people who had hired him knew he was under suspicion. Whatever his reasons, he provided authorities with strong evidence. His confession sounded almost too good to be true, so he had to prove he had made the bomb.

"We had to convince a jury that he was telling the truth," according to Ronay. "So we went out and got an identical car, except for the color, and had Townley build us a bomb. He assembled it and showed us where to put it on the car. We followed all his instructions and blew up the car. The results were incredible. The damage was exactly the same, exactly, something that even the best bomb maker in the world couldn't do on the first attempt unless

he knew exactly how the bomb had been made and where it had been placed. This demonstration proved Townley's credibility to the jury. There just couldn't be any doubt about it, he'd built the bomb that had killed Letelier.''

While explosives used responsibly can be a valuable tool, a bomb is simply a weapon, and is often used like any other weapon in the commission of a crime. Bombs are used in robberies and extortions and to commit murder. And sometimes the bomb maker is identified through traditional methods of crime solving.

"Our intent is to collect $1,000,000 or make you wish we had," wrote "J. Hawker," who was threatening to blow up the Portland, Oregon, power transmission system with his dripping-water-can bombs unless that ransom was paid. The bomb was the weapon, but the crime was extortion, and "Hawker" had to make arrangements to pick up his ransom payment. He created an elaborate communications scheme in which he issued instructions about the money drop over a citizens band radio frequency. He responded to questions by tooting on a birdcall: once for yes, twice for no. During his transmission FBI agents triangulated his location using direction-finding equipment—and found themselves driving behind a car being driven by a man with a radio in one hand and a duck call in his mouth. David Heesch was arrested, and in his refrigerator agents found copies of the threat letters. Asked by the judge during his trial about his intent, Heesch replied, bluntly, "To extort a million dollars." He was sentenced to twenty years in prison.

The threat of a bomb is every bit as effective as a real bomb during a robbery, and hoax bombs, devices built to look like real bombs, are often used in holdups. For investigative purposes these bombs, which can be very sophisticated, are treated exactly the same as real weapons, and can be traced through their signatures and components.

Bombs are used to kill for the same reasons any other weapon would be used: for vengeance, for passion, and for money. But a bomb offers the killer the advantage of being far from the scene when the murder is done. Jack Gilbert Graham coldly killed his mother and forty-three other people to collect her insurance policies and a sizable inheritance. Twelve years later, in 1967, and for the same reason, Earl Cooke put a bomb aboard an American Airlines flight on which his wife was a passenger. Although Cooke's bomb went off in the baggage compartment, it did only minimal damage. Cooke became a suspect when charred luggage tags were found to have come from the suitcase in which the bomb had been hidden. The bomb consisted of two sticks of dynamite to be detonated by four blasting caps. The timer was an alarm clock; when the alarm rang a metal hammer would hit a bell and complete the circuit, causing the bomb to go off. Toolmarks convicted Cooke. Agent-examiner Charles Killion was able to positively identify marks found on the alarm-clock bell as having been made by the jaws of a vice in Cooke's workshop. Added to other evidence, this led to Cooke's conviction and a sentence of two concurrent twenty-year terms.

A year later Sam Hammons, a NASA employee with a top-secret clearance, was killed by a package bomb sent to his Avon, Ohio, home. In Hammons's office FBI agents found letters written to him from a woman he had known in high school, and with whom he had recently became reaquainted. Agents were intrigued by this relationship when they discovered that the briefcase in which the bomb was mailed had been purchased not far from her home. Surprisingly, though, it hadn't been bought by this woman but by her boss, a man named Albert Ricci. The evidence against Ricci quickly piled up. He had been on vacation near Salt Lake City, Utah, the day the bomb was mailed from there. He had purchased parts of the bomb in a local hardware store and had persuaded a friend to get him eight

sticks of dynamite. The motive was passion: Ricci was infatuated with his secretary, Hammons's high school friend, and his insane jealousy caused him to murder his supposed rival, an innocent man who didn't even know he existed. Before Ricci could be arrested, he drove his car into a deep pond and died.

In a bizarre 1993 San Francisco case, two male lovers tried to kill the third member of their love triangle, the estranged wife of one of the men, because she would get a sizable portion of the couple's $3 million estate in their divorce. The men sent her a lovely bouquet of flowers— with a pipe bomb planted in it. The woman and a co-worker were seriously injured, but survived. When police looked for a motive, they uncovered the love triangle, and the woman's husband and his lover became suspects. Doug Deedrick of the Hairs and Fiber Unit was able to match pieces of dried flower found on the floorboard of one of the men's cars with bits of the bouquet. A toolmarks exam proved that the nails used in the bomb had been fabricated on the same machine and within a few minutes as nails found in the apartment of one of the suspects. And smokeless powder that could be associated with the victim's husband was identical to the explosive used in the bomb. One of the men was convicted of delivering the bomb, but not making it. The victim's husband remained under investigation.

Perhaps the most complex bomb ever encountered by the Explosives Unit was the massive thousand-pound steel box used in an attempt to extort $3 million from Harvey's Wagon Wheel Resort Hotel in Lake Tahoe, Nevada. It was the kind of bomb usually seen in movies, a seemingly impregnable box made by a mad genius, ticking down the hours until a ransom was paid or it was detonated.

The device was wheeled into the casino in 1980, hidden under a cover with "IBM" stenciled on it to make it ap-

pear to be a business machine. Once it was in place on the second floor, the bomb was armed and an extortion note was left: "This bomb is so sensitive that the slightest movement either inside or outside will cause it to explode," read the note. "This bomb can never be dismantled or disarmed without causing an explosion. Not even by the creator."

"He was certainly right about that," admitted Chris Ronay, who supervised the case in the lab. "This was quite a bomb. It had twenty-eight toggle switches and it was designed so that if two specific switches were put in the correct position it could be moved. Supposedly when the ransom was paid, the bomb maker would tell us which two switches would make it safe, not that anyone would have dared move it, even with those instructions.

"It had eight different triggering mechanisms, each one designed to prevent us from using traditional methods to disarm the bomb. In the movies you see people disarming a bomb by cutting a wire or putting it in a bucket of water. You never cut wires. A lot of bombs have shunts so that if a wire is cut the bomb will go off; if anything, you might try to short-circuit it. And if you put a bomb in a bucket of water you're likely to be hit with sharp fragments of that bucket when the bomb goes off. To disarm a bomb you need to separate the power source from the detonator; if it doesn't have power it isn't going to go off. And that can be done in several different ways.

"In this case we started by X-raying the bomb. We thought we might be able to disrupt the wiring, but it was like spaghetti in there. The bomb maker had put in all kinds of relays and switches to confuse us, and it was impossible to trace the wires from the battery to the blasting cap. We couldn't move the bomb because he'd also put in a motion detector, a PVC tube lined with tinfoil that had a pendulum consisting of a piece of wire weighted with a nut and bolt. If we moved or shook or jolted the bomb in any

way, the nut would hit the foil, completing the circuit. Sometimes you can disarm a bomb by filling it with liquid nitrogen foam, which freezes the parts and prevents them from moving. This bomb had a tinfoil membrane around the inside, so if you cut into it with a drill, the bit would make contact with the casing and the foil, completing the circuit and . . . He also had a toilet plunger in there, so if we filled the container with foam, the plunger would have been lifted, activating a switch that would detonate the bomb. And he had three different timers operated by the toggle switches.

"You can also render safe a bomb by shooting it with an explosive charge, a bullet, a high-impact water cannon, or anything that takes out the battery. That may cause the device to start functioning, but any initiator has to have a certain amount of current for a certain duration. If you're quick enough, it may start to get current, but you can disrupt it before it reaches full current. In this case the detonator was inside a smaller box sitting on top of the bomb. What we finally decided to try to do was disarm the bomb by taking out the detonator with a seven-pound shaped charge of C4. Pressure waves move off an explosive at right angles, so by shaping the charge you can actually aim the force of the explosion. We hoped we could rip off the top of the bomb faster than the current could get to the explosive. We knew it was a big gamble, but we really had no choice. There was no way of moving that thing."

Meanwhile, during the thirty hours that all this was going on, the other casinos in town were taking bets on what hour the bomb would explode. At the same time agents were trying to make arrangements to pay the ransom. The agents were told to fly over an area in a helicopter and land when they spotted a strobe light. They never saw the light. As it turned out, the extortionists had left the battery for the strobe light home and couldn't signal, so the drop was missed the first night. They stole a battery for the second

night, but the helicopter flew over a different area. So the drop was never completed.

"In theory, the method we chose to disarm that bomb should have worked," Ronay said. "In reality, it toppled the bomb over and a thousand pounds of dynamite blew out the inside of Harvey's Casino. In this business, lives come first, then property. Disarming the bomb in place was the most reasonable approach toward risking the minimum number of people. The bomb blew a five-story cavity into the building, and I remember looking up and seeing bathtubs and TVs dangling in midair, but not one person was hurt. When the bomb went off, any plans we had to pay the ransom were abandoned, and the extortionists disappeared.

"We began our investigation by trying to trace pieces of the bomb. We found the manufacturer of the casters and tried to trace their customers. We looked for someone who'd recently sold twenty-eight or more toggle switches. The bomb was coated with four layers of paint; we looked for a common source. We went through the bomb piece by piece, looking for that one object that would put us on the track. And we didn't get anywhere.

"FBI agents and local police went to every motel within about a hundred miles, asking about guests who had been driving a vehicle large enough to transport the bomb. A reward was offered, and authorities finally got a tip from an individual who was friendly with the former girlfriend of a man named John Birges, Sr. According to this man, Birges's former girlfriend claimed he had been talking about the bombing. Police started looking for other evidence that might implicate Birges, and bits and pieces began coming together. One of Birges's two sons had gotten a speeding ticket in the Lake Tahoe area at the time of the bombing. Birges's girlfriend had been involved in a minor traffic accident and had been taken to the hospital. Finally, Birges's sons were subpoenaed by a grand jury and under oath denied having been near Harvey's when it was

bombed. Confronted with evidence they claimed they were scouting for fields in which to plant marijuana. When they were indicted for perjury and threatened with prison, they rolled over. They confessed and agreed to testify against their father in exchange for immunity from prosecution. John Birges, Jr., established his credibility as a witness when he correctly identified the two switches that would have disabled the motion detector.

"When I testified at the trial," Ronay recalled, "the senior Birges couldn't resist asking me if I wanted to know how the bomb could have been disarmed. Of course I did. He took out an automobile headlight with two alligator clips attached to it and told me how to hook it up to the full scale mock-up of the bomb we'd made for the trial. I did, the light went on, and he asked, 'If you leave it there for a long time, what'll happen?'

" 'Eventually it'll drain the battery and make it useless,' I said. 'Theoretically, that would disable the bomb.'

"I didn't want to get into a discussion with him, but even after the battery had lost power there were ways that bomb could've been detonated. For a man that intelligent, he was very simplistic in his approach to disarming it. But he had made some bomb. Birges was sentenced to two twenty-year terms without parole. And Harvey's? They rebuilt the whole place. It's bigger than it was before the bombing."

In most cases people make one bomb to achieve one purpose; they're amateurs and they make mistakes. But just as there are serial killers and serial rapists, there are serial bombers, individuals who make and place many bombs over a long period of time. They are professionals, they are very good at their work, and they are very difficult to catch. One bomb maker, known to the Bureau by his Major Case name, Unabomber, has killed two people and injured at least twenty-three with letter bombs since 1978.

In 1979 an explosive device aboard an American Airlines flight from Chicago to Washington went off and caused a small fire in the baggage compartment. Chris Ronay and the case agent, Tom Barrett, were intrigued by the unique improvised detonator and began showing it to other people in the explosives world. They found two similar devices that had been detonated within the past eighteen months that made it clear they were dealing with a serial bomber. Named Unabomber because the targets of his first bombs were university professors and airlines—more recently his letter bombs have also been sent to individuals associated with scientific and computer research as well as airline production—this bomber makes almost every component of his bombs. He makes his own boxes and hinges, his own endcaps and pipes and switches. He files down wire to make nails, and files away screws to eliminate toolmarks. He carves parts out of wood and uses old lamp cord for his wiring, and he has used several different types of powder in each bomb, possibly so he doesn't have to obtain his explosive from one source which might attract attention. In many of the bombs the initials ''FC'' have been stamped into a piece of metal. Officials believe ''FC'' stands for an obscene phrase used to belittle computers. This craftsmanship has become his signature. In December 1994, his most powerful device, about the size of a VCR cassette, killed advertising executive Thomas Mosser when he opened it in the kitchen of his New Jersey home.

In many cases bomb makers claim credit for their work, or at least reveal a motive. With the exception of a single letter received by *The New York Times* that is believed to have been written by Unabomber, he has remained silent about his motive. In 1987 he was seen in Salt Lake City placing the bomb that resulted in his first killing, and law enforcement officials describe him as white male, about six feet tall, in his late thirties or early forties, with a medium build, ruddy complexion, and reddish-blond hair. The best

clue was found with one of his bombs in June 1993; in indented writing, an impression made in paper by writing on a top sheet, the lab discovered a message reading, "Call Nathan R—Wed. 7 pm." Treasury Department investigators, admitting they are no closer to catching Unabomber than they were in 1978, have offered a million-dollar reward for information leading to the bomber. One additional intriguing bit of information: there were no bombings between 1987 and 1993. This leads investigators to suspect that Unabomber was in some sort of institution at the time, most probably a prison.

Not all bombers are as difficult to catch as Unabomber. Donald "Pee Wee" Gaskins, for example, who claimed to have killed as many as sixteen people, was on death row in South Carolina. The prisoner in the cell next to his, Rudolph Tyner, had killed several members of a South Carolina family, and friends of the victims were irate that he might live there indefinitely as his appeals moved through the legal system. Somehow they managed to smuggle bomb components, including high explosives, to Gaskins, who constructed a crude radio bomb. He strung a wire from his cell into the ventilation duct. The radio bomb was delivered to the killer in the next cell, who was told to open the vent, where he would find a wire, and hook it up to the radio, which would enable him to speak to Gaskins. He did just that, and when he put the radio to his ear, Gaskins blew him up.

The entire investigation was about three feet long, the distance between the two cells. Although previously sentenced to ten life sentences, for this murder Gaskins was executed by the state of South Carolina in 1991.

4

Threads of Evidence:
The Hairs and Fiber Unit

U.S. ATTORNEY: In addition to Mr. Camarena's blood and hair type, did you find at the crime scene any other hair that matches anyone else in this courtroom?

FBI LABORATORY TECHNICIAN: Yes, sir, we found hair that matches samples labeled as coming from Mr. Verona in the bathroom of the Lope de Vega house, from the rear bedroom where Mr. Camarena was held. . . . These were recovered from drains into the main sewer line.

CBS-TV EMMY AWARD-WINNING MINI-SERIES,
Drug Wars: The Kiki Camarena Story

Look at the shirt or blouse or sweater you are wearing. Somewhere on this garment you are probably going to find some hairs—perhaps your own, perhaps someone else's—and some very small fibers. Grasp one of those hairs or fibers in your hand. It isn't very big; it weighs almost nothing. You didn't even know it was there. But in that hair or fiber there exists a world of information about you and about your life. Given samples for comparative purposes, it would be possible to determine through those few hairs and fibers how you have spent this day: where you have been, how you got there, whom you saw, what you did.

For some people, for some very unlucky people—DEA agent Kiki Camarena, who was tortured and murdered in a Mexican hacienda; five-year-old Melissa Brannen, who disappeared from a Christmas party and was never seen again; Nathaniel Cater, who was murdered by Atlanta child-killer Wayne Williams—a few hairs and fibers, ex-

actly like those you are holding, allowed detectives to determine how they spent the last moments of their lives, and led directly to their killers.

Sherlock Holmes would have searched a crime scene with his magnifying lens and perhaps a fine-toothed comb. Today he would probably use a handheld vacuum cleaner adapted to trap hairs and fibers in a special filter, or he would "sweep" the area with wide transparent tape. The tiny bits of debris he collected might allow him to connect the victim to a place, to other victims, or to the killer.

A hair is simply a filament growing out of the skin of a mammal, while a fiber is the smallest unit of textile material. Thousands of tiny fibers are twisted together to make thread or yarn, which in turn is woven into fabric.

Hairs have been used to link criminals with their crimes for more than 150 years. As early as 1938, French and British investigators were using hairs found at crime scenes to try to link a suspect to the crime. The first known use of hairs as evidence in an American courtroom took place in Massachusetts in 1869, when hairs found stuck to the dried blood on the end of a club helped convict a man of beating his wife to death. Fiber evidence was rarely valuable to investigators before the 1950s because there was little variation among natural fibers and colors available at that time. But the post-World War II explosion of synthetic fibers finally made it possible for investigators to make strong connections between fibers found at a crime scene and fibers that could be linked to a suspect.

The use of hairs and fibers as evidence is based on the work done by French criminologist Dr. Edmond Locard, whose theory of transfer states that when a person comes into contact with another person or place, some human hairs or fibers are going to be transferred to that person and that environment. It also states that they are easily shed, so the hairs and fibers found on an individual will reflect the most recent contact or environment.

When a person is involved in a crime, there is a significant chance that he will leave some of his hairs and fibers at the crime scene and he will take with him some hairs and fibers from that place. The objective of the Hairs and Fiber Unit in the FBI's sci-crime lab is to link hairs and fibers from an unknown source to hairs and fibers from a known source, thereby proving a connection, and once that connection has been made, figuring out how that exchange took place.

Sometimes a single hair can be sufficient to link a killer to his victim. In a Jackson, Tennessee, case, an escaped convict killed the priest who caught him burglarizing a church rectory. He was captured a short time later and denied both the burglary and the murder. The Tennessee Bureau of Investigation sent his clothes to the Hairs and Fiber Unit to be examined. Although the suspect was black, several brown Caucasian hairs were found on his jacket. Hairs known to have come from the priest—the "K," as items from known sources are referred to in lab reports, matched the hairs from an unknown source, the "Q," which were found on the suspect's clothing. This proved the two men had been in contact. The suspect was convicted of murdering the priest and was sentenced to death.

That's the way it's supposed to work. But rarely is it that easy. Often there are so many factors complicating a case that the value of hairs and fibers as evidence depends almost entirely on the ingenuity of the examiner. Making hair and fiber comparisons is a learned skill, but figuring out how to use them is an art.

On December 3, 1989, five-year-old Melissa Brannen disappeared from a Christmas party in Fairfax, Virginia. She just vanished, seemingly without a trace. Police learned that a man named Cal Hughes had abruptly left the party at the same time the child disappeared, although no one had seen them together. When police arrived at Hughes's home about one o'clock in the morning, he was

busy washing and drying all the clothes he had been wearing that night, including his shoes and belt. It was an odd thing to be doing, especially at that hour, and Hughes became a prime suspect.

Hughes denied having any contact with the little girl and gave police permission to search his car. Detectives swarmed over the car, dusting it for fingerprints, searching for bloodstains, confiscating the floor mats for further testing and carefully running pieces of transparent tape over the seats to pick up the thousands of tiny hairs and fibers collected there, searching for any evidence that Melissa Brannen had once been in that car. All the evidence was sent to the FBI lab, as were the clothes Hughes had been wearing that night, strands of hair from both Melissa Brannen and her mother (taken from their brushes), and articles of clothing worn recently by the child.

There are no shortcuts in hair and fiber examinations. Even the most sophisticated computers can't help. An experienced examiner looks at hundreds, sometimes thousands, of hairs and fibers under a microscope, maybe makes some notes, and tries to remember as much as possible. Then he begins making comparisons, trying to find two or more hairs or fibers found in different places that came from the same source. Depending on the ability of the examiner to make those comparisons, lives will be changed forever.

The agent-examiner assigned the Melissa Brannen case was Doug Deedrick, who had joined the lab in 1972 as a clerk and tour guide, becoming an agent in 1976 and a lab technician a year later. With his neatly combed graying hair, his glasses, and his white lab coat, Deedrick looks more like a scholarly university professor than one of the most respected investigators in the sci-crime business.

In most cases submitted to the sci-crime lab, the Hairs and Fiber Unit gets the evidence first. Because the minuscule hairs and fibers can easily be shed and lost, the evi-

dence is taken into a scraping room—a temperature-controlled, humidity-controlled, sealed environment—and hung on a rack. A clean sheet of white paper is laid under the evidence and a technician then scrapes it with a metal spatula. Clothes are scraped both inside and out. Hairs and fibers that might be of value are mounted on slides to be looked at under a microscope by an agent-examiner. Certain fibers—white cotton, for instance—are so common that they are worthless for comparative purposes, so they are never collected. But everything else goes to the examiner.

Deedrick began his investigation by trying to compare samples of hair recovered from Melissa Brannen's hairbrush and previously worn clothing to hairs found on the front seat of Hughes's car. Because children's hair changes drastically over short periods of time, he was unable to make any good matches. But when he examined the little girl's nightshirt he found several short black hairs stuck in the fabric. "That was the first break in the case," Deedrick explained matter-of-factly. "One of the things you have to have when working these cases is good recall. You have to log in your mind everything that you've seen as best you can. These particular hairs caught my attention because I knew I'd seen them among the submissions taken from the suspect's car. They were easily identifiable: they were black rabbit hairs. And they could be positively compared with hairs found in the car. I didn't know where they came from, but I knew I had a link between the little girl and the suspect's car.

"An agent spoke with Mrs. Brannen, who told us that she had worn a dyed black rabbit coat to the party, and that Melissa had previously played with that coat at home. We got the coat, and I compared the hairs found on Melissa's nightshirt, the hairs found in the suspect's car, and the hairs from the coat. They were the same hairs. It could have been a coincidence, we'd found only two or three of

those hairs in the car, but I don't believe in coincidence that much. I felt we'd made a positive link to the suspect. But it wasn't nearly enough to make a case.''

The few rabbit hairs found on the front seat of Hughes's car provided a tantalizing clue, but a defense attorney could argue that Hughes had picked up those hairs by accidentally brushing against the little girl or her mother at the party, then shed them as he drove home.

Deedrick also found one hair, one slender hair, on the passenger-side floor mat that exhibited all the characteristics of hair found in Melissa's brush. All his experience told him that Hughes had been with that little girl, but he still didn't have enough evidence to make a case. To prove that Melissa Brannen had been in that car, Deedrick had to find a way of linking the clothes she was wearing when she disappeared to the debris recovered from the front seat—a seemingly impossible task when you don't have those clothes. As Deedrick explained, ''You look at the questioned debris and see if you can find fibers that might have come from the clothes the victim was wearing. It's kind of experienced guesswork and it's a real long shot. But we didn't have too much else. Melissa's mother told us she was wearing an outfit with a blue sweater. In the tapings from the car I'd seen a number of blue synthetic fibers. So I decided to try to recreate the clothes she was wearing.''

The Hairs and Fiber Unit works almost 2,500 cases a year. Murder is just another faceless crime, another pair of pants to be examined. There are just too many cases, too much violence for people working in the unit to become emotionally involved in every case. But violent crimes involving children get the full attention of the lab. Many of the agents and technicians working there have their own kids. Doug Deedrick has three little girls, one of them born the same year as Melissa Brannen. And the disappearance of Melissa three weeks before Christmas got special attention.

The night Melissa disappeared she had been wearing a Sesame Street outfit consisting of red tights, a red plaid skirt, and a blue acrylic sweater with a picture of Big Bird on it. The outfit had been given to Melissa by her grandmother, who couldn't remember where she had bought it. Deedrick discussed this case with his wife, who by pure luck had saved an old J.C. Penney catalogue that featured children's clothing. And in that catalogue Deedrick found an outfit consisting of red tights, a red plaid skirt, and a blue acrylic sweater with Big Bird's picture on it. Melissa's mother identified it as the outfit her daugher had been wearing. As things later turned out, the outfit had been manufactured exclusively for Penney's, and this catalogue was the only place it had been advertised or sold. If Deedrick's wife hadn't kept her old catalogue, this case might never have been solved.

Meanwhile Deedrick painstakingly examined clothing Melissa had worn within the previous year. And on a pink coat he found one blue acrylic fiber, just one, that he could positively associate with the fibers found in Hughes's car.

Penney's obtained an outfit from a customer in another state. "It arrived in the lab about five-thirty," Deedrick recalled without any emotion in his voice, "and I'll never forget that night. The sweater was actually purplish-blue. As soon as I looked at the fibers under the microscope, I knew we had a match. Without question they were the same fibers that we'd found in the car. We'd found a total of fifty acrylic fibers on the passenger seat and one on the driver's seat. We'd also found ten red cotton fibers that I matched to the red cotton in the skirt. There was no longer any doubt that Melissa Brannen had been in that car, but we still had to prove it to a jury."

There are more than a thousand manmade fibers currently being manufactured, and more than 7,000 different dye formulations. Manufacturers do not duplicate each other's dyes; dye formulas are closely guarded trade

secrets. So the chances that two dyed synthetic fibers from different sources would match are statistically almost nil. Said Deedrick, "We had three things we needed: the transfer of the fiber from the victim to the suspect; the persistence of the fiber, meaning we'd found a lot of them; and, finally, the uniqueness of the fiber. What we still had to demonstrate was that these fibers were so unusual that realistically they couldn't have come from an unrelated source. We had to show that it was much more than an amazing coincidence that they had been found in Hughes's car, that these fibers were proof he had abducted Melissa Brannen and taken her somewhere in that car."

Deedrick conceived a dramatic way to illustrate to a jury how unlikely it would be that these fibers had come from any other source but Melissa's sweater. He asked his co-workers in the lab to bring in any blue acrylic clothing they owned. Eventually he received 107 garments, from caps to socks, and identified 126 different blue acrylic fibers. He made 7,938 comparisons—and could not make a single match. No two of those blue acrylic fibers from different sources could be matched either visually or instrumentally.

"We proved that Melissa Brannen had been sitting in the front seat of that car," Deedrick said, a note of satisfaction in his voice. "The fact that Cal Hughes had denied speaking to her and had denied being with her were statements he just couldn't overcome. Although we were never able to discover what had happened to the little girl, Hughes was convicted of abduction with intent to defile and received a fifty-year sentence."

Making a hair or fiber match is a skill that can't be learned from a textbook. "There's really only one way to learn it," explained Agent-examiner Mike Malone, who spent almost two decades in Hairs and Fibers, "and that is to do it and do it and do it. You look at thousands of hairs

and fibers and eventually you begin to see patterns, you learn what to look for.''

An individual being trained to conduct hair and fiber examinations will spend at least a year in the unit assisting experienced examiners. The on-the-job training is supplemented with some classroom work, extensive reading, and several moot court sessions. "The object of our work is to be able to testify in front of a jury that a known and an unknown item came from the same source, to be able to convince a jury that the comparison we've made has real meaning,'' according to Agent-examiner Wayne Oakes. ''And who better to teach this than the people who have testified collectively in more than a thousand cases?''

To assist in identifications, the unit maintains several large collections, among them a hair collection that includes samples from every part of the body from every race of people, as well as from almost every animal and rodent. The largest hair in that collection, and the toughest, is from an elephant, and it's so thick it can barely be mounted on a slide. That sample proved valuable when people charged with illegally bringing elephant-hair bracelets into the country falsely claimed that the material in their possession was a plastic facsimile.

Perhaps the most unusual request for an animal-hair identification came from the Spokane, Washington, sheriff's office. A local farmer reported seeing Bigfoot, the legendary beast whose existence has never been proven, running across his field. According to the farmer's story, Bigfoot escaped by leaping over a barbed wire fence. When the sheriff's office investigated they found a tuft of unusual black hairs caught in the wire and sent them to the lab for identification. Was this proof of Bigfoot's existence? Only if Bigfoot is actually a black horse, which was where the hairs came from.

The unit also maintains an extensive fiber collection, which includes most common and many unique fibers as

well as doll-hair fibers and human wig-hair fibers, one of the largest feather collections in the world, a large wood collection, and a rope and cord collection.

Hair and fiber identification is not an exact science. This just isn't the kind of evidence that allows examiners to testify that two hairs or two fibers came from the same source to the exclusion of all other possibilities. "It's not fingerprints," Wayne Oakes said. "It's extremely rare that we see hairs from two different people that are so close we can't tell them apart, so this is the basis of a strong association. We can't testify that two hairs came from the same person. What we can say is that two hairs or two fibers are consistent in every measurable way and that it is highly likely they came from the same source."

Still a lot of information can be learned from a single hair: whether the donor was an animal or a human, Caucasoid, Negroid, or Mongoloid; what part of the body it came from; whether it fell out naturally or was forcibly removed; even whether the donor suffered from certain diseases or drank too much or used certain drugs. It's even possible to determine how long ago the hair had been dyed or bleached. Surprisingly, it isn't possible to determine if a hair came from a man or a woman unless the root is attached, or the age of the donor. Only head hairs, pubic hairs, and facial hairs are suitable for comparative purposes, as there just isn't enough difference between your body hair and someone else's to make a good basis for comparison.

Fibers are never unique. There are just too many of them. So in most cases it's not as important to trace a fiber to a single garment as it is to show that fibers found in different places came from the same source. There are four types of fibers: naturally occurring animal fibers, such as wool; vegetable fibers, such as cotton; minerals, such as asbestos; and manmade fibers. Manmade fibers are used in the production of about 75 percent of all textiles. There are

twenty-one generic classifications of manmade fibers, among them the six most people are familiar with: acetate, rayon, nylon, acrylic, polyester, and olefin.

Although hairs and fibers exist in abundance, every hair and every fiber exhibits a combination of characteristics that makes it different from most others, and those are what examiners look at when making comparisons. A hair, for example, has external features such as length, color, degree of curliness or straightness, texture, thickness, diameter of the shaft, shape and condition of the root, appearance of the tip, and whether it has been dyed or chemically altered in any way. Numerous internal characteristics are also used for comparative purposes, including the width of the medulla (the hollow core running down the center of a hair), the type and condition of the scales that make up the cuticle, or outer layers, and the size, shape, and density of the pigment, which gives hair its color.

A lot of foreign material, from dirt to lice, is also found on hairs, and that material will often enable examiners to connect a suspect to a crime. Doug Deedrick had a murder case in which a woman was kidnapped and shot in the head at close range. When he looked at several strands of her hair, he found a bluish material he couldn't identify. Whatever it was, it was something he hadn't seen before, and unusual enough to make a good basis for comparison. When police arrested a suspect they discovered a loaded semi-automatic weapon under the front seat of his car. The first round in that gun was an unusual type of ammunition called a glaser round, a bullet with a Teflon shell that disintegrates upon impact and releases several small pellets. It's sort of a shotgun shell for handguns. Tests conducted by the Firearms Unit confirmed that the bluish material Deedrick had found on the victim's hair was Teflon that had fused to it on impact. That allowed Deedrick to make a strong association between the suspect and the victim.

In many cases it's important to prove that hair has been

forcibly removed. If a hair has been torn out, its root will be stretched rather than bulbous, it may have skin tissue still attached to it, and it will probably contain some pigment because it's still in the growing stage. Hal Deadman, who worked in Hairs and Fibers for sixteen years before joining the DNA Analysis Unit, once received a pair of shoes worn by a suspect in an Indiana robbery-murder case. Several of the victim's hairs were found stuck to the dried blood on the tip of the suspect's shoe. The suspect claimed that the victim had been shocked when she found him in her house and had suffered a heart attack, striking her head when she collapsed. He testified that he had stepped in the blood from her head wound when he fled the house. But from the condition of the roots, Deadman was able to determine that the woman's hairs had been forcibly removed; this led to the inevitable conclusion that the suspect had stomped her to death. The suspect was convicted of murdering the woman.

The main characteristics of fibers used to make comparisons are the type and generic classification, the diameter and coarseness, the presence of additives used in production, machine marks made during processing, the cross-sectional shape—artificial fibers are made by forcing molten liquid through a spinneret, something like a shower head; the cross-sectional shape is determined by the shape of the holes in the spineret—and changes due to use, such as sun-bleaching or discoloration from repeated washings. Perhaps most important is color. In the sci-crime business, blue is never blue; it's a color produced by mixing various dyes. While to the naked eye two colors may appear to be identical, they have probably been made from different dyes, or different proportions of dyes. The presence and amount of different dyes can be determined by an instrument called a microspectrophotometer, which basically produces a "spectral" fingerprint of the color. Identical

color fingerprints make a very strong basis for association between two fibers found in different places.

With the exception of the microspectrophotometer, almost all examinations in the Hairs and Fiber Unit are done visually. Most comparisons are done on the compound microscope, which magnifies a sample up to four hundred times, and the comparison microscope, which consists of two compound microscopes bridged together to allow an examiner to look at two specimens simultaneously.

What makes a match? Absolutely everything. There is no minimum number of characteristics that must match, no hard and fast rules of evidence that require a standard be met. Simply, everything that can be seen or tested must be the same for a match to be made. As soon as one difference in characteristics is seen, the examination is over: the two specimens are not the same.

Every examiner has his or her own standards. "If you can't find at least fifteen identifiable characteristics," Mike Malone said, "then it's not unique enough to be of value for comparisons. For me, I always looked for twenty characteristics to match, which is about as many as you're going to find if you don't include things like bleaching, dyeing, and damage."

"When I'm asked on the witness stand how many characteristics matched," Wayne Oakes explained, "my answer has to be, 'All of them.' People have tried to quantitate this for a long time, but no one has been able to figure out how to do it."

Although you never see Detective Columbo vacuuming a crime scene, every complete crime-scene search includes a collection of hairs and fibers. "It's all there," Deedrick said. "It's always there. The pieces always fit if you look carefully enough. You find the body of a murder victim along the side of a road. What you want to establish is where she was when she died, who she was with, and how

she got to this ditch. It's there, and with enough experience you can figure it out. You can determine the race of the person she was with, whether they had sex, whether they had a fight. Maybe she was on a carpeted surface; was she in a car or a residence? Was it an old carpet or a new one? Did she have pets, or did the suspect have pets? Was it a dog or a cat or something unusual? There's a tremendous amount of information right there, but only if you know how to look for it.''

Hairs and fibers can be found anywhere and everywhere. They can be found on every type of clothing, but particularly on socks and stockings. Hairs and fibers are found inside pockets, in pants cuffs, under fingernails. In the controversial Tawana Brawley case, for example, charred cotton fibers found under the girl's fingernails matched the fibers in a washcloth that had been used to write racial slurs on her body, proving she had written them herself. In a Wilkes-Barre, Pennsylvania, case, Deedrick matched blue-jean fibers found underneath a murdered woman's fingernails to her husband's clothes, providing strong evidence that they had fought during the last few moments of her life.

When a victim is hit with a blunt instrument—a hammer or frying pan, for instance—head hairs can often be found stuck to the instrument's surface, proving this was the weapon used in the crime. The lab once received a five-hundred-pound rock with blood on it, sent air express. The victim had apparently been thrown against the rock during a fight, and the submitting agency wanted the unit to check the bloodstain for hairs and fibers. It took a forklift to get the rock in and out of the building.

Hairs and fibers are found on knives and screwdrivers and guns. When a gun is fired, a vacuum is created, and this "blowback" instantly draws anything close by into the muzzle. So when a weapon is used to commit suicide, hairs are often found in the muzzle.

Hairs and fibers can also be found in fecal material, and when a body decomposes they are found in deposits of body fats. Contrary to the popular myth, hair does not continue growing after death; rather, the scalp shrinks and often slips off the skull intact, forming what is known as a hair mask. The unit occasionally receives a hair mask with a request for as much information as possible about the donor. Because Hairs and Fibers serves as the liaison unit between the lab and experts in esoteric subjects at the Smithsonian Institution, at one time the Hairs and Fiber Unit received a lot of bones, particularly in the spring when winter snows melted and bodies were discovered. Since the Smithsonian would not accept skeletal remains with flesh still attached, someone had to remove that flesh. "I had a nice operation set up," Agent-examiner Chet Blythe remembered. "I'd have a leg boiling in sodium hydroxide or an arm in enzymes. I tried everything to remove the flesh. I even had a head once. But eventually people started sending us entire torsos, which we weren't equipped to handle, so we had to stop it."

In one serial murder case the unit received the entire contents of the suspect's apartment, shipped to Washington, D.C., in a twenty-seven-foot long trailer, with a request that it examine all his furniture, even the tires from his car, to search for hairs or fibers that might be linked to one of his victims. In other cases the unit has received sections of walls, carpets, dirt, and just about every part of a car—including the entire car.

Smashed automobile windshields are sent to the unit because hairs and fibers found embedded in the broken glass can help determine who was driving the car. In rape cases, hairs and fibers have been found on dildos. In a North Carolina case, the wing of an Air National Guard F-4 jet sliced through a civilian aircraft. The civilian plane crashed into the sea, killing everyone aboard, while the F-4 managed to land safely. There was some question about how many peo-

ple had died in the crash. Several human hairs were found on the leading edge of the F-4's damaged wing, enabling the unit to prove that at least three different people had been on the airplane that crashed.

Hairs can be linked to a specific person and can be used simply for purposes of identification. When the space shuttle *Challenger* exploded, Doug Deedrick examined hairs recovered from the wreckage to help identify the bodies, as well as to try to determine if there had been a fire in the cabin before it crashed into the ocean. He found no evidence in the hairs of a fire.

Because hairs can be linked to one person, their presence at a crime scene makes extremely good evidence. In the most common type of case, a North Carolina bank robber discarded a nylon stocking mask that had been worn during the robbery. Hairs were found inside that stocking and when a suspect was arrested, samples of her hair were sent to former unit chief Allyson Simons for comparison. Simons was able to make a positive association between the hairs found in the stocking mask and the suspect, thus proving that she had worn the mask while committing the robbery.

To prevent that kind of match from being made, suspects have been known to shave off all their hair or dye it or bleach it. But the courts have ruled that law enforcement agencies have the right to obtain hair samples, and suspects have actually been prohibited by court order from getting a haircut or changing hair color.

Connecting the victim to the crime scene can be just as important as proving the suspect was there. When newly married Patricia Giesick was killed by what appeared to be a hit-and-run driver while on her honeymoon in New Orleans in 1974, her new husband, Claude Giesick, Jr., stood to collect $350,000 on a double indemnity life insurance policy. But suspicious investigators discovered that Giesick had rented two cars the day before the accident, and they

traced the second car to the rental agency. Although there was no visible damage to the car, two strands of hair were found stuck to the tie rod underneath the car. Two thin strands of hair. The Hairs and Fiber Unit found that those two hairs "were consistent in all microscopic characteristics to Patricia Giesick's hair." The car that had killed her had been rented by her groom. Her death had not been an accident. Tied firmly to the murder by those two hairs, Giesick confessed that he had pushed his wife in front of the car and testified against the driver. The driver was eventually sentenced to life in prison without parole, while Giesick received a twenty-one-year sentence for manslaughter.

The ability to connect victims to the crime scene through a few hairs and fibers proved invaluable in convicting the murderers of Drug Enforcement agent Kiki Camarena and pilot Alfredo Zavala. During unauthorized flights in Zavala's plane, Camarena had located several large marijuana plantations outside Guadalajara, Mexico, forcing the embarrassed Mexican government to destroy a marijuana crop with a street value of about three billion dollars. Soon after this, Camarena and Zavala were kidnapped. Witnesses saw Camarena being driven away in a large automobile. Two well-known Mexican drug traffickers, Rafael Caro-Quintero and Ernesto Fonseca, immediately became the primary suspects, but because the were paying huge bribes to government officials, it became impossible to develop any evidence against them.

Tremendous pressure was exerted on the Mexican government to cooperate in the search for Camarena and Zavala. The border between San Diego and Mexico was practically shut down. Every car was painstakingly searched, laborers couldn't get into this country, and the long, long lines caused fresh produce to start rotting in trucks. Finally the Mexican police, the MFJP, received information that Camarena and Zavala were being held at a

ranch owned by the Bravo drug gang, a rival of Caro-Quintero and Fonseca. After misinforming the DEA about the time the raid would begin, the MFJP raided the Bravo ranch, killing all the members of that gang. Two days later the bodies of Camarena and Zavala were found on the ranch, wrapped in plastic bags lying near a road. A team of investigators from the sci-crime lab was sent to Mexico to examine them.

Both men had been tortured before they were killed. A metal rod had been driven into Camarena's skull. Zavala may have been buried alive. But from the dirt and other debris found on their bodies, agents from the Materials Analysis Unit determined that they had been buried elsewhere and then dug up and left at this site. The obvious intent was to shift responsibility for their murders from Caro-Quintero and Fonseca.

Agent Jack Dillon of the lab's Firearms Unit took hair samples and small cuttings from the clothing of each victim, as well as a piece of the rope and tape that had been used to bind and blindfold them. Mike Malone found a light-beige nylon carpet fiber in the cutting from Zavala's sweatshirt. "That was just about the first lead we got," Malone remembered. "It wasn't much, but it told us that the last thing Zavala had been in contact with was probably a light-beige rug. Early on we told the DEA that they would find a light-beige rug in the room in which Zavala had been killed."

A source informed DEA agents that one of Fonseca's most trusted assistants had parked a brand-new car in his garage and then bricked up the door. The brick wall was torn down and the car, a Mercury Marquis, was searched; Malone was able to match a single hair found on the rear floor mat with Camarena's. Kiki Camarena had been in that car.

In April 1985, two months after the kidnapping and murders, the MFJP claimed that it had located the villa

where Camarena and Zavala had been held. It was a luxurious house hidden behind high walls at 881 Lope de Vega in downtown Guadalajara, a house owned by Rafael Caro-Quintero. "We wanted to get in there right away," Malone said, "but they wouldn't let us in. By the time we were finally allowed to search it the place had been scrubbed down, every wall had been repainted, and just about all the furniture had been replaced. A squad of Federales was living there, supposedly to protect the place. They were actually living in the crime scene. We weren't supposed to find anything. But just in case we did, armed Mexican soldiers watched us, ready to confiscate anything we might find."

The search team got one big break. New carpets had been installed just before the kidnappings, and they hadn't been replaced. Malone started his search in an unattached guest house that had unusually thick walls and a steel door with iron bars on it; the guest house was a perfect place to hide a prisoner so no one would know he was there. The first thing Malone saw when he walked into that house was a light beige rug. Malone divided the room into four quadrants, vacuuming each quadrant with a different filter. The fibers found in Zavala's sweatshirt matched the carpet fibers. But Malone also found tangled in that rug two head hairs, so small that even the most thorough cleaning hadn't dislodged them, two head hairs consistent in every way with head hairs taken from the corpse of Kiki Camarena. Both men had been held in that room.

A car parked next to the house was thoroughly searched. Two more of Camarena's hairs were found on the back floor, suggesting that he had been transported in both cars to or from the villa. But before the search could be concluded, Malone and Agent Ron Raywalt spotted a folded license plate at the bottom of a hole covered by a grate; it was the license plate witnesses had seen on the car driven by Camarena's kidnappers. This discovery caused anxious Mexican officials to end the crime-scene investigation, and

only after months of negotiations was the FBI team permitted to return and complete their search.

The Mexicans had tried to erase all evidence from the crime scene, but hairs and fibers are so small it's almost impossible to get all of them. So in a bedroom inside the main house, a hair that had been forcibly removed from Camarena's head was found. The sheet in which Camarena had been buried was matched to linens in another bedroom. Pieces of the cord with which Camarena had been bound were matched to cord found on the property. Kiki Camarena and Alfredo Zavala had been held and probably killed at 881 Lope de Vega; they had been buried and exhumed, then left to be discovered in an attempt to satisfy the protests of the American government. "They never allowed us to take hair samples from Caro-Quintero or Fonseca," Malone said with obvious regret. "We've still got about five hundred hairs from those crime scenes that are unknowns. But I have no doubt that among them would be Caro-Quintero's and Fonseca's."

Additional evidence was developed linking those men and members of their drug gang to the crime scene. In several trials held in Los Angeles, during which hundreds of witnesses testified, six members of the Caro-Quintero organization were convicted of crimes connected to the kidnappings and murders and sentenced to life imprisonment. In trials held in Mexico all of the major members of the Caro-Quintero organization were tried and convicted and are currently in prison.

Hairs and fibers often connect the suspect directly to the victim. Among the most compelling evidence against serial killer Ted Bundy were ninety-eight cross-transfers of fibers between Bundy and a twelve-year-old victim named Kimberly Leach. Fibers from Bundy's coat and from the carpet of a van he had stolen were found on the young girl's clothing, while fibers from the girl's clothing were found

on Bundy's. This convinced the jury that Bundy had been in close contact with Kimberly Leach, and helped convict him.

In a Wooster, Ohio, case two men were charged with the rape and murder of a little girl when orange carpet fibers found on her body appeared to be similar to orange fibers found in their environment. But when Agent-examiner Alan Robillard compared those fibers he discovered they were quite different. He eventually testified for the defense. "The DA attacked me pretty severely on the stand," he remembered, "because I was saying that these fibers were not the same. I didn't say the two suspects didn't do it, I just said no association could be made based on those fibers. But they were convicted anyway.

"Ironically, while these guys were in jail, another little girl was murdered, and the same orange carpet fibers that had been found on the first victim were found on her body."

Almost a year later a terrified woman was found running down a highway. The driver who picked her up thought she was wearing denim; in fact she was naked, but she had been beaten so severely her body was completely bruised. She had escaped from the home of a man named Eric Buell, and she was able to bring the police back to the house in which she had been held and tortured. In Buell's van, police found an orange carpet. Robillard said: "How many pieces of carpet like that exist in the world? We were able to show that the carpet had been made by J.P. Stevens, and because of the recession they'd made only four thousand yards. They had sold about a hundred and fifty yards to a store in Worcester, and that carpet was so ugly the store still had a hundred and twenty yards in stock. That allowed us to make a very strong association to Buell's van."

Robillard testified again, this time for the prosecution. Buell was convicted and sentenced to death.

The more unusual hairs and fibers are, the more valuable

they are as evidence. When Green Beret Dr. Jeffrey Mac-
Donald was accused of murdering his wife, Colette, and
their two daughters—in the famed "Fatal Vision" case—
he insisted that his family had been killed by a drug-crazed
band of hippies led by a woman wearing dark clothes, a
floppy black hat, and a long blond wig. After being convicted of the murders, MacDonald appealed several times
on various issues. In 1992 his new attorney, Alan Dershowitz, claimed that blond wig hairs found in Colette Mac-
Donald's hairbrush had never been produced at earlier trials and supported MacDonald's claim that a woman in a
blond wig had been in his home that night.

At least five hairs found in the MacDonald home have
never been identified, but the crime-scene search conducted
by the military police was done quite carelessly. People
were constantly going in and out of the house—someone
even stole a wallet from the house during the search—so
those hairs could have belonged to anyone. But the evidence against MacDonald was overwhelming. There was
extensive blood-spatter evidence and a multitude of fiber
evidence. MacDonald claimed that he had taken off his
pajama top and used it to defend himself when the hippies
tried to stab him, but a determined sci-crime lab technician
named Shirley Green spent weeks working with that pajama top, folding it and refolding it, until she was able to
align the numerous cuts in it to the twenty stab wounds in
Colette MacDonald's chest, proving it had been laid over
her while she was being stabbed.

Still, there were those unexplained blond wig hairs. Dershowitz's appeal for a new trial was based on his contention that these wig hairs, some hairs found on Colette's
body, and some dark wool fibers constituted hard, scientific
evidence to support MacDonald's story that intruders had
been in his house. Mike Malone got the case.

"We ended up finding two different types of wig fibers," Malone said. "One of them we'd never seen before.

Examiners in the Instrumental Analysis Unit did a spectro-graphic exam and identified it as a fiber called saran. We checked all our files, we checked our collection, we didn't know anything about it.

"So we did a lot of research and discovered that saran is a very unusual fiber, and it's never used in human wigs. It's used almost exclusively for doll and mannequin hair, dust mops, and patio screens. With two little girls we could assume there were some dolls in the house, but no one had kept them so we had no basis for a comparison. Eventually we found a woman who works for Mattel and has what might be the largest doll collection in the world. She's got thousands of dolls. We were able to find two different Barbie dolls with hair made of fibers similar to the fibers found in Colette's brush. We couldn't testify that they'd come from those dolls, but we could tell the court that they had not come from any known type of human wig. Those fibers were unique."

Malone was also able to match the questioned dark wig fibers to a fall owned by Colette MacDonald that had been kept by her father. One of the hairs found on Colette's body came from Jeffrey MacDonald; the other hairs were limb and body hairs and were therefore unsuitable for com-parison. And finally, the dark wool fibers had probably been picked up by Colette when she collapsed onto a shag carpet and most likely came from her own clothing. On the basis of Malone's report, Dershowitz's appeal for a new trial was rejected.

In most cases hairs and fibers become significant only when they can connect a suspect to a place or person he denies having had any contact with. If the victim and sus-pect are known to have been in contact, or if there was a legitimate reason for them to have been at the crime scene, hair and fiber evidence has very little value. But there are exceptions, and this is where the agent-examiners become detectives. Generally it's extremely difficult to determine

when the transfer of hairs and fibers took place. In the Camarena case the rugs in the villa had been installed just before the kidnapping. Therefore Camarena had to have been in those rooms after a certain date.

In 1987 Doug Deedrick had a triple murder case in Alaska in which he had to prove that a suspect had been in an apartment at a specific time through hair and fiber evidence. A woman and her seven-year-old daughter had been strangled, and her two-year-old daughter's throat had been slit. The woman's nephew, who had lived in the apartment for about a month, but had been thrown out ten days before the murders, immediately became the primary suspect. A substantial number of his hairs were found in the apartment, but because he had lived there they had very little value as evidence.

"The most compelling evidence was a rag that had been wadded up and left in the bathroom sink," Deedrick remembered. "I found a pubic hair with a partial egg case from pubic lice on it. I found the same egg cases on the nephew's pubic hairs, so we could pretty much conclude that the pubic hair found on that rag was the nephew's. My problem was establishing when he'd left that hair."

Just as Sherlock Holmes might have done in this case, Deedrick decided to find out how hairs moved through a house in a normal situation, then contrast those results to what had been found in that apartment. "I started by doing a pubic-hair study at home, just to see if pubic hairs were easily transferred out of one room and where they would most likely be found. I took a crime-scene vacuum home and for two weeks I vacuumed every room every night and preserved the material I found. Then I examined every hair and compared it to known samples from my wife and myself. I kept track of where I'd found hairs and how many I found. The results seemed to prove that there was a migration of hairs from room to room, mostly by getting stuck on clothing, particularly socks."

An important element in the case was the cleaning habits of the dead woman. Her friends testified that she had vacuumed the apartment often, and in fact had done so the day before she was murdered. Deedrick did a stratum search of the vacuum cleaner bag, estimating how much dirt might have been picked up each time the vacuum cleaner was used, then searching the dirt layer by layer, day by day, inch by inch. "I had to go down pretty far just to find hair that matched the suspect. The fact that I found none of his hairs in the top layers supported the contention that there weren't a lot of hairs left in the apartment from the time he was living there, and that most of the hairs we found had been left there while he was in the apartment committing the crimes."

Most, but not all. Obviously some of the hairs found there had been lying on the floor for weeks. Deedrick had to show a difference between those old hairs and newly deposited ones. "Hairs that have been in a particular environment for any length of time," he said, "especially hairs that have been on carpeting, tend to pick up residual dirt and debris. They get dirty. I looked at thousands of hairs found in that apartment and divided them by their condition. The pubic hairs we found on the children's bodies were clean; there was no dirt or soot or debris on them. The pubic hairs we found on the washrag in the sink were also extremely important because the washrag was still damp, and it wouldn't have been if it had been put there ten days earlier."

By tracking the movement of hairs and fibers in the apartment, Deedrick was able to determine how the crime might have happened. The suspect was wearing green wool gloves when he entered the apartment. He fought with the woman and grabbed her by the hair. This was proved by the forcibly removed hairs found on the gloves. Then he sexually assaulted her and strangled her with a towel. Fibers from that towel were also found on the green gloves. It

was at that point he probably decided to clean himself, so he had to take off the gloves. In addition to finding pubic hairs on the washcloth, Deedrick also found green wool fibers from the gloves, fibers from the woman's nightgown, and fibers from her bed on the cloth.

After killing the woman he strangled her older daughter. This was shown by the fact that Deedrick found fibers from her mother's nightgown on the little girl's body, as well as several green wool fibers, probably remnants left on the suspect's hands after taking off the gloves. And finally the nephew killed the younger girl.

Deedrick had built a strong case against the suspect, who tried to flee, but was caught. Deedrick testified before the grand jury, then spent two days on the witness stand during the actual trial. The nephew was convicted of the three murders and received three one-hundred-year sentences.

Unlike hairs, which can be traced to a specific person, fibers are extremely difficult to trace back to a specific source—that blouse or those pants. But because fibers are transferred in such large numbers they are much more likely than hairs to be found at a crime scene. They are particularly valuable in allowing investigators to create links between victims, suspects, and places.

In recent years fibers have often enabled police to link the victims of serial killers. Over an eight-month period beginning in May 1984, ten young women were raped and murdered in the Tampa Bay, Florida, area. The first victim had been strangled. She was found naked, her hands tied behind her back, her legs tied spread-eagled. A single bright-red fiber was found on her clothing. From the size and shape of the cross section, investigators determined that it was probably an automobile carpet fiber. On the basis of Locard's theory that fibers generally reflect the most recent contact, the Hairs and Fiber Unit informed

Florida police that their suspect was probably driving a vehicle with red carpeting.

Two weeks later, the second victim was found. Her throat had been cut and she had been bludgeoned. She was naked from the waist down, her hands had been tied behind her back, and the same red fiber was found on her clothing. But this time there were additional clues. Several fibers from a second red vehicle carpet were also found on her clothing, suggesting that the killer was driving a vehicle with two different red floor mats. Some strands of medium-length brown Caucasian hair were found: the suspect was probably white and had medium-length brown hair. And finally, from tire impressions left at the scene, FBI lab examiners determined that the suspect's car had a Goodyear Viva tire with the whitewall facing inside on the right rear, and a somewhat unusual Vogue tire, which was made by a small manufacturer primarily for Cadillacs, on the left rear. The size of the tire indicated the suspect was driving a medium or full-sized car.

In June the decomposing body of a woman was found lying in an orange grove. Because she was fully dressed and her hands were not tied, she was not linked to the other victims. So the evidence was sent to a different examiner in the sci-crime lab, and to this examiner the red carpet fibers that were found meant nothing.

The murders seemed to stop for several months, but in early October the naked body of a young woman was found lying in a dirt field. She had been shot to death about five weeks earlier. Exposure to the elements had caused her scalp to slip off her skull, and this mask was found next to her decomposing body. Telltale red carpet fibers and a brown Caucasian pubic hair were recovered from her clothing. A week later the body of the fifth victim was found in a field. Two weeks later the sixth victim was found, just off a highway. The remains of the seventh victim were discovered several days later; her bones were scattered over a

large area, but a single red carpet fiber was found tangled in her hair. Eventually ten murders were attributed to the serial killer, linked together by these red carpet fibers and strands of brown hair.

While the physical evidence was accumulating, there was nothing solid to lead police to the killer. They needed a break, and they got one. Very early on the morning of November 3, as a seventeen-year old girl was riding her bicycle home from her job at a doughnut shop, a man leaped out of a car, knocked her off her bike, and kidnapped her. He covered her eyes with a blindfold and took her to an apartment, and for the next two days he sexually assaulted her. "This girl was very sharp," Mike Malone said admiringly. "She never lost her composure. She did exactly what he wanted her to do and, over time, he took a liking to her. On the second night he told her he was going to let her go. Once again she was blindfolded and he put her back in his car. She remembered two things: She could see under the blindfold and read the word "Magnum" on the dashboard; and before he let her out of the car, he had stopped at an automatic teller machine to get some cash.

"The Hillsborough County sheriff's office and the Tampa police department did a real good job on this case. Although this kidnapping didn't fit the killer's pattern, just to cover every possibility they sent her clothing to the lab. As always, my technician got the clothing and started to process it for hairs and fibers. A few minutes later she came running into my office, telling me that all kinds of red fibers were falling off the clothing. Most of our cases are routine, but every once in a while there's a moment of tremendous excitement. This was certainly one of them.

"I examined those fibers under a microscope; then, just to be sure, I analyzed the red dye. Bingo! I could make an exact match to the fibers found on the murder victims. There was no doubt about it. The same person who'd kidnapped this girl had committed those murders."

The only car manufactured that had the name "Magnum" on its dashboard was the 1978 Dodge Magnum. A team of detectives began compiling a list of every 1978 Dodge Magnum registered in the Tampa Bay area. At the same time, a second team of detectives began checking all the bank ATMs that had been used at approximately three o'clock in the morning of the day the girl had been released. Only one name appeared on both lists: Robert Joseph Long. Bobby Joe Long. The rape victim was shown a photograph of Long and positively identified him as the man who had kidnapped and assaulted her.

Long was put under around-the-clock surveillance. While he was in a movie theater an agent crawled underneath his car and examined the tires. On the left rear was a Vogue, on the right rear was a Viva. When Long came out of the theater he was arrested and charged with murder.

His car and apartment were thoroughly searched, and Malone flew to Florida to make the hair and fiber comparisons. The fibers taken from the two different red carpets in Long's car matched the fibers found on eight victims. Long's head hair and pubic hair matched the brown Caucasian hair found on several victims. Head hairs from six of the victims were found inside the Dodge Magnum.

When police confronted Long with the evidence he said, "I think I may need an attorney." Later, after accepting his situation, he admitted, "You got me."

For his crimes Bobby Joe Long received twenty-six life sentences—and the death penalty. "I guess the thing that was most surprising to me," Malone said, "is that when we finally got this guy, he wasn't some kind of monster. He was just an ordinary guy who liked to kill people."

While the fiber evidence provided the vital link between Long and his victims, detectives eventually compiled an abundance of hard evidence against him. Hairs and fibers have rarely been enough on which to base an entire prose-

cution, but in one of the most chilling cases in recent American history, the Atlanta child murders, it provided the only physical evidence needed to convict Wayne Williams, who was accused of killing at least twelve of the thirty victims.

During a twenty-two-month period beginning in July 1979, thirty black children and young men either disappeared or were murdered in the Atlanta, Georgia, area. The string of killings made headlines around the world, and a large task force, consisting of representatives from several different law enforcement agencies, was formed to investigate. The victims were murdered in different ways, causing investigators to believe that more than one person was responsible. But several of the victims could be connected to the same killer or place by the presence of greenish-yellow and violet acetate fibers found in their clothing and hair. The fibers indicated that each of these victims had been in the same environment either just prior to or after their death. Identifying the source of the fibers might lead police to the killer. Fibers can rarely be traced to a single source—it had never been done before—but there were absolutely no other clues.

By the time the FBI sci-crime lab became involved in the case, in 1981, most of the murders had already been committed. The greenish-yellow fibers had already been identified by Georgia investigators as carpet fibers. Because carpet fibers have to withstand continuous weight and pressure, they are usually thicker and larger than other fibers. But these fibers were different. "I'd been doing hairs and fibers work for a long time," remembered Agent-examiner Hal Deadman, who did the hair and fiber comparisons in this case, "and these fibers were unique. Every company makes its own fibers, but certain cross-sectional shapes and sizes are pretty common in the industry. These fibers had an unusual triangular cross section; they were unlike anything I'd ever seen before." The fact that the fibers didn't

come from a common type of carpeting was good news to investigators, because the less common a fiber, the more valuable it is as evidence.

Agents eventually identified the manufacturer of the fiber as the Wellman Corporation, a Massachusetts company. Wellman had sold yarn made from this fiber, called 181B, to a Dalton, Georgia, carpet company, West Point Pepperell. West Point Pepperell had used 181B in the production of its Luxaire line for only one year, and among the colors it had produced was something called English Olive, a greenish-yellow identical to the color of the fibers found on some of the victims. A very small number of English Olive Luxaire carpets had been sold in the Atlanta area; theoretically, it might have been possible to track down everyone who had purchased them. If this had been done, eventually agents would have knocked on the door of twenty-three-year-old Wayne Williams.

But just before the FBI located the carpet manufacturer, an Atlanta newspaper reported that police had found unique fibers on the bodies of several victims. Until that story was published, the victims had been found fully clothed; after it appeared, the victims were stripped and dropped off bridges into the Chattahoochee River, presumably to allow the river to wash away any hairs and fibers. Because the killer's pattern had changed, the Atlanta task force began staking out bridges over the river. And one morning, at about two A.M., officers heard a loud splash. Minutes later they stopped the only car on the bridge at that time. The driver was a young black man, a music promoter named Wayne Williams. Police reported that Williams told them he had just dropped some garbage in the river; Williams denied telling them anything. But two days later the body of a man named Nathaniel Cater was pulled from the river near the bridge. And in his hair police found a greenish-yellow carpet fiber.

Williams's home, in which he lived with his parents, was

searched for the first time. Eventually several searches would be made and hundreds of thousands of hairs and fibers would be collected and examined. But that first night Larry Peterson of the Georgia state police crime lab made the initial comparisons between the fibers found on the victims and fibers taken from the Luxaire carpet in Williams's home. "Peterson called me at about one-thirty in the morning," Hal Deadman recalled, "and told me very matter-of-factly, 'I've made some matches. You'd better come over here.' I went right over to the lab and looked at them. They looked fine. At that point both Larry and I were convinced that someone in the Williamses' environment was involved in the murders. The chance of this being just a coincidence was essentially zero."

Williams vehemently denied any involvement in the murders, and police found no other physical evidence that would connect him to the victims. This pile of fibers, not even enough to withstand a strong breeze, was all prosecutors had. But the killings had stopped with Williams's arrest, and prosecutors were convinced he was guilty of at least some of them. Proving that was going to be very difficult. Hairs and fibers had never been used as the primary evidence in a murder trial, and no one knew if a jury would convict someone of murder, beyond a reasonable doubt, on the basis of hair and fiber comparisons.

Prosecutors decided to try Williams for only two murders, those of Nathaniel Cater and Jimmy Payne, but under Georgia law evidence from other murders that can be shown to be related to those crimes also can be introduced at trial. The carpet fibers proved the relationship between Cater and Payne and the other victims.

The hair and fiber evidence was initially used to link Williams and his victims. Twenty-eight different fibers, in addition to dog hairs, found on the bodies of one or more victims were matched to nineteen different objects found in Williams's home and his car. Connecting one fiber to an

environment and a victim has very little significance, but the ability to make multiple associations is extremely important. "On some of the victims we found as many as ten fibers that could be directly related to Williams's home or a car he had in his possession at the time of that murder," Deadman said. "The chances that those ten fibers could have come from a place other than Williams's home or car are just about impossible."

That would be true even if all the fibers that could be associated with Williams were commonly found, but they weren't. Twenty-seven of those fibers could be classified as unusual or uncommon, meaning they formed the basis of a strong match. Prosecutors used statistical evidence to emphasize the importance of these fiber matches. To show how unlikely it was that the 181B fibers came from anywhere except the carpet in Williams's home, agents traced the entire production line of Luxaire carpets. Considering the number of yards manufactured and sold, and assuming that every carpet sold almost a decade earlier was still in use, there was still only a 1-in-7,792 chance of finding a similar carpet.

And those odds were multiplied by every different fiber found on the victims that could be linked to Williams. In addition to the carpet fibers, hairs that could be associated with Williams's dog, and violet acetate fibers that could be matched to a spread found in his bedroom were found on ten victims. Prosecutors used charts to show that it was virtually impossible that those three different fibers could all be found anywhere except Williams's home.

In addition to being used to link Williams to the victims, fibers were also used to establish a time frame. Nine victims were linked by automobile carpet fibers to three different cars used by Williams. When Williams was using a rented car, fibers that could be matched to carpeting from that car were found on victims. A noose comprises millions of fibers woven together to make an extremely strong rope.

The hair and fiber evidence was forming a noose that was tightening around Williams's neck.

"There was no question that we tied his household and his automobiles to the victims," Deadman stated flatly, "no question about it at all. And while his mother and father also lived in that house, Wayne Williams was the only one who drove some of these cars. I testified for several days, trying to explain to the jury the significance of all these associations. But you never know if they really understand this evidence until the verdict comes in."

The knowledge that police had found a few fibers on his victims had forced Wayne Williams to change his killing patterns, and caused him to be caught on that bridge above the Chattahoochee River. And it was those small fibers, fibers no different from those you can pick off your clothing right now, that resulted in Williams's being convicted of murder and sentenced to spend the rest of his life in prison.

While it's not possible to claim that a fiber came from a specific source to the exclusion of all other sources, it is possible to make precisely that claim with pieces of fabric. Fabrics consist of millions of woven fibers, and examiners can show that pieces of torn fabric fit together by matching rough edges, tears and cuts, broken patterns, any kind of damage that allows an end-to-end comparison. "Fabric matches are part of our training," Wayne Oakes said. "Fabric matches make very compelling evidence. No matter how hard someone tried, they just couldn't reproduce the randomness of a cut or a tear or a ripped edge."

In a particularly brutal Port Orchard, Washington, case, three hitchhiking teenagers, two girls and a boy, were picked up by a man driving a van. After buying wine and beer, the man drove them out into the country. And there he pulled a gun on them and tied them up with strips torn from a sheet in the rear of his van. He sexually assaulted

all three of them, then shot and killed one of the girls, killed the boy by slicing his throat and cutting out his tongue, then shot the other girl in the eye and ear, leaving her for dead. She survived, and when he went back to his van, she tried to escape through the woods. He tracked her down and slit her throat. Still she fought to live. And she was very, very lucky. She fell onto an upturned tree stump and the dirt and debris stemmed the flow of blood from her throat. Miraculously, she survived.

She was able to provide police with a good description of the killer and his van, and he was captured. Oakes testified that he was able to make a perfect match between the strips of cloth used to tie up the victims and the sheet found in the back of the suspect's van—important corrobative testimony to support the survivor's story. "Doing fabric matches is a lot like putting pieces of a jigsaw puzzle together," Oakes said, "but it's something a jury can see and understand. In this case it was such a strong match that it certainly helped convict him."

"Calling what we do just hairs and fibers examinations really isn't sufficient," Mike Malone pointed out, "because this is kind of a catch-all unit. While the majority of our work is done with hairs and fibers, we also do a little bit of everything else that might be considered trace evidence, things that are hard to see with the naked eye. If you have to use a microscope to look at something, we're probably going to get it. That might include plant material, glass chips, paint chips, even soil examinations."

And feathers. Those soft fluffy things that float on a breeze and are used to make people laugh. The body covering of birds. There's something pleasant and whimsical about feathers that may seem out of place at a crime scene, but feathers have unique characteristics that can be used to provide a strong link between a suspect and a crime.

Hairs and Fibers was once known as the Microscopy Unit because of the variety of exams conducted by the unit.

And still, in addition to conducting hair and fiber examinations, most agent-examiners have at least one additional area in which they have qualified to testify in court as an expert. Doug Deedrick's is feathers. He is recognized as one of the leading feather experts in the sci-crime world. "I always wanted to get into something that's a little different," he admitted, "something that not everybody else was doing. I got interested in feathers and I nurtured that interest and eventually, without even realizing it, I'd accumulated all the information I needed. Then I built a substantial reference collection for the lab."

Feathers are often found at crime scenes. Down clothing is easily damaged in shootings and stabbings and beatings; bedding is damaged in sex crimes; Deedrick has even found feathers inside hoax bombs. He began learning about feathers in 1978 from the Smithsonian's feather expert, a remarkable woman named Roxy Laybourne. Now in her eighties, Laybourne has been working with the FBI for more than fifty years, and has worked with Deedrick in a variety of cases, from providing evidence against killers to helping discover the cause of airplane crashes.

Although it's possible to identify from a feather the family and body area of the bird from which it came, it isn't possible to prove that a specific feather came from a specific bird or, more important, a specific pillow or mattress or vest. But feathers still make strong evidence. In a Naples, Florida, case two people were shot to death at almost point-blank range. They were found sprawled on a bloody bathroom floor. A pillow with several bullet holes in it was lying nearby; it had been used to muffle the gunshots.

The vacuum that is created when a weapon is fired will suck all kinds of debris into the gun barrel. Sometimes the victim's blood or brain matter will be found, but in this case, when a suspect was arrested, several tiny feathers were found inside the barrel of his gun. Deedrick testified

that the feathers found inside that gun exhibited the same microscopic characteristics as the feathers found inside the pillow, testimony that helped convict the suspect of murder.

Periodically, Deedrick receives feathers that have been ingested into airplane engines, particularly in cases of unexplained engine failure. When one of the Air Force's most sophisticated planes, a billion-dollar B-1 bomber, crashed, feathers found inside the engine were identified as coming from a brown pelican. Because of that finding, the Air Force changed the path of its test flights away from the migration route of the brown pelican.

The weapons used to commit crimes generally evolve with the times and technology, but criminals have been using ropes and cords throughout the annals of crime. While duct tape is now frequently used instead of rope, rope is still used quite often to tie up victims and on occasion can provide valuable evidence.

In the early 1980s two young newspaper boys in a small town just outside Omaha, Nebraska, were abducted and murdered while making their Sunday-morning deliveries. One of the boys was found bound with what appeared to be an ordinary white nylon rope, which is just too commonly used to make a good basis for comparison. But ropes are made by winding many different yarns around a center cord called a tracer, and when the unit's rope expert, Wayne Oakes, began unraveling this rope, he found it had been made from 106 different yarns and twenty-four different fiber types. It was mostly what is known as junk filler, yarns and fibers that have no real value, and it didn't affect the quality of the rope, but as a basis of comparison it was like discovering a vein of gold. "This was a unique rope," Oakes explained. "I'd never seen anything quite like it. I had photographs of it distributed to all the law enforcement people in the area, and emphasized that whenever they did

a crime-scene search they should look for a white rope. If they found one, open it up; if it looks like the rope in the photograph, send it in. I knew if we found it we'd be able to make a very strong association between the killer and those kids.''

The murders had caused a heightened sense of suspicion in the town. One morning, a worker at a day-care center noticed an unfamiliar car in the parking lot and wrote down its license-plate number. The driver spotted her and chased her, but she managed to get away. She immediately called the hot line that had been set up by the task force investigating the murders. The FBI agent who received the call traced the plate number to an automobile dealership. The car, he learned, had been loaned to a customer whose own car was being serviced. The agent immediately went to the dealership to investigate. He looked through the window; lying in plain sight was a short length of white nylon rope.

The suspect, an Air Force enlisted man, was questioned by both local police and the FBI. He gave authorities permission to search his quarters. Another length of rope was found there and sent to Oakes. The comparison was time-consuming, Oakes remembered, "We microscopically compared every one of those one hundred and six yarns and then we chemically tested them to make sure they'd been colored with the same dyes as the rope found on the boy's body. It was an identical match." Faced with this evidence, the suspect confessed. It was an old rope, he said, a rope he had had since his days as a Boy Scout volunteer. It was this rope that tied him tightly to the murder of two children. He was sentenced to be executed by lethal injection.

A few slender strands of hair, fibers almost invisible to the naked eye, the fluff of feathers, bits of cord, a torn piece of fabric: in terms of size and weight none of this adds up to very much, but as evidence it's strong enough to

support the full weight of the law. It's the stuff that's always there but rarely seen, the stuff that proves, as the Chinese proverb warns, "Everything may depend on the difference between two hairs."

5

The One and Only:
The Latent Fingerprint Section and DNA Analysis Unit

Every human being carries with him from his cradle to his grave certain physical marks which do not change their character, and by which he can always be identified—and that without shade of doubt or question. These marks are his signature, his physiological autograph . . . and this autograph cannot be counterfeited, nor can he disguise it or hide it away, nor can it become illegible by the wear or mutations of time. . . .

This autograph consists of the delicate lines and corrugations with which Nature marks the insides of the hands and the soles of the feet. If you look at the balls of your fingers . . . you will observe that these dainty curving lines lie close together, like those that indicate the borders of oceans in maps, and that they form various clearly defined patterns, such as arches, circles, long curves, whorls, etc. and that these patterns differ on different fingers.

MARK TWAIN, *Pudd'nhead Wilson*

Just before midnight, on October 1, 1993, twelve-year-old Polly Klaas and two girlfriends were having a slumber party in her family's Petaluma, California, home. Suddenly, without warning, a man dressed in dark clothing and carrying a knife walked into the room and threatened to slit their throats if they screamed. The intruder ordered them to lie down on the floor; he tied their hands and pulled pillowcases over their heads. And then he kidnapped Polly Klaas.

"When I hung up the phone after being notified I just stared outside," remembered Captain Pat Parks of the Petaluma police department. "I realized it was a dark, cold night out there, and somewhere a terrified little girl was depending on us."

Within an hour Petaluma police were searching the Klaas home inch by inch, looking for the smallest clue. "We used all the traditional investigative techniques," explained Detective Michael Meese, "including the various fingerprint powders. But we came up with almost nothing."

An FBI evidence response team—crime-scene experts— got to the Klaas home about an hour after Petaluma police. After receiving permission from the local police, they began an intensive search. "When they got to her bedroom," Detective Meese continued, "they began by applying red fluorescent powder to precisely the same surfaces I'd just dusted for prints. I hadn't found a thing. But then they turned out the lights, put on tinted goggles that looked sort of like a chemist's safety glasses, and turned on a light that looked like sort of a wand."

This light was an alternate light source, ALS, as it is known. Viewed through filtered goggles, the light illuminates objects that cannot be seen with the naked eye. "Many different prints that we hadn't found were suddenly visible," Captain Parks said, "but there was only one that we could not account for. That was a partial palmprint found on the upper rail of Polly's bunk bed. We had a print, but initially it didn't do us much good. There isn't too much you can do with a palmprint until you have a bad guy to go with it."

Almost two months later some tattered children's clothing was found on a hillside. A computer search disclosed that on the night of the kidnapping two sheriff's deputies had reported that a car driven by a man named Richard Allen Davis had been stuck on a private road near this site.

Further investigation revealed that Davis had served fifteen years in prison for burglary, assault, and kidnapping. Finally, here was a bad guy whose palmprints could be used as a comparison.

After Davis was arrested his palmprints were sent to fingerprint specialist Mike Smith at the sci-crime lab in Washington, D.C. It was a difficult comparison to make—the latent print found on the bunk bed wasn't very clear—but it was enough. Smith was able to make a positive comparison; he was able to say that the only person in the world who could have left that print in Polly Klaas's bedroom was Richard Allen Davis.

Eventually additional evidence against Davis was developed. The Materials Analysis Unit made a positive fracture match—it matched the torn edges of the strips of cloth found in Polly's bedroom and at the site where Davis's car broke down. Hairs and Fibers identified a single beard hair found in the bedroom as consistent with Richard Davis. But when Davis heard news reports that his palmprint had been positively identified, he asked to speak to Detective Meese. In that interview he admitted kidnapping and killing Polly Klaas. And then he led police to her body.

The most important piece of evidence was the partial palmprint. A square inch of wavy lines. And had this crime been committed only a few years ago, that print probably would not have been found.

Mark Twain was right. From the day you are born until the day you die the only physical aspect of your body that won't change is the shape of those funny lines in your skin. Prints—fingerprints, palmprints, footprints—are the only physical means of establishing your identity to the exclusion of everyone else who has ever lived. No two people—no two fingers—have ever been found that are identical. "And the day we find two prints that we can't tell apart," explained Danny Greathouse, the Latent Fingerprint Sec-

tion chief, "that'll be the day we close the door and walk out of here forever because we'll be out of business."

Look at the undersides of your fingers. You'll see that they are covered with slightly raised areas of skin, called ridges. If you look a little more closely, you will see that these ridges aren't continuous; they stop, they start, they divide, and they make formations. It's the arrangement and relationship of these ridges that make your fingerprint unique and identifiable. And what makes that more than just a curiosity is the fact that almost everybody sweats. Sweat is secreted from the body through billions of microscopic pores in the skin. About 99 percent of perspiration is composed of water, with the remaining 1 percent composed of salt, amino acids, and other chemicals. That 1 percent makes all the difference. When someone touches an object, perspiration—or in some cases other substances that the person has touched, such as grease, oil, food products, dirt, even blood—is transferred from the ridges of the fingerprints to that object, leaving an impression. Because no two prints are alike, this impression can be used to prove that a particular person was in a specific place or handled a specific object. If that impression is visible to the naked eye, as on a glass, it's a patent print, while an invisible print is a latent print. Depending on what material the print consists of, it can be made visible in a variety of ways. It's generally latent prints that put people in prison.

These strange lines in the skin have fascinated people for thousands of years. Ancient Indians in Nova Scotia etched pictures of hands with raised ridges into the side of a cliff. Clay tablets depict Babylonian officials taking fingerprints from criminals. And throughout history charlatans have thrived by predicting people's future on the basis of the lines on their hands.

Fingerprints as a means of identification can be traced back to eighth-century China, when they were used to seal business contracts. In fourteenth-century Persia, all official

government documents were required to include fingerprint impressions. But it wasn't until 1858, when Sir William Herschel, the British administrator of a large district in Bengal, India, required Indians to seal contracts with their fingerprints as well as their signatures, that fingerprinting became an accepted means of identification in the modern world. Fingerprints were used for official purposes in the United States for the first time in 1882, when an officer of the U.S. Geological Survey engaged in mapping the continent used his own print to prevent forgery of his supply orders.

It was also around this time that fingerprints were first used in law enforcement. One of the basic problems faced by early law enforcement officials was how to register and identify criminals. Early civilizations branded criminals with tattoos or cut off a finger or a hand. In the early 1800s policemen with photographic memories would visit prisons and look at newly arrived convicts to see if they were familiar and to memorize their faces for the future. Newly invented photography was used for the first time in Belgian prisons in the 1840s, but since there was no means of reproducing photographs the work had very limited value. So, simply by taking an alias or slightly altering their appearance, repeat criminals most often went undetected.

In 1879 Frenchman Alphonse Bertillon invented a method of identifying people by measuring different parts of their bodies, ranging from the spread of their arms to the length of their left foot. As many as fourteen different measurements were taken; the odds against two people having the same Bertillon measurements were estimated at almost 300,000,000 to 1. The Bertillon Method became the primary means of criminal identification throughout Europe and America, and it might still be in use today if Will West hadn't been sentenced to serve time at Fort Leavenworth Prison in 1903.

When West arrived at Fort Leavenworth, his Bertillon

measurements were taken—and when a clerk checked the files he found that a prisoner named Will West, who had essentially the same measurements, was already there serving a life sentence for murder. Improbable as it seemed, a second William West was indeed hard at work in one of the prison shops. Incredibly, although the two men did not know of each other's existence, they bore the same name, they looked like identical twins in prison photographs, and their Bertillon measurements were just about the same. In fact, the only thing about them that was remarkably different was their fingerprints. The next day the prison at Leavenworth abandoned the Bertillon system and began fingerprinting inmates.

A year later, a national fingerprint bureau, which included all federal prisoners, was established at Leavenworth. And in 1924 Congress established the Identification Division of the Bureau of Investigation as the national repository of all fingerprint records. For the first time, by comparing inked prints taken in association with various arrests of the same people, officials were able to connect crimes committed in different cities and states to the same criminals.

Fingerprinting caught the fancy of the American public during the gangster era, when it became the G-men's—as FBI agents were popularly known—first major scientific tool for tracking public enemies like Ma Barker, Jake Fleagle, and John Dillinger.

The Identification Division eventually became the largest operating unit within the FBI, employing more than 2,600 people. If your prints have ever been taken, they probably will be among the more than 200,000,000 prints representing more than 68,000,000 people on file in the bureau's Criminal Justice Information Services Division. About seventy percent of all people arrested already have their prints on file somewhere in the operations branch of this division.

But when Detective Columbo wants to know if a partial

print found on a car radio button tuned to a rock-and-roll station belongs to a world-famous classical violinist, he submits it to the Latent Fingerprint Section, which officially was separated from the Ident Division and became part of the sci-crime lab in 1993. "Latents" works all criminal cases. The fact is that it's just about impossible to commit a crime without touching something at the crime scene. So the prints are there, but they're often invisible to the naked eye. To be of any investigative value, they have to be found and made visible, developed enough to be suitable for comparison, then compared to the known prints of a suspect. All that happens in the Latent Fingerprint Section.

Knowing where to look for prints and how to develop them is a fine art learned mostly through experience, and many of the nearly one hundred specialists in Latents have been on the job more than thirty years. "Often an entire case will hinge on the ability of the crime-scene investigator to find prints," explained Danny Greathouse, one of only five fingerprint specialists to become an agent. "The problem is that most of the time prints are invisible, so you have to know where to look for them.

"I always begin at the point of entry: Where did that unknown person come into the room? How did he get into the car? And the point of exit—how did he get out of there? Then I look around to see what's been disturbed, what's been moved. I look for footprints, which not only make good evidence, but they allow me to follow an individual's movements around an environment.

"There are always logical places to look. In motel rooms we often find prints on the wall next to the front window because someone has leaned on it while moving the curtain to peek outside. I remember one major drug case in which dealers hid out in an apartment and before they left they wiped down the whole place. The only print we found was on the bathroom mirror over the toilet; one of the men had

leaned on it while going to the bathroom. In a bank robbery case the gang had carefully wiped down every inch of the apartment they'd lived in for weeks while planning the robbery, but when they left, someone forgot to turn on the dishwasher and we got all their prints off dirty dishes and glasses and silverware.

"When I was working in the field we had a case in which a young Wisconsin couple was kidnapped, the woman was murdered, and her husband was shot in the head but miraculously survived. While we were searching the area outside their apartment I picked up a cigarette butt and we were able to get a latent print off the filter. When the victims' car turned up at O'Hare Airport in Chicago, we found a different print on the inside of a window. I eventually developed two suspects and those prints enabled us to prove that one of them had been at the crime scene and the other one had been inside the car, evidence that certainly contributed to their convictions."

What makes fingerprints both unique and valuable is that they are usually invisible and can be found just about everywhere: Prints are found on paper in white-collar crimes, on ransom notes in kidnappings, and in blood at shootouts. In a car they are found on radio dials and seat levers and mirrors. Men's prints are often found on the underside of a toilet seat, made when they lifted it. In one murder case prints were found on the ear stem of a pair of glasses and proved the suspect had been in the victim's car. They have been found on a single match at a bank robbery. They have even been found on used toilet paper and used sanitary napkins and used condoms. They are found on all types of garbage, as well as on currency.

Sometimes the place prints are found is key to solving the case. In a Midwestern murder case, the prime suspect denied having access to the gun used in the killing—until his prints were found inside the gun, apparently left there when he cleaned it. Prints have been found inside bombs.

In a New York City murder case the suspect's prints were found in a telephone book next to the listing of the victim's address. In a 1985 Mideast airplane hijacking in which five people were cold-bloodedly shot in the head by the hijackers and fifty-eight others died when commandos stormed the plane, one of the masked hijackers was identified and convicted from a print found in the charred remains of the cockpit. In a questioned suicide case the victim's own print was found on the plunger of the syringe used to inject the fatal overdose.

In a truly baffling Philadelphia robbery, an armored car picked up a locked sack filled with cash from the headquarters of a large bank, but when that bag was opened at a branch office, it was filled with rolls of toilet paper. Witnesses had seen the cash put in the bag, and the seal was still intact when the bag was delivered, but the cash had been replaced with toilet paper. The bag, the seal, and the rolls of paper were submitted to Latents. Everything was searched for prints, but the substitution remained a mystery until a specialist cut open the cardboard centers of the rolls and examined them. And on one of them he found a single fingerprint.

It belonged to a guard working on the armored car. Knowing the route the truck would follow, the guard had filled a money bag with toilet paper, sealed it, and stashed it in a trash can, and when the truck made a scheduled stop he had exchanged that bag for a cash bag. And except for that single print found on the inside of the toilet paper roll, he might have gotten away with it.

In one of the most unusual fingerprint cases, a print was found burned into a murder victim's pantyhose. When the body of a woman who had been tortured, raped, and then murdered was discovered floating in a creek, her clothing was sent to the lab for examination. Usually fingerprint specialists don't even look at fabrics because the weave obliterates ridge detail, and whatever oils might be present

are rapidly absorbed. But in this case a specialist named Jerry Withers happened to notice an unusual pattern in the victim's pantyhose. When he looked at it a little more closely, he realized that a fingerprint had been burned into the nylon fibers. Rereading the details of the case, he learned that the victim had been tortured with a hot knife before she had been killed. The killer must have used the victim's pantyhose to protect his hand. The heated blade had melted the fabric; he had touched it while it was in a liquefied state, and when it cooled, his print was clearly and permanently impressed into the fabric—a print that led directly to a murder conviction.

Obviously, the more irregular the surface, the more difficult it will be to get the ridge detail needed for a comparison. It's difficult to get a print from a stucco wall or a cinderblock, for example. A lot of guns have rough or checked surfaces to make them easier to grip, especially when the shooter is sweating, and those surfaces pretty much eliminate the possibility that prints will be left on the weapon.

Once it was believed that it was just about impossible to develop prints on human skin, but under specific conditions it can be done. After a triple murder and rape in a Miami health club, for example, a local crime-scene technician decided to examine those areas that had to have been touched during the crime. One of the victims had been dragged across the floor by her feet and then raped, so the technician put fingerprint powder on her ankles and hips. Amazingly, he was able to develop several partial prints. In her terror, the victim had been sweating and had exuded various body oils. The killer had held her tightly, making clear prints in those oils. When she died her body had stopped absorbing the oils, leaving them on the surface of her smooth skin. The prints were eventually identified as those of a former club employee, who was convicted of the murders.

Prints can't be dated; there's no means of determining from a print how long it's been there. So other evidence has to be used to prove that a given print was made during the commission of a crime. In a Pennsylvania case, three men shot and killed the elderly owner of a grocery store during a holdup. When their prints were found on a glass counter, their defense attorney claimed the defendants had been in the store the day before. But the victim's wife testified that she had cleaned the counter the morning of the robbery, as she did every morning, so that the prints had to have been made after she had cleaned. The jury believed her and convicted the three holdup men of the murder.

The first rule of all latent-fingerprint examinations is that there are no rules. Where prints are involved, anything is possible. Nothing should be overlooked. For example, when labor leader Joseph Yablonski challenged the powerful leadership of the United Mine Workers union, he and his entire family were murdered. Pittsburgh police searching the area around his house found several discarded beverage cans. They had been lying in the rain and snow for at least a day, perhaps longer, and the freezing cold and wet weather certainly should have destroyed any latent prints. But this was a major case, so the cans were processed anyway—and to everyone's surprise several good prints were developed. It was later learned that the killers had waited patiently outside the Yablonski home, eating and drinking, until the family had gone to bed. Presumably grease or oil from the food had gotten on their hands and been transferred to the cans—substances that are particularly resistant to moisture. The prints enabled police to place the suspects at the Yablonski home at the time of the killings and contributed significantly to their conviction.

Making latent prints visible is really where fingerprinting becomes a science. Developing latent prints was once pretty simple. There were only four methods that worked. Dusting powder was used on nonporous surfaces, such as

glass, plastic, or metal, while the chemicals iodine, ninhydrin, and silver nitrate were used on porous surfaces like paper, cardboard, and unfinished wood.

It was discovered almost a century ago that iodine fumes react with body fats and oils to make prints composed of those substances temporarily visible. In the 1950s scientists found that ninhydrin, the chemical most commonly used in fingerprint developing, reacts with amino acids or protein matter usually found in perspiration to make them visible. And silver nitrate combines with invisible body salts to form the very visible sodium chloride. These chemicals must be used in this order, or whatever latent prints might exist will be destroyed. And if these methods failed to produce prints on porous surfaces, it was generally accepted that they just weren't there.

That wasn't entirely true. The most historically significant exception took place on November 22, 1963, in Dallas, Texas, when President John F. Kennedy was assassinated by Lee Harvey Oswald. Less than two hours after Kennedy had been shot, Dallas police found a rifle lying next to a window in the Texas School Book Depository. A barricade of cardboard book cartons had been built around the window. Although Oswald's right palmprint was found on the rifle's stock, someone could have left the rifle there to implicate him. Following standard crime-scene procedure, detectives searched the area for latent prints. Oswald's fingerprints and palmprints were developed on three of the cardboard boxes and on a paper bag.

That proved nothing. If prints are to be connected to a crime, they have to be found in places they shouldn't be found. Oswald worked in the building, so it was not at all unusual that his prints would be found there. What the police had to prove was that these were fresh prints, that Oswald had been at that window within the last few hours. Since prints can't be dated, that was an almost impossible

job. But not in this case, in which Dallas detectives had made one of the luckiest mistakes in sci-crime history.

Cardboard is a porous, or absorbent, surface. Detectives should have sprayed chemicals on the boxes, but they mistakenly used dusting powder—and they had developed several prints. The question was, why? The boxes were sent to the lab in Washington for a more complete examination. By experimenting with dusting powder on similar boxes, specialists discovered it would develop prints for up to three hours after they had been made, but then the body fluids would be absorbed into the cardboard, keeping prints from being developed. The fact that Oswald's prints had been developed with dusting powder proved he had been at that window within the time frame of the assassination.

The once-prosaic world of dusting powder and three chemicals began changing drastically in the 1970s as new chemicals and new techniques were discovered to make visible prints that once would have remained undetected. More than forty new methods of developing latent prints have been found, ranging from lasers to fumes from superglue—the same stuff you buy in the store and can't get off your fingers.

With so many different techniques available, the challenge in each case becomes picking the right process. Tim Trozzi, who joined the Bureau in 1979, said, "It's a combination of skill, experience, and intuition, and quite frankly, sometimes it's a bit of luck. You have to start by considering the nature of the object you're examining, how long the print might have been there, what type of atmospheric conditions it's been subjected to, and what else might have happened to it. If it's a car, for example, we'd want to know if it had been washed.

"Then we have to consider the properties of the different methods. I know, for example, that if I use iodine fumes first and that doesn't work, I can still go back and try superglue and fluorescent dyes. But if I use superglue first,

I'll ruin it for iodine, and it might even inhibit me from using lasers. The problem is that every case is unique. What worked perfectly last time might not work at all this time.''

In the past, making that decision was pretty simple: powders for nonporous materials, chemicals for porous ones. But now just about everything, porous or nonporous, is examined first under the laser. If prints cannot be seen under a laser, other methods are used.

Dry powders, which are available in a variety of colors to provide contrast against the surface, adhere to whatever moisture or chemicals remain on a nonporous surface.

If the evidence is fresh—if technicians are on the scene within hours of the crime's commission—the first thing they may try on a porous surface is iodine fuming. It used to be that prints developed with iodine fumes disappeared when the fumes dissipated, but now they can be fixed with a chemical spray and remain visible for as long as two days before fading. Liquid iodine has proved to be particularly effective in bringing up prints left on rubber gloves.

Ninhydrin is still used in a large percentage of cases. It works best in humid conditions, so many more prints are developed with it in the summer than in the winter, and it doesn't work very well at all in places with dry climates— Arizona, for instance. To produce humidity in the lab, after applying ninhydrin to a surface, specialists put the specimen in a ''humidity cabinet'' or apply heat and humidity with an ordinary steam iron.

Ninhydrin is especially good for developing prints on paper. In an Ohio murder case, the victim's body was found in his car, which had been pushed into the Ohio River. The only item found in the car that the victim's family couldn't identify was a map of the local area. The victim had grown up in that town; there was no reason he would need a map. So this map was put in a toaster oven and slowly dried. Once dry it was sprayed with ninhydrin

and then steamed; several good prints immediately materialized. Those prints were linked to a suspect, who had apparently needed the map to find the river. The prints allowed the prosecutor to prove that the suspect had been in the victim's car, evidence that proved crucial in his conviction.

Silver nitrate is still used occasionally to develop prints on paper, but in many cases it's been replaced by a more effective multistep process called physical developer, in which the evidence is exposed to several different chemical solutions, much like developing a photograph.

Some chemicals will work only on very specific substances. Gentian violet, for example, that old purple dye used for a variety of medicinal purposes, is very effective in developing prints left on adhesives, particularly on the sticky side of tape. Multi-metal deposition develops prints left on photographs. Prints are often left in blood when a violent crime is committed, but when the blood dries it loses its color and the prints disappear. Diaminobenzidine reacts with the enzymes remaining after the color is gone, to produce visible prints.

Like many of these new techniques, the fact that common, ordinary superglue will cause prints to become visible was discovered by accident. In 1979, a British policeman used superglue, scientifically known as cyanoacrylate, to repair a cracked film-processing tank in a darkroom. To his surprise, he noticed that the glue illuminated fingerprints left on the side of the tank. When he tried it on other surfaces he found that it produced distinct, raised prints. Although it's now known that superglue adheres to the moisture found in latent prints, no one really knows why. It just does.

Superglue fuming quickly became one of the most efficient and productive means of developing latent prints. It works best when the glue is heated in a dry, enclosed area—inside a sealed room or a car, for example. Small

evidence is fumed in a vacuum chamber, while a tent is built around larger pieces of evidence. Colored dyes or powders may then be used to make the prints stand out against the background.

In a San Mateo, California, case, a Taiwanese informant who was about to reveal details of a major Taiwan government scandal to American reporters was murdered. His killers made their getaway on bicycles, which were later abandoned. Traditional means of bringing up prints on nonporous surfaces failed, but when the bikes were super-glued, a single print became visible. The State Department then provided samples of the prints of several high-ranking Taiwanese government officials, among them some of the people who would have been implicated in the scandal. And one of them was a perfect match. This official couldn't be linked directly to the murder, but he was in-dicted for conspiracy. On the basis of that single print, which only a few years earlier would not have been found, he was convicted and sentenced to twenty-seven years to life in prison.

The fact that lasers would make certain prints visible was accidentally discovered in Canada in the mid-1970s. It seemed as if every time Canadian researchers turned on their lasers, which are basically a high-energy light source, the experiment was complicated by the presence of finger-prints. Lasers were quickly adapted to law enforcement purposes. Lasers are nondestructive—unlike powders or chemicals, their use leaves no residue and won't damage the evidence. For that reason the first thing that happens when evidence arrives in the lab is that someone turns out the lights and turns on the laser.

No one knows why a laser will make some prints visible when other processes have failed to develop the same print. It's not known what the laser is reacting to in the print, but for some reason the method seems to work better on older evidence. For instance, in 1975 the U. S. Department of

Justice initiated deportation proceedings against Valerian Trifa, a former archbishop of the Romanian Orthodox Church of America, claiming that when applying for naturalization he had concealed his World War II membership in the fascist Iron Guard, Romania's pro-Nazi party. Trifa denied these accusations and, after more than three decades, it was almost impossible to find any hard evidence against him.

But in 1982 the West German government produced a postcard Trifa sent to a high-ranking Nazi official in 1942; on it he pledged his loyalty. Trifa denied having written the postcard. The West Germans refused to allow the FBI lab to use any potentially destructive processes on this historic document, so powders, chemicals, and superglue couldn't be used. The laser was the only tool left. And under the intense laser beam, a left thumbprint, a print made forty years earlier, became visible. That print was identical to the inked print Trifa had voluntarily given when he became an American citizen. There was no question about it: the former archbishop was a Nazi war criminal. Technology had finally caught up with him, and he was deported in 1984.

In addition to the powerful lasers used in the lab, smaller portable lasers are used to search crime scenes. When a Vancouver, Washington, man was suspected in the abduction of several young children, authorities received permission to search his house. With the lights turned on brightly, investigators found nothing that could link the suspect to the missing children. But when the lab's Tommy Moorefield searched the house with the portable laser, he found a tiny footprint on a closet ceiling, a place no footprint should be found. That section of ceiling was cut out and sent to the lab for further processing with a more powerful laser; the footprint was identified as that of one of the missing children. It was later discovered that when the killer left his house, he would tie up his victims and leave them on the shelf at the top of this closet. One of those kids, strug-

gling for his life, had left his footprint. The print was enough to link the suspect to the missing children.

Lasers are expensive; the laser used in the sci-crime lab cost $65,000, far beyond the budget of most law enforcement agencies. But among the new techniques now being used to develop latent prints is a combination of chemicals and alternate light sources. RAM, a fluorescent dye stain developed in the Latent Print Section, causes some prints to become visible under ultraviolet light, for example. So rather than needing a $65,000 laser, a police department can use a solution costing a few bucks and a hundred-dollar ultraviolet lamp.

Each process makes prints visible for a different length of time. Blowing on certain prints will make them visible as long as your breath lasts, for example. Prints made visible by a laser can be seen only as long as the laser is on, while superglued prints are almost permanent; they practically have to be chiseled off some evidence. Whatever method is used, a permanent copy of the print has to be made while it's visible. That means "lifting" it, or photographing it.

In the 1920s, when most prints were developed by powders, prints were lifted, or transferred from the evidence into a more permanent and transportable form, by using the sticky side of rubber patches made for automobile inner tubes. Those rubber patches have been replaced by rubber lifting tape.

But in almost every instance the preferred means of making a permanent record of a print is to photograph it. By placing various filters over the camera lens, it's possible to photograph prints that are invisible in ordinary light. For example, if a print left on a soda can is visible only when seen with filters under a laser, a photograph of that will show only the print—the can will disappear, because the camera simply doesn't "see" it at that wavelength.

Contrary to popular belief, finding a print at a crime

scene or on other evidence is not enough to identify a suspect. The work really begins once the print is found and developed. Without the name or alias of a suspect, it's extremely difficult to find, among the more than two hundred million criminal prints on file, the part of one finger that matches.

Attempts to automate fingerprint searches so as to identify a suspect from a latent print began in the 1930s when the Bureau tried to create a database on punch cards, but that file was soon overwhelmed by the huge number of submissions. So until sci-crime entered the computer age, automated searches were rarely attempted and even more rarely successful. The art of fingerprint identification entered the computer age in 1968, when a rudimentary computer was used for the first time to assist in identifying the man who had assassinated Martin Luther King, Jr.

When Dr. King was murdered in Memphis, Tennessee, in 1968, detectives found latent prints on the rifle from which the fatal bullet was believed to have been fired, and on a pair of binoculars. When investigators find only a single print or a fragmentary print, it's very difficult to figure out which finger left that print. Sometimes that can be determined from the location of the print on the object. For example, people generally rip paper by holding it between their thumb and forefinger, so when a print is found on torn paper, it's generally assumed to be either a thumb or forefinger. In this case, because of the position as well as certain other characteristics, the prints were identified as that of the killer's left thumb. As Specialist Bobby Erwin explained, "We had a left thumbprint, we had the alias the killer had used when he checked into the hotel—'Eric S. Galt,' I believe it was—but we had nothing to match that print to. We needed a real name so we could find a card in our files.

"Memphis police and federal agents had developed a lot of suspects right off. But we just couldn't make a match.

The police tracked this Galt to shoddy hotel rooms in several states, and we got a lot of paper items—newspapers and maps—and we developed more prints from those. We got one good print off a map found in a flophouse in Atlanta, identical to the prints found on the rifle and binoculars, that gave us a lot more detail.''

Investigators checked the prints of known members of subversive groups like the KKK and the Minutemen, but were unable to make a match. With no other suspects, it was decided to compare that latent print to those of all current fugitives known to the Bureau. This turned out to be about 53,000 people. ''But we had a physical description of the assassin and an identifiable thumbprint,'' Erwin pointed out, ''so we asked our people, 'Can we narrow it down by physical description and a description of the type of print in the number six finger?' Using that information they conducted a computerized search and successfully narrowed it down to nineteen hundred individuals.

''Then we requested that the assembly section pull all those cards a hundred at a time and we were just going to sit there and go through them one by one. It was less than a needle in a haystack, because we didn't even know if the needle was there. So they brought the first hundred cards and I started going through them and I looked at the fifth card and there it was. The fifth card. I didn't have to compare it to our latent thumbprint. I'd looked at that print so often it was embedded in my mind. I saw this one and I almost fell out of my chair. The funny part of it was that the assistant supervisor, Dan Bailey, sat right across from me and at times during the search, just to shake things up, I'd say every once in a while, 'Hey, Dan, I got the guy.' He'd get excited and I'd confess I was kidding. This time though, I looked at him and said evenly, 'Dan, I got him.'

''He didn't believe me. 'I'm not kidding,' I said, 'I got him. It's him.' The fifth card. I handed the card to him and he just stared at it, then said softly, 'By God, it is him.

Here goes the ball rolling.' That's how we finally identified James Earl Ray as the man who killed Dr. King.''

Ray's prints were in the fugitive file because he had escaped from a Midwestern prison where he was serving time for robbery. He eventually pleaded guilty to Dr. King's murder and was sentenced to ninety-nine years in prison.

The procedure used to identify Ray has become far more sophisticated. Once it's determined which finger or fingers made a latent print, a computer search can be conducted. Prints are stored in the computer on the basis of the unique identifying characteristics found in a small portion of the center of the finger. The computer has a sort of digital map of that part of the finger. Obviously, the ability of the computer to identify an unknown individual by matching a latent print increases tremendously when additional information about the suspect is available, for instance his height or race, enabling investigators to be more specific in their search.

This system can be very effective. When an off-duty Harrisburg, Pennsylvania, policeman was murdered, his stolen van was spotted in Virginia. After a wild shootout on a highway, the killers escaped and abandoned the van in North Carolina. Several days later a van stolen from the North Carolina town in which the policeman's van had been recovered was found in Tallahassee, Florida. The same prints were found on both vans. Using a partial description of the killers, the Latent Print Section ran an automated search for those prints—and scored a hit. One of the killers, positively identified through his prints left on the vans, was subsequently convicted of the murder.

Every comparison between a latent print and a known print is done pretty much the same way, whether prints are being compared to try to find Martin Luther King's killer, or to identify putrefying remains from Jonestown, or simply to determine if an applicant for a civil service job has a

criminal record. A specialist looks at one print and then another, back and forth, back and forth, comparing the shape and relative position of those thin lines.

The only thing that can be learned from a fingerprint is whether it matches another print. Prints aren't hereditary; there's absolutely no relationship between prints made by relatives, even identical twins. Neither race nor sex nor age can be determined from prints, although women generally have thinner ridges than men. It's impossible to determine health or occupation from a print, though some people who do manual labor tend to wear down the ridges of their fingers.

Prints either match or don't match, and that's all you can state positively about them. A print comparison is a subjective examination, it's a matter of expert opinion. One of the very first pieces of equipment adapted for sci-crime fingerprinting work, in the 1920s, was a linen counter, a handheld magnifying glass used in the textile industry to count threads. Many examiners still rely on a simple handheld magnifier, which enlarges prints three or four times, but they also have available a macroscope, which will magnify prints as much as $87\frac{1}{2}$ times as well as enhance the contrast; the comparison microscope, which enables them to look at two prints simultaneously; and the image enhancer, the first piece of equipment designed specifically for this work.

Prints that are just not clear enough to be used for comparative purposes can be further developed on the image-enhancer computer system, which converts the print into a digital image to make it suitable for a comparison.

A print comparison is based on ridges, the raised part of the skin, and their relationship to each other. Ridges start and stop, they change direction, they make circles and slopes, they make formations. A single ridge that branches off into two ridges is called a bifurcation. A ridge that stops suddenly is an ending ridge. A short ridge is, in fact,

called a short ridge. A ridge that doesn't show direction is a dot.

For an examiner to decide that two prints have been made by the same person, every single characteristic of every identifiable ridge must be exactly the same. Most examiners begin by locating a similar point, a focal point, on each print. According to Greathouse, "We'll look at the thickness, the location of the pores, the breaks and changes in direction, everything. When we're confident we've found an identical point on each print we're comparing, then we'll look to see the relationship between that ridge and other formations. Maybe two ridges over and to the left there is a bifurcated ridge, and one ridge over and down from that there's an island formation, and three ridges over and to the right there might be another ending formation. Points begin to fall into place. Once two points of identity are located, the next step is to count the number of intervening ridges between them; if you've found two similar ridges, for two prints to be the same there must be the same number of intervening ridges between them, whether it's two or four or ten."

Most comparisons are based on the portion of the finger above the first joint. In that small area there are as many as three hundred identifiable points, known as minutiae, that can be used as the basis for comparison. There is no minimum number of points that must be identical for a match to be made; when a specialist decides that two or more prints are the same, for all legal purposes they are the same. British law mandates that at least sixteen points must be matched before a suspect can be indicted or an expert can testify in court. The sci-crime lab has matched prints with as few as seven points. But there only needs to be a single unexplainable dissimilarity between prints for them to be considered different.

* * *

For as long as law enforcement agencies have been using fingerprints to link suspects to crimes, criminals have been trying to find ways to destroy, disfigure, or disguise their prints. They have often tried to obliterate their prints with sandpaper, dental sanders, even acid, but ridges are several layers of skin deep and are not easily destroyed. Perhaps the most-publicized attempt to destroy prints was made by Public Enemy Number One, John Dillinger, who in the early 1930s paid a surgeon $5,000, plus $25 a day room and board at the doctor's house, to cut off his fingerprints and perform some minor facial surgery. The operation succeeded in creating scars that obscured the ridges in the center of each finger above the first joint, but the ridges outside that small center section were left intact, and that was more than enough to make a match. Legend has it that the man shot and killed by G-men outside Chicago's Biograph Theater was not Dillinger, but rather an unknown man who had been set up by the arch-criminal. But Special Agent Gerry Engert, one of the first agents assigned to the lab—and the man who took the prints from the dead body—said flatly that it wasn't true. "I know that was Dillinger's body," he said, "because I had the prints in my hand and I made the comparison to his known prints myself. There was absolutely no question about it."

In 1941, a criminal named Roscoe James Pitts gained a painful place in sci-crime history by having the skin surgically removed from his fingertips, which were then sewn onto his chest until they healed. That actually worked. Pitt's fingertips had no ridge pattern; he had successfully destroyed his fingerprints. But unfortunately for him, both his original print card, as well as the prints taken when he was arrested, included portions of the ridges just below the first joint, allowing him to be positively identified by a comparison of the ridges in the middle of his fingers.

No criminal has ever escaped prosecution by obliterating his fingerprints, although they continue to try. In 1990

Miami police arrested a suspect in a drug case whose prints were severely scarred. Latent-print experts soon discovered that the suspect had actually sliced his fingerprints into small pieces and transplanted those pieces onto other fingers. His fingertips had healed, leaving him with new prints in which broken ridges ran in all different directions, making it impossible to link him to previous crimes by comparing his prints.

Or so he thought. Latent-print specialist Tommy Moorefield was intrigued by the problem. He cut photographs of these prints into small pieces and began trying to fit these ridge patterns together; it was literally a human jigsaw puzzle. Nights and weekends, working at home and in his spare time in the office, Moorefield painstakingly restored small sections of several prints to their original pattern, until specialists in the Technical Section were able to match them to those of a fugitive convicted in another major drug case. That comparison led directly to the man's conviction.

Fingerprints are also a primary means of identifying a dead body. After 913 men, women, and children were murdered or committed suicide in Jonestown, Guyana, each one of their decomposing bodies had to be identified. When the shriveled body believed to be another victim of Atlanta child-killer Wayne Williams was pulled from a river, he had to be identified before police could trace his relationship to Williams.

Identifying a body is often a routine task. A local police department finds a body in the woods and needs to confirm its identity. So a set of fingerprints is taken from the body and submitted to the lab for comparison with prints on file in the Technical Section. But at times the job can be extraordinarily gruesome. Terrible things happen to bodies, things that make them unrecognizable as human beings, and those thin lines on their fingers may be among the very few physical clues to their identity.

In addition to the psychological problems caused by dealing with charred or mutilated or decaying bodies, it can be very difficult to obtain a print suitable for comparison. Very often the hands of people who die in accidents are found clenched into tight fists, and while that might be beneficial to specialists because the fingerprints are somewhat protected, first the hands have to be pried open. This can be done forcefully, it can be done by making small cuts in the base of the fingers, or it can be done by severing the hand from the body and heating it in a microwave oven for several minutes.

To return shriveled or badly wrinkled skin to a natural, rounded shape so as to obtain a print, investigators can soak it in water, heat it for a short time in a microwave, or inject it with a chemical substance called tissue builder. Conversely, if the finger is swollen, as it might be if the corpse was a "floater"—a body that has been in the water for a long time—sidelighting will create shadows in the fingerprint valleys, which can then be photographed. If the top layer of skin, the epidermis, has been destroyed or damaged or charred in a fire, it can be cut off, and usable prints can be obtained from the second layer of skin, the dermis. If it's intact but too soft or flabby to be printed, it can be sliced off, and after being briefly bathed in alcohol, slipped over the specialist's own finger, and printed as if it were part of that finger. Sometimes the ridge detail on the outer part of the skin has been mutilated but is still visible on the inner side. In that case the skin can be cut off and turned inside out and printed, but the valleys will show up as dark lines and the ridges will be the blank areas between them.

Very few law enforcement people are qualified to do this kind of work. So when a body is found, the necessary legal permissions are obtained, and the entire hand or the fingers are severed from the body and submitted to the lab. There they are processed in a neat, quietly respectful place called

the Dead Room, officially known as the Deceased and Special Processing Room, room number 10986. There is nothing unique or special about the Dead Room to set it apart from the other offices in the lab. It's neat and clean and very quiet and has an antiseptic look about it. There are several long work counters, the microwave, and a large refrigerator in which the body parts are stored. Body parts are supposed to be submitted to the lab in a protective container; perhaps the most unusual submission came from a Texas sheriff, who sent a hand in a Kentucky Fried Chicken bucket.

The agents and examiners and specialists and technicians who work in the sci-crime lab have become accustomed to dealing with the horrors human beings can inflict upon each other. But of all the jobs in the lab, perhaps the most difficult assignment is working on the FBI's Disaster Squad. This is the front line of horror. In August 1940, a Pennsylvania Central airliner carrying twenty-five passengers, among them an FBI agent and an FBI stenographer, crashed into a Virginia cornfield. Most of the bodies were burned beyond recognition, so local FBI agents, wanting to give these victims their names back, volunteered to fingerprint the corpses and submit them to the Bureau for identification. That crash marked the birth of the little-known Disaster Squad. Since that time more than one hundred print specialists have worked almost two hundred disasters. They were in Puerto Rico to try to get prints from the charred bodies of the ninety-seven people who died in an arson fire at the DuPont Plaza Hotel; in Lockerbie, Scotland, to identify the victims of Pan Am Flight 103. They printed the Jonestown victims, the marines who died in the bombing of their Beirut, Lebanon, barracks, soldiers killed in Operation Desert Shield and Desert Storm, and Americans who have died in floods, fires, volcanic eruptions, and airplane crashes around the world. They even identified the

remains of the astronauts who died in the explosion of the space shuttle *Challenger*.

As Carl Collins, a member of the Disaster Squad for more than two decades, explained, "The most important thing is not to think of a hand or body as being a person. It's a job to do."

"You just learn to cope with it," said Ron Hurt, who has been doing fingerprint work for more than three decades. "We know what to expect before we go in, and with the exception of the odor—you never get used to the odor, and once you've smelled it you never forget it—you find a way of dealing with it."

Just as in criminal cases, after a victim's print has been obtained it has to be compared with a known print for a positive identification to be made. If a victim's known print isn't on file, law enforcement personnel will go to the victim's home or office and lift prints off objects that person was known to have used: a telephone, a cosmetics case, a glass-top desk. Almost 60 percent of all remains examined by the Disaster Squad have been positively identified.

While fingerprinting remains the primary means of positively identifying an individual, it isn't the only way. In many cases, blood will tell. And, in fact, so will every other body fluid: semen, vaginal fluid, saliva, perspiration, and urine. There are grand tales written in blood, tales of passion and horror and murder, tales accessible only to those with the knowledge to read them. It's the job of the lab's DNA Analysis Unit to decipher these tales told by body fluids.

"We deal in violent crime," unit chief Dave Bigbee said; "that's all we have time to do. We're the people who get bloody clothing with bullet holes and knife tears in them, rocks covered with blood and hair and brains, a cinder block that's been dropped on somebody's skull. That

evidence can give us a lot of information about what happened.''

In violent crimes—murders and rapes, assaults, child molestations—body fluids are recovered more often than any other type of evidence, including fingerprints. Serial killer Ted Bundy was conclusively linked to one of his victims through saliva found in a bite mark on her body.

As the discoveries of science are applied to law enforcement, different areas of sci-crime take on a new significance. Until recently only a limited amount of information could be learned from body fluids. But now these fluids are the focus of the most significant advances since the amazing discovery more than a century ago that people could be positively identified by the lines on their skin.

Throughout history blood had often been found at the scene of violent crimes and on suspects, but it wasn't until 1901 that it even could be proved that blood had come from a human being rather than an animal. A few years later it was discovered that all human blood could be typed into four groups, A, B, AB, and O. Blood-group typing allowed police to associate suspects with a crime, but since so many people shared the same blood group, it was still not possible to identify a specific person from blood found at a crime scene.

While most often blood typing served to eliminate suspects, in very specific cases it could be valuable. In a 1955 case, a dishonorably discharged marine driving a stolen car was stopped by California highway patrolmen, who found both the marine's clothes and the car's interior covered with blood. A few hours later the body of the car's owner was found in the Nevada desert. Tests confirmed that the blood found on the suspect marine and in the car was type A, the same as the victim's, while the suspect himself was type O. The blood couldn't have been his. Additional evidence was found and the suspect pleaded guilty to murder.

Other body fluids—semen, saliva, perspiration, and vagi-

nal fluids—had almost no value to law enforcement until researchers discovered in the 1950s that about eighty percent of all Americans secreted certain chemicals into those fluids, chemicals from which their blood group could be determined. These people are known as secretors, while the remaining twenty percent are known as nonsecretors. When an elderly woman was raped and murdered in Baltimore, for example, seminal stains found on her slip showed that she had been raped by a type B secretor. Eight suspects were identified—but only one of them was a type B secretor. Although the suspect had been linked to the crime by other evidence, it was when he was confronted by those test results that he confessed.

But this was still "class evidence," limiting the number of potential suspects to a small group rather than to a single person. It remained the dream of sci-crime researchers to find a method other than fingerprints by which a specific individual could be linked to a crime. That method was finally developed in the mid-1970s; surprisingly, it wasn't DNA.

Blood is partially composed of enzymes and proteins, which are collectively known as genetic markers. While they function exactly the same way in all human beings, they don't have the same chemical makeup. For example, the enzyme phosphoglucomutase, known as PGM, is found in everybody's blood, but thus far ten different types of PGM have been identified. Two people may share the same blood type, but statistically it is much less likely they would share a blood type *and* a PGM marker. Thus far scientists have identified twelve different genetic markers, each of them containing between three and ten types. Although all twelve are rarely identified in a blood sample, finding even three or four makes it possible to prove that a sample had come from one person in a million—in some cases, one in a hundred million.

In the small Tennessee town of Maynardville, a young

married woman was abducted and beaten to death. A friend of her husband was suspected but there was little physical evidence to link him to the murder. Because he was often in their house, the fact that his hairs and fibers and fingerprints were found there had no value. Police searched his house, and in a clothes hamper they found the new Levi's jeans he'd been wearing earlier that day.

The jeans were sent to Dave Bigbee for examination. "Usually it's very difficult to do anything with blood found on Levi's jeans because the blue dye interferes with testing," Bigbee said. "But in this case we got lucky. One of the first things we routinely do is turn clothes inside out and cut them open at the seams. Sure enough, we found a dime-sized bloodstain in one of the pockets. The pockets are made of white cotton, and white cotton is a terrific material for typing. The suspect claimed that he'd been in a fistfight and had skinned his knuckles.

"We ran tests for all twelve enzyme systems, but we were able to get results in only five or six of them. Three of the enzymes could not possibly have come from the suspect, but were consistent with the victim's blood. The assumption was that he'd skinned his knuckles when he punched her and, probably without even thinking about it, had put his hands in his pockets. Statistically, chances were extraordinarily high that this was the victim's blood, and that's exactly the way I testified in court. This was the evidence that ultimately led to the suspect's conviction."

Genetic markers make very strong evidence. While serial killer Wayne Williams was convicted of two murders, authorities believe he may have been responsible for as many as thirty deaths in the Atlanta area. For example, some very small bloodstains were found underneath the seat of his car. The genetic markers developed from those stains were consistent with the markers found in the blood of two victims who had been stabbed to death. Had Wil-

liams been tried in those cases, this would have provided almost insurmountable evidence against him.

Chances that two people would have twelve identical markers are estimated at about 1 in 1,300,000,000. But the problem with genetic markers has turned out to be that they are not very stable; once blood is outside the body, the enzymes immediately begin deteriorating. By the time a bloodstain dries, several of the markers will have disappeared completely. And since most blood samples are submitted to the lab for analysis in the form of dried bloodstains on a piece of cloth or on other evidence—liquid blood is rarely received in the lab—from which small pieces can be removed for examination, many of the genetic markers have been lost by the time the samples arrive in the lab.

Enter DNA—deoxyribonucleic acid, the human genetic blueprint, the stuff that makes each of us each of us. DNA is extraordinarily valuable to scientists all over the world in investigating the secrets of life and death, but in sci-crime labs DNA is the long-sought connection between body fluids and the specific person from whom they came. DNA is the biological equivalent of fingerprints.

Basically—very basically—DNA is an extremely complex chemical consisting of four sub-units, called bases, that combine in various proportions to form molecules called nucleotides. There are three billion nucleotides in the nucleus of every one of your cells, linked in a chainlike sequence in an almost infinite variety of arrangements. Except for identical twins, each arrangement is unique; no one else in the world will have the same arrangement as you. And in every one of your cells, cells in your blood or your skin or your hair roots or your sperm, that arrangement will be exactly the same.

Different segments of that chain are responsible for different things—your eye color, whether you go bald or not—but for law enforcement purposes none of that is im-

portant. What matters is that a small segment of the chain can be isolated and printed on a sheet of photographic film. The result, called an autorad, looks just a bit like an out-of-focus bar code. But, unlike the countless cans of tomato soup that all bear the same bar code, no two people—again, except for identical twins—will have the same genetic code. So by developing an autorad from materials connected to a crime and comparing it to DNA taken from a suspect, investigators can link that suspect to that crime, or clear him of suspicion.

Like fingerprints, DNA can be used to make a positive identification. When an arm and hand were found in a shark's belly, the lab was able to identify the victim from a fingerprint. But fingerprints were of absolutely no value when part of a leg was found floating in a Florida river a few days after a woman college student had disappeared. However, because DNA from any part of the body is identical to DNA from any other part of the body, the lab was able to determine that this was not the missing student's leg. Even if a DNA specimen from the student hadn't been available, the examination could have been conducted by comparing DNA taken from the leg to DNA taken from a blood relative. Unlike prints, DNA is inherited, so a small segment of the DNA chain will be identical in all blood relations. Incredibly, in 1993 British DNA experts were able to confirm that a skeleton was indeed that of Czar Nicholas II of Russia, who had been slain in 1918 by Bolsheviks, by comparing DNA taken from those bones to a DNA sample volunteered by England's Prince Philip, a distant blood relative of the czar.

One of the many advantages offered by DNA is that it's found everywhere white blood cells are found. Obviously, it's found in blood; it's found in semen in rape cases; it's in the skin found beneath a victim's fingernails after a struggle; it's in hair root follicles; it can even be found in

saliva cells left on the mouthpiece of a telephone after a conversation.

But contrary to what has often been written, it isn't actually part of the composition of saliva or perspiration or urine or tears. DNA is found in only one place, the nucleus of cells. It is these cells that are often carried by body fluids, floating like weeds in a river. So while the best place to obtain a DNA sample might be from blood, it's much more easily obtained from the inside of the cheek. The epitherial cells on the inside of the cheek are among the loosest in the body; when you speak or cough or chew gum or smoke cigarettes or spit or dribble, some of these cells are expelled in your saliva, and a DNA profile can be developed from them. After the bombing of the World Trade Center, the FBI received a letter claiming responsibility for the explosion and threatening further attacks. A DNA profile was developed from cells found in the saliva used to seal the envelope flap. When a suspect in the bombing was identified, that profile was successfully matched to his known sample.

In another case, when Exxon executive Sidney Reso was kidnapped from his New Jersey home in April 1992, detectives traced ransom calls to the public phones from which they had been made. They not only dusted these phones for fingerprints, they also wiped them with cotton swabs to try to find DNA samples on the mouthpieces. Their hope was that when they found a suspect they would be able to use this evidence to prove he or she had used these phones. Unfortunately, matters never got that far. Reso died from a bullet wound suffered during his kidnapping, and his killers were captured when they tried to collect the ransom.

The use of DNA for sci-crime purposes was pioneered in the early 1980s in England by Dr. Alec Jeffreys at the University of Leicester. Britain's national sci-crime lab, a branch of the Home Office, began working cases in 1986. The FBI lab officially began accepting requests for DNA

comparisons in December 1988, and its value so quickly became obvious that the lab ceased testing for genetic markers and changed the name of the unit from the Serology Unit to DNA Analysis.

Historically rape cases have been the most difficult of all violent crimes to solve. Only half of all reported rapes ended in arrests, and less than half of the people arrested were convicted; this is by far the lowest conviction rate for any violent crime. Part of the reason is that there was no way to connect the most important evidence in a rape case—the semen—to the suspect. DNA changed all that. In Tacoma, Washington, for example, a suspect confronted with DNA evidence pleaded guilty to the rape of an elderly woman suffering from Alzheimer's disease, even though the victim had no memory of the crime. In Cheyenne, Wyoming, a five-year-old girl was abducted and raped, and her body was found floating in a river. Three suspects were identified, among them her natural father. Her father's contribution to her DNA showed up clearly on the autorad, but his DNA did not match the semen found on her body. He was innocent. But the profile of his best friend's DNA did match. Confronted with this evidence, the suspect admitted that he had kidnapped and raped the little girl while he was drunk, but claimed she had died when she ran away from him and fell from a bridge into the river. He was sentenced to life in prison.

Conversely, in many cases DNA has provided defense attorneys with proof of their client's innocence. In fact, one of the early cases worked in the DNA Analysis Unit was eerily similar to the 1903 Will West case that established fingerprints as the accepted means of positive identification. It began one night in a dark bedroom when an intruder raped and beat a Parkville, Maryland, woman. Although in the dark she never got a good look at her attacker, she positively identified him as the man with whom she had recently ended a stormy four-year relation-

ship. She had lived with this man and she said he had done it, and that was about as close to an open and shut case as possible. The man was arrested and charged with assault and rape.

The accused man had dark, curly hair and a dark, bushy beard. While in prison awaiting trial, he encountered the former boyfriend of the victim's roommate. This man, who had lived in the same neighborhood, also had dark, curly hair and a dark, bushy beard—in fact, he bore an uncanny resemblance to the suspect. In a dark room, in the terror of an attack, these two men easily could have been mistaken for each other. The suspect pleaded with detectives to investigate the second man.

Four months after the victim's boyfriend had been arrested, DNA tests conducted by the FBI lab proved he was not the rapist. The victim's positive identification had been wrong. Prosecutors then obtained a court order allowing them to take a blood sample from the second man. This time the DNA profiles matched; the second man was the rapist. Just as fingerprints had been the only means of telling the two William Wests apart, DNA was the only means of keeping an innocent man out of prison, and of putting the man who could have passed for his twin brother in prison for assault and rape.

In a similarly bizarre case, after five female college students were brutally murdered in Gainesville, Florida, in 1990, an eighteen-year old suspect diagnosed as a manic-depressive confessed to the killings, claiming they had been committed by his evil alter ego. But three of the victims had been raped, and DNA comparisons proved the confessed killer could not have committed the crimes. A week after the last murders a man named Danny Rolling was arrested on burglary charges in Ocala, Florida. Rolling was wanted in Shreveport, Louisiana, for attempted murder, and authorities there informed Gainesville police that several unsolved killings in that city were similar to the

Florida murders. A DNA comparison proved that Rolling had raped the victims. He was subsequently tried and convicted of murder and sentenced to death.

Another advantage offered by DNA is that, unlike genetic markers in blood, it's remarkably durable. Although DNA will deteriorate if exposed to radiation—sunlight, for instance—under proper conditions it can remain viable for thousands of years. Researchers have extracted DNA from body lice found on Egyptian mummies and from American Indian hair follicles hundreds of years old. This property allows examiners to reopen particularly heinous cases that occurred before DNA typing was available.

In 1972, an Oklahoma man named Gene Leroy Hart was charged with sexually assaulting and killing three Girl Scouts. The girls were on a camping trip when their killer cut his way into their tent, raped them, and murdered them. Hart had been tried for the crimes, but acquitted. Oklahoma authorities firmly believed he was the killer, but they hadn't been able to prove it. The triple murder had officially remained unsolved. It was possible the killer was still on the loose.

Hart was later convicted in another rape case and died of a heart attack while in prison. The Oklahoma state crime lab, anxious to finally close this case, sent the DNA Unit a sample of Hart's blood and the pillowcase with which the killer had wiped himself after raping the girls. Amazingly, specialists were able to develop a DNA profile from the twelve-year-old semen on the pillowcase. It was identical to the profile from Hart's blood. There was no longer any doubt about it: Gene Hart was the killer. The case was finally closed.

Often the only source of DNA is a drop of perspiration found on the sweat band of a cap or the saliva used to lick a stamp or left on a cigarette butt. Rapists have even attempted to destroy DNA in semen by pouring bleach or vinegar on their victims. But while a dime-sized blood

sample is needed to detect some genetic markers, scientists can now develop a DNA profile from just a few human cells.

Researchers at Quantico have been working with a technique called polymerase chain reaction that allows them to amplify, or make copies of, that portion of the DNA chain needed to produce a profile. With this technique they can take one small cell found on the back of a stamp and, as if they were using a biological copying machine, reproduce it until they have the quantity needed to create a profile. This is about as close as law enforcement has ever gotten to being able to identify a criminal from the air he breathed.

In criminal cases DNA can be used only to either include or exclude a suspect. Presently there is absolutely no way of using it to develop a suspect. But several states are participating in the establishment of a national database in which the DNA profiles of convicted felons, especially sex offenders, will be stored. In addition to allowing police to identify repeat offenders from DNA left at a crime scene, the database will enable them to associate rapes committed in different places to the same man, and to coordinate investigations. In Indiana, for example, seven rapes were committed in the same area within a brief period of time. Authorities believed the crimes had been committed by a single serial rapist, but DNA typing proved that while five of the rapes had indeed been committed by one man, another man was responsible for two of them.

The embryonic database proved to be of extraordinary value when a twenty-four-year-old Ritchie, Illinois, man was murdered and his twenty-one-year-old wife was raped, shot in the head at point-blank range, and left for dead on a cold November morning in 1991. A year and a half later police still had no solid leads in the case. But in June 1993, Illinois sci-crime specialists entered the DNA profile developed from the killer's semen in their data bank. The Illinois state program was so new that it contained only six

hundred DNA profiles developed from the blood of convicted sex offenders. Incredibly, the computer identified the DNA from the murder scene as that of an individual who had previously served time for sexually molesting a seventeen-year-old girl. Further testing confirmed the match. The individual was arrested and charged with the crime. A year later he was still awaiting trial.

The only information included in the planned national database will be the short chain used for comparisons. The FBI lab doesn't even develop the more complex profile needed to determine the race or sex of individuals, other physical attributes, or their medical history. They simply create an autorad, the bar code, and it either matches another submission or it doesn't.

There is a misconception that DNA eventually will replace just about every other sci-crime technology, particularly fingerprinting. This isn't true. DNA provides evidence that has never before been available in violent crimes, but it's complementary to prints. DNA is rarely found on paper, for example, but prints found on paper provide valuable evidence in a variety of crimes from money laundering to bank robberies to kidnapping.

It isn't only what's in blood that tells a tale. There's much to be learned from the patterns made by blood, the bloodstains and blood spatter. Sherlock Holmes once determined a man's height by measuring a bloodstain found on a wall, and perhaps that was the beginning of the study of blood spatter. Blood spatter is based on the fact that blood is a fluid and will act according to the laws of physics, like any other fluid. It will act the same way under the same circumstances every time.

According to Agent-examiner Bob Spaulding, one of the sci-crime world's most respected blood-spatter experts, "By observing the spot size, quantity, shape, distribution, location, angle of impact, and the target surface of a blood-

stain, a lot of valuable information can be learned about what took place.'' Certain things will be true in every case. If an individual has blood spatter on himself, he was at the scene when a bloody object was being struck in some way. The more force with which someone is hit, the smaller the size of the resulting spatter. So a low-velocity impact, a punch in the nose causing blood to drip straight down to the floor, will leave larger spots, while a medium-velocity impact, perhaps from a stabbing or beating, will result in smaller spots. Bloodstains caused by the high-velocity impact of a bullet will be mistlike in appearance, with droplets about $\frac{1}{25}$ of an inch in diameter. This mist will travel only a very short distance from the point of impact and will be dispersed in a conelike shape.

A path of elongated droplets several feet apart indicates that the victim was running; rounder droplets closer together mean he or she was walking. Some bloodstains will show directionality, and by drawing a line from the center of several stains, it's possible to determine where the assailant was located when he struck or shot the victim. A large stain on a surface—clothing, in many cases—is called a contact stain and means the surface was in touch with a bloody object.

A large bloodstain with an area void of blood means that something blocked the spray of blood, and therefore that it will be on some person or object. Several relatively straight lines of elongated bloodstains are called cast-off or in-line staining, and are caused by blood being thrown from a moving object, a knife or a club, as it changed direction. Castoff is often found on a ceiling in particularly brutal assaults, when each time the attacker drew back his weapon he threw off another line of blood. Castoff allows investigators to determine how many times the victim was struck—the total of blows is always at least one more than the number of stains, because at the first blow the weapon

has no blood on it—and the direction from which the attack came, because blood is almost always cast off during the backswing.

The value of blood-spatter evidence was probably best exemplified in the case of Green Beret Dr. Jeffrey MacDonald, who claimed that drug-crazed hippies had broken into his home at the Fort Bragg Army Base in North Carolina, and murdered his pregnant wife and his two young daughters. MacDonald told a chilling story of what had happened that night, explaining that he had been stabbed and knocked unconscious, and on awakening found that his family had been slaughtered. All three victims had been stabbed repeatedly, and MacDonald's two daughters had also been beaten with a blunt instrument. He was the only survivor.

But the blood told a very different story. Although there was a great deal of hard evidence that contradicted MacDonald's version of the murders, Agent-examiner Paul Stombaugh, then chief of the Chemistry/Toxicology Unit, was able to use bloodstain and blood-spatter evidence to reconstruct the crime. What made this case so unusual was the fact that each of the people involved—MacDonald; his wife, Colette; and their two daughters, Kristen and Kimberly—had a different ABO blood type. By identifying the blood type found in each room and on the knives, ice pick, and clubs, Stombaugh was able to show where each person was struck and with what weapon.

Stombaugh's riveting testimony at a grand jury hearing in 1975 formed the key part of the prosecutor's case. Point by point he refuted MacDonald's story. "This is Kristen's room . . . ," he said matter-of-factly as the grand jurors were shown a color slide of the bloodied room. "This is the top sheet on that bed and it has a huge bloodstain on it. Yet there was no bloodstain underneath, on the bottom sheet. In reading the reports, it was reflected that the huge

bloodstain on the top sheet in Kristen's room was type A blood—Colette's blood type. Kristen had type O blood, and the rest of the blood in that room, the bulk of it, was type O. . . .

"The only way you can get staining such as this is from a steady flow right down onto it. . . . At one time this had a very heavy flow of blood from a type A person directly onto it. . . . Now, if this bedspread had been placed down on the floor of Kristen's room, and Colette's body were lifted off the bed where she was bleeding, she would have bled directly on the spread. Then her body could have been covered with this sheet. . . . The spread, you see, is very heavy and blood does not soak through it. It acts like a bit of a well in there, and holds it. . . ."

The bedspread also had blood on it, but this was type AB, Kimberly's blood type—and the same type found on the club that was used to beat her to death. "This stain is not the result of direct bleeding," Stombaugh continued. "It's been a transfer of blood. In other words, a very bloody object having AB blood on it was placed there. It could have occurred by resting the club, in a bloody condition, on the bedspread."

Later in his testimony, Stombaugh told the jurors, "I think he picked Kim up, carried her into her bed and, due to the AB blood spatters on the wall, I believe he hit her again with the club and killed her."

Asked if he had any response to Stombaugh's testimony, MacDonald replied, "No, except that by my being unable to explain blood spots you make me guilty of the homicide of my family." Exactly what bloodstain and blood-spatter evidence is supposed to do.

MacDonald was indicted by the grand jury for the murder of his wife and children. Prosecutor James L. Blackburn told jurors during his summation, "I can only tell you from the physical evidence in this case that things do not lie. But I suggest that people can, and do. . . ."

And later Blackburn concluded, "[MacDonald's attorney] said earlier that the physical evidence doesn't mean anything—it doesn't speak. It is only the attorneys speaking. I say to you that physical evidence simply cries out an explanation."

The evidence spoke forcefully. MacDonald was convicted of the second-degree murder of Colette and Kimberly, and the first-degree murder of Kristen. He was sentenced to three consecutive life sentences, the most severe penalty the law could impose.

Reading blood spatter is an inexact science; there are a lot of variables involved, and rarely is blood-spatter evidence as significant as it was in the MacDonald case. But bloodstains and spatter can be particularly valuable in determining whether a death was a suicide or homicide. To the uneducated observer, it can also be very misleading. During a Texas heat wave, the body of a man was found hanging in his home; the walls and ceiling of the room were covered with tiny drops of blood. It looked as if he had been brutally beaten, then hanged. But only to the untrained eye.

"He'd been hanging there three or four days before they'd found him," Agent-examiner Linda Harrison said, "and during a Texas heat wave, that's a long, long time. His body had begun decomposing. When I first took a look at the photographs of the walls and ceiling, it did look like it might be blood spatter. But as I looked a little more carefully I could see that it wasn't. What it was all over those walls was fly excrement.

"Flies had been feeding on the body, then landing on the walls and ceiling with blood on their legs and excreting the blood they'd digested. One of the things that had made that obvious was a photograph showing a lightbulb that had been left on. There wasn't a spot on it. The flies hadn't gone near it because it was too hot for them. If we had been dealing with blood spatter, we certainly would have

found some there. We couldn't tell them for sure that this was a suicide, but we could tell them that the scene was not the result of a beating.''

Once again, the blood had told the story.

6

The Match Game:
The Materials Analysis and Elemental Analysis Units

Elementary.

SHERLOCK HOLMES,
in Sir Arthur Conan Doyle's ''The Crooked Man''

"Evidence is sacred," Fred Whitehurst, an agent-examiner in the Materials Analysis Unit, said frankly, "because it can lead to me taking away your life and your liberty. So if society is going to use it to take away your most basic privileges, it better be damn good."

In a quiet, well-groomed suburban neighborhood just outside Tucson, Arizona, an eight-year-old girl rode her bike around the corner and was never seen again. In El Salvador, three American nuns and a lay worker arriving on a peace mission were murdered by government troops, who claimed that they had driven through a blockade. In Michigan, the bones of a fifteen-year-old girl were uncovered ten years after her murder, and the two men who had watched her die each swore the other had killed her. In Texas, the naked body of a young woman was found in a ditch at the edge of a highway, her hands and legs bound with tape; she was the victim of a serial killer.

Dead men do tell tales; evidence speaks for them. And anything, absolutely anything, can become evidence. Pause for a moment and look at your surroundings. If a crime

were to occur right here, which of the things you see would you expect to become important evidence?

Evidence is anything that can be used to connect someone with a crime, a crime scene, or a victim, and you have probably overlooked the most obvious things. What you saw when you looked around is the world of the FBI's Materials Analysis Unit and the Elemental Analysis Unit. "In most other crime labs we'd be referred to as the trace evidence unit," explained Jim Corby, the trim, soft-spoken chief of Materials Analysis. "We work with paints, glass, plastics and polymers, tapes and adhesives, soil and building materials, explosive residue, gemstones, cosmetics, lubricants, and just about anything else that doesn't seem to readily fit into another unit's expertise.

"We use them to try to put a suspect back at the crime scene by associating him with something he left there or something he took away with him. And we do that with some pretty good science. We compare samples microscopically, microchemically, and instrumentally. Everything we identify has to be confirmed by two different scientific methods following established protocols before we'll go into court with it. If we conclude that two samples came from the same place, you can be certain they did. And if we can't make an identification, we try to provide some information about a sample that might be of probative value to investigators. We try to tell them what it is and where it might have come from. To do that we've established sample collections in several different areas, ranging from our first collection, the National Automotive Paint File, which was started in 1932, to our newest collection, which consists of eighty-five different types of petroleum jellies."

Objects that the Materials Unit doesn't analyze, Elemental Analysis does. Elemental Analysis looks at the nuts and bolts of crime. Literally.

The unit was formed in the mid-1970s to take advantage

of neutron activation, a sophisticated technology that allows examiners to determine the elemental composition of a substance in parts per billion—to get down to its basic chemical makeup. While the unit originally specialized in identifying gunshot residue—proving that someone had recently been very close to a fired gun—it has expanded to include the identification, comparison, and behavior of metals.

The substances frequently submitted to crime labs for identification and analysis are paints, glass, and soil. Paint may well be the most commonly encountered manmade substance in the world. We have covered our world in color. Pause again and think of a color, any color, then look around for objects that color. All sorts of things will jump out at you. And even though so much of the world is painted, the paint from a specific place may be unique. White paint is not just white paint. It's composed of organic and inorganic pigments to give it color, the solvent that carries the pigment, a binder to hold it to a surface, and additives that make it waterproof or shinier or longer-lasting. It may have been put on with a brush or a roller or a spray gun. And it has been exposed to environmental conditions ranging from bright sunlight to a kid with a crayon. Every one of these characteristics can make a given sample of white paint different from all other white paints, and also make it possible to establish that a sample came from a specific place or object and to connect that place or object with a suspect or victim.

While to most people the only important characteristic of paint is its color, the fact that paint is durable, chips or breaks easily, can be unique, and is transferred from one object to another makes it terrific evidence. In September 1984, in the small town of Flowing Wells, Arizona, eight-year-old Vicki Hoskinson went for a ride on her pink bicycle and disappeared. The bicycle was found hours later lying in the street, its frame slightly damaged, but the little

girl seemed to have vanished. Seven months later some of her remains along with her crushed skull were found in the desert, the rest of her skeletal remains having been carried away by animals. There were no clues, no suspects.

The first break in the case came when a jailhouse informer claimed that a prisoner named Frank Jarvis Atwood had told him that he had bumped a little girl off her bicycle, then taken her into the desert, where he had sexually molested and strangled her, leaving her for dead. According to this story, Atwood had left the scene, but had dropped his car keys during the assault and had returned to find them. To his surprise the little girl was still alive, so he beat her to death with a rock.

It was an incriminating story, but without corroborating evidence it had little value. A good defense attorney would rip the informant's story apart, claiming that he had invented it to get his own sentence shortened. But proving that Atwood's car, which was in police custody, had hit the little girl's bike would put Atwood at the scene. Both the bicycle and the car's bumper were submitted to the sci-crime lab. On the bumper, Agent-examiner Tim Carlson found specks of pink paint, no larger than the dot over an "i." Carlson compared those specks with the paint on the bicycle. They were identical in every measurable way. And it was enough evidence to indict Frank Atwood for kidnapping and murder.

"It really wasn't more than a trace," Jim Corby remembered, "but it was enough to make a comparison. It had required extraordinary detective work by the local law enforcement to come up with this evidence. We work with minute amounts of evidence and if we handle it carelessly or touch it the wrong way it might literally jump across the room. A breeze from an air vent can blow away the most important evidence in a case. At one time or another probably every person in this unit has been down on his knees searching the floor for a chip of paint."

Tim Carlson died of cancer before the trial began. In order to have an expert witness testify about the significance of the evidence, it was resubmitted to the lab and examined by Corby. Much of the prosecution's case rested on this trace of pink paint. Atwood's attorney tried to stop the tests, claiming, "The State will readily admit that they have absolutely no connection between Vicki Lynn Hoskinson . . . and Frank Jarvis Atwood, except insofar as the State alleges that the paint on the bumper of Frank Jarvis Atwood's vehicle originated from the bicycle of Vicki Lynn Hoskinson or another similar source."

The court permitted Corby to proceed with his examination, and he began by using a microscope to compare the pink paint from Atwood's bumper to a paint sample from the child's bicycle. The samples were the same color and had the same general physical appearance, that of an enamel paint. If anything about them had been different, Corby would have reported that they had not come from the same source. As in almost all other types of comparisons, there is no minimum number of characteristics that must match. Everything that can be measured or observed must match.

If Corby had been conducting this examination as he would have when he first joined the lab in 1965, he then would have applied various solvents to the two samples to see if they reacted the same way, and he would have reported that they had the same general class characteristics. But modern science has made it possible to go much further, to look at substances on a molecular level. Corby took a tiny piece of the speck and put it in the pyrolysis gas chromatograph mass spectrometer, which burned it at 760°C. The mass spec separates and charts the gases released by a substance as its organic components are vaporized, providing a detailed analysis of the chemical makeup of a sample. The chemical makeup of the pink

paint from Atwood's car and the paint from the bike were alike.

Finally, Corby took the sample to Dennis Ward in Elemental Analysis, who examined both substances under a scanning electron microscope, which enabled him to identify the metallic elements present in the paint. As Corby testified at Atwood's trial, these tests could not prove that the pink paint on the bumper and the pink paint on the bicycle had come from the same source to the exclusion of all other possibilities. It simply meant they could have come from the same source.

But Ward suggested that if there had been a transfer of paint from the bicycle to the bumper, there also might have been a transfer of the bumper's nickel coating to the bicycle. Although to the naked eye there was no nickel present, in three different places on the bicycle the scanning electron microscope detected traces of nickel similar to the nickel plating on the bumper of Atwood's car. The very unusual two-way transfer of paint and nickel enabled Corby to tell the jury, "In my opinion the pink paint on the bumper came from that bicycle or another source that had to be painted exactly like that bicycle." Legally, that was the strongest statement he could make. It was strong enough. Atwood's attorney called it "the most damning testimony in the case." The jury found Atwood guilty of the murder of Vicki Lynn Hoskinson, and he was sentenced to death.

A few chips of paint don't seem like very much, but in hit-and-run cases they are often the only evidence found at the scene. Compared to more highly publicized crimes, hit-and-run accidents have become so common it's easy to forget how brutal they can be. But the people who investigate them never forget. "We've gotten the clothes of hit-and-run victims in here that are like soup," Corby said. "They're just drenched with blood and body fluids. Sometimes a victim's body will be thrown more than a hundred

feet from the point of impact, and when a body is hit with that kind of force it just explodes.'' Paint chips have been found embedded in victims' clothes, on their eyeglasses or belt buckles, in their shoes, under their fingernails, even on their false teeth. Almost no chip is too small to be useful; the basic rule of the unit is that if you can see it, you can work with it.

The National Automotive Paint File, which consists of more than 40,000 original paint finish samples, enables examiners to identify the year, make, and model of a car by comparing the physical characteristics and chemical composition of paint found at the crime scene with that of known specimens. For example, when a ten-year-old Los Angeles boy was killed by a hit-and-run driver, his clothing was sent to the lab. It was processed in an airtight scraping room and carefully scraped with a metal spatula. Several tiny sparkling paint chips fell from his pants, perhaps having been held there by the boy's dried blood. Using the paint file, these chips were identified as a gold metallic acrylic paint used on three car models by the same manufacturer. The lab reported to Los Angeles police department that the killer would be driving one of these models.

It didn't take the LAPD long to discover that one of the boy's neighbors drove a gold sports car. The suspect claimed he had recently replaced the hood of his car because it had been damaged in a traffic accident. When the hood was recovered and submitted to the lab, examiners were not only able to match the paint chips found in the victim's clothes to the car, they also found fibers caught in the metal that could be matched to the boy's jacket. Faced with this evidence, the owner of the car confessed to the crime.

The paint file includes only factory-applied paint. Obviously it isn't possible to use a sample from that collection to identify the make of a car that has been repainted. But once a suspect is identified, repainting does make it easier

to prove that paint came from a specific vehicle. Each layer of paint makes a car just a little more unusual. The more layers of paint, the more remote the possibility that a paint sample came from any other source. In a Wisconsin hit-and-run case, the lab's ability to identify the eight layers of paint from a chip found at the scene allowed police to make an extremely strong association to the suspect's car. The chances of finding two cars that had been painted the same eight colors in the same sequence were considered very remote.

Ironically, as the ability of the lab to match evidence to samples has improved, car manufacturers have begun changing their paint systems to combat environmental hazards like acid rain, with the result that less paint is being found at crime scenes. As for Jim Corby, who probably knows as much about automotive paint systems as any sci-crime examiner in the world, he still relies on the old method of protecting the paint on his gray car: "I let a thick coat of dirt protect my paint. Washing it too often wears down that protective coating."

Paint can provide key information in any crime in which a car is involved. As a San Diego bank robbery team made their getaway from a parking lot, for example, they accidentally bumped into a parked car. The paint smudge left on that car enabled lab examiners to identify the make and model of the car the robbers were driving. The motor vehicle bureau provided a list of everyone in the area who owned that model, and that enabled police to identify the suspects. The foreign paint found on the car in the parking lot led directly to the apprehension of the bank robbers.

While a significant percentage of paint exams involve automotive paint, the Materials Analysis Unit also provides assistance in cases in which information can be learned from any kind of paint. For example, the lab's understanding of how paint is transferred when two objects collide provided valuable evidence for investigators trying to deter-

mine exactly what had caused an Air Florida jet to crash into Washington, D.C.'s, Fourteenth Street Bridge. Particles of automotive paint and glass found embedded in the fuselage of the plane were matched to the cars that had been on the bridge at the time of the crash. By comparing the places on the fuselage where paint and glass were found to the areas of the cars from which they had come, investigators were able to determine the angle of the plane as it skimmed over the bridge. That angle was an important clue to the cause of the crash.

While most paint examinations involve the comparison of two submissions, the expertise of the unit's examiners has been applied to several unusual and difficult cases. When a Navy helicopter crashed, for instance, investigators wanted to verify the craft's maintenance logs, which reported that several key parts from the rotor assembly had been stripped of paint, examined for cracks and metal fatigue, and then repainted. Some of these parts were sent to the lab and were examined by Jim Corby. "The question was how could we determine if the examinations recorded in the log had actually been conducted," Corby remembered. "Well, we know how certain paint formulations migrate, and we knew that if the cracks had been present when the parts were repainted we'd find a trace of that paint inside those cracks. And that's what we found. In at least some instances, the stress fractures, the tiny cracks, had been present when the parts were repainted, meaning that if the proper maintenance examinations had been done, those cracks should have been detected and the critical parts replaced or repaired."

Like any substance in use for centuries, the paints we apply today have evolved slowly and can often be dated by their components. If a paint contains a certain chemical compound, it must have been manufactured after that compound was in production. That can be very useful information. One of the great mysteries of this century is the fate

of aviator Amelia Earhart, who vanished while on a flight around the world in 1937. So when parts of an airplane were discovered on a remote Pacific island in 1991, the FBI lab was asked to determine whether the paint on those parts could have come from Earhart's plane. The difficulty in conducting this type of examination is that there is no paint sample known to have come from the plane to use as a basis for comparison. The Materials Analysis Unit confirmed that the paint contained pigments and resin consistent with those known to have been used in paints in 1937. The parts could have come from her airplane, but without having other parts painted at the same time in the same place, it wasn't possible to conclude that they in fact had come from that airplane.

By finding chemicals in the paint that were not in use in 1937, the lab could have proved that the parts hadn't come from Earhart's plane. This is precisely what happened when the lab was asked to authenticate a painting purportedly by Renoir. Had it been a Renoir, it would have been worth a fortune. Using X-ray diffractometry, a process in which compounds are identified by the way X rays react as they pass through a substance, it was discovered that the pigment contained titanium dioxide and barium sulfate. Renoir had lived and painted long before titanium dioxide was used in pigment, so its presence in the sample proved that this painting was a forgery.

After paint, glass may well be the most ubiquitous man-made substance in our world, and glass fragments are found at a surprisingly large number of crime scenes. While people think of glass as fragile, in fact it is one of the hardest substances in the world, harder than steel—on geologists' scales, that is, in which substances are rated by their ability to scratch other materials. But glass breaks easily. And because it reacts in a highly predictable man-

ner, detectives who understand the properties of glass can learn a great deal about what happened at a crime scene.

While a piece of glass may shatter into countless fragments of all sizes, every one of those fragments, the largest and the smallest, will have identical properties. The color will be the same and the density, dispersion, and refractive index will all be the same, allowing investigators to prove the tiniest sliver came from a specific picture window.

Among the many properties of glass that make it so valuable to detectives is that it adheres to almost any surface without people being aware of it, and it stays there for a long time. If you break a pane of glass, for example, tiny shards from that glass may get caught in your clothing, your hair, even the soles of your shoes, and may still be there after showering or laundering. In a classic example of the importance of glass as evidence, Chris Fiedler was assigned a case that involved what appeared to be a pretty ordinary examination of glass found on a suspect after an attempted rape in Baltimore. "Several elderly women in the area had been raped, and everybody in the neighborhood was very scared," he recalled. "One night a man broke into the home of an older woman and was confronted by her son, who had been staying there to protect her. The rapist panicked, dove through a window, then ran several blocks before he was captured. Baltimore police submitted samples from the window he'd dived through, as well as numerous slivers of glass that had been found on his body, in his clothing, and on a pair of leather gloves he was wearing when they caught him.

"I was able to associate some of the glass found on the suspect and the glass from the broken window, but what surprised me was that some of the glass found on the suspect hadn't come from that window. Who knew how long he'd been carrying it around? The police went back to several other houses where the rapist had gained entry by smashing a window. The broken glass had been replaced,

but by wiping down the windowsills with a damp cloth and searching the floor inside and the ground outside they were able to come up with fragments from the broken windows. No matter how hard you try to clean up broken glass, there are usually going to be a few slivers left behind. By measuring the refractive index, the dispersion, and the density of the glass, and then by looking at it instrumentally to determine the elemental composition—how much of which elements made up the glass—I was able to connect the suspect to three other rapes. This significantly contributed to his conviction and he was sentenced to a long prison term.''

Few people realize how hard and durable glass is. Because it is stronger than most other substances, glass is often found embedded in hammers, crowbars, and other tools used to smash into a home or building. Even if the suspect knows that the chips are there, it's just about impossible to remove them all. That fact turned out to be the key to the solution of a mass murder in Georgia. An entire family, six people, were shot and killed by an intruder. Local police had no clues, no suspects, no apparent motive—no place to start their investigation. But several weeks after the murders, a young boy fishing in a pond snagged a .22 Magnum, the same caliber as the missing murder weapon.

Police were able to trace the gun back to its owner, who admitted knowing the murdered family but provided a reasonable alibi for the night of the slaughter. The gun and the bullets recovered from the victims' bodies were sent to the Firearms Unit. The bullets had been too badly damaged for a match to be made, but a Firearms examiner noticed several long scratches on the gun barrel. There was nothing really special about them, but he was curious. So he brought the gun over to Chris Fiedler to see if those scratches might be significant.

Fiedler found tiny bits of glass and powder in the

scratches. There wasn't even enough glass to cause a small cut on your finger, but it was still more than enough to use as a basis for comparison. To gain entry into the victims' home, the killer had smashed a small pane of glass with an unknown object. A gun, maybe? Even though the gun had lain at the bottom of a pond for weeks, the glass was still firmly embedded in the barrel. Fiedler was able to make a match between those slivers and the broken glass from the victims' back door. The gun had been used in the killings. To escape the death penalty, the suspect pled guilty to murder and was sentenced to life in prison.

In many violent crimes, bullets are fired through glass, and an examination of that glass can reveal certain details about the crime. In an ideal situation, three things about a shooting can be determined from a sheet of glass: which side the shooter was standing on; the angle from which the bullet was fired; and, if more than one shot was fired, the sequence in which they were fired.

It's logical to assume that when someone shoots through glass the fragments will be found on the opposite side of that glass. Logical, but wrong. Glass is elastic, and when a projectile of any kind hits it or goes through it, glass will bend like a tree in the wind, then snap back violently. This phenomenon is called blowback. Glass will blow back as far as eighteen feet in the direction from which the projectile came. In many cases police have been able to place a suspect within twelve to eighteen feet from a piece of glass through the particles found on his clothing or body.

In addition to knowing how far from the glass the shooter was standing, it's possible to approximate his location by determining the angle at which the bullet struck the glass. If the bullet hole in the glass is symmetrical, perfectly round, the bullet was fired at a right angle to the glass; the shooter was standing directly in front of it. As the angle of the shooter to the glass increases the hole will

become elongated; the greater the angle the more elongated the hole will be.

It's also possible to determine from a sheet of glass the order in which shots were fired through it. This has proved to be particularly important in cases in which suspects claim that a law enforcement officer had fired first, and they returned fire in self-defense. In just about every TV shootout, a single bullet causes a window to burst into countless pieces. Most of the time that isn't what happens. Tempered glass or glass that is held securely in a frame will usually crack but not shatter. In fact, you can shoot several bullets through a pane of glass before it falls apart, and under certain circumstances it's possible to examine that glass and determine the sequence in which the shots were fired.

When a wounded suspect was charged with attempted murder for shooting at a California highway patrolman, he claimed he had fired in self-defense, after the officer had fired at him. It was the suspect's word against the officer's, with the suspect's freedom and the officer's career at stake.

Several shots had been fired through the windshield of the suspect's car. It looked a bit like a crazed spider's web, and long thin cracks emanated from each bullet hole, turning the windshield into a glass maze. Figuring out the sequence in which the shots had been fired meant finding a path through that maze. Cracks will radiate from anything that pierces a sheet of glass, but they will stop when they meet another crack. So the first shot will cause many uninterrupted cracks. The cracks created by the second shot will terminate wherever they cross paths with cracks from the first shot; cracks created by the third shot will stop when they meet cracks from either of the first two shots; and so on. The cracks must make contact; there is no way to determine when an isolated shot was fired. But once two or more bullet holes are put in sequence, the size of the hole, the angle of the shot, and the residue found around

the point of entry together enable investigators to determine which gun fired what bullet. In the California case it was proved that the suspect had fired first, and had been hit when the patrolman returned his fire.

Proving that pieces of glass have the same composition makes for a strong association, but showing that they once fit together makes for a positive match. In hit-and-run cases, in particular, the fitting of a shard of headlight glass found at the scene to the broken headlight on a car means that this car, to the exclusion of every other car in the world, was involved in the crime. But glass fracture matches can be made in other types of cases, too. In Butte, Montana, the badly burned body of a murder victim was found smoldering in the woods. From the lack of blood at the scene and the fact that there were no signs of a struggle, it was obvious that he had been killed elsewhere, then dumped in the woods and set afire. His clothing had been destroyed, but police found several pieces of glass that had not been damaged by the fire.

A suspect was identified and in his garbage pail investigators found several pieces of glass from a broken window. Agent-examiner Bruce Hall was asked to try to link the fragments. "The first thing we usually do when we get large fragments of glass in here is try to fit the pieces together," he said. "That's about the most meaningful evidence there is. In this case we got lucky. The pieces found on the body fitted perfectly to pieces found in the suspect's trash. It was like putting a jigsaw puzzle together. Apparently a window in the suspect's trailer had been smashed during a fight and the suspect never realized that some fragments of glass had struck his victim. We got a guilty plea in that case."

Because bits of glass are small and just about impossible to trace, glass is often used to contaminate consumer products. In many instances consumers claiming to find bits of glass in a product have demanded payment from the manu-

facturer. In these cases, the fault might lie with the manufacturer, the glass might have been put into the product by someone tampering with it in the store, or the consumer might be committing fraud, hoping for a quick payoff.

One of the most publicized product-tampering cases occurred in 1988, when mothers around the country began complaining that they were finding tiny pieces of glass in jars of Gerber's baby food. That kind of publicity can ruin a company, even if it's not responsible, by destroying consumers' confidence in the safety of a product. Dozens of jars of baby food in which glass particles supposedly had been found were submitted to the lab from all over the country. Chris Fiedler got the case. The fact that supposedly contaminated jars had been found in so many different places made it very unlikely that this was a true product-tampering case—unless somebody was doing a lot of traveling just to put glass in baby food—so the presence of the glass was either the fault of the manufacturer or consumer fraud. "We spent a tremendous amount of time looking at those jars," Fiedler said. "We knew that if the contamination had occurred at the plant level, we would find the same type of glass in different jars. Well, we didn't. Instead we found many different types of glass—mirror glass, headlight glass, lightbulb glass—but we didn't find the same glass in two different jars. The glass in every single jar was unique. We have had cases in which a bulb broke over a packaging line and bits of glass got in several boxes or cans, but this wasn't one of them. In my opinion, the fact that different glass was found in the jars meant it had been put in there by different consumers, presumably because they thought the company would pay them."

Because glass is so common, people often forget that it can be extremely valuable, valuable enough to be counterfeited. One of the largest product-counterfeiting cases in recent history involved high-quality crystal. The manufacturer estimated that over a five-year period more than $40

million in counterfeit crystal was sold to consumers. To the consumer the products, including the packaging, looked exactly alike, but tests performed in the lab showed that the counterfeit crystal had a lower lead content than the authentic crystal. That didn't mean the glass was weaker, but rather that it wasn't as clear. Nor was it worth what consumers had paid for it. In this examination it was relatively simple for the examiners to see right through the fraud.

Sometimes dirt can make the facts of a case as clear as glass. In March 1975, a fifteen-year-old Michigan girl about to give information to authorities about two men with whom she was involved in a bad-check scam disappeared and was never seen again. In April one of the two men was sent to prison for an unrelated crime. A decade later, the other man involved in the check-passing scam claimed that his former partner had strangled the girl in his car, shot her in the head, then buried her. He didn't know exactly where she had been buried, he explained, because when his partner took her body into the woods, he had fled. On the basis of this testimony, the first man was tried and convicted of the murder, even though the girl's body was never found.

After being sentenced to prison for the murder, the first man appealed, invoking the classic "The other guy did it" defense. According to his story, in August 1975, while he was behind bars, the second man had thrown the girl off a railroad trestle onto the rocks below, then buried her in the area. Thus two men each claimed that the other had committed the murder. There were no other witnesses. How do you determine which man was telling the truth? How do you know either man is telling the truth?

Among the discrepancies in the conflicting stories was the claim that the girl had been shot in the head. If she hadn't been, the second man's testimony, the testimony that had sent his partner to prison, would be discredited. In

order to prove that she hadn't been shot, the man convicted of the murder finally told authorities where her body had been buried. Her skeletal remains were found precisely where he said they would be, and there was no bullet wound in her skull. She had not been shot. Which man was telling the truth: the man convicted of the crime, who had supposedly shot her in March, or his accuser, who had supposedly killed her in August? If she had been killed in August, the convicted killer could not have committed the crime because he had been in jail.

The victim's decayed clothing and several pounds of dirt found at the grave site were submitted to the lab. The case was assigned to Chris Fiedler, who enlisted the help of Wayne Lord, the Bureau's entomologist, the bug expert, who was working in the Research and Training Unit in Quantico, Virginia. Fiedler and Lord visited the grave site in late spring. As Fiedler remembered that trip, "She'd been buried in a swampy area and when we were there, there was a tremendous amount of insect activity. The mosquitoes were just awful; we were getting bit all over.

"Back in the lab the first thing we did was send her clothes over to Hairs and Fibers to determine what they were made of. We only had some scraps, but we knew that if she had been wearing winter clothing—wool socks, a jacket—we were probably talking about March rather than August. Then Wayne Lord started examining the soil for evidence of insect activity. Soil is very predictable; we knew what we should find. The soil in the area was very sandy. It was soft when we were there, meaning insects would have been able to get into the ground pretty easily—unless, of course, it had been frozen when she was buried.

"There were no insects in the soil. And she had been wearing heavy clothing. The combination of the Hairs and Fibers exams and the fact that Wayne Lord found no insect activity in the soil led us to conclude that she'd been killed and buried in March. We never found out why there was a

discrepancy about the gunshot wound to the head. Maybe the guy took a shot at her and missed, but it didn't make any difference. His appeal was denied and he's still in prison for her murder."

Specifically, in the sci-crime business, "soil" or "dirt" means any type of natural ground cover that has accumulated over a period of time, whether it comes from a fertilized field in the country, a park in the city, or a sandy beach. The fact that soil has predictable properties—it freezes, it migrates, it absorbs fluids—makes it valuable in cases like the Michigan murder. But its primary value is that it allows investigators to associate a person or an object with a specific place because, while one soil sample may look like any other, soil is unique to a specific location. And as every mother with a once-clean floor will attest, it's very easily transported.

Soil is naturally composed of four parts: minerals, organic matter—anything once part of a living organism—air, and water. It's also subject to changes wrought by the environment or by humans: bird or animal droppings, floods, the presence of fertilizer, building materials, or even particles from roof shingles. And all of these things combine to make soil from a specific place unique and identifiable.

The first step in a soil comparison is to compare the color of the soils under different light sources. If two samples are different in color, they came from different places. Why they're different isn't important for law enforcement purposes; the fact that they look different under the same conditions means they are different. A nationally used color chart allows soil comparisons to be made by telephone so investigators will know if they are, literally, on the right track.

Next, the texture of the soil samples and the presence of any peculiarities—things like plants, seeds or droppings, building materials—are compared. If they match, the soil is

then washed in an ultrasonic cleaner. Washing dirt with high-frequency sound waves enables examiners to isolate the minerals or extraneous matter like glass or bricks that might be there. The washed samples are then dropped into a heavy liquid called bromoform, a chemical with a high specific gravity; the lighter minerals, like quartz, float on the surface, while the heavier minerals sink to the bottom. If two samples came from the same place, they will contain essentially the same type and density of minerals in addition to all the other matter.

If soil samples from two things found in different places match, they prove that the items were once in the same place. And that can cover a lot of ground. A month after Adolph Coors of the Coors Brewing Company was kidnapped in Colorado in 1960, a car belonging to the prime suspect was found burned in an Atlantic City, New Jersey, dump. The fire had destroyed just about everything that might have provided clues to Coors's whereabouts. But four different types of soil were found under the front fender. One of the soils came from the dump, but the other three were consistent with soil from the Rocky Mountain area. When Coors's buried body finally was found several months later, one of those soil samples from the car could be matched to an area not far from the grave site. It was enough to show that the suspect had been in that area, and it became one of the key pieces of evidence at the trial. The suspect was convicted and sentenced to life imprisonment.

Much more recently, when DEA agent Kiki Camarena disappeared along with the pilot who helped him discover large marijuana plantations near Guadalajara, Mexico, the primary suspects in the kidnappings were the owners of the plantations, who were known to be paying large bribes to Mexican government officials. But two days after a government raid on a smaller plantation, in which all the members of that drug gang were killed, the bodies of Camarena and his pilot were found wrapped in sheets lying in a ditch.

Agents from the FBI lab were given a few minutes to examine the bodies, which were covered with dark soil. The agents were surprised that the bodies had suffered no animal or insect damage. An exposed body normally will be attacked by animals and insects very quickly. These bodies showed no signs of such activity.

The reason for that became obvious the next day, when the agents were permitted to visit the spot where the bodies had been found and where they had allegedly been lying for several weeks. Even a casual look at the site made two things clear. No body fluids had seeped into the soil, and the dirt was light-gray in color. The lack of body fluids proved that the bodies had not been buried there for any length of time, and the fact that the dirt found on the bodies was not light gray indicated that they had been buried elsewhere first and then brought to the ditch to be discovered. The Mexican government's attempt to blame the murders on the smaller drug ring had failed.

Contrary to the TV-created myth, it's just about impossible to trace soil back to its source without a lot of additional information. Finding soil on a shovel doesn't do detectives much good if they don't know where the grave is. When a dirt-encrusted packet of the ransom money paid to skyjacker D. B. Cooper turned up near the mouth of the Columbia River, investigators studied the layers of hardened dirt in an effort to pinpoint the area in which the money had landed; the hope was to find some evidence of Cooper's fate. Certain clues can be obtained from a soil sample, among them whether it was close to a road or near a structure of some kind, how close it was to fresh water or salt water, what type of plant and animal life might be found nearby, whether the area was urban or rural, whether it had been fertilized or planted, and while some information was elicited from the Cooper sample, no additional money or evidence of Cooper's fate has yet been found.

Sometimes it's the manmade materials found in a soil

sample that enable detectives to link a suspect to a crime. A realistic pipe bomb used in a Miami extortion case turned out to be filled with soil, to give it the necessary weight, rather than gunpowder. Among the extraneous materials found in the soil were bits of solder and tiny green chips from roof shingles. When a suspect was identified, his attorney pointed out that the soil found in the bomb could have come from anywhere on the suspect's block. That was true, but the only house on the block with green shingles belonged to the suspect. Every other house had red shingles. Additionally, the suspect had recently installed an outdoor faucet and the solder used in that job was consistent with the solder found in the soil. The combination of the type of soil, the green chips, and the solder allowed prosecutors to show, within a few feet, the source of the soil found in the dummy bomb.

While detectives often speak of tying a suspect to a crime, they are much more likely to be able to tape him to it. One of the most common denominators of violent crimes is the use of duct tape. In fact, criminals use it so often that it's commonly referred to as crime tape. Duct tape is used to bind victims' hands and feet; it's used to cover their mouths or blindfold them; it's used to hold bombs together; it's used in burglaries—in the Watergate burglary, for instance—to keep doors open; and, while it usually isn't the murder weapon, it often plays a significant role in killings. In an Indiana case the victim was taped to railroad tracks. He was killed by the train, but he was held in place by the tape. The killer was tied, or taped, to the crime when the tape used in the murder was proved to have come from a roll of tape found in his pickup truck.

Because tape is so often found at crime scenes, the Materials Analysis Unit has set up a tape collection, which currently consists of approximately one thousand samples from around the world. According to chemist Roger

Keagy: "When we get an unknown tape in here, we want to be able to tell the contributors what they should be looking for. Generally we can tell them who manufactured the tape, what color filler yarns it'll have, whether it was made for consumer or industrial use, and in some cases, if it's a specialized tape, even the type of industry. We can at least provide some leads."

When a piece of tape used in a crime, and tape from a known source that might be linked to that piece, arrive in the lab, the examiner first tries to match their ends. That's the strongest of possible matches. In the mid-1980s a serial killer was raping and murdering women in several Southwestern states. Each of his victims was found nude, her hands and feet bound together with duct tape. Police estimated that he had murdered as many as ten women. Soon after a body was found just off an interstate highway in Amarillo, Texas, a truck driver named Herbert Benjamin Boyle became the prime suspect. In the cab of Boyle's rig, police found a strip of duct tape that he had used to make a temporary repair. Jim Corby examined the evidence. "We got the tape in from the body of his last victim and the sample from his truck. And we were lucky. I was able to fit the torn end of the tape found on the victim to the piece found in his truck. It was an absolutely positive association.

"But then I was able to go further than that. As his other victims were found, we were able to prove, either by an end match or by the chemical composition of the tape, that the suspect had used the same tape on several of his victims. When I testified, I had about fifteen segments of tape, and I demonstrated to the jury how they all fit together—and how every one of them could be matched to the tape found in Boyle's truck. It was as if the string of murder victims was being held together by this tape. Boyle was sentenced to death."

Linking segments of tape together is valuable only if the

tape can be associated with a suspect. Otherwise all you have is a torn roll of tape. After the examiner attempts to make an end match, the crime tape will be sent to Hairs and Fiber, where they look for bits of hair or material in the adhesive, and to the Latent Fingerprint Section, where examiners try to find fingerprints. It's pretty difficult to use tape without touching the adhesive, so prints are often found on tapes. In the Boyle case, for example, his thumbprint, found on a segment of tape used to bind one of his victims, provided very strong evidence that he had used the tape in his killing spree.

If an end match isn't possible, then investigators compare the tape's physical characteristics—color, width, thickness, number of work yarns (the threads that run the length of the tape) and fill yarns (the threads that run across its width)—and, finally, the chemical composition of the tape backing and the adhesive. A primary difference between various brands and grades of duct tape is the type and amount of the adhesive. While not as conclusive as an end match, a characteristic and compositional match is still significant evidence. In a Garrison, Texas, case that received national attention because the police officer involved videotaped his own murder, three men were stopped by Constable Darrell Lunsford on a lonely highway. While a camera mounted in Lunsford's police cruiser recorded the scene, the officer searched the suspects' car for drugs. Suddenly one of the men grabbed the officer's gun and, off-camera, shot and killed him.

The videotape was sent to the Materials Analysis Unit, and after it had been enhanced by the lab's Video Support Unit, it was probably enough to ensure the conviction of the suspects, who had been captured. But it was still important to tie the suspects to drugs, because that would provide their motive for shooting the police officer and would make a life-or-death difference in their sentences.

While no drugs had been found in the suspects' car, sev-

eral bags of marijuana were found in a nearby field. The bags were sealed with tape, and a roll of similar tape was found in the suspects' car. Proving that the tape on the bags had come from the roll in the car would link the suspects to the drugs. The ends of the tape didn't match, and no fingerprints or fibers were found, so a compositional exam was done.

The adhesive was analyzed on a pyrolysis gas chromatograph. This instrument separates the different chemicals that make up an organic substance. As each of the components of a substance turns into a gas, it registers a peak on a printed graph. By comparing the time at which a given sample's peaks occur with the known reactions, it's possible to characterize the sample's chemical makeup. The tapes found on the marijuana bags registered three more peaks, or components, than the tape found in the car. There was no match. This could have been invaluable to the defense.

Agent-examiner Richard Buechele, a chemist who prior to joining the lab had worked in private industry researching explosive residues and developing a method for extracting toxins from body tissue, then worked three and a half years as a street agent in New York City, did the analysis. "Using other techniques I was able to identify the additional chemicals," he said. "I just didn't know what they were doing there. And as long as I couldn't figure that out, I couldn't testify that these tapes were the same. I couldn't link the drugs to the suspects. The detective who had found the bags told me they'd been wrapped in the sweet-smelling paper sheets used in washing machines to eliminate static cling, which are used by drug smugglers to help prevent dogs from smelling the drugs. I tested several different brands of those sheets, but they weren't producing the extra peaks. I thought: Maybe it's just a fragrance. So I contacted fragrance manufacturers. A chemist at Custom Essence in New Jersey finally suggested that my unknown

chemicals could be the volatile organic compounds found in marijuana. Suddenly it became very clear. The scent of the marijuana had been absorbed by the adhesive and was being detected and recorded by the gas chromatograph. Eliminating those peaks not only allowed me to make a match between the tapes, it also allowed me to demonstrate that the tape had been used in the transportation of drugs. All three men were convicted, and I know the work we did here contributed to those convictions.

Sometimes it just seems as if the world is made of plastic. Once again, wherever you are, look around and see how many things right in front of you are made out of plastic. So much of our world is plastic, from rigid automobile panels to flexible wire coating, that plastics have become a substantial part of the Materials Analysis Unit's workload. But even though so many things are made of plastic, a given plastic can be unique. Some plastics, or polymers as they are known scientifically, are produced for only one specific product or application. Nothing else in the world is made of that polymer; this fact allows examiners to prove that a piece of plastic came from that item.

The best way to associate two pieces of plastic is to show that they fit together. For example, a woman in Chicago was severely injured when she was bashed over the head with a large radio. A chip found at the scene fit perfectly into a radio found in the suspect's home, providing the critical physical evidence needed to convict him of assault.

As plastics replace metal in automobile panels, it's becoming common to find small pieces of plastic rather than paint chips and fragments of metal in crimes committed with cars. In a case eerily similar to the Vicki Hoskinson murder, an eleven-year-old girl in Louisiana disappeared while riding her bicycle. When a suspect was identified, investigators found a small colorful chip, which they be-

lieved to be paint, on the trunk latch of his car. The little girl's bike was eventually recovered from the bottom of a lake, but it was not the same color as the chip found on the trunk latch. Finally, lab examiners realized that the chip wasn't paint, but rather a thin plastic material that appeared to be part of a label. Examiners matched it by color, texture, and chemical composition to a plastic label on the seat post of the bicycle. That turned out to be the only hard evidence to link the suspect to the little girl, but it was proof that her bike had been in the trunk of his car, and was enough to contribute to his conviction.

When pieces of plastic don't fit together, a compositional match is attempted using something called differential thermal analysis. Often the best way to show that two substances are either alike or different is to determine their basic chemical makeup; different substances will be made of different chemicals. That method doesn't always work for plastics. Sometimes two plastics will have the same chemical makeup, and the only difference between them will be that they were molded under different pressures, depending on how much flexibility was desired. So the best way to chemically compare two pieces of plastic is to reverse the manufacturing process—to unmake them.

When a plastic object is made, certain chemical changes take place at specific temperatures. When the process is reversed, when plastic is heated rather than cooled, those transitions will be reversed. If two pieces of plastic have the same source, those transitions will take place at precisely the same temperatures. If they are different, even though they may look the same, feel the same, and even consist of the same polymers, the transitions will occur at different temperatures. While this process allows examiners to show that two pieces of plastic have the same characteristics, it doesn't prove they came from the same specific item.

But sometimes similar characteristics can be enough. In

an Indiana murder case a young woman was shot in the head at point-blank range during a robbery. When Doug Deedrick of Hairs and Fibers examined her clothing, he found some unusual blue dots, which he sent over to Materials Analysis to find out what they were made of. They turned out to be a pretty common plastic, polyvinyl chloride (PVC), which is used in numerous products from garden hoses to household items.

Those blue dots formed a trail. When a suspect was developed, the same blue dots were found on the floor of his car, in his gym bag, which had been tossed into a Dumpster, and, finally, on the plastic-coated palms of a pair of old work gloves found in his possession. The gloves had dried out; when they brushed against something, little blue dots fell off the coating.

Jim Corby first tried to fit some of the dots back onto the gloves to prove they had come from those specific gloves. Although he wasn't able to do that, by analyzing the PVC he was able to show that the plastic dots found on the victim's pantyhose, scarf, and clothing, and the dots found in the suspect's car and in his gym bag, were identical in composition to the textured blue plastic dots on his gloves. Those little plastic dots let police follow the suspect's trail from the murder scene to his own home, a path that led directly to a guilty verdict and a death sentence.

Among the most common plastic items regularly used are plastic garbage bags. And while they all may look alike, in some small way every garbage bag is different. Because garbage bags are heat-sealed (in this process, an impression is made in heated plastic) most cases in which plastic garbage bags are evidence are sent to the Document Section. Perhaps the best-known case in which a plastic garbage bag comparison proved significant was the brutal murder of a baby in Illinois. Four days after a woman named Paula Simms reported that her baby had been kidnapped, the baby's nude body was found in a garbage bag

that had been tossed into a trash container not far from Simms's home. An examination showed that the baby's body had been frozen before being discarded. This was Paula Simms's second child to be murdered, so she immediately became the prime suspect. There were many inconsistencies in her story, but the only physical evidence was the garbage bag in which the body had been found. Somehow that garbage bag had to be linked to Simms.

Police found two rolls of garbage bags in Simms's house. One was still sealed. Forty-four bags remained on the second roll, while three other bags were in the house. Jim Gerhardt did the examination. "It's hard when you look at evidence like this not to think about the baby," he said softly, "but all we can really do is examine the evidence and bring out what's there. The first thing I tried to do was match the ragged edges on the hem and mouth ends of the bag in which the baby was found to other bags in the house through what we refer to as fish eyes, the dark dye lines that run from one bag to the next in an irregular pattern. They can be very strong evidence. For example, if we can link three plastic bags filled with drugs found in different locations, we can prove they came from a common source. In one case I was able to put four hundred plastic meat-packing bags back in the right order to prove they'd all come from the same roll. But I wasn't able to do that in the Simms case. Either this was the first bag on the roll or the bags on either side of it were missing. So we had to find a different way to do it."

One of the many things that make the FBI's sci-crime lab unique is the freedom given examiners to thoroughly research unusual subjects, to make themselves experts in very narrow disciplines. In this case Gerhardt learned all he could about plastic garbage bags by visiting manufacturers. "I learned how these bags are made and I found out what the unique aspects of the manufacturing process were. It turned out to be the method used to close the bag on the

hem end, the seals. As the bags go down the line, a heated bar presses down on the plastic and melts it into a seal. It's sort of like typewriter keys making an impression on paper. I could see that there were imperfections in the sealing process, that when the bar hit the plastic it left tiny impurities, burrs and creases and pinholes. What made them valuable to me was that they were transient: they would appear for a number of bags, then disappear. These impurities would change drastically every minute, which meant that only a limited number of bags were going to have similar imperfections. If we could match those imperfections found on the bags in Simms's home to those on the bag in which the body had been found, we could positively link Paula Simms to the murder.

"Once we knew what to look for, it was a pretty straightforward examination. There were several transient imperfections present on the bags found in her home and in the bag used in the murder. During the trial we used enlarged photographs to show the jury just how the bags matched. In fact, we were able to show that the bag in which the body had been found was made within ten seconds of the last bag left on the roll. So either this bag had come from that roll, or the killer had come into the Simms house, kidnapped the baby and put it in the garbage bag, then left it in the park. The jury didn't believe that had happened. They convicted Paula Simms of the murder of her baby."

Originally Materials Analysis and Elemental Analysis were combined as the Instrumental Analysis Unit; while they are now independent, they often collaborate. In many cases, after Materials has determined the physical characteristics and organic composition of a substance, it is sent over to Elemental, where people like chemist Charlie Peters are able to measure how much of each chemical element is present down to parts per billion, and Dennis Ward puts it

in the lab's scanning electron microscope to look at the distribution of the elements. By the time these units have finished analyzing a submission, they have developed a complete chemical profile—and a positive comparison made on these levels is very strong evidence that two samples have a common source.

In addition to assisting other units in their examinations—for example, doing gunshot-residue tests for the Firearms Unit and bomb-residue tests for the Explosives Unit—Elemental Analysis has responsibility for all metals exams. And while gunshot-residue cases make up a significant part of the workload, it also includes any case in which questions about metals or stress systems have to be answered. How long has this gun been in the water? Did a gunshot cause this helicopter to crash? Has this foil pack been opened and then resealed? As Agent Bill Tobin, the lab's metallurgist, said, "We just never know what kind of case is going to come through the door. I might work a plane crash today, a product-tampering case tomorrow, a serial killing the next day. When I first came into the lab, I intended to put in the required time, then get back on the street as an agent. But after I was here a little while, I realized that this was where I wanted to be."

Most crime labs rely on chemists to perform their metals examinations, and that can make a big difference in the results, according to Tobin. "A chemist might get a bullet that has been taken out of a body and find iron and titanium on it. But a metallurgist will look at that same bullet and realize there isn't just iron on it; there are iron, manganese, carbon, and some sulfur. And he'll know that titanium is an important component of many paints, so there's a strong possibility this bullet ricocheted off a painted surface before it struck the victim. Unless, of course, the victim had an artificial limb or medical implant in his body that might have contained the same elements."

For sci-crime purposes the most important properties of

metals are that their behavior is predictable—metals react the same way to external forces all the time—and that they "remember," retaining a shape or chemical change for a very long time. These properties proved to be particularly important in one of Tobin's most unusual cases, the well-publicized murder case in which a trauma caused a woman to suddenly remember that more than two decades earlier she had witnessed her father killing her playmate by bludgeoning her with a rock.

How do you begin to substantiate a twenty-year-old murder that might never have happened? There was almost no physical evidence to support the woman's story, so it came down to her memory against her father's denial. But among the very few pieces of potential evidence was the victim's ring. Tobin discovered that it had been struck with enough force by an object with an irregular surface to cause substantial damage to the metal band. The marks left by the blow were not uniform, as they would have been had it been hit by something with a smooth surface, a hammer, for example, or an automobile fender.

"That ring told me several things," Tobin explained. "I could see it had been subjected to forced contact with an aggregate surface. I could see that the damage was not typical of normal servic abuse—it didn't just happen in day-to-day wear. And I could see that the damage was very typical of what we expect to see when metal has been in forced contact with an object having an irregular surface profile. Based on all that, the best inference I could make was that it had been hit by a rock. To me, it looked like the person wearing the ring was probably raising her hand to ward off the blow.

"I see a lot of this type of damage. When people are being hit, they'll raise their hands to protect themselves, and whatever object they're wearing—rings, bracelets, watches—get smashed in the attack. The damage to this ring was consistent with that sort of assault."

While Tobin's finding could not prove conclusively that the woman's memory was true, it provided physical evidence to support it, and may well have been a key factor in the eventual conviction of the father for the murder of the little girl.

Commonly encountered items like screws, drapery hooks, paper clips, staples—just about every type of metal fastening device—may not seem very important or exciting; in fact, they are often used in crimes and can be the evidence that links a suspect to a crime scene. One of the most important cases in which the lab helped nail the suspect was known as the Boston hitchhiker murders.

In the late 1970s several young women last seen hitchhiking in the area of Boston University were found brutally murdered. As Bill Tobin described the case, "Among the most remarkable things about these murders was that the crime scenes were almost pristine. We never found hairs or fibers, any serological evidence, no fingerprints. These were almost perfect crimes."

Boston police eventually charged a man named Anthony Jackson with the killings. Jackson was a genius, a Ted Bundy type. In half of his trials he handled his own defense. Although officially he was a suspect in ten murders, unofficially police believed he might be responsible for twice that number. By the time Tobin got involved in the case, Jackson had been tried for four murders and had been found guilty of two of them, for which he had received two separate life terms. What made this fifth trial so important was that in Massachusetts a felon serving a life sentence was eligible for parole after six and a half years, but under a recidivist statute an individual convicted of three felonies was considered a career criminal and lost all rights to parole. So it was three strikes and out, forever.

"I don't usually speak to a suspect when I'm testifying," Tobin remembered, "but during one recess, a Boston

detective and I approached him and asked, 'Off the record, Jackson, how many women are you responsible for in the Boston area?'

" 'Just in Boston?' he answered. 'I left my mark in Detroit, too. They're not gonna forget me up there for a while.' He paused, then admitted, 'All together, twenty-seven.' " Only one man, John Wayne Gacy, had admitted killing more people.

Tobin had been brought into the Jackson case because one victim's body was found stuffed into a closet that had been nailed shut. In Jackson's garage police had found a collection of nails, screws, and drapery hooks, the jumble that anyone who makes minor home repairs might have. They had sent the lab this collection and the nails removed from the closet door, to see if an association could be made. What made the hardware collection more important was that it had been accumulated over time rather than purchased all in one store and all at the same time, so it was unlike any other collection in the world.

In a universe of billions of nails, how do you prove that two of them came from the same collection? "Nails are not high-spec items," Tobin explained. "There's no big deal if there's a tenth-of-an-inch difference. So I began by separating them by size. That really narrowed down the community. Then I examined the composition of the plating with an X-ray fluorescence spectrometer. Every element on the periodic chart responds differently to X-ray bombardment; it gives off a certain amount of energy. The X-ray fluorescence spectrometer measures that energy, allowing me to interpret which elements are present. Two nails manufactured at the same time are going to have the same plating. So that further narrowed the community.

"Finally I looked at fabrication characteristics. Metal is formed into a final shape by either forced contact with another metal or by casting the molten metal. The manufacturing process is going to leave a 'fingerprint' on the

workpiece, the nail, that is unique to that piece of equipment. Even better, it's transient because the die that is making the nail is wearing down with every nail it makes. So whether it's a nail or a spoon or a screw or a paper clip, if I get the right samples I can show that two items were made by the same manufacturer with the same specific equipment at just about the same time.

"In this case I was able to show that three different and unrelated nails found in the door, and three different and unrelated nails taken from Jackson's garage, were made by the same manufacturers on the same equipment at about the same time. Those nails had come from Jackson's garage or another collection of nails exhibiting similar characteristics. The latter possibility was concluded to be extremely remote."

Attempting to diminish the importance of Tobin's testimony, the defense bought nails in fifteen different hardware stores—but failed to find even two series of nails that matched each other. With Tobin's testimony playing an important part, Jackson was convicted and will spend the rest of his life in prison.

Metals bend and break, they deform, and they corrode, but in a predictable manner. Things happen to metal for a reason that can be learned by examining it. When a government helicopter on a top-secret mission in Europe mysteriously crashed into the ocean, for example, a computer analysis of the damage to the rotor blade indicated that it had been struck by a bullet. The helicopter had been shot down. And that might mean that terrorists operating in the area had escalated their attacks on American military targets. If so, some sort of forceful response would be required. The blade was delivered to the lab for an exhaustive examination. No residues of bullet constituents were found, so the rotor might not have been hit by a bullet. And rather than the unpredictable and continually changing marks caused by a bullet striking metal, there was an elongated groove in

the blade with unchanging marks. Finally, the absence of rust in the groove indicated that the damage had taken place after the chopper crashed. So, rather than confirming the report, the lab suggested that the damage to the rotor blade had occurred after the crash, probably during recovery operations. Further investigation proved that this was precisely so. The helicopter had crashed because of an engine malfunction, and the blade had been damaged when a grappling hook slipped while lifting the craft out of the sea.

The first clue a detective looks for, and one of the most important, is what time the crime took place. Knowing that allows detectives to begin piecing together events. Sometimes it's an easy thing to determine: watches are broken during assaults; clocks are knocked over in a struggle. In a Florida case a man sneaked away from a party for the sheriff's department to kill his wife, his in-laws, and his business partner—but his party alibi fell apart because a stray bullet smashed through a wall into a clock in the next room, stopping it at the precise moment of the murders. While the suspect could prove he had been at the party slightly before and just after the killings—several of the guests remembered his being very specific about the time—no one recalled seeing him at the time pinpointed by the clock. So it became important to prove that the clock had been working until the moment of the murders.

Although the bullet had missed the clock's mechanism, it had struck the case with enough force to knock the workings out of alignment. Since there was no real damage, the prosecution had to show that the bullet had stopped it. In the trial's most dramatic moment, Bill Tobin explained to the jury why the clock had stopped—then proved it had been in perfect working order by putting a gear wheel back on its track, then stepping back as the clock started ticking. The suspect was convicted of murder.

It's also possible to tell time by understanding nature. A metallurgist can make important determinations from the presence of rust. While at best it's only an approximation, measured in weeks and months rather than minutes and hours, the amount of corrosion enables the examiner to figure out how long a metal object has been exposed to the elements. Evidence like this is rarely conclusive, but it can help police corroborate testimony or piece together the details of a crime.

In one of the most complicated and potentially explosive cases in Boston history, a white man named Charles Stuart claimed that he and his wife had been robbed and shot by a black man while they were stopped at a traffic light. Mrs. Stuart had been killed, and her husband had suffered a superficial gunshot wound. A black suspect was arrested, but as the city of Boston tensed for a racial confrontation, Stuart's story started falling apart. Just as it became obvious that he had invented the tale, he committed suicide by jumping off a bridge.

According to Stuart's brother, Matthew, the crime had been planned as an insurance scam, a fake robbery. Matthew claimed he had taken the gun from his brother, not knowing his sister-in-law had been murdered, and had thrown it into the Charles River. Boston Police scuba divers recovered the rusty gun and submitted it to the lab. Obviously the case wasn't going to turn on this evidence. It was just another small piece in a very complex case. But it was important to determine if the gun had been in the river as long as Matthew Stuart claimed, or if he had tossed it in the river more recently to back up his story.

All rust is not created equal; objects rust quite differently when subjected to different conditions. So corrosion is a useful tool for determining how long anything metal, from a gun to an airplane, has been underwater. Tobin began by examining the environment in which the gun had been found, to make sure it was consistent with the type of

rust he had found on the gun. In addition to looking at hydrological—water-analysis—data, he studied a video-tape, made by the divers, of the place where the gun had been recovered. As he explained, "Probably the most important thing I need to know is whether this is an aerobic environment, meaning oxygen is plentiful, or anaerobic, which means little oxygen is present. I can usually figure that out by looking at the biological activity, the plants and the fish. Then I look at the condition of other submerged objects, the things we generally find in urban rivers, like box springs, cars, and wheelchairs. If they have a light whitish coating, I know the environment probably contains calcium carbonate, magnesium, and some silicate. If they have a darker coating, I'd expect to find sulfur compounds there.

"Everything matters, everything that contributes to corrosion behavior, and if the corrosion I find on a submerged object isn't compatible with the environment, then I know we've got a problem. I know it probably hasn't been in that environment or hasn't been there for the period of time in question. But if everything is consistent, then the extent of the corrosion will give me a good idea how long it's been in the water.

"In the Stuart case I found that the amount and type of rust was consistent with the testimony."

In product-tampering cases, if a metal object is found in a package, or if the question is whether a foil seal has been opened after leaving the factory, the evidence goes to the Elemental Analysis Unit. Perhaps the first major product-tampering scare in America took place in the 1970s, when consumers around the country began reporting that they had found various metal objects in boxes of Girl Scout cookies. Hundreds of boxes of cookies were submitted to the lab; almost without exception they contained either a needle, a straight pin, or a razor blade—and almost without

exception the object had been put there by the consumer after the product had left the factory.

Usually it was obvious. There was a cookie with a bite taken out of it and a pin bisecting the missing portion, like a bridge, something that couldn't occur naturally. In some instances, the needle was longer than the cookie; in others, two or three bites had been taken out of the cookie, leaving only a narrow sliver with the object in it. And in almost every case the consumer had expected a "settlement" payment from the manufacturer or was seeking publicity.

Not every submission was fraudulent, however. Accidents—and sometimes crimes—take place at the factory level. A few of the cookies contained bits of tungsten carbide and tool steel, alloys commonly used on production lines and rarely found in the home. Thus it was likely that damaged machinery had contaminated those cookies.

The primary means of separating true product-tampering cases from manufacturing problems is to inspect the packaging. People will often go to great lengths to conceal the fact that a package has been opened, then resealed, but it's impossible to reseal a package perfectly. When poison was discovered inside a bottle of Tylenol, it was vital to determine whether it had been put into the container at the factory—perhaps by a disgruntled employee—or whether someone had taken the bottle off the shelf, opened it, added the poison, then resealed it.

Using a scanning electron microscope, an instrument capable of magnifying an image sixty thousand times, chemist Dennis Ward examined dozens of factory-sealed bottles to familiarize himself with the structure of a properly sealed bottle. When Tylenol is bottled, a foil seal is heat-welded to the polyethylene bottle; the bottle cannot be opened at the top without breaking that seal. Whoever had put the poison in the bottle had tried very hard to conceal his work. After slitting open the foil and adding the poison, he had used heat to reseal it, perhaps an iron. To the naked

eye the bottle looked normal, but under the scanning electron microscope, it was very easy to see that some of the
polyethylene had been melted and had flowed down the
side of the bottle. Although the poisoner was never found,
the lab proved that this case was one of true product tampering rather than the manufacturer's fault.

In a Lakeland, Florida, murder case, a man named
George Trepal, angry at his neighbor, put the odorless,
tasteless poison thallium into eight bottles of Coke and
managed to get those bottles into his neighbor's home.
Peggy Carr died; five members of her family were also
poisoned, but recovered. A Florida state lab examined
more than four hundred different items taken from that
home, from food to wall scrapings, before discovering
traces of the poison in three empty Coke bottles. Four other
bottles appeared to have been unopened. Once again the
question became whether the poison had been put into
the bottles before or after leaving the factory. So while the
U.S. Centers for Disease Control, in Atlanta, began to consider ordering the recall of millions of bottles of Coke,
executives and scientists from the company worked with
examiners in the sci-crime lab to answer that question.

It was decided that the best way to determine if the bottles had been opened after being shipped was to measure
the pressure inside the four bottles that appeared to be intact and compare it to other sealed bottles. After a frantic
search, Coke located several bottles that had been sealed in
the same plant at about the same time as the questioned
bottles. The caps of all four sealed bottles were punctured,
the soda was shaken up, and the pressure was measured.
Each of the bottles found at the Carr home showed a reduction in pressure. Once the caps had been pierced, the Toolmarks Unit discovered striation marks on the inside of the
caps, confirming that they had been pried open and then
crimped back into place.

And George Trepal? After he moved out of his house,

FBI agents moved in and found a small vial of thallium. He was convicted of murder, attempted murder, and product tampering.

Although it might seem unusual for the Elemental Analysis Unit to be involved in poison cases, heavy metals like arsenic, thallium, mercury, and lead make excellent poisons because they are odorless and colorless and are just as fatal when ingested in small doses over a long period of time as they are when taken in a single massive dose. The disadvantage of using heavy-metal poisons is that while almost every other poison deteriorates over time, elemental poisons remain in the body forever. In a chronic-poisoning case—one in which the poison has been administered over a period of time—traces of heavy-metal poison can be found in tissues and bones, even in hair and nails.

In most cases the submitting law enforcement agency suspects that a specific poison has been used and simply wants to confirm its presence, but on occasion an unknown sample needs to be identified. Chemist Charlie Peters, who joined the lab in 1975, remembered one case like that very well. "We had a man in the hospital dying and no one knew why. It was later learned that drug killers believed the victim was a narcotics agent and tried to kill him by giving him a white substance he believed to be cocaine. He collapsed, and when we got the substance he was in a coma. We were able to look at the particles under the electron microscope and tell them pretty quickly that it was thallium. That enabled them to save his life."

Often questions of physics need to be answered by the lab. Basically anything to do with stress or strain is assigned to the metallurgist. When a prisoner in a New Jersey jail hanged himself with his shoelace, the question was whether a shoelace could really have supported his weight.

Using a tensile tester, an instrument that measures force, it's possible to answer that question. The shoelace was more than capable of supporting that prisoner's weight. In

a Southwestern murder case a man wrapped a sphygmomanometer, a blood-pressure cuff, around his sleeping wife's neck and then inflated it, strangling her while leaving almost no marks on her neck. The question local investigating police wanted answered was whether the cuff could generate enough force to choke someone to death. "That's not as simple an examination as it sounds," said Bill Tobin, who did the testing. "It's a tricky physics question to isolate the forces constricting the neck. I did some research and found out that it takes six point seven pounds of force to occlude the carotid artery in the neck and cause unconsciousness. I asked a somewhat frail female technician to pump up the cuff with her weak hand, her left hand. I put the cuff around a simulated "neck" designed with electronic force-measuring capability. I found out it's pretty easy to generate three hundred and fifty pounds of force, more than enough to kill someone."

Escaping prison by sliding down tied-together bedsheets is an old, if not particularly honorable tradition. While it's occasionally successful, more often the sheets rip or knots come undone and prisoners are injured or killed in the fall. In one New York City attempt, a prisoner was killed when the sheets came apart and a second prisoner fell on him. So when an Illinois prisoner weighing 390 pounds escaped by sliding down a length of sheet, a very suspicious warden wondered if the sheets were meant to divert attention from a friendly guard who had simply opened the door. The sheets were submitted to the lab with a request to determine if they could have supported the prisoner's weight. Tensile-strength tests were stopped at 2,238 pounds; the sheets probably could have supported more than two tons, so the prisoner could have lowered a Volkswagen down the sheets without difficulty.

The most elementary of all structural examinations done in the sci-crime lab are conducted by chemist Dennis Ward on the scanning electron microscope. While other analyti-

cal instruments provide numerical, quantitative analysis of composition, the SEM, as it is known, can provide the examiner with a picture of the distribution of elements in a material. This is a very effective tool for comparing materials with a complex internal structure such as multiple-layer paint chips. Using the SEM, Ward was able to visualize the nickel from Frank Atwood's bumper on the fender of Vicki Hoskinson's bicycle. "We perform practical, nuts-and-bolts electron microscopy," he said. "We adapt the procedures to fit the needs, because every problem that comes through the door is different and requires a different approach."

Electron microscopes, which can cost as much as $250,000, were first adapted to sci-crime use in the 1960s. Very simply, they work by scanning an electron beam over an object, then imaging the signals that the sample produces. Everything examined under an electron microscope has to be electrically conductive so usually a conductive layer, carbon or gold, is added to the object. "We're actually imaging at the gold," Ward explained, "but it's so thin that it conforms to the object underneath. It's like looking at a snow-covered mountain range. You're looking at the snow, but you're really seeing the shape of the mountain range."

While scientists in other fields use the scanning electron microscope to take extraordinary photographs of the inner structure of the world, Ward usually ends up looking for debris on the nose of a bullet, or studying a particle found on a shirt. Usually he is searching for supportive evidence, but there are times when he can make a case. In a Midwestern rape-murder, for example, a tiny silver spot was found on the victim's blouse. It was much too small to be analyzed by other techniques. A pair of gloves found on the suspect appeared to carry traces of the same silver material. "I tried to associate the spot and the gloves," Ward said, "although I knew it was a long shot.

"We could have performed a bulk composition analysis, which would have determined only what chemicals were present. With the SEM, however, I was able to identify all the particle types present, including their frequency, their size, and their composition. By showing correspondence on that level, I could state that it was likely that those gloves touched that blouse. It wasn't quite so important where that silver material came from or even what it was, as to determine the association."

The SEM can be a means to look into the eyes of a bug or examine life forms found within a raindrop. "There's an extraordinary structural beauty in nature that you can't see with your naked eyes or even through a light microscope," Ward said, "and sometimes when I'm looking at the symmetry of crystals, or the diversity of biological structures, I can't help but admire this world. But the fact that I evaluate traces and change people's lives with the smallest of all evidence constantly fills me with wonder."

To Conan Doyle's Sherlock Holmes, of course, that was elementary.

7

The Paper Chasers:
The Document Section

This writing is of extraordinary interest. . . . These are much deeper waters than I thought.

SHERLOCK HOLMES,
in Sir Arthur Conan Doyle's "The Reigate Puzzle"

What can you never do precisely the same way twice?

Who wrote the Bill of Rights?

How did a paintbrush help convict Patty Hearst of armed robbery?

How can you see through a sealed envelope?

And finally, what is the one thing that the vast majority of all crimes have in common—all crimes, from murders to multimillion-dollar bank swindles? Motive? No, crimes are committed for every conceivable reason. Modus operandi? No, crimes are committed in every conceivable way. Here's an important clue: the answer is in your hands.

The vast majority of crimes involve paper. Numerous types of crimes are committed *on* paper: forgery, fraud, counterfeiting, embezzlement, money laundering, swindles, insider trading, espionage. Every crime that requires record-keeping requires paper: gambling, drug trafficking, smuggling, prostitution. Some violent crimes involve paper: kidnappers write ransom notes, bank robbers use demand notes; bombs are sent through the mail; extortionists write down their threats; arsonists use paper matches to start fires. And even the most clever criminals can be traced by the paper trail they leave: receipts for bullets and

bomb components, credit card vouchers, car-rental forms, motel registers.

That paper trail can lead directly to a conviction just as certainly as footprints in fresh snow. For example, over a holiday weekend robbers drilled into the vault of a Laguna Niquel, California, bank and stole $14 million. They left absolutely no physical evidence at the crime scene. But one aspect of the robbery was unique: they filled the alarm system with liquid styrofoam, which immobilized the system when it hardened. FBI agent Stan Renquist recognized this as the method previously employed by a gang operating out of Youngstown, Ohio. Using handwriting samples obtained from gang members during earlier prosecutions as a basis for comparison, investigators learned that the gang had bought plane tickets at a Youngstown travel agency and flown to California. Other handwriting comparisons confirmed that they had rented cars and a van in Los Angeles under assumed names—and in the trunk of one of those cars, agents found a rare coin that had been taken in the robbery. Handwriting comparisons proved that the gang had leased an apartment for several weeks, and when they'd left, someone had forgotten to turn on the dishwasher and their prints were found on glasses and plates. These thieves had traveled, rented cars, and leased an apartment under assumed identities; no one saw them enter or leave the bank, and they left no hard evidence. But the one thing they couldn't disguise led directly to their arrest and conviction: their handwriting on pieces of paper.

The Document Section of the sci-crime lab includes seven different units, which have responsibility for investigating anything to do with paper, from white-collar crimes to breaking written codes, as well as the machines used to create those documents: typewriters, computers, fax machines, photocopiers, and all kinds of printers; and, by extension, the impressions made by footwear on a surface. Everything about paper is potentially a clue: the paper it-

self, the ink, the handwriting or typewriting or printing, alterations and obliterations, smudges; things that aren't easily seen with the naked eye, such as watermarks, indentions caused by writing on a top sheet, or copy-machine gripper marks; the meaning of words or numbers; even the ragged edges.

From the day the Bureau's crime lab opened in 1932, document examinations have been one of the most effective means of linking a suspect to a crime. Probably the first great case in which the lab played a significant role was the infamous "crime of the century," the kidnapping and murder of aviator Charles Lindbergh's baby son. More than two years after the baby's body was found, a man named Bruno Richard Hauptmann was caught after spending some of the ransom money. Substantial circumstantial evidence linked Hauptmann to the crime, but he swore he was innocent. After his arrest, he voluntarily gave authorities a handwriting sample, which Charles Appel, the founder of the crime lab, compared to the writing on the ransom notes.

Testifying before a grand jury, Appel explained that he had examined fifteen hundred different handwriting samples without finding any of the peculiarities that he had found in both Hauptmann's writing sample and the ransom note. "Remarkable similarities in inconspicuous personal characteristics and writing habits" were found, Appel said, forcing him to conclude that "it is inconceivable that anyone but Hauptmann could have written the ransom notes."

Appel's startling testimony captured the fancy of the public and helped convict Hauptmann of the kidnapping and murder. Although Hauptmann's conviction remains one of the most controversial decisions in American judicial history, Appel's handwriting comparison is considered so strong that it is still used in the training of document examiners.

Handwriting comparison is the most common type of

document examination. And it is a very inexact science. Every individual's handwriting is unique. Even you can't write your own name precisely the same way twice. Write your signature on two separate pieces of paper, then lay one over the other and hold them up to a light. They will be close, but one will never exactly cover the other.

Your handwriting is as unique as your fingerprints. No one in the world writes exactly the way you do. Even identical twins will not have identical handwriting. And barring illness, your writing style will be identifiable for the rest of your life.

On occasion you are able to identify a letter writer because you recognize the writing on the envelope. You've seen that writing often enough to recognize its distinctive characteristics. Handwriting comparison works basically the same way. Examiners familiarize themselves with an individual's normal writing by looking at as many samples of that writing as possible, then compare the writing style on a questioned document. The basic tools of this trade are a low-power microscope, a magnifying glass, and various light sources. For more sophisticated work, a camera with various filters will be used.

To make an accurate comparison examiners must have several samples of the subject's natural handwriting. Each person has a normal range of writing characteristics—no one signs a gas-station credit card receipt while standing at a pump the same way he would sign a million-dollar recording contract—and the examiner has to familiarize himself with that range of possibilities. The writing instruments have to be the same; the known document should have been written at approximately the same time as the questioned document; cursive writing has to be compared with cursive writing, and printing with printing. When New York was terrorized by a killer who identified himself in letters to newspapers as Son of Sam, the Questioned Documents Unit in the section had in its anonymous-letter file

threatening letters written to a Brooklyn resident by a man named David Berkowitz—later identified as Son of Sam. But because the letters to newspapers were printed while the threatening letters were in script, it simply wasn't possible to make a match.

There's no standard procedure for making a handwriting comparison; it always comes down to a side-by-side comparison of a known document and a questioned document. A person's writing is a combination of class characteristics—the remnants of the type of handwriting he was taught in school—and the individual characteristics he has acquired. A document examiner—there are only about 180 certified document examiners in the country—will look for those individual characteristics and subtleties that make one person's writing different from every other person's.

Using magnification, examiners look at writing skills and style; the slant of the letters; how far above or below the line letters are formed; the size and height of the letters, their angularity, and the way they are connected; the distance between words; the height of the letters, the amount of pressure on the paper, the way in which a word begins when the pen is put down on the paper or is lifted at the end of a word, the way the ''i''s are dotted and the ''t''s are crossed. They will determine the width of the margins and the length of the indention at the beginning of a paragraph. They will note how much room the writer leaves at the top of a page and how far from the bottom he or she ends. There are no rules to follow, and there is no minimum number of characteristics that must match or be different. The examination is completely subjective, based on the examiner's experience; every examiner has established his or her own set of standards. Examiners have the option of giving a positive opinion, as Appel did in the Lindbergh case, stating that a specific person wrote a specific document; a qualified opinion, meaning that he or she

probably wrote it; or a negative opinion. Or he can fail to reach any conclusion at all.

The impossibility of establishing universal standards for all comparisons makes handwriting analysis seem more speculative than scientific, but when Document Section chief Ron Furgerson was asked how many of the 180 certified document examiners would reach the same conclusion in a case as he would, he stated flatly, "All of them."

While handwriting comparison is most often used in the cases of questioned documents or to link a suspect to a crime, on rare occasions it has been used to identify a suspect. One of the few cases solved through a document comparison was the 1956 Westbury, New York, kidnapping-murder of a one-month-old baby named Peter Weinburger. The case began with the most horrifying scenario a parent can imagine: the baby was taken from the front porch of his home when his mother went inside to get him a clean diaper. The only hard evidence found at the scene was a hastily scrawled ransom note warning, "Don't tell anyone or go the Police about this, because I am watching you closely. I am scared stiff, & will kill the baby, at your first wrong move . . ." The kidnapper demanded $2,000 and signed the note: "Your baby sitter."

Several phone calls and additional letters were received, and the family agreed to pay the ransom, but the kidnapper failed to show up at the planned payoff location. The largest manhunt in local history began. Because of the nature of the crime and the small ransom demanded, detectives suspected they were looking for a petty criminal.

Lacking any other clues, desperate investigators under the direction of FBI lab document examiners began an exhaustive search of public records in the metropolitan area, hoping to match the distinctive handwriting on the ransom notes. More than two million public documents were examined at municipal offices, schools, public agencies, defense plants, anywhere a large number of public documents

was kept on file. And in the U.S. probation office in Brooklyn, New York, an agent noted a strong similarity between the writing on the ransom notes and papers found in the file of a man named John La Marca, who was on probation for making and possessing untaxed alcohol.

FBI document examiners confirmed that the ransom note had been written by La Marca. Confronted with this evidence, La Marca confessed to the kidnapping and led police to the baby's body. Two years later he died in Sing Sing's electric chair. In effect, he had written his own death warrant.

Even the smallest idiosyncrasy in handwriting can be enough to identify a specific person. Weeks before "God's banker," the internationally respected financier Michele Sindona, who handled the Vatican's money, was to go on trial in New York for bank fraud in connection with the failure of the Franklin National Bank—at that time the largest bank failure in American history—he was supposedly kidnapped. Although his family received ransom notes, authorities were skeptical. Many investigators believed that Sindona had arranged this disappearance to avoid trial. Two months later, Sindona showed up in New York just as mysteriously as he had vanished, claiming that he had escaped from his kidnappers.

Prosecutors knew they would have a difficult time making a jury understand Sindona's extraordinarily complex financial dealings, particularly since the key witness against him, an officer of the Italian finance police, had been murdered in Milan. But they also knew that if they could prove Sindona had faked his kidnapping, a jury would be more likely to convict him. If they could prove he had run, the assumption would be that he must be guilty.

Sindona couldn't identify his kidnappers, and he had no idea where he had been held. About the only thing he knew for certain was that he had been transported by automobile; he had never been taken anywhere on an airplane. So

agents knew that if they could prove he had been on an airplane his story would collapse.

Information developed in a parallel organized-crime investigation led agents to believe that Sindona had been in Italy during at least part of the time he was missing, and had returned to New York during the same two-week period as several members of the Brooklyn Gambino crime family. Acting on that hint, agents asked the customs bureau to supply all the customs declarations submitted by people traveling from Italy to New York during that period. They suspected that the card they were searching for, if it existed, would be made out in the name of an Italian man in his fifties, probably with a Brooklyn address, probably traveling alone, probably declaring nothing of value. It was a lot of "probably"'s, and investigators had only one clue to guide them: Michele Sindona habitually put a small dot inside the bowl of the number 9.

Agent Joe Holliday sat hunched over a small desk at Kennedy Airport for days, examining thousands and thousands of white cards. Meanwhile, Sindona's trial began in Manhattan. As Holliday's search continued, the impeccably dressed Sindona sat impassively in the courtroom, going home each night to his lavish New York apartment, confident of acquittal. Then one afternoon Holliday picked up a card and stared at it—and inside the bowl of the number 9 in an address he saw a dot. Sindona's dot. The card was flown to Washington, where experts in the lab's Identification Division were able to develop a partial fingerprint: Sindona's. Proof that he had been on an airplane, proof that he had been out of the country.

The trial was in session when prosecutors dramatically requested a recess. They presented this evidence to the judge in his chambers. Sindona was immediately remanded into custody. He never spent another free day in his life. The U.S. jury convicted him of bank fraud; two years later an Italian jury convicted him of masterminding the murder

of the primary witness against him. He died in prison, claiming with his last words to have been poisoned, but more likely a suicide. One of the most powerful men in the world had been convicted by a dot no larger than the period at the end of this sentence.

Often the crime itself is committed on paper. Frauds and forgeries can be traced back hundreds of years, when criminals would forge the king's seal on documents to give them the full power of the crown. Any writing or printing that gives value to paper, from an ordinary check to Adolf Hitler's diaries, might be forged. And any document that is prepared with the intent to deceive or defraud is considered a forgery.

The most common forgery is a signature. A "freehand forgery" consists of someone signing another person's name in his own handwriting, with no attempt to disguise it. It's very easy to determine that this is a forgery, and it can usually be linked to an identified suspect. A "traced forgery" is made by writing over the actual signature with great pressure, then tracing the indented writing made on the page underneath. A "simulated forgery" is an attempt to duplicate another person's handwriting. It's usually done freehand; the forger simply practices someone else's signature until he or she can simulate it. Sometimes it is extremely well done, and it's very difficult to link a suspect to the forgery because he isn't writing in his own style.

Document examiners usually insist on working with original papers because photocopies help disguise certain elements of forgeries. It's impossible to do an ink examination of a photocopy, or restore erased or obliterated marks, or find an impression in the paper known as indented writing, or develop latent fingerprints. Forgeries can be made by punching tiny holes in a real signature, then simply connecting the dots, which will disappear on a photocopy. Forgeries made with carbon paper will look genuine on a

copy. A rubber-stamp copy of a signature can easily be made and used, and on a photocopy it will be almost impossible to determine that the signature isn't real.

But there are several different ways to prove a document is a forgery. Traced forgeries can be detected by comparing the questioned signature to the original from which it was copied. Because no two signatures can be precisely the same, if a signature is completely covered when a second signature is laid on top of it, one of them is a forgery. The Justice Department once asked the FBI lab to examine a document that purported to be a previously unknown seventh draft of Lincoln's Gettysburg Address. Agent-examiner Jim Gerhardt, who joined the Bureau in 1971, was assigned the case. "I discovered that of the six known drafts of that speech, the one that most resembled the document I had was kept in the Lincoln Bedroom at the White House. I went over there with a photographer and we took pictures of that draft; then I did my comparison. The document I'd gotten from the Justice Department matched the White House draft perfectly. When I laid one on top of the other, the bottom copy was not visible. That's impossible; a human being can't function with the precision of a machine. So I knew it was simply a good reproduction of the genuine document."

Proving that Howard Hughes's will was a forgery was slightly more difficult. After the reclusive multimillionaire's death, a previously unknown will turned up, purportedly leaving one-sixteenth of the estate to a Gibbs, Nevada, gas station owner named Melvin Dummar. Agent Jim Lile was asked to examine the document. "The media immediately rushed out to meet Dummar," Lile remembered with a hint of a smile, "and when Melvin heard about this, he fainted. He claimed he had no idea why Hughes had left him this fortune. Of course, when he found out that the will had been sent to the FBI for examination, he remembered picking up an old man hitchhiking in the desert one

day. He even remembered somebody giving him this document in an envelope and that he had dropped it off on a desk at the Mormon church.

"I eventually testified for fourteen hours in this case," Lile remembered. "When I first looked at the will I could see it had a lot of problems, but I've been doing this for a long time, and I'd examined a lot of documents in which the writer's style had changed because of age or infirmity or drugs or alcohol or some kind of physical disability. So I couldn't just dismiss this because the contents seemed so unlikely. I still had to do a complete examination. The difficulty I had was that no one knew for sure what the status of Hughes's health was at the time this will supposedly had been written. The only way to solve that problem was to find as many documents as possible written contemporaneously with the will. Because Hughes was practically a hermit, it was difficult to get those samples.

"The State of Nevada eventually provided me with about a hundred pages of Hughes's handwriting. Using them for comparative purposes, I could state positively that the will was a poorly prepared simulated forgery. The first stroke of a pen on paper can either be tapered or blunt, but after that, most end strokes are tapered. The pen is moving when it leaves the paper and flows right into the next word. Between the time most people start writing a word and finishing, the pen rarely leaves the paper. If people do stop within a word, it's usually because they forget how to spell it and pause to think about it. If there is any retouching, it's invariably for legibility. The Hughes will was full of those things I would expect to see in a simulated forgery: blunt endings, retouches as the forger attempted to correct mistakes, illogical stopping places where the forger had to go back and look at the model he was copying, very poor line quality. It was a bad job.

"To prepare a simulation, forgers will create a model alphabet, they'll find all the letters in the hand of the writer

and copy them. The difficulty comes in finding examples of the connecting strokes; the way letters are connected is as important to an examiner as how they are formed. *Life* had run a copy of a letter Hughes had written that showed his handwriting, how he made his margins, some characteristics, the kind of paper he used, everything a forger would need to make a model. Using that letter I made my own model to see which letters and connectives were not present, so the forger couldn't know what they looked like. Sure enough, in the will those letters and connectives were totally fabricated—the forger had to fake them—so I was certain that this letter had been used as the model for the forged will.''

Ironically, there was no way Lile could prove from the document who had actually written it. Since Dummar was copying Hughes's writing, none of his own writing characteristics were present. But the accumulation of other evidence made it clear who'd forged the will, and Dummar eventually confessed that he had made up the whole thing.

On occasion the lab is asked to authenticate historical documents. The only way to prove that a historical document is genuine is to compare the handwriting and the materials to documents known to have been written at about the same time in the same place by the same people. So when the National Archives wanted to establish who had actually written out the Bill of Rights, it sent to the lab a facsimile of that document as well as samples of the writing of William Lambert, a clerk in the House of Representatives when these amendments to the Constitution were adopted. A basic handwriting comparison proved that the Bill of Rights had indeed been written out by William Lambert.

But most historical exams are not that easy. Because there are rarely sufficient handwriting samples to allow a comparison to be made, the materials used to create the

document have to be analyzed. Paper is made of fiber, water, and chemicals, but the specific components vary depending on the time and place the paper was produced. By comparing the components in a sheet of paper to what was known to be available when and where the document was purportedly written, examiners can often prove that a document was forged. When diaries supposedly written by Adolf Hitler were discovered, for example, an analysis showed that the paper contained chemical optical brighteners and that the bindings had rayon fibers. Since neither material was used during the period these diaries covered, they could not possibly have been written then.

Almost all written or printed documents consist of ink applied to paper. Since 1969, several ink manufacturers have included a chemical tag in their formulations, allowing investigators to date an ink by the presence of a certain chemical. Prior to that, dating an ink was a difficult process. An enormous variety of natural and manmade stains have been used to write on paper, and identifying the components of an ink can provide vital clues about the validity of a document. Ink changes as time passes: it fades, it chips, it changes color, it reacts with the chemicals in paper, it responds to environmental conditions—and every one of those changes can be used to determine the authenticity of a document.

One of the most ingenious attempted forgeries in recent history was the so-called Salamander Letter. The case began when a Salt Lake City rare-documents dealer named Mark Hofmann, who had previously sold several historic documents to the Mormon church, came into possession of a letter supposedly written in 1830 that contradicted some of the basic tenets of the church and connected founder Joseph Smith with occult beliefs. If this letter was real, the entire history of the Mormon religion would be challenged. Church officials sent it to the FBI to be authenticated. In addition, they sent several other documents from their

archives known to have been written by the author of this letter, a wealthy farmer named Martin Harris.

Lab examiners tested the Salamander Letter for the presence of more than one ink; multiple inks might indicate that it had been altered. Only one ink formulation was found. Microscopic examinations revealed no alterations, obliterations, or erasures. The paper and the ink were consistent with the materials available when the letter supposedly was written. The results of the handwriting comparison were inconclusive. While examiners did not confirm the authenticity of the letter, they also did not discover that it was a forgery. That was left to two document examiners in Salt Lake City.

George Throckmorton was Utah's only licensed document examiner, and William Flynn was one of the most respected examiners in the nation. Working with eighty-one contemporary documents provided by the church, they tested everything from the method used to cut the paper to the presence of chemical additives. And they noticed that on some of these documents the ink was uniform, while on others it had developed minuscule cracks and fissures. Something was wrong; all of these documents had supposedly been written at about the same time with the same materials, so it was odd that the ink had aged differently. Throckmorton and Flynn began experimenting, trying to discover if it was possible to create ''old'' ink in a modern kitchen.

At one time finely ground iron ore was added to ink to make it more permanent, but iron gallotannic ink, like iron, will rust when exposed to oxygen. Over time it will turn reddish brown and eventually flake off the paper. That is what is happening to the Declaration of Independence. But there are means of speeding up the oxidizing process, of making a document appear much older than it actually is. Throckmorton and Flynn discovered that the addition of a substance called gum arabic to ammonia and sodium hy-

droxide successfully aged the ink—although it also cracked it. In one afternoon they had produced "century-old" ink. They had proved that the letter could have been forged.

But Hofmann had known that the authenticity of this letter might be challenged. And that was the real genius of his plan. His fraud had been years in preparation. Unknown to the sci-crime lab, the sample documents provided to the Bureau by the church as a basis for comparison had *all* been created by Mark Hofmann. He had forged the documents on blank pages carefully removed from old books. Because these documents were of minor historical significance, hence not valuable enough for anyone to go to all the trouble of forging them, they were accepted as genuine. Now the real value of these documents had been revealed. They were created to salt the files, to be used for comparative purposes when potentially valuable documents were offered for sale. And except for those tiny cracks in the ink, Hofmann would have gotten away with his plan, and perhaps changed the history of the Mormon church forever.

In the world of document examinations, seeing is often deceiving. Imagine being able to see inside a sealed envelope or read invisible writing. Forgers often change the monetary value or the designated recipient of a document—a check, for example—by altering numbers or changing the signature. This is done in several different ways: adding numbers in similarly colored ink; erasing; using ink eradicators, bleaches, inorganic solvents, or masking materials such as white-out; even photographing the document, changing features on the negative, and then printing it.

And this is where seemingly routine document examinations get into light physics. Basically, ink consists of a pigment to give it color and a solvent to carry the pigment. When you write on a sheet of paper the pigment remains on the surface, while the solvent is absorbed into the fibers. The visible part, the pigment, can be removed or covered or

will fade, but the solvent will remain in the fibers. The trick is to make it visible.

Ink on paper either absorbs or reflects energy to become visible. Lightwaves are measured in nanometers, and absolutely all the light we are capable of seeing with the naked eye measures between 400 and 750 nanometers, not a very large segment of the spectrum. But by adding or subtracting different types of light and filters, it's possible to make the invisible visible—if not to the eye, at least to the camera. There's no real way of predicting how an ink will react to light; it's completely a function of the chemistry of the ink. Ink can reflect light, absorb light, transmit light, or luminesce, meaning glow. Below 400 nanometers, X rays and ultraviolet light will cause some solvents to luminesce, while above 700 nanometers infrared lighting will make others visible. But a camera with the appropriate lens and filters can see light up to 1200 nanometers and display it on a photograph or a screen, thus making something invisible, visible.

The camera will see only what is visible within a desired wavelength and nothing else. Thus it can "see" through white-out, for example, because the correction fluid is not visible at the same wavelength as the ink material beneath it. The camera can even "see" through paper, which makes it possible to photograph documents inside a sealed envelope, or read through the carbon on a charred piece of paper. It's a long way from comparing the way two "t"s are crossed.

So by manipulating lights and filters, document examiners can look at what appears to be an ordinary check and see that the signature has been eradicated and written over, or that the check's value has been changed by the addition of zeros in an ink that appears to be the same color but which luminesces at a different wavelength.

There are ways to protect yourself from forgers. Many signature blocks include "safety patterns," extremely thin

decorative lines. While it's possible to eradicate a signature, it's extremely difficult to reconstruct the lines that had been covered by that signature and were removed with it. In fact, document examiners have been able to reconstruct the original name and numbers on a check by closely examining the places where the pattern was broken. "Closely examining" is actually not right—in these cases, the farther away you stand the more discernible the broken pattern becomes.

To prevent your documents from being changed, write on top of as many printed lines on the page as possible, such as the ones underlining the signatures, and use ink of the same color as the printing. Forgers can use filters just as examiners can; if you use blue ink to sign a document that's printed in black ink, someone can easily filter out the blue ink to create a photo of a "clean" document. Using black ink to sign a document printed in black forces forgers to painstakingly remove your entire signature by hand, a tedious and often difficult task.

Writing or printing on paper also makes an impression in the fibers, not only on that page but on several pages beneath it. These impressions are called indented writing. On television, detectives like Columbo lightly brush over a blank sheet of paper with a pencil to fill in the impressions in that paper. That's about the last thing a good detective would do, because it's more likely to cover up whatever image is there than to make it visible. Indented writing can be made visible with oblique lighting or with a fascinating machine called an electrostatic detection apparatus (ESDA).

One of the basic principles of sci-crime investigation is that things that aren't immediately obvious will become visible when the angle of the light source is changed. If you lay a flashlight on the floor or on the seat of a piece of furniture, its beam will illuminate all sorts of hairs and fibers and other objects you hadn't previously noticed. Or

if you lay one sheet of paper on another and write something on it, then look at the bottom sheet under normal lighting, you may see some barely perceptible indentions. But if you lay a flashlight at the side of the paper and look at it again, the oblique (or "raked") lighting highlights shadows in any depressions in the paper and makes them readable. So rather than brushing a sheet of paper with a pencil, Columbo should have been looking at it with an angled light source.

Indented writings have provided key evidence in numerous cases. People often destroy the paper on which they have written, but just as often they forget that they have made an impression on the sheets beneath it. In 1986 Jim Gerhardt worked on a Massachusetts murder case in which a woman's ex-lover was suspected of killing her new boyfriend. The victim was murdered on his birthday, his head practically blown off by a shotgun fired at point-blank range. A note found next to his body read, "Happy Birthday, Friend." Local police wanted the Document Section to compare the printing on that note with samples from the ex-boyfriend. They obtained a search warrant; in the ex-lover's car they found an envelope with the woman's name and address printed on it. They submitted it to the lab for comparison with the note.

"My job was to put the note and the envelope side by side and examine the handwriting characteristics," Gerhardt remembered. "It was a basic writing comparison and I had no reason to examine the envelope for indented writing. I was working in an office with a window looking east. I was there about seven o'clock in the morning and the envelope just happened to be lying on my desk. As the sun rose behind me, sunlight streamed into my office at a very low angle. I just happened to glance at the envelope—and I saw that there was indented writing on it. When I looked at it more closely, I could see that the indentions read, 'Happy Birthday, Friend.'

"It was incredible. I had the Special Photography Unit photograph the envelope using oblique lighting, then prepared an overlay for the trial showing that these indentions had been made when the note was written. It's possible that the suspect would have been convicted of murder without this evidence, but we were able to show that he'd sat in his car and written this note, and then had gone inside and killed the victim. That proved this was premeditated murder, and he received the death penalty."

As improbable as it may seem, Gerhardt actually had an even more unusual indented-writing case. After breaking up with her boyfriend and starting to see another man, a young New England woman began receiving neatly typed threatening letters. The eleventh letter warned, "If you don't quit seeing him, you're going to get shot." Soon after that letter arrived, a shot was fired at her while she was driving her car. Local police began surveillance of the woman's former boyfriend, and one cold winter night they saw him go out in his backyard and bury something wrapped in a plastic garbage bag. Several days later the woman received a twelfth note six lines long, concluding with the promise, "Next time I won't miss." And he didn't. As she paused at a stop sign, a rifle bullet ripped through her car door into her spine, paralyzing her for life.

Police immediately obtained a search warrant and dug up the suspect's yard. Buried in the frozen ground they found a manual typewriter, presumably the typewriter on which the threatening notes had been written. It went to Gerhardt for comparison. "Just looking at the typewriter I could see that the type was the same size and design as the letters on the notes, so it seemed probable the notes had been written on it," Gerhardt said. "But to identify a typewriter as the one on which a document was written to the exclusion of all other typewriters, you need some unique identifying characteristics like damaged typefaces or bent type bars of a peculiar alignment of characters, and this

typewriter didn't have any of those. I really wasn't sure I could make a positive identification.''

Once again, Gerhardt was sitting at his desk very early one morning, the rays of the rising sun coming in from behind him, but in this instance the light illuminated indentions in the rubber platen of the typewriter. ''Normally you can't read typewritten characters on the platen because they're continually being pounded on top of each other,'' Gerhardt said. ''But in this case the characters were clearly visible. I put better lighting on the platen and with a bit of magnification I could read six lines that were identical to the wording and spacing of the twelfth note. This was the hard evidence needed to connect the suspect to the shooting. So I made some notes and sent the platen to the Special Photography Unit to be photographed as evidence.

''The next morning I got a call from one of our photographers. 'What do you want us to photograph?' he asked.

'' 'The indentions in the platen,' I told him.

'' 'There aren't any,' he said. Apparently when I received the typewriter the rubber platen was still frozen from having been buried in the ground. But as it warmed up in the lab the indentions disappeared, and before we could photograph it they were gone completely. The only thing I could do was write a complete report stating that I had seen the impressions on the platen, and that they were identical to the twelfth note. Fortunately, my report was enough. The suspect pled guilty to the shooting.''

In fact, the colder the environment, the more likely that indentions will be found in paper. Humidity tends to swell the fibers in paper and make indentions disappear.

The most unusual thing about the electrostatic detection apparatus is that no one can figure out why it works. It just does. The ESDA was developed by the British as a means of enhancing latent fingerprints on paper, but it wasn't very effective for that purpose because indented writing kept showing up and interfering with the prints. The ESDA is

very simple to use. A sheet of paper that might have indented writing on it is laid on top of a glass plate. A sheet of Mylar is laid on top of that. The lid of the machine is charged with about eight thousand volts of current, and there is a brass plate in the bottom. An electrostatic material, usually copy-machine toner, is sprinkled onto the paper. When the ESDA is turned on, these tiny charged pieces of toner migrate to the places closest to the brass plate—the depressions in the paper—fill in those indentions, and make whatever writing is on the page legible.

That's the theory. But fingerprints will also show up when the machine is turned on, and since fingerprints do not make impressions in paper, the theory doesn't hold up very well. Still, however ESDA works, it does work, and it can be a very valuable sci-crime tool. For example, an Oregon woman with two small children fell in love with a man who didn't like kids. So one night she drove her children to a lonely spot and shot them. One of them died. Although she claimed that a bushy-haired stranger had attacked her family, she was convicted of murder and attempted murder.

Amazingly, she managed to escape from prison. Among the few things found in her cell was a blank notebook. Tiny scraps of paper along the spiral edge indicated she had torn out some pages, so Oregon detectives, who did not have access to an ESDA, rushed the notebook to the FBI lab. Document analyst Joanna Neuman examined the notebook page by page. And on the fourth page down the ESDA magically revealed a roughly drawn map and a street address. Oregon police obtained a search warrant for that address and found the woman hiding there. Within days of her escape she was back in prison.

Being able to prove that a sheet of paper came from a specific notebook has enabled police to link a suspect to crimes in several cases. Bill Bodziak, who joined the Document Section in 1973 with degrees in biology and chemistry, was assigned a Massachusetts murder case in which a

man and a woman were accused of killing another woman. "The police had found a map at the crime scene," Bodziak remembered. "It was a diagram of the barn that the victim would go to every night to feed her horses. Each of the stalls was indicated, and the speculation was that it had been drawn by the female suspect to show her male accomplice where to hide in wait for the victim. One of the items I was asked to examine was a blank notebook found among the female suspect's possessions.

"If we could prove that this drawing had come from that notebook we could link the woman to the murder. That kind of paper is usually cut with long knives, and the edges are nicked off in a random pattern. It leaves a pretty rough edge, and if you look at it under a microscope you can see a pattern. In addition, the knives also leave a striation pattern along the side of the notebook. You can't see it if you look at one sheet of paper, but if you look at most notebooks from the side that pattern is visible.

"These pages had been cut at a slight angle. If I put the map in the back of the notebook the edge would protrude ever so slightly. But if I put it between the twelfth and fourteenth pages it fit perfectly. When I looked for indentions on the fourteenth page I found not only the map we had, but evidence that an earlier version of the map had been drawn. So by putting that incriminating map back in her notebook, we proved she'd been involved."

One of the major problems the Document Section faces in dealing with paper is that paper can be easily destroyed. It can be torn, shredded, burned, or crumpled up; it can even be soaked until the fibers separate and it disappears. Part of the Document Section's responsibility is to restore damaged paper documents so that whatever information is on them can be recovered.

Occasionally that becomes a gruesome task. In an Indiana case, an elderly woman was murdered by paper. The

killer had stuffed wadded pieces of paper down her throat and in her nostrils, suffocating her. Those wads of paper were submitted to the lab on the slim chance that the killer might have brought the paper to the crime scene with him, and that there was some information on it that might help pinpoint a suspect. Each wad of paper was painstakingly opened and examined, but the paper turned out to have come from the victim's home and had no value as evidence.

Obviously the technique used to restore paper depends entirely on its condition. Wet paper, for example, must be allowed to dry slowly at room temperature or, preferably, put in a freezer and allowed to dry there. Papers burned or charred in a fire might appear to be hopelessly destroyed, but if they haven't disintegrated into ashes, they probably can be restored and read. When a pile of papers burns the pages in the middle are protected because there is little oxygen around them to feed the flames—that's the reason the center of an artificial fireplace log takes hours to ignite. So after being separated they can be read. Even those pages completely charred can be read with infrared lighting and photography, the light allowing the carbon to become transparent and the ink opaque.

Often the difficulty in restoring damaged pages is that when touched they crumble into tiny pieces. To prevent that, at one time each page was placed between two layers of glass. This worked, although each page weighed about a pound. Plexiglas made it a little lighter. But when the Document Section was asked to restore a brittle sheet of paper found glued to the back of a painting recovered from art thieves, a new solution to that problem was found at the Library of Congress. Librarians there had been encasing fragile documents in a remarkably thin polyester film that enabled them to take a brittle sheet of paper and, once it was enclosed, bend it, fold it, crumple it, even bake it with-

out harming the document. The film absorbed the stresses created by movement without harming the paper at all.

Some papers are so badly crumpled that any attempt to flatten them would destroy them. A seemingly magic potion, called parylene, actually rebuilds the paper. Originally developed to give strength and resiliency to extremely brittle materials ranging from thousand-year-old fabrics to spiderwebs, parylene comes in granular form and is baked onto the surface of whatever is to be protected in a special chamber. The process can be thought of as injecting silicone into a butterfly's wings to give them added strength. A sheet of paper that has been crumpled into a ball in a fire can be coated with parylene while still in that shape, then opened and smoothed out and read.

There are no miracle devices when it comes to putting back together torn or shredded papers. Restoring them is like solving an intricate jigsaw puzzle. Someone has to sit at a desk for hours and hours matching up tiny scraps of paper. There are no shortcuts, and the work is as arduous as it sounds. But often the recovered documents prove invaluable.

When a landlord in Portland, Oregon, was cleaning out a house he had rented to a group of college-age kids, a torn scrap of paper drifted to the floor. It looked like a portion of map, and an arrow on it pointed to a local bank that had recently been robbed. The landlord contacted the FBI, and agents began sifting through a large Dumpster near the house. They discovered thousands of tiny scraps of paper, and examiners from the Document Section flew to the site for what they assumed would be a few days' work. Seven weeks later the restored pages provided evidence—and fingerprints—in five bank robberies, the planned kidnapping of the mayor of Portland, and the attempted bombing of an army induction center. Four suspects were identified by name. Three addresses were found that assisted authorities in their efforts to track down the gang. Eventually eight

people were arrested in connection with these crimes, and almost every scrap of evidence came right out of the garbage.

Even the most experienced detectives have to piece together scraps of paper the same way they would solve a jigsaw puzzle: they start with corners and edges; they look for matching colors or similar handwriting; they find unusual patterns or smudges or coffee stains; they look for clues in the way the pages have been ripped. They do the work scrap by scrap; there is no easier or faster way.

Some types of paper are made to be instantly destroyed. Gambling and drug records, espionage documents, and records of just about any type of criminal enterprise are sometimes kept on flash paper or water soluble paper, both of which can be destroyed instantly without leaving any trace evidence. Nitrocellulose, commonly known as flash paper, is simply ordinary paper treated with a nitrate to make it highly flammable. Stage magicians use it to make their tricks disappear in a puff of smoke. It's dangerous, unstable stuff. A ream of flash paper has the destructive power of a small bomb. When the sci-crime lab was located in the old FBI headquarters in the Justice Department building, an agent working gambling cases locked a pile of flash paper in his metal desk when he went to lunch. The heat from the sun ignited the papers, blowing up the desk and moving a temporary wall back several inches.

Flash paper should be kept refrigerated. About the worst place to store flash-paper evidence is in the evidence room. Many cases have literally gone up in smoke when a seemingly spontaneous fire broke out in a sealed evidence storage room.

Water-soluble paper isn't dangerous; instead of disappearing in a flash, it instantly dissolves. When dropped into water the paper is transformed into a murky cloud and then disappears, leaving absolutely no trace evidence. Most large-scale gambling operations keep a pail of water on the

floor next to each desk so that records can quickly be destroyed. Water-soluble paper is used in a variety of commercial products from laundry-detergent packaging to pipeline cleaners, so that the entire package can be dropped into the water. But blank water-soluble paper has so few legitimate uses that possession of it has been accepted in trials as evidence of participation in a gambling operation.

Whatever the condition of the paper, a lot can be learned about a suspect from the particular words written on the document. Examiners don't rely on any type of graphology—handwriting analysis—because generally it isn't possible to determine, on the basis of handwriting, a person's sex, age, general health, race, religion, educational or professional background, or even which hand they wrote with. (However, there are some indications of handedness in the slant of the letters and the way the "t"'s are crossed.) But the choice of words on a document can be used to draw a portrait of the person who wrote them.

Penny Pickett is the lab's forensic linguist. By examining the way writing is structured and the words the writer chooses, a forensic linguist is able to derive a general description of the writer. While there is no way short of a signature or a telltale clue to identify a specific individual, a forensic linguist can give investigators strong clues about the type of person who prepared a particular document. From a friendly letter or a ransom note, a forensic linguist can confidently deduce the writer's gender and age, educational level, racial and religious background, nationality, and sometimes even professional history or military background. Although forensic linguistics sounds like some New Age technique, document examiners in the Lindbergh kidnapping were able to determine from the ransom notes that the person who wrote them was a German national who had spent several years in the United States—an accurate description of Bruno Hauptmann.

* * *

As technologies have evolved, the Document Section has had to keep pace with them. The fountain pen was replaced by the ballpoint pen, which in turn was replaced by the felt-tip pen. At one point the only personal writing machine was the manual typewriter. The lab still maintains the largest collection of typewriter samples in the world, and can determine from typeface and spacing exactly what make and model of typewriter was used to produce a document. By focusing on the unique characteristics of the questioned document—bent keys and spacing and type bars—it is even possible to prove that a document has been written on a specific typewriter. As far back as 1933, in one of the very first cases worked by the lab, a woman who had mailed poisoned fudge to a relative in a veterans' hospital was caught when examiners were able to match the typing on the package to the L.C. Smith typewriter she had left in a repair shop.

One of the most controversial cases ever worked by the lab, the Alger Hiss espionage case, turned on a typewriter identification. Examiners proved that negatives found hidden in a pumpkin were photographs of sensitive State Department documents that had been written on Hiss's typewriter. Legend has it that Hiss's attorney tried to have a duplicate typewriter made that exhibited the same unique characteristics as the one used by Hiss—which would demonstrate that it wasn't unique after all—but that proved impossible. Hiss was sent to prison for denying under oath to a congressional committee that he had prepared and hidden those documents.

The once-ubiquitous manual typewriter was replaced by the electric typewriter and the electronic typewriter, which in turn are now being replaced by the computer disk and personal printers. But the machine that has really changed the work of the Document Section is the photocopier. The copy machine has enabled everyone to become a printer. In the early 1970s examiners realized that more and more

often the original evidence they had to work with was itself a copy. Just as with typewriting, a technique had to be developed to link copies to the machine on which they had been made.

Try to find copies of two different documents and look at them. Were they made on the same copy machine? If you had to trace them back to the copier on which they were made, where would you start? What would you look for? "People believe photocopies are not traceable," Jim Gerhardt pointed out, "and that's just not true. With a little luck, we can not only prove a document was made on a specific machine, we can determine within a narrow period of time when it was made."

If you look carefully at copies of documents, marks you didn't notice before suddenly become obvious: black dots, thread shadows, dirt, tiny star-shaped smudges caused by cracks in the machine's glass. Idiosyncrasies like these make it possible to prove that a specific document was copied on a particular machine to the exclusion of all other copiers. They are the "fingerprints" of that machine. The combination of the design and location of these marks is unique; no other machine in the world will produce them. The problem is that many of these defects are transient— they disappear when the machine is cleaned—and that new characteristics can be created.

Occasionally a copier's unique characteristics are obvious. In the 1980s an individual who identified himself, in notes left at crime scenes, as "El Condor" exploded small bombs against the walls of several federal buildings, including the FBI office, in the Miami area. The notes were identified as photocopies that had been made on different copiers. Since no two copies were made on the same machine it was assumed the bomber didn't have access to a copier and was therefore using coin-operated machines. Immediately following a bombing, detectives searched the surrounding area for stores with coin-operated copiers. In a

7-Eleven convenience store, a detective opened the lid of a copier and found a banana peel squashed against the cover. The banana peel appeared as a dark stain on copies made on that machine, and it matched the dark stain found on the note left at the scene of the last bombing. A general description of "El Condor" was obtained from a clerk in the store and eventually he and his partner, "El Tigre," were apprehended.

The illegal copying and distribution of confidential documents has became a major problem in both the business and political worlds, making it very important that a method be found to identify the individual who provided the original documents. Look very carefully at this page. It consists of ink printed on paper. But no two sheets of paper are alike, and copiers will reproduce the unique characteristics of a sheet of paper, enabling investigators to prove that a document has been copied. Mike Noblett, who joined the sci-crime lab in 1976 when photocopies were just beginning to be accepted as evidence, helped develop the investigative methods used in copier examinations. When a major tire manufacturer somehow obtained a copy of a confidential Department of Transportation report critical of its new product, for example, the DOT wanted to find out who had leaked the report. Copies of the report had originally been distributed to ten people; each of these copies, in addition to the copy retrieved from the manufacturer, was sent to the lab. Noblett conducted the investigation. "On one page of one of the original copies I found a single unbleached fiber in the paper," he said. "On the white paper it was just a brown speck, but in exactly the same position on the leaked document I found a black mark. The unbleached fiber was completely random in nature, but it was the fingerprint of that page. It enabled me to show that this was the document that had been copied and identify the office that had leaked it."

The quality of color copiers has gotten so good that it's

possible to make copies of currency or stock certificates that can pass as originals. In a major stock scam a share of Walt Disney stock was reproduced several times on a copy machine and the forgeries were put up as collateral against a large bank loan. The name and serial number were obliterated before the copies were made, and each copy was numbered and signed as though it were an original. The lab was asked to show that one specific certificate, and no other, had been the source of the copies. What made this one certificate unique was a slight wearing of the ink where the certificate had been folded. Folds or creases are entirely random and no two will match precisely, even if the sheets are folded inside each other. The fold on a particular original certificate was matched to the copies, proving they had been made from that document.

Anything that makes a document different from every other document can be the source of identification: the tiny holes left by the removal of a staple, a fold in one corner, a speck of dirt, even stains will enable a copy to be linked to the original.

The American greenback is the most counterfeited currency in the world, because it is the most easily recognizable; and the twenty-dollar bill is the denomination most often counterfeited because it is the largest one easily passed. Anything larger is very carefully scrutinized. The quality of currency produced on some advanced color copiers is so good that the counterfeit bills can actually be used in change machines, while most other color copiers will produce bills just good enough to be accepted in dark bars or foreign nations. Hold a twenty-dollar bill up to a light. To prevent American currency from being easily copied, a translucent vertical strip has been embedded in each bill between the presidential portrait and the left end of the bill. Printed in microprint on that strip is the denomination of the bill. This security strip has been added specifically to prevent counterfeit bills from being produced on copiers,

because even the most sophisticated machines can't reproduce the microprint.

As the nature of crime has evolved, the structure of the sci-crime lab has also evolved to reflect those changes. During World War II and throughout the Cold War, for example, the cryptanalysts had their own section, but now, because codes involve the use of paper, cryptanalysis is within the Document Section's purview. When Ron Furgerson joined the lab in 1971, as many as fifteen people still worked almost full-time on breaking codes in the Cryptanalysis, Gambling and Translation Section. But as the need for code breakers diminished, that section was incorporated into Documents. Currently the two people working codes average about two cases a month. The majority of Bureau cases involve criminal activity rather than espionage, so most of the work once performed by crime lab cryptologists is now done by the CIA and National Security Agency. The spy business just isn't what it used to be.

"We still see a lot of codes," Furgerson pointed out, "because people involved in a clandestine activity, whether it's criminal or espionage, are going to try to protect their communications from law enforcement, and they do this by creating codes. The fact that we still do work in this area makes us unique among crime labs."

A criminal organization is run just like a big business. Records of orders and deliveries and payments and bets and payoffs have to be kept, and most of those records are kept in code. These records can be used to prove ongoing criminal activity, but to have any real value the codes have to be broken. The lab first got into the code-breaking business in the early 1930s, when rum runners violating Prohibition encoded their records. But then and now, most criminal organizations—and most criminals—don't use the ingeniously complicated codes used to transmit military in-

formation. They have neither the time nor the need. Rather they use the most basic types of code. And here's your chance to be a code breaker: Decipher the letters AZCGLMQGQI.

The key to deciphering a code is figuring out the key, which is the explanation of what each cipher represents. The most common type of code is the substitution code, in which another letter, an abbreviation, or a symbol is used in place of the actual letter or number. The most basic substitution codes use the first, second, or third letters above the numbers on a telephone dial as substitutes for those numbers, while the two letters that do not appear on the dial, Q and Z, represent the numbers 1 and 0, which are not accompanied by letters on the dial. Hence AZCGLMQGQI is 202-456-1414, the telephone number of the White House.

According to Furgerson, criminal codes are still cracked the traditional way—with a lot of hard work. "Unlike espionage or military cryptanalysis," he said, "we're often working with a very small amount of text. We probably don't even get a complete alphabet, maybe just a few records. If we were trying to break a Russian navy code, we'd have tons of intercepts and we could apply all types of computer techniques to try to break it. But in criminal work the computer is usually of little help."

A basic method used to find the key is to apply mathematical probabilities to the code. Each letter of the alphabet appears in written English with a known frequency. Matching that to the frequency with which ciphers appear in the code might give code breakers a clue to the identity of some of those ciphers. But because criminal codes are generally brief, sometimes just a heading at the top of a column of numbers, the frequencies don't manifest themselves. "It's trial and error," Furgerson said, "assumptions based on experience, some guessing, trying one thing, then trying something else, then trying again. There's a lot

of educated guesswork involved, and then, if you're lucky, the guesswork slowly evolves into probabilities until you find that one element that cracks open the door just a bit. Sometimes you can work on something for days and days and days and then in the middle of the night, when you're not consciously thinking about it, the light will go on. It's the most joyous feeling you can imagine.''

What makes breaking criminal codes even more difficult is that often the cryptologist is working blind; he doesn't know what the code might be about. If it were that Russian navy code, a cryptanalyst would assume that it had something to do with ships and water and that military terminology would be present. A criminal code can be about almost anything, so one of the first things a cryptologist will do is try to make a comparison between actual events that have occurred and the encoded material. Knowing the type of information that might be contained in a code is extremely important in solving it. After heiress Patty Hearst was kidnapped by the Symbionese Liberation Army, she participated in several robberies. When she was caught, the question arose whether she had been forced to participate in those crimes or had done so willingly. There seemed to be no way to determine a definitive answer to that question.

But among the items found on Patty Hearst when she was arrested was a slip of paper on which were written some seemingly random letters. The importance of that paper didn't become obvious until SLA sympathizers Bill and Emily Harris were arrested and the same letters were found written on a piece of paper in their home. Obviously this was encoded material. But how would you begin to figure out what a line of seemingly random letters means? First, by making some assumptions. ''We tried to figure out what information these people would need to carry with them,'' Furgerson said. ''What would they need that they wouldn't want other people to know? Eventually, we realized that they had to have a means of getting in touch with

each other if they were separated, a way to regain contact. So our first assumption was that these were telephone numbers. But they were longer than normal phone numbers, so our second assumption was that some nulls, some meaningless letters, had been added to the code. That led us to believe that it was what is called a keyword code."

A keyword code uses as its source a ten-letter word or phrase in which no letters are repeated, with the first nine letters representing the numbers 1 through 9, and the tenth representing 0. "Once we decided these were phone numbers, we looked at the rules regarding such numbers," Furgerson explained. "We knew they didn't start with a one or a zero. We were certain it was a California number so we had some idea what the first three numbers might be. We just worked at it and worked at it until it began to make sense." One member of the SLA was a painter; as it turned out, the keyword for this code was "paintbrush"—ten letters, no repeats, each letter representing a number. The "p" was 1, the "a" was 2, and so on up to 0. When the code was broken it turned out to be a list of phone numbers through which SLA members could safely regain contact with the group if they were separated. At Patty Hearst's trial, the fact that the SLA trusted her enough to give her these encoded numbers was evidence that she had become a willing member of the group and had voluntarily participated in the robberies.

Keyword codes are used frequently in criminal activities because the keyword is easy to remember and the code is relatively simple to decipher. In one major drug case, for example, the memorable keyword was "money talks."

Ironically, while advanced computers have made it possible for governments to create codes that realistically can never be broken, the most difficult codes submitted to the Document Section for decoding are those created by individuals for use by a small group of people. A chemist who was making PCP, angel dust, in his laboratory disguised

his notes in a code based on the periodic table of the elements. Many codes are created in prisons to allow inmates to communicate privately with each other. In one case a man killed a police officer, spray-painted the doors of his police car white so he could use it for his getaway, and stole the officer's weapon. When arrested he claimed he had been insane when he committed the crime. Two slips of paper were found in his pocket. On one was written a meaningless series of letters, while the letters of the alphabet with tiny pencil marks below them were written on the other.

Those tiny pencil marks were the key to breaking the code. To an experienced cryptanalyst, they indicated that the person who prepared the code was counting something and that the code had a mathematical basis. It turned out to be what is called an auto-key generation code, in which each letter is determined by the letter that precedes it. When the code was broken the first plaintext word was "rifle." The "r" was in plaintext; it was an "r," and "r" is the eighteenth letter of the alphabet. The next letter should have been "i"; the code's creator began with "i" and counted eighteen letters, so the "i" was represented by the letter "z." "Z" is the twenty-sixth letter of the alphabet; "v" plus twenty-six became "u." When decoded, the note laid out the suspect's entire plan for killing the police officer and escaping. It proved that the killing had been premeditated, and so it destroyed the insanity defense. The suspect ended up pleading guilty.

Usually when police break up a drug or gambling organization, they get to see only a piece of the action: a major drug dealer might get caught holding only a single kilo of cocaine. But his records will show the entire scope of his organization. Knowing that, criminals often try to protect such records by hiding them inside computers. Law enforcement had to develop means to get that information out of the computers. When the first request to break into a

computer and retrieve business records came into the lab in 1985, only two people, Mike Noblett and Betty James, knew anything at all about computers, and Betty James was completely self-taught. "We worked two cases that year," she remembered, "and in 1992 we worked a hundred and twenty cases, many of them involving systems consisting of several computers."

The Computer Analysis Response Team, CART, which was enlarged in 1993 to include eleven people, was made part of the Document Section because hard and soft disks generate documents. "The computer is a repository of records," James explained, "an electronic filing cabinet. In the old days an agent would be able to execute a search warrant by opening file drawers and looking through them. Now he sends the computer to us and we open it up for the accountants, who try to make sense out of whatever we find stored there."

Many people mistakenly believe that when data are erased from a computer they're gone forever. In every case the computer unit begins by copying all the data on the hard disk onto a new disk, and all work is done on that copy. As James said, "The one thing we're careful not to do is tamper with evidence. We don't change anything. We just go in there and browse around and then print out whatever we find. We never leave footprints." That also enables the investigators to avoid traps left by clever programmers that will delete information if the wrong command is given.

Most of these programs are password protected, meaning the only way to get into them is either to figure out the password or find a means to bypass it. Figuring out a password is the latest example of code breaking. People, even criminals, often use as a password something that is part of their lives and therefore easy to remember: their nicknames, the name of their pet, the street they live on, or the

team they root for. One large drug operation used the password "drugs."

While the vast majority of cases consist of finding and printing out records and spreadsheets, occasionally other crimes will be documented on computers. When paintings worth several million dollars were stolen from a private art museum in Boston, the museum computer that ran a sophisticated security system was sent to the lab. "It was obviously an inside job," Noblett said. "It took us about two months to figure out what the computer was trying to tell us. Finally, we could determine when the alarms were turned on and off, what doors were open at what time, and where the guards were at every moment. By working backwards, we were able to figure out which guard was at the door that was opened when it shouldn't have been, how long it was open, and when he returned to his assigned post. The computer solved that crime for us."

Killers occasionally like to record their crimes. A Virginia murderer kept a chilling computer diary in which he wrote of stalking his victim for more than a year. At the end of this file he wrote that if he couldn't have this woman, no one would, and then he killed her.

Computers have provided the hard evidence in several violent crimes. While most of the computers sent to the lab are IBMs or IBM clones, an old Atari system was submitted in a Midwestern case in which an entire family was murdered. With the help of the manufacturer, Betty James was able to break into the family's system. Among the documents she found was a letter supposedly written by one of the victims and dated weeks before he was killed, in which he approved the transfer of valuable stock options to another man. But computers can't lie; the internal clock on the hard disk proved that this letter had actually been written after the murders. The motive for the killing was right there in black and white. The murderer had broken into the house and killed every member of the family, then coldly

sat down and written the letter on the computer, transferring the stock options to himself and making sure to backdate the letter. He never realized that the internal clock would destroy his alibi.

While the use of computers is one of the most advanced methods of tracking a suspect, probably the oldest of all detection techniques is simply following a suspect's footprints. Even now, in a world covered by concrete and tiles and carpets and hardwood surfaces, these lasting impressions will provide surprisingly valuable evidence. Because footwear makes an impression on a surface in the same way as a printer makes impressions on paper, these investigations are assigned to the Document Section. For similar reasons, so are tire impressions.

Bill Bodziak, a compact, dark-haired man who has a ready smile and is the recognized expert on footwear evidence in the sci-crime world, believes that such evidence can be found at just about every crime scene. "The criminal had to walk around to commit the crime," he said. "In homicides and assaults, rapes and robberies, violent crimes of any kind, footwear evidence has been the sole basis for a conviction. And believe me, no pun is intended. Simply, if we can show through a footwear or tire tread impression that an individual was present at a crime scene, that person is going to have to come up with a pretty good reason to explain why he was there. And if that impression is made in the victim's blood, as often happens, then he's got a real problem."

Footwear impressions are made when someone walks on a soft surface, like snow or sand or mud or even dirt, when someone tracks material from a dirtier surface onto a cleaner surface, or simply when someone walks in the dust. Impressions can be made from any material—water, blood, or grease, for example—and they are found almost anyplace you can imagine: on countertops (the prints are made

when robbers leap onto a counter and walk on papers); on tiny pieces of broken glass from the windshields of cars (victims push their feet against the glass as they struggle); in blood on concrete steps; even on the skin of a human being.

When a six-year-old Florida girl was brutally raped and murdered, Bodziak was able to find evidence in the bruises the killer left on her skin. "There was a contusion, a bruise, made by the heel of the killer's shoe when he kicked her," he said. "Normally contusions will give you some detail, but they rarely show the small details, cuts and scratches in the shoe, that enable us to match it to one shoe to the exclusion of all others. But this was unusual. I could determine the size and the design of the shoe, and I could even see evidence of wear. I was able to determine that the contusions had been made by a deck shoe whose heel was worn down, and I could see precisely where the stitching had gone into the heel. Stitching is done randomly; no two shoes are alike. Using the stitching holes, I was able to match the impression on that little girl's skin to the suspect's shoe. It was the footwear impression that really got us the conviction."

Although there are tens of thousands of different shoe types and styles, footwear comparisons can be narrowed down to a specific shoe. Comparisons are based on class characteristics—the design, size, and shape of the shoe—and then on more individual characteristics, which include anything that has been added to the shoe or taken away from it. Such characteristics might be produced by normal wear and tear, a nail embedded in the heel, gum stuck to the bottom, a pebble wedged into the sole, cuts and scratches, the location of the stitching holes—anything that makes that one shoe different from all other shoes. "People often use the phrase 'DNA fingerprint,'" Bodziak said, "meaning it could come from only one person. I'm trying to convince people to say 'DNA footprint.'"

When a footwear impression is found at a crime scene investigators begin by photographing it. Then, if it is a depression, a cast is made using hard dental stone. If a photograph won't provide enough detail and it's not possible to make a cast of the print—for example, if the footprint is made in blood on a tile floor, often that section of the surface is actually lifted up and submitted to the lab. When the young woman who managed a New York City Gap store was murdered, a large slab of concrete flooring and tile was sent to Bodziak, who was able to enhance a barely visible athletic-shoe print that had been made in the manager's blood. That impression was eventually matched to a sneaker worn by a former employee of the store, and led to a conviction in the murder.

"We're one unit that gets everything sent in," Bodziak reported, "including the kitchen sink. We get sent entire countertops, staircases, slabs of concrete. In a Maryland murder case a woman's body had been dumped from a car, and the car then backed up through her blood, leaving three distinct impressions of the tire tread on the road surface. Three large sections of macadam were brought in by hydraulic lift, and from those we were able to enhance some faint impressions and make a positive match to her husband's car."

The most difficult problem with any latent evidence is making it visible. Like latent fingerprints, footwear impressions that aren't visible can be enhanced with chemicals or powder, then "lifted" with tape. Shoeprint impressions made in the dust are the flimsiest of all evidence, fragile enough to be blown away by a soft breeze, yet powerful enough to send someone to prison. This is fate at play; an open door on a windy day might be enough to prevent a killer from being convicted.

Finding and preserving evidence in the dust is the stuff of the finest fictional detectives. The best way to find prints in dust on hard surfaces is not to turn on the lights but to

turn them out, and examine the surface with oblique lighting, something as simple as a flashlight laid on the floor. But almost any impression left in the dust can be materialized and preserved by a remarkable instrument, the electrostatic dust lifter, which is one of the really great "toys" of the sci-crime world: a tool to make the invisible visible. Unlike most instruments, which are adapted for sci-crime work from another field, the electrostatic dust lifter was developed specifically to do precisely what it does: transfer impressions made in the dust from a surface to a sheet of paper for preservation. It was invented in the 1960s by a Japanese policeman who worked part-time as a TV repairman. He noticed that dust was invariably attracted to the high-voltage source in the back of the set and realized that this property could be adapted to sci-crime purposes.

It's simple to use. If there is reason to believe prints might be present—if, for example, someone had to move from a dirty surface to a clean one to commit the crime—a sheet of black lifting material is laid down over the surface and a high-voltage charge is run through the material. The material is drawn down tightly against the surface and the dust is transferred to the lifter. The impression is actually made by the dust. The process is nondestructive, and usually enough dust is present to enable several lifts to be made from the same area. And the method works on just about any surface.

In a Wilmington, Delaware, rape case, an impression left on the floor was just about impossible to photograph because the tiles were old and dirty. When Wilmington detectives tried lifting the concrete it broke in small pieces. Bodziak took a two-inch-by-three-inch fragment of tile and, using the electrostatic dust lifter, was able to bring up a portion of an athletic-shoe sole bearing several unique wear marks, more than enough evidence for prosecutors to make a positive, and incriminating, match to the suspect's sneakers.

That's the way footwear evidence is developed and used in an ideal situation; unfortunately, few cases are so straightforward. About the strangest shoeprint Bodziak ever saw wasn't even a print, but rather the negative impression of a print. After a string of armed robberies in convenience stores, on a freezing winter afternoon New York City police got lucky and interrupted a holdup in progress. The suspect started running over snow-covered rooftops and down alleys, just as in the movies. When police finally caught him the gun he had been carrying, the gun that might connect him to several robberies, had disappeared. Investigators retraced the chase route, and in a dry area behind a roof vent they found a gun that was eventually linked to the holdups. The challenge was to find a way to connect that gun to the suspect.

Not far from the gun, police found several ridges of snow in a recognizable pattern. When captured, the suspect was wearing boots with an indented ripple pattern on the soles. During the chase snow had been packed into those indentations; when the suspect bent down to hide the gun behind the vent, his soles bent and the snow popped out, much like ice cubes popping out of a plastic tray. It left an almost perfect negative impression of the boot soles. Although there was not enough detail to make a perfect match between the ridges of snow and the suspect's boots, there was enough to allow Bodziak to testify that the ridges had very likely come from those boots. That testimony connected the suspect and the gun, and it took the jury about twenty minutes to convict him of the series of armed robberies.

Contrary to the plotting of detective fiction, it isn't possible to estimate someone's height by the distance between steps—his gait—because during the commission of a crime, a suspect is usually moving very fast; he is running or backing up or moving sideways or struggling, attacking or defending, even sneaking around. The thing he isn't do-

ing is moving normally. But it is possible to make a good estimate of someone's height from the size of his shoes, and the size of a shoe can be determined from a shoeprint.

Tire tread impressions are almost as useful as shoeprints. There are thousands of tread designs, and every tire wears differently or picks up debris from the road, making it unique and therefore identifiable. Tire treads are made of what are called elements, which are small sections of the tire with a specific design that is repeated over the entire tire. Some tires have as few as three different elements, while better tires have as many as nine. These elements are designed to improve traction and cut down on the noise the rubber makes as it is squeezed against the road surface. Tread design—the size and location of the elements—is what makes a tire identifiable. Sci-crime detectives can not only identify a specific tire from a tread impression, they can often find the portion of the tire that left the impression.

Oddly, anecdotal evidence shows that most violent crimes in which tread marks are found have been committed by people driving older cars with various brands of replacement tires. So even though there are thousands of identical tires on the road, the combination of different tires makes a car unique. For example, Florida police searching for a serial killer knew that he was driving a sedan with two somewhat unusual rear tires, one of them put on backward so that the whitewall faced inward. When Bobby Joe Long was identified as a suspect, a quick examination of the tires on his car proved that it had been used in at least two murders.

As you might suspect, tire impressions are often found on the bodies of hit-and-run victims. But, surprisingly, these are not tread impressions. Rather, as a car runs over a body, clothing wraps around the tire so that the imprint of the sidewall, the part of the tire on which the brand name and model number appear, is pressed into the cloth.

Bodziak has worked several cases in which he could read the name of the tire manufacturer on the victim's clothing.

The Document Section will use absolutely anything found at a crime scene to make a match to a suspect—even a match. Since the section has responsibility for anything involving paper, upon request it will conduct cigarette or matchbook examinations—paper matches only; wood matches are examined by Hairs and Fibers. Jim Gerhardt is the lab's matchbook expert. "It's not really much of a competitive field," he admitted, "and I guess I've sort of cornered the market. We only get four or five cases a year, but sometimes these comparisons can be very useful. Naturally, matches are most often found at fires in which arson is suspected. The object is to somehow connect those matches to a suspect.

"Turn a match on its side," Gerhardt explained, "and you'll see little particles sticking out. That's because paper matches are produced from junk filler consisting of everything from rag threads to paint chips. Those particles will fit perfectly with the adjoining matches in a matchbook, enabling us to make a microscopic comparison to prove that a match came from a specific matchbook to the exclusion of all other matchbooks ever made. I can often find as many as thirty different points of comparison in one match."

When burned matches were found near the place where a suspicious fire had started in Los Padres National Forest in southern California, Gerhardt was able to link them to a matchbook found on a suspect by showing that the ragged edges of the burned matches fit together perfectly with the ragged edges in the matchbook.

Matches may seem to be the most common thing in the world, but they are unique enough to provide telling evidence of a crime. When a large Boston building burned down in 1986, police at the scene found a matchbook with

all the matches torn out. The property owner was questioned and denied having been near the building. In his pockets police found two unused matchbooks. Gerhardt couldn't link burned matches to the empty matchbook; instead, he was able to show that the matchbook found at the scene had been made between the two matchbooks found in the building owner's pocket. Gerhardt showed that the empty matchbook shared a ragged edge with each of the other two. The owner pleaded guilty to setting the fire to collect insurance on the building.

In years past it was considered important to be able to identify the brand of cigarette found at a crime scene, and the lab maintained an extensive cigarette sample collection. It was rarely used and even more rarely valuable, so it was disbanded. But cigarettes can still make strong evidence. Police found a bloody cigarette butt at the scene of a 1986 murder in Allentown, Pennsylvania, and asked Gerhardt to try to associate it to a pack of cigarettes found on the primary suspect. Gerhardt could show that the butt was the same brand as the pack; that proved nothing. But he also found a filter in the bottom of the pack, and he was able to show microscopically that this filter had been detached from the butt found at the crime scene. It was a simple—and incriminating—association. Apparently the filter had been knocked off the cigarette during the fatal brawl and by chance had fallen back into the pack. It was a one-in-a-million oddity that led directly to a murder conviction, perhaps proving once again that smoking can be hazardous to your health.

While the cigarette collection was one of the first maintained by the lab, it became outdated as more conclusive means of linking a suspect to the crime scene were found. But with the recently developed ability of examiners to make DNA comparisons, cigarette butts, which might contain saliva from which DNA can be extracted and compared to DNA from a suspect, have once again become

important pieces of evidence. The world of sci-crime goes around and around.

And finally, the old saying promises that good things come in small packages. But in the Document Section, the good thing often *is* the package. After a Washington schoolboy found what appeared to be a rock with perfectly rounded edges at the mouth of the Columbia River, it eventually found its way to the Document Section. This "rock," in fact, consisted of hard cash—very, very hard cash. It turned out to be made of calcified layers of currency, $6,000 in twenty-dollar bills that had been compacted over time into a rock-hard substance. When agent Lou Senter pried apart the layers with a tweezer and read the serial numbers of the bills, the "rock" turned out to be part of the $200,000 ransom paid to America's first skyjacker, the infamous D. B. Cooper, who had parachuted out of an airplane with a satchel filled with cash. The money was the first clue to Cooper's fate after he leaped out of that airplane and was never seen again.

8

Number One with a Bullet:
The Firearms and Toolmarks Unit

Do you know, Watson, I believe your revolver is going to have a very intimate connection with the mystery which we are investigating.

SHERLOCK HOLMES,
in Sir Arthur Conan Doyle's
"The Problem of Thor Bridge"

"The President's limousine arrived back in Washington about six o'clock. Around one o'clock the next morning Cort [Cortlandt Cunningham] and I started sifting through the blood looking for lead fragments. It was tough; it was very tough." Bob Frazier, believed by many experts to be the finest firearms examiner who has ever lived, was speaking for the first time outside a courtroom about the assassination of President John Kennedy. "The yellow roses that Mrs. Kennedy had been holding were scattered all over the back of the car along with Mrs. Connally's bouquet of red roses, and we had to move them, we had to get them out of the way. We'd just reach down into the clots of blood and scoop it up in our hands and let it dribble through. Whenever we felt something gritty, we'd clean it up and if it was lead, we'd save it in a pillbox. We didn't really recover a lot of the lead."

"Guns don't kill people," proclaims the slogan of the National Rifle Association. "People kill people." Actually, bullets kill people: bullets shot from guns, fired by people. This is an unbreakable chain, a chain that can be traced

from either end. From a bullet found in a victim, it's possible to determine precisely which gun fired it, and from that gun, the person who pulled the trigger can be identified. In perhaps the classic example, when the bullets that killed Dr. Martin Luther King, Jr., were proved to have the same rifling characteristics as a rifle found nearby, fingerprints found on that rifle eventually led to the identification of the assassin, James Earl Ray.

A bullet makes a fuss. It leaves plenty of information in its wake, and finding and interpreting that information is the basis of sci-crime ballistics. It's the work of the Firearms Unit, and it is one of the oldest applications of science to crime solving.

The proliferation of guns in America is a subject of great controversy. Guns have become the primary means of murdering human beings in this country, and the issue of gun control has become a central focus of American political debate.

Firearms examiners don't take sides in this debate, at least not officially. By the time sci-crime investigators get involved the weapon has already been fired, the victim has been shot. Their work is devoted to answering one question: Who pulled the trigger?

The use of a bullet to connect an individual to a crime dates back to 1835, when a member of London's Bow Street Runners, the predecessor to Scotland Yard, was able to match a ridge found on a bullet removed from a victim's body to a gouge in a bullet mold found in a suspect's home. When confronted with this evidence the suspect confessed to the shooting, and the science of ballistics was born. The first recorded firearms case in America took place in 1879, when a man charged with murder was acquitted after a gunsmith testified that the suspect's gun hadn't been fired in more than a year. In a 1902 murder trial, Judge Oliver Wendell Holmes enlisted the services of a gunsmith to determine if the fatal bullet had been fired

from a suspect's gun. The gunsmith fired several shots from the weapon into a basket of cotton, then used a magnifying glass and microscope to show the jury that marks found on the fatal bullet were identical to marks on the test bullets. Thus he proved that this gun had been used in the murder, proof that led to the suspect's conviction.

Basically, that's still the way firearms examinations are conducted. The equipment has become a lot more sophisticated, but the premise is exactly the same: bullets fired from the same gun will exhibit many of the same unique characteristics. So by comparing a bullet fired in a crime to a bullet fired in a test, investigators can prove that a specific weapon was used in the commission of that crime.

Almost every firearms case handled in what is officially known as the Firearms and Toolmarks Unit begins with the submission of a gun or bullets. Sometimes the bullets have been pried out of a wall or a tree, but many of the ones that reach the lab have been taken out of a body. The Firearms Unit deals almost exclusively in violent crimes, and its examiners have plenty of work.

Generally, the first information that can be gotten from a bullet is the type of gun from which it was fired. A weapon fires a certain size of bullet, a certain caliber, but many different guns fire bullets of the same caliber. What makes each make and model unique is its rifling, the grooves inside the barrel. It was discovered hundreds of years ago that spiral grooves cut into the barrel of a weapon will significantly improve both its range and its accuracy. When a weapon is fired, a tiny explosion caused by the hammer striking a primer inside the cartridge ignites the gunpowder which propels the bullet through the barrel. The grooves in the barrel cause the bullet to spin rapidly, greatly increasing its stability in flight. The raised areas between the grooves are called lands, and as the bullet spins down the barrel, these lands and grooves make an imprint on it. The rifling, the number of lands and grooves, the direction

of the "twist"—the spiral that makes the bullet spin clockwise or counterclockwise—and the width of the lands and grooves are the gross characteristics that make it possible to determine what kind of gun fired that bullet.

These microscopic marks left on a bullet were the strongest evidence in one of the most controversial trials in American history, the 1921 murder trial of Nicola Sacco and Bartolomeo Vanzetti. In April, 1920, the paymaster and a guard carrying the $16,000 payroll for a South Braintree, Massachusetts, shoe company were shot and killed in a daylight robbery. Within days the getaway car was discovered abandoned in nearby woods. A man seen in that car was traced to a second car then being repaired in a garage in West Bridgewater. Then this suspect showed up to pick up the second car; police raced to the garage, but by the time they got there the man had grown suspicious and fled on a motorcycle. He eventually escaped to Italy. But two other men who'd accompanied him to the garage, Sacco and Vanzetti, were arrested. A .32-caliber Colt automatic was found on Sacco, while Vanzetti was carrying a .38-caliber revolver. The guard had been killed by a .32.

Sacco and Vanzetti were poor Italian immigrants who spoke little English. But both men were anarchists, members of an international movement that believed that true social justice for the poor and oppressed could be achieved only by the destruction of established governments. In America, anarchists had purportedly been responsible for numerous bombings, among them attempts on the life of John D. Rockefeller and the attorney general of the United States. The government had responded with mass arrests and deportations. So what began as a local robbery and murder case grew into an international political event, and Sacco and Vanzetti were seen as martyrs in the struggle of the downtrodden against the rich and powerful. Throughout the world many people believed that their arrest was simply a crude effort by the ruling class to crush political dissent.

The entire case turned on a single bullet. Six .32-caliber bullets had been taken from the bodies of the victims. The chief of the Massachusetts state police fired fourteen test shots from Sacco's pistol into a box of oil-soaked sawdust, then compared them to the six bullets fired in the robbery. The rifling on the test bullets matched one of the bullets recovered at the crime scene. It was assumed that the other five bullets had been fired from another pistol, perhaps by someone else involved in the robbery.

Although several cartridge shell cases found at the scene could also be associated with Sacco's pistol, the prosecution's case really came down to that one bullet. Had it been fired from Sacco's gun? Two self-taught "experts" testifying for the prosecution said the marks proved it had been; two self-taught "experts" testifying for the defense said it had not.

During their deliberations, jurors requested a magnifying glass so that they might examine the bullets themselves. This rudimentary examination was apparently enough to enable them to conclude that the bullet had been fired from Sacco's gun. Both men were convicted of murder and sentenced to death.

The saga of Sacco and Vanzetti became a major international cause. Millions of dollars were raised in their name. Huge demonstrations were held in Paris and Moscow and cities throughout South America. The French Chamber of Deputies, the British Labour party, and the German Reichstag asked that they be released. American embassies around the world were bombed, and government officials were threatened. Artists drew inspiration from the case, producing books and articles and plays, paintings and sculptures. The convictions became even more controversial in 1925 when a condemned killer claimed that the murders had actually been committed by his gang. Finally, in 1927, Massachusetts governor A. T. Fuller bowed to the pressure and appointed an independent three-man commis-

sion to advise him whether or not to grant clemency to Sacco and Vanzetti. In effect, this was a new trial.

But while the case was making headlines around the world, several significant advances had been made in sci-crime ballistics. Phillip Gravelle invented the comparison microscope, which allowed two bullets to be examined side by side; physicist John Fisher developed a microscope that measured lands and grooves and angles with unprecedented accuracy, as well as the helixometer, a lighted "telescope" that could be inserted into the barrel of a weapon to make a detailed inspection of the rifling.

It was during the 1927 hearing that the comparison microscope, which eventually became the essential tool of sci-crime examiners, was first used in a courtroom. Dr. Calvin Goddard, a pioneer in the study of ballistics, examined the bullets and stated that the fatal bullet had been fired from Sacco's gun and that at least one of the shell casings found at the scene had also been fired by that gun. A defense expert who had previously claimed that Sacco's gun could not possibly have fired that bullet peered into the comparison microscope and said, after a long and dramatic silence, "Well, what do you know about that?" He then withdrew from the case.

On August 23, 1927, as millions of people around the world protested, Sacco and Vanzetti were executed. That ended their lives, but not the controversy, which continued to rage through the decades. But even more sophisticated tests conducted by ballistics experts in 1961 affirmed the original conclusion that the questioned bullet had been fired from Sacco's .32-caliber Colt automatic.

Not only do rifling characteristics permit a bullet to be linked to a gun, but because each arms manufacturer uses its own land-and-groove design, it is possible to work backward, to determine from the impressions on a bullet exactly what make and model of weapon has fired it. In the early 1920s a man named Charles Waite traveled around the

world recording the number of lands and grooves and the direction and angle of the twist for almost every gun that had been mass produced. So when police recovered a .32-caliber bullet with six lands and grooves and a left twist, they knew precisely what type of gun they were looking for.

That capability helped solve one of the most infamous crimes in American history, Chicago's St. Valentine's Day Massacre. On February 14, 1929, two men disguised as policemen walked into a garage with guns drawn and ordered seven members of bootlegger Bugs Moran's gang to put up their hands and stand against the wall. The gangsters did as ordered, confident that Moran would clear up any problems with the law. But as they stood facing the wall, two other men came silently into the garage and mowed them down. Within seconds six of the men were dead and the seventh was dying. The cold-blooded slaughter horrified—and titillated—the American public and made Al Capone, the man believed to have masterminded the killings, the nation's most celebrated gangster.

More than seventy cartridges found at the scene were identified by firearms experts as having been fired from .45-caliber Thompson submachine guns. The police knew what type of weapons to look for. Ten months after the killings, a policeman in St. Joseph, Michigan, was shot by a motorist he had stopped for a minor traffic violation. The shooter escaped, but his license-plate number was traced. When police broke into the apartment of the man to whom the plates belonged, they discovered a small arsenal hidden in a closet, and among the weapons were two .45-caliber Thompson submachine guns.

Using his comparison microscope, Dr. Goddard proved that these were the weapons used in the St. Valentine's Day Massacre. The motorist, Fred Burke, was eventually captured and, primarily on the basis of Goddard's testimony, convicted of murder and sentenced to life imprisonment.

Goddard's work on the case so impressed two wealthy Chicago businessmen who had served on the coroner's jury that they hired him to establish the first Scientific Crime Detection Laboratory in America. It opened on the Evanston, Illinois, campus of Northwestern University in 1929.

It was the success of Goddard's laboratory that convinced director J. Edgar Hoover that the Bureau of Investigation needed its own crime lab. When the Criminological Laboratory, as it was officially known, opened in 1932, the very first piece of equipment purchased specifically for the lab was a comparison microscope to be used for making bullet comparisons.

While the world of sci-crime has been revolutionized in so many ways since then, bullet and cartridge case comparisons remain as valuable as ever. In the 1980s Jack Dillon, who became Firearms Unit chief in 1988, headed a five-year project that created an updated database of firearms rifling. This database, available on computer software to law enforcement agencies, contains the general rifling characteristics of more than eighteen thousand different weapons. That's not every make and model produced by arms manufacturers, but it does include the weapons police officers commonly encounter.

These class characteristics provide excellent information. In San Antonio, Texas, for example, a federal judge named John Wood came out of his house one morning to discover that his car had a flat tire. As he bent down to inspect it, a bullet ripped into his back and killed him. The bullet was shattered by the impact, but several fragments were submitted to the lab. The class characteristics of these fragments enabled the lab to report that the bullet could have been fired from one of only four different weapons, among them the expensive .240 Wetherby Magnum Mark 5 rifle.

The investigation proceeded on several paths. Judge "Maximum John" Wood, as he was known, had made a lot of enemies by handing out the longest possible sen-

tences, particularly in drug-related crimes. It was eventually learned that a woman named Jo Ann Harrelson had recently purchased a Wetherby Magnum Mark 5 rifle, and she became a suspect in the killing. Gradually other evidence was developed, and her husband, Charles V. Harrelson—the father of actor Woody Harrelson—was convicted of the assassination of Judge Wood. He had been hired by drug dealers who were about to be tried in Judge Wood's courtroom and wanted to ensure that he would never pass the maximum sentence on them.

While rifling enables examiners to state the make and model of the weapon that fired a bullet, it can't be used to prove that a specific weapon fired a specific round. To link a bullet to a particular gun investigators must compare the unique marks found on the inside of the gun barrel with the marks imprinted on a bullet.

Arms manufacturers use a very sharp, very strong tool to cut grooves into the metal barrel of a gun, and just like a knife being continually rubbed against a rock, this tool is worn down. Because it changes microscopically with each cut, it leaves slightly different marks, usually striations, inside the barrel. These marks are unique: no two guns will ever have the same ones. They are the weapon's fingerprint, its DNA profile.

Usage also leaves marks inside a gun barrel. Sometimes these marks are transient, like rust or dirt, but more often they are permanent and will be found on every bullet fired through that barrel. Additionally, other machine-made parts of weapons—the firing pin, the breechface, the extractor, and the ejector—all make contact with the cartridge case and imprint distinctive marks that enable a gun to be positively linked to cartridge cases found at a crime scene.

These unique marks are reproduced every time a gun is fired and they provide indisputable evidence that a bullet was fired from that gun. To make a bullet comparison in

the lab, a weapon suspected of having been used in a crime is fired into a water tank. Then the marks made on the test bullet are compared with the marks on the bullet recovered at the crime scene. At least, that's the way it is usually done. "The most unusual case I ever worked took place in the early 1980s," recalled Agent-examiner Bob Sibert, who has spent two decades in the Firearms Unit. "I'd gotten fired bullets and cartridge cases in a case we called Tribal Thumb. That was the name of an extremist group in San Francisco that had assassinated two people who were sitting in a parked car. The bullets were in pretty good shape and I was hoping to determine from the rifling the make and model of the gun that had fired them. We keep as many different bullet cartridge cases as possible, both specimens submitted to us for examination and specimens we've test fired, in a file for comparison purposes. I started going through that file looking for class characteristics, lands and grooves, type of twist, firing pin shape, all types of marks. I pulled out a cartridge case that had been fired during a bank robbery. Some of the robbers had been caught, but they hadn't been tried yet. I looked at this cartridge case, and not only were the class characteristics identical to the cartridge case found at the murder scene, but so were the unique markings. It was very hard to believe; the odds against that happening are astronomical, beyond calculation. I examined the cartridge case under the comparison scope and sure enough, they'd been fired in the same gun. When I made that identification, my jaw dropped so hard it just about left an impression on my 'scope. It was the most incredible coincidence." Sibert's discovery provided the link between the bank robbers and the killings, and resulted in their conviction for murder.

On television, when a detective finds a gun at a crime scene, usually he will very carefully and professionally pick it up by sticking a pen or pencil into the barrel so that he won't mar any latent fingerprints on the gun. In fact,

that's about the last thing a real detective would do. The most important information that can be obtained from a gun is inside the barrel, and sticking any object in there may alter or destroy telltale marks. On occasion criminals will try to alter these markings by scratching the barrel with a sharp object or pouring a caustic substance, battery acid for instance, into it. And that will work; it will change the markings enough to prevent that gun from being linked to a bullet fired from that gun. (Incidentally, the proper way to pick up a weapon that might have been used in a crime is to put on cotton gloves, pick it up touching only the scored, or rough, surfaces—usually the grips—and dropping it into a bag. That will preserve any latent prints that might be on the weapon.)

Bullets are a lot more difficult to find at a crime scene—unless they are in the victim. As Agent-examiner Gerald Wilkes, who has spent more than two decades in Firearms, pointed out, "Once bullets start flying, where they're going to end up is almost random and haphazard. Bullets don't follow a predictable path. They do strange things, seemingly for no reason. In an Oklahoma case, I remember, an individual drove a hundred and fifty miles from his house to rob a bank. And lo and behold, the teller turns out to be a girl he went to high school with, and she recognizes him. So he has to eliminate all the witnesses. There were three people in the bank and he took them out back and made them kneel down. He shot the first two in the back of the head. But then he took that same gun and put it against the back of the girl's skull and fired it at point-blank range. It was a .357 Magnum, a very powerful weapon. The bullet entered the back of her skull, took a ninety-degree turn, and went all the way around her head, then exited from her forehead. It knocked her unconscious. He rolled her over and saw the exit wound and assumed she was dead. She wasn't; she wasn't even badly hurt. She suffered no brain damage and was able to testify against the guy in court.

That bullet didn't even go into her skull, and there is no one who can tell you why that happened.

"But we had another case in which the victim was shot by a .22 bullet. That's a small caliber, and he was hit in the wrist, which normally is not very serious. But the bullet went into his vein, traveled through the vein up his left arm and into his heart, and killed him. With bullets, you just never know."

In a shootout inside a house in St. Louis, Missouri, a suspect fired five shots, killing FBI agent Doug Abrams and wounding two other agents. Four bullets were quickly accounted for, but the fifth bullet, which had passed through an agent's leg, could not be found. A week later it turned up in six inches of water in the kitchen sink. By comparing damage to the bullet to damage to objects, Firearms examiners determined that the bullet had passed through the agent's leg, gone through an indoor-outdoor carpet in the kitchen, hit the floor and bounced up through the carpet, hit a chair leg, which deflected it upward, bounced off the ceiling, and finally landed in the sink, where it was found. You just never know.

There are many ways to search for bullets at a crime scene. Obviously, if a bullet is in the victim the doctor or coroner will find it. If the shooting took place indoors, the bullet will usually be found embedded in the walls or furniture. But when a shooting takes place outdoors, a flat trajectory can send the bullets absolutely anywhere, and often they're never recovered.

Even in what is certainly the most carefully investigated shooting of all time, the assassination of President Kennedy, the first bullet fired was never found. "From the Zapruder film we knew when the first shot was fired," Bob Frazier, who headed the firearms investigation, remembered. "It obviously missed, and hit the limb of a tree or something. There was a man standing a couple of hundred yards away who said he got hit with a piece of cement and

there was blood running down his cheek. Nobody could account for it except that the bullet might have hit the curb and knocked a piece of cement out of it which cut him in the cheek. Nobody ever found that bullet. It could have gone to pieces. But it just disappeared.''

Detectives use metal detectors, underwater metal detectors, crime-scene vacuums, even X-ray machines to find spent bullets. They are found embedded everywhere imaginable: in the ground, inside utility poles, inside flattened automobile tires. They are found smashed into fragments next to a brick wall. One examiner received a tree trunk; still embedded in it was a bullet from a murder committed thirty years earlier. In those cases in which bullets cannot be found, the spent cartridges become the best evidence.

One of history's most controlled crime-scene searches took place not far from the lab when John Hinckley attempted to assassinate President Reagan. Gerald Wilkes and Rick Crum were two of the first agents on the scene. "The first thing we had to do was account for all the shots," Wilkes explained. "We wanted to know where each bullet was, which would eliminate the possibility that there was a second shooter. We knew six shots had been fired because there were six fired cartridge cases in the cylinder of Hinckley's gun, and the sound of six shots being fired had been recorded on videotape. We knew that four people had been hit, so that's four bullets. Another bullet had hit the right rear window of the limousine, the fifth bullet. But we couldn't find the sixth bullet anywhere.

"We walked through the crime scene, then we crawled through it on our hands and knees, and finally we went through there with brooms and swept up everything. We collected gum wrappers, bottle caps, cigarette butts, everything. And finally we found that bullet. It had missed everything, gone across the street and hit a second-story window, and shattered. We found tiny bullet fragments on the

pavement outside the window and on the floor inside the building. There was only a small hole in the glass.

"Agents at the hospital where the President was being treated gathered up all his belongings and sent them to us so we could do residue tests. Now we believed we really did have everything we needed. In fact, two nights later, I was fast asleep when the assistant director in charge of the lab, Tom Kelleher, woke me and asked, 'You still got all of the President's stuff?' When I told him I did, he asked, 'Did you happen to get a little flat card with an orange band on it?'

" 'Yeah,' I said, 'it's in my locker.'

"I could hear him breathe a sigh of relief. 'Would you get out of bed right now and go to your office, please. Two White House staffers will meet you there.'

" 'Couldn't this wait till the morning?' I asked.

" 'Uh, no,' he said firmly. 'That thing you stuck in your locker box is the encoding card that arms all of our nuclear warheads. You've had it for two days and they'd really like it back.' "

It often requires a great deal of skill as well as luck to find a bullet at a crime scene. When a flight carrying gamblers between San Francisco and Las Vegas crashed for no obvious reason in the 1950s, there was speculation that the pilot had been shot. The lab sent Agent-examiner Bill Magee to the site to investigate the crash. "My job was to go out there and try to find out if a gun had been fired on that airplane. It turned out to be a nightmare. As I discovered, a rivet hole is just about the size of a .38-caliber bullet. And when a plane crashes, those rivets start popping out. I looked at thousands of holes, almost any one of which could have been made by a bullet. When I went back to the lab and reported that I hadn't found any evidence to support the shooting theory, they told me to go back and look some more.

"This time, before I went back, I developed a spot

chemical solution that would turn purple when exposed to lead. I knew that when a bullet hits metal it leaves a lead deposit, so I figured this solution might help us find the evidence we needed. I went back there and began demonstrating the procedure we were going to use to the agents who would be helping me with the search. I picked up a piece of metal tubing with a dent in it and applied some of my solution to it—and the damn thing turned purple! I sent this piece back to the lab, and in addition to the lead we found some antimony. Antimony is used in bullet metal to harden it. The piece turned out to be part of the frame from the pilot's seat. There was no question about it, at least one shot had been fired on that plane, at the pilot.''

Finding a bullet at a crime scene can also help determine its point of origin. In some instances firearms experts can trace the trajectory of a bullet to find the spot from which it was fired. This can't be done often, because once a bullet hits something, whether a brick wall or a human bone, it changes direction and its path can't be traced. To successfully establish the trajectory of a bullet, investigators need two different surfaces that the bullet has passed through. Then it's simply a matter of lining up the holes, which can often be done by aiming a laser beam through them and seeing where it ends up. Sometimes this is done the old-fashioned way, by sticking a dowel through a hole and determining the angle of penetration with protractors, a carpenter's level, and a plumb line.

When a shot was fired through a window and into the wall of the Israeli consulate in Washington, D.C., government officials feared that it was a terrorist act. Lab examiners aimed a laser beam from the point of impact in the wall through the hole in the window. The beam went straight between other buildings to a spot several blocks from the consulate. An investigation discovered that at the time the shot had been fired, a security guard was chasing a purse snatcher and had, in fact, taken a shot at him. The rifling

on the bullet was consistent with the guard's gun. This proof that the episode had been just an unlucky shot perhaps averted an international incident.

In a similar case, Supreme Court justice Harry Blackmun, who wrote the majority opinion in the controversial *Roe v. Wade* case, which established a constitutional right to abortion, was sitting in his Virginia apartment near the Potomac River when a bullet crashed through the window and lodged in his chair. This certainly could have been an assassination attempt.

The first thing examiners noted was that the bullet, which was made of soft metal and should have been badly damaged, in fact was almost intact. That meant it had been fired from a substantial distance and had been slowing when it went through the window and into the chair. By retracing the path of the bullet, the point of origin was determined to have been more than a half-mile away, across the Potomac. That was far too great a distance for a handgun to be fired with any accuracy. Although the gun from which the bullet had been fired was never identified, some police officers in Georgetown admitted they had been shooting at an opossum at just about the time the bullet went through Blackmun's window, and it is probable that this was the source of the stray shot.

A popular misconception about bullets is that the angle of incidence—the angle at which a bullet strikes an object—will equal the angle of rebound, as it does when a ball is thrown against a wall. If that were true, experts would be able to plot the path of a bullet even after it struck an object. But when a bullet hits something, its shape is altered; and that change in shape will cause it to deflect at a different angle. In fact, if someone is shooting at you, about the worst thing you can do—contrary to TV or the movies—is lie on the ground or hide behind a car, because when a bullet strikes the ground it will generally rebound or rise only about a few inches and travel close to

the surface. So if you're hiding behind a car, all the shooter has to do to hit you is aim at the ground directly in front of you.

The first thing that happens when a gun arrives in the firearms lab is that an examiner or technician looks inside the barrel. When a gun is fired, a small but very powerful vacuum, the blowback, draws anything close by into the barrel. On occasion blood, hairs, or fibers from the victim are found in the gun barrel. In a double homicide case in Florida, the killer tried to muffle the sound of the gunshots by shooting through a pillow. When a suspect was arrested, parts of a feather were found in the barrel of his gun—a feather that Doug Deedrick of the Hairs and Fiber Unit could positively associate with the feathers in that pillow.

Once the barrel has been cleaned the gun is test-fired. Just about every gun that comes into the lab is fired twice, to produce two bullets and two cartridge cases which can be used for comparisons. In the FBI lab guns are fired into a water-filled steel tank four feet wide, five feet deep, and ten feet long. The water makes the bullet decelerate and drop to the bottom of the tank, which is painted a light color to make it easy to find the bullet. Water is the ideal medium to use to slow down a bullet, because it won't affect any of the microscopic markings. Historically, fire-arms examiners have test fired bullets into boxes filled with cotton or oil-soaked sawdust, fifty-five-gallon drums, even a ten-foot-long row of telephone books. While those materials might stop a bullet, they are not particularly efficient; it can take a long time to find a small bullet in a big box of cotton.

Guns arrive in the lab in every conceivable condition, and sometimes have to be repaired before they can be test-fired. In some cases, this has to be done despite great diffi-culty. In December 1987, a Pacific Southwest Airlines commuter flight from Los Angeles to San Francisco sud-

denly dove into a hillside, killing all forty-three people aboard. Initially National Transportation Safety Board officials suspected the plane had been destroyed by a bomb. But one of the cockpit tape recorders picked up several screaming voices and what sounded like gunshots seconds before the plane crashed. And in the debris police found an airsickness bag on which someone had written, "Hi, Ray, I think it's sort of ironical that we end up like this. I asked for some leniency for my family, remember. Well, I got none and you'll get none." Among the people killed in the crash were an airline supervisor named Raymond Thompson and a passenger named David Burke, whom Thompson had fired three weeks earlier for purportedly stealing $69 from cocktail sales. Speculation began that Burke had shot Thompson and the pilots, causing the plane to crash. The bodies of the victims were so badly mutilated that it was impossible to find evidence to support that theory. But FBI agents located one of Burke's former co-workers, who admitted loaning him a .44 Magnum pistol and twelve cartridges a month earlier.

"In the crime scene we found a .44 Magnum broken into two pieces," explained Agent-examiner Robert Murphy, firearms expert with more than two decades experience in the lab. "The barrel had been broken off the frame and the pieces were found about a hundred yards apart. The frame was beyond repair; it was twisted and distorted. The cylinder had frozen into the frame and we had to pound it open to see if there were fired cartridges in the chambers. There were; all six cartridges had been fired.

"So we had a gun, but we didn't have any bullets. While the gun and the note and the cockpit recording were strong circumstantial evidence that some event had taken place aboard the aircraft just before it crashed, we really couldn't prove anything."

Eventually a member of the search team found a copper bullet jacket in the wreckage and gave it to Murphy. "I

looked at it," he recalled, "and sure enough, it was a .44 Magnum bullet jacket. We knew that if we could positively link that jacket to the gun, we could prove bullets had been fired on the plane.

"But the gun was mutilated, there was no way we could fire it. Fortunately, the barrel was intact, and the barrel was the critical part, the part with the markings. I thought that if we could put the barrel on another gun and somehow fire it, I might be able to make an identification and close this thing out.

"Every day we receive guns for disposal, guns that were used as evidence in court cases that weren't returned to the owner, guns that were confiscated from criminals, guns that have been surrendered or just turned up somewhere. A few of these weapons are added to our gun collection, but most of them are taken up to a steel plant and melted down. I looked through the disposal collection and found a Smith & Wesson .44 Magnum revolver. Our armorers at Quantico fit that barrel onto the frame for me. From that point on it was just a routine examination: I test-fired the gun into the water tank, then examined both bullet jackets under the comparison scope. The markings were so good it took me just a few seconds to make a positive identification. There was no longer any question about what had caused that airplane to crash."

Most of the guns submitted to the lab for examination are pretty common weapons, but occasionally unique specimens will turn up. They are usually handmade guns taken from prisoners, and while they may not be very sophisticated, they are as deadly as the best store-bought weapons. They are made of wood and pipe fittings, rubber bands and elastic. Nails become bullets. One particularly ingenious prisoner constructed the barrel of his gun out of paper. For safety reasons, homemade guns are always fired into the tank by remote control.

Silencers are also submitted to the lab. A silencer is any

device that, attached to the end of a gun, will muffle the noise when the gun is fired. Even a poorly made silencer can be effective, as every six-decibel reduction will cut the sound of a gunshot by half. So if a silencer reduces a gunshot sounding by twelve decibels, it cuts the sound by 75 percent.

Many years ago a sport called parlor shooting—target shooting in the living room—was a popular pastime. At that time silencers could be legally purchased—presumably so as not to disturb the neighbors—but since then they have become illegal. With the exception of soldiers and police officers, no one can legally possess a silencer. That means silencers can't be bought; they have to be made. And they can be made very easily, out of basic household products ranging from plastic bottles to lawn-mower mufflers. Among the most popular materials are two-liter plastic soda bottles.

Silencers work by containing, then gradually dissipating, the gases released when a gun is fired. One of the most unusual—but still effective—silencers submitted to the lab was made out of a plastic baby bottle filled with rubber nipples. When the gun was fired the plastic expanded; after the bullet exited the plastic contracted, while the nipples caused the gases to slowly dissipate.

A silencer can also be used to link a bullet to a weapon. Anything through which a bullet passes, especially a silencer, will leave its mark, and these traces can be used exactly like barrel markings. Probably the most important case in which silencer marks provided decisive evidence was the murder of Alan Berg a very controversial radio talk-show host in Denver, Colorado. Berg had received several death threats from the right-wing groups he regularly attacked on his show; one night, as he got out of his car in front of his home, he was gunned down by an automatic weapon. As many as fifteen shots were fired in a few seconds. A neighbor who heard the firing said it hadn't

sounded like gunshots, but rather like a muffled chain being dragged off the back of a pickup truck: an apt description for the sound of a silencer.

Berg's murder went unsolved for several months. Then an informant told police that members of the Silent Brotherhood, a right-wing white supremacist group in Washington State, were responsible for the killing. An investigation eventually narrowed down the numbers of suspects, and search warrants were obtained. Among the weapons found in one house was a .44-caliber automatic with a silencer welded to its barrel. It was sent to the lab, where Bob Murphy examined it. "I think we were a little surprised when we found this weapon," Murphy said. "Why they didn't just get rid of this gun I have no idea. The only thing we could figure out is that they were so enamored with guns that they couldn't bring themselves to get rid of it.

"When I got the gun the silencer was still attached to the muzzle. It was a homemade silencer made out of a grease-gun tube. Truthfully, it was the strangest-looking weapon I've ever seen. It looked just like a submachine gun with a grease gun welded to the front. But it reduced the sound level almost twenty-four decibels, which meant that the gun made only about ten percent of the normal sound. A portion of the silencer made contact with the bullets when they were fired, and it left some very rough, very coarse striations. Anyone with experience would have known immediately that the marks were too rough and too haphazard to have been made by the barrel. No barrel is rifled that roughly. So the marks had to come from an external source, and there was that big thing stuck to the end of the barrel. When I test-fired bullets through the silencer, I was able to duplicate those marks and make a positive identification. There was no question about it, this was the gun that had been used to kill Alan Berg."

Four members of the Silent Brotherhood were eventually

convicted of crimes associated with Berg's murder and received sentences of up to one hundred years.

Of course, even after a bullet has been linked to a gun, the gun has to be linked to a suspect. That can be done in many different ways, including fingerprints, but as Bob Sibert pointed out, "Whoever is caught holding the gun is the guy with the problem. It's either help us link it to the person who fired it or be indicted as a co-conspirator. And if he doesn't want to help, he might end up facing the whole rap by himself."

The Firearms and Toolmarks Unit works about eleven hundred cases annually, many of them involving multiple weapons. After a disastrous fifty-one-day confrontation with the Branch Davidian religious cult in Waco, Texas, ended in the deaths of four federal agents and at least seventy-five members of the cult, for example, the unit examined more than three hundred weapons. The majority of these guns are eventually destroyed, but a few of them are added to the Bureau's weapons collection, the most complete and fascinating collection of weapons anywhere in the world. It includes more than five thousand handguns and shoulder arms of just about every conceivable type, from miniature revolvers to sawed-off shotguns and grenade launchers, and almost every one of them has been used in a crime. The collection includes common weapons, like the two-dollar Liberators the Allies air-dropped to guerilla fighters by the tens of thousands during World War II, and unusual weapons, like the seven-shot cylindrical revolver used in the Wild West and a survival weapon in which all the parts fit into a floating stock. It even includes historical curiosities like the guns used by John Dillinger and Ma Barker and a shotgun that Pretty Boy Floyd unsuccessfully tried to convert to an automatic weapon. Examiners use the collection to identify parts of weapons recovered at crime scenes, to familiarize themselves with

weapons they will be examining or testifying about, and simply to see how certain weapons work.

While the best piece of evidence in a shooting is always the gun, much useful information about the crime can be learned from the bullet. A common misconception is that the bullet is the thing that's put into the gun and fired. Technically, a bullet consists of a cartridge case that holds everything together, plus a primer that is struck by the weapon's firing pin to cause a tiny bit of explosive powder to burn and drive the projectile—the bullet—through the air. It's the bullet that causes the damage.

The first thing examiners try to determine from a bullet is its class characteristics, which identify the type of weapon that could have fired it. If all bullets arrived in the lab in pristine condition this would be a very simple examination, but they don't. The function of a bullet is to hit something, and when it does so it's going to be damaged. The examiners in the Firearms Unit are among the most expert in the world, but with more than fourteen thousand different types of ammunition available, sometimes even they can't readily identify a bullet from a few shattered fragments. And when John Hinckley attempted to assassinate President Reagan, their inability to quickly identify the type of bullets he fired almost proved fatal.

The bullet that hit President Reagan had ricocheted off the presidential limousine. It was a million-to-one shot. The bullet had gone through the tiny opening between the open rear door and the car body; it was deflected by the frame and struck the President under the arm. "When I got the bullet that night," said Gerald Wilkes, who did the examinations, "it was as flat as a dime. It had been flattened when it hit the car. One side was completely caved in, while the other side was intact. The hole in the President's garment was more of a little slit than a bullet hole.

We didn't know it at first, but the fact that the bullet hit the car the way it did may have saved the President's life.

"This bullet had limited marks on the undamaged side. They weren't the greatest, but they were enough to allow me to link it to bullets I test-fired from Hinckley's gun.

"A second bullet had hit Press Secretary James Brady in the head. That one was in a million pieces. All that was left of it was the very bottom portion of the base. My first thought when I looked at it was that I'd rarely seen that type of mutilation. There was no way we could make an identification on that bullet. There just wasn't enough of it left.

"The third bullet had struck Secret Service agent Tim McCarthy. It had been damaged but we were able to identify it. The fourth bullet had hit DC Police Officer Thomas Delehanty. It had lodged so close to his spine that doctors had decided it was too risky to operate, that he could live with it in his body, so we couldn't identify it.

"Two days after the shooting we got a box of ammunition that had been found in Hinckley's hotel room. As soon as I opened the box I got this terrible feeling in the pit of my stomach. These bullets were called 'Devastators.' They carried a tiny explosive charge in an aluminum canister in the nose—and they are designed to explode upon impact. That's why there was so little left of the bullet that hit Jim Brady. It had exploded in his brain. In each case the soft nose had been flattened, and the lead had folded over the canister, preventing me from seeing this.

"Right away I knew we had two serious problems. First, we needed to know what the explosive charge was. That stuff is potentially poisonous. And if some of it had leaked into the President's body, it was possible he was being slowly poisoned. And second, we had a police officer with a bullet in his body that could explode at any moment.

"We immediately informed the doctors at Bethesda Naval Hospital that they had a serious problem to deal with.

Then we sent agents to Norcross, Georgia, where these bullets were made, to learn as much as possible about them. We didn't know if they were heat sensitive, shock sensitive, we didn't know anything.

"It didn't take us too long to find out that they were dangerous. One of the examiners in Neutron Analysis, Rod Asbury, was very carefully dissecting a Devastator with a scalpel under his microscope when the bullet exploded. The microscope shielded him from serious injury. He had some cuts and the scope was ruined, but he was very lucky. That told us for certain we were dealing with a very unstable explosive.

"We learned from the manufacturer that the explosive charge was lead azide. It doesn't take much to cause azide to explode. The obvious question was, Why hadn't the bullet that hit the President exploded? No one will ever know for sure, but there were probably two reasons. First, these bullets needed to be traveling more than nine hundred feet per second to develop enough force to detonate, and when the bullet glanced off the limo it had slowed down. Second, the nose had been flattened when it hit the car, sealing the canister inside. We weighed the amount of azide remaining in the bullet removed from the President's body and compared it to the weight of an unfired Devastator. The weights were almost identical—none of the azide had leaked into President Reagan's body.

"But when we told Officer Delahanty's doctors what kind of bullet they had in there, they accused us of inventing the story so we could get the bullet as evidence. The situation really got pretty nasty. Finally, I told the doctor, 'You do what you want to do. It's your call. I'm just telling you what's in the guy's neck.'

"The doctors wanted answers we couldn't give them. 'All I can tell you,' I said, 'is that this stuff is very dangerous. There's a real danger to your hands and eyes. It's

possible that if you touch this stuff with a metal tool it'll explode. We just can't rule out anything.'

"The final decision was left to Delahanty, who wanted them to operate. The operation took place in an isolated wing of the hospital, and it was performed by volunteers. Everyone wore special glasses to protect their eyes, and although it was an intricate and complicated procedure, the bullet was removed without incident and the patient was fine."

The fact that bullets can be flattened or smashed on impact often makes it impossible to link them to the shooting weapon, but there are situations in which that damage can actually be beneficial. When a bullet passes through a substance it picks up and carries with it microscopic particles of that substance. Pieces of bone, hair, dirt, drywall, brick and mortar, paint, glass, fibers, even blood are found on bullets and can be very helpful in figuring out the path of a gunshot. In the St. Louis shootout in which Special Agent Doug Abrams was killed, a bullet found in a hallway had a fiber impression that matched Abrams's pants. Another bullet carried paint and drywall, confirming it had bounced off a wall.

When a Pennsylvania police officer was charged with killing an innocent motorist, he faced the almost impossible task of proving the death had been a terrible accident. The officer claimed he had tripped and his gun had gone off, striking the victim, but there were no witnesses, just one scared police officer and a body. Then an examiner found microscopic bits of cement and glass embedded in the nose of the bullet. This evidence supported the officer's story that his gun had accidentally discharged, and that the bullet had ricocheted off the pavement, through the car window, and into the unfortunate victim.

When a bullet's nose is distorted, it may lock materials and fibers inside; by prying it open, investigators can see, in order, every substance that bullet passed through. This

kind of evidence can be particularly useful in determining whether victims have been shot in the front or back, which is sometimes very difficult to figure out from their wounds. In another St. Louis case, when Doug Deedrick in Hairs and Fibers opened up the nose of a bullet he found fibers from the victim's jacket and jacket lining—and, to his surprise, orange fibers that didn't match the victim's shirt or T-shirt, and a tiny piece of a feather. Deedrick realized that this meant the victim had been wearing a down vest, a fact that hadn't appeared in any police reports because the vest didn't look damaged. But when police took a more careful look at it, they discovered a small rip on the seam—which changed their reconstruction of the position in which the victim had been standing when he was shot.

When a bullet is too badly damaged to be linked to a weapon, or if the bullet is in good shape but a gun is never recovered, a strong case can still be made by linking the elemental composition of the fired bullet to the composition of unfired cartridges found in a suspect's possession. All arms manufacturers use their own mixtures when making ("loading") ammunition, and that mixture changes with different batches. Antimony is used to harden metal, and bullets will consist of between one half of 1 percent to $2\frac{1}{2}$ percent antimony, depending on the manufacturer. The fact that a bullet recovered at a crime scene has the same composition as bullets that can be associated with a suspect makes strong circumstantial evidence. The odds that two people randomly purchased the same type of ammunition made by the same company in the same batch are statistically very slight.

Linking crimes committed by the same person in different jurisdictions has long been a basic objective of law enforcement agencies, but except for the sensational cases headlined by the news media, they have never been able to do it on a regular basis. Incredible as it might seem, even if the same weapon was used in murders in jurisdictions as

close as Washington, D.C., Virginia, and Maryland, there was absolutely no way for police departments in those areas to associate the killings. To help local departments link crimes committed by the same person, in 1992 the Firearms Unit initiated its Drugfire program. Originally started to connect drug-related shootings, Drugfire was expanded to include all crimes in which a weapon is fired.

The only way to link shootings is to compare the markings on recovered fired ammunition components, and until recently that meant physically examining all the specimens that might have been fired by the same weapon under a comparison microscope. That rarely happens. But a new computer process has made it possible to create a digital image of the marks on the surface of a cartridge case and to characterize them in detail by means of numbers. When a computer matches the digital image of two or more cartridge cases, these images can be transmitted between different sci-crime labs, and if they still appear to be similar then the specimens will be physically examined.

Drugfire enables investigators in different jurisdictions to enter the description of fired ammunition components in a shared database, in which they are stored until matched to items recovered in other crimes. In the program's first, experimental year of operation in the Washington, D.C., and Maryland area, seventy pairs of cases that previously would not have been associated were found to involve the same weapon. This allowed different departments to pool their resources in their investigations.

"I know I'll never forget the first hit we got because it was so strange," remembered Bob Sibert, who was instrumental in setting up the program. "One day we were training some officers from the Metro Washington police department. There were a limited number of cases in the system. So to show them how the thing worked, we put in the description of a cartridge case that had been recovered from a homicide that had taken place in March—and the

computer matched it to a cartridge case that had been test-fired from a firearm that had been recovered in January. Well, it looked like we had our first problem with the system. How could a gun that was in police custody in January have been used in a homicide two months later?

"It was a very good comparison. I called over one of our managers and told him that I'd been looking at firearms evidence for twenty years and if that wasn't an identification I'd eat it. So we called the Metro Washington police department and asked them to pull the cartridge cases from evidence and physically compare them. They did, and agreed it was an ident. Then we asked them to get the gun out of the property room. And that's when we found out the gun was missing.

"They discovered that a number of firearms had been stolen from the property room and had found their way back onto the street. Internal Affairs jumped all over this and eventually arrested an individual for stealing guns out of the property room and trading them for drugs."

Drugfire is one of the very few technological break-throughs in firearms identification since the development of the comparison microscope in 1925. "As the program expands regionally," Sibert said, "local police departments are going to be able to associate shootings, and that's going to save time and money. And cause a lot more dangerous people to be taken off the streets."

While the evidence in a shooting is still a smoking gun, sometimes the smoke is enough. Residue, smoke, can be used to show that someone has recently fired a weapon and, more significantly, it can also be used to approximate the distance between the victim and his assailant.

When a weapon is fired, two metals present in the primer, barium and antimony, survive the burning process and are often found on a shooter's hand. Often, but not always: the shooter might have been wearing a glove; the

residue might have been blown away by the wind or washed away by rain; the weapon might not have left any residue because of the way it was held; the shooter might have rubbed off the residue by putting his hand in his pocket or by washing his hands. Or, for a reason no one can explain, in some instances there isn't any residue. Even in ideal conditions residue rarely remains on a shooter's hands longer than a couple of hours. So lack of residue isn't exculpatory evidence—not finding it doesn't prove that a subject wasn't near a gun when it was fired. But finding it is a strong indication that he was.

This invisible residue becomes particularly valuable when it can be used to refute an individual's claim that he wasn't near a fired weapon. In a South Carolina homicide, a woman denied being in her home when her husband was shot to death. But when primer-residue tests on her hand turned out positive, she collapsed and confessed that she had shot him.

The traditional method used to detect residue after a shooting was to wipe the back and side of a subject's hand with a cotton swab which would then be chemically tested for the presence of barium and antimony. But barium and antimony are also found in fertilizers and paper products and other sources of environmental contamination. In fact, at any time about one percent of the general population would test positive for these metals. So defense attorneys would argue—sometimes successfully—that the presence of these metals had no meaning at all. But several years ago it was discovered that primer residue is actually composed of microscopic particles, little balls, containing these elements, and that they can be seen under an electron microscope. More important, barium and antimony combine this way only in primer residue, so finding them in this form is considered strong evidence that an individual was near a weapon when it was fired. The microscopic particles put the shooter at the scene.

For a long time the presence of primer on a body was considered the best way of determining if an individual had committed suicide or been murdered. No more—not since it has been shown that a shooter may have no primer on his hands, while victims shot at close range may well have a measurable amount on their bodies.

Suppose two people go into the woods and the one who comes out claims that the other person was shot during a fierce struggle and that he had fired in self-defense. Or suppose a dead person is found gripping the gun that killed him. It looks like suicide but no note is found and some valuables are missing. How do you figure out what really happened? Gunshot residue. It's different from primer residue in that it's found on the victim rather than the shooter. And it can be used to approximate the distance between the weapon and the victim; that's often the key piece of evidence in a claim of self-defense or a questioned suicide.

When a bullet passes through any material, an invisible residue, consisting mostly of lead, is deposited around the bullet hole in a very specific pattern. If the area around that hole is treated with chemicals that react to lead, a residue pattern emerges as a purple stain. It makes good evidence because its size varies according to the distance from the weapon to the victim. Imagine that you're throwing a handful of powder against a wall. The closer you are to the wall, the smaller the area the powder will cover; the farther away you are, the larger the pattern. Residue patterns are produced exactly the same way. If the gun is fired within a few feet of something a small, dense pattern will be left on it; beyond a certain distance, about ten feet, there won't be any residue at all. Because the size of the pattern will be the same every time the same weapon is fired with the same ammunition from the same distance, it's possible to figure out how far the shooter was from his victim by reproducing the pattern in test firings.

This is evidence that can destroy a defense. In one early-

1980s case, a woman and her boyfriend were camping out in Yosemite National Park. It was just the two of them, the stars above, and a high-powered rifle. The seemingly distraught woman claimed that her boyfriend had been cleaning the rifle when it accidentally went off, striking him in the chest and killing him instantly. One survivor, one story. The rifle, several rounds of ammunition, and the victim's clothing were submitted to the lab. Chemicals were applied to his shirt, and a gunshot residue pattern developed. On a firing range, the rifle was fired at a similar shirt from various distances to try to produce a similar residue pattern. Repeated tests proved that a pattern of the size found on the shirt could have been created only if the weapon was fired from between five and a half and six feet away. No one can clean a rifle from six feet away. That evidence proved the woman was lying, and a jury convicted her of murder.

In many cases a shooter claims that the gun went off during a struggle. This happens, though it happens most often on television. Without witnesses, it's a very difficult claim for a prosecutor to disprove. But a bullet fired at almost point-blank range will leave several clues. For example, a contact shot will actually melt certain types of cloth fibers around the edges of a bullet hole, and that melting can easily be seen under a microscope. A contact shot may also leave powder burns or deposits of unburned gunpowder.

Gunshot residues are far better at proving that a weapon was fired within a few feet of someone or something than they are at proving that a shooter was several feet away. The lack of residues really doesn't prove very much. Residues are pretty easily blown away or washed away, or they just aren't left when a shot is fired from a long range. The residue of a given shot might even have been deposited on some intervening material—a curtain, a piece of glass, a car door. But when police find a compact residue pattern,

powder burns, or unburned gunpowder on a victim, that victim was shot at close range, and could have been shot during a struggle or committed suicide.

Many shooters claim that their gun fired accidentally: They were cleaning it, and somehow it went off. They tripped, and it went off. They dropped it, and it went off. As Rick Crum said, "We're asked quite often, 'Could this weapon have been fired accidentally?' The answer is always yes. Any weapon that can be fired can be fired accidentally. But what they really want to know is, 'Was it fired accidentally?' And there is almost no way we can answer that question."

The first thing lab examiners will do when a shooter claims his gun fired accidentally is try to reproduce the action. They will drop it and shock it and bang it and try many different ways to make it go off. Even if the gun doesn't fire, the strongest conclusion the lab will report is that they were not able to make this weapon discharge, but they can't eliminate the possibility that some external force caused it to fire.

A Georgia man accused of shooting a friend in the head claimed that the victim had been twirling the cocked weapon Western style when it went off. The victim had survived, but had no memory of the incident. "We tried it in the lab," Crum remembered, "and we found that it's extremely difficult to make a weapon fire by spinning it by the trigger guard. To keep that gun spinning, your finger can't be on the trigger, it has to be on the trigger guard. The force is being exerted downward, not forward. So we reported that it was difficult to make this weapon discharge in the direction of the person spinning it by the trigger— but once again we couldn't rule out the possibility."

Generally, other evidence has to be used to either support or disprove a claim that a gun fired accidentally. In a Florida retirement community, a seventy-year-old woman was shot to death by a single blast from a shotgun as she

sat in her rocking chair. Her distraught husband claimed he had found her body when he returned from a fishing trip, but detectives noted that he appeared to be drunk, and they questioned him carefully. Not buying his alibi, they arrested him and charged him with his wife's murder. The shotgun and a shell casing were submitted to the lab.

Two days later the man changed his story. This time he admitted that he had killed his wife, but he claimed it had been a terrible accident. As he walked into the kitchen, he said, he tripped on the edge of the rug; the shotgun went off, killing his wife, who was sitting on the other side of the room.

One survivor and one story, but the evidence spoke for the victim. The kitchen door and the edge of the rug were approximately thirty-five-feet from the rocking chair. The wound in the woman's left cheek was about an inch and a half in diameter. By test-firing the murder weapon with the same type of ammunition the husband had used, examiners were able to prove that the only distance from which a wound that size could be produced was five feet. The husband's alibi was destroyed and he was convicted of murder.

All the information that can be learned from guns and bullets and residue is put together in the reconstruction of a crime scene. Few of the other units in the lab ever go to a crime scene; even firearms examiners rarely see a body, but they do often visit shooting scenes to try to reconstruct the crime. "What we try to do," explained Rick Crum, an expert in such reconstructions, "is determine what happened, how it happened, the sequence of events, and the location of the shooters in relationship to each other. And we do this by applying just about every firearms technique we use."

In 1988, a polygamist clan known as the Singer-Swapp family bombed a Mormon church in Marion, Utah, then barricaded themselves into a house on the family farm. The

standoff lasted thirteen days, and when the shooting started, Utah Department of Corrections officer Fred House, a dog handler, was killed, an FBI agent was shot in his bulletproof vest, and Adam Swapp was wounded. After this shootout the family surrendered.

Crum was assigned to go to the site to try to reconstruct the shooting. "We began by walking over the whole scene. The shooters had been in the main house. A second house, seventy-five yards away, which we called the greenhouse, was where Officer House had been killed. The neighbors, the Jepsens, lived in the third house, which was a hundred and fifty yards from the main house. Timothy Singer admitted being the shooter, but he claimed that he had been firing at Fred House's dog, which was about twenty feet in front of the officer, and that the killing was accidental. The question I had to try to answer was whether Timothy Singer was aiming at Fred House or the dog.

"The people on the scene gave me a good idea of what they thought happened. Eyewitnesses aren't completely reliable, because people don't necessarily try to remember things when the shooting starts; they try to keep themselves from getting shot. A total of ten shots had been fired from the main house. Four shots had gone through the door where Fred House was standing, each of them between waist to neck high and lodged in a wall. A fifth shot had struck him in the side and killed him. Two more shots passed through the open doorway, traveled through the house and out through a rear window, and hit the Jepsens' garage.

"Initially we believed that Timothy Singer had done all the shooting. But when I positioned myself in the window from which he reportedly had fired the shots that hit the Jepsens' garage, I couldn't see the bullet holes. I thought that was pretty strange." Crum requested a survey team be brought to the site to determine if the shots could have been fired from that window. The team reported they could

sight an area about six inches to the left of the holes, but the holes themselves were blocked by a corner of the greenhouse. This was the first indication that there might have been a second shooter. Crum knew he had to find out where those shots had been fired from.

"Two bullets had gone right through the Jepsens' garage wall, across a three-foot storage space, and into a second wall," he explained. "I took some steel rods and stuck them through the holes, right across the storage area. I could have used a laser beam, but it would have been difficult because these holes were so small. I could tell the bullets had traveled straight through the walls, because the rods were not bent. Using a protractor I could very accurately measure the angle of penetration of each shot. Then I asked the surveyor to project these angles backwards in the direction of the shooter. Very surprisingly, these holes projected backwards through a broken window in the greenhouse, through the doorway in which Fred House had been standing, to a position at the corner of the main house. This told us that Timothy Singer could not possibly have fired these shots.

"It had snowed heavily since the shootout, and more than two feet of snow was on the ground, but using metal detectors we recovered several cartridge cases from that position. There had been a second shooter. Lab tests confirmed that the shot that had killed Officer House had been fired from Timothy Singer's .30 carbine, but that three bullets had been fired from a second .30 carbine. Eventually the people in the house admitted that Jonathan Singer was the second shooter.

"One of the determinations we had to make before the trial was whether or not these rifles hit where they were sighted. Could the shooters have been firing at a target twenty feet in front of Officer House and accidentally hit him? When I test-fired these rifles I found nothing that would have caused a shooter to miss by that wide a margin.

I fired these weapons with the sights in every possible position, and they always shot just about where you aimed them.

"None of this told us whether Timothy Singer had been shooting at Officer House or the dog—I couldn't put myself in his mind—but during the trial the jury had to wonder, could it possibly have been a coincidence that two shooters using two accurate firearms had fired at the same time, and that their aim had been so bad that seven of the ten shots had passed through the doorway in which Officer House had been standing at waist to shoulder height?" The jurors convicted four of the people in that house of homicide and other charges.

The most significant firearms determination, that a recovered bullet was fired from a specific weapon, is made possible by the fact that each time a hard object strikes a softer object it leaves a characteristic impression. Tools act precisely the same way: they mark objects, making it possible to prove that a specific tool was used to perform a certain task. Firearms examiners conduct toolmark examinations pretty much the same way they link weapons and ammunition.

Toolmarks may seem mundane, but toolmark evidence can be found in just about every type of crime. Bombs are made with tools; safes are broken open with tools; people who poison consumer products open packages with tools. Toolmarks rarely provide enough evidence to make a case without additional proof, but they can make a significant contribution toward a conviction.

Like every firearm, every tool is unique. Every hammer, every screwdriver, every tool has some sort of defect in its striking surface, cutting surface, or bit; these defects are produced when the tool is made or result from wear. Some of these marks are transient, but others are permanent and will appear every time the tool is used. These marks don't

affect the quality of a tool—most of them are not even visible to the naked eye—but they can be identified under a microscope. And they can be used to connect an individual to a crime.

When a tool is found that may have left identifiable marks on evidence, an examiner will use it on a piece of metal or wood, then compare the marks it makes to the marks left on the evidence. Just as in firearms, the proof is in the re-creation. For example, in 1982 a California highway patrolman named George Gwaltney reported finding the body of a woman, later identified as Robin Bishop, who had been shot and killed by the side of the highway. There was no sign of a robbery, just a body with a bullet hole in it. Inside the woman's body medical examiners found semen they could characterize as having come from a man who had once had a vasectomy but later had a second operation to have it reversed.

Eventually, key evidence was submitted to Jim Cadigan, who had joined the Firearms and Toolmarks Unit in 1976 and had worked briefly in the lab with his father, who spent thirty-seven years there as a documents examiner. "What made this case difficult was the fact that there didn't seem to be any motive," Cadigan said. "But a police officer remembered seeing a highway patrol car in the area at just about the time of the murder. As a precaution, homicide detectives decided to examine the service revolvers of all the highway patrolmen on duty at that time. Everybody turned in their weapon except George Gwaltney, who claimed he'd left it at home. The detectives followed Gwaltney to his house, but he beat them there and by the time they arrived the gun was gone. Gwaltney told them it'd been stolen. So these detectives, not being dumb, got a search warrant, and in a locked box in his truck they found the frame of his service revolver.

"Somebody had tried to destroy the gun," Cadigan continued. "The cylinder and barrel had been ripped out of the

frame, and without the barrel, it was almost impossible to prove the fatal bullet had been fired from this weapon. A local crime-lab examiner identified some toolmarks on the frame, especially a deep cut that looked like it might have been made by a screwdriver blade, but he was unable to associate any tools found in Gwaltney's house with the marks. Gwaltney was twice tried for murder in his hometown, and both trials ended with a hung jury. Federal prosecutors took over and charged him with violation of the victim's civil rights, and we finally got involved in the case."

The evidence against Gwaltney was all circumstantial. For example, he had had a vasectomy, which had subsequently been reversed. But lab investigators knew that if they could prove he'd destroyed his own service weapon, he'd have a real problem explaining the fact. Innocent people don't do things like that. The case against Gwaltney was built in the lab. Robin Bishop had been found lying face down; Gwaltney claimed he hadn't touched her body. But Alan Robillard in the Hairs and Fiber Unit was able to match a few tiny strands of fur found on her stomach with the fur collar of Gwaltney's uniform jacket, proving he was lying about that. Rick Crum was able to associate Gwaltney with the bullets found in the victim's body by matching machine marks, made on the base of the bullet itself during manufacturing, to other bullets in his possession. Cadigan did the toolmark exam. "The marks on the frame hadn't been made by a screwdriver at all," he said. "They weren't pressure-type marks; they were gripping marks, the kind that might have been made by a tool holding the gun tightly while the barrel was unscrewed. I decided it was a vise or a pipe wrench.

"Among Gwaltney's tools we found a pipe wrench with a broken tooth. I tested it on a piece of metal and it left a very similar mark. Using that mark for orientation, I was able to positively identify other marks found on the gun

frame with marks made by other teeth in the pipewrench. I could show exactly how the wrench had held the frame, and the broken tooth gave us the unique mark we needed to prove it had been held by this particular tool. The jury had to wonder why he'd taken the gun apart and then lied about it. With the additional evidence we were able to develop in here, the prosecutors finally got a conviction on the third attempt. Gwaltney was sentenced to ninety-nine years in prison.''

Toolmarks can be large scrapes in the ground made by a shovel, or tiny nicks on a bottle cap. Toolmarks can be impressed into any kind of material; wood and steel and even human skin and bone. Pliers, for example, have been identified from marks left on nipples. A knife was identified from marks left on an esophagus. After Milwaukee police arrested the serial murderer Jeffrey Dahmer, they submitted parts of several human skulls, in which holes had been drilled, along with a set of drill bits found in Dahmer's home, to see if examiners could make a comparison. Not all tools leave marks; saw marks are almost impossible to identify because the edges are continually cutting and ripping, which destroys individual marks. Occasionally drill bits can be matched to holes if those holes do not completely penetrate a material. In the Dahmer case the holes went through the bone, and the best the lab could do was report that the holes drilled in the skulls were consistent in diameter with the recovered bits. That type of class evidence has very little value, because Dahmer's were standard-sized bits that might have been found in any tool collection.

Toolmarks examiners are also qualified to make fracture matches, to testify that at one time two pieces were part of the same object. For example, several Virginia bank robberies in which thieves used crowbars, screwdrivers, and hammers to pull out night-deposit drawers were positively connected through toolmarks found in the debris. But from

the type of crime and the method they used, that was pretty obvious anyway. And it didn't help identify the gang. After one of the robberies, however, detectives found the broken tip of a screwdriver at the scene. It didn't seem like much, just a tiny piece of broken metal. But eventually several suspects were identified and a search warrant was obtained. In the suspect's possession police found several broken screwdrivers, and toolmark examiners were able to positively link the broken tip to one of the broken blades. That tip connected the thieves to that specific robbery, and other toolmark evidence connected that robbery to several others. Primarily on the basis of toolmark evidence, the entire gang was convicted of bank robbery.

Throughout history people have set out to make their marks in the world, but when weapons or tools are concerned, marks have often led to their undoing.

In the Singer-Swapp family case, Rick Crum proved there had been an unseen second shooter. But in the most controversial crime in American history, the assassination of President John Kennedy and the wounding of Texas governor John B. Connally, Jr., the conclusion reached by the lab's Firearms Unit that there was one assassin has been challenged and debated for more than three decades. This was probably the most extensive firearms investigation in history. The official determination of the commission chaired by Supreme Court chief justice Earl Warren was that a single gunman, Lee Harvey Oswald, firing a C2766 Mannlicher-Carcano rifle from a window in the Texas School Book Depository, had killed the President. Almost immediately, though, that conclusion was challenged. The possible existence of an unseen second shooter became the basis for countless conspiracy theories. Since that time much of the evidence has been questioned, dozens of books have been written, additional hearings have been

held, and a majority of Americans continue to believe that there existed a conspiracy to assassinate the President.

Bob Frazier, then chief of the Firearms Unit, and examiners Cort Cunningham and Charles Killion conducted the original investigation. And while the crime was sensational and the result heartbreaking, the procedures the men followed were relatively routine. "We worked exactly the same way we did in every other case," Frazier remembered, "except it was decided that in this case there would be three examiners—myself, Cort Cunningham, and Charles Killion—and each of us would do his own work. All three of us came out with the same results, and those were the results that were furnished to the Warren Commission."

The actual investigation was divided into two phases: the initial firearms comparison and the crime-scene reconstruction. "We heard about it at noon," remembered Frazier, who in a career that began in 1943 has conducted more than twenty thousand firearms investigations. "That evening we got the rifle from Dallas. I think we received two cartridges at that time, and we got a third one later. We also got a loaded round that came out of Oswald's rifle. Between the time of the assassination and the time we got the rifle, we were looking for the same type of ammunition [Oswald had used]. It was Western 6.5 millimeter and we got three different lots of it. I don't know if this came out or not, but I think the CIA furnished Italy with three or four million rounds of this ammo. Italy didn't use it, so it was sold back to the U.S. on the open market. Believe me, holding that rifle was emotionally upsetting, 'cause we knew it was the rifle that had been used. I know it affected me and it still does, it still does."

Practically the first thing Frazier and Cunningham had to do was recover as much of the fired ammunition as possible from the President's limousine. "We didn't really recover a lot of the lead," Frazier said. "One bullet went

through his head, caught him behind the ear. It blew out a large piece of skull that was found in the gutter. And two big pieces of that bullet came out the top of his head; one fragment hit the chrome above the front window on the windshield, and the other one hit the windshield. It definitely hit it because we found lead on the glass."

"They appeared to be two pieces of one bullet," added Cunningham, who also did the firearms investigation of the revolver Oswald had used to kill Dallas police officer J. D. Tippit.

"What happened," Frazier continued, "I think probably in the confusion when they got to the hospital, everybody jumped out of the car and if there were lead fragments on their clothes or in their pockets or anywhere else, they fell on the ground and were just trampled on and that was the end of it. But we found core fragments that accounted for practically all of the bullet that hit the President in the head. The other bullet that was found [lying on a stretcher in Dallas] was the one that went through the President and through Connally . . . That was the one they called the pristine bullet, but it wasn't pristine at all. The commission came up with that term, 'pristine,' meaning it was undamaged. What they meant was that the nose hadn't been mutilated like the one that hit the bone and broke into pieces. But this one was flattened; if you'd taken a hammer and hit that bullet on the side, you could have flattened it just like it was flattened."

As soon as the lab received the evidence, the rifle was test-fired and the unique markings on the test-fired bullets and cartridge cases were compared to those on the bullets and cartridges recovered from the shooting. "We had a long cotton-filled box that we fired into at that time," Frazier said. "One very interesting thing about the microscopic marks is that in one of the groove impressions there was a defect to the extent that it produced a little deeper groove in the bullet. The muzzle might've had a little tick

in it or something. That particular groove was later used by an outside examiner to say that in all probability Oswald had also shot at General Edwin Walker in April that year. A bullet recovered from that shooting had that one groove on it. He found other marks that he said probably came out of this gun. We did not. We felt there weren't enough marks on it to reach any conclusion at all in the Walker shooting. Bureau policy has always been if it's not positively identified it's no conclusion.''

On the basis of microscopic rifling marks, the examiners were able to conclude that the whole bullet, the bullet fragments, and the cartridge cases had come from the rifle, found in the book depository, on which Dallas police had identified Lee Harvey Oswald's fingerprints. The firearms examination proved that this rifle and no other was the one from which the fatal shots had been fired. "And when it comes to the firearms part," Frazier pointed out, "there have never been any changes.''

The investigation's conclusions, rather than being the end of the case, were the beginning. Almost every other aspect of the assassination scenario has been challenged. Among the many claims made by skeptics are that a second shooter fired from behind a grassy knoll, that more than three shots were fired, that Oswald could not possibly have fired his rifle three times within the necessary time frame and certainly not with enough accuracy to hit a moving target, that one bullet could not possibly have wounded both Kennedy and Connally and ended up in Connally's knee, and, finally, that Kennedy's movements when shot prove that the fatal shot had come from in front of him, rather than behind.

In this crime-scene reconstruction, the FBI examiners had the advantage of a home movie of the shooting, taken by a spectator named Abraham Zapruder. Cunningham said that the crime-scene reconstruction began with that film. "We kept going over and over and over the film. Once

we started looking at it, we watched it a hundred and fifty times if we watched it once.''

"I remember the first time we looked at it," Frazier said. "There were about six or eight of us watching. That first time was pretty rugged because the President's head just explodes. The room was absolutely silent. Then we discovered that there was information on the Zapruder film we saw that didn't appear on the screen when the film was projected. The frame is eight millimeters, and another two millimeters is film that's exposed in the drive wheel—and you can actually see the rest of the picture. You'd be surprised how much information is out in the perforated edge. We had eight-by-tens printed of every frame. In prints you can see a woman standing on the steps of the School Book Depository who doesn't show when it's projected. Or it will show somebody over on the other side taking a picture at a certain point. The way the reconstruction was handled, we got together all the pictures that had been taken that could be located, and using the Zapruder film for timing, we triangulated the car in a particular place at a specific moment. We were trying to pick out when the bullets were fired, where the car was hit, the direction the bullets came from, everything."

Frazier and Cunningham did not investigate the possibility of a conspiracy. They simply examined the evidence they had, and from that reached their conclusions. As for the second assassin supposedly shooting from the grassy knoll in front of the President, Frazier explained, "All this talk about someone seeing a puff of smoke, what they forget is that the charge used in bullets is smokeless powder and the word 'smokeless' means smokeless; it doesn't produce a puff of smoke. It produces a little dark residue possibly, but not like you would take a puff on a cigarette and blow it out."

Key evidence for those people who believe that someone fired at Kennedy from the grassy knoll is the fact that on

the film the President's head seemed to jerk backward when he was shot, rather than being driven forward as would seem logical if he was shot from behind. "There's no doubt where the bullet struck the President in the back of the head," Cunningham said. "That frame can be pinpointed."

"And the fact that his head moved backwards can be explained by the jet effect of all the liquid leaving his skull," Frazier continued. "It was like a jet effect created by the material leaving. . . . People say, Well, the motorcycle people behind were all covered with blood and brain tissue. Of course they were. They were moving forward at fifteen miles per hour; this material went up in the air and they drove underneath it. You can look at the President's car and find blood and brain sprayed all over the front windshield and even on the hood of the car."

When President Reagan was shot, a videotape with audio made it possible to prove how many shots had been fired. Zapruder's film did not have sound, and the number of shots witnesses heard was disputed. "They had people who practically heard a machine gun going off," Frazier said. "But there were three people in the Book Depository building on the floor right under Oswald and they said definitely they heard three shots, and they definitely heard cartridge cases hit the floor. And when the shots went off, the floor shook and little particles of sawdust and cement fell down, so they knew where the shots came from.

"Some people [standing outside] underneath the shots said they heard three or four or five shots, but what they were hearing was the crack of the bullet going overhead because it was traveling faster than the speed of sound. They heard the sound of the bullet going overhead and then a half second later, boom, they heard that same shot going off back there in the building. If you hear that second shot, it means you haven't been hit by the bullet. Later, investigators returned to Dealey Plaza and fired a weapon and

people heard echoes off the grassy knoll, off the stone work, the railroad embankment. They were hearing reverberations. Eyewitness testimony is not the most accurate there is, and earwitness testimony is even worse."

According to the Zapruder film, the three shots had to have been fired in a minimum time span of 4.8 seconds if the second shot missed, or between 7.1 and 7.9 seconds if either the first or third shot missed. Many people believe that Oswald's rifle simply could not be fired three times within that time span. Frazier and Cunningham disagreed. Frazier, Cunningham, and Charles Killion test-fired the rifle for speed and accuracy within days of the assassination. The examiners proved it was easy to fire three aimed shots from Oswald's rifle within any of those time frames. "We fired that gun several times," said Frazier. "Cort fired it, Killion fired it, and I fired it. The minimum amount of time it took me to fire three shots was four point six seconds; the maximum time was six point five seconds. And I wasn't familiar with that gun. The problem with most people is that they forget the clock starts running when you fire the first shot. The cartridge is already in the rifle, you don't have to load it. You're really only loading two shots while you're firing the three. Those two shots had to be fired in a minimum of four point eight seconds, which is twice as long as it takes to shoot carefully aimed shots."

As for accuracy: "This is something that just about every expert has ignored," Frazier said. "The scope of the rifle had been taken off by Dallas police to search for latents, and when we got it, it was loose; we had to tighten the screws down. I think there were shims under the scope when it was used and the Dallas police lost them when they took it off.

"Cort and Killion and I went down to the range and fired at fifteen-yard targets and twenty-five-yard targets and later at hundred-yard targets. At twenty-five yards you

could cover our shots with a quarter; at a hundred yards we were within two inches, and the longest it took was six point five seconds. When we tightened the scope we found that it was arranged so that it was shooting a little bit high and to the right. The car was moving, so if you aimed right at the President, then the car would actually move right into the line of fire. If you aimed right at him with the first shot you'd hit low, but with the car moving, the second shot would have hit him the way it did."

Finally, the so-called magic bullet, the "pristine" bullet. This bullet supposedly passed through the President, passed through Governor Connally, hit him in the wrist, and then penetrated into his leg. More than any single piece of evidence, it is the damage attributed to this one bullet that raises doubts about a single shooter. "There's no such thing as that magic bullet," Cunningham said flatly. "Bullets are not predictable. I remember I testified in a case in Baltimore where a man sitting in a bar got into an altercation with someone else, who took out a .22 and shot him right between the eyes. A police officer arrested the shooter and called the ambulance to remove the body. Halfway to the morgue the victim sat up and started complaining that he had a hell of a headache. This bullet struck his skull, went under his scalp and over the top of his head, and ended up in the back. The doctors took it out, patched him up, and he went back to the bar where the same astonished officer saw him later in the day.

"But you have to understand that in the Kennedy assassination we're talking about military-type bullets which have a solid nose, a jacketed nose, and they're crimped around the base of the bullet. That makes it much stronger, and you get much more penetration with it."

"When the Zapruder film showed the President had been shot," Frazier said, "he was sitting straight up in the car. He'd been waving and he'd just lowered his hand when he got shot in the back. The reason the bullet was squashed

was because it went through the President's body and came out through the buttonhole area of his shirt. It just nicked his tie. It didn't hit anything hard next to the backbone, but the pressure would've damaged the central nervous system. That caused the President to jerk up his hands in front of him. In the films you could see he was frozen in that position.

"Connally had been facing forward. When the bullet came out of Kennedy, it was traveling sideways, because the wound in Connally's back was an elongated hole. So the bullet was tumbling when it hit him and it went through him still tumbling, knocked a piece of rib out and came out of his chest. Then it went through his wrist backwards. It had to be backwards because the bullet didn't mutilate and there was lead found in Connally's wrist. And then it buried itself in his leg, still traveling backwards, because when they X-rayed him they found a couple of pieces of lead there. None of this was unusual. It got squashed flat and slowed down. That's why it didn't completely shatter his wrist bone. At the instant of the shot, Connally was facing just exactly right for the bullet to follow a straight line through the President, through Connally's body, to hit his wrist and go into his left leg.

"When we hear this called the magic bullet, we kind of laugh."

Neither Frazier nor Cunningham has ever doubted the conclusions they reached in the days after the assassination. "At first I got angry when I heard these stories," Cunningham said, "but now I just shrug. They start out with a false premise or a 'Let us suppose,' and three pages later, it's no longer 'Let us suppose,' it's a fact. I mean, it would send a logic professor to his grave. It's the most ridiculous thing."

"Same with me," Frazier agreed. "You know they don't have their facts straight, but I'm not going to straighten them out. I almost wrote Walter Cronkite once because he

twice made a serious mistake about the amount of time it took to fire three shots—they developed a big TV program on that basis—but if they want to do that they will, regardless of what I say.''

"I don't mean to be insulting to people," Cunningham added, "but these people are not taking the facts into account, because if their story isn't sensational, it doesn't sell books.''

Neither man has seen *JFK*, director Oliver Stone's movie based on numerous conspiracy theories. And the investigators have read very few of the dozens of books on the subject. "I had to read the first few," Frazier admits, "because Mr. Hoover said, 'Read these books and tell me whether they're right or wrong. Go through it and write in the margins.'' So I wrote a memo saying, 'He's wrong here, he's wrong here, he's wrong here,' and then I forgot about it. That's the way we handled the controversy.''

And finally, when asked the seemingly obvious question—"Was this the greatest case of your career?"—Frazier smiled and said, "When you're dealing with firearms cases, you get a case of a lifetime every week.''

9

Frame-ups and Downright Lies:
The Special Photography Unit, the Video Enhancement Unit, and the Polygraph Unit

"I am immensely indebted to you. Pray tell me in what way I can reward you. This ring—" He slipped an emerald snake ring from his finger. . . .

"Your Majesty has something which I should value even more highly," said Holmes.

"You have but to name it."

"This photograph!"

SHERLOCK HOLMES,
in Sir Arthur Conan Doyle's
"A Scandal in Bohemia"

We are a world of picture takers. In the United States more than two billion still photographs are taken annually—pictures of weddings and parties and parades, beautiful pictures of the Grand Canyon and historic monuments, pictures of family and friends and lovers, and pictures of accidents and tragedies and rapes and assaults and bank robberies, pictures of mutilations and decapitations and simple murder. We record what we do, the good and the bad. We make a permanent record, on film and on videotape, of the most beautiful and horrific moments of our lives. The FBI's Special Photography Unit works mostly with the horror.

While photography and, by extension, video are generally believed to be modern crime-fighting tools, in fact photography is one of the oldest. Within years of the inven-

tion of photography in France in the 1820s, daguerrotypes, photographs printed on silver plates, had replaced branding as the preferred means of identifying felons. The problem was that the pictures could not readily be reproduced, and criminals would change their expressions while being photographed, making it difficult to positively identify them. In 1885 Alphonse Bertillon, the creator of the Bertillon Method of identification by body measurement, insisted that all French prisoners be photographed from the front and in profile, under good lighting and from the same distance. Bertillon thereby invented the mug shot.

A photograph was first used as evidence in an American trial in 1859, when it was used to prove that a property title was fraudulent. The first traffic-accident photo was entered as evidence in 1875, when a plaintiff tried to prove that he had been forced to drive his horse and buggy off an embankment to avoid a deep mud hole. When technology finally made it possible to reproduce photographs in large quantities, almost every major American police department established its own ''rogues' gallery,'' as photofiles of wanted criminals were known. Today, the very first thing that happens at a crime scene, before anything is touched, before the body is examined, before prints are developed, is that it is photographed. A permanent record is made to be used in the investigation and perhaps as evidence.

In 1935 the FBI set up its Photographic Operations Unit, which was eventually split into the Photo Processing Unit, which mass-produces almost four million documents annually, and the Special Photography Unit—the picture detectives.

Special Photo, which officially is part of the Document Section, has management, service, and investigative responsibilities. The unit purchases and maintains the four thousand Nikon camera bodies and eleven thousand interchangeable lenses used in field offices, photographs all the evidence submitted to the lab and conducts all of the eso-

teric photo work—including surveillances, aerial photography, and the placement and supervision of concealed cameras. But its day-to-day investigative function consists of trying to squeeze every last bit of information out of a photograph. The photographs submitted to the lab for examination are often overexposed or underexposed; they're out of focus; the subject is partially out of the frame or is too far away to be identified or is even obscured by reflections. Special Photo's task is to overcome these problems so the people or objects in the picture can be identified.

There's often a wealth of information to be found in photographs that is too small to be seen with the naked eye. What time is showing on the victim's watch? Can that bracelet be identified as part of the stolen property? What's the license-plate number of that truck? Is that a man crouching behind the bushes on the grassy knoll?

In sci-crime photography, bigger is much better, so photographs are either enlarged or are examined under magnification. But there is a limit. A photograph is actually a mosaic. It consists of thousands of minuscule grains of light-sensitive minerals. When these minerals are exposed to light, they get darker; the more light they're exposed to, the darker they get. A negative simply regulates the amount of light hitting the grains. Different films consist of different amounts of grain; the more grains there are, the better the quality of the print. But when you enlarge a photograph, you will eventually see each of these grains, as well as the white spaces between them. Enlarging or magnifying a photo doesn't produce additional information, it just makes it easier to identify what's already there.

A lot of crucial evidence is developed just by making a portion of a photograph larger. In a 1984 case, for example, a suspect indicted for producing and distributing child pornography freely admitted he had made the films, but claimed to have made them more than seven years earlier. If this was true, he was protected from prosecution because

the statute of limitations would have expired. The films were sent to the lab to see if that claim could be challenged. In the lab a persistent technician went through the films frame by frame until he found a sequence in which several books were visible in the background. He enlarged those frames and looked at them under a high-magnification lens, then enlarged them again. And again. And finally he was able to identify a 1979 J. C. Penney catalogue. In 1984, the year of the indictment, that catalogue was only five years old. The statute of limitations on those frames hadn't expired, and on the basis of that evidence the suspect was successfully prosecuted.

In a Fort Lauderdale, Florida, murder case, a coroner apparently misidentified the bullet he removed from the victim, stating that its caliber differed from that of the bullet entered as evidence against the known shooter. The defendant's attorney moved for a dismissal, claiming that someone had tampered with evidence to frame his client. All that stood between a murderer and freedom was a photograph taken during the autopsy, in which the fatal bullet could be seen lying on a tray. "A bullet is a bullet," explained Gerry Richards, who served as unit chief from 1985 until his retirement in 1993, "and generally you can't see the striations because there isn't enough resolution in the photo. But we started blowing up the frame, we magnified it as far as it would go before it started falling apart, and I noticed what appeared to be random spots on the bullet. Some kind of stains. We couldn't do a firearms comparison, there wasn't that much detail, but we could see that the relationship between the stains and lines and grooves on the bullet were exactly the same as we saw on the bullet in custody. That enabled us to show that the coroner had made a simple mistake. It was the right bullet all the time."

Perhaps the most extensively examined blowups in history are those made from the Zapruder film of President

Kennedy's assassination. One particularly controversial frame has been interpreted by some people as showing a man mysteriously crouching behind bushes on the grassy knoll overlooking the scene. Other viewers see nothing more than innocent shadows. The lab has looked at the Zapruder film several times since 1963 as photo enhancement technology improved, but as Richards said, "Often making it bigger isn't the answer. What's behind that bush is a lot of skepticism. In many cases this kind of work is like cloud writing. You look up at a cloud and if you wait long enough you can see anything you want to see. You look through those leaf patterns on the Zapruder film and people are convinced that things are there, and in their mind they are. But they're not."

Because people tend to believe things they see with their own eyes, photos are often doctored, or changed. Enlarging and magnifying are among the tools used by photo examiners to help determine if a picture or a document is genuine. The examiner will look for the unusually sharp edges produced by cutting; differences in contrast or brightness; differences in proportion or scale between people or objects; differences in the direction of shadows; background information; even changes in the dot patterns. In perhaps its most controversial case, the lab was asked to determine whether a photograph printed in a Russian magazine in the late 1980s was genuine. It seemed to show two American airmen who years earlier had been listed as missing in action in Vietnam. If the picture was real, it would prove that Americans were still alive and being held captive more than two decades after the war had ended. A private sci-crime lab concluded that the photograph was real. "That was a tough one," Richards admitted. "A lot of people wanted it to be true, but there was no way that could be determined from that photograph. It was a really bad photograph to begin with; it had obviously been copied many times and then it was badly printed in the magazine. We

looked at the shadow detail, we looked at the edge detail—they were very sharp where they should have been soft. We looked at clothing patterns. But there was no way we could give a definitive answer. The best we could say was that in all probability the photograph had been altered, but it was so poor we really couldn't say much of anything.'' Several years later researchers found the original photograph from which the doctored version had been produced, finally proving that the questioned photograph was fraudulent.

Digital photography, in which images are generated by a series of numbers that can be changed by computer, has made it possible to doctor photographs without leaving any traces. Want to sail a boat in the desert? The computer can make it look real. But this same technique, digital image processing, has also made it possible for the lab to rectify problems with contrast, brightness, even focus. ''It doesn't work all the time,'' said Dick Swing, a mathematician with an expertise in optics who was fifty-five years old when he joined the lab in 1983 and has since become the oldest person working there. ''It doesn't even work most of the time, but when it does, there's usually no other way to solve the problem. It's us or nothing.''

Special Photo began adapting digital image processing to sci-crime work in 1979. The technique is based on technology created by NASA and the Jet Propulsion Laboratory for the space program, and it's actually a simplified version of the process used to clear up the blurred photos taken by the Hubble Space Telescope. The computer divides a photograph into more than 300,000 tiny squares called pixels, meaning picture elements: 480 in a row, 640 in a column. Every one of the squares is considered to be a shade of gray measured on a scale ranging from 0, which is pure black, to 250, pure white. If there isn't enough contrast, the pixels will be bunched within a relatively narrow range. So 166 on the scale will be slightly lighter than 163, but much too close for the human eye to detect any differ-

ence. By manipulating the gray scale with the computer, one can make desired portions of a photograph lighter or darker, thus creating contrast between different areas and making selected images stand out from the background. The result isn't going to be a very pretty picture, but suddenly small details like the license plate number of a truck in the distance become visible.

In a Cayce, South Carolina, murder case, the killer stole his victim's ATM card and code number and began making withdrawals. ATMs routinely photograph each person making a transaction. The photo of the killer was taken in poor light by an old camera on sixteen-millimeter film; it was so dark that local police weren't even sure there was an image on the film, but they submitted it to the lab anyway. As Swing remembered proudly, "We tried all the photographic techniques and we could see that there was something there, we just couldn't see what it was. The picture was badly exposed and badly processed, but the focus was good. We could see there was a man's face there, but we couldn't make an identification from it. And we could see that the picture had all kinds of garbage on it, things like scratches and dings and marks. We used a computer program we have called an eraser in which the computer averages the gray marks of the pixels around the marks and uses that number to correct the damage. After we cleaned it up, we stretched the contrast as much as we could and we began to see a face. Eventually we got an identifiable image; we could see the person who used the victim's card.

"Cayce police had developed a suspect. Apparently when he saw this picture, he rolled right over. He claimed that his brother had actually committed the murder, but admitted that he and his wife had been accessories. Our ability to turn that mud into a usable photograph made all the difference."

Digital image processing is also used to take out a blur or correct the focus. The problem with most criminals is

that they refuse to stand still long enough to allow sharp pictures to be taken by a surveillance camera. So their images are blurred. What the computer does, in essence, is push everything back into focus. It squeezes the image together. But to do this, it needs to find a single point of light.

After John Hinckley shot President Reagan, the lab received a series of badly blurred photographs purportedly showing Hinckley shooting at the President over the top of a limousine. But the pictures were so blurry it was impossible to even be sure the shooter was a man. The point of light was a reflection on the limousine's bumper. And while in actuality it was a point, on the blurred film it appeared to be a line. The computer "knew" that the amount of blur in the picture was equal to the length of that line, so when the line was compressed back into a point, the rest of the images also should become sharp. And that was precisely what happened. Even with this process Hinckley couldn't be positively identified—faces are very difficult to identify—but it was clear that the shooter was a man, and many of his features could be distinguished. In other cases digital imaging has allowed investigators to read license-plate numbers, logos on bank robbers' caps and shirts, and parts of documents.

In the sci-crime world a photograph isn't art, it's evidence, and it's only as valuable as what it can be used to prove. The strongest possible connection between an individual and a crime is a picture of that person committing the crime. But even when a criminal act is captured on film, from a distance the criminal will look enough like many other people to create a reasonable doubt. Making facial identification even more difficult is the fact that most photographs taken by surveillance equipment are terrible. While it isn't unusual for a camera to take as many as a thousand photographs, or a long roll of video, during a

robbery, rarely are more than a few frames usable. The lighting is bad; the robber is wearing a disguise or never looks at the camera; the image is too small; the lens is scratched; or the roll of videotape has been reused so often that the metal oxide on which the image is produced has worn off. The lab actually got a request to examine and return a video of a bank robbery in progress as quickly as possible, because the bank didn't want to have to buy another roll of tape.

The few physical identifications that can be made from photographs are made on the basis of unique characteristics. Everybody's got a head; that's a class characteristic. But a tattoo is different; it's a unique characteristic. Examiners look for permanent, unique characteristics that can be used to pick out one person from everyone else in the world, and the more of them someone has—the more scars and tattoos and freckles and birthmarks and missing teeth examiners find—the stronger the identification will be.

Marks found on any part of the body can serve as the basis for identification. Killers and rapists often take photographs of their victims so they can relive the excitement of the crime. When Baltimore police raided the apartment of a man suspected in several rapes, they found his photograph collection. Although he had carefully hidden his face from the camera in pictures taken with his victims, the lab was able to positively identify him from moles and birthmarks on his leg.

But the great majority of identifications from photographs are made by clothing comparisons. This is a real art. The shirt or blouse you are wearing may have been mass-produced—thousands of seemingly identical garments may have been made—but the clothing you are wearing right now is unique. No matter how carefully a garment is made, different garments will never be identical at the seams. Seams are random, and while great care may have been taken to ensure that, for instance, stripes on a

shirt pocket are aligned with the stripes on the shirt's body, manufacturers aren't as careful at the shoulders or in the back, places that aren't easily seen, and variations at these spots generally supply the basis of the easiest clothing identifications. The more intricate the pattern the easier it is to make an identification. The results of wear—stains, tears, loose threads, damage of any kind—are also unique and make an excellent basis for comparison.

To make a comparison between a garment seen in a photograph and a similar garment that can be associated with a suspect, Special Photo takes its own photographs of that garment being worn by a member of the unit. They will try to match the crime-scene photo as closely as possible, re-creating the lighting and posing the model in the same position. Then an examiner will compare the two photos. Finding a single unique characteristic in one garment but not in the other is enough to conclude that they are different; and while there are no specific parameters, examiners usually want to find at least three identical, unique characteristics before making a positive ident. All the stripes have to come together at the seams in precisely the same way, the rip has to be just *there,* the same scuff mark has to be on a shoe. An examiner once positively linked a suspect with an ordinary dark-blue wool cap that had been worn as a mask in a bank robbery, by counting the number of rows of threads between two holes cut for eyes.

Clothing identifications are most often made in robberies, but they have also provided significant evidence in several murder cases. After a young Indiana girl had been kidnapped, tortured, and finally strangled with a strip of cloth, police developed a suspect but had no hard evidence to connect him to the crime. They needed something, anything, that would link him to the victim. They eventually found a photograph, taken weeks before the murder, in which the suspect was standing in front of an unmade bed in a motel room. The sheet on the bed looked a lot like the

strip of cloth used to strangle the girl. The photograph was blown up so the sheet could be examined in detail. The way the pattern met at the seam was identical in the photograph and on the piece of cloth recovered with the body. The murder weapon had been the sheet seen in the photograph. This comparison was just about the only hard evidence against the suspect, but it was enough to lead to his conviction.

Years ago the legendary photographer Alfred Stieglitz reportedly told Pablo Picasso, "I don't understand your paintings. They don't look like anything." With that he showed the artist a photograph of his wife, the painter Georgia O'Keeffe. "This is my wife," he continued. "This is exactly what she looks like."

Picasso looked at the snapshot, then replied politely, "Small, isn't she?"

Among the most important clues that can be extracted from a photograph is the size of a person or an object. This is particularly good lead information in bank robberies. Sometimes a bank robber's height can be established simply by putting a height marker precisely where he stood, then photographing it with the same camera and doing an overlay, but most often it requires the use of a technique called photogrammetry. The science of photogrammetry, making measurements from photographs, was born in 1859 when a French army colonel mapped the terrain of a battlefield from a hot-air balloon. Topographic mapping is still the primary use for photogrammetry—the U.S. Geological Survey uses it, exclusively, to map this country—but Special Photo began adapting it to crime fighting in 1979 and is the only lab in the country providing this service.

Most photogrammetry is done with stereoscopic photography, in which two pictures are taken at the same instant from slightly different points. But no one ever takes stereoscopic pictures of crimes in progress, so Gerry Richards

and several co-workers in the unit pioneered the use of single-image photogrammetry, which allows measurements to be taken from a single photograph. While you see objects in all three dimensions, a photograph captures only two dimensions. The result of that is perspective: for example, railroad tracks that are actually parallel appear to converge in the distance. To determine the height of a person in a photograph, examiners have to know the exact sizes of several other objects in that photograph, including at least one object that's vertical and touching the floor. In a bank, for example, the known object might be the counter, which can be measured accurately after the robbery.

Photogrammetry uses complicated geometric formulas and permits the height of a person or object to be calculated within an inch. And that inch can mean the difference between freedom and years in prison. After a Los Angeles bank was robbed, the tellers described the robber as very tall, and police subsequently charged a six-foot-eight-inch man with the crime. He was positively identified by the tellers, none of whom was taller than five foot three. The problem was that in the photographs taken by the surveillance camera, the robber appeared to be no taller than six feet. The LAPD insisted it had the right man, but Gerry Richards insisted just as vehemently that the man seen in those photographs was only six feet tall. Eventually he flew to Los Angeles to take a new set of measurements and check his calculations. "And then I told the police, if the guy you got in jail is six-eight, he's not your man," Richards said. "He may be a bad guy, but he didn't do this one. I finally told the prosecutor, 'If you put this guy on trial, I'm going to testify for the defense.' Finally, and reluctantly, they decided to let him go."

Photogrammetry played a supporting role in the *Twilight Zone* case, in which actor Vic Morrow and two young children were killed when a helicopter crashed during the filming of a scene in which a Vietnamese village was being

bombed. Director John Landis was indicted for criminal negligence for ordering the helicopter to hover too close to the explosions, but in fact no one really knew how close to the ground the helicopter had been before it crashed. The National Transportation Safety Board asked Special Photo to determine where the helicopter was at all times and whether the crash had been caused by debris from the explosion flying into the rotor, delamination of the rotor (in which several layers that make up the rotor come unglued due to excessive heat), or simply a faulty rotor.

"Let me put it this way," Richards remembered. "After we got done laughing, we told them it was impossible. Then we started figuring out how to do it. The techniques we normally use to make photogrammetric measurements depend on having manmade objects that are straight and level and either vertical or perpendicular. Here we were dealing with round thatched huts. There was nothing straight, nothing level. We eventually figured out that the only thing in the pictures that we might be able to use were the helicopter's landing skids. They weren't square, but they were parallel to each other. We also had about twenty known factors: the camera speed, the size of the frame, the focal length of the lens, the distance between the skids, and so on. By combining all of this information, we were able to draw rays, or vertical lines, from the ground to the helicopter, and we plotted its position as each explosion went off. We figured out that it was about twenty-four feet above the ground and its tail rotor was directly over the fourth and fifth explosions when they went off, and that's when they lost control.

"Was that too close to the ground? There's no legal definition of that, but the jury decided there was no criminal negligence. Could we isolate the cause of the crash? No. The prosecutors wanted me to testify that bamboo flying up from the hut had hit the rotor and caused it to detach. When we enlarged the film and slowed it down, we could

see all sorts of junk flying up there. I said it looked like bamboo and it was shaped like bamboo, but there was no scientific way of concluding that it *was* bamboo. The only thing I could say was that there was a lot of garbage flying around after the explosion, and in one frame the rotor was there, and then it was gone.''

Another difficulty often encountered in working with still photographs is that they are still: they have been taken from one position, sometimes the wrong position. But in some cases it's actually possible to change that position after the photograph has been taken. The technique is called warping, or rubber sheeting, and it's done to eliminate the distortion caused by perspective. At many crime scenes the photographer stands in the doorway and shoots the entire room, meaning everything in that room is distorted. And later, when examiners inspect the photographs, they may find something that had been overlooked—a shoeprint in dust under a television set, for example. Potentially there's a lot of good lead information in that print, but it's only valuable to investigators if it can be seen at actual size, as if it had been photographed from directly overhead so that it might be accurately measured. Two methods are used to rectify the image, to make it look as if it had been photographed from above in what is called an orthographic, or ''true,'' projection.

A special rectifying enlarger, which works by tilting both the lens and the image, can be used if the angle to be corrected is less than fifteen degrees. But if it's greater than that, and it almost always is, then the work has to be done by computer. The computer rotates the image of the shoeprint, recalculates its size on the basis of the degree to which it had to be stretched or compressed, and then fills in the missing areas. This is a sort of futuristic trick photography, and it turns dust into evidence.

Valuable clues can also be found in shadows. Special Photo receives photographs from local police departments

that want to know when the photos were taken. In fact, one of the tests given to photo examiners in training is to determine from a picture the time of the day and the day of the year it was taken. Shadow analysis, which is used by military intelligence to decipher aerial photographs, can often answer those questions. Shadows move with the sun, so there are only two days each year during which a person or an object in a specific place will cast exactly the same shadow. If an examiner knows where a photograph was taken, he can figure out the latitude and longitude, and from that determine on which two days a shadow would have a given length. Other clues in the photograph—the type of clothing worn, whether the trees are bare or the flowers are blooming—allow it to be narrowed down to a specific date. If the relationship of the shadow to true north is known—if it is known which way the camera was pointing—it's relatively simple to determine from the length and the angle of the shadow what time of day the photo was taken.

Conversely, shadows can be used to determine where a photograph was taken if you know when it was shot, although obviously the real key to figuring that out comes from the images in the picture. When a known terrorist was arrested in Washington, D.C., several photographs of the city were found in her possession. From the view, it was obvious they had been taken from the dome of the Capitol. This is a restricted area, with very limited access; whoever took those pictures shouldn't have been there. Since it could be determined when the pictures were taken, finding exactly where they were taken might lead to the associate of the terrorist who took them, or at least to the person who provided access to the area. An examiner taped a negative inside a camera so he could see it when he looked through the viewfinder, then walked around the dome until he found the exact spot where he could align the negative with the view. The photo had been taken from a walkway on the

second level, and by checking security logbooks agents learned who had been in that area when the picture was taken.

One of the Bureau's most important responsibilities is covert surveillance. It secretly watches bad guys: spies, members of organized crime, drug dealers, money launderers, crooked politicians, and anyone else conducting illegal activities in this country. Such surveillance often requires the use of specialized cameras, lenses, and film, some of which were developed by the military for intelligence work. The FBI "air force" includes several small airplanes equipped with high-resolution aerial cameras capable of both daytime and nighttime surveillance. Long lenses are used to photograph objects from as far as a quarter mile away. When inmates rioted and took control of Talladaga Prison in Alabama, photographs taken from a great distance provided vital information about the location of the hostages, the types of weapons the prisoners had, the weak points in their security, even the way the doors opened and how they were hinged.

"Concealments"—hidden cameras—were once limited by the size of the camera required to produce usable photographs, but technology has made it possible to hide cameras just about anywhere. Concealments can be as small as a pinhole in a wall or as large as the entire wall. Special Photo has built cameras into books and briefcases and heating ducts and lamps and light fixtures; it has put them in tie clips and gift-wrapped packages. For one bribery investigation a camera was built into a hand-carved wooden state seal that eventually hung in the office of the state treasurer.

The ideal place to hide a camera is somewhere that will cause people to stare right into the lens. Television sets make excellent concealments because people look directly at them. In a New York City undercover operation being

run out of a bar, a camera was hidden behind a painting of a beautiful nude woman hung in a back room; the sensible assumption was that every man coming into that room was eventually going to take a long look at that painting. When a nurse in a Virginia veterans' hospital was suspected of stealing from patients, a camera installed behind an exit sign above the door caught her in the act. Concealed cameras are capable of operating for months without being serviced, and can shoot as many as sixteen hundred pictures on a single roll of film. The shutter can be triggered manually, by remote control, or even by sensors set off by the subject.

Among the special equipment employed by the lab is a thermo-camera, or thermoimager, which enables investigators to photograph differences in temperature. These cameras produce an image on a monitor, rather than a traditional print. They are often used in searches to find hiding places. Walls are heated, usually with a hair dryer; because recesses hold heat longer than the rest of the wall will, they show up on the monitor. Electronic thermo-cameras are used to locate wall safes, for example, but an imager was also used to search the apartment of a Dallas, Texas, serial killer who was believed to have hidden a jar filled with his victims' eyeballs in a recess in a wall. That jar was never found.

Infrared and ultraviolet filters and lighting enable investigators to see through things, to read documents through sealed envelopes, to read writing that has been obliterated, and to see other things that can't be seen under normal light with the naked eye. The human eye sees only a portion of the entire light spectrum; in that visible portion, four things can happen to an object. It can reflect light, in which case it will appear white. It can absorb light, and appear black. It can reflect some of the light and be visible as a color. Or the light energy passes through it, so it appears transparent.

Alternate light sources—X-ray, infrared, and ultraviolet—make it possible for human beings to see portions of the light spectrum not normally visible. The importance of this to detectives is that different objects, among them inks, respond differently to the various forms of light. Some will get lighter, some will get darker, and some, because they are not visible at that portion of the spectrum, will become transparent. They will just disappear. While alternate light sources and filters are most often used in document examinations, they have also proven valuable in a variety of applications. After a San Diego woman was brutally beaten and raped, police sent the FBI lab the filthy paisley blouse she had been wearing. Her attacker had left a muddy shoeprint or palmprint on the blouse, but the multicolored fabric made it impossible to see the print clearly. When the blouse was photographed using infrared lighting and filters, the fabric seemed to disappear, leaving a clear photograph of the muddy shoeprint.

When the battered body of a Des Moines woman was found on a lonely gravel road, police searched the home of the man last seen with her. Although he claimed that she was alive when he dropped her off, in his home police found burnt fragments of what seemed to be the strap of a woman's pocketbook, and a few charred pieces of a photograph. With infrared lights the camera could see right through the blackened crust coating the photograph, and the victim's relative identified it as a picture of her niece. Presumably, the photo had been in the victim's pocketbook. The fact that it was found in the suspect's possession was enough for a jury. The suspect was convicted of second-degree murder and sentenced to fifty years in prison.

The lab's permanent setup for photographing evidence under alternate light sources is the only one of its kind in regular use. The camera provides high-quality resolution and a very permanent record—you get the hard evidence that can be used in a courtroom—and with a time exposure

the camera can take a good picture of a very weak image. This became important when the body of a Texas woman was found clutching a ballpoint pen. Police, discovering some marks on her hand, believed that before she died she had written the name of her killer on her hand. But the printing was too faint to be read. At the suggestion of an examiner, the police severed the victim's hand, packed it in dry ice, and sent it to the lab. Under alternate lighting some writing could be seen, but still not clearly enough to be read. Then examiners tried photographing the hand with night scopes, which are extremely light-sensitive. While that made the printing slightly more legible, it still couldn't be deciphered. This was terribly frustrating; the killer's name was right in front of the investigators, but they just couldn't see it. Finally, they used the night scope to make a time exposure; they left the lens open for hours, which allowed the faint light emanating from the writing to "burn" an image into the film. After several hours they were able to read the name the woman had written on her hand in the final seconds of her life, providing a vital clue for investigators. They had successfully photographed something that didn't seem to be there.

The Video Enhancement Unit, seven people working in a $4 million broadcast-quality studio located in the basement of the headquarters building, began in the early 1980s as part of Special Photo and became an independent unit in 1990. "What sets us apart down here," said unit chief Don Brager, who joined the Identification Section in 1978 as a clerk and eventually became the first non-agent to head a lab unit, "besides the fact that we're down here, of course, is that we're all young, we're all ambitious to the point of being aggressive, and we run our unit like a committee. There's great teamwork and camaraderie elsewhere in the lab, but I think we go further than anybody else. We're certainly the most informal unit in the lab. We dress nice

when we have to, but mostly we're crawling around running cables, so generally we're pretty informal.''

In the early 1980s video cameras cost as much as $10,000, well beyond the budgets of most police departments, but as the equipment became affordable, the world of Special Video changed drastically. For the first time accidents and crimes were being taped as they happened, creating a new kind of hard evidence. Video enhancement specialists, or analysts, as the members of this unit are officially titled, are responsible for converting videotapes into usable evidence, and that can mean restoring it, enhancing it, interpreting images, or adding information like time codes or subtitles. Occasionally, they even produce tapes.

Tapes arrive in the lab in every conceivable condition. They have been burned and scratched and scraped and stretched and twisted and cut into pieces. They have been erased and flushed down toilets and retrieved from plane crashes and garbage dumps. In some cases the only request is to try to find anything, even one frame, on the tape. ''We do a lot of things in here that no one else has tried,'' said Bob Keller, a TV and radio major at Ball State University who started in the Bureau's office of public affairs. ''Basically, we find that there's a need to do something unusual, then we try to figure out how to do it. There are really no textbooks to go to; our best sources are the people who manufacture this equipment. We had a case in here in which a military aircraft flew into a mountain, and no one had any idea why. The pilots gave no indication that they had a malfunction; they just ran into the mountain. There was a three-quarter-inch video recorder in the nose of this plane that records what the pilot is seeing on his radar screen. The military came to us with some mangled tape that had been retrieved from the wreckage and asked if there was anything we could do with it. I didn't think there was. I mean, this stuff looked like strands of spaghetti.

''One of the things we're proud of in here is that we

never say no. This whole area is still so new even we're not sure what's possible. The tape looked awful, it had kind of shriveled up in the fire, but experts from the 3M Corporation advised us to try putting a wet cloth over it and then iron it. We did, and it spread out somewhat. It turned out that the tape wasn't as damaged as it originally appeared to be and we were finally able to play it. I didn't know what I was looking at, but there were two military pilots working with us, and as soon as they saw this thing, they knew exactly what had happened. And basically, it turned out to be pilot error. They saw one mountain; unfortunately, they never saw the other one.''

Sometimes tape damage isn't accidental. Sometimes people realize that a tape they have made could put them in prison, and try to destroy it. For example, a Baltimore, Maryland, crack addict calmly set up a tripod and taped himself raping a young girl in her living room. Then he killed her mother. Later, when he realized that the police were closing in on him, he dowsed the tape with lighter fluid and burned it. A few fragments were recovered by police and delivered to the FBI lab in a plastic bag. Most of the magnetic oxide, the part of the tape that carries the image, had been burned off. But examiners were able to develop partial images on a few frames; these showed the rape in progress. It wasn't very much, but it identified the suspect clearly, and when these bits of tape were shown in a courtroom, they were enough to convict him of rape and murder.

While most of the units in the lab deal with brutality and death on a daily basis, only the people in Video Enhancement actually see people dying. As camcorders have become ubiquitous in society, it's no longer rare for a deadly accident or a murder to be recorded. In a typical case, two teenaged boys taped themselves on an all-day drinking spree. They were having a great time; they were laughing, mugging for the camera. But the tape ended abruptly in

their car when they crashed head-on into another vehicle. The crash resulted in the death of three people. The lab got the case because police wanted to know how fast the boys were driving when they lost control of the car. The Video Unit reconstructed the tape, then enhanced it so as to be able to read the speedometer just before the impact, and reported the car was approaching ninety miles per hour.

Another tape showed a happy family on their small boat, out on a lake for a summer afternoon of waterskiing. Over the shoulder of a child on water skis, another boat can be seen coming toward them. That tape also ends suddenly and tragically: that other boat, being driven by a drunk boater, crashed into the family and killed everyone except the skier. Three months after the accident, the tape was recovered from the lake bottom; when the lab restored it, the details of the fatal accident became chillingly clear.

"It's really sad sometimes," Brager said softly, "really sad. You just have to learn to separate yourself. We see things in here . . . A guy robbed a convenience store, we see him on the surveillance camera. The security guard comes out and the robber shoots him in the head. You're actually seeing the gunshot on tape. You see the guard's body reel back, you see him collapse on the ground, and he's huddled against a wall. Just sitting there, and then his body goes limp. You just saw a man die. It's not TV or the movies; it's not easy to watch. Sometimes I try to make myself believe it isn't real, that it was just a TV show."

Police investigating that murder wanted the lab analysts to enhance the video, to see if they could produce a clear picture of the killer or determine what kind of gun he used. The video unit, like Special Photo, can use several techniques to improve the quality of a tape. They can lighten or darken it; the image can be sharpened or enlarged; a small section of the image can be isolated; the speed of the action can be changed; and much of the "noise," the graininess and scratches caused by the metal head of the recorder

grinding off bits of magnetic oxide, can be reduced. While the unit was able to produce a better picture of the convenience store, there just wasn't enough information on the tape to lead to the gunman.

The unit was a lot more successful in helping Garrison, Texas, police solve the 1991 murder of Constable Darrell Lunsford. After a suspect apprehended by Lunsford in a drug-smuggling case was released by the court because of a lack of evidence, Lunsford mounted a video camera on the dashboard of his patrol car so he could record his arrests. The camera was running the night he stopped three men who appeared to be driving recklessly. As videotaped in the headlights of his patrol car, Lunsford started to open the trunk of the other vehicle—which was later found to have contained forty thousand dollars' worth of marijuana—when the three men grabbed his gun, pushed him into a ditch, and shot him in the head. While the actual shooting was not on tape, the initial struggle was recorded. Lunsford's body was found in that ditch; his video camera was still running.

Although the three men couldn't be seen clearly enough in the dim light to be positively identified, the video enabled police to develop a general description, and the men were arrested within the next few days.

The first thing that happens when a tape arrives at the lab is that copies are made. Original tapes are evidence; they can't be changed in any way. Working on the copies prevents defense attorneys from claiming that someone has tampered with the evidence. In the Lunsford case, the unit was able to substantially improve the contrast, eliminate much of the "noise," and sharpen the focus. The three men, who could barely be seen on the original tape, were clearly identifiable on the enhanced tape. There was little other hard evidence to link the three men to Lunsford's murder. No weapon was found, and there were no witnesses. There was just this videotape. The jury watched it

in complete silence, then convicted all three men of murder.

There have been several well-publicized cases in which the unit has been asked to make an identification from a poor-quality tape. In 1989, when terrorists announced that they had hanged Marine Lieutenant Colonel William Higgins in retaliation for the Israeli kidnapping of a Shiite Muslim clergyman, they released a badly blurred video of a man hanging from a rope in a prison cell. From that video it was almost impossible to be certain the body was really that of Lieutenant Colonel Higgins. The Defense Department wanted two questions answered: Was that Higgins's body in the video? And if so, when had he been killed?

Certain clues seen on the tape made it likely that the victim had been killed long before the video was released, before the clergyman was kidnapped. Although supposedly hanged in midsummer, the victim was dressed in winter clothing. Also pathologists noted that the body did not exhibit the usual results of hanging: open mouth, bulging eyes, protruding tongue, darkened eyes, loosened bowels, and elongated neck. This indicated that the man had been killed earlier, and not by hanging, and that his body had been preserved until the tape was made.

Proving that it was the body of Lieutenant Colonel Higgins was more difficult. Unit analysts decided to try to compare Higgins's facial features to those of the victim. They began by making a video of the last known photograph of Higgins ever taken. "We wanted to do an overlay," Bob Keller explained. "But because the body was in a different position in the two videos we had to change its position. We can do that with a video image. We can move a video frame on its axis. We can turn it and twist it and flip it. It's just as if you were holding a photograph in your hand; anything you can do with that photograph we can do with a video frame. They do it all the time on television.

But we can't create information that isn't there. If you turned over a photograph you'd see a blank side. We can't turn an image around and look at the other side."

When the figures in the two videos were about the same size and in the same position, lab examiners created an overlay and slowly went back and forth between the two images, using what is known as a wipe pattern. Starting at the very top of the head, a horizontal strip from the photograph was superimposed over the video. Then a second strip, then a third . . . As the strips moved down the screen, it became obvious that the facial features were just about identical. Everything matched: the recession of the hairline, an indentation in the forehead, the depth of the eye sockets, the ear orifice and the nose. The figure in the terrorist video had tape over his mouth, so that was as much of a comparison as could be made. But it was enough to allow the FBI to announce, "A positive identification could not be made, but numerous observable characteristics were noted indicating that the person in the videotape was Lieutenant Colonel Higgins."

In a somewhat similar case, when the body of an American airman supposedly washed up on a beach in a hostile country, the State Department obtained a videotape and asked the lab to confirm that it was one of two men listed as missing in action over that nation. It was an almost impossible job because the body apparently had been floating in the ocean for quite some time: it was bloated and decomposing. "When you look at something like this tape you just sigh and go to work," Bob Keller said. "We did some research and found out that there's only one part of a body that doesn't swell up in the water, and that's the ear, which is basically all cartilage. We also learned that while most facial characteristics change through life, the shape of the earlobe remains the same. So we wondered if we could do an ear comparison.

In Higgins's case that wasn't possible because not

enough of the victim's earlobes were visible in the original video, but in this case the position of the victim's head allowed this comparison to be done. After obtaining recent photographs of both of the missing airmen, Keller remembered, "We decided to try to do an overlay. We wanted to lay the ears in the photographs right over the ear visible in the video. We were able to turn the body slightly; it was enough. Once we'd put the ears in about the same position and made them about the same size, doing the layover was pretty basic. We just dissolved back and forth between the video and the photo. Now, this might not have worked if we'd been asked to identify the ear on the video from millions of others, but we didn't have to. It was just whether or not it was one of two known airmen. And when we did the comparison, we could be almost one hundred percent positive that it was."

In addition to enhancing the quality of a tape, the Video Unit will use basic technical means to make it easier for a jury to understand what it is seeing. During surveillance of a drug operation, for example, Washington, D.C., police taped two men passing a briefcase filled with cocaine, but the exchange was made so smoothly and so quickly it was hard to really see it happening. Video normally runs at 29.9 frames per second, but when the tape was slowed to a few frames per second, it was very easy to see the briefcase being passed. When one of the suspects saw himself on the tape, he immediately confessed, and implicated other members of the drug organization.

Perhaps the most famous homemade video in history was a very badly lit, grainy, black-and-white tape showing Los Angeles policemen brutally clubbing a man named Rodney King. Solely on the basis of this tape, the officers were indicted for assault with a deadly weapon. When the tape was submitted to the lab, it was copied onto high-grade broadcast tape, which preserves the quality far longer than most commercially available tapes, and then a

time code was added, enabling jurors to see exactly how much time elapsed between blows and how long the entire attack lasted. It was a routine job and probably didn't affect the outcome of the case at all. The first trial resulted in a hung jury, a decision that sparked the devastating riots in South Central Los Angeles, and in the second trial, a federal trial, the officers were convicted of violating King's civil rights.

The Bureau's audio work—planting microphones and enhancing soundtracks—is done by a unit in the Information Resources Division, but as videotape generally carries an audio track, these two units often work together. More than a year after $7 million was stolen from Wells Fargo in West Hartford, Connecticut—at that time this was the second-largest robbery in U.S. history—agents from the San Juan office planted a microphone in the apartment used by members of a Puerto Rican pro-independence group believed to have participated in the heist. As several members of the gang, Los Macheteros, watched a Boston PBS documentary about the unsolved robbery, they made incriminating comments that were picked up by the bug. They were arrested and Video Enhancement was asked to synchronize this audiotape with the documentary, so a jury would understand the meaning of their comments. But the gang members had been speaking in Spanish, and what really made this tape valuable to prosecutors were the English subtitles added to it, then synchronized with the action. It suddenly became very clear to the jury what one of the suspects meant when he said, as he watched a dramatization of the crime, ''Remember that?''

A videotape contains much more information than immediately meets the eye—if an examiner knows what to look for and how to use it. Far in the background of a tape made by a security camera during a Dover, Delaware, bank robbery, an examiner noticed, was a car parked in front of the bank. The car remained there throughout the robbery,

and when the robber fled, it disappeared. Police weren't even aware of this getaway car until it was spotted on the tape, and it subsequently became an important lead in their investigation.

In a case that required the video unit to use almost all of its technical capabilities—enhancement, comparison, the addition of information, even production—three blurry frames shot by an ATM time-lapse videocamera were turned into the hard evidence needed to convict a man named Robert Auker of the murder of his wife.

On May 24, 1989, nineteen-year-old Lori Ann Auker simply disappeared from the face of the earth. The next day her car was found in the parking lot of a Northumberland County, Pennsylvania, mall, where she worked in a pet shop. She had gone to work, but she never got there. Nineteen days after she was last seen alive, her body was found at the bottom of an embankment. She had been stabbed at least seven times. Her estranged husband, with whom she was involved in a custody suit over their child, immediately became the prime suspect. But for more than a year police were unable to find enough evidence to link him to the crime.

As it turned out, there had been a silent witness to her abduction. A time-lapse video camera hidden in an automated teller machine outside the Northern Central Bank in the mall took a photograph in which a specific section of the parking lot could be seen in the background. Although the bank had several surveillance cameras, they were all connected to a single video recorder which alternated between the different cameras, so the image seen by this camera was recorded at ten-second intervals. The tape had been reused so often that most of the oxide had been worn off. It was almost transparent, so a Northumberland detective brought it to the lab to see if it could be enhanced and examined. Regular video shoots almost thirty frames a second, but time-lapse video, which is used in place of still

photography, shoots only one or two frames a second. So there might be a week's worth of information on a two-hour tape. Bob Keller watched the blurry tape with the detective. "The police were interested in seeing what was on this tape because they'd found her car in the parking lot," Keller remembered. "They wanted to know if we could see anything unusual. Maybe she'd been taped pulling into the lot or walking toward the bank. They were looking for any leads.

"When the detective and I watched the tape we didn't see her pull in, but he pointed out to me where her car had been found. We looked at the few frames they wanted me to see, and in the last frame I saw a blurred person way in the distance—it might have been a woman—walking toward the camera. For some reason the police hadn't associated this person with the victim. So I decided to watch a little more of the tape than they had. Three frames in particular caught my attention. In the first frame I saw a figure coming toward the bank. In the second frame, taken ten seconds later, a car had backed out of a parking spot and the door on the passenger side was open. The figure was just barely visible. But ten seconds later both the car and the figure were gone. That was really strange, I thought. Logically, within that time frame the car might have been gone, but we still should have seen that person coming closer. The probable explanation was that the person had gotten into the car. I told the detective, 'It looks to me like whoever was driving that car is the person you want to speak to.'

"The problem we had was that the quality of those frames was awful. When a tape is playing in a time-lapse mode, or when it's on pause, the metal heads just grind against the oxide. So you get very few plays in the time-lapse mode. In this case the images were just barely visible. An ATM camera is focused on the person using the machine; that's who the bank wants to get a good look at. We

were looking beyond that into the parking lot, so the image was out of focus, it was blurred, and the oxide was just about worn off the tape. In fact, there was a potentially important frame that we saw only once; then the last of the oxide fell off and we never could get it back again.''

Although the car was visible on only one frame, it was identified from the taillight assembly as a Chevy Celebrity made between 1982 and 1985. Robert Auker's father owned a 1984 Chevrolet Celebrity, and he admitted that his son had been using it the day Lori Auker disappeared.

The day after Lori Auker's disappearance, the car had been sold, and subsequently had been resold several times. By the time the police found it, it was owned by a Pennsylvania state trooper. This was a long time after the murder; although the car was thoroughly searched, all police found were a few hairs and a little bit of blood, nothing that enabled them to associate the car with either the suspect or the victim.

"The police were sort of out of ideas," Keller continued, "So I told them, 'If you think the car in the video is the car you have in custody, why don't you recreate the video using the same ATM machine. Put the car in the same spot and try to recreate those three frames. That way you'll have a known and a questioned, then you can do a comparison to see if they really are identical. That's the way we work in the lab.' "

At that time Video Enhancement did not have some of the more sophisticated video equipment available, so Don Brager contacted Al Teitjan, a video expert who had done most of the video enhancement work for NASA after the space shuttle *Challenger* exploded. Teitjan agreed to help produce the reconstruction. After the second video had been shot, someone realized that the car mistakenly had been put one parking spot farther away from the ATM machine than the questioned car, a problem Teitjan corrected by enlarging the image to make it appear closer.

Before making the comparison, Teitjan used computerized digital enhancement—the same method used by Special Photo—to remove some of the blurriness and improve the contrast in the original video. He divided the image into pixels and changed selected gray levels to make the person and the car stand out from the background. After that Teitjan and Brager did a wipe, just as had been done in the Higgins case, replacing the car seen in the questioned video with the known car. As Keller recalled, "We put one on top of the other and you could see the similarities were very great. And we never had to say it was the same car. The jury saw this tape and made that determination for itself."

There was additional circumstantial evidence against Auker. He claimed to have been at a store in another mall when his wife was abducted, yet clerks in that store testified they hadn't seen him that day. He had taken out a life insurance policy on his estranged wife just weeks before her murder, but had tried to backdate it. The jury deliberated slightly more than an hour before convicting Robert Auker of kidnapping and murder, then took just a little longer in the penalty phase to recommend death.

While you may not realize it, your picture is probably being taken several times every day. Due to the availability of inexpensive camcorders, point-and-shoot cameras, and throwaway cameras and to the increasing use of security cameras, surprisingly good evidence has been provided in many cases. To take advantage of this new source of hard evidence, the FBI is currently considering establishing regional imaging centers at many of its field offices. These computer-based systems will enable agents to enhance, focus, or sharpen potential evidence right on the spot rather than being dependent on the lab. The Video Enhancement Unit, like Special Photo, will manage and support these systems as well as actively participating in the most sensitive cases.

* * *

Another small unit in the Document Section, the Polygraph Unit, does that right now. In addition to maintaining quality-control responsibility over the fifty-one field agents trained to conduct polygraph examinations, the unit performs the most important tests itself. The polygraph, popularly known as the lie detector, may be the most misunderstood of all sci-crime instruments. Most people believe the polygraph is used almost exclusively to determine guilt or innocence, that it can be "beaten" by sociopaths, and that information obtained in polygraph examinations isn't admissible in court.

Not true. The lab uses the polygraph as an investigative tool to help develop leads and evidence and to verify information; only on occasion is it used to help determine guilt or innocence. According to Document Section chief Ron Furgerson, who previously ran the Polygraph Unit, "We're never testing for ground truth. We're testing what the subject believes to be the truth, which is very different. Anybody who believes he is telling the truth is going to pass this test." For this reason, anybody—sociopaths, psychopaths, schizophrenics, the toughest prisoners, experienced espionage agents—can be tested, and the results may prove useful in the investigation. And while the results of a polygraph exam are permitted to be introduced in a trial only by prior agreement of both the prosecution and the defense, a confession made during the test is admissible as long as the polygraph exam itself is not discussed.

Rudimentary versions of the modern polygraph have been used by various cultures for thousands of years. Lie detection is based on the fact that people worry about being exposed when they lie, and that fear or anxiety causes measurable physiological changes.

The ancient Chinese made suspects chew dry rice, then spit it out. Fear causes the digestive system to slow down, producing a dry mouth, which in turn makes it difficult for

guilty people to generate enough saliva to spit out the rice. Arabs would put a donkey with a greased tail in a darkened tent, then would warn suspects that when the donkey's tail was pulled by a guilty man the animal would bray. Those who emerged from the tent without grease on their hands were presumed guilty.

The very first lie-detecting machine, the hydrophygmograph, was invented in 1895 and measured changes in the pulse rate and blood pressure of a subject being questioned. In 1921 John Larsen developed an instrument that continuously recorded changes in blood pressure, pulse rate, and respiration during questioning; he named this instrument the polygraph.

For a time it was believed to be infallible. It caused banner headlines in the early 1930s when Bruno Hauptmann, the accused kidnapper and killer of Charles Lindbergh's baby, failed a crucial polygraph test. But in 1938, when lie-detector tests given in a Florida kidnapping-murder indicated that an innocent man was guilty and that the person who later confessed to the crime was innocent, FBI director J. Edgar Hoover ordered agents to "throw that box into Biscayne Bay."

The Bureau continued using it on an occasional basis—after Jack Ruby shot Kennedy assassin Lee Harvey Oswald at point-blank range on national TV, he demanded a lie-detector test to prove he did not know Oswald—until 1964, when Hoover banned it from the FBI completely. That proved embarrassing in 1971 when, directed by President Richard Nixon to find the source of leaks of sensitive material from the State Department, the Bureau was forced to borrow polygraph equipment from the New York City police department. That episode rekindled interest in the polygraph, which, ironically, proved its value two years later when tests given to White House aides Jeb Magruder and Gordon Strachan helped expose the Watergate cover-up.

The sci-crime lab's Polygraph Unit was established in

1978. Since then the lie detector has proved to be an extremely valuable investigative tool. It's a tool, not the answer, and that's the key to its use in the lab. "We interview and obtain information from a wide variety of sources," explained Jim Murphy, the tall, distinguished-looking chief of the Polygraph Unit. "This information needs to be corroborated, and the polygraph is a very cost-effective way of doing that. We know it's not perfect, it's not equal to the truth; but, for the most part, it's a reliable indicator of the truthfulness of what someone says. Simply put, it's an effective way to get a confession from somebody or develop information that's going to solve a crime for you. We need people to tell us what happened."

The success of a polygraph examination is directly related to a subject's fear of detection. Sometimes the test isn't even necessary. After four guards were killed during the attempted robbery of an armored car in Denver, thirty-six of the thirty-eight company employees who had the insider's knowledge required to plan the holdup agreed to take the test. In the belief that innocent people have little to fear from the machine, police immediately focused their investigation on the two men who refused to be tested, and within a short period of time they developed enough evidence to charge one of those men with masterminding the crime.

People's beliefs about what the polygraph is capable of doing are sometimes more valuable than what it actually can do. After three American nuns and a lay worker had been raped and murdered in El Salvador, the U.S. State Department put tremendous pressure on that country's government to allow Salvadorian National Guard troops known to have been in the area to be tested. Special Agent Sinecio Gutierrez conducted the tests in Spanish. The guardsmen were understandably nervous, and the test was set up to magnify that fear. Gutierrez began by warning them that the machine would know when they were lying.

To prove this, he conducted what's called a stimulation test. He had the men write down a number between 10 and 20 and hide the paper in their pocket. When the test accurately determined the number they had picked, the troops were convinced of the machine's powers. Four of the guardsmen confessed to their participation in the crime, implicated high officers, and told agents exactly what had happened. Their fear of being caught lying was enough to trigger their confessions.

Often the Bureau relies on the machine to determine the value of a subject's information. "When an FBI agent was murdered in Kansas City," Jim Murphy said, "a fifty-thousand-dollar reward for information was offered. So we had a lot of people coming forward with information. Obviously, they wanted that money. We could have wasted a lot of time tracking down all those leads. Instead we put them all on the machine, which enabled us to determine the value of their material. We had one woman who came in with very detailed information. She claimed to have been with the men who killed the agent; she even drew a diagram. Well, we really thought we had something. But after reluctantly agreeing to take a polygraph test, she failed it. And then she admitted that she'd made up the whole story to collect the reward." The killers were eventually caught by other investigative means, but the polygraph played an important role by eliminating suspects.

At the very beginning of New York State's Tawana Brawley case, in which a black teenager claimed to have been kidnapped, sexually assaulted, and otherwise abused by four white men, a woman said she had seen Brawley climb into the plastic trash bag in which she was found, the bag Brawley later said she had been forced into by her tormentors. When the woman voluntarily took a polygraph test and passed it, the Bureau began to question the teenager's tale, and other evidence was developed that disproved it.

In 1992, Haitian army captain Stagne Doura, a former commander of the national penitentiary, claimed that deposed Haitian president Jean-Bertrand Aristide had personally ordered him to kill a prisoner named Roger Lafontant. Lafontant had been a member of dictator Jean-Claude Duvalier's cabinet. Doura said that Aristide had threatened to kill him if he failed to carry out this order. Lafontant was murdered that night. This was a very sensitive case because the U.S. government was actively trying to restore the democratically elected Aristide to power. The U.S. State Department asked the FBI to administer a polygraph test to Doura. The Bureau reported that the tests showed ''no attempt at deception.'' Doura was telling what he believed to be the truth: Aristide had ordered a summary execution. Even though his claims were probably true, the State Department took no further action in this case.

But sometimes, however, polygraph screenings unexpectedly reveal crucial information that does lead to prosecution. One day a woman named Barbara Walker contacted the Boston field office and claimed that her ex-husband was a Soviet spy. She hadn't lived with the man for more than a decade, and she seemed to have some personal problems, so initially agents were quite skeptical. But certain parts of her story were too detailed to have been made up. Only after she volunteered to take a polygraph test—and passed it—did the Bureau begin to take her accusations seriously. As a result, they were able to smash a major espionage operation, and John Walker was convicted of spying for the Russians and sentenced to life imprisonment.

But the polygraph test that provided the most stunning result began as a simple confirmation of an FBI agent's sworn statement. After a young woman in Pikeville, Kentucky, disappeared, her relatives told police that the last person known to have been with her was an FBI agent named Mark Putnam. Putnam had worked in the Pikeville

office for several years before being routinely transferred to Miami. During that time, the woman had been one of his informers. She had disappeared at about the same time Putnam was back in Kentucky testifying in a trial. Putnam admitted that the woman had worked for him, but denied her relatives' claims that they had had an affair. He gave a sworn statement to investigators in which he said he had no knowledge about her disappearance.

To prove to Kentucky authorities that the FBI had conducted a thorough investigation, the Bureau's Office of Professional Responsibility, Internal Affairs, asked Putnam to take a polygraph test. It was routine, perfunctory, the kind of test given every day. Except on that day, to everyone's astonishment, the examination results indicated that Putnam had indeed had an affair with the woman and had probably killed her. When told that he had failed the test, Putnam broke down. He admitted that he had had an affair with his informer, had panicked when she became pregnant, and had strangled her to death. Because the only evidence against him was his own statement, which was compelled by the results of the polygraph exam, his lawyer was able to arrange a plea bargain, and he was sentenced to only eight years in prison.

The fact that Putnam confessed after failing the test wasn't unusual. A complete examination consists of three phases: a pre-test interview, the exam, and the post-test interrogation. If the results of the post-test interrogation indicate that the subject has not been truthful, the examiner will explain that and give him the opportunity to talk about it. At that time, according to statistics, more than half the people who have failed will either confess or change their story. That's precisely what happened when Special Agent Salvador Escobedo tested an employee of the DuPont Plaza Hotel in San Juan, Puerto Rico, after a deliberately set fire killed ninety-six people and caused $10 million in damage. After the employee had failed the test, Escobedo gently

asked him if he wanted to talk about it. He broke down, admitted starting the fire, and named the two other men who had been with him. Eventually all three men confessed and received prison sentences of a minimum of seventy-five years.

A polygraph exam is not nearly as dramatic as it's made to be in movies. When possible, it's conducted in a small, quiet room with nothing hanging on the walls that might distract the subject. "The atmosphere's created to give us every possible psychological advantage," explained Murphy. "When a subject comes in, we start by talking to him about the facts of the case, and we take down his statement or alibi. But right at the beginning, we warn him that if he doesn't tell the truth he's going to fail the test. I always suggest that if he's going to lie to me, he shouldn't waste my time or his time. He should just get up and leave. And I don't care who it is, no matter how guilty that person is, he never leaves. Never. He knows that leaving at that point would be an admission of guilt. So now I've got a captive subject.

"We try to be natural and sincere and friendly. I usually tell them that my job is to help them get through the test, but that to do so they're going to have to cooperate with me. One case I had, a Washington, D.C., man was accused of having committed a rape about six months earlier. In the pre-test, he denied it completely, but he remembered exactly where he'd been that night, which I thought was unusual. I mean, how many people can tell you where they were on a particular night six months earlier? When I actually conducted the exam, I asked him if he'd been at the place he mentioned on the night of the rape, and he answered yes. I took a deep breath, a loud deep breath, and told him, 'Look, I want to help you get through this, but that alibi just isn't going to work. You're going to have to give me a better one.' So he said, 'Okay, let me try this one. . . .' Gradually I was able to get him to admit that

he'd had sex with the victim, but he insisted it was consensual, that she was accusing him of rape to get even with him for something. But he was the rapist and eventually he was convicted of the crime.''

Before the examiner begins the test, he will rehearse with the subject the questions he is going to ask. He will go through the questions one by one and explain exactly what they mean. Every question will be answered yes or no. Exams generally are limited to ten questions, which are repeated two or three times in order to collect enough physiological data to draw a conclusion. Several control questions are asked, and questions like ''Are you wearing shoes today?'' enable the examiner to establish a normal baseline with which to compare the subject's reaction to the pertinent questions. Examiners never ask surprise or trick questions, although they may vary the order in which they ask the questions.

The modern polygraph is a long way from a greased donkey's tail. The subject wears a blood-pressure cuff on his arm, rubber tubing around his chest, and electrodes on the ring and index fingers of his left hand. The polygraph records the responses of the autonomic nervous system: his blood pressure and pulse rate; his breathing; and changes in his galvanic skin reflex, which is his resistance to electricity. In a 1987 study conducted to assess the accuracy of polygraph exams, the Bureau's Inspection Division compared test results with subsequent investigative developments. After looking at more than twenty thousand tests, the evaluators determined that less than one percent were probably wrong. And in the ninety-one cases in which the polygraph results were eventually proven wrong, only twenty-seven involved exams in which people who were lying beat the machine.

When used by an experienced operator, the polygraph can provide a great amount of information. After World War II, for example, polygraph tests were given to Nazis in

an attempt to locate art treasures stolen from Paris. Even when subjects refused to respond, their physiological reaction often provided the answer. While the machine is rarely used to pin down a location, in certain instances it can be very effective in doing just that. It was used that way when a Newark, New Jersey, woman claimed her baby had been kidnapped, but told a story that made little sense. Once she was hooked up to the machine, the examiner began "searching" for her baby. When the woman was asked if the baby was in New York State, she replied that she didn't know, but the polygraph indicated she was lying. Working slowly and methodically, the examiner eventually narrowed the location to somewhere in New York City, but couldn't get any more specific. The test reversed the focus of the investigation from kidnapping to abandonment, and the subject finally admitted that she had left the baby in a Macy's washroom. Macy's had turned the baby over to the city's child welfare department, and she was found quite safe.

A polygraph exam is always voluntary. No one can be compelled to take the test. But refusal to take a test does cast doubt on an individual's credibility. When Arkansas state troopers claimed that they had arranged sexual encounters for President Clinton, they offered to take a lie detector test. But when a New York newspaper made arrangements to take them up on that offer, they quickly changed their minds. While the effects of their charges lingered, the story quickly dropped out of the headlines.

Conversely, the fact that a subject voluntarily takes a polygraph test does lend credibility to his or her claims. When figure skater Tonya Harding's estranged husband, Jeff Gillooly, was arrested and charged with plotting an assault on Harding's rival Nancy Kerrigan, prior to the 1994 Winter Olympics, Gillooly decided to make a deal with prosecutors by implicating Harding in the plot. As a prerequisite for any agreement, the prosecutors wanted Gil-

looly to take a polygraph exam. The questions focused on whether Gillooly was telling the truth when he said that Tonya Harding was aware that there was going to be an assault on Nancy Kerrigan and had approved the plan. When Gillooly passed the test, the focus of the investigation shifted to Harding, who eventually confessed her involvement in the bizarre plan to keep Kerrigan out of the Olympic games.

While the question-and-answer phase of a polygraph test is always straightforward, examiners have been known to use a variety of techniques to convince subjects to tell them the truth. When two suspects in the same crime are being interviewed in separate rooms, for example, the examiners will often play them against each other. They might have a pizza delivered to one room and nothing to the other, and let the second suspect draw the obvious conclusion from that. Or they might use bits of information obtained in one interview to convince the second suspect that they know more than they really do. And finally, they might simply say, "We really don't need to spend any more time here. Your partner told us that he got the watch and the wallet, but that you did the shooting. So we're going to take a statement from him." It's all legal, as long as the subject is not coerced into making a statement, or told what to say. Then it's up to the machine to determine if he is telling what he believes the truth to be.

The roster of cases in which the polygraph has been used to verify information, develop investigative leads, or clear innocent people reads like the history of crime in modern America. One of the most dramatic exams in recent history was that given to Jack Ruby, the man who shot and killed Lee Harvey Oswald before Oswald could be questioned about the assassination of President Kennedy.

Oswald's murder is the pivotal point in just about every Kennedy assassination-conspiracy theory. According to many of these theories, Ruby knew Oswald and killed him

to prevent him from revealing details of the plot to kill Kennedy. Ruby vehemently denied this until the day he died of cancer, and demanded the opportunity to prove, by taking a polygraph exam, that he was telling the truth. The Warren Commission charged with investigating the assassination finally acceded to Ruby's pleas, and Special Agent Bell Herndon was assigned to conduct the test. The test took place in Dallas, Texas, on July 18, 1964. "I'd been working right along on various aspects of the assassination; just about everybody in the lab was," Herndon recalled. "Oddly enough, what I remember most were the President's shoes. They were very old and very worn, they'd probably been resoled several times, but they were so well polished. So by the time I interviewed Ruby, the exam was just another aspect of the case.

"I prepared the questions with several people, including Arlen Specter, later to become a senator from Pennsylvania but then a lawyer working for the Warren Commission. We formulated questions for Jack Ruby to see if we could get to the crux of the matter. Did Ruby know Oswald? Was Ruby involved in a conspiracy? Was there premeditation on the part of Ruby and Oswald to get together to do something about President Kennedy? Was Ruby possibly linked to an organized-crime element out of Chicago and paid off to silence Oswald? Was there a conspiracy? Was Ruby paid off by the Mafia? Was Ruby a member of the Communist party? We were aware of all the theories going around and we tried to cover them all in my interrogation.

"The test was very lengthy, which I objected to, and I do think there came a time when Ruby was desensitized. He was showing some fatigue. When the test began I tried to establish a rapport with him. I felt like I had the best chance with him if I treated him very respectfully, if I was very sympathetic, if I didn't make him feel like he was a subject, but rather just an individual trying to clarify his involvement in the assassination. I didn't want to be the

heavy, which is sometimes necessary when you're sitting down with a hardened criminal and you have to dominate the situation.

"I think I was probably correct, because Ruby was co-operative. He seemed to understand the intent of the questions, he didn't move, he didn't fidget, and he answered the questions as he was instructed. I think that Mr. Ruby felt that by taking this test, by being candid and cooperative, he could convince the world that he shot Oswald because he was so mad that Oswald had killed our beloved President. The one question I never asked him was, 'Did you shoot Lee Harvey Oswald?' because that was pretty well resolved. He'd done it on national television; it just was beyond being a relevant question.

"I've always considered the polygraph to be a scientific interrogation technique, but there's more to it than the machine. The Bureau's position is that subjective impressions by the interrogator are just as valuable as what the chart or pen tracings show. I always look for body language, eye expressions, nervousness, whether he's deliberately trying to defeat the machine by flexing his muscles or by moving, clearing his throat; it's all part of an innate sense a good interviewer gets after conducting years of exams.

"I believed Jack Ruby when he told me he did not know Oswald and that he was not part of a conspiracy. I had asked him several control questions where I knew he was not telling me the truth, but I didn't see that same kind of reaction to the relevant questions that I asked him. There was also a question of Ruby's mental stability. His doctor was present because I had been warned that maybe Ruby was not quite what we would call fully sane. But he appeared to be physically fit to me, and he wasn't under any medication.

"My conclusion was that he was a valid subject. I felt that although maybe he had some mental aberrations, and who wouldn't in his situation, I thought that there was no

indication of deception to relevant questions. But I also stated that if a doctor said that this man was a manic-depressive, I wasn't going to be foolish enough to contradict him. And if that were true, then I would have to render my conclusion nonconclusive. But on that day, I felt he understood the intent of my questions, that he was not divorced from reality and he was fully cooperative, and that he was telling the truth as he believed it to be.''

Is it possible to beat the machine? To get away with deception? Absolutely. The Russians, Cubans, Bulgarians, and other former Eastern bloc countries had extensive programs in which they taught their agents and military officers various ways of handling a forced polygraph exam. Because Eastern bloc nations did not commonly use the polygraph, our government did not have such a program. But in one instance an American operative moving freely between West and East Germany was accused by the East Germans of working for American intelligence and given a polygraph test. He failed the test, and was ordered to return the next day for a retest. This operative could easily have returned to West Germany and safety, so when he voluntarily returned the following day the East Germans decided the polygraph could not possibly be accurate and ignored the results.

Some people are untestable because of their physical makeup or diminished mental capacity, in which case examiners will not get consistent specific and significant responses and the results will be inconclusive. And some people do attempt to beat the machine by using drugs. An experienced examiner can usually read that in the charts, which come out flat as opposed to going up and down. In those cases the examiner may request a urine sample to test for the presence of drugs.

And finally, there is one foolproof way to beat the machine. A man from the hills of West Virginia was suspected of involvement in a bank robbery and was tested in the

Fredericksburg, Virginia, field office. During the test he denied that he had robbed the bank. At the conclusion of the test, the examiner looked him right in the eye and told him, pointing to the polygraph, ''I have proof right here that you did it!''

With that, the subject ripped the chart off the machine and ate it.

I guess you can say law enforcement officials have come a long way since the days of Sherlock Holmes and his magnifying glass.

— NORTHUMBERLAND COUNTY DISTRICT ATTORNEY ROBERT SACAVAGE,
at the conclusion of the Robert Auker murder trial

ACKNOWLEDGMENTS

Exploring a new world requires guides and helpers, and I was extremely fortunate to have many of these in the preparation of this book. I cannot sufficiently express my gratitude to the men and women of the FBI crime lab who welcomed me warmly and gave of their time and expertise. I hope the recognition they receive from this book in some small way repays them for their efforts in my behalf. I hesitate to name any of them for fear I won't name all of them, but they have my appreciation as well as my admiration.

This project began at dinner one night with my friend FBI Special Agent Joe Pistone, better known as "Donnie Brasco." I value his friendship, as I do that of Lou DiGiaimo, the motion picture casting director who introduced Joe and me and helped create this project.

I would not have been able to embark on this endeavor without the efforts and sacrifices of my literary agent, Jay Acton, a man of many talents and remarkable understanding, and I am grateful to him. My editor, Fred Hills, was unfailingly supportive, in addition to being an extraordinary editor and a very good guy. Of course, he had the benefit of his superb assistant, Laureen Rowland, who helped speed the process with professionalism and strong doses of good cheer.

I needed an enormous amount of assistance in the preparation of my research materials, which included 180 hours

of interviews. I was so terribly lucky to find Ann Bartlett and the people she enlisted, Grace DiCamillo and Mary Ann Rebori, and I hope they know how grateful I am for their efforts. It's impossible to enumerate the many tasks accomplished in my behalf by Laura Vertullo, but each of them was done with expertise and enthusiasm, and I thank her for that work. Every author needs help in stepping back from his work when the shaping process begins, and at that time I was fortunate to have had the help of two friends, the best-selling author Berry Stainbeck and editor Ellie Kossack, and for their assistance and the way it was offered I will be forever appreciative.

In a long process such as this one any writer needs friends willing to put up with him, or more specifically in this case, to put him up. I am so lucky to have such friends in Iris, David, and Jordan Kai Burnett; and Trish, Paul, and Jessica Reichler.

And finally, a very special note of appreciation of Margarey Tremblay of the FBI Office of Public Affairs. Marge Tremblay, who recently celebrated her thirtieth anniversary with the Bureau, was the finest guide any adventurer could wish to find, and she does the FBI proud. For those taxpayers who complain about government waste, I offer Marge Tremblay. Believe me, with her we're getting our money's worth.

DAVID FISHER

INDEX